FLASH-BANG!

A shadow against the smoke resolved itself into an Iranian soldier. Murdock fired a single round from chest high that snapped through the man's throat, then punched a neat hole through the glass of the large bridge window at his back.

Murdock fired again as a second Iranian rose from the track-mounted, sliding bridge chairs. A triplet of rounds from Roselli's H&K slammed him out of the chair and into the bridge console, arms flailing before he slumped to the deck in a spreading pool of blood. A Japanese merchant sailor leaped behind a hostage, threw an arm around the man's throat, and held the muzzle of a SIG-Sauer P-220 automatic pistol against the man's skull.

There was no time for negotiations. Murdock shifted the aim of his H&K slightly and squeezed the trigger . . .

KEITH DOUGLASS

BERKLEY BOOKS, NEW YORK

SEAL TEAM SEVEN

A Berkley Book / published by arrangement with
the authors

PRINTING HISTORY
Berkley edition / August 1994

All rights reserved.
Copyright © 1994 by The Berkley Publishing Group.
SEAL TEAM SEVEN logo illustration by Michael Racz.
This book may not be reproduced in whole or in part,
by mimeograph or any other means, without permission.
For information address: The Berkley Publishing Group,
200 Madison Avenue, New York, New York 10016.

ISBN: 0-425-14340-6

BERKLEY®
Berkley Books are published by The Berkley Publishing Group,
200 Madison Avenue, New York, New York 10016.
BERKLEY and the "B" design
are trademarks belonging to the Berkley Publishing Corporation.

PRINTED IN THE UNITED STATES OF AMERICA

10 9 8 7 6 5 4 3 2 1

FOREWORD

Created by Presidential order in 1962, the U.S. Navy SEAL (SEa-Air-Land) Teams are today among the foremost elite special-operations forces in the world. During the war in Vietnam there were two Teams, SEAL One and SEAL Two, each composed of a number of fourteen-man platoons, the basic SEAL operational element.

During the 1980s, the Reagan Administration recognized that the changing face of modern warfare demanded a greater emphasis on special forces and covert operations, and the Teams were expanded accordingly. By 1990, the number of Teams had grown to seven. SEAL Teams One, Three, and Five were headquartered at Coronado, California, under the auspices of Naval Special Warfare Group One, for deployment to the Pacific and the Far East. SEAL Teams Two, Four, and Eight were located at Little Creek, Virginia, under NAVSPECWARGRU-Two for deployment to the Caribbean, the Mediterranean, and the Middle East. SEAL Six, commissioned in November 1980 as the Navy's covert anti-terrorist unit, was listed under NAVSPECWARGRU-Two for administrative purposes only; in practice it answered directly to the U.S. Special Operations Command—which includes the Army's Delta Force and the Air Force's First and Seventh Special Operations Squadrons—and to the Joint Chiefs of Staff.

For reasons of both security and politics, the SEALs' TO undergoes periodic revision. As of this date and to the best of the author's knowledge, however, SEAL Team Seven is completely fictitious. It was the author's decision to employ a fictional unit in order to show as many of the missions and activities of modern SEALs as possible, including operations that in real life might have been undertaken by Group One, Group Two, or SEAL Six.

—Keith Douglass
August 1993

PROLOGUE

0945 hours
Freighter *Yuduki Maru*
Cherbourg Harbor, France

A blast from the freighter's horn sounded across the water, momentarily drowning the shrill calls of circling sea gulls as the 7,600-ton freighter began her ponderous acceleration toward the open sea. Echoes bounced back from Cherbourg's waterfront, mingled with the thunder of noise from an angry crowd.

Ashore, beyond the chain-link fence separating Cherbourg's military port facilities from the civilian docks, a thin line of troopers drawn from the French Gendarmerie Nationale faced a sea of protestors, who answered the ship's horn with a wild, drawn-out wail of noise. Placards danced above shouting, angry faces; fists punched the sky in time to chanted slogans. Near the military base's main gate, a scuffle broke out between police and the mob.

Tetsuo Kurebayashi leaned against the railing on *Yuduki Maru*'s starboard side, a ghost of a smile tugging at his normally impassive face. International Greenpeace had made *Yuduki Maru* and her sister ships the focus of a whirlwind of controversy. The publicity of her departure from France would ensure plenty of attention from a watching world later, once Yoake-Go, Operation Dawn, was fully under way.

Kurebayashi was fourth officer of the *Yuduki Maru,* but his

1

first loyalty was not to the ship, nor to the company that owned and operated her, nor even to Captain Koga. As he turned from the railing, he caught the eye of Shigeru Yoshitomi, a deck division cargo handler, and he gave the man a slight nod, an exchange unnoticed by their shipmates nearby. Though of mutually alien social classes, both men were Ohtori, and brothers in blood.

In the harbor, less than one hundred meters off the *Yuduki Maru*'s starboard beam, a two-masted sailing ketch, a gleaming, white-hulled, rich man's toy, matched the freighter's slow pace. A banner had been unfurled on the yacht's port side, bearing legends in French, English, and Japanese: BAN THE SHIPMENTS and GREENPEACE. *Yuduki Maru*'s escort, the sleek cutter *Shikishima,* was already moving up to position herself between the freighter and the Greenpeace yacht. According to the news stories Kurebayashi had heard while he was in France, the yacht, a forty-meter motor sailer named *Beluga,* was to be *Yuduki Maru*'s watchdog for the entire length of her voyage from Cherbourg to Japan, following in her wake and making certain the freighter did not break the international agreements that had shaped her planned course.

Kurebayashi smiled again at the thought. Only a handful of men aboard the Japanese freighter knew it, of course, but the *Yuduki Maru* would not be completing her voyage to the home islands.

Excitement quickened within. All of his training, all of his dedication to the Cause, all of his long-bottled desire to strike back at the hated American imperialists, would soon find outlet in action, and in purpose.

Soon, the Ohtori commando thought. *Only three more weeks . . .*

1

Tuesday, 3 May

2245 hours (Zulu +3)
Hawr al-Hammar, Iraq

A shadow against shadows, the black-hooded form silently broke the water's surface scant meters from the indistinct shoreline where lake gave way to marsh. The commando had removed his face mask underwater to avoid telltale reflections. For long seconds, he remained motionless in the water, eyes alone moving in his heavily blacked-out face.

Nothing. The wind whispered through the forest of marsh grass ahead, where unseen hordes of nameless creatures chirped and keeked and buzzed, undisturbed by the intruder. A crescent moon had set an hour before; the only light came from a dazzling spill of stars overhead and from a faint glow against the southeastern sky.

Moving gently to avoid making even the slightest splash, the figure pressed forward, swim fins seeking leverage in knee-deep muck, elbows braced across the black canvas of a gear flotation bag clutched to his chest like a swim board, gloved hands tight on his sound-suppressed subgun, an H&K MP5SD3. His movements against the bottom stirred the mud, which bubbled to the surface as an oily scum and a ripple of dull, sulfur-heavy plops. The stench—petroleum, decay, and the rotten-eggs stink of hydrogen sulfide—was thick enough to bring tears to the eyes, but the swimmer ignored it, sliding through the mud toward the cover of the marsh.

A stroll in the park. He'd waded through worse than this plenty of times before in Florida, Panama, and Virginia's Great Dismal Swamp.

Gradually, the deep, clinging muck thinned beneath his fins, rising to meet the ill-defined shore. Among the clumps of reeds and marsh grass, he found what passed for solid ground—a water-logged patch of tangled roots and mud inches above the *lap-lap-lap* of the surface of the lake. Silently, with a precise and practiced economy of motion, the black figure removed his swim fins, which were strapped on over his combat boots. Next, he unzipped the waterproof satchel and began breaking out various pieces of equipment. AN/PVS-7 night-vision goggles slipped over his face. The pound-and-a-half device transformed darkness to flat, green-lit day and gave him the surreal aspect of some alien, half-mechanical creature. For a full three minutes, the figure crouched at the edge of the swamp, scanning his surroundings through the NVGs, listening to the night noises and the steady lapping of the water.

Still nothing. Good.

Switching off the night goggles and sliding them up on his head, he broke out a GPS receiver and flipped up the plastic-housed antenna on the side. Thumbing the button marked POS, he studied the cryptic line of alphanumerics displayed on the instrument's small, lighted screen, then nodded satisfaction. Outstanding! Dead on target to within twenty meters, and that after an underwater swim of almost three klicks!

Pivoting on his heels, the figure aimed a finger-sized pencil flash toward the lake and squeezed it—once, twice . . . pause . . . a third time—the red glow too dim to be seen more than a few dozen meters across the water. In silent response, almost magically, other dripping, night-clad figures began rising from the sheltering water where they'd been awaiting the signal. Each man was outfitted like the first, in black fatigues, rebreather gear, and numerous waterproof pouches and rucksacks hooked to load-bearing harnesses; each too sported subtle distinctions of garb and equipment. One carried the waterproof backpack that housed the squad's HST-4 sat-comm gear and KY-57 encoder. Another was already unshipping the long-barreled deadliness of an M-60E3, the lightweight version of the machine gun with an auxiliary front pistol grip mounted between the legs of its bipod. A third pulled the mud plug from the suppressor barrel of his H&K MP5.

In all, six more men joined the first at the swamp's edge. Two donned NVGs and slipped away into the reeds, providing security for the other five as they broke out the rest of their gear.

Blue Squad, Third Platoon, SEAL Team Seven, had arrived, armed and ready for war.

1455 hours (Zulu −5)
Meeting of the House Military Affairs
Committee
Capitol Building, Washington, D.C.

"The name SEALs," Captain Granger explained, sitting alone at the long table and reading from his notes, "is an acronym standing for 'Sea, Air, Land' and symbolizes the three elements the teams infiltrate through in pursuit of their mission objectives. The first two teams were formed in January of 1962, at the order of President John F. Kennedy. Their commission called on them to operate up to twenty miles inland, serving as naval commandos with the express missions of gathering intelligence, raiding, capturing prisoners, and generally raising havoc behind enemy lines."

Opposite Granger's table, the members of the House Military Affairs Committee sat listening or spoke together in low-voiced murmurs. There were cameras in the room as well. These hearings were being reported by CNN and C-SPAN, and much of the speechmaking and posturing was for their benefit.

"Their baptism of fire came in Vietnam," Granger continued, "where they served with distinction. Between 1965 and 1972, forty-nine Naval Special Warfare personnel were killed in action in Vietnam. During this same period, naval records credit SEAL direct-action platoons with over one thousand confirmed kills and nearly eight hundred probables, as well as close to another thousand enemy personnel taken prisoner.

Three SEALs won the Navy Medal of Honor during the Vietnam conflict, while five SEALs and two UDT frogmen won the Navy Cross. Immediately after the war—"

"Ah, Captain Granger." Congressman Rodney Farnum, head of the House Military Affairs Committee, leaned closer to his microphone. "If I may interrupt."

"Yes, Mr. Chairman?"

"The House Military Affairs Committee is second to none in its, ah, deep admiration for members of America's special-warfare community, and we recognize their significant contributions to this nation's defense in the past. However, as the purpose of this special meeting is to review *future* funding levels for the Navy's special-warfare needs, and since several of the congressmen on this panel have commitments elsewhere this afternoon, perhaps it would be helpful if we could limit the session this afternoon to the present and to the, ah, future in the near term."

"As you wish, Mr. Chairman. I thought an overall background might be useful."

"I think we're all adequately familiar with the subject. Are there objections from my distinguished colleagues at the table? No? Then perhaps we could cut straight to the chase in this matter, Captain Granger. Let us begin by hearing your views on the necessity for maintaining an expensive and force-redundant unit like the U.S. Navy SEALs in this modern, post-Cold War era. . . ."

2301 hours (Zulu +3)
Hawr al-Hammar, Iraq

Chief Machinist's Mate Tom Roselli, the SEAL squad's point man and the first one ashore, donned his communications headset, fitting the earpiece snugly inside his left ear and securing it beneath his knit cap. The wire ran down the back of his neck and through a slit in his black fatigue shirt, where it plugged into the Motorola unit secured to his combat harness. The filament mike rested below his lower lip. He touched the transmit key and *tsked* lightly twice. A moment later, he heard an answering *tsk-tsk* through his earpiece as the squad's CO replied. Radio check okay.

Excitement burned, *burned* in Roselli's veins like liquid fire. He was pumped, he was psyched, he was ready to kick ass and take names. This was it, the real thing, the combat mission he'd been training endlessly for throughout his seven years as a U.S. Navy SEAL. He'd been on combat ops before, during the Gulf War, but never one like this.

Less than an hour earlier, Chief Roselli and thirteen other hard, combat-ready men, each shouldering over one hundred pounds of equipment, had stepped into darkness thirty thousand feet above southern Iraq. Silently, they'd fallen through the thin, cold air over the Hawr al-Hammar, a long and meandering, swamp-bordered lake that stretched for sixty miles along the lower reaches of the Euphrates River, from An Nasiriya to where the Euphrates joined the Tigris just above the city of al-Basra. Opening their steerable, parasail chutes at eight thousand feet, they'd glided for miles above the silent waters, splashing at last into the eastern end of the lake. From there, the fourteen men, one SEAL platoon organized into two seven-man squads, had made their way to the southern shore.

Roselli was with Blue Squad, six enlisted men under the platoon's CO, Lieutenant Vincent Cotter. Gold Squad, if all had gone according to plan, should be forming up separately about a mile further to the west.

By 2310 hours, the squad was ready to travel, its high-altitude breathing equipment and swimming gear wrapped up and stashed at the water's edge, the men rigged out in their first- and second-line CQB rigs. Lieutenant Cotter lightly touched Roselli's shoulder. *You're on point.* Roselli nodded, pulled his NVGs back down over his face, and started off, taking the lead.

They moved south, wading through mud and silt that gradually thinned beneath their boots until they were pressing ahead across firm, almost-dry ground, their passage screened by the dense sea of man-high reeds that stretched away endlessly into the darkness on all sides. They spaced themselves at five-meter intervals. Next in line after Roselli was

Master Chief George MacKenzie, a long-legged, man-mountain Texan big enough to hump the squad's sixty-gun and carry an MP5SD3 slung over his shoulder as well. The number-two man was also the squad's navigator, checking compass and GPS frequently to keep the team on course. Cotter, the L-T, walked the number-three slot, and behind him came Electrician's Mate Second Class Bill Higgins, the team's commo man. Slot five was walked by the squad's medic, Hospital Corpsman Second Class James Ellsworth; inevitably, everyone just called him "Doc." The niceties of the Geneva Convention meant little to a SEAL team deep in enemy territory; Doc wore no red crosses and he packed an H&K MP5SD3 like Roselli's, though his personal favorite for a primary weapon was a full-auto shotgun. Behind him, lugging an M-16/M203 combo, was Hull Technician First Class Juan Garcia, "Boomer," the squad's demo man. The tail gunner slot was occupied by Quartermaster First Class Martin "Magic" Brown, a black kid from inner-city Chicago whose expertise on the range with a Remington Model 700 had earned him a position as the squad's sniper.

Though each man was a specialist, their training and their skills overlapped. Two of them, the man on point and the man bringing up the rear, wore NVGs at all times, while the rest relied on night-adapted, Mark-I eyeballs. They traded off those positions frequently, though, to prevent night-goggle-induced eye fatigue, so the only slots that remained unchanged throughout the hike were three and four, the CO and the commo man.

No words were exchanged between the members of the team. Communications were limited to hand signs, touch, and rare, nonvocalized clicks and cluckings over the technical radios. Mutual trust and coordination within the group were perfect, almost effortless. These men had worked, trained, slept, and practiced with one another for months, until each could sense the others' positions and movements even in total darkness.

Sometimes Roselli imagined he could even sense their thoughts.

At the moment, of course, he didn't need psychic powers to know what the others were thinking. Everyone was focused completely on the mission, and on their objective, now some ten kilometers to the south.

1515 hours (Zulu –5)
Meeting of the House Military Affairs
Committee
Capitol Building, Washington, D.C.

Congressman Farnum leaned forward, one hand clutching the base of the microphone as he played to the cameras in the room. "But Captain Granger, isn't it true that these SEALs, these, ah, 'NAVSPECWAR' people, as you call them, isn't it true that they present the Navy with special administrative and discipline problems?"

"Of course, Mr. Chairman. As I'm sure there are similar administrative difficulties with other elite military forces."

"Ah. But is it not true, Captain, that there have been numerous incidents near SEAL bases involving disorderly conduct? Drunkenness? Sexual harassment of both civilians and female military personnel?"

"It's true, Mr. Chairman. There have been some incidents. But I should point out, sir, that these are very special men, highly trained, dedicated, *motivated* to a degree I never would have dreamed possible before I saw them in action."

"That hardly excuses their actions, Captain Granger. Ah, you are not a SEAL yourself, are you?"

"No, sir. But I have worked closely with the Teams on several occasions."

A congressman several places to Farnum's left looked up from the papers on the table before him. "When was it that you last saw SEALs in action, Captain Granger?"

"During the Gulf War, Congressman Murdock. I was a commander at the time, attached to the boat squadron that put a SEAL detachment ashore off Kuwait City the night before General Schwarzkopf began his end run around the Iraqi right. It was a damned impressive operation, let me tell—"

"I'm certain it was, Captain," Farnum interrupted. "Some of these elite units make a point of carrying off flashy, showboat missions that grab the public eye."

"I'd hardly call that op 'showboating,' Mr. Chairman. The SEALs worked in complete secrecy, and their involvement in Desert Storm did not surface until some time after the war. In that particular instance, they swam ashore onto a heavily defended beach at Kuwait City and planted a large number of demolition charges. When those were set off, the explosions convinced the Iraqi commanders that the U.S. Marines were coming ashore there, at Kuwait City, rather than across their trenches and minefields in the south. In fact, our records show that several Iraqi units were moved *back* from the front lines to Kuwait City that morning, in anticipation of Marine landings there."

"Ah, yes, Captain Granger," Farnum said, shuffling through his notes. "We're aware of all that. However, the point here is that *all* of our military services maintain—at great expense, I might add—elite special-warfare units. The Air Force has their First and Seventh Special Operations Squadrons. The Marines claim their whole corps is an elite force, but they reserve a special distinction for their Special Operations Capable units. The Army, ah, well, the Army has Rangers, the Delta Force, Airborne units, Special Forces. Is it not true, Captain Granger, that these units perform many of the same tasks as the Navy's SEALs?"

"Well, yes, it is, Mr. Chairman, but—"

"Marine Recon teams could have planted those demolition charges in Kuwait as easily as SEALs, am I right?"

"Yes, sir."

"Why is it that the U.S. Marines, the FBI's Hostage Rescue Teams, the Rangers, Delta Force, the SEALs, and God knows who else all train extensively to carry out, for example, hostage rescue missions? How many hostage situations has our nation been faced with in the past, Captain Granger?"

"I'm afraid I'm not qualified to answer that question, sir."

"The point is that we simply do not need so many units all designed to perform the same basic tasks. This is an appalling and incredibly expensive duplication of effort, training, equipment, and budgetary allocation that this nation can ill afford in these times of fiscal challenge. It is our purpose here today to determine just why Congress should permit continued funding for the U.S. Navy SEALs."

"Well, Mr. Chairman, the SEALs add a unique and valuable dimension to our special warfare capabilities. Their ability to work underwater, for instance—"

"Is duplicated by the Special Forces. Actually, I must admit that the old Underwater Demolition Teams did provide a useful service in surveying beaches, blowing up obstacles in advance of a landing, and that sort of thing. But the UDTs were closed out in 1983, when they officially became part of the SEALs, correct?"

"Yes, sir."

"Now we have SEALs who do everything the UDT did, but who also conduct raids, rescue missions, even intelligence ops many miles inland. I submit that, for all of the branches of the armed forces, special operations are, ah, sexy. They have seduced all of the services, who see them as a means of securing for themselves larger and larger portions of the military appropriations pie.

"Now, in my understanding, Captain, the historic role of the U.S. Navy is ships and sea lanes. They support our ground forces overseas and, through our ICBM submarine force, maintain one leg of our nuclear-deterrence triad. I fail to see why we need these naval commandoes, these Rambos who carry out missions that can just as easily be assigned to Army Special Forces.

"In short, Captain, we simply do not *need* the SEALs. They are an expensive luxury we can easily do without. . . ."

0145 hours (Zulu +3)
South of Hawr al-Hammar, Iraq

Once the marsh had extended for most of the twenty kilometers between the motionless black waters of the Hawr al-Hammar and the ancient city of al-Basra to the southeast. North of the lake, the swamps had covered hundreds of square miles between the Tigris and the Euphrates River, stretching almost halfway to Baghdad.

In the years since the Gulf War, however, Saddam Hussein's

engineers had been busily carving a system of canals and man-made or man-improved rivers throughout the area in an attempt to drain the entire region. The Qadissiya River—dug in 1993 by 4,500 workers in just forty-five days—drained much of the southern Iraq wetlands into the Euphrates, and together with the Saddam River and the Mother of Battles River had already transformed the age-old topography of this part of the Fertile Crescent. Officially, the project opened new land for agriculture. It was pure coincidence that the south Iraq marshes had long provided refuge for Shi'ites, dissidents, and rebels.

As the intruders worked their way south through the dying marshlands, they encountered more and more signs of habitation. Twice they halted, then took wide detours to avoid *sarifas,* traditional marsh dwellings woven from the omnipresent reeds with ornate, latticework entrances. The huts, and the slender, high-prowed canoes called *mashufs* by the locals, were identical to huts and canoes built in this region for at least the past six thousand years.

Twice too the squad went to ground as Iraqi military patrols blundered past, crashing through the reeds and calling to one another with sharp, guttural cries in Arabic. Another time, as the squad was wading along the muddy banks of a canal, they froze in place, as unmoving and as invisible as moss-covered logs, while an ex-Soviet Zhuk-class patrol boat motored slowly past.

At last, reeds gave way to clumps of grass and scrub brush bordering an area of dry, sandy soil. At the swamp's edge, the squad paused once again to rest, and to strip and clean their weapons right down to the springs and followers of their magazines. A blaze of light glared against the sky to the southeast, harsh and intrusive after the silent darkness of the marsh.

Roselli's pulse quickened as he studied the source of that light through a powerful pair of binoculars. Five hundred meters ahead, the modern airport of Shuaba had been constructed on land reclaimed from the dying swamp. From a low rise in the ground, Roselli could see the control tower and hangars of the civilian airport. To the right were more buildings and a smaller tower, as well as the barracks belonging to a military air base. Beyond that, against a hillside and barely visible against the glare from the airfield lights, was a small town, the village of Zabeir.

Directly in front of the civilian tower, pinned in the cross fire of a dozen powerful searchlights, sat a transport, a C-130 Hercules. Prominent on the plane's high tail was the pale blue flag of the United Nations.

Roselli let out a pent-up breath as he lowered the binoculars, but at the same time the fire in his veins burned hotter. The SEALs had reached their objective, parachuting into a lake, then trekking through Iraqi-controlled territory across kilometers of swamp, and they'd done it unobserved.

Now, however, the real fun was about to begin.

2

Lieutenant Vincent Cotter studied the UN C-130 through his binoculars, carefully searching for the guards he knew must be there. The rear ramp was up and the cargo doors closed, but a civilian-type boarding ladder was still rolled up against the port-side door forward. Had Iraqi troops entered the aircraft? Were the hostages still on board? There was no way to answer either question from out here.

Third Platoon had been carefully briefed on the situation the previous afternoon at Dahran, and Cotter had looked at photographs of Shuaba Airport shot both from an orbiting KH-11 spy satellite and from a high-altitude Air Force Aurora reconnaissance aircraft.

Both sources indicated that the Herky Bird was heavily guarded outside. As of the last radio contact with the UN plane's crew, some eight hours ago, the Iraqi troops had still been respecting the technical claim of extraterritorial sovereignty for the aircraft and had not gone aboard. That, Cotter reflected, could easily have changed in the past few hours. The SEAL team would have to proceed carefully, working on the assumption that armed Iraqi soldiers were now on the plane. As for whether the UN inspectors were still on board, that would have to be settled by a closer look.

The crisis had begun at 0930 hours the day before, when the

C-130 had left Baghdad's Al Muthana Airport for Shuaba and an unscheduled inspection of a reputed chemical and biological weapons plant outside al-Basra. The tip that had led the UN weapons inspectors to that fourteen-hundred-year-old city on the west bank of the Shat Al-Arab River had been as solid as they come; German engineers who had helped build the facility ten years earlier had come forward with both the blueprints and photographs. The al-Basra facility was almost certainly being used to make and store CB agents, and the presence of an unusually thick concrete floor under part of the plant suggested that it might be tied in with Iraq's nuclear program as well.

Arriving unexpectedly at Shuaba, twenty kilometers east of al-Basra, fifteen UN inspectors had unloaded their Land Rovers and descended on the suspected facility, built halfway between al-Basra and Shuaba Airport and masquerading as a machine tool-and-die plant. There, the inspectors had brushed past surprised Iraqi guards and impounded a number of files and other physical evidence, then driven with them to the airport. They'd been in the process of loading the documents aboard the aircraft when Iraqi troops—reportedly members of the Republican Guard—had arrived, demanding the return of classified documents. When the Swedish commander of the UN team refused, a standoff had ensued. The Iraqis were point-blank refusing to allow the Hercules to take off unless the stolen files were returned.

Similar standoffs had occurred before in the wake of the '91 Gulf War. Until now, all had been resolved peacefully. This time, however, the situation was more urgent, and more deadly. Iraq's ruling military council, calling the incident a gross violation of national sovereignty, was threatening to destroy the plane rather than allow it to leave the country. Adding to the confusion, one of the UN inspectors aboard was an American, a CIA case officer named Arkin; the Company wanted Arkin out of Iraq and on his way to Langley for a debrief ASAP. From the tone of his operational orders, Cotter guessed that the Agency spook had stumbled across something in al-Basra pretty damned important.

SEAL Seven had been tapped by the Pentagon to carry out the mission, code-named Operation Blue Sky, a covert insertion into Iraq followed by a hostage rescue.

Cotter turned his binoculars toward the east, where two aging, rust-bucket buses had been parked across the runway, effectively preventing takeoff. A couple of jeeps were parked there as well, and the SEAL lieutenant could see the telltale orange sparks of a couple of lit cigarettes. He could smell them too. When the wind was right, it was possible to detect the odor of a cigarette at two miles; these were harsh and pungent, either Turkish or Russian, he thought.

"I make four hostiles at the roadblock, Skipper," Martin Brown whispered at his side. Brown had his Remington Model 700 unpacked, with an AN/PVS-4 nightscope already mounted over its breech.

"Let me have a peek, Magic." Cotter's night goggles could only distinguish human-sized targets to a range of about 150 meters. Taking Brown's sniper rifle, the L-T peered through the starlight scope, which extended his view to better than four hundred meters.

Yeah . . . there they were, revealed in an eerie glow of greens and grays, four Iraqi soldiers lounging by their vehicles, smoking, talking, but not appearing particularly alert.

Shifting the rifle-mounted scope to the C-130, he spotted two more soldiers sitting on the bottom steps of the boarding ladder. He counted three troops resting on the ground beneath the aircraft, and another on the control tower, standing on a railed outside walkway up near the top of the building. Ten in all . . . with the certainty that there were more nearby, possibly inside the terminal building or the hangars, possibly inside a trio of Iraqi army trucks parked next to the control tower's entrance.

He handed the rifle back to Brown, then checked his watch, carefully shielding its face with his hand as he uncovered the luminous numbers: 0215 hours. It was almost time.

Vincent Xavier Cotter, reserved, soft-spoken, oldest son of a devoutly Catholic family, seemed an unlikely warrior. During high school he'd actually considered becoming a priest, but then his father had died and he'd dropped out, going to work to support his mother and two younger brothers. Eventually he'd gotten his G.E.D. equivalency, then gone on to enlist in the Navy, figuring that he could send most of his pay home while the government provided him with room and board.

Navy life had agreed with him. Four years later, as an engineman second class, he'd "shipped for six"—re-enlisting for another six years—and put in for Basic Underwater Demolition/SEAL school at Coronado, California, at the same time.

He still wasn't entirely sure why he'd volunteered for BUD/S training, though he suspected it had something to do with proving himself *to* himself, a challenge to mind and body. SEAL training had been a challenge, all right, a nightmare of mud, exhaustion, humiliation, and grueling hard labor beyond anything he'd ever imagined, a hell-course designed to weed out the less than physically and mentally perfect.

He still dreamed about that damned bell sometimes.

It had been set up on a post at one end of the parade ground, "the grinder," as it was better known to the recruit boat crews who'd drilled and exercised there. All any BUD/S trainee had to do to quit, at any time of day or night, was walk over to the bell and ring it three times. During the sleepless days of physical challenge officially known as Motivation Week—it was never called anything but Hell Week by the trainees—two BUD/S recruits had actually been detailed to *carry* the bell everywhere the boat crews went. He'd wanted to ring it. Oh, how he'd wanted to ring it! There'd been times when Cotter had wanted a shower and clean clothes and an uninterrupted eight-hours sleep so badly he would have done anything, *anything* to win them.

Except quit. He'd stayed the course and graduated, one of twelve out of an original complement of sixty. After the usual six months' probation, he'd finally won the coveted "Bud-weiser," the eagle/trident/flintlock-pistol emblem of the SEALs worn above his left breast.

For the next year he'd served with SEAL Team Two,

stationed at Little Creek, Virginia, and participated in the
SEAL raids on Iranian oil rigs during the so-called "Tanker
War" of the eighties. In 1986 he'd qualified for NESEP, a Navy
education program that put him through four years of college,
with ten weeks of OCS the summer before his senior year.
After BUD/S, college had been a vacation, and his stint of
Organized Chicken Shit in Providence, Rhode Island, had been
sheer luxury. He'd even managed to find time to get married
and have a daughter. Graduating as an ensign in 1990, he'd
immediately returned to the Teams, serving with SEAL Four in
the Gulf War, then going on to command the newly formed
SEAL Team Seven's Third Platoon.

He checked his watch again: 0230 hours.

It was time.

Switching on his Motorola, he spoke quietly into his lip
mike. "Gold, this is Blue. Authenticate, Sierra Tango one five."

"Blue, Gold" sounded in his headset. The voice belonged to
Lieutenant j.g. Ed DeWitt, Cotter's 2IC, his second-in-command.
"Copy. Authenticate, Tango Foxtrot three niner. Lockpick."

DeWitt's squad was in position and ready to go. "Roger that,
Gold. Stand by."

Slipping quietly through the darkness, he joined EM2
Higgins, who was putting the finishing touches on the unit's
tiny satellite transceiver, plugging the HST-4 sat comm into the
KY-57 encryption set. The antenna, a folding umbrella just
twelve inches across, had already been set up and aligned with
a MILSTAR satellite 22,300 miles above the equator.

"So, L-T," Higgins said quietly. "Is it going down?"

"That's a roger. Unless Washington has something else to
say about it." He took a handset the size of a cellular car phone.

"Fairyland, Fairyland," he called softly. "This is Blue
Water."

"Blue Water, Fairyland" sounded over his headset a moment
later. "We read you."

"Fairyland, Blue Water. Lockpick. I say again, Lockpick."

"Blue Water, Lockpick confirmed. Cold Steel. I say again,
Cold Steel."

Adrenaline coursed through Cotter's veins. The mission was still go! "Roger, Fairyland. Cold Steel. Blue Water out."

Cotter replaced the handset in its rucksack, locking eyes with Higgins as he did so. "Looks like it's a go," he said.

Higgins—known as "Professor Higgins" for his bookish habits between missions—replied with a killer's maniacal grin, teeth gleaming in a black-painted face out of nightmare.

1835 hours (Zulu −5)
Joint Special Operations Command Center
The Pentagon

During the first hours of the Desert Storm land campaign, one observer had wryly pointed out that Iraqi spies might have noted that something was afoot by the large number of pizza deliveries to both the White House and the Pentagon. True or not, this night several delivery cartons were open on the table, revealing half-eaten pizzas. The room's occupants, however, were paying less attention to their dinner than they were to a large television monitor on one console. The uniforms represented several services, Army, Navy, and Air Force, and the civilians among them included liaison officers with the CIA and one undersecretary to the Secretary of Defense.

Captain Phillip Thomas Coburn felt somewhat out of his league with the suits and the flag-rank brass, but he took comfort in the fact that he was a SEAL, and what was going down on the screen was a SEAL op. A twenty-five-year veteran, he'd started out with SEAL Two in Vietnam. Now he was the commanding officer of SEAL Seven, an elite and highly classified unit organized into four platoons of fourteen men each.

The room's lights were out, and watchers' faces were illuminated by the eerie phosphor glow of the screen. In the background, a whispering murmur of many voices could be heard, the relayed comments of aircraft pilots and of the SEALs themselves as they spoke to one another over their tactical radios. Operation Blue Sky was a large and complex mission, one involving far more assets than just the SEAL platoon now on the ground.

The scene on the television monitor was a bird's-eye view of an airport; a large, four-engine aircraft, seen from almost directly overhead where it sat on the runway, was clearly visible. The points of light moving toward it were antlike in comparison.

But Coburn felt a thrill as he watched the screen. Those were *his* men moving like shadows across the television monitor. God, how he wanted to be with them!

"Feeling your age, Phil?" a soft voice murmured at his side.

"Stuff it, Paul," he whispered back, and the other man grinned in the darkness.

Captain Paul Mason was Coburn's single friend and confidant in the room, and another veteran of the Teams in Nam. A training injury had knocked Mason out of the jump and PT quals twelve years back, though he still thought of himself as a SEAL. The Teams were like that. Once you were one of them, you never left, no matter what your current duty assignment might be. Now Mason was a staff officer, serving as a voice for the Teams with USSOCOM, the U.S. Special Operations Command that managed all SPECWAR groups, including the Army Special Forces and Delta Force, as well as the Navy SEALs.

Shared experience had made the two men friends. Mason was no longer qualified as a SEAL, while Coburn, though he'd maintained his quals over the years with a fiercely dedicated daily regimen of running, exercise, and workouts, was stuck behind a desk. His last field assignment had been Grenada, and at fifty years of age he could feel the inner clock ticking away. *Damn it,* he thought, staring at the monitor. *I should be there, not nursemaiding a bunch of suits and flags in a Fort Fumble basement!*

"I'm still not sure what the hell I'm seeing," a Navy admiral complained. His name was Thomas Bainbridge, and he was the commanding officer of NAVSPECWARGRU-Two, the Little Creek-based headquarters of the East Coast SEALs.

"Real-time thermal imaging, Admiral," Mason said smoothly. "Computer-enhanced and corrected to give a steady image from a single angle. Right now our Aurora is circling above Shuaba at ninety thousand feet . . . so high up you couldn't even see it from the ground in broad daylight, much less in the middle of the night. Its scanning infrared sensors are incredibly sensitive. What you're seeing is the body heat from our SEALs as they deploy for the assault. This lone guy here on the control tower is probably an Iraqi soldier. These white glows up here look like warm engines, probably a couple of jeeps parked there in the past couple of hours. And . . . looks like four more guards by the jeeps."

"There they go," an Air Force general said, pointing to the left side of the screen. "Can you get a close-up of that?"

A computer technician typed several characters, and the image on the screen changed, zeroing in on four ghostly shapes moving with short, leapfrogging rushes across the dark blue ground toward a cluster of green buildings. Three other shapes remained in place in the rear. Close inspection revealed one of them to be a man bracing a dark, elongated object atop a low hill.

That would be the team's sniper.

"The detail is absolutely amazing," an Army colonel remarked.

"Welcome to the twenty-first century, Colonel," one of the suits, a CIA liaison officer, said. "Warfare with all the comforts of home." He took a bite from a slice of pepperoni pizza, and some of the others chuckled.

Coburn said nothing, but continued to watch the stealthy deployment of his men on the screen. The comment about warfare in comfort rankled, but then, as friends of his in the Teams had often told him, "When an asshole gives you shit, you gotta consider the source."

Almost as though he'd read Coburn's thought, Mason winked at him.

Coburn rolled his eyes toward the ceiling, then leaned closer to the screen. "Could we see a wide-angle shot, please?" he asked quietly. The tight view requested earlier showed nothing but a single team sprinting toward the aircraft; there was a full platoon on the ground now, fourteen men, and he wanted to see the entire plan unfolding, not just one small part of it.

The technician typed in a command, and the C-130, huge on the screen, dwindled to a toy outside a tiny cluster of buildings.

According to plan, the two SEAL squads had approached the objective separately. Gold Squad was to neutralize the guards at the runway roadblock and in the control tower; Blue Squad would hit the guards outside the Hercules and board the aircraft itself. Coburn could just make out the flitting heat shadows of the two SEAL groups as they dispersed across the airfield. Two men appeared to be creeping up on the Iraqis at the roadblock. The others were moving to jump-off positions closer to the C-130.

"Fairyland, Tally Three" sounded over the room's speakers. *"Hot Iron, repeat, Hot Iron."*

General Bradley, one of the Air Force officers, cocked his head, listening to the murmured transmissions, relayed through an Air Force AWACS aircraft over northern Saudi Arabia. "Ah! There's Tally Three. Here we go!"

Tally Three was a pair of F-117 Stealth fighters circling south of al-Basra. When informed that the SEALs were going in, the black, arrowhead-shaped aircraft had swung north and commenced their approach. Their target was an Iraqi SAM site and command bunker dug into the hillside above the village of Zabeir. When the bunker went, the SEAL platoon would launch their assault.

The tension in the room was growing, tightening. Even here, in a darkened room thousands of miles from where the action was going down, Coburn felt the old combat reflexes kicking in. His senses were sharpened; it seemed that he could smell not only the pizza, but the breath and sweat and aftershave of each of the men present in the room. He could hear the tick and hum of the room's computers, the sigh of the air conditioner, the excitement in the anonymous radio voices of the AWACS crew as they noted the time and confirmed that Cowboy One, Two, and Three were all airborne.

He desperately wanted to be in the field again, on the ground with Third Platoon.

"Man, oh, man," the spook said, grinning. "*This* is the way to fight a war!"

Somehow, Coburn resisted the urge to drive that pizza slice down the man's throat with his fist.

0236 hours (Zulu +3)
Shuaba Airport, Iraq

"You got him?"

"He's dead meat, Skipper. He just don't know it yet." Brown lay prone at Cotter's side, the Remington braced on his left hand, motionless, his right eye pressed tight to the rubber shield of his starlight scope to keep the device from casting a telltale glow on his face. "Say the word 'n' I cap him."

Cotter checked his watch again. Tally Three ought to be sounding the starting gun almost any moment now. Invisible to radar, silent as death, an F-117 should have already loosed its Paveway II, sending the one-ton smart bomb gliding in along an invisible laser beam and right through the SAM bunker's front door. . . .

A yellow flash lit up the southeastern sky, sudden, startling, and utterly silent as it billowed skyward into an orange fireball unfolding from the hillside above Zabeir. Cotter kept his binoculars on the Iraqis near the C-130. All were standing in the open now, staring into the flames with gaping mouths.

"Knock, knock," Higgins said. "Avon calling."

Then the sound of the bomb blast thundered down from the hill, and Cotter's hand touched Brown's shoulder. "Do it!"

The sniper's rifle bucked in the SEAL's hands, its crack swallowed by the distant waterfall roar of the explosion. On the control tower's deck, the lone Iraqi guard pitched backward, dropped his weapon, then collapsed unmoving onto the walkway. Brown had already shifted targets, aiming toward the Hercules where the guards were pointing at the explosion and calling to one another. He fired again, and one of the Iraqis, the red triangle of the Republican Guard plainly visible on the sleeve of his fatigues, spun back into the boarding steps, arms akimbo.

Before his comrades could react, four night-clad figures,

torsos bulky with unfamiliar gear, faces painted black and heads shrouded by balaclavas and the insect-glitter of night-vision goggles, materialized out of the shadows and opened fire.

Brown shifted targets again and, one by one, began knocking out the spotlights surrounding the plane.

3

Hollywood depictions to the contrary, no sound-suppressed weapon is completely silent. The MP5SD3s carried by the three SEALs in the aircraft assault element came close, though, the high-speed whirr of their bolts louder than the stuttering cough of their firing. Roselli sent two quick three-round bursts into the center of mass of one of the Iraqi soldiers at a range of fifty meters, jerking the man back and tossing him aside like a string-cut puppet. To either side, Doc Ellsworth and Mac MacKenzie loosed sharp, controlled bursts in synch with Roselli's, taking down the last three Iraqi guards in the space of a couple of heartbeats. Boomer Garcia backed them up, ready with his M-16/M203 combo as he scanned the darkness encircling the C-130.

Roselli raced to the parked Hercules, feeling vulnerable. The terminal building loomed beyond the aircraft, the slanted windows of the control tower dark and empty and threatening. He ducked beneath the C-130's wing, pausing to put another three-round burst into the sprawled body of one of the Iraqi soldiers. Nearby, Doc made sure of another one.

During the mission planning, there'd been some discussion as to whether or not they should take prisoners, especially at this stage of the operation when some hard intel about whether or not the Iraqis had already boarded the aircraft would be

25

damned useful. The final decision had been that there would be no time to interrogate prisoners, no time to cross-check their stories for confirmation. Better to just hop-and-pop, relying on speed and surprise to overcome any bad guys waiting aboard the Herk. As for taking prisoners, well . . . shooting POWs was a direct violation of the Geneva Convention. Third Platoon's written orders directed them to handle prisoners "according to SOP," which everyone understood to mean that there would be none.

"Clear!" Ellsworth called from the other side of the aircraft.

"Clear!" MacKenzie called from the foot of the boarding ladder.

One Iraqi body lay on its back, left arm thrown across its chest in an awkward position. As Roselli approached, the arm slipped down and flopped limply onto the tarmac. Instinctively, he triggered a burst into the man's chest. "Clear!"

"Alfa, Bravo," MacKenzie said over his tactical radio. "Stage one, clear. Five tangos, five down. Going to stage two."

Tangos—SEAL talk for terrorists. These Iraqis weren't terrorists, Roselli knew. They were just soldiers, doing what they'd been told to do.

Unfortunately for them, the same could be said of Third Platoon, SEAL Seven. And the SEALs were *very* good at what they did, better, he thought with a natural and unassuming arrogance, than anyone else in the world.

"Let's move it, Razor," MacKenzie said, using Roselli's squad handle. "Up the ladder! Go! Go! Go!"

"Right, Big Mac." Slapping a fresh magazine into his H&K, Roselli braced himself, then sprinted for the boarding ladder at the side of the Hercules. It was dark—the searchlights aimed at the Herky Bird were gone now, courtesy of Magic Brown—and he'd slid his NVGs up on his head so that he wouldn't lose his peripheral vision in combat. He nearly fell headlong when he stumbled across the body of the Iraqi lying on the stairs, but then he was past and climbing, with Doc and Mac at intervals behind him, and Boomer mounting guard at the bottom with his 203 grenade launcher. The C-130's crew-access door was closed, but Roselli had the T-shaped key that opened it.

Slamming the heavy door back on its mount, he paused outside to see if anyone was going to react to his arrival with gunfire, then lunged through and into the interior.

Aboard the C-130 Hercules, the forward, port-side access opens onto a fore-and-aft passageway on the aircraft's port side. To the right, the passageway leads straight aft to the aircraft's cavernous cargo deck; to the left, it goes forward a few steps, then takes a sharp twist to the right and up several steep steps to the flight deck.

Roselli turned right, then went prone, MP5 at the ready and extending into the plane's hold. Behind him, Mac went left to clear the flight deck. Doc followed Roselli to help secure the hold.

On the cargo deck the only light came from a couple of battle lanterns hanging from the starboard bulkhead. In their pasty glare, Roselli could see a number of men milling about in confusion, some already on their feet, others just rising from blankets or sleeping bags scattered about the deck. Some wore civilian clothing, others military fatigues, though all had the blue armband of the UN. There were a couple of Land Rovers parked aft in front of the tail ramp, piled high with cardboard cartons.

Hours of practice in SEAL Team killing houses had trained Roselli to take in a room at a glance, separating the bad guys from the good in an instant. No one visible in that crowd was holding a weapon, though some wore pistol holsters. None had the look of focus or concentration that suggested he was carrying out some prearranged plan. To a man, they looked frightened, confused, and a more than a little dazed.

"What the hell's goin' on?" someone yelled in English. He was answered by an excited voice in French, then by someone else speaking what might have been Swedish.

"Everybody down!" Roselli bellowed, hoping the tone of his voice would carry the meaning to those who didn't speak English. "We are American Special Forces! Everybody down!" The babble of voices increased, and Roselli shouted again, his voice echoing in the hollow compartment. "American Special Forces! Everybody down!"

A big, blond man wearing a uniform and a blue beret approached, hands raised. "You are . . . Americans?"

"Please get down, sir," Roselli replied crisply, still on the deck, his MP5 unwavering. "I don't want to have to shoot you. *Now!*"

The man complied, and he barked an order at the others as he did so. In a few moments, everyone was lying flat on the deck. In moments more, the C-130 was secure. The UN inspectors looked terrified, and as Ellsworth moved past him to start checking the rest of the hold, Roselli could certainly understand why. The black fatigues and combat vests, heavy with pouches, grenades, magazines, and equipment; the faces painted black with only the eyes and lips showing through the greasepaint; the commo gear and NVGs pushed back on their heads, all combined to create a terrifying, nightmare image. The SEALs looked like invaders from some other, darker world.

As Ellsworth covered the plane's occupants, Roselli ran a quick count. There were fifteen UN inspectors aboard, plus the four-man crew of the Hercules. Nineteen for nineteen, and no ringers hiding among the hostages.

"Did any Iraqis come aboard?" Roselli asked the inspection team leader.

"N-no, sir! They gave us until dawn to surrender the records."

"Looks like we came just in the nick then," Ellsworth said, teeth showing very white against his black-painted face.

"Cargo deck clear!" Roselli called over the radio. "Hotels secure!"

Hotels meant hostages. Had there been bad guys on the plane the SEALs would have had to tie the hands of everyone aboard with plastic restraints and clear them one by one, but that wasn't necessary now. MacKenzie appeared a second later. "Flight deck's clear. Regular cakewalk." He touched his Motorola's transmit key. "Alfa, Bravo!" he called. "Stage two clear, negative tangos. We have the package! No damage!"

0239 hours (Zulu +3)
Shuaba runway, Iraq

"We have the package! No damage!"

Cotter heard those welcome words over the tactical channel and loosed a pent-up sigh of relief. The code phrase meant that all of the UN people were safe, the first half of the mission successfully accomplished.

Which left only the getaway.

"Alfa, this is Charlie!" That was Nicholson, one of the two Gold Squad men sent to take down the guards at the roadblock. "Clear! Four tangos down!"

That left one element of the assault still unspoken for. Delta, consisting of the rest of Gold Squad—DeWitt, Wilson, Fernandez, Holt, and Kosciuszko—had been assigned the daunting task of clearing the airport terminal facility, together with the attached air traffic control building that glowered over the parked Hercules like a prison guard tower.

"Delta, this is Alfa. Report."

For answer, there was only a series of clicks, a signal that element Delta was busy right now.

0242 hours (Zulu +3)
Shuaba control tower, Iraq

Electrician's Mate Second Class Charles Wilson, "Chucker" to his squad mates, braced himself on one side of the door, while Chief Kosciuszko took the other. This was the deadliest part of clearing a building, going through a closed door with no idea what was waiting for you on the other side. Reconnaissance by grenade was the preferred room-clearing technique, but the assault so far had been carried out in near-perfect silence, and the longer the SEAL assault team let the neighbors sleep, the better.

So Kos nodded to Chucker, and Chucker nodded back. The chief took a step back, kicked at the flimsy, hollow-core door, and smashed it open. In a smooth roll around the door frame, Wilson burst into the room, his H&K held high, tight, and ready.

Nothing. Several beds, one of which looked as if it had been slept in recently.

Neither man wore NVGs. Even low-light gear requires *some* light to work, and it had been decided before the mission that individual IR goggles, which "saw" heat instead of visible light, were too heavy to make bringing them along as well worthwhile. Instead, both men had flashlights taped underneath the heavy, sound-suppressor barrels of their MP5SD3s; they provided both light for searching darkened rooms, and a quick-and-dirty aim-assist device in a close-quarters firefight.

Chucker crouched to one side of the door, H&K still at the ready, as Kos rolled in and began searching the room. They moved swiftly and with few words. "Clear," Kosciuszko said, and withdrew from the room. Chucker noticed a closed door and tried the knob. Locked. He put his shoulder to it and the cheap lock gave easily. Inside, his flashlight revealed a tumble-down of empty cardboard boxes, a mop and a wheeled, metal bucket, piles of rags and cleaning supplies.

"Chucker!" sounded over his radio. "Move! Move!" Kos sounded worried. Time for the search was sharply limited.

"On my way."

"Kos, this is Rattler." That was Fernandez. "We're in traffic control. Negative, negative. No hostiles."

"Roger that," Kos said, still standing by the splintered door. "Extract. Two-IC, this is Kos. Terminal clear. Dry hump!"

"Copy," the squad leader, Lieutenant j.g. DeWitt, replied. "Move 'em out, Kos."

"On our way."

0245 hours (Zulu +3)
Shuaba runway, Iraq

"Alfa, Delta!" DeWitt's voice called over the tactical frequency. "Clear! Dry hump!"

Meaning they'd not found any guards inside the terminal complex. Cotter gave the scene another scan with his binoculars as worry tugged at his awareness. Had there only been ten Iraqis to begin with? To guard the UN Herky Bird and its treasure trove of stolen intelligence? Shit, there ought to be more, a *lot* more. Even if they hadn't heard the death-silent assault by the SEALs, they ought to be reacting by now to the explosion in Zabeir. Where the hell were they?

"You see any movement out there?" he asked Brown.

"Negative, Skipper. Nothin' but our own people."

"Stay on it. Gimme the sat comm, Professor." Higgins handed him the radio. "Sky Trapper, Sky Trapper," he called. "This is Blue Water."

"Blue Water, Sky Trapper" sounded over his headset a moment later. "Copy. Go ahead."

Sky Trapper was a Saudi Arabian AWACS aircraft manned, at least for tonight, by U.S. Air Force personnel. The airborne communications and radar early warning plane was orbiting over northern Saudi Arabia, serving as a command center for the far-flung assets of Operation Blue Sky.

"Sky Trapper, Blue Water. Cold Steel, authentication Charlie India two-three. We have the package intact, repeat, we have the package intact. We're ready for delivery. Tell Cowboy and Shotgun to get their asses in gear!"

"Ah, roger that, Blue Water. Be advised that Shotgun should be over your position any time now. Cowboy is en route, ETA six minutes."

"Copy, Sky Trapper. We'll be waiting. Blue Water out."

Handing the sat-comm handset back to Higgins, Cotter paused and listened, straining against the darkness. Yes . . . he could just hear it now, the faint and far-off *whup-whup-whup* of approaching helicopters.

He changed channels on his Motorola, switching to a frequency that would link him to the entire SEAL platoon. "Blue and Gold, this is Papa One. Helos are inbound. Don't shoot 'em down, they're on our side. Two-IC?"

"Copy, Papa One," DeWitt replied. "Go ahead."

"Start bringing your people in, two at a time."

"Roger, Papa One, wilco."

"Out."

The plan was moving like clockwork now, each man with an assignment, each man with a place. Right now, Cotter's place was at the Herky Bird with the rest of his unit. He touched

Higgins's shoulder. "I'm going in there. You two stay put until Cowboy One touches down, then hustle on in, okay?"

"Right, L-T."

"Magic?"

"Yeah, Skipper?"

"You did good. Real nice shooting on those two tangos. Two for two."

Brown's face split in a wide grin. "Hey, thanks, Skipper!"

Cotter believed in giving praise where praise was due. He'd been concerned, naturally enough, about the cherries in the platoon—and Magic Brown had been one of them. The quartermaster first class had been in the Navy for ten years, but he'd only been a SEAL for one, and this was his first time in combat. No matter how hard a man trains, no matter how grueling his indoctrination, there is no way to tell how he will act the first time he has to actually kill another human being. Brown had come through his baptism of fire and blood splendidly.

Rising, Cotter left the shelter of the low ridge and trotted toward the C-130. In the distance, the glare from the exploded SAM bunker had dwindled to a sullen flicker, and the aircraft was almost lost in the darkness. Damn. Where were the rest of the Iraqis, partying in town? Fleeing toward al-Basra? Getting ready to spring their trap? Cotter didn't like this situation one damned bit.

0245 hours (Zulu +3)
Shuaba control tower, Iraq

The rumbling boom of the explosion had brought him wide awake in an instant. While his partner Ibrahim had stood guard on the walkway outside, Sergeant Riad Jasim had been catching a brief nap in a duty room inside the control tower; but now fire stained the sky, Ibrahim was dead, and strange, black-garbed men were swarming among the shadows beneath the UN aircraft.

Terrified, Jasim had hidden inside a second-floor storeroom as someone banged up the control tower steps outside. He cringed as they slammed open the door to the storeroom, but he was hidden behind a pile of empty boxes and—praise be to Allah!—the intruders had no time for a thorough search.

When they left, he sagged back against the concrete block wall, trembling with relief.

Jasim spoke no English, but he had a good ear. He'd heard the language spoken before, during the heroic Mother of All Battles when his supreme commander, the glorious Saddam, had halted the enemy invaders at the gates of Iraq with the mere threat of his terrible weapons. "Terminal clear! Dry hump!" was English, Jasim was sure of it, even if the words themselves were gibberish. The Americans were here, attempting to liberate their spy plane!

When the heavy-booted intruders had left, Jasim had slipped out of the storeroom and up the steps to the glassed-in control tower. There, flat on his belly, heart pounding, he edged toward the glass door leading out onto the circular walkway that encircled the tower. He'd left his AKM assault rifle outside, with Ibrahim.

He was no hero. He'd been a simple farmer from al-Kut until the army had drafted him, but he believed in Saddam Hussein as the soul and savior of the Iraqi people, and he knew that Paradise awaited him if he died fighting the infidel Americans.

Slipping through the open door, he crawled onto the walkway. Ibrahim lay across his path, eyes open and staring, blood soaking the front of his uniform.

"My friend," Jasim told the corpse. "I will avenge you!"

But the brave words could not stop the trembling weakness he felt within. Somehow, he forced himself to go on. Retrieving his rifle and chambering a round, he inched himself closer to the edge of the walkway.

0248 hours (Zulu +3)
Shuaba Airport, Iraq

By the time Lieutenant Cotter reached the C-130, the platoon was already deploying in a loose perimeter about the aircraft. Two Gold Platoon men, Fernandez and Holt, were already setting out four strobe beacons in a Y-shaped pattern, the top of the Y marking a safe LZ for a helicopter, the tail indicating the wind direction. MacKenzie met Cotter at the perimeter. The big master chief had slung his H&K and broken out his machine gun. Crouching there on the tarmac with that big gun in his hands and a belt of 7.62mm ammo draped over his shoulder, the Texan looked a bit like a black-faced, black-fatigued Rambo.

Except that Rambo never would have stood a chance against these night-clad killers. They moved with an efficient deadliness Hollywood could never portray and which movie-going audiences would find frankly unbelievable. Cotter felt a swelling, glowing pride for his men as he entered the perimeter. They were the best, absolutely and without qualification.

"Platoon, this is Blue Five!" Ellsworth's voice snapped over the radio. "I've got movement. Two . . . maybe three hostiles. Bearing one-seven-five, range one-one-zero meters. Near the big hangars."

Side by side, Cotter and MacKenzie dropped prone, scanning the southern end of the airfield with their NVGs.

"Don't see 'em, Skipper. You?"

"Negative." Cotter replied. He thumbed his Motorola. "Boomer! This is Papa One! Toss 'em a package, will you? Let's see if they'll party."

"Sure thing, Skipper. On the way!"

There was a hollow-sounding *thunk* nearby, and the 40mm grenade from Garcia's M203 arced into the shadows, then exploded with a flash and a savage roar. The thin sheet metal of the hangar buckled and tore, and one uniformed body flopped out onto the tarmac in a bloody sprawl. From the other side of the hangar, an assault rifle opened up with the characteristic flat cracking of an AKM, the muzzle flash flickering and stabbing against the shadows.

MacKenzie returned fire with his M-60, sending a burst of green tracers streaking into the night. Someone over there in the shadows shrieked in agony. The 203 *thunk*ed again, and this time the hangar was engulfed in a flaming maelstrom of exploding white phosphorus. Flaming fragments arced across a hundred yards onto the tarmac, streaming contrails of twisting white smoke.

"Nice'n neat with ol' Willie Pete," Boomer called.

Half of the hangar was burning furiously now. Several Iraqis ran screaming out onto the runway, their uniforms ablaze, only to be put down by sharp, short bursts from the waiting SEALs. The fire revealed a large number of other Iraqis running wildly in the opposite direction, up the hill toward Zabeir, most without rifles, belts, or helmets, many without shirts, a few without clothing.

"I think we popped their barracks," MacKenzie observed dryly. A trio of armed Iraqis broke across the tarmac, angling toward the Hercules, and he shifted the M-60, then cut them down one, two, three. "Looks like they've decided it's time to *di di mau*."

"Roger that, Mac. Keep knocking 'em down. Our choppers are incoming."

With a roar, a machine like a huge, metallic dragonfly thundered over the airstrip, the light from the burning hangar glinting from the angled sides of its canopy. Painted dark olive, the aircraft was a U.S. Marine AH-1W SuperCobra, fitted with an infrared night-vision system and an M197 undernose turret.

"Blue Water, Blue Water" sounded over Cotter's air-ground channel. "This is Shotgun One/one. What's going on down there, Navy? Bit off more'n you could chew? Over."

"That's a negative, One/one," Cotter replied. "But we do have some unfriendly types who want to party. How about taking down those hangars one hundred meters south of the landing beacons, over."

"Roger, roger. Never fear, the Marines are here, and the situation is well in hand." The SuperCobra clattered overhead again, its skids at telephone-pole height above the runway. When the three-barreled 20mm Gatling cannon in its nose turret cut loose, it sounded like the high-pitched rasp of a chain saw. Downrange, sheet-metal hangars, maintenance sheds, and storehouses disintegrated in shrieking storms of whirling fragments.

A second SuperCobra arrived seconds later, call sign Shotgun One/two. The pair split up and began orbiting the SEAL perimeter, flying low both to spook hidden Iraqis into showing themselves and to discourage further attacks on Blue Water. Any Iraqi sniper in the area was going to think twice before opening fire with those birds of prey circling, talons exposed and ready.

The Marine SuperCobras had been stationed on a Marine helicopter carrier, the *Tripoli,* now with II MEF in the Arabian Sea south of Pakistan. As soon as word of the crisis at al-Basra had reached Washington, they'd been directed to hopscotch from the *Tripoli* to al-Masirah to Masqat, then up the Gulf coast to Dubayy to Dahran to al-Kuwayt, refueling at each stop along the way. They were gunships, not transports, their nose cannon, rocket pods, and Hellfire missiles designed to give close support to the troops on the ground.

Half a mile away, a concrete bunker dissolved in orange flame as Shotgun One/two speared it with a Hellfire. The night was bloody with flame and roiling smoke and the thunder of high explosives.

Iraq certainly knew they were at Shuaba now. At this point, the SEALs had scant minutes to extract before the full weight of Saddam's war machine moved to crush them.

4

Coming in behind the first SuperCobras, and escorted by two more, were three CH-53D Sea Stallions—Cowboy One, Two, and Three—the Marine helicopter transports that would take the SEALs and the rescued UN inspectors to safety. Their unmistakable racket was clattering out of the west now, coming in at treetop height.

"Blue Water, Blue Water" sounded over Cotter's radio. "This is Cowboy. Please authenticate."

"Boomer!" Cotter yelled. "Pop 'em a six-sixty-two!"

"Roger, boss!" A moment later, Garcia's grenade launcher thumped again, and an M662 red flare popped into gleaming, bloody visibility high overhead, drifting back toward the airfield on its parachute.

"Blue Water, I see a red flare. I'm coming in."

"Roger that, Cowboy. We're ready to ramble. You should see the beacons any time now."

"Roger, Blue Water. Beacons in sight. Looks like you boys have a hot LZ down there."

"We're not taking any fire at the moment, Cowboy. You're clear to land."

"Copy, Blue Water. We'll send in Cowboy Three first." One of the Sea Stallions loomed out of the night, huge and noisy.

37

"Okay!" Cotter called over the platoon channel. "Start sending them out!"

His orders laid down the evacuation procedure. The records from the al-Basra "factory" would go out on the first helo, with the UN inspectors doing the loading while the SEALs held the perimeter. The inspectors would extract on the second helo, and the SEALs on the third. The orders had a certain amount of built-in flexibility. One Sea Stallion could carry up to fifty-five troops and all their gear; if two of the Sea Stallions broke down or were disabled, nineteen ex-hostages and fourteen SEALs, plus the hijacked Iraqi records, could all be easily transported aboard the third helo. One of the lessons learned at Desert One during the failed rescue of the American hostages in Iran was to allow plenty of redundancy in a rescue mission's helicopter assets.

The first Sea Stallion was touching down now, its rotors howling, dust swirling up from the tarmac in a blinding, stinging cloud. Two more CH-53s circled with the gunships, vague yet menacing shadows against the night.

0249 hours (Zulu +3)
Shuaba control tower, Iraq

Riad Jasim had never been so terrified in his life, not even when the American B-52s had bombed his encampment in northern Kuwait during the Mother of All Battles, churning up the desert like some monstrous, demonic plow turning the soil. Helicopters clattered and circled, great, evil insects waiting to pounce, and he was convinced that they saw him, they *must* see him, lying here in the open on the control tower walkway. He played dead, praying desperately. The hangars at the south end of the field were blazing furiously, and Jasim knew that the rest of the Republican Guard company that had quartered there was dead or in flight. He was alone, more alone than he'd ever been in his life.

But somehow, somehow he had to do *something*!

Cautiously, Jasim raised his head, peering down over the edge of the tower walkway. . . .

0250 hours (Zulu +3)
Shuaba Airport, Iraq

"Let's go! Let's go!" Cotter pumped his arm in an urgent hurry-up as the two Land Rovers rumbled down the rear ramp of the Hercules and onto the tarmac. In single file, the UN inspectors trotted after them, shepherded along by Roselli and Ellsworth. There'd been no further gunfire from the nearby airport buildings for several minutes now, and the other SEALs stood or crouched at various points encircling the C-130, their attention focused on the flame-shot darkness around them.

"Are you in charge here?"

Cotter turned. A slight, bearded man in civilian clothes, khaki slacks and a safari jacket, stood behind him, a briefcase clutched incongruously in one hand.

"What the hell?"

"I gotta talk to you," the civilian said. The roar from the grounded Sea Stallion was deafening, and he had to shout to make himself heard. "I'm Arkin! I imagine you have special orders concerning me!"

Cotter sighed. This must be the spook from the CIA—the intelligence organization the SEALs derisively called Christians In Action. He didn't have time to screw with this shit now.

"Everything is under control, Mr. Arkin," he said. "If you'll go back with the others and—"

Arkin hefted the briefcase. "I've got important intel here, fella, and it's got to get out right away. I can't wait for the rest of that shit to be loaded on the helicopters."

"You'll go out with the others on the second helo, Mr. Arkin. You'll go faster if you help your friends load number one."

"No! I can't wait! I want—"

Cotter reached out and closed his left hand on the front of Arkin's collar, pulling him up on his toes and bringing his face to within inches of his own. "I don't give a fuck *what* you want, mister! Get your ass back with the others, and I mean *now*!"

He released the man with a shove that nearly sent him sprawling. Arkin gaped at Cotter, looked as though he was about to say something more, then apparently thought better of it, shrugged, and turned away. . . .

0250 hours (Zulu +3)
Shuaba control tower, Iraq

From his vantage point fifteen meters above the ground, Sergeant Jasim could see the bustle of activity on the runway below. The two Land Rovers were approaching the big helicopter transport, which was squatting now on the runway with its rotors still turning. The UN spies with their blue armbands were trotting along behind their vehicles, as the black-suited commandos in their weird, bug-faced masks stood at the ready, their weapons probing the encircling night. Could they see him? Apparently not. At least they were not shooting at him, but appeared to be simply standing guard, watchful and deadly.

Jasim would get only one good burst from his rifle. He knew and accepted that. But at which target? There were so many.

Visibility was poor with the airport's lights shot out, but there was enough illumination from the burning hangars to reveal two men off to one side of the UN aircraft, obviously engaged in a heated conference. One was dressed like the other commandos in black, anonymous. The other, in light-colored civilian slacks and jacket and a blue armband, was an easy target, and the briefcase he was holding suggested that he might be a man of some importance.

The circling helicopter gunships were farther away now, searching for Jasim's comrades in the surrounding hills. Breathing a final prayer to Allah, Riad Jasim aimed his AKM carefully, taking his time to align the sights as he'd been taught, hold his breath, and slowly squeeze the trigger. . . .

0250 hours (Zulu +3)
Shuaba Airport, Iraq

Cotter watched the Agency spook stalk back toward the line of UN people still emerging from the Hercules. The self-important little bastard would probably file a report back at

Langley, contending that he'd not received the necessary cooperation from the SEAL platoon tasked with extracting him.

Screw him. Cotter had gone rounds with the Agency's Christians before, and the exchange had never been pleasant. . . .

He caught the wink of a full-auto muzzle flash in the corner of his eye, felt rather than heard the savage snap of bullets cleaving the air inches above his head. Arkin was ten feet away, his back to the SEAL lieutenant, completely unaware that they were being shot at. Without thinking, Cotter launched himself forward, tackling the CIA man from behind just as the unseen gunner corrected his aim. Arkin *oof*ed as he went down hard beneath the SEAL and the briefcase skittered loose across the tarmac.

Something slammed into Cotter's side, then his right arm, then his back, the impacts painless but savagely hard, like hammer blows. For a dazed moment, he didn't know where he was. Why was he on his back, on the ground? . . .

0250 hours (Zulu +3)
Shuaba Airport, Iraq

Roselli had seen the Lieutenant knock the UN guy flat, then seen Cotter plucked from the man's back by an unseen hand and rolled off onto the tarmac. He'd not heard the gunshots above the roar of the helicopter, but he could tell from the way the Lieutenant had been thrown that they'd come from high up and *that* way, from the top of the terminal building tower.

He cut loose with a long burst from his MP5, screaming "Cover! Cover! Sniper on the tower!" as loud as he could. Other SEALs reacted in the same instant. MacKenzie sent a stream of green tracers slashing through the terminal's windows, and then Garcia's M203 spoke, slamming a 40mm grenade into the tower walkway, where it detonated with a flash and a bang and a sparkling shower of steel fragments and broken glass. Bodies . . . no, *pieces* of bodies spun lazily through the air, accompanied by an avalanche of shattered bricks and concrete.

Roselli was beside the Lieutenant in a second, crouching over him. "L-T! L-T! Can you hear me?" Oh, God, his blacks were sticky with blood. Shit, shit, *shit*! Where was all the damned blood coming from? The Skipper was wearing a Kevlar bullet-proof combat vest, of course, but it looked like he'd taken a round in the right shoulder. That was okay . . . sure. A ticket home and his arm in a sling, but he'd be up and back in full working mode in a few weeks, just like in the fucking movies. . . .

"Outa my way, Chief!" Doc Ellsworth was there, shoving him aside. Roselli didn't want to leave. "Damn it, Chief, out of the way! I've got him!"

Turning, Roselli stared up at the control tower. The large, slanted windows had been blown out, and one side looked as though a giant had taken a hungry bite out of it. "Two-IC!" he yelled over the tactical channel. "This is Roselli!"

"DeWitt here," he heard. "Go ahead."

"The L-T's down! Damn it, I thought you said that fuckin' tower was fuckin' *clear*!"

"Okay, Razor. Chill out." He heard a click as DeWitt changed channels. "Platoon, this is Two-IC. The Lieutenant's down. I've got command. Acknowledge!"

"I hear you," MacKenzie's voice replied. "Blue copies."

"Acknowledged, Lieutenant," Chief Kosciuszko's voice added. "Gold copies!"

The man Cotter had knocked down was sitting up nearby, cradling his arm and rocking back and forth. "I'm hit! I'm hit! God, I'm hit!"

Roselli crouched beside him. It looked like a round had punched through the guy's safari jacket sleeve, bloodying his arm. A graze, nothing more. "You'll live," he said bluntly. "Hold still." He popped open one of his pouches, pulled out a roll of gauze, and quickly wrapped the man's arm.

"My attaché case. Where's my attaché case?"

Roselli retrieved it. "Here. Now get the fuck back with the rest of your people."

"But—"

"*Move* it, you numb-nuts dumb-ass son of a bitch!" The UN man blinked at him in shock, then scrambled away, clutching his briefcase to his chest. Roselli turned back to Ellsworth.

"How's the L-T, Doc? Just a shoulder, right?"

"Shut up, Razor." Something in his voice, the intensity of his expression as he lifted Cotter's arm and probed his side with bloody fingers, told Roselli that it was more than a flesh wound. He could see the blood welling up beneath the Lieutenant's bullet-proof vest, coming through the vest's arm-hole just beneath his arm. Ellsworth started packing the space with whole rolls of gauze.

Cotter's head rolled to one side. "Doc . . ."

"You lay still, Skipper. You took a round in the side."

"Can't . . . feel m'legs."

"Shit." Ellsworth looked at Roselli. "Damn it, Razor, make yourself useful! Get me a Stokes from the helo!"

"Right, Doc."

The UN people had finished off-loading the cardboard boxes from the two Land Rovers onto the first Sea Stallion, then pulled back as the pilot fed power to the rotors and lifted from the tarmac with shrill thunder. Seconds later, the number-two Sea Stallion touched down in the beacon-lit spot evacuated by the first. As the crew chief lowered the rear ramp, Roselli ran up and jumped aboard. "We got a man down!" he yelled. "Gimme a Stokes!"

The crew chief pulled a Stokes stretcher off the bulkhead, a lightweight, open coffin-shape of wire mesh and white canvas straps used for transporting wounded. Roselli carried it back to Ellsworth on the double, then helped the corpsman gently lift Cotter into the basket.

"He took a round right through the armhole in his vest," Ellsworth said as they strapped him down securely. He spoke rapidly, and Roselli had the impression that he wasn't even speaking directly to him. "Collapsed his right lung and I think it went out through his spine! Damned, damned bad luck the Kevlar didn't catch it! Shit! Shit! Friggin' blood loss. Did it nick the post-caval? Gotta get him BVEs, stat." Doc looked up at Roselli suddenly. "C'mon! Help me with him. Easy now."

Wildly, fragments of first-aid training flitted through Roselli's mind. *Don't move a victim with a back injury!* Except when leaving him where he was would be more dangerous.

The second Sea Stallion was loading now, the rescued UN inspectors and Hercules crewmen filing aboard between two SEALs standing guard. Among them, Roselli glimpsed the man Cotter had saved, marked by the white bandages on his arm, his briefcase clutched to his chest like a shield. Good riddance to the bastard. If the L-T hadn't been trying to save his ass . . .

Commands crackled over Roselli's radio, but none included his call sign and he ignored them. The SEAL platoon was starting to pull back from the airport buildings. The Sea Stallion was loaded, its ramp closing like the jaw of some gape-mouthed fish. The helo rose from the tarmac in a whirlwind of noise and dust, then swung low across the runway, angling toward the west and vanishing into night. One of the SuperCobras paced it.

Ellsworth and Roselli positioned themselves on either side of Cotter's Stokes, grabbed the carry straps, and lugged him toward the LZ where the third transport chopper was just touching down. Together, with an assist from the Marine crew chief, they hoisted him onto the Sea Stallion before the rear ramp was all the way down, then scrambled aboard themselves. Two by two, the rest of the SEALs followed. Three savage explosions ripped through the night as the trucks parked next to the terminal exploded one after the other. Garcia and Frazier, Gold Squad's demo man, had been busy setting charges while the rest of the SEALs covered the perimeter.

That perimeter was shrinking now as more and more of the SEALs climbed up the Sea Stallion's ramp. MacKenzie and Lieutenant j.g. DeWitt were the last two men aboard.

"Let's go!" DeWitt yelled, holding his microphone to his lips, making a circling motion with his free hand. "All aboard! Haul ass!"

With a roar, the Sea Stallion lifted into the night sky, turning toward the west. As Roselli stared out the still-open rear doors, he watched the C-130 parked in front of the Shuaba terminal, kept watching as the Hercules crumpled, an orange flower blossoming from the root of its port wing. Then the fuel tanks touched off, and in seconds the UN C-130 was a single sheet of flame, its fuselage and wings a wire-work skeleton half glimpsed through the raging, hungry blaze. Smaller explosions took out the two Land Rovers an instant later, tearing out their guts and scattering smoking bits of engine across the runway. When the Iraqis returned with the dawn to reclaim their airport, they would find not one vehicle, not one piece of American equipment left behind intact for them to claim as spoils of war. With a whine, the ramp slid up and the rear doors clamped shut, cutting off Roselli's view of Shuaba.

He turned back to Ellsworth, who was still working on the L-T. The Stokes was lying in the center of the chopper's cargo deck, and a clear plastic oxygen mask had been strapped over Cotter's paint-blacked face. There were bubbles of blood clustered around the Lieutenant's nostrils, and more blood at the corner of his mouth. His breathing beneath the mask was rasping and labored, audible even over the roar of the Sea Stallion's rotors. MacKenzie was kneeling beside the Stokes, holding a plastic bottle filled with clear liquid aloft as the Doc threaded a thick needle into a vein in Cotter's left inside elbow. The other SEALs of Third Platoon, along with the helo's Marine crew chief, watched from a circle about the tableau, impassive. They all knew that if Doc couldn't save the Skipper, nobody could.

"Shit," Doc said, rocking back on his heels. His arms were bloody, clear to his elbows. He pried up one of Cotter's eyelids, staring at the pupil. "How long to Kuwait?"

"It's almost a hundred miles to Kuwait City," the Marine crew chief said. "Call it thirty minutes."

"Shit, shit, *shit*!" Doc started unzipping and unhooking the L-T's combat gear and discarding it on the helo's deck, using a pair of blunt-tipped bandage scissors to cut away his fatigue shirt. Roselli helped, as MacKenzie continued to hold the IV bottle in the air. By the light of the helo's battle lanterns, the L-T's skin looked death-pale where it wasn't crusted with blood.

Roselli felt a creeping, nightmare presentiment. He'd seen death before.

He'd had been in the Navy for twelve years and in the Teams for seven. His first time under fire had been in Panama, where he'd been wounded in the assault at Paitilla Airfield. Four of his squad mates had been the very first American fatalities of Operation Just Cause, four good friends killed in a clusterfuck where elite SEALs had been thrown like cannon fodder against barricaded defenders with machine guns, then ordered to hold the position all night for reinforcements that were late in arriving.

The bond between members of a SEAL platoon is close, closer than any other human relationship Roselli could imagine. Though he wasn't married, he knew SEALs who were . . . and to a man they seemed to value the camaraderie of their fellow SEALs and swim buddies more than they did their own wives.

Thinking of wives reminded Roselli of Donna, Cotter's wife. And they had a kid. Oh, damn . . . *damn!*

0305 hours (Zulu +3)
Helo Cowboy One

Cotter awoke, aware of faces bending over him, fuzzy against the glare of lights. Pain . . . he felt pain . . . but it wasn't as bad as he'd thought it would be. Funny, he couldn't feel a thing below his diaphragm.

"Where? . . ."

Was that Doc's face peering down into his? Hard to tell. "We're aboard the helo, L-T," Doc's voice said. "You just rest easy."

"The . . . men?" It was hard to speak, hard to make himself heard. Each breath was a small agony, and he wasn't sure Doc could hear above the background roar of the rotors.

Doc's face dipped lower, turning. "What was that, sir?"

"The . . . the men. Get them . . . out. . . ."

"Everybody got out, Skipper. You're the only one who stopped a bullet. Why the friggin' hell didn't you duck?" Doc's voice was light, bantering, but Cotter could hear the tightness behind the words. "Damn it, what kind of example is that for you to set for your men?"

"Mission? . . ."

"All three helos made it out, Skipper. Everybody made it out.

Mission complete. Now shut the hell up and let me work. You've got a hole in your side and you're losing blood. Understand me? Skipper? Do you hear me?"

Cotter heard, though the faces and lights had blurred to a soft and indistinguishable white haze. Was he dying? His thoughts touched lightly on Donna and Vickie, but they slipped away. Somehow, he couldn't hold onto the memory of their faces, and that raised a small stab of guilt. He tried to draw a breath, bracing against the pain . . . but nothing would come. He tasted blood, hot and thick and choking, weighing down his throat and chest. Couldn't breathe. . . .

His boys were all out safe. That was good. And the mission a success . . . what had it been? He tried to think, couldn't remember. Oh, yeah. Training mission, working with the Marines at Vieques, the big island east of Puerto Rico. It was nice there, a tropical paradise. Sunny beaches. Warm water. He loved Puerto Rico. Training session. How had he been hurt? Accidents happened, even in training . . . especially in SEAL training.

Goddamn, he was proud of his boys, every one of them. The best warriors, the best men in the whole God damned world.

The white haze was turning dark around the outside, like a tunnel. Funny. He couldn't even remember Donna's face, but he could see the SEALs he'd worked with and commanded over the years, every one of them, like they were right there with him.

"Proud . . . of . . . you," he said.

Damn he was proud of his boys. . . .

0306 hours (Zulu +3)
Helo Cowboy One

"Lieutenant!" Ellsworth was kneeling over the Stokes, both hands on the center of Cotter's chest, pumping down on a heart that stubbornly refused to beat. "God damn it, don't you die on me! Lieutenant!"

Roselli, at the L-T's head, had pulled off the O_2 mask at Doc's instructions and was holding an AMBU mask over

Cotter's bloody nose and mouth, squeezing the inflated bag to ventilate the Skipper's lungs.

Doc kept pumping at the Skipper's chest. "L-T! SEALs don't quit! They don't know *how* to quit! They're too *stupid* to quit! Lieutenant!"

At last, though, Ellsworth slumped back on his haunches, a stricken look on his face. "Goddamnit," he said, his voice empty. "God damn it to *hell*!"

"You did what you could, Doc," MacKenzie said.

Roselli stared at the L-T's face, stunned. The Lieutenant *couldn't* be dead . . . he couldn't!

Abruptly, Ellsworth shook off Mac's hand and resumed pumping at Cotter's heart, but Roselli already knew it was too late. They would keep working at him until they got him aboard a medevac at K-City, but it wasn't going to do one damned bit of good.

The Skipper was dead. *Dead.* Blown away by some half-assed rag-head who probably barely knew one end of a rifle from the other.

Roselli felt like he wanted to cry.

5

Friday, 6 May

0950 hours (Zulu −5)
SEAL Seven Administrative Headquarters
Little Creek, Virginia

It was an informal hearing, though the two naval officers and one senior enlisted man sitting at the panel flanked by the U.S. and U.S. Navy flags gave the proceedings the air of a court-martial. Captain Coburn sat at the folding table between his Exec, Commander Monroe, and Senior Chief Hawkins. Morning sunlight filtered through the venetian blinds drawn over the windows. Chief Roselli stood in front of them at parade rest, feet braced apart and hands behind his back, but otherwise as rigid as if he'd been at attention.

"But when Lieutenant Cotter was hit," Coburn said, "it *was* your impression that the terminal building had already been cleared, was it not, Chief?"

"I don't know, sir. Things were kind of confused there for a bit."

"Sky Trapper was recording your communications at the time, Chief. Your exact words to Lieutenant DeWitt were, I believe . . ." He picked up a paper on the table and read from it. "Yes. 'The L-T is down. Damn it, I thought you said that fucking tower was fucking clear.'"

"Actually, Captain, I think I said something more like, uh, 'The L-T is down. Damn it. I shoulda snuck in, uh, snuck in and made sure it stayed clear.' Something like that. You know, sometimes it's kind of hard to make out what's being shouted over the Motorolas. Sir."

"Mmm. Understood." Coburn dropped the transcript and leaned back, his weight causing the folding metal chair to creak beneath him.

Coburn had been a SEAL for a long, long time, and he knew that Roselli was covering for DeWitt. SEALs always took care of their own. *Always*.

Monroe stirred at Coburn's side. "So what was your assessment of the tactical situation, Chief? Why wasn't the tower properly cleared?"

"Aw, shit, sir. It was a big building, lots of rooms. We only had one platoon with a shitload of objectives. We just had four guys in the Delta element, plus Lieutenant DeWitt, to clear the tower. They could've missed someone, or a bad guy could've sneaked in after they'd gone through."

"In your opinion, should someone have been posted on that tower after it was cleared?"

Roselli shook his head. "That would've been hard to manage, sir. We were stretched damned thin as it was with only fourteen guys. And we would've had to abandon the terminal anyway when we started pulling in the perimeter. I don't think we should've done things any differently than we did."

"I see," Coburn said. "Very well, Chief. Thank you very much. You're dismissed."

"Aye, aye, sir." Roselli turned, then stopped himself. "Uh, Captain?"

"Yes, Chief?"

"I just wanted to say that every man in the platoon did a wizard job on that op. And that includes Lieutenant DeWitt. If we'd had more men, maybe the L-T wouldn't've bought it. I don't know. But I don't think we can second-guess any of that now."

"We'll keep that in mind. Thank you, Chief."

After Roselli had left, Coburn looked at the papers on the table before him. "Is that it, George?"

"Yes, sir," Monroe replied. They'd spent most of the previous day and all of that morning interviewing the men of

Third Platoon. Their report, the result of the inquiry, would go up the chain of command to Rear Admiral Bainbridge, CO-NAVSPECWARGRU-Two.

The responses from the men had been interesting. Ellsworth was blaming himself for not being able to save Cotter, while DeWitt, naturally, had assumed responsibility for Cotter's death because Delta had missed the sniper in the terminal building. Every man in the platoon except DeWitt had formed a united front, insisting that DeWitt and Delta were not to blame for Cotter's death. Garcia, Frazier, Holt, and Nicholson had all suggested that the terminal *could* have been blown up after it was searched, but admitted that the sniper could well have slipped in from someplace else, in which case he could have capped the Lieutenant from the rubble as easily as from the tower walkway. Coburn knew from long experience that there was no way to second-guess the men on the ground from the safe and sane security of some CONUS headquarters basement.

He had a feeling, though, that there was going to be one hell of a lot of second-guessing this time around. Ever since the new Administration had come in, the political climate in Washington had turned distinctly chilly toward the military, and *especially* toward the military's elite forces. There were people in the House and on Capitol Hill, including the current head of the House Military Affairs Committee, who distrusted the elites, who associated covert operations with black, dirty, or illegal ops, with "wetwork" and lying to Congress. Hell, there were admirals and generals at the Pentagon who hated the special-operations forces, who claimed the elites grabbed the best men, the best equipment, and the lion's share of dwindling military appropriations. Together, the anti-special-forces people in the Pentagon and the anti-military people in Congress had formed an unlikely alliance with the goal of eliminating the elite military forces entirely. To that end, the HMAC had been holding special, televised meetings all week on the subject of special-forces appropriations, and the way things were going so far, it was all too likely that the SEALs were going to be closed down.

Coburn's entire naval career had spanned most of the SEAL Teams' existence. It hurt to think they might soon be cut. *God damn it to hell,* he thought. *I'd like to see a* battleship *pull off what Third Platoon just did!*

"So, Captain?" Senior Chief Hawkins said, jolting Coburn's darkening thoughts. "What's the verdict?"

"Oh, DeWitt's in the clear. I have no doubts about that. You two?"

"Agreed," Monroe said. "My God, jerking nineteen men out from under the noses of a Republican Guard battalion, with only one wounded among the hostages?"

"And only one casualty among the raiding forces. That's pretty damned good, no matter how you look at it. The whole platoon did magnificently. I'll stress that in my report."

"Roger that, sir," Hawkins said dryly. "But will they buy it up on the Hill?"

"God knows, Ed. The way things have been going up there lately, we're going to be lucky if we have a Navy left when they get done with their cuts." He stood, gathering his papers. "Well, gentlemen, let's get squared away and get the hell out of here. We have long drives ahead of us if we're going to make that funeral this afternoon."

1615 hours (Zulu −5)
Arlington National Cemetery

Rank upon rank upon gleaming white rank of tombstones graced those gentle, tree-shaped slopes of the Arlington National Cemetery. At the top of the hill among ancient, spreading oaks rested the brooding, white-pillared facade of the Custis-Lee Mansion, while opposite, across the dark, bridge-spanned reach of the Potomac, the white marble government buildings and monuments of Washington, D.C., shimmered beneath the haze-masked afternoon sun. Southeast, masked by trees, was the five-sided sprawl of the Pentagon; a mile to the northwest, also invisible, was the Iwo Jima Memorial. Arlington seemed suspended in time, removed somehow from the clutter and rush of the modern world, even when its stillness was broken by the roar of commercial airliners thundering over the Potomac from Washington National . . .

. . . or by the sharp report of volleyed rifle fire.

The last echoes of the military salute hung suspended above the lines of tombstones and the grassy hillsides. As the final crack of the third volley faded, a Navy bugler in dress blues raised his instrument to his lips and began intoning the mournful, drawn-out notes of Taps.

A casket rested above the open grave, attended by sailors and officers who stood in ranks in full-dress whites, and a smaller group of civilians. Much of SEAL Team Seven was present, all who could make it up from Norfolk, over fifty officers and men standing motionless in white-clad ranks.

The leaders of each formation held their hand salutes as Roselli and Holt lifted the American flag from the casket and, with crisp, precise movements, folded it corner over corner from fly to hoist, ending with a thick, white-starred blue triangle with no red showing.

Taps wavered to a lonesome end, and Chief Boatswain's Mate Kosciuszko snapped *"Two!"* As one, hands held rigid in salute dropped with a crack. Holding the flag, Roselli pivoted ninety degrees, took two steps, and pivoted again in a right-angle turn. Three more steps and another squared-off turn put him directly in front of Captain Coburn, commanding officer of SEAL Team Seven, and the presiding officer for the morning's solemn service.

Master Chief Engineman George MacKenzie watched, face hard, as the captain accepted the folded flag, waited for Roselli to return to ranks, then turned sharply and walked the few paces to the waiting huddle of civilians. Donna Cotter, in black, waited for him with lifted chin. Little Vickie, grave and somber in a dark gray dress, stood quietly at her mother's side, looking up at Coburn with large eyes.

Still at attention, MacKenzie strained to hear the old, proud, and formal words as Coburn leaned forward and spoke to the widow. "On behalf of a grateful nation and a proud Navy, I present this flag to you in recognition of your husband's years of honorable and faithful service, and his sacrifice for this nation."

Coburn handed Donna the folded flag, then saluted her. Across the neatly landscaped grass, the officer in charge of the rifle salute party rasped out, "Port . . . *harms!* Order . . . *harms!*"

Ritual. History. Tradition. Men died. The service went on.

"Honor detachment, dis . . . *missed!*"

The neat blocks of white dissolved. Small groups of two or three or four gathered here and there, talking in low voices. Others began the long walk back up the hill to the parking lot beyond Halsey Drive.

MacKenzie waited, uncomfortable in the stiff and unaccustomed embrace of his whites, as a small mob of people, military and civilian, filed up to Donna Cotter, speaking to her, clasping her hands, touching her pain. It was a long line. The Navy community was close, the Navy's Special Warfare community closer still. There was no one present on that hillside, military or civilian, who didn't know what being a SEAL—or a SEAL's wife—meant.

George MacKenzie, born and raised far from the sea in Midland, Texas, had been in the Navy for eighteen years, a SEAL for fourteen. Tall, lanky, normally quiet almost to the point of invisibility, he was the son of an air-conditioning repairman who'd never been in the service. He'd joined the Navy because by the time he'd graduated from high school, he'd been sick to death of the endlessly flat, barren-brown monotony of the West Texas plains, and because he'd imagined the Navy would give him his best chance at seeing something of the world beyond Midland.

He'd never imagined in his wildest dreams just how much of the world he would see . . . or from what vantage points.

As an engineman second class, he'd volunteered for BUD/S. Duty in the engine room of the U.S.S. *Guam* was boring, but he'd been fascinated by the dangerous look of a SEAL platoon assigned to the ship one day for an exercise. After that, the Navy had never seemed boring again. Serving with SEAL Team Two, he'd seen combat in Grenada. After that, he'd transferred to the super-secret SEAL Six—"The Mob," as its members called themselves—a small and tightly knit Team designed as the Navy's counter-terrorist unit. In 1985, he'd taken part in the aftermath of the *Achille Lauro* hijacking, surrounding the Egyptian 737 with the terrorists aboard when Navy F-14 Tomcats off the *Saratoga* forced it to land at Sigonella. Unhappy at the social breach opening between SEAL Six and the rest of the Navy SPECWAR community, MacKenzie had transferred again in 1987. After a tour as an instructor at BUD/S in Coronado, he'd shipped out with SEAL Four in Just Cause and Desert Storm.

Then, right after the Gulf War, Lieutenant Cotter had called him up and offered him the chance to become a plank owner of the newly formed and highly secret SEAL Seven. He'd been with Seven since the beginning, right there alongside the L-T and Captain Coburn and Senior Chief Hawkins, lending his long experience to the unit's training and organization.

How many men had he known along the way who'd been killed in action? How many friends? Somehow, he could imagine all of them, standing there on that Arlington hillside with him that morning, the dead in ranks with the living, their dress whites heavy with the medals they'd won in actions from Colombia to the Persian Gulf. He could remember each one of them, their names, their faces, their totemic warrior's nicknames like "Shark" and "Gator" and "Mad Dog."

Losing friends like those was never easy. If anything, it got harder each time.

June, MacKenzie's wife, was standing alone beneath a tree on the far side of the funeral party, but he couldn't go to her, not yet, not before he'd discharged this one, final duty. The group of friends and supporters around Donna Cotter was thinning out. Steeling himself, back ramrod stiff, MacKenzie walked toward the widow. Vickie, he was relieved to see, had already been led away by a relative.

"Hello, Donna."

She was an attractive, dark-haired woman of about thirty, heavyset but with a proud, no-nonsense bearing. Her green eyes locked with his. "Mac. Thanks for coming. For being here."

"I'm sorry about Vince, Donna. I really am. The guy was one in a million."

She looked down at the grass for a moment, then raised her eyes to his once again. She held the folded flag pressed against her breasts like a talisman . . . like a shield. "You've got to tell me, Mac. What happened?"

It was his turn to look away. Across the Potomac, the cherry blossoms had exploded in a sea of pink around the white dome of the Jefferson Memorial, their colors captured by the Potomac's sluggish waters. "You've seen the official letter, Donna. You know I can't say anything else."

"*Damn* you, Mac. If you think I'm going to buy that old 'training accident' line, you're nuts. Was it that thing in Iraq the other day? It was, wasn't it?"

Operation Blue Sky had rated a page-two couple of columns in Wednesday's *Washington Post,* with a shorter follow-up yesterday. All that had been said was that Iraqi troops had tried to stop a UN inspection team from leaving, and that U.S. military forces had rescued them. An unnamed member of the inspection team had told the press they'd been rescued by "American Special Forces." Iraqi sources claimed that the UN people had been released, the situation resolved "in the interests of international peace and cooperation," but that American aircraft had nevertheless bombed a school outside of al-Basra, killing two students and wounding a third. The Navy SEALs had never even been mentioned.

Which, of course, was exactly the way they preferred it. When their C-130 had touched down at NAS Oceana on Wednesday, there'd been no one waiting to meet the grim coterie of commandos as they filed off the transport, a thirteen-man honor guard to a lone, flag-draped coffin. No press, no cheering crowds, no speeches.

And that was as it should be.

Sometimes, though, that could be cold for the families who'd been waiting back in the world of bridge clubs and shopping malls, of the formal functions and the politics of naval social life.

How many times had he been over at the Cotters', barbecuing ribs on Vince's backyard grill, drinking beer and swapping stories with SEALs and SEAL wives. The formal gulf between officers and enlisted that existed through most of the rest of the Navy was all but nonexistent in the Teams. Vince and Donna Cotter were his friends. Damn, he *couldn't* lie to her, not about this.

And he couldn't tell her the truth either.

"Donna," he said, choosing his next words carefully. "If the munchkins say he died in a training accident, then as far as I'm concerned that's exactly what happened. But I can also tell you that Vince was the best warrior, the best leader, the best officer, the best *friend* I've ever known. He was a hero, and I'm proud to have known him."

The woman started to say something, then stopped, her face creasing with iron-held grief that could no longer be denied. "Oh, Mac, Mac, what am I going to do without him?"

MacKenzie opened his arms and enfolded her in an embrace, holding her close as she sobbed, the flag, Vince's flag, trapped between them. After a while, June came up and put her arm around Donna's shoulders, leading her away up the hill.

MacKenzie turned his back on the tombstones and spent a long time after that just standing there on the grass, staring at the Washington skyline.

Damn. Third Platoon would *never* get another CO as good as the Skipper. DeWitt might pass inspection, but he didn't have enough time in grade for promotion to full lieutenant. That meant they'd bring in someone else, an outsider.

He wondered who the newbie was going to be.

6

Monday, 9 May

Hell Week had begun that morning at precisely 0001 hours—
one minute past midnight—and the men of BUD/S First
Platoon, class 1420, were running. The sun was just beginning
to cut through the chill that had lingered over the Silver Strand
throughout the predawn hours, and the surf was breaking in
long, emerald-green rollers that sparkled enchantingly in the
morning light. First Platoon was less interested in the picturesque beauty of the ocean, however, than in remaining upright.

Organized into six boat teams of seven men each, the
platoon numbered forty-two men, and they were running along
the beach through soft sand that shifted unpredictably beneath
their boondockers. Each team carried an IBS—an Inflatable
Boat, Small—balanced on their heads, a black rubber craft that
had long been a mainstay of both the SEALs and the old UDTs.
Twelve feet long and six feet in the beam, the boat could carry
seven men and one thousand pounds of gear. Fully equipped, as
they were now with everything save motors, each weighed 289
pounds.

Each boat crew struggled to run together, supporting the
balky mass of its IBS on their heads, bracing the boat
unsteadily with arms aching from endlessly repeated push-ups
earlier that morning. The shorter men in each team held empty

coffee cans wedged between their heads and their boat so that they could carry their share of the load. The exercise appeared to be mindless harassment, but it had the positive benefit of providing yet another excuse for the recruits to learn to work together . . . or else.

As did nearly every other aspect of BUD/S training.

Lieutenant Blake Murdock trotted easily alongside the lead boat crew. Tall, lean, powerfully muscled, he paced the recruits with an easy gait in deliberate contrast to their exhausted stumblings. In a malicious addition of insult to injury, while the recruits wore shorts and white T-shirts already drenched with sweat, Murdock wore a khaki uniform, flawlessly, crisply pressed and creased, the railroad tracks of his rank gleaming in highly polished gold on his collar, his eagle-trident-pistol badge shining above two rows of colorful ribbons. The only concession he'd made to the morning's workout was his boondockers, identical to the footgear worn by the recruits. Dress shoes did not stand up well to sand and salt water, nor was it a good idea to run in them. The boondockers were spit-shined, however, until they shone like dress Corfams. Murdock had made a point of running with the trainees throughout the past weeks, effortlessly pacing them without showing a wrinkle, without showing even a single stain of sweat in his uniform as the recruits struggled to match his pace.

The other instructors wore blue staff T-shirts and olive drab shorts as they harried the trainees. *"Get in step there! Hup! Two! Three! Four! Pick up your feet, you tadpoles! Come on, come on! Get together!"*

Tomorrow, the boat crews would start running with their instructors as passengers in the rubber boats, paddling the air as they shouted "encouragement," standing up, moving around, and in general doing everything they could to upset the crews' physical and mental equilibrium.

Keeping the recruits off balance was a key part of the program. Reveille that morning had been a dark, smoky, and piercingly noisy chaos of automatic gunfire, smoke grenades, and flash-bangs detonating outside the barracks windows as the instructors screamed confusing, often contradictory orders into the ears of the dazed recruits. *"Fire! Fire on the quarterdeck! Fire party lay to the quarterdeck! Down on the deck! Give me one hundred! Outside! Outside, you pussies! Get wet! Into the surf! Fall in on the grinder in boondockers and jockstrap! Move! Move! Movemove*move*!"* They'd stampeded from the barracks into the night, most of them half dressed, as a SEAL chief petty officer fired bursts from his M-60 over their heads.

For these recruits, those able to stick it out anyway, the next five days would be an endless and agonizing round of mud, exhaustion, pain, and humiliation, a grueling trial of fitness and stamina during which they would be lucky to get a total of four hours' sleep.

Hell Week. This was the end of BUD/S Phase 1 training, the culmination of weeks of running, boat drills, running, push-ups, running, swimming, more swimming, and running, running, and more running. Phase 1 was partly for physical conditioning, of course, but far more than that it was deliberately designed to eliminate the quitters, to weed out that seventy percent or more of each SEAL class that did not have the peculiar twist of mental conditioning, stamina, and determination that was vital for service with the Teams. It had been suggested more than once that BUD/S training was two-percent physical and ninety-eight-percent mental.

"Ladies," Murdock had told the class during formation the evening before, "the next five days and nights have been lovingly crafted to make you do just three things: quit, quit, and *quit*! We are going to do our level best to make all of you see the error of your ways and give up this crazy idea you have that you could actually become SEALs. We've lost a few people already, but hey, we were just getting warmed up with them. They were the lucky ones, sweethearts, the guys who looked deep down inside their souls and realized that they just didn't have what it takes to be a Navy SEAL.

"I can promise you that we're going to lose a hell of a lot more of you before this week of fun and games is over. The United States Navy invests something like eighty thousand dollars in each and every man who finally pins on the trident-and-pistols." For emphasis, he'd tapped his own SEAL pin as he walked down the line of young, skin-headed recruits standing rigidly in their underwear in front of their racks.

"It is our solemn duty to ensure that all those taxpayer dollars are not wasted in this new era of government fiscal responsibility," he'd continued, "that those of you who finish this course—*if* any of you finish this course—are truly the elite, the very best men in body and spirit we can produce. In short, ladies, *SEALs*.

"Of course, I very much doubt that any of you have what it takes to be SEALs. . . ."

It was a canned speech, one that Murdock had delivered numberless times before to numberless SEAL recruits. He'd been stationed with the Training Division at Coronado for almost two years now.

When, he wondered, was he going to get his transfer? He wanted a combat platoon, had been applying for one for the past six months. He strongly suspected that the dread hand of his father was somehow involved.

Blake Murdock had been a SEAL for five years now, but he was one of the unlikeliest SEALs in the Teams. Eldest son of a wealthy Virginia family that had gone into politics three generations ago, he'd long since grown tired of the questions leveled at him almost every time he came aboard a new duty station. "Murdock? Are you any relation to *Charles* Murdock?"

"Yes," he would always answer, a little wearily when he admitted to it at all. "He's my father."

Blake had grown up on the rambling Murdock estate outside Front Royal, half a mile from the banks of the slow-flowing Shenandoah. He'd attended local private schools, then Exeter, with the clear expectation that he would go on to Harvard, followed by a career in law or politics. Indeed, from the very beginning he'd had the feeling that his entire future, from school to marriage to career to internment in the St. John's Episcopal family vaults, all had been carefully planned out with all the care and attention to detail of a well-crafted military campaign.

Murdock knew exactly when he'd begun wanting more, *needing* more than the stuffy wood paneling and elitist snobbery of Exeter's hallowed halls. It had been during the summer before his senior year, when he'd somehow ended up in the mountains of Colorado with an Outward Bound group. At school he'd been a star track and field man, as well as making first string on the football team, and he'd thought he was in pretty good shape, but a summer of long hikes, rugged climbing, and orienteering through the Rockies had convinced him otherwise.

And, of course, that was where he'd met Susan.

His parents had never quite accepted her. She'd been Jewish, for one thing, and for another she came from a military family. Her girlhood had been spent growing up in such diverse places as Yokosuka, Subic Bay, and Pearl Harbor; her father had been a Marine gunnery sergeant who'd lost a leg at Da Nang, her oldest brother a Navy chief stationed aboard an attack sub.

Not exactly the sort of people the Murdocks could easily seat at a dinner party with the landed gentry of Warren County at their Front Royal estate, or worse, at the Chevy Chase Country Club inside the Washington Beltway.

By the time he'd graduated from Exeter, he'd decided that he didn't want any part of Harvard, and Susan had had a lot to do with that decision. Certainly, Outward Bound had generated in Blake a fierce and burning need to keep proving himself physically, and in more challenging ways than joining Harvard's football or track teams.

His parents had not been happy with his decision to join the Marines. There'd been considerable discussion on the matter, ending at last, in the best tradition of Washington politics, in compromise. Blake would attend Annapolis and become an officer in the U.S. Navy.

That would never have been possible, of course, without the direct intervention of his father, Congressman Charles Fitzhugh Murdock, former Virginia state legislator and a three-term member of the House of Representatives. A member of the House Military Affairs Committee, the elder Murdock had considerable leverage both on Capitol Hill and among the higher echelons of the Navy establishment. He'd all but guaranteed Blake a comfortable and promising military career, as a line officer in the fleet, as a Pentagon staff officer, even one day, possibly, as a military liaison officer to Congress.

"We want nothing but the best for you, Blake," his mother had told him the day he'd left for Annapolis. *"The Navy's lucky to get you. Why shouldn't your father pull a few strings to help smooth the way?"*

Why not indeed?

All Blake Murdock knew was that suddenly, somehow, his life was being planned for him again.

Turning sharply away from the surf, the platoon trotted inland, struggling over the crest of a dune, rubber boats still balanced on their heads. Over the top, they descended onto a muddy flat, where a number of logs lay in ominous rows. Each was a section of telephone pole, soaked in creosote and weighing three hundred pounds.

At an instructor's bellowed orders, each boat crew lowered its IBS to the sand, then filed into line behind one of the logs. They'd begun this exercise during the first week of Phase 1, and all the men knew the drill by now.

"Okay, ladies," Murdock shouted. "I think some of you are still a bit sleepy. You need some warm-up exercise to make the day go right. One!"

At each log, seven men in line stopped and seized it.

"Two!"

As a unit—more or less—each team straightened upright, hoisting the log to waist level.

"Three!"

Up the log went to shoulder level.

"Four!"

Muscles bulging, backs straining, teeth gritted in seven-times-repeated agony and concentration, the team shoved the log aloft. There was some wavering, but no one collapsed. No one gave up.

"Three!"

The logs dropped back to shoulder level.

"Two!"

Waist level.

"One!" Onto the ground . . . and woe to the man who straightened up without waiting for the command to be given.

"One!" It started all over again, but with interesting variations. "Two! Three! Four! Three! Four! Three! Four! What's our creed?"

They shouted the answer back at him. *"Sir, the only easy day was yesterday, sir!"*

"Anybody want to quit? The bell's right over there with Petty Officer Simmons. All you have to do is walk over and ring it."

No answer.

"Three! Four! Three! Four! . . ."

Murdock watched the boat crews heaving their telephone poles, but his thoughts were on Susan. He'd been thinking about her a lot lately, probably more than was healthy. The only easy day was yesterday? Right . . .

Somehow it seemed to keep getting harder.

Susan had been killed on Route 50 when a seventeen-year-old kid with a Corvette and a cocaine habit had jumped the median barrier and taken her out head-on. She'd been on her way to attend his graduation ceremony at Annapolis, three days before they were to have been married.

"I know it's hard, dearest," his mother had said after the funeral. *"But you know, it must all really be for the best somehow. Susan was a nice girl, I'm sure, but I'm afraid she just wouldn't have fit in. I still don't think she would have been happy in our family. . . ."*

So shallow. So self-centered, as though the universe revolved about her and her money- and privilege-centered point of view. And so like her, and like his father too, for that matter. That conversation had been the final, the irrevocable straw. A week later, Ensign Murdock had cut short his graduation leave and put in for BUD/S SEAL training at Coronado. After a week of physical fitness testing he'd been accepted. The training had been hellishly difficult, but he'd thrown himself into each new physical and mental challenge with a wholeheartedness he'd not even known he possessed. The alternative, he'd thought, was to brood . . . and in that direction lay only destructive self-pity, possibly suicide, certainly a betrayal of everything he and Susan had hoped and planned for.

When he'd completed both SEAL training and the follow-up airborne course at Fort Benning, Georgia, he'd specifically requested a West Coast assignment. So far as he was concerned, the further away he could get from his family and their plans for his life, the better.

As a member of SEAL Team Three, he'd missed out on seeing action in Panama, but had participated in the Gulf War. As a squad leader the following year, he'd run some highly classified missions along the North Korean coast before being promoted to lieutenant and getting assigned back to Cornado as a senior instructor.

"Three! Four! Three! Four! . . ."

Turning away for a moment as he continued counting the cadence, Murdock spotted a familiar figure leaning against the hood of a jeep parked by the Strand highway. Maybe? . . .

"Three! Four! Three!"

He waited then, a long, long silence during which the waves crashed against the sand just beyond the dune at his back, and sea gulls screeched and shrilled at one another as they circled overhead. He could hear the gasping breaths of the recruits as they strained against their chest-high burdens.

"Anyone want to quit?" he called, his voice almost friendly. There was no reply from the waiting trainees.

"Ah, well. Thought I'd try. Four!" The logs went into the air and stayed there.

"Two-IC!" Murdock called.

One of the instructors jogged up and saluted. "Sir?"

"Take over, Kaminsky. You know the drill."

The petty officer grinned, a death's-head rictus. "Aye, aye, sir. We'll make 'em sweat!"

As Murdock strode away, Kaminsky started the cadence anew. "And . . . three! Four! Three! Four!"

Leaving the grunting, heaving platoon to their telephone poles, Murdock walked over to the man standing by the jeep. Chief Frank Bowden was a thickset black machinist's mate who'd been in the Navy for eighteen years and in the Teams for twelve.

"Morning, Lieutenant," the chief said, saluting crisply. "My, oh, my, but you're up bright and early."

"Out with it, Bow. You look like the proverbial cat with the proverbial canary feathers on his snout."

"Could be. I just came down from Admin. Seems there's a packet for you there, swim buddy."

"What . . . orders?"

"All the way from BUPERS. Word is they came through Saturday."

"God damn! And nobody told me?"

"I just did, man."

"How 'bout running me back there?"

"Hop in, Lieutenant. It'll be my pleasure."

A quick cruise down Silver Strand Drive brought Murdock back to the cluster of buildings that was the heart of SEAL school. The main building was a light tan, brick structure, Above the doors in front of the glassed-in foyer were the words:

NAVAL UNDERWATER DEMOLITION
SEAL TRAINING DIVISION

To the right of the walk leading up to the building was a life-sized replica of the Creature from the Black Lagoon, a net draped over his right hand, a trident in his left. A sign on the trident read, "So you want to be a frogman?" A plaque recorded the statue as a gift from an earlier SEAL training platoon upon graduation.

As Bowden parked the jeep, a platoon of trainees marched past. These were Phase 2 men, wearing olive-drab fatigues and caps instead of shorts and white T-shirts. At this stage of their training, they were less into mud than they were into demolitions and weapons training.

"Gee, I want to be a SEAL!" the petty officer in charge of the column singsonged.

"Gee, I want to be a SEAL!" came the chorused reply.

"Eat seaweed with every meal!"

"Eat seaweed with every meal!"

"Hoo yah!"

"Hoo yah!"

"Sound off!"

"One! Two!"

"Sound off!"

"Three! Four!"

"Cadence count!"

"One! Two! Three! Four! One, two . . . three-four!"

SEALs spent far less time marching than they did running, since traditional drilling on the parade ground was useful only to instill cooperation and esprit de corps. Still, Murdock thought, these men looked sharp, damned sharp. Lean, hard, and ready to kick ass and take names.

"Bein' a SEAL just can't be beat!"

"Bein' a SEAL just can't be beat!"

"Get more ass than a toilet seat!"

"Get more ass than a toilet seat!"

Mother, Murdock thought wryly, *would not approve.* He returned the salute of the formation's leading petty officer, then crossed the road behind them, past the scowling Creature, and up to the training center's front door.

"See that girl all dressed in green?"

"See that girl all dressed in green?"

"She goes down on SEALs like a submarine!"

"She goes down on SEALs like a submarine!"

No, Mother would *definitely* not approve.

A second class yeoman in whites manned the front desk in the headquarters foyer. "Hey, Burman. What's the word."

"Good morning, Lieutenant Murdock," the yeoman replied. "I guess you're looking for this." He handed him a thick manila envelope. Murdock rapidly opened it, broke out the top sheet, and began reading.

ON RECEIPT OF THESE ORDERS, YOU WILL
PROCEED TO THE U.S. NAVY AMPHIBIOUS
BASE, LITTLE CREEK, VIRGINIA, WHERE YOU
WILL TAKE COMMAND OF THIRD PLATOON,
SEAL SEVEN, UNDER COMMAND AUTHORITY
USNAVSPECWARGRU-2.
YOU ARE AUTHORIZED SEVEN DAYS' LEAVE
IN WHICH TO MAKE ARRANGEMENTS FOR
TRANSFERRING PERSONAL EFFECTS. . . .

Murdock looked up, stunned. He was going to NAVSPEC-
WARGRU-Two, to *Norfolk?* It was hardly credible. There was
a long, long history of rivalry, even outright animosity between
the two SpecWar groups. The West Coast SEALs thought their
East Coast counterparts were too hidebound, too tied to rules,
discipline, and spit shine; the East Coast SEALs thought the
Californians too laid back and easygoing, without a proper
respect for attitudes and traditions military.

"Where you headed, Lieutenant?" Burman asked.

"Son of a bitch, they're sending my ass to Shit City,"
Murdock replied, using an old Navy term for Norfolk. "I'm
going to be running a platoon at Little Creek."

"Bummer," the yeoman said, shaking his head. "Course, that
could mean you're going up against the Rags."

"Maybe." Murdock was too stunned to even begin to unravel
his own feelings at the news, but already a nasty suspicion was
forming in his mind.

So help me, he thought, clutching the orders as he turned
and strode toward the Bachelor Officers' Quarters, *if my father
had anything to do with shanghaiing me back to the East
Coast . . .*

7

Tuesday, 10 May

Headquarters, SEAL Seven
Little Creek, Virginia

There was a sharp triple rap on the door, and Captain Phillip Coburn looked up from the battered gray metal government-issue desk from which he ran SEAL Seven operations. "Come."

He was pretty sure he knew what was about to happen.

Electrician's Mate Second Class Charles "Chucker" Wilson opened the door and centered himself before the desk. The young SEAL was immaculate in his whites, with his white hat neatly folded and tucked into his waistband. Uncovered, he did not salute, but he stood at attention with his eyes focused on the big print of the *Bon Homme Richard* fighting the *Serapis* on the bulkhead at Coburn's back.

"Sir!" Wilson snapped out. "Request permission to speak to the Captain, sir."

"Aw, knock off the boot-camp crap, Chucker. Stand easy and tell me what's on your mind."

Wilson relaxed, but only slightly. "Uh, yessir. I mean, thank you, sir. I . . ."

Coburn sighed. "Spit it out, son."

The petty officer fumbled for a moment with the gold Budweiser on his white jumper. Damn. Coburn had thought this was why Wilson had requested the interview, but he'd still been hoping he was wrong.

69

Wilson dropped the SEAL badge on Coburn's desk. "I want to put in for a transfer. To the fleet."

"Shit, Chucker, you know what you're saying?"

"Yes, sir. I think I do."

"You just got your Budweiser . . . what? A month ago?"

"I didn't deserve it, sir."

"Bull. The officers who reviewed your record after your probationary assignment didn't agree. You questioning their judgment?"

"With respect, sir, they weren't at Shuaba."

"You *don't* want fleet duty."

"Yes, sir. I do."

"A SEAL? Scraping paint and flemishing lines? You'll be so bored you'll be climbing the bulkheads inside of six weeks. What the hell makes you think you want to stop being a SEAL?"

"Sir, I was the guy tasked with going through that control tower at Shuaba. I don't know what happened, but somehow I missed a hostile. And that hostile nailed the L-T."

Coburn tipped his steel, straight-backed chair, balancing on the two rear feet as he considered how to answer. "Chucker, we went through this at the inquiry last week. What happened was not your fault. It was not Lieutenant DeWitt's fault, it wasn't anybody's fault. There weren't enough men with Blue Water's ground element to adequately search that tower. As I see it, you did your best, you—"

"Begging the Captain's pardon, sir, but I was *there*. That last room we checked . . . I should've gone in and taken a harder look."

"You told us all of that at the inquiry."

"Captain, that whole building was dark and empty. It, well, it *felt* empty, and I must have gone in assuming that it was empty."

"Okay. So you screwed up. Made a bad call. That doesn't mean you can't be a SEAL. Even SEALs make mistakes."

"I screwed up, and the best officer I've ever known bought it. Sir, I've given this a lot of thought, and I'm looking at it like this. What happens next time I'm on a combat op? With some new platoon leader? I'm going to be there trying to keep my mind on the mission, and I'm going to be thinking about Shuaba. Maybe spend too much time checking a room. Wondering if I'm going to screw up again. Sir, you know as well as I do that you can't stop to think about stuff in combat. If you do, you're dead. And maybe some good guys are dead with you."

"And you think dropping out of the SEALs is the answer?"

"Yes, sir. I do. It's . . . what's best. For me. And for the Team. Look at it from the guys' point of view, Captain. They know what I did at Shuaba, and they know what I didn't do. Think they're going to want to go into a free-fire zone with a fuckup like me backing them up? I sure as hell wouldn't."

"Bullshit, Wilson," Coburn snapped, dropping the father-figure approach in a sharp change in tactics. "The Navy's got eighty-some thousand bucks tied up in your training, and you want to chuck it all the first time you run into some rough sailing? What are you, a quitter? If Hell Week didn't make you chuck it all, why should this?"

"This is different, sir."

"Bullshit. Once you're a SEAL, you're always a SEAL. I don't think you'd be happy any place but with the Teams!"

"Maybe not, sir. But I think it's better if I get out."

Coburn considered the youngster for a long moment. Wilson was just twenty-three years old, and though he had the lean and deadly look worn by most SEALs, there was a vulnerability about him as well. As though something inside had snapped.

Maybe the kid knew himself, knew what was best for himself and his buddies after all.

"Mmm. Tell you what. I'll approve a transfer for you, Wilson, but *not* back to the fleet. There're plenty of spots open in the Teams where you can make yourself useful. Admin. Intelligence. Parachute packing. How about the SDVs?"

Wilson's lip curled at the mention of the Swimmer Delivery Vehicle teams. Most SEALs thought of an assignment to the SDVs as real dead-end to their career tracks, a purgatory to be escaped at the first opportunity.

"I'd . . . prefer to go to the fleet—"

"Since when does the Navy give a shit what you *prefer,* mister? You claim you're thinking about what's best for the Teams? Well, so am I. We have a lot invested in you, son. *You* have a lot invested in you too. I'm not going to let you throw it all away, at least not without a chance to think about it. You read me, son?"

"Y-yes, sir." He looked broken, as though he'd just been sentenced to life at hard labor. "If you say so, sir."

"I say so. I'll have personnel draw up your orders this afternoon. I will also write up a recommendation for your next CO that you be allowed to return to a direct-action team once you've had a chance to think things through. Because I think you're combat SEAL material, and you won't be happy doing anything else."

"Yes, sir."

"Now get out of here." He tossed the badge back to Wilson. "And take this thing with you."

"Aye, aye, sir."

Coburn sat there, rocking back and forth on his chair for a long time after Wilson had gone. The kid would be back, he was sure of that much. But in the meantime, he'd left Coburn with yet another administrative headache, an open slot in Third Platoon's Gold Squad.

The real problem was Third Platoon's morale, which had been at rock bottom since Cotter's funeral. They would be lucky, Coburn thought, if Wilson was the only team member who quit.

He reached out and touched a button on his intercom. "Lamb!"

"Yes, sir," replied the voice of his yeoman in the outer office.

"What do we have in the replacement pool? E-4 or E-5."

"Not a thing, sir. I'm afraid the cupboard's bare. At Little Creek, anyway."

Damn. He'd been pretty sure that that was the case. "Okay. Looks like we'll have to tap Coronado."

He wondered who Seven would draw as a replacement for ET2 Wilson.

1045 hours (Zulu −8)
La Jolla, California

This early on a weekday the beach on the rocky coast north of
San Diego was nearly deserted. Though the southern California
sun was warm, a chilly breeze off the ocean had kept all but
the most dedicated sun worshippers at home. The coastline
here consisted of smooth, sandy beach stretching out from the
base of a rocky bluff. North, at the top of the bluff, the roof of
the Scripps Institution of Oceanography was just visible behind
a screen of palm trees and shrubs. South, the shore grew swiftly
steeper in a rugged headland rising in a sheer, black and red
cliff above the crashing surf.

Machinist's Mate Second Class David Sterling was a
SEAL . . . almost a SEAL, at any rate. He'd completed his
twenty-six weeks of BUD/S and several weeks more in
airborne training at Fort Benning. Now he was assigned to
SEAL Team One's headquarters platoon at Coronado, where he
was serving out his six months of probationary apprenticeship
before winning the coveted eagle-trident-and-pistol Budweiser.

This week, he was standing night duty, which left his days
delightfully free. He'd brought Christine Jordan, his girlfriend
of the past two months, to the beach for a picnic. She was
nineteen and a freshman at San Diego State, a gorgeous, tanned
California girl with fantastic long legs, long, sun-blond hair,
and a face and body right out of *Playboy*. His tactical plan for
the day called for considerably more than lunch and a swim. So
far, their relationship hadn't passed the heavy petting and
fondling stage, though they'd talked about going further often
enough. With no other beach-goers closer than half a klick off,
Sterling had decided that now was the time to make his move.
He might show up for duty tonight without having slept in
thirty hours, but what the hell? He'd done worse stints during
Motivation Week, and man, this was going to be worth it!

"C'mon, babe," he told her. They were lying face to face on
a beach blanket. Minutes before, he'd coaxed Christine into
slipping off her black and red bikini top, and for emphasis now
he reached over and delicately kneaded her left nipple until it

popped up like a bullet. "SEALs do *everything* in the water! You know that!"

"David," she said, dimpling. "You are absolutely nuts!"

"That's what you love about me, right?"

"But suppose someone sees us!"

"Who's to see? The beach is deserted! We've got the place to ourselves, at least until school lets out."

"Gee, David, I don't know . . ."

Bending his head to her breast, he gave her nipple a long and lingering kiss. Chris moaned, her head back, her mane of long blond hair spilling across the beach blanket.

"Ooh, David . . . you *are* persuasive. . . ."

"Come on, Chris! Let's get naked and get wet! It'll be fun!"

Impulsively, Christine stood up. She stood there for a moment, hesitating, her arms crossed protectively over her bare breasts as she looked first one way up the beach, then the other. Then she stooped, skinned off her bikini briefs, and scampered toward the water, her long brown legs scissoring in the surf.

"Yes!" Sterling tugged off his own swimsuit, dropped it on the blanket, then raced into the waves in close pursuit. She squealed as he grabbed her from behind and dragged her down. A wave crashed over them, knocking them together as he encircled her with his arms. Their lips met.

Clinging to one another, they made their way to a point about one hundred yards off the beach, beyond where the surf was breaking. Each wave lifted them high as it surged beneath them, then sent them plummeting into its trough, a wild and exhilarating ride with Christine shrieking in his arms. It was probably too rough today for any serious seaborne docking operations, but the clinging and grappling were tremendous fun and promised better things for later.

He was trying to maneuver himself between her thighs despite the ocean surge when Christine gave another scream, this one of a sharply different timbre from the others. "What's wrong?"

Eyes wild, her wet hair plastered across her face, she pointed past his shoulder toward the beach. "David, look!"

Turning, he saw the people winding down the path from the

road where they'd parked Sterling's VW. It was a fair-sized crowd, five or six adults and at least that many children. Some of them carried beach umbrellas, coolers, blankets, and the other paraphernalia of an afternoon's outing at the beach. A teenager sent a frisbee sailing across the sand, and a small dog yapped after it.

They were setting up shop less than five yards from the towels, picnic basket, and swimsuits that Sterling and Christine had left on the beach.

"Oh, God, David!" She was trembling in his arms. "What are we going to do now?"

"That's okay. They can't see anything but our heads out here."

"No! I mean what about our clothes! We can't go back now!"

"Why not? We just go ashore, walk over to our stuff, get dressed, and leave. What can they do?"

"David!" She pushed back against his embrace, staring into his face. "You can't be serious!"

"I'm perfectly serious."

"I can't walk up onto the beach in front of people *naked*!" A wave carried them higher, and she turned to stare at the beach again. "Oh, God, no! No!"

"Now what?"

"I *know* some of those people! They're from my church! And that . . . that's Pastor Kline! David! It's a church picnic! What am I going to do?"

"Okay, listen. I'll tell you what. You stay here. Just tread water. I'll swim back, get our suits, and bring yours out to you."

"No!" The word was nearly a scream.

"Why not?"

"They might know you! They know I've been going out with you! If they saw you come out of the ocean like this, they'd know I was with you, and they'd know what we've been doing! You can't!"

"Well, we sure as hell can't stay out here all day." The water was pretty cold. Sterling was feeling fine so far, but Christine's lips were already blue, and her teeth were starting to chatter. "Look, it's easy. Just ignore them. What can they say? Just go up and—"

"God, David, sometimes you can be so damned *arrogant*!"

He blinked. "Arrogant? Me? I'm just being practical! Christine, you're freezing. Come on. I know you're a bit embarrassed, but—"

"It's so *humiliating*! David, I can't possibly let my pastor see me like this! I'll never be able to show my face again! He'll tell my *father*! Oh, why did I even listen to you? I knew this was a mistake!"

Sterling sighed. Impasse. Christine wasn't going back to the beach, she wasn't going to let him go back to the beach, and if she stayed where she was she'd succumb to hypothermia in thirty minutes or less. Her fingertips and the dusky aureoles around her nipples were already starting to wrinkle up like prunes.

There had be another solution. A SEAL solution . . .

"Okay," he told her. "I've got it."

Turning in the water, he presented his back to her. "Grab hold. Hold onto my neck."

Reluctantly, she slipped her arms around his neck, and he felt her body pressing against his back and buttocks. "What are you going to do?"

"We're going for a little swim, babe."

Launching into a powerful breast stroke, Sterling began swimming south, moving parallel to the beach and in the general direction of the La Jolla headlands, which rose from the sea about half a mile away.

It would have been a stiff swim for anyone but a SEAL, but Sterling made it seem almost effortless, hauling Christine through the water with a sure and practic͏ͅ they drew farther and farther away from the picni͏ͅ ͏ͅch, he could feel her starting to relax a little.

The rough part came when he reached the surf line just below the cliffs, where the waves broke in savage, white fury over the boulders scattered along the beach. "Wrap your legs around my waist," he called to her. "And for God's sake, hang on!"

Somehow, he plunged out of the crashing water and sprinted up a narrow shingle of wet sand without being smashed against the rocks. In the distance to his left, the picnickers were visible as a cluster of colored dots, too small for faces to be made out. South, around the headland, Sterling had thought he'd glimpsed some fishermen on the rocks as he'd come in, but if they'd seen the two swimmers they gave no sign. And apparently Christine hadn't seen them either. Her face was buried against the back of his neck.

"Okay," he told her, straightening a bit and bracing her legs with his hands. "We're ashore, but I want you to stay where you are. We have a little climbing ahead of us."

"Why? If we find someplace to hide in the rocks . . ."

"Babe, in another hour or so this beach is going to be wall-to-wall people, okay? Besides, I can feel you shivering. We've got to get you warmed up before you catch pneumonia."

It was a grueling climb up a slanted rock ledge that ran along the face of the bluff like a narrow path. Fishermen had probably used this route for years to get down to the beach from Torrey Pines Road, which followed the headland around its crest, overlooking the ocean. Or it might have been a beach maintenance access path, a part of La Jolla Heights Park. Christine weighed perhaps 120, close to the weight of a SEAL's full HAHO gear, and it was a struggle to keep moving.

"David, where are we going?"

"We left the car on the road," he told her. "It's just a hundred yards or so up the road. All we have to do is get to the top of this hill."

"And walk down the road like, like *this*?"

"I don't   too many options, Chris. Should be okay, though   won't be heavy this time of day." He staggered on,   ks and gravel pressing against the bottoms of his bare feet. He thought of all the long, long runs—as much as fourteen miles in the sand—supporting a 300-pound log with six other guys, and knew he could make it. Piece of cake.

At last they reached the top, where a metal guard rail

separated Torrey Pines Road from the edge of the cliff. Far
down the road to the north, Sterling could see his blue
Volkswagen parked where he'd left it in the shade of a palm
tree. He let Christine down, but picked her up again when half
a dozen steps on the hot gravel at the side of the road reduced
her to tears and a slow and painful hobble. Carrying her
piggyback again, he trotted along the side of the road. A truck
thundered by, the driver happily leaning on his horn. Sterling
could feel Christine trembling against him, hiding her face,
certain that the whole world was staring at them.

And she may have been right. There were lots of houses in
view up here, mostly the elegant, architectural dream homes of
the wealthy southern Californians who inhabited this strip of
prime, ocean-view property. If any of them happened to be
looking out those big, expensive picture windows now, Sterling
thought, they were getting one hell of a great view.

"David!" Christine wailed. "I just remembered! We locked
the car! Your keys and everything are down on the beach!"

"Don't worry about it. I'll get us in."

A Cadillac drove past, and the driver beeped his horn. "Oh,
this is awful!"

At last they reached the VW. Sterling let Christine down, and
she immediately scampered for the partial shelter behind the
car's body. "How . . . how are we going to get in? Can you
pick the lock?"

"Easier than that, Chris. I left the trunk open." Walking to the
front of the car, he opened the hood. "Shit," he said conversationally. "I thought I had a blanket stowed in here. Guess not."

"David, what are we going to *do*?"

He hesitated, faced now with the moment of truth. That
battered, blue VW was something of a classic, an ancient car
dating back to the years when they actually manufactured the
VW Beetle in the United States, lovingly preserved and rebuilt
through a long succession of enlisted Navy and Marine
personnel, passed down from owner to owner each time a tour
of duty was up. Sterling had lavished hundreds of hours on the
vehicle until it ran like a Swiss watch. Damaging it was a kind
of sacrilege.

"David!" Fists clenched, face red, Christine bounced rapidly up and down on her toes, a movement that communicated her urgency while doing delightful things to other parts of her anatomy. *"There's a bus coming!"*

He sighed. "Okay." Balling up his fist, Sterling smashed through the back of his glove compartment, a dark brown box shaped in thick, heavy cardboard like the material egg cartons are made of. Reaching into the hole from the trunk side, he fiddled with the latch for a moment until the glove compartment door popped open. Then, leaning in as far as he could, he reached through the open glove compartment and pushed open the small ventilation window on the passenger's side. "I hated it when they stopped putting these on cars," he said conversationally as he moved to the side of the car, reached through the open window, and unlocked the door. Christine slipped in through the door just before a yellow high school bus loaded with cheering students roared past. It looked like a field trip of some sort. Sterling cheerfully waved as the bus groaned past them and on up the hill. Christine was huddled on the VW's floor, possibly in an attempt to crawl beneath her seat.

Sterling reached across to unlock the driver's side door, walked around to the trunk, where he fished out a screwdriver, then slammed the hood shut. Sliding into the driver's seat, he turned his attention to the VW's ignition.

Damn but he hated doing this. Well, it could be repaired. In seconds, as Christine watched from the floor with wide eyes, he popped the ignition mount out, engaged clutch and gas, and pressed two lengths of bare wire together. The VW's engine gunned into life.

"Thank God," Christine said. "Now what?"

"Now we get you home," he said, backing into the road, then turning south. "I'll let you out in your driveway where it's pretty well screened from the street. You run in and get dressed, then bring me something to wear. A pair of your brother's shorts maybe."

"Okay."

"Then I'll hightail it back here, grab our stuff, and pick you up in plenty of time for us to have lunch. How about Delaney's? Sound good?"

"David Sterling! If you think I'm going out with you after what you've just done to me, exposing me to the whole world and humiliating me in front of God knows how many people—"

"Hey! Would you rather walk home? You can get out now, if you want."

"No! You wouldn't!"

"Try me!"

Christine lived in La Mesa, a San Diego suburb twenty miles from La Jolla, nestled into the hills between Route 8 and Route 94. Once they pulled onto the main highway, traffic was fairly heavy. Christine got off the floor and onto her seat, but she held her arms awkwardly to cover her breasts and lap. The VW was pretty low to the ground, and plenty of truck drivers seemed to be doing their best to peer down at her from their cabs as they drove past. The last part was the worst, when they actually had to drive through downtown La Mesa, getting stopped by three traffic lights in a row.

At last, Sterling turned into Christine's driveway. Her home was a small, neat ranch house where she lived with her parents. Turning in his seat, Sterling checked the street at their back. "Okay. Looks clear. Go!"

She slipped out of the car and scampered up the walk toward the door. Just as she reached it, the door opened wide. Her father was standing there waiting for her, his face like a darkening thunderhead.

"Oh, *shit*!"

Sterling had a feeling that Christine wasn't going to be bringing her brother's shorts out to him. As Christine's father advanced down the walk, he decided that a tactical withdrawal was definitely the order of the day. Throwing the VW into reverse, he backed swiftly onto the street, straightened out the wheel, then headed back the way he'd come.

Forty minutes later he was parked once more on Torrey Pines Road, just above a beach that had grown considerably more crowded in the past hour and a half. He really had no alternatives now, for he couldn't get back on base without showing his ID card to the sentries at the gate, and that was in his wallet on the beach with his clothes.

Climbing out of the VW, he started picking his way down the path toward the beach.

The police officer who arrested him a few minutes later was very nice about it. At least she allowed him to get dressed, but she was most unreasonable when he tried to suggest that the incident had been perpetrated by a couple of Sterling's friends who'd stolen his clothes and abandoned him on the road as a crude prank. Apparently, there'd been a number of complaints from residents in the area about a couple of nudists along the highway.

Eventually, and after a long and unpleasant phone conversation with the Officer of the Day at Coronado, the La Jolla police agreed to relinquish the case to the military authorities.

The Navy would deal with David Sterling.

8

Friday, 13 May

1915 hours (Zulu −7)
C-141 military flight
Over the Rocky Mountains

"So at the captain's mast, my CO tells me he was of a mind to ship my ass off to Adak," the young sailor was saying. "Fortunately, this request for a warm body had just come through from Norfolk, and he decided the easiest course was to put me on the first available flight out of Diego."

Blake Murdock leaned back in the uncomfortable bucket seat and grinned. "What about your Volkswagen?"

"Aw, I arranged to have the Navy ship it to the East Coast. It wouldn't have made it over the mountains anyway. What I'm really gonna miss is my boat."

"Boat?"

"Yeah. A sweet little twenty-one-foot sloop I kept at the base marina. Her name was *Docking Maneuver*. I ended up selling her to a lieutenant commander in Admin."

"There is nothing," Murdock said, "like sailing."

"Yeah. I did a lot of racing too. Out to Catalina and back. You sail, sir?"

"Used to. My family had a yacht on Kent Island, on the Eastern Shore. Sometimes I think I'm just a frustrated Captain Ahab, three years before the mast and all that. I did some racing too back when I was at the Academy."

"Man. How the other half lives, huh?"

Murdock decided to change the subject. "So what about Christine?"

"Aw, that's ancient history. She wouldn't talk to me." He shrugged, then grinned. "Probably just as well. I don't think she appreciated everything I did for her up there on that hillside. Women!"

Murdock didn't answer that one, but turned and peered out the tiny window in the bulkhead at his back. The two of them were the only passengers on an Air Force C-141 Starlifter en route from Miramar Naval Air Station to Andrews Air Force Base outside of Washington, D.C. From there, they'd find another military flight down to Norfolk, or if necessary, hire a cab with the money from their travel allotments. It promised to be an uncomfortable five hours or so, sitting on the narrow bucket seats grudgingly installed for the odd passenger, sharing the cargo deck with stacks of chained-down crates, but space-available seating aboard military transports was one of the perks of military service. Murdock preferred these flights to the crowds aboard commercial airliners.

He wondered if all SEALs were just a little paranoid, nervous when there were too many strangers about.

"Hey, Navy," an Air Force sergeant, the Starlifter's crew chief, said. "Either of you guys want some coffee?"

"Sure," Murdock replied. "Black."

"Same here," Sterling added.

They waited for the Air Force sergeant to bring their coffee and leave before resuming their conversation, a reserve that was almost second nature among SEALs. Both men were traveling in civilian clothes, and neither knew a thing about the other save name, rank, and the fact that both were SEALs, but that alone formed a solid bond and a man-to-man rapport that frankly excluded all outsiders.

"So it sounds like you're E&Eing just in time," Murdock said after the sergeant had left. Their conversation was easy, despite the difference in ranks. Rank meant far less in the Teams than it did in the rest of the Navy.

"I guess you could say that, sir. You know what I'm really glad to be escaping, though?"

"Christine's Dad?"

"Very funny. I could've taken him, no sweat."

"Yeah, right." He took a sip of the bitter black brew. "What, then?"

"Well, ever since I made it through Phase 1 of BUD/S, I've been wondering what my handle would be. Once I was a full-fledged SEAL and all. I mean, 'David Sterling' is kind of blah, know what I mean? I always thought 'Shark' would be a great nickname."

"So?"

"So I was telling some of the guys about what happened with me and Christine. I mean, they knew I was up for captain's mast, and they'd heard scuttlebutt about what had happened. So I told them." He made a wry face. "And they started calling me something."

"What?"

" 'Jaybird.' "

"As in 'naked as a,' " Murdock said, laughing. "Hey, it fits!"

"Yeah, well, it don't any longer, sir. You see, by getting shipped to the East Coast, nobody there'll know about me. I can tell 'em anything. 'Jaybird' will be safely buried back in Coronado."

"Don't be too sure about that, David. The Navy's a tight, close community, and the SEALs are tighter and closer yet. Hell, there probably aren't many more than a thousand SEALs in the world today. You're always running across some guy you knew at another duty station."

"Aw, you know how East and West Coast SEALs are always running each other down. I figure I'll be safe enough in NAVSPECWARGRU-Two. Don't you think?"

"It's possible, I guess." Murdock had been thinking a lot lately about that rumored chasm between east and west. How readily were the men in his new platoon going to accept him? "Where are they putting you anyway?"

"I don't know yet, sir, but I hear there's an opening in one of the action Teams. I've still got about two months to go on probation, so I've really got to keep my nose clean after all the fuss back at Coronado."

"I should damn well think you'd better, Jaybird," Murdock said, grinning.

"Aw, Lieutenant, don't call me that. Hey! What's your new station?"

"They've got a platoon waiting for me. Don't know any more than that."

"Huh. Maybe we'll be seein' each other again at Little Creek!"

"Could be. Anything's possible. Especially for SEALs."

2130 hours (Zulu −5)
Sarnelli's Bar
Norfolk, Virginia

They'd come to Sarnelli's to do some serious drinking, a part of the ongoing wake for the Lieutenant. MacKenzie ordered his usual Bombay gin, a taste he'd acquired during his tour with SEAL Team Six back in the eighties, then turned to face the gloomy cavern of the bar.

Things were just getting warmed up. Radioman First Class Ronald "Bearcat" Holt was on the floor of the bar, braced in push-up position on his fingertips. Lucy, one of the waitresses at Sarnelli's, was stretched full-length face-up on his back, bracing herself by gripping his belt. She looked tiny, and a little apprehensive.

"Okay!" Fernandez shouted, waving a fistful of money. "Gimme a hundred! Ready . . . go!"

"Hold it!" Roselli called, waving his hands. "Hold it!" Reaching down his leg, he slipped the black, double-edged leaf-blade of a Sykes-Fairbairn commando knife from a boot sheath.

"Hey, hey!" one of the bartenders warned. "No weapons in here! You guys know the rules!"

"It's all right!" Roselli replied, grinning. "Everything is perfectly under control. We must observe all the propri . . . all the propri . . . Everything's got to be kosher here! But this here op is turnin' into a damned sneak-and-peek!" Lucy's short skirt had hiked up on her thighs, exposing white panties.

Delicately, without touching her legs, Roselli used the point of his knife to tug the skirt back into a less revealing position.

"Looks like real delicate surgery, Razor," Boomer said.

"Well, yeah," Roselli replied. "But we wouldn't want no Tailhook charges brought against us, fellas, now would we?"

Some of the SEALs cheered, while others booed him. "You're a real gentleman, Razor," Lucy said sweetly. Several SEALs groaned at that, and Boomer hit him with a fistful of popcorn.

"Hey, I can't help it if I'm just too impossibly cool to be believed," Roselli said. "Right, the bets are covered, the lady's covered, are we set, gentlemen? Okay, go!"

Holt began performing push-ups at the rate of one per second. Some of the other SEALs began counting cadence. "One! And two! And three! And four!"

"C'mon, Holt, no cheating! All the way down!"

"I'm goin' all the way down!"

"I don't think she's heavy enough!"

"Yeah, why don't you try it with a telephone pole?"

"Or Big Mac!"

"Screw you, Razor!" Holt called out.

"An' twelve! An' thirteen! An' fourteen!"

Another quiet Friday night at Sarnelli's, MacKenzie thought, wrapping his big hands around his glass of Bombay gin. Sarnelli's, a little bar and restaurant on Little Creek Road in east Norfolk, had long been a popular watering hole for naval personnel, but since the creation of Team Seven it had become virtually a private domain, SEAL territory, and all others enter at your own risk.

"He's gettin' tired. Look at his face!"

"Aw, he's just gettin' warmed up!"

". . . twenty! An' twenty-one! An' twenty-two!"

Actually, MacKenzie reflected, it *was* rather quiet tonight, and that worried him. There were only seven SEALs in the whole place, counting him, all wearing civvies and none of them even bothering with the handful of Marines and Navy personnel already there when they arrived. Outwardly the boys were as rambunctious as usual, and as determined to get drunk, but there was a hard edge to their laughter, a bitterness to their jokes and banter that typified what MacKenzie had been noticing all week.

The platoon's morale was way the hell down. Lately, good-natured hazing or kidding was more likely to be taken as an insult, and there'd been a number of fights during the past few days. In a booth over in one corner, Doc Ellsworth was ignoring the push-up contest. He'd picked up two pretty SEALettes, a blonde and a redhead, and was demonstrating his famous double-beer-drinking trick, holding two open bottles of Budweiser upended in his mouth at once, no hands, and chugging the contents down in a steady series of gulps. The girls, a couple of military groupies MacKenzie had seen hanging out at Sarnelli's with his boys before, watched wide-eyed. The rest of the SEALs were clustered around Holt and Lucy.

"Forty-three! Forty-four! Forty-five!"

Doc spit out the two empty bottles, then leaned across his table. "Aw, shit, guys!" he called. "Wouldn't it be better if Lucy was underneath him while he was doing that?"

"Yeah Doc's right! Hey Holt, you dumb ass! You got it backward! The girl's s'posed to be *under* you!"

"Fifty-two! Fifty-three! Fifty-four!"

"Wait! Wait!" Garcia shouted. "I'll fix it!" The SEAL positioned himself, then dove head-first toward the two people on the floor, landing on top of Lucy, who squealed and wiggled beneath him. Holt *oofed* and staggered a bit under the impact, then continued pumping away.

"Sixty! Sixty-one! Sixty-two!"

"Hey, it's a Lucy sandwich!" Nicholson called. "Sarnelli's house specialty! Looks real good!"

Roselli laughed as Garcia kissed Lucy on the cheek. "Looks like fun, anyway. Can anybody play?"

"What the fuck's goin' on back there?" Holt demanded from the bottom of the pile, though he never missed a beat. "Garcia! Get your ass off of there! That ain't in the bet!"

"Yeah, get the fuck out of there, Garcia!" Miguel Fernandez shouted, his dark face flushing darker as he advanced on the unlikely, heaving trio. "I got money riding on Ron and you're screwin' up the bet!"

"That ain't all that's riding on Ron," Roselli said, snickering.

Fernandez grabbed Garcia by his waistband and hauled him off Lucy bodily. She gave a loud scream and almost fell off Holt.

"Put me down, you pussy!" Garcia bellowed.

"Who's a pussy, you piss-balled, penny-pricked little son of a bitch?" In an instant, the atmosphere had transformed from camaraderie to vicious, flaring anger. Fernandez launched a swift right hook that connected with the side of Garcia's head and sent him tumbling across a table.

"Knock it off, you two!" MacKenzie bellowed, moving toward the two antagonists. On the floor, Holt kept doing his push-ups with Lucy still clinging to his back.

Garcia scrambled up off the floor and came back, fists clenched, but when he threw a punch it was only a feint. His foot came up instead, slamming into Fernandez's side.

MacKenzie suddenly stepped between them, reaching out with two long arms and snagging both combatants by their collars. "I said knock it off, shitheads!" He didn't raise his voice, but the cold deadliness behind the words somehow penetrated the two SEALs' blind anger. "I don't give a shit, but the L-T wouldn't like to see you two kill each other. You boys read me?"

"Mac," Garcia said, panting. "That bastard—"

"Stow it, Boomer! Chill out!"

"Chief—"

"You too, Rattler. I said the L-T wouldn't like it!"

That stopped them cold. MacKenzie could feel the fight drain out of both men.

"Now shake hands."

They shook . . . then embraced, hugging each other warmly. MacKenzie stepped back, nodded approvingly, then turned to face the bar again.

"Aw, now ain't that sweet," he heard from the front of the restaurant. "The SEALies're hugging."

"Must be springtime," another voice said, a bass, gravelly rumble. "Mating season fer fuckin' SEALs."

"You boys listen to your momma there and be nice to each other!"

The SEALs went dead quiet at the intrusion. A dozen strangers had entered the bar, and now they were closing slowly around the tight-knit group. They too wore civilian clothes, but the close-trimmed hair above their ears, "white-walls" in military parlance, gave them away.

Marines. Marines out on liberty and cruising for trouble, from the look of them.

"You SEALies're making too damned much noise," one of the Marines growled. He was drill-sergeant lean, recruiting-poster handsome, and had the cold look of a competent killing machine.

"Yeah," a second man chorused. "A man can't hear hisself think." This one stood six-two and must have weighed two-fifty, all of it workout honed, chiseled, and sweat-polished slabs of muscle. When he lunged his blond head forward and scowled, he forcibly reminded MacKenzie of that wrestler guy on TV . . . what was his name? Hulk Hogan, yeah.

"Shouldn't be a problem for you shit-for-brains jarheads then," Fernandez said, his argument with Garcia forgotten now. "Seein' as how you guys can't think anyhow."

"Ooh," the first Marine said, shaking his hand as though he'd burned it. "We got us a wise-ass tough-guy SEAL here, men. I think maybe we'd better housebreak it, don't you guys?"

"Hey, no fighting in here!" a bartender called from behind the bar. "Take it outside before I call the SPs!"

"Aw, this won't take that long, Pops," another Marine said. "We just gonna do a little after-hours moppin' up for you here."

"Yeah, no fuckin' Navy puke SEAL alive can take on the Marines," the big guy said. He curled his forearm up, flexing it, and muscles popped and rippled impressively from wrist to bull-massive neck.

"So you grunts figure you're better'n SEALs, huh?" Roselli demanded, stepping closer. There was a nasty glint in his eye.

The big Marine apparently didn't see that glint or else was

too drunk to care. "Fuck! All you SEALs are pussies! Right, guys?"

"Right on, Fred!" There was a chorus of assent, but Fred probably never heard it. Roselli had turned slightly, his hands had blurred, and then the Marine was hurtling through the air upside down, touching down neatly and briefly in a big bowl of popcorn on the bar, then somersaulting behind the bar with a shattering crash and a sudden snow flurry of snack food. Lucy screamed and scrambled to get off Holt before another flying body landed on her. The two SEALettes with Ellsworth shrieked and ducked under the table, while other Sarnelli's patrons ran for cover. A second Marine slammed face-first into a decorative wooden pillar, clung to it lovingly a moment, then slid limply to the deck.

Sipping his gin, MacKenzie briefly considered the tactics of the situation. Clearly, it was his duty as senior man present to break up the fight before someone got hurt or Sarnelli's suffered any more wear and tear to the crockery. The men of Third Platoon looked to him for leadership, and to set a good example. He was, in fact, a father figure for these younger boys, and he took his position in that regard quite seriously.

Picking up his glass, he turned and leaned against the bar, watching approvingly as Nicholson dropped into a perfect Hwrang-do defensive stance, lightly touched a charging bull-Marine, then stepped aside as the Marine hurtled past and collided noisily with a chair. MacKenzie had been worried about the platoon's morale, but as he thought about it, maybe what the boys needed most was a good fight. He winced as Holt, risen now from the barroom floor like a fury from Hell, seized two leathernecks and slammed them together, head to head. Yeah, something to get the adrenaline flowing, something to remind them of how good it was to work together.

Fernandez and Garcia were back to back now, covering each other as they took on separate frontal assaults. Good . . . *good*! A Marine brought a chair down on Boomer, smashing him to the floor. Fernandez whirled, leaped, and brought the assailant down with a slashing kick to the face.

A Marine grabbed Doc Ellsworth in a bear hug. "Watch it,

fella," Doc said. "I'm a non-combatant." Suddenly the Marine's face turned purple and he crumpled to the deck at Doc's feet, gasping for breath. Doc fastidiously brushed himself off, looked down at his writhing victim, and said, "If that pain persists or if you notice any blood in your urine, come see me during sick call tomorrow."

Holt slammed into the bar next to MacKenzie. "Damn it, Big Mac, ain't you gonna help?"

"I am helping," MacKenzie replied. He took a sip, then lowered his glass. "I'm not putting you all on report for fighting. Oh-oh, watch it there."

A few feet away a Marine grabbed Fernandez from behind and was trying to hit him with a bottle. Holt roared, the sound startling enough that the Marine dropped the bottle just as Holt lunged forward, tackling both men and driving them to the deck.

And suddenly, it was very, very quiet in Sarnelli's.

"Clear!" Boomer called, standing astride a limp Marine.

"Clear!" Holt said.

"Clear!" "Clear!" "Clear here!" "And clear!" The other SEALs chimed in from various parts of the bar, and MacKenzie did a quick head count. Six SEALs, still on their feet. Counting him, seven. Twelve Marines down. *Very* down.

MacKenzie sighed, then reached down and turned the head of one unconscious Marine so he wouldn't drown in a puddle of spilled liquor on the deck. Straightening up again, he reached for the wallet in his hip pocket. "Awfully sorry for the mess, Pete," he said, handing a fifty and five tens across the counter to the owner. "That cover things?"

Sarnelli glanced around the room. The actual breakage wasn't bad. The men had been surprisingly restrained this time. Only the Marines had stooped to throwing furniture around.

"That'll be fine, Mac. Thanks. Better scoot, though. The boys called the SPs when it started getting rough."

"On our way. Thanks." He gathered his SEALs with a glance. "C'mon, you heroes. E & E, on the double."

"Aw, Chief," Doc said. He was already back in his booth

with his arms around the two girls. "I was just getting to the good part!"

"Move your ass, Doc. Unless you want to spend your liberty in the brig. Move it! Hop 'n' pop!"

"Prowl 'n' growl!"

"Shoot 'n' loot!"

It was more of a victorious saunter out of the bar than a retreat. They scrambled into the pair of cars they'd come in and roared back onto Virginia Creek Drive before the wailing sirens drew close.

The new lieutenant was supposed to show up tomorrow, MacKenzie thought as they raced east toward Little Creek. Maybe that was excuse enough to go ahead and make tonight a *real* celebration. In Lieutenant Cotter's memory, of course. Because it was one sure-fire definite affirmative that the new guy, whoever he was, would never be able to take the L-T's place.

"C'mon, guys," he yelled over the roar of Doc's Chevy. They were in the lead. "Let's reconnoiter. Left at the light!"

"Now you're talkin', Boss!" Roselli called from the back seat. "Hell, I thought you'd lost it for a minute there!"

The Chevy turned sharply, and Holt's car followed.

It was going to be a long night for the citizens of Norfolk's east side.

9

Saturday, 14 May

"Lieutenant Murdock reporting for duty, sir."

"At ease, Lieutenant. Hand 'em over."

Murdock handed his sheaf of transfer and travel orders and his personnel record folder across the desk to the lean, bronzed captain sitting there.

"Okay . . . Murdock," the captain said, leafing through the first few pages. "I'm Captain Coburn, commanding officer of SEAL Seven. Welcome aboard."

"Thank you, sir."

He indicated a battered gray-painted metal chair nearby. "Grab a seat. Drop anchor."

"Thank you, sir."

"Coffee?"

"No, thank you, sir."

Coburn leaned back in his chair, studying Murdock with a critical eye. "So, Lieutenant. How much do you know about SEAL Seven?"

"Not all that much, sir. I tried to look up its history before I left Coronado, but there's not much to be found."

"Figures. Some of that is the usual SEAL secrecy, of course. SEALs don't say nothing to nobody when they don't have to, and they say even less to people who aren't in the Teams. But

SEAL Seven is new, and it's a new idea. A lot of the people you'll be meeting around here are plank owners, including myself."

Plank owners—personnel aboard for the first cruise of a new ship, or who'd been in on the mustering of a new command. It was a special distinction, one worn with quite a bit of pride. Of course, the SEALs had expanded a lot during the eighties, from two Teams to seven, and with new Special Warfare bases appearing from Japan to Puerto Rico to Scotland, so there were plenty of plank owners still about. But from what Murdock had gathered so far, SEAL Seven was brand-new, only recently brought on-line.

"SEAL Seven has been operational now for about six months," Coburn said, confirming Murdock's thoughts. "It was created as our first rapid-deployment SEAL combat team."

"I thought all SEAL Teams were expected to be rapid-deployment, sir."

Coburn's mouth twisted in a wry grin. "They're supposed to be, and they are. Still, the logistical tail tends to slow things down quite a bit. That's where the Army's Delta Force has been running into trouble, as I'm sure you know. All the super-sophisticated sci-fi hardware in the world won't help you when you can't deploy to a trouble spot halfway around the globe in less than forty-eight hours. Tell me what you know about SEAL Six."

Murdock blinked at the sudden shift in the topic. "Um . . . organized in 1980 as the Navy's response to the hostage crisis in Iran. Put together by a guy named Marcinko. Something of a nonconformist, if what I've read is true."

"That doesn't say the half of it. Go on."

"He conceived of SEAL Six as a special anti-terrorist unit. Go anywhere, do anything. Dress as civilians and blend in with the local population. Hit the terrs on their own home turf. They took part in the *Achille Lauro* incident, didn't they?"

"That's affirmative. One of the men in your platoon used to be with SEAL Six, and he was at Sigonella when it all went down. MacKenzie, a master chief. He'll be able to tell you some stories."

"I should imagine."

"Okay, you know the basic layout of the SEALs, the Teams' TO as it was developed in the eighties. Two Navy Special Warfare Groups, Group One on the West Coast, Group Two headquartered here at Little Creek. Teams One, Three, and Five at Coronado. Teams Two, Four, and Eight here. And SEAL Six is still located across the way at Dam Neck, but they answer directly to the Joint Chiefs.

"While we've tried to keep the SEALs flexible overall, a certain amount of specialization has crept in over the years. Units grow larger, acquire more equipment. They become more difficult to move on short notice. SEAL Two, for instance, runs Navy Special Warfare Unit Number Two out of an advance SEAL deployment base at Machrihanish, in Scotland. They do a lot of training with people like the SAS and GSG-9, and if something goes down in northern Europe or the North Sea, they're the ones who'll go. SEAL Four works with Special Warfare Unit Three, down at Roosey Roads, in Puerto Rico. They handle things that come up in the Caribbean.

"SEAL Seven is basically an experimental concept, like the Army's light infantry, a Team that can be deployed anywhere in the world on a few hours' notice. We can draw on equipment stashed at other SEAL prepositioning sites, of course, but the key to making the notion work is mobility. In fact, we're not even tied down to the traditional Group One and Group Two theaters of responsibility. Seven was originally slated to set up shop in Coronado, which is why we got the odd number. The Pentagon decided they wanted us closer at hand, at least to begin with, especially with things so bad in Europe and the Middle East right now."

"So the idea is we could be sent anywhere in the world."

"Right. If a crisis goes down in Iraq, let's say . . . some UN weapons site inspectors are being held hostage, for example . . . a SEAL platoon from Seven can be on-site within twenty-four hours to act as forward controllers for air strikes, gather intelligence for a major military operation to follow, or if the opportunity presents itself, grab the hostages and beat it for home."

Murdock had looked up sharply at the mention of Iraq. Now he smiled slowly. "Are you saying, sir, that that 'Special Forces' op in Basra the other day was us?"

"More than that, Lieutenant. It was your new platoon."

The news stunned Murdock. He'd not seen that one coming. "I'll be God damned. . . ."

"Hours after Iraqi ground troops blocked the takeoff of the UN transport, fourteen men under the command of Lieutenant Vincent Cotter inserted by parasail into Hawr al-Hammar, crossed several kilometers of salt marsh and swamp, assaulted Republican Guard elements guarding the aircraft and Basra airport, and extracted all of the UN personnel by helicopter. A textbook operation, well planned, well executed. The platoon suffered one KIA: Lieutenant Cotter."

"Damn." Murdock closed his eyes. "I'm sorry to hear that, sir."

"Cotter was a good officer. One of the best. You're going to have to hit the deck running just to keep up with his shadow."

"You know, I had the impression that my transfer was something of a hurry-up affair," Murdock said. "They tagged me smack in the middle of a BUD/S class in Phase One."

"Our replacement pools have been run down with the personnel cutbacks recently," Coburn explained. "And the established Teams have priority for replacements and material. You'll find Seven is still in the process of learning how to fit into the scheme of things out here."

"I understand, sir."

"You know, back in the eighties, SEAL Six was notorious with the rest of the SEALs because they always got the best and hottest of everything. The hot new toys, the nifty James Bond gadgets, unlimited funding. Not to mention the sexy, covert missions. There was a lot of jealousy among the Teams over that." Coburn grinned suddenly. "Well, at Seven it runs the other way. We're like the Marines here, Murdock. We make do with what we have, travel light, and count on the men instead of the gadgets.

"And speaking of men, you've got some of the best in Third Platoon. Your two senior CPOs are Ben Kosciuszko and

George MacKenzie. I told you about MacKenzie. He's the guy who was with Six for a couple of years. Kos came in with the UDT, so you know *he's* been kicking around for a while."

Murdock nodded. The SEALs had been an outgrowth of the old Underwater Demolition Teams, which had formally been swallowed up by the SEALs in 1983.

"You can rely on them," Coburn continued. "I suppose you'll want to meet the rest of your people yourself. You want me to walk you over?"

"That's okay, sir. I think I'd just as soon drop in on them unannounced and see just what I have to deal with."

"Well, they know you're getting in sometime today. God knows what you'll find waiting for you. They're a high-spirited bunch."

"I'll take my chances, sir."

"Fine. We have an office for you in this building, just down the hall. The BOQ is just down the road. Anything you need, let me know."

It was clearly the end of the interview. Murdock stood. "Thank you, sir."

"Glad to have you with the Team."

0915 hours (Zulu −5)
Norfolk City Jail
Norfolk, Virginia

"Aw, c'mon, Ray," MacKenzie said. "I'm sure the boys were just blowin' off a bit of steam. You know how it is!"

"Blowing off steam, huh?" Captain Raymond Nagel of the Norfolk Police favored MacKenzie with as dark a glower as the SEAL had ever seen as he tapped a stack of reports on his desk with a bony forefinger. "Look, Mac. I've got thirty-seven complaints here from various parts of Norfolk's east side. Your boys were busy last night."

MacKenzie was already tallying up the possible damages in his head. Thank God that the cop on at the duty desk was an old friend. He'd known Ray Nagel back in Viet Nam—he'd been Gunnery Sergeant Nagel of the U.S. Marines then—and since MacKenzie had been transferred to Little Creek, he'd more than once had official dealings with Nagel as representative of the Norfolk City Police Department.

"Are you sure it was my people, Ray? I heard some Marines went off half cocked and—"

"It's *your* people we've got back there in the tank, Mac." Nagel picked up another sheet of paper and studied it judiciously. "Chief Machinist's Mate Thomas Roselli. Radioman First Class Ronald Holt." He glanced up. "They *are* yours?"

MacKenzie sighed. "They're mine."

"Just wanted to keep the record straight. Okay, at nine-forty last night we got a call from a bar that a fight was in progress. We get there just behind the Shore Patrol and find twelve Marines that look like they'd had a run-in with a steamroller. No one'd say what happened, but these little tiffs between gyrenes and the SEALs are getting kinda routine, ain't they, Mac?"

MacKenzie spread his hands. "Ray, I can't even say for sure it was my guys who did it. Were they at that bar?"

"You don't know?"

"Hey, I'm asking you, right?"

"Yeah, okay. Fine. At ten-fifteen last night, we get another call from the Night's Rest Hotel up on Ocean View. Seems several guys were seen climbing up the *outside* of the hotel. Five stories, straight up. Some of the guests thought the place was being burglarized and called the police. There were also complaints about an unusually loud party on the fifth floor, and reports of several young ladies running down the corridor naked, rather loudly pursued by several naked or indecently exposed men.

"By the time the police arrived twenty minutes later, we'd already received another call, this one from hotel security. They said the hotel manager'd gone up to a room on five in response to complaints about the party. When the police reached the fifth floor, they about tripped over a man and a woman copulating in the hall in front of the elevator. Four more men were in a room registered to a 'Mr. Smith,' threatening to throw the manager out of the fifth-story window and into the hotel swimming pool below. Your man Holt had him by the ankles and was dangling him out of the window upside down. That's assault, Mac. It's damned serious."

MacKenzie groaned. After the dustup at Sarnelli's the night before, they'd hit a bar or two more before Garcia passed out, dead drunk on the sidewalk. MacKenzie had driven him back to the base. This new round of fun and games must have started after he'd left. Damn it, he'd *told* them . . .

"What's my boys' story, Ray?"

The police captain made a face. "That they were just having a quiet little get-together with some, ah, friends, that the manager used abusive and threatening language, and that they were just trying to reason with him."

"Uh-huh. That sounds about right."

"The room was a shambles. The bed frame had collapsed, and the thing was disassembled and stacked in one corner along with the mattresses, which I suppose explains why that couple was going at it out in the hall. The bathtub had been filled with something later identified as liquid lime Jello. And there were colored balloons hanging from the ceiling panels that turned out to be inflated condoms. 'Mr. Smith' was identified by the manager as your Chief Roselli. The arresting officers took Holt and Roselli into custody. Both men were under the influence and resisted arrest."

"Uh-oh. How badly did they resist?"

"One of my men may have a broken wrist, Mac. Four others have an assortment of bruises and contusions."

"That's a relief. Shit, Ray, you know as well as I do that if my boys had *really* been resisting arrest—"

"They also broke five nightsticks with karate blows and chucked two revolvers, a pair of handcuffs, and one of my men into the Jello."

MacKenzie sighed. "You sent five men to answer that call?"

"Eight. Hell, the dispatcher called in a 10-34, Mac. That's 'riot in progress.' We finally managed to subdue Roselli and Holt, but the other three got away. The one in the hall slipped out a window and climbed down the outside of the building. The other two went through the open window in the hotel room. They dove—*dove,* mind you—five stories into the hotel pool. Damned lucky for them the deep end was beneath their window. But one older lady ended up in the hospital."

"My God. They landed on her?"

"No. Just shock. The guests at the poolside were rather, ah, startled, shall we say, by the sudden appearance of two naked men landing in the water."

"Is the woman okay?"

"Yeah. No thanks to your SEALs. The ones that got away were last seen barreling across the hotel's golf course in a '91 Chevy, taking out a palm tree and an ornamental fence on the way. The hotel's tallied up a bill of, let's see . . ." Nagel consulted another paper on his desk. "Two thousand, three hundred ninety-five dollars. Damage to the bed, the grounds, the tree, the fence. Christ, Mac, this really is the final straw. We could hit your people with assault, unlawful restraint, resisting arrest, malicious destruction of property—"

"Ray, I'll give it to you straight. These boys just came back off a mission. A *real* mission. And they lost their CO. I mean it. It really hit 'em hard."

Nagel's eyes widened. "No shit?"

"Ray, you know I wouldn't shit you. We lost a good man."

"Where was it, Mac? Iraq?"

"You also know I can't tell you anything."

Nagel took a deep breath. "Look Mac, I understand, and I wanna do you a favor, you know I do. But this is a decent town, and I can't have your boys trashing the place just because they need to cut loose. I've covered for your SEALs before, but . . ."

"Have you filed charges yet, Ray?"

"No, but—"

"Is the hotel manager pressing charges?"

Nagel glowered, then shook his head, almost reluctantly. "If they get paid, they won't file. I think the manager was so relieved to get them out of his place he, well, sorta forgot."

MacKenzie pulled out his checkbook and began writing. The senior chiefs at Little Creek maintained a discretionary fund against just such emergencies. Roselli, Holt, Doc, Fernandez, and Nicholson would be encouraged to "contribute" to that fund, as they had a time or three in the past. He filled in the amount for three thousand, tore it off, and passed it to Nagel. "That's for the damages, Ray. If there's any change left over, maybe the Policemen's Fund? . . ."

Nagel accepted the check and tucked it into a desk drawer. "Thanks, Mac. The boys'll appreciate it. But I can't keep sweeping up the mess your SEALs leave behind them. . . ."

The lecture that followed was rough, but not as rough as MacKenzie had feared. At least this time around there would be no civil charges against his men, and he thought he could handle the military end of it informally, through extra duty and that "contribution" to the chief's fund. Of course, if they wanted a captain's mast, he'd let them have one.

He wondered, though, what the new CO would make of all this. Maybe it was better that he never know. . . .

They brought Roselli and Holt out to him, both men showing some nasty blotches around puffy eyes. "*You* two," he said ominously, "have a shitload of explaining to do!"

Damn, what was the new lieutenant going to think?

0945 hours (Zulu −5)
Headquarters, SEAL Team Seven
Little Creek, Virginia

Murdock stood appalled inside the barracks wing set aside for SEAL Seven personnel. There were going to be some changes made here if he had anything to say about it. . . .

Not all of the men of Third Platoon "lived aboard" at the Navy's Little Creek Amphibious Base. Kosciuszko and Mac-Kenzie were both married, Murdock had noted while going through their records a few minutes earlier, and lived off base. Brown and Frazier were also married and lived in base housing, while Lieutenant j.g. DeWitt stayed in the Bachelor Officers' Quarters, the BOQ Coburn had mentioned.

The rest of the Third Platoon, however, was quartered here in the barracks, a large, two-story cinderblock affair painted a depressing olive drab and overlooking the dumpsters arrayed along the back of the enlisted mess across a dusty street. Large signs decorated the bulkhead outside the door: "To err is

human. To forgive is not our policy." "SEALs have nerves.
They just ignore them." There was trash on the floor, several
beer cans and a plastic Diet Coke bottle. More alarming was
the white bra dangling like a pennant from an overhead light,
and the sheer panties on the deck just inside the door.

Otherwise, the place was similar to other enlisted barracks
Murdock had seen. A fair amount of ingenuity had been used to
turn a spartan and utilitarian open barracks into living quarters
offering a semblance of privacy. The original dormitory space
had been divided into "cubes" by plyboard partitions, each with
two racks in a bunk-bed arrangement, plus gray, upright
lockers, a table or battered government-issue desk, and occasional human touches like a guitar case or a stereo or a nude
centerfold taped to bulkhead or open locker door. Each cube
was separated from the world by improvised curtains hanging
across its entrance, old sheets or blankets.

There were beer cans scattered about the barracks deck, and
one body, a man clad in boxer shorts and a T-shirt. Murdock
stooped to check the guy's breathing; he appeared to be
sleeping off a binge, and didn't move when Murdock nudged
him twice. He was clutching a woman's bra, a lacy black one,
in his right fist.

Murdock stood as another man entered the passageway, a
short, dark-skinned Latino with a thin, black mustache. He was
wearing a towel and shower clogs and carried a bar of soap.

"What's your name?" Murdock asked.

"Boomer. Ah . . . Garcia. Sir."

"I could be mistaken, Garcia," Murdock said slowly, "but I
thought the usual procedure was to shout 'Attention on deck'
when an officer walked in."

Garcia stiffened, hands at his sides. "Attention on deck!"

Murdock nudged the body with the toe of his shoe. "What's
this?"

"That's Doc," Garcia said. "Uh, HM2 Ellsworth. Sir."

"He always rack out in the passageway?"

"No, sir. We, ah, we had a bit of a party last night, sir."

Murdock looked at the woman's undergarment in Ellsworth's
hand. "So I see."

Two more men stumbled from behind two of the curtained-off cubes, one wearing civilian clothing, the other in boxer shorts. Their reactions were definitely running a bit on the slow side. It took several beats for them to realize that Murdock was there and to shuffle into a position approximating attention in front of their cubes.

"Names?"

"Torpedoman's Mate Second Nicholson, sir." He was the one in his underwear. He had the hard-muscled body of a SEAL and a face that looked too young to shave.

"Gunner's Mate First Class Fernandez. Sir." Another Latino, stocky, heavier than Garcia, with black hair beginning to curl over his ears.

"And this is that crack SEAL platoon I've been hearing about?" He crossed his arms and shook his head in mock exasperation. "I don't believe it!"

"Sir," Nicholson said. "It's Saturday."

"I know what day it is, Nicholson. Thank you. Next time the Iraqis decide to take hostages, you can pass 'em the word that we won't attack until regular working hours.

"In the meantime, and before the Norfolk City Department of Health comes in and closes this establishment down, you're going to square this shithouse away. Understood? I said, 'Understood?' "

"Yes, sir!" the three chorused.

"Garcia!"

"Yes, sir."

"Lose the face fuzz."

"But—"

"You're a SEAL, Garcia. You know that facial hair can break the seal on a swim mask."

"But Lieutenant Cotter said—"

"I don't give a shit what Lieutenant Cotter said! Strip the lip!"

"Aye, aye, sir." Murdock heard the resentment in Garcia's voice.

"Fernandez?"

"Yes, sir."

"Haircut."

Fernandez looked startled. "Aye, aye, sir."

"Just in case there was any question, ladies, I am your new platoon leader, and we will be seeing a lot of each other in the next few days. Where's the rest of the platoon?"

The men traded uneasy, sidelong glances. "I ain't sure, sir," Garcia said. "Maybe they left early."

Murdock glanced at his watch. It was almost 1000 hours. "When you see them, you can tell them I will be holding an inspection of this barracks tomorrow afternoon. I will expect the flotsam cleared away, the contraband off the bulkheads and lockers, the personal gear stowed, and the deck waxed and shined." He looked meaningfully at Nicholson. "And I don't give a shit if tomorrow *is* Sunday. Beginning Monday, I will begin talking to each of you individually. I want to get to know you, find out what the hell makes you think you're decent SEAL material. And . . ." He stopped, and nudged Ellsworth again. "Will two of you pick this up and get it to its rack? I have this thing about gear adrift. That is all."

Murdock turned to make a dignified exit and nearly collided with a familiar figure in civilian clothes who was just coming through the door, a big, olive-green seabag balanced on one shoulder.

"Uh . . . Third Platoon?" the newcomer asked uncertainly, looking around.

"Jaybird!" Murdock said, taking a step back and smiling. "You're just in time!"

Sterling's eyes widened. "Oh, no . . ."

The SEALs stared after the lieutenant for several long moments after he'd gone.

"What the fuck was *that*?" Fernandez wanted to know.

"A prick," Garcia replied. "Mickey Mouse himself with delusions of grandeur."

"You guys notice his hand?" Nicholson asked. "He's a ring-knocker."

"No shit?" Garcia said. "An Academy grad?"

"I don't care if he's John Wayne in drag," Fernandez said. "We're SEALs. We don't hafta' take that shit."

"Scuttlebutt is he's from Coronado," Nicholson added. "A fuckin' BUD/S instructor."

"He is," Jaybird put in. "I flew out from California with him last night."

"Aw, man," Garcia said, disgusted. "I did my hard time in BUD/S. What *is* this shit anyway?"

"Yeah," Fernandez added. "I wonder if that dude's always so full of sweetness and light, man." He pointed at Jaybird. "I thought you California SEALs were 'sposed to be laid back and mellow, man."

"Hey, don't blame me," Jaybird said. "I hardly know the guy!"

"Obviously," Nicholson pointed out, "he's an officer an' a gentleman. Far above us enlisted pukes. Say, how'd you get a handle like Jaybird anyway?"

On the deck, Ellsworth gave a mournful groan. "Hey," Garcia said. "Couple a' you guys gimme a hand here."

Together, they got Doc to his rack.

For a long time after that, they discussed the new lieutenant's manner, bearing, attitude, and probable ancestry, comparing it point by point with those of Lieutenant Cotter.

So far, the new guy didn't measure up well at all.

10

Wednesday, 18 May

1145 hours (Zulu +3)
Freighter *Yuduki Maru*
Indian Ocean, south of Mauritius

The sun glared with brassy heat from the flat swells of the Indian Ocean, as two ships, the *Yuduki Maru* and her escort, *Shikishima*, plowed steadily eastward at eighteen knots. Twenty days out of the French military port at Cherbourg, she had another four weeks' voyage ahead of her. Her course lay due east across the Indian Ocean, south of Australia and New Zealand, then turning northwest, passing through Micronesia and the empty waters of the western Pacific until she entered her home port of Tokai, ninety miles northeast of Tokyo.

Yuduki Maru's long-way-around voyage had been dictated by the volatile rumblings of international politics. Like some twentieth-century Flying Dutchman, she was pledged to remain always at least two hundred nautical miles from land. Forbidden outright to enter the waters of South Africa, Indonesia, Chile, or Malaysia she had a sharply limited choice of courses. The Straits of Mulacca, twenty-three miles wide at their narrowest, and the South China Sea, a den of modern-day pirates, both had been closed to her.

In the interests of secrecy, her final course had been set only days before she'd left Cherbourg. Not that secrecy remained absolute. The Greenpeace vessel *Beluga* had dogged the tiny flotilla since their sailing, remaining just over the horizon, making certain that the Japanese ships did not break their international quarantine.

Captain Chuichi Koga, *Yuduki Maru*'s master, was unconcerned with the *Beluga,* as he was with the quarantine and with the crowds of protestors who'd mobbed the fences at the naval base perimeter at Cherbourg. The total voyage, Cherbourg to Tokai, should take seven weeks. Koga, a professional, confident, and supremely competent officer of the merchant marine who demanded absolute punctuality of himself and of his crew, had no doubts whatsoever that they would arrive in port on schedule.

Yuduki Maru was small for so long a voyage, with a length overall of 119 meters, a beam of less than eighteen meters, and a full-load draft of just over six meters. She had a displacement of 7,600 tons.

Nevertheless, she was an impressive vessel. Like her sister ship, the *Akatsuki Maru,* she had been an American cargo ship—sailing under the name *Atlantic Crane*—before her conversion to her new and highly specialized task. She'd been refitted in a Belfast shipyard, her hatches strengthened, her huge, forward deck crane removed, and her electronics suite upgraded and modernized. Large sections of her cargo hold had been sealed off and converted to carry extra reserves of diesel fuel so she could manage her forty-thousand-kilometer voyage without refueling. Some of her cargo space had also been converted into accommodations. Besides her usual crew of forty-five, the *Yuduki Maru* carried thirty armed guards.

And, of course, there was the comforting presence of the *Shikishima* a kilometer to port. Captain Koga, like most of his superiors, would have been far happier if a couple of Japanese Navy destroyers could have escorted *Yuduki Maru* on her long passage. Unfortunately, Japan's postwar constitution specifically prohibited any of her 125-odd military vessels from being deployed outside Japanese waters. For that reason, escort duties had been assumed by the Kaijo Hoancho, an organization analogous to the U.S. Coast Guard. *Shikishima* had been specially built for this task at a cost of twenty billion yen, a 6,500-ton cutter armed with machine guns and one of the

American Phalanx close-in point-defense systems. She also carried a Kawasaki-Bell 212 helicopter on her fantail landing platform.

The Americans had been involved with planning for the security of these voyages from the beginning. They were, naturally enough, keenly interested in the security of *Yuduki Maru*'s precious and deadly cargo.

Two tons of plutonium, after all, was prize enough to attract the eye of dozens of governments, political factions, terrorist groups, environmental activists, and outright criminals all over the world.

It was enough to provoke a war, and more than enough to finish one. It was also a symbol of Japan's national honor.

Japan's interest in plutonium was strictly peaceful and economic. Ever since the 1960s, the country had been committed to achieving energy self-sufficiency through an aggressive and high-tech atomic power program. In particular they'd sought the promise of fast-breeder nuclear reactors.

There were already forty-one conventional nuclear power plants fueled by uranium in the Japanese home islands. For years, the spent nuclear fuel from these reactors had been shipped to reprocessing plants in Europe, notably the French company Cogema, in Cap de la Hague, Normandy, and a British plant in Sellafield, Cumbria. There, high-grade plutonium was extracted from the radioactive ash left over from the conventional nuclear plants; a special type of power plant, the so-called fast breeder, generated power from plutonium and, in a process that seemed to defy the normal laws concerning something from nothing, actually generated *more* nuclear fuel as an end product. Ultimately, Japan could be completely self-sufficient, generating all of its own power needs, even exporting power to other nations.

It was a worthwhile goal, given that Japan was currently almost entirely dependent on outside sources for energy, and she had some grand and energy-intensive plans for future technological growth. Unfortunately, there were some serious drawbacks as well.

First and foremost, plutonium is without question the deadliest substance known. Quite apart from its high levels of radioactivity, it is so toxic that a microscopic amount can kill a man, while a gram or two in a water reservoir can wipe out an entire city. And, of course, there is the nuclear genie; the hardest part of building an atomic bomb is processing the uranium in the first place, or getting hold of enough plutonium to provide the fissionable material. Just eight kilograms of plutonium is enough for the manufacture of a quick-and-dirty nuclear device as powerful as the one that burned the heart out of Nagasaki.

Too, there were the political problems that buzzed around the stuff like flies over garbage. A sizable percentage of Japan's home population resisted any manifestation of nuclear power, for obvious reasons, and the outcry from environmentalists and antinuclear activists around the world had been startling. Transporting so much plutonium was perceived as an unacceptable risk, one threatening thousands, even millions of people, should something go wrong.

Nor was breeder technology proven. Monju, a prototype breeder reactor, was still a year away from producing electricity. America, France, Great Britain, and the other major industrial powers had long ago abandoned the breeder concept as too risky for commercial use.

The creation of so much plutonium had proven to be a public relations nightmare for Tokyo, but there was no other way for the country to achieve its goals. Suggestions from the international community that Japan use plutonium extracted from the post-Cold War world's nuclear stockpiles instead of shipping it halfway around the world was no solution at all, since something still had to be done about all that plutonium piling up in Europe. Besides, the Japanese public insisted, understandably if somewhat irrationally, that only plutonium that had never been used in nuclear weapons was acceptable as a power source at home.

Fears of what would happen if Japan's plutonium stockpiles at home or abroad fell into the wrong hands dogged the nation like a shadow. Antinuclear groups were swift to point out that while a serious malfunction in a conventional reactor could lead to meltdown and the release of radiation, a disaster in a breeder plant *could* result in a very large bang indeed.

Since the United States had sold the original nuclear fuel to Japan, Washington, under the provisions of the nuclear non-proliferation treaty, maintained a say over what happened to it and how it was handled. Unfortunately, the U.S. government was far more sensitive to pressure from the environmentalists than Japan was. A 1989 plan to fly the plutonium back to Japan had been vetoed outright by the U.S., which dreaded the political, ecological, and literal fallout of a plane crash.

The ideal, of course, would have been to process the original spent fuel cores at home, in Japan, but the first such reprocessing plant, now being constructed at Rokkasho, in northern Japan, was not due to begin operation until 1997, and would only have an output of five tons of plutonium a year. Besides, Britain and France had already served notice that they would not store Japan's accumulating stores of plutonium indefinitely. The stuff was difficult to keep, took up a lot of space, and provided a dazzling target for terrorists and activists of any of several political persuasions.

And so, the only alternative for Japan, hedged in by a bewildering array of political threats, treaty and constitutional obligations, and public relations problems, had been to transport the stuff back to the home islands by sea. Tokyo had consulted with Washington on the operation and accepted the American directives regarding security. These had included the structural upgrades to the freighters, the addition of an on-board security force, and the building of the *Shikishima* herself, since Japanese naval vessels were not allowed to leave their home waters.

The first shipment of 1.7 tons had left Cherbourg early in October of 1992, arriving without incident in Tokai fifty-eight days later. Several shipments had made the passage since, the start of the biggest sea lift of plutonium in history. The timetable ultimately called for a total of some ninety tons of plutonium to be shipped from Europe to Japan by the year 2010.

Koga wondered if his government was tempted by so much

plutonium to abandon its stance of nearly fifty years and become a nuclear power. The idea didn't bother Koga as it did many of his countrymen; *he* didn't remember Hiroshima, and as Japan became increasingly isolated in a hostile world, it would have to learn to protect itself, without relying on the vacillations of a fragmented and unreliable West.

In the meantime, it was enough to carry out his duty, which was to deliver two tons of plutonium safely to port in Tokai.

Raising his binoculars to his eyes, he scanned an empty horizon for a moment, then turned them on the lean, white hull of *Shikishima,* still maintaining station to the north. The Kaijo Hoancho emblem, a triple blue stripe on the hull forward, like a squared-off Roman letter S lying on its back reaching from scupper to waterline, was clearly visible, as were the sailors lounging in the gun tub on the forward deck. They seemed unconcerned about the proximity of *Yuduki Maru*'s cargo.

And in fact, there was little to worry about. The cargo was safely stowed in hundreds of individual lead pigs in the freighter's holds, divided into carefully measured and separated quantities to avoid critical mass and a chain reaction. So far as any external threat was concerned, *Yuduki Maru* and *Shikishima* were alone on that wide, empty ocean. The nearest land at the moment was the southern tip of Madagascar, one thousand kilometers to the north, and the weather, a serious concern during the initial planning, was exceptionally and spectacularly calm.

Koga turned his attention to the *Yuduki Maru*'s deck below the bridge. The freighter was designed along the lines of a tanker or bulk carrier, with the blocky, white superstructure far aft, and hold access through deck hatches in the long forward deck. A number of men were visible at the moment, mostly off-duty crewmen basking in the sun. One man, a galley worker, was perched bare-legged on one of the hatch covers, dutifully slicing up vegetables, which he removed one by one from a large sack at his side, and dropping the pieces in a bowl in his lap.

Also visible were five of the ship's security people, wearing brown uniforms and carrying Beretta submachine guns. *Yuduki*

Maru's security force had been drawn from one of Tokyo's Police Special Action Units, again to avoid the restrictions of Japan's postwar constitution. They were the best there was, however, tough, disciplined men who had trained extensively with the British SAS, Germany's GSG-9, and Israeli paratroopers.

There was simply no way any enemy could get at the plutonium in *Yuduki Maru*'s hold. Koga allowed a rare smile to crease his lips. It promised to be an extraordinarily boring voyage.

"Captain!" the helmsman shouted, pointing to port. "Look!"

Koga looked, and had trouble absorbing what he was seeing. A column of water hung suspended at *Shikishima*'s side, descending across her deck like a blanketing mist. In the next instant, the escort vessel seemed to arch from the water like a stretching cat; the thunder of the detonation reached *Yuduki Maru* a second later, a piercing roar that assaulted the ears and rattled the glass in the bridge windows. *Shikishima* dropped with nightmare slowness back into the sea, her back snapping as she struck, mingled black smoke and orange flame mushrooming into the sky above her deck.

Koga watched, transfixed, horrified. What was happening? Contradictory thoughts chased one another through his head. The *Shikishima*'s boilers had blown up. She had struck an old mine adrift since some long-ago war. She had been torpedoed. . . .

Torpedoed! A second blast tore through *Shikishima*'s stern quarter, hurling fragments—boat davits, life rafts, stanchions, men—hundreds of meters through the air. The Safety Agency's escort could not possibly have struck *two* mines. Somewhere in that empty sea, a submarine was firing torpedoes at the flotilla!

"Captain!" the helmsman wailed. "What should we do?"

Do? If they stopped to pick up survivors, the next torpedo might well slam into *Yuduki Maru*'s hull, with disastrous results. Indeed, a torpedo might already be on the way, streaking unseen toward the freighter beneath the ocean waves.

"Speed . . . more speed!" Koga said. He reached for the

intercom microphone hanging on its hook beneath the forward bridge window, and froze, hand extended, as he saw the drama unfolding on the forward deck.

The five security men down there had raced as one to *Yuduki Maru*'s port railing, staring at the stricken *Shikishima,* pointing and calling excitedly to one another. At their backs, unnoticed, the lone galley hand had reached into the burlap bag of vegetables and was extracting the gleaming black length of an AKM assault rifle.

Before Koga could react, before he could think of shouting warning, the crewman opened fire on full automatic from a range of less than five meters. Security personnel jerked and twisted. One lurched forward and fell over the side, as the others groped for slung weapons, dropped twitching to the deck, and died.

The intercom forgotten, Koga reached instead for the ship's alarm button. He slapped it, and the raucous blast of the emergency alarm blared from the bridge speakers and throughout the ship. The security officer stationed on the bridge unholstered his pistol and took a step forward. "Captain—" he said, and then one of the doors leading onto the bridge from aft burst open, and two wild-eyed men exploded from the passageway behind it. One held an Israeli-made Uzi submachine gun, the other an AKM. The one with the Uzi triggered the weapon, and 9mm slugs tore half the security officer's skull away, pitching him against the bridge window in a spray of blood and shattering glass. The other ignored the rest of the bridge crew, but hurried to the door leading to the ship's communications center.

"Come out! Come out!" he shouted, but the communications officer and those standing watch with him must not have moved quickly enough to suit him, for almost immediately the AK opened fire, a hammering fusillade that was deafening in the confines of the bridge. There was a long, drawn-out scream, a second burst of automatic fire, and then only the rasp of the ship's emergency alarm.

"Kill that noise," the man with the Uzi growled, and he held the weapon's muzzle a few centimeters from Koga's head.

Koga complied instantly. He had no doubt that these madmen would kill everyone on the bridge if they showed the slightest resistance.

It dawned on Koga, belatedly, that the man with the Uzi was his own fourth officer, Tetsuo Kurebayashi. The gunman emerging with a sadist's grin from the communications center was Shigeru Yoshitomi, a lowly cargo handler.

"Chikusho!" Koga said as the alarm strangled into silence. "Damn you!" It seemed inconceivable, impossible. Terrorists on his ship, members of his own crew! "What is it you want?"

"Silence!" Kurebayashi snapped. His face was twisted with mingled joy and battle-lust, and looking into those eyes, Koga was terrified. "Hands up! And the rest of you! Get down on your knees! Hands over your heads! *Now!*"

Koga dropped to his knees with the rest of the bridge personnel. From where he kneeled on the deck, he could just glimpse *Shikishima*'s final death throes above the bridge window sill. Fire boiled from the sea, and only the bow and part of the helicopter pad on the fantail were visible, jutting at sharp angles from the sea and separated by a sea of burning oil. Black smoke stained the cloudless sky.

In the distance, somewhere below decks, he could hear the muffled pounding of automatic gunfire. Gods, how many terrorists *were* there? How had they infiltrated his crew? Koga was filled with a sudden, sad foreboding.

Despite all of his care and professionalism, *Yuduki Maru* and her deadly cargo were not going to make her scheduled port of call.

1520 hours (Zulu +3)
Motor yacht *Beluga*
Indian Ocean, south of Mauritius

Though she desperately wanted to acquire the casual international sophistication of her German friends Gertrude and Helga, Jean Brandeis still felt uncomfortable going topless in front of the men aboard the *Beluga,* even if one of them was her husband. Her modesty, she'd decided, was a last, conservative vestige of her Midwestern American upbringing, one she'd not been able to shake after years of living both in Los Angeles and in France. Throughout *Beluga*'s long cruise from Cherbourg down the Atlantic coast of Europe, she'd compromised each time Gertie and Helga stripped down for sunbathing by lying face down on a towel spread out on the deck, and always with her bikini top within easy reach.

By the time *Beluga* had entered African waters at the end of the first week of the cruise, she was so badly sunburned that she'd had a decent excuse to cover up. Then, during the passage around the Cape of Good Hope, there'd been a stiff, cold wind, with weather and temperatures appropriate to November in northern latitudes.

Eventually, though, about the time *Beluga* again crossed the thirtieth parallel somewhere south of Madagascar, Jean's burn had darkened to a delicious California-girl tan, and the days had warmed enough that Helga and Gertrude had begun their daily regimen of nude or half-nude sunbathing again. Afraid of seeming prudish or provincially unsophisticated, and encouraged by her husband, she'd joined them.

She wanted so much to make a good impression on their new friends.

Jean Brandeis had considered herself to be a liberal activist ever since she'd married her husband, Paul, five years earlier. Paul Brandeis, a Hollywood producer who'd won international acclaim with his films on a variety of ecological and animal-rights causes, had swept her into a whole new world of celebrities, parties, and popular activism. Encouraged by a well-known French producer, both of them had joined Greenpeace International two years earlier.

That was when they'd met Karl and Helga Schmidt and Rudi and Gertrude Kohler, all long-time members of both Greenpeace and Europe's International Green Party. Karl had had a hand in organizing the huge protest in Cherbourg; the yacht *Beluga* was Rudi's, though he'd registered it as belonging to Greenpeace. Jean had been thrilled by the urbane sophistication of Paul's new friends and excited by the prospect of activist work, a *cause* she could fight for.

Somehow, though, she'd never expected that work to carry

her across ten thousand miles of open ocean, dogging the heels
of a Japanese freighter. Focusing world media attention on the
threat presented by the *Yuduki Maru* and her cargo was a
worthwhile cause certainly, but the voyage had rapidly degen-
erated into an unending tedium dragging on for day after day
after sunbaked day. Quarters aboard were cramped; *Beluga* was
a forty-meter, two-masted schooner, a millionaire's yacht, but
after three weeks with ten people aboard—the six of them plus
a four-man crew—her dimensions had somehow shrunk to
those of a twenty-foot day sailer. Helga and Gertrude, who
three weeks ago had seemed so witty and smart and vivacious,
were revealed as shallow gossips who talked of little but sex,
celebrities, and themselves.

To make matters worse, lately Karl had started hitting on her,
his casual and friendly flirtations becoming more insistent,
more open. It seemed to Jean that when he bumped into her in
Beluga's narrow passageways, the contact was deliberate, and
more lingering than was strictly necessary to get by.

And Paul wasn't making it any easier on her either, damn
him, with his fiercely whispered admonitions that she should
be nice to their hosts. She knew he saw Karl and Rudi both as
contacts who could open some important doors in the European
entertainment industry, but she wondered if he had any idea
what Karl's idea of *nice* might be.

She wished this cruise were over. More than that, she wished
something would happen. It was so boring, plodding along in
the wake of that damned, unseen Japanese ship, day following
day, each day the same. . . .

A cry from the bow snapped her from the warm lassitude of
her thoughts. Karl and two of the crewmen were running
forward, and she could feel the pitch of *Beluga*'s diesel engine
change in the ever-present throb transmitted through her deck.
Something *was* happening . . . something that had the yacht's
crew excited.

Karl ran aft again, heading toward *Beluga*'s wheel. "Karl!"
she called as he passed. "What is it?"

"I'm not sure, honey," he said. "Viktor thinks it could be a
shipwreck."

A shipwreck, hundreds of miles from the nearest land? That made no sense. Forgetting her partial nudity, she scrambled to her feet and hurried forward. A small crowd was gathering at the starboard railing near the foremast, chattering to each other in German and gesturing at the water. Viktor, the *Beluga*'s mate, was studying the water ahead though binoculars.

"What is happening?" Helga asked, coming up behind her. "What do they see?"

Peering past Viktor's shoulder, Jean could see a darkening on the sea a hundred yards off. An oil slick, probably. She knew about oil slicks . . . but there was lots of floating debris as well.

Helga screamed, pointing.

The man was floating face-up twenty feet off *Beluga*'s starboard side. Despite the burns on his face, he was clearly Oriental.

He was also clearly dead.

Paul was beside her, a Geiger counter in his hand, a grim expression on his face as he swept the instrument back and forth in the air.

"Is it . . . was it . . ."

"No radiation," Paul Brandeis replied curtly. "I don't know if it was the *Yuduki Maru* or not. It could have been her escort." He turned to Viktor. "We'd better call this in."

"Ja, Herr Brandeis."

Jean folded her arms across her breasts and shivered. Her wish—that something would happen—had been granted.

Somehow, though, *this* wasn't quite what she'd had in mind.

11

Thursday, 19 May

1512 hours (Zulu −5)
NAVSPECWARGRU-Two Briefing Room
Little Creek, Virginia

Captain Paul Mason strode into the briefing room, back straight and almost pain-free. It had been several years now since he'd needed a cane to walk, and he continued to skirmish with the Navy doctors who'd originally predicted that he'd be driving a wheelchair for the rest of his life.

Someday, Mason knew, he would not only walk, but he would jump out of airplanes again as well, don the heavy tanks of a SCUBA apparatus, and even pull a five-miles-plus endurance swim with fins.

He was a SEAL.

Waiting in the room were several of the important ops-level people in the Norfolk SEAL Community; the skippers of SEAL Teams Two, Four, Seven, and Eight; Captain Kenneth Friedman, commanding Helicopter Attack Squadron Light Four, the Red Wolves; and several staff, logistics, and support officers. Rear Admiral Bainbridge, CO-NAVSPECWARGRU-Two, was there as well, chewing on the stem of an unlit pipe and looking distinctly unhappy as he reviewed a sheaf of computer print-outs just handed to him by his meteorological officer. Also present was Rear Admiral Kerrigan of MIDEASTFOR. The Middle East Force, under the operational umbrella of the Sixth Fleet in the Med, was headquartered in Bahrain, but Kerrigan

served as staff liaison to the various naval commands based in
Norfolk, including NAVSPECWARGRU-Two.

And at the end of the table, isolated by his civilian clothes,
was the suit from Langley. Brian Hadley didn't *look* like a
spook—small, rumpled, and nearsighted, with the frizzy white
hair of a university professor—but he was supposed to be one
of the best analysts in the CIA's Intelligence Directorate, head
of the Office of Global Issues.

Hadley had arrived, Mason knew, only moments ago from
the Executive Office Building, where the National Security
Council staff had been meeting round the clock since this
current crisis had broken loose.

Mason walked to the end of the long mahogany table, taking
his place behind the podium there. The other men in the room,
most of whom he knew well, watched him attentively.

"Very well, gentlemen," Mason said, gripping the sides of
the podium. "You've all been following the situation, and you
know why we're here. For the past twenty-four hours, the
Japanese plutonium ship *Yuduki Maru,* with two tons of
weapons-grade plutonium aboard, has been off course. She is
out of radio contact and, until we can determine otherwise, we
are assuming that this is a terrorist incident and are classifying
it as a Broken Arrow."

The men around the table shifted uncomfortably. Broken
Arrow was the code phrase for any accident with nuclear
weapons—specifically with U.S. weapons accidentally launched
or jettisoned, such as had happened back in the sixties with the
crash of a U.S. aircraft carrying nuclear weapons off the coast
of Spain.

The provisions for calling a Broken Arrow alert, however,
included the theft or loss of any nuclear weapon or radiological
component, or any situation where there was a real or implied
public hazard from that component. The fine points had been
debated in both the Pentagon and the White House already; the
plutonium aboard the *Yuduki Maru* belonged to Japan and was
not the direct responsibility of the U.S. government. Still, the
United States had assumed an indirect responsibility for the
plutonium. American firms had sold the original uranium to

Japan in the first place, and perhaps more to the point, two tons of radioactive plutonium represented a terrific danger, both to American interests and to America's allies. If terrorists had indeed hijacked the *Yuduki Maru,* they were not likely to be sympathetic to U.S. interests.

Reinforcing this, Mason went on to discuss the evidence that this was the act of terrorists. "The *Shikishima,*" he said, "the freighter's Maritime Safety Agency escort, has been confirmed sunk. At about 1530 hours yesterday local time, the Greenpeace yacht *Beluga* encountered the oil slick and some floating bodies. *Beluga* and other vessels in the area have been alerted to keep an eye out for survivors, but at this point we are not hopeful.

"We were able to pinpoint *Yuduki Maru* immediately and confirm that she is now cruising almost due north at eighteen knots. As of 1300 hours our time today, she was two hundred miles off Pointe Itaperina—that's the southeastern corner of Madagascar. Our intelligence on the situation so far is limited. There has been no communication from her crew, and attempts to contact her have been ignored. We have no idea who is in command now, what group, faction, or government is responsible, or what the freighter's new destination might be."

"How the hell was the escort sunk?" Captain Whittier, of SEAL Two, wanted to know. "Sabotage?"

"Possibly, though security was extraordinarily tight on both vessels before they left Yokohama. At the moment, we're operating on another, rather disturbing possibility." Mason opened his briefcase and removed a folder stamped Top Secret. Inside were two eight-by-ten-inch black-and-white photographs, which he passed around to the other men at the table.

"As you can see from the inscription," Mason continued, "both photographs are of the Iranian naval facility at Bandar Abbas, right on the Straight of Hormuz. The first one was taken on 4 May. Note the two submarines in the upper left."

"Kilos," Captain Harrison, the CO of SEAL Eight, said. "The Iranian Kilos."

In 1992, amid considerable international controversy, Russia had delivered to the Republic of Iran two conventional attack submarines of the type known in the West as Kilo. Displacing 2,900 tons submerged, with a top underwater speed of twenty knots, they'd been designed by the old Soviet Union primarily as a commodity for export. Algeria, Poland, Romania, and India all had Kilos in their fleets, and possibly Cuba and Libya as well. Each was armed with twelve 533mm torpedoes.

"The second photograph was taken by a KH-12 satellite two days later, on 6 May. One of the submarines, note, is gone. We have identified the missing boat as the *Enghelab-é Eslami.* That's Farsi for the *Islamic Revolution.*"

"Let me get this straight, Captain," Admiral Bainbridge said. "You're saying that the goddamn *Iranians* could be behind this?"

Mason faced him squarely. "There is no hard evidence to that effect, Admiral. At least not yet. But one possibility we must consider is that an Iranian submarine torpedoed the *Shikishima,* and that at the same time, a terrorist component aboard the plutonium freighter seized the ship. The *Yuduki Maru*'s new course is consistent with a port in Iran."

"And this Iranian boat has been missing all this time?" Bainbridge asked, "Almost two weeks?"

"You know it's never as easy as it looks in the movies, Tom," Admiral Kerrigan told him.

Bainbridge scowled. "I thought we had subs in the Gulf watching the sons of bitches?"

"We did," Kerrigan said. "We've had an attack boat stationed in Bahrain ever since the Iranians took delivery of those boats, a blanket warning to them not to get cute with shipping in the Gulf. But tracking a submarine in the open ocean's tough, especially a conventional boat. They're quieter than nukes. No cooling pumps for the reactors. Our sub, the Sturgeon-class attack boat *Cavalla,* headed out after the *Revolution* as soon as we realized the Iranian boat was gone. We also have other attack subs converging on that area, but, well, it's a big ocean. Remember the flap a few years back, when that North Korean freighter carrying missile parts to the Gulf just disappeared? And that was with subs searching for her, satellites, the whole nine yards."

"Yeah, but I have a sneaky suspicion you'll find the bastard if you concentrate on the area around that Japanese freighter," Captain Whittier observed.

"I must stress again that Iranian involvement at this point is strictly hypothetical," Mason said. "We did not see the actual sinking of the *Shikishima,* and our tracking of the *Yuduki Maru* so far has been through strictly electronic means."

"Electronic means?" Captain Friedman, the helo squadron skipper, asked. "What, radar?"

"An electronic transponder built into her superstructure," Hadley said. His speech, the way he said "transpondah," had the nasal twang of upper-class Massachusetts. "We used the same trick back in the eighties, tracking a load of fifty-five-gallon drums of ether we thought might lead us to a secret cocaine cartel lab in the Colombian jungle. The transponder's small, the size of a book, but it puts out a steady signal that can be pinpointed by an ELINT satellite in orbit. It was the change in position registered by our satellite that first told us yesterday something was wrong."

"My God," Bainbridge said slowly. "Didn't we have any spy sats following that tub? We should have been watching that ship twenty-four hours a day!"

"Our technical assets are limited, Admiral," Hadley said. "More than most people realize. We never have been able to provide full twenty-four-hour coverage of any one potential target."

"But damn it, this is the Jap *plutonium* ship!"

"We can still only watch the thing when our satellites are above the horizon, Admiral, and frankly, there just aren't enough satellites to go around. For the past few days, most of our watch time had been allotted to southern Iraq, following up on the aftermath of Blue Sky.

"Now, on the direction of the President, the National Reconnaissance people have shifted the bulk of our observation time to the *Yuduki Maru.* I'd estimate that we have about forty percent coverage now."

"In other words, we can see her two hours out of five, is that it?"

"Essentially, Admiral, yes."

"Damn." Bainbridge glowered a moment more, then glanced up the table to where Mason was waiting. "Sorry, Captain," he said. "Please continue."

Shepherding one of these high-level briefings was always a challenge, Mason thought. The admirals were used to running their own shows . . . while the SEAL commanders had less than the usual respect for rank, privilege, or decorum. It made for some lively sessions sometimes.

"Thank you, Admiral," he said. "Okay, judging from the *Yuduki Maru*'s transponder track and where it departs her scheduled course, we believe that the raid took place at approximately noon yesterday, Zulu plus three, about 0400 hours our time. The National Security Council has been in almost constant session since we received news yesterday morning of *Yuduki Maru*'s possible capture.

"This morning, the President gave the authorization to begin working on ways to get that ship back. Since it's a ship and it's at sea, gentlemen, it looks like this one's going to be a SEAL op."

There was a stir around the table at his words, though obviously the news was not a complete surprise. Mason saw a smile or two among the SEAL skippers. Only Kerrigan and some of his staff officers looked displeased. Kerrigan, Mason remembered, was not a fan of special-ops forces. Well, there were plenty in the military community who agreed with him—the usefulness of elite units like the SEALs and the Army Special Forces was still being hotly debated, as the ongoing Congressional hearings on SEAL funding proved—but there wasn't much choice this time around. Only the SEALs could reach *Yuduki Maru* before she got close to a populated coast. Sure, a submarine or an airstrike from a carrier would stop that freighter in her tracks.

But at what terrible cost?

"All SEAL commands will be responsible for drawing up preliminary plans for the operation. Assume a ship-boarding action, aimed at securing the ship and holding it for the arrival of a NEST team." The Nuclear Emergency Search Team was one of America's most secret units. Operating under the Department of Energy, it had the sophisticated equipment necessary for finding, handling, and safing nuclear material.

"The code name assigned to the mission will be Sun Hammer," Mason continued. "My staff will provide you with whatever you need in the way of background intel. I also want your assessments, your honest assessments, of each of your Teams' readiness and capabilities. Some of you are stretched damned thin right now. Two, most of your people are in Germany right now, aren't they?"

"Hell, Captain," Whittier replied easily, "that just means they're halfway to the Indian Ocean already."

"This isn't a competition. I know all of you want to participate, but the final decision will be based on who is best able to handle this. Let me have a preliminary work-up by 0900 tomorrow.

"Now, we have one potential wild card in the picture," Mason continued. Opening the folder again, he extracted another photograph. It was a file photo of a battered-looking vessel, rust-streaked and decrepit, tied up to a crumbling pier. Her forward well deck was so low it seemed a fair-sized wave might swamp her. The number 43 was painted on her bow beneath her high forecastle deck.

"Looks like one of our old yard oilers," Admiral Bainbridge observed.

"She is," Mason said. "She used to be the YO-247. Launched in 1956, and turned over to Iran under the old U.S. Military Air Program. I'm not sure of the year, but pre-1979 obviously. Not really a seagoing vessel at all, but the Iranians have modified her heavily. She's the *Hormuz* now. One hundred seventy-four feet long. Top speed nine or ten knots. Cargo capacity of about nine hundred tons."

"Modified her for what?"

"Under the Shah she was a fleet oiler. Since the Iranian Revolution, she's been laid up at Bandar Abbas most of the time, but there's evidence they've been upgrading her for long-range work. Possibly as a *Milchekuh*."

The word, German for "milk cow," was drawn from the

Germans' use of disguised ships for at-sea replenishment of their submarines in World War II.

"Which is how that Kilo could operate so far out of Iranian waters," a staff officer observed.

"Exactly," Mason agreed. "And . . . it could be coincidence, but the *Hormuz* left Bandar Abbas late last month. We haven't found her yet."

"You're looking, of course," Bainbridge said, turning to the CIA man.

"Of course," Hadley replied. "Although in her case, we don't have the advantage of a transponder. But if we find the *Hormuz* anywhere between Socotra and Madagascar, we'll have a pretty good idea of what happened to the *Shikishima*. And we'll know that Iran *is* behind the hijacking."

"We are also concerned," Mason added, "about whether or not the *Yuduki Maru* could rendezvous with the *Hormuz*. Right now, we're probably dealing with a relatively small number of terrorists, presumably members of the freighter's crew. If she meets up with the *Hormuz,* though, the terrorists could be reinforced by troops. Worse, all or some of *Yuduki Maru*'s cargo could be transferred to the other ship."

"Is that likely, Captain?" Admiral Kerrigan asked. "The Japanese freighter has twice the speed of the *Hormuz* and is a hell of a lot more seaworthy to boot. The Iranians wouldn't be crazy enough to put the cargo in . . ." He let the thought trail off as he considered the possibilities.

"As you've just guessed, Admiral," Mason said with a grim smile, "we don't have the faintest idea what the Iranians are going to do. Maybe they wouldn't care if the plutonium was scattered across half the Indian Ocean. Maybe that's the whole point of this operation, to call attention to some political grievance they'll announce over the course of the next few days. Or maybe they figure we won't dare attack because any damage to the vessel would cause the very eco-disaster we're trying to prevent. The surface currents in that part of the Indian Ocean all run east to west, toward the East African coast, then down the Mozambique Channel. Huge areas of the coast, from

Mogadishu to Cape Town, could be contaminated if the *Yuduki Maru* sank or caught fire.

"As you SEAL Team COs work up your operations drafts, keep in mind that we may have to deal with both the *Yuduki Maru* and the *Hormuz,* as well as the possible presence of an Iranian Kilo.

"But—and I can't stress this enough—we still don't have any hard proof that the Iranians are behind this incident. That's strictly a worst-case scenario. *Shikishima* could have been blown up by a bomb somehow planted on board in Japan. The absence of both *Hormuz* and *Enghelab-é Eslami* from Bandar Abbas could be coincidence. If the Iranians are not involved, we're probably looking at a strictly terrorist act, probably by something like the old Japanese Red Army."

"They've been out of the picture for a good many years now," Hadley pointed out.

"One of their leaders formally renounced the use of force in 1981," Mason said. "But they maintained a headquarters in a PFLP camp outside of Beirut throughout the eighties. They could have decided to become active again. Or we could be dealing with another Japanese terrorist organization, an off-shoot, or some group we haven't heard of yet."

"Lovely thought," one of Bainbridge's staff officers muttered.

"My people will provide all of you with everything we know about the JRA and other terrorist groups that could be involved. And of course, if we have any communication with the hijackers—demands, threats, whatever—we'll set up an intel conduit to keep all pertinent material flowing your way."

"So," Eight's Captain Harrison said thoughtfully. "We're basing out of Diego Garcia, I suppose."

Diego Garcia was the tiny coral atoll, some one thousand miles south of the southern tip of India, which was the United States Navy's sole outpost in the vastness of the Indian Ocean.

"We're already putting our transport assets together toward that end," Bainbridge said. "Air Force C-5s will carry your helicopters and whatever other gear you need to the island. The

State Department is also in touch with the Sultan of Oman, trying to get permission to use Masirah as a staging area."

An island located just off the Omani coast, Masirah was close to the southern approaches to the Strait of Hormuz. Though the traditionally touchy Arab sensibilities objected to American troops on their territory, Masirah had been used in the past, beginning with the Iranian hostage-rescue attempt in 1980. Obtaining permission to use the former British base there would probably not be difficult, so long as the Americans kept a low profile.

Which SEALs were very good at doing.

"That's all I have at this time, gentlemen," Mason concluded. "Other questions?"

There were none.

"Okay." He scanned the faces of the group until his eyes met those of Captain Coburn, of SEAL Seven. "Phil?" he said. "Don't leave."

In small groups, already discussing the operation, the others filed from the room. Phillip Coburn remained.

"What do you think, Phil?" Mason asked.

"Could be hot, Paul." Alone, they reverted to first names. "If those terrorists planted explosives around the ship, there may not be any way to get at them with any kind of reasonable chance of success."

"Gambling on the odds will be up to the politicians," Mason said. "How's Seven fixed right now?"

"Second and Fourth Platoons are in the Caribbean," Coburn said. "Training deployment to Vieques with the Marines. One and Three are here. They could be ready to leave on twenty-four hours' notice."

Unlike the other SEAL Teams, SEAL Seven, brand-new and still growing, had only four platoons.

"How would you handle the deployment? Just in rough."

"Two platoons," Coburn said without hesitation. "I'd put Third Platoon in the lead, with one squad for the *Yuduki Maru,* a second for the *Hormuz.* They're my most experienced people, with the most actual combat experience. They'd go in and secure both vessels at once, then hold 'em for the NEST guys.

First Platoon in reserve, probably at Masirah. As backup to Three in case something goes wrong."

"Third Platoon just got back from Iraq."

"Right. And they just got kicked in the gut too. I need to put them back in ASAP."

"This is too damned important a mission for you to use it to build up your people's morale, Phil."

"They can handle it, Paul. They're the best people I have." There was fire in his eyes and in his voice as he said the words, and Mason could feel his excitement.

"Well, the final decision hasn't come through yet, but there's a good chance we're going to have to use Seven on this one. I had to go through the motions with the others, but Two, Four, and Eight are all pretty well committed elsewhere right now."

"What about Six?"

Mason smiled as he shook his head. "That's USSOC territory, and outside my bailiwick. But Six is under a cloud right now, and I have a feeling the Joint Chiefs aren't going to want to use them. The size of the appropriations for their toys are part of the reason Congress is looking so hard at the SEALs just now.

"In any case, we're still looking at the Seven concept of a unit that can deploy outside of established operational areas. And Seven's pre-positioned gear is still handy at Bahrain. Unlike SEAL Six."

"That's right," Coburn said eagerly. "Like I said, twenty-four hours. All you have to ship are my boys."

"Draw up your plan, Phil. Have it on my desk tomorrow morning."

"Aye, aye, Captain!" He looked as delighted as a kid at Christmas.

Mason sighed. He just wished that he could be going along.

12

Friday, 20 May

1330 hours (Zulu −5)
NAVSPECWARGRU-Two Training Center
Little Creek, Virginia

Lieutenant Murdock stood with the men of Blue Squad, Third Platoon. "Okay, people," he said, his voice devoid of emotion. "Hit it again. Four-man entry, door center, buttonhook."

They were standing outside the NSWG building variously called the "fun house" and the "killing house," part of the SEALs' Little Creek training facilities. They were tired, all of them, and their faces were coated with greasepaint and gunpowder. Their bodies seemed bent beneath the weight of their gear, combat blacks and full harness, Kevlar vests, safety helmets, and tactical radios. Murdock had been running the platoon since daybreak, literally and figuratively. Gunfire banged and crackled in the distance—First Platoon practicing on the outdoor firing range. It had been a long day already, and it would not be ending at five o'clock.

"First four up," Murdock continued. "Let's have Roselli, Garcia, Higgins, and Brown."

"Aw, man, Lieutenant," Brown said. "I'm a sniper, not a God damned door kicker."

"You heard the lieutenant," MacKenzie said softly. There was no threat or anger in his voice, but the men complied immediately, filing into place beside the fun house south wall,

129

where a couple of construction ratings were hammering the wooden framework of another practice door into place.

The subtleties of MacKenzie's line had not escaped Murdock. He'd noted that the men, when they referred to Cotter, called him "L-T," while Murdock was still "the lieutenant." The distinction spoke volumes of the gulf between him and his men.

Or am I just being paranoid? Murdock wondered. He'd not yet worked up the courage to actually discuss the situation with MacKenzie.

He was in a hell of a tough position. In the SEAL Teams especially, the differences between enlisted and officer were almost nonexistent. The men followed the officer not so much because of his rank, but because they knew he'd been through everything they'd been through, Hell Week included, and that he was as good a man as they were. He had to earn their respect, not demand it as a right.

There was an almost overwhelming tendency for new lieutenants joining a platoon to try winning that respect by familiarity, by being "one of the guys," but that approach was dead wrong from the start. The platoon's survival could hinge on whether or not the unit had one absolute leader; he had to be obeyed instantly, without argument or discussion. "Respect" in this context did not mean "like."

He'd held inspection on Sunday, as promised, and been pleased to see the barracks had been cleaned up, as ordered. He'd also noted the fading bruises on the faces of Holt and Roselli but refrained from commenting on them. Keeping order in the ranks was MacKenzie's job, and Murdock had already decided to let the master chief keep running the platoon his own way. If any serious deficiencies cropped up, well, that would be the time to pounce. *Not now* . . .

He knew they didn't like him, and after five days he still felt like he was wrestling with Cotter's ghost. But if he drilled them hard enough, by God, the respect would come.

If it didn't, they'd never survive as a team.

The workers had finished with the door and stepped back out of the way. The killing house, constructed of plywood, Kevlar, and concrete blocks, was designed to allow rapid reconfiguration for any desired room layout, with or without windows, with one or multiple doors in any location, with or without interior partitions. Except for Higgins, who was carrying a shotgun, all of the men carried Beretta 92M pistols loaded with Glaser safety slugs, frangible rounds that would not punch through walls and kill someone half a mile away . . . or ricochet from concrete and kill someone in the room.

Safety rounds or not, SEALs took their training with deadly seriousness. Men had died in this exercise. MacKenzie had told them all about the time he'd actually seen a kid shot and killed in the fun house when the guy behind him tripped going through the door.

"Right," Murdock said. He held up his clipboard and read the notes he'd scrawled there. "The situation is three suspected terrorists and at least one hostage. Nothing known about position or disposition. Go in, take 'em down, and try not to shoot the hostages or each other. Ready?"

There were some murmured assents.

"I said, 'Ready?' "

"Hoo yah!" The old SEAL battle cry seemed to draw the tired men together, to focus them. *But God,* Murdock thought, *they're still operating at the ragged edge. Are they going to be ready in time?*

He'd learned about Operation Sun Hammer only that morning, when he'd first seen the wall-sized blueprints and detailed scale models of the *Yuduki Maru* that the team would be using for their briefings. He was at once excited by the prospect, and scared. Was the platoon ready so soon after Cotter's death? Could it be *made* ready? He still didn't know.

The four men took their positions, careful to stay outside the possible fire zone through the door. Roselli was to the left of the door, with Higgins and the shotgun next to him and a step out from the wall. Brown and Garcia were to the right, squeezed up against the wall with Brown in the lead.

Room entries provided a special tactical challenge for a small assault team. Only one or, at the most, two men could go through a door at a time, and while they were in the doorway they were trapped in what was known as the "fatal funnel," where gunmen inside had a clear shot at them while they were still processing what their eyes and ears told them as they burst through the door. Their decisions had to be both immediate and correct. A misstep or a momentary hesitation could result in two men getting tangled up in the doorway or tripping over an unexpected piece of furniture. A bad call could get a hostage killed or give the bad guys time to open fire. Room entries were carefully choreographed, with different dances for different situations, and each was rehearsed time after time after time, until the decision-making and the movements were all automatic.

Murdock checked the men's positions, nodded, then said, "See you inside." Opening the plywood door, which was centered in the south wall of the structure, he stepped into the killing house.

The dummies had already been positioned by the range captains. Each was a fairly lifelike mannequin similar to those in a department store, though all showed signs of wear and tear and roughly patched bullet holes. The sitting figures slumped with the peculiar lifelessness of propped-up store dummies; the standing figures, suspended on thin wires from the rafters overhead, swayed a little with the air currents in the room. The lighting had been arranged so that it would be in the assault team's eyes, and it cast larger-than-life shadows against the bare, chipped walls.

A male mannequin in civilian clothes sat on a battered sofa directly opposite the door, his wrists handcuffed behind him. At his back, standing behind the sofa, was a female figure, also in civilian clothes and distinguishable as a terrorist only by the automatic pistol taped to her hand and resting inconspicuously on the sofa's back. To the right, near the northeast corner, were two standing figures, a woman in jeans and sweater, her hands fastened behind her back, and a man holding an AK-47 behind her, positioned in such a way that he was partly blocked by the hostage from the vantage point of someone coming through the door. A third terrorist, wearing army fatigues, hung from the ceiling in the southeast corner; and finally, by the west wall, a single uniformed male terrorist sat slumped behind a card table, an AK propped up next to him.

Murdock took a quick look around to make certain that everything was ready. As a final touch, he quietly picked up the low coffee table from its place in front of the sofa and positioned it carefully about two feet from the door. Then he took his place in the northwest corner—well out of the line of fire, he hoped—took out a stopwatch with one black-gloved hand, and switched on his radio.

"Okay, MacKenzie. Ready."

"Yes, sir. Blue Squad! Stand ready . . . go!"

Murdock hit the stopwatch timer button. Almost simultaneous with the word "go," he heard the deep-throated boom of Higgins's Remington shotgun, the snick-snack of a manually pumped round, and a second boom as thunderous as the first. The door's hinges, impacted by one-ounce slugs, disintegrated into bits of metal, loose screws, and splinters, and the door smashed back into the room an instant later. A small, black object the size and shape of a cardboard toilet-paper tube bounced across the floor, then gave off a loud crack, a simulation of the flash-bang grenade that would have stunned and blinded everyone in the room if it had been real.

The SEALs came through before the simulator's echoes in the small room had died. Roselli was first, "buttonhooking," or rolling around the door frame to the right, toward the southwest corner; Brown was a split second behind him, buttonhooking left as Garcia came through the center, vaulting both the coffee table and the wreckage of the door as lightly as any world-class gymnast. Gunfire crashed in tight groups of three, so quickly triggered they sounded like full-auto shots. The terrorist in the southeast corner jerked and spun on his wire, half of his head blown away by three fast shots from Brown; Garcia, far enough into the room to see past the female hostage, took down the man with the AK, while Brown pivoted into the southeast corner, aimed across the room, and put three rounds into the female terrorist behind the sofa. Roselli shot the terrorist behind the table, spun, and put three more rounds into the female terrorist an instant behind Brown's shots, blasting the mannequin's head to fragments and severing it from its wire. A piece of the mannequin's head, a clump of curly yellow hair still attached, bounced off Murdock's flak vest. Garcia leaped across the sofa, checking behind it for any nasty surprises—a hidden terrorist, say—then spun with his Beretta still extended rigidly in front of his body, shifting from corner to corner of the room. "Clear!" he yelled.

"Clear!" "Clear!" Brown and Roselli chorused in almost perfect unison.

Higgins, crouched in the doorway behind the coffee table, his shotgun covering everyone in the room, joined in. "Clear!"

Murdock's thumb came down on the stopwatch button.

"Five-point-one-eight seconds," he said, reading the numerals off the watch. "That's still slow, people. Damned slow. We can do it in four and a half easy!"

Collectively, the SEALs sagged as they came down off their combat high. Thumbs dropped half-loaded magazines into gloved hands, and then slides were ratcheted back, expending chambered rounds that clinked on the concrete floor. MacKenzie and Ellsworth stepped into the room, squeezing past Higgins and the ruin of the door.

"Assessment," Murdock snapped. He walked over to where the female hostage was slowly turning on her wire. Her right shoulder had been neatly popped from its socket, and a bullet hole showed in her sweater. "Let's take a look at what went wrong. Garcia, I think you cut it a little close on this one. You killed the tango but you also crippled his hostage."

"I was a little rushed, Lieutenant. I was a bit off balance after jumping that fucking table, and I triggered while I was still bringing my aim up."

"I also noticed you turn away from Tilly the Terrorist over there behind the couch. Didn't you see her?"

"I saw her, sir," Boomer said. "But I thought the guy with the AK, coming in behind the girl, was the bigger threat. His gun was up, Tilly's was down. Besides, she had a hand gun while he had an assault rifle."

"She was also right next to a hostage and she was the last one to die. How could you have taken her down faster?"

The analysis went on for several more seconds before it was interrupted by a sharp, steady beeping. Murdock reached down to his harness and thumbed off the pager. "Excuse me, people. Duty calls. Master Chief, walk them through again, will you?"

"Aye, aye, sir."

Making his way out of the killing house, Murdock walked across the barren dirt outside to a small command center, where a telephone had been set up. Punching in a number, he held the receiver to his ear. "Murdock."

"This is Doubleday in HQ," a voice said. "Sir, you have a visitor here."

"Who? Oh, never mind. I'll be right up." He sighed as he cradled the receiver. Probably Captain Mason and someone from the Pentagon, with the final word on Sun Hammer. What was he going to tell him, that the men were ready? That they could take down a ship at sea loaded with two tons of the deadliest poison known to man?

Ten minutes later, he walked through the front doors of SEAL Seven's headquarters, his boondockers tracking the recently mopped and waxed linoleum deck. He felt sweaty, grimy, and tired, and if this was some bigwig from Fort Fumble, as the Pentagon was sometimes called, he hoped he wasn't being graded for neatness.

He recognized his visitor's back as soon as he walked into the officers' lounge, and felt a sharp twist in his gut. This was no Pentagon VIP.

The man, an old, white-haired, craggy-faced version of Murdock, turned, his back as ramrod stiff, as *unyielding* as the younger man remembered. "Hello, son."

"Father! What the hell are you doing here?"

"I heard you'd been transferred. I thought I'd come down and look you up." He looked around the lounge, at its peeling paint and shopworn, fifth-hand furniture, nodding as though it met all of his expectations. "This is where you work now, eh?"

Murdock's lips compressed into a tight white line. "I was seriously wondering if you had anything to do with this. They yanked me out of the middle of a Phase One class in Coronado, had me about bust a gut to get out here."

"And you thought I arranged it to get you back to the East Coast?" The older man shook his head. "I'm afraid not. I *could* arrange a transfer, you know. . . ."

"We've been over that ground, Father. You know how I feel."

"Yes. You seem to have this idealistic notion about your career path. Damn it, Blake, didn't anybody ever tell you that these special-forces units like the SEALs are a dead end career-wise?"

"It's what I want. I'm very good at what I do. Sir."

"Um. I daresay you are." He looked Murdock up and down. "You're looking fit enough. Nice southern California tan."

"What did you want to see me for, Father? My platoon has a heavy training schedule today."

"Well, actually, I heard you might be going overseas soon. On, ah, business."

Murdock glanced about the empty room. Even here in SEAL headquarters there were things that weren't openly discussed. And he wasn't sure what his father's security clearance was.

Hell, the man was a member of Congress, for God's sake, and on the House Military Affairs Committee to boot. Still, the reserve that had built up between the two men, an impenetrable wall for the past five years, remained. Murdock did not immediately reply.

"Look, Blake," the older Murdock said. He spread his hands, as if to demonstrate that he was unarmed. "I know this must be a bad time. But I wanted . . . I wanted to see you once, before you left."

"I don't know that I'm leaving, sir." He was dying to know what his father knew . . . and unwilling to be the one to ask.

"Son, this mission coming up is going to be dangerous. And thankless. Definitely a case of damned-if-you-do-and-damned-if-you-don't."

"How the hell do you know about this?"

"The Joint Chiefs have been keeping Congress informed, of course. Some of us, at any rate. I'm on the mailing list."

"What about Farnum?"

The older Murdock cracked an uneasy smile. "My esteemed

colleague from California has, ah, such a pressing schedule, I believe it was decided that it was unnecessary to add to his work load."

Murdock knew how it worked. Notification of Congress about upcoming military operations had long been a sore point in the tug-of-politics between Capitol Hill and the Pentagon. The actions of some congressmen during the debate over Nicaragua during the eighties had, in Murdock's view, been nothing less than treasonous. More than once, covert operations had been given away to Managua by left-leaning representatives, and American advisors and other personnel had died as a result.

The elder Murdock appeared to read his son's thoughts. "I know how you feel about some of my colleagues. There are quite a few powerful men and women on the Hill who are no friends of the military. But you can't lump me in with men like Farnum."

"Of course not. You've been doing your bit to keep the bastards from disemboweling the armed forces. And I appreciate that. All I want is to be able to live my own life. All I have lined up for my 'career path,' as you call it, is to do what I want to do. I'm not going to be some politician's trained, uniformed poodle, okay? I happen to think the SEALs are important, that they're needed."

"I understand that, Blake. I don't think you realize it, but I do understand. And I'm trying to tell you that the SEALs have some pretty powerful enemies, and not just on the Hill. I'm talking about the Pentagon, here."

"Nothing I haven't heard before." A substantial number of the decision-makers and policy-setters in the military still disagreed with the whole idea of elite special forces. General Norman Schwarzkopf, the strategic mastermind of Desert Storm, had been well known for his mistrust of units like Delta or the SEALs. Most military commanders disliked them for the simple fact that they skimmed off the best troops from conventional forces and often got priority treatment when it came to funding and special equipment.

People actually within the Special Warfare community, of course, had a different perspective on the problem.

"Well, it looks like the hammer's going to come down pretty hard in my committee," the congressman said. "Farnum and some of the others have latched onto the SEALs like bulldogs, and they aren't going to let go. And I'm damned worried about this business in the Indian Ocean. . . ."

"Uh, I really don't think it's a good idea to talk about some of this stuff. Not here."

"Maybe you're right. But look at it from my point of view for once, Blake, okay? I'm on a committee that is examining the role of Navy special forces. Now, a crisis comes up where those forces have a chance to do what they've been trained to do, and it just happens that the son of one of those committee members is leading the team. If you succeed, it's going to look like the whole operation was set up to give me support. I won't have a power base I can rely on. What I have to say up there will be discounted. Follow?"

"I think so."

"But if what I hear is true, your chances of succeeding are, well, they're not good. Like damned near impossible. What happens to your precious SEALs if the son of a congressman on the Military Affairs Committee comes back a corpse?"

"I don't think—"

"What happens if half of Africa gets contaminated with radioactivity because the SEAL son of the congressman *screwed up*? It'll mean the end of everything you say you believe in, Blake, not to mention my own political career."

"Not to mention your son."

"Well, yes. Of course. I didn't mean to imply that—"

"The hell with your politics, Father, and the hell with you. The SEALs have a damned important role to play, more so than ever with the world falling apart the way it is." He looked down at his dirty combat blacks, then wiped at the greasepaint smeared on his face. "They're not interested in appearances or tact or appropriate social behavior. They're concerned with the way the world *really* works. I'm a SEAL. I'm going to carry out my orders to the best of my ability and I'm going to do what I've been trained to do for as long as the Navy will let me do it. And I am not going to let you or Mother or anyone else not in my immediate chain of command tell me what to do with my life. Not any more. Clear?''

Murdock sighed. "Clear. Speaking of your mother, Blake, she sends her best.''

"I'm sure she does.''

"You really ought to bury the past, son. She does love you, you know, and you've managed to break her heart. All she ever wanted was what's best for you. As I do.''

"Then stay out of my life. Sir. Even if you manage to kill the SEALs, I will set my own course. I will not accept a nice, safe posting to some congressional staff because I am not a lapdog, and I most certainly will not refuse a mission because it might be politically inconvenient for you. Now, sir, I have that training schedule to complete. If there's nothing more?''

When there was no answer, Blake Murdock turned crisply on his heel and strode from the room.

He had to struggle to maintain his composure. Obviously, things had not changed between him and his father. The congressman was still looking to get him into some nice, safe niche inside the Beltway, some place with a political future for the heir to the Murdock dynasty.

Outside the headquarters building, he checked his watch. Yeah, there was still time. He wanted to put himself on a four-man break-and-enter team and run through the killing house a few more times before breaking for chow.

It might help him burn off some of his anger.

He knew one thing, though, if he knew nothing else. He was more determined now to carry out Sun Hammer than he'd been before, if only because of his father's opposition.

Damn the man . . .

13

Saturday, 21 May

0215 hours (Zulu +3)
Yuduki Maru
Off the Madagascar coast

Tetsuo Kurebayashi had bow lookout this night. He enjoyed the night watches, for the ship was silent and still, empty save for the pounding of the big freighter's screws churning up the wake astern. When he stood on the foredeck, with his back to the light from *Yuduki Maru*'s towering white bridge and with the night air in his face and darkness all around, it was like stepping into another universe, where he was alone, a solitary Mind and Will in a dark and eternal cosmos.

Craning back his head, he stared up into the star-glorious sky overhead. Here, well beyond the circle of light spilling from the *Yuduki Maru*'s bridge windows, the night was a wondrous immensity. The Milky Way arced overhead from horizon to horizon, diamond dust gleaming against black velvet. Alpha Centauri shone like a beacon high up, near the zenith, while other stars, alien to men raised in northern latitudes, burned in the south. Kurebayashi's eyes traced out constellations unknown in Honshu but familiar to mariners who sailed the southern seas: Centaurus; Vela; the four, tightly clumped jewels of Crux.

He searched for Orion and the Martyr's stars, but that constellation had long since set in the west.

No matter. The spirits of the *Junkyosha,* the Martyrs, were here, as much a part of this operation as were Kurebayashi and his comrades. He thought about how close he and his brothers were to their goal, to final victory, and excitement quickened within.

So far, everything had gone perfectly according to Isamusama's plan. The most difficult aspect of Operation Yoake had been smuggling eight of the brothers aboard, disguised as members of the Police Special Action force assigned to *Yuduki Maru*'s security contingent, and two more as members of her crew. The Tokyo organization had taken care of all the details. Rumor had it that they had people planted inside the police personnel office who'd been able to reassign security force members, plant false IDs and fingerprint records, and even buy some of the officers of the government-subsidized company that owned *Yuduki Maru* and her cargo. It was the old, old story playing itself out once more: The technology, the planning, the security arrangements themselves might all be perfect, but the strongest walls were always exactly as strong as the weakest men guarding them. When *Yuduki Maru* had set sail from Cherbourg, ten of the seventy-five men aboard had been members of Eikyuni Shinananai Tori.

It had been more than enough. The other twenty-three security men aboard had been killed within seconds of *Shikishima*'s destruction, those on duty gunned down by their supposed comrades from behind, those off duty below deck killed by poison gas and gunfire as they slept. Five members of the ship's crew had also been shot, but so far, at least, the rest were cooperating with *Yuduki Maru*'s new masters. The officers had been separated from the men, and both groups were kept locked in carefully searched compartments below, released a few at a time under close guard to carry out their shipboard duties. They'd been promised their lives if they cooperated.

Kurebayashi wondered how many of them seriously believed they would be allowed to live once *Yuduki Maru* made landfall. The stakes in this game were so fantastically high. . . .

Since the takeover, there had been only one significant threat to *Yuduki Maru*. For the past three days they'd been steaming steadily on a heading of 012, almost due north. The coast of

Madagascar, however, slants from south-southwest to north-northeast, so the plutonium freighter had been steadily drawing closer and closer to the huge island's eastern shore. At this moment she was just 150 miles southeast of Cape Masoala, and needless to say, her abrupt change of course had not gone unnoticed.

Ever since they'd left Cherbourg, the Greenpeace vessel *Beluga* had dogged the freighter's northbound wake. Perhaps because they hadn't been sure whether the course change was according to plan or not, Greenpeace had made no immediate announcement about the change in course, but as the *Yuduki Maru* had steadily neared the Madagascar coast, violating her pledge not to approach any coastline by less than two hundred miles, *Beluga* had radioed the news to the world.

As expected, once the news had gone out, governments along the *Yuduki Maru*'s new course had panicked. The 235-ton coastal patrol boat *Malaika,* largest ship of the Malagasy Republic's tiny navy, had attempted to rendezvous with the freighter late on Friday afternoon but had been scared off by warnings broadcast over the radio. In two more days, they would be passing through the Seychelles and Amirante Islands, a thousand kilometers northeast of Madagascar, and there would almost certainly be another attempt then.

Well, Kurebayashi and his comrades were ready. He hefted his AKM, comforted by its reassuring bulk.

Nothing, he thought, *not all the navies of the world, can possibly stop us now!*

0720 hours (Zulu −5)
Headquarters, SEAL Seven
Little Creek, Virginia

Maps of various scales of the western Indian Ocean had been tacked up on every wall of SEAL Seven's briefing room, mingled with blown-up black-and-white aerial photos of two ships. KH-12 satellites had been tracking the *Yuduki Maru* almost continually since Thursday; holes in the spy sat observation time had been filled in by relays of Air Force high-altitude Aurora reconnaissance aircraft.

Things had been moving quickly since the Broken Arrow alert had gone out. Most of SEAL Seven's energies had been directed toward gathering intelligence. Early Friday—Friday afternoon, Madagascar time—the missing Iranian oiler *Hormuz* had been picked up and photographed as well, less than six hundred miles north of the Japanese freighter and plodding south on an intercept course. During the past twenty-four hours, the two ships had closed the gap to a few dozen miles. By now, everyone assigned to Operation Sun Hammer was working on the assumption that the Iranians must be behind the hijacking of the *Yuduki Maru*. Iran, of course, had denied the charges.

There were orbital snapshots of other vessels as well, the motor sailing ketch *Beluga,* registered with Greenpeace, and a small Malagasy Republic coastal patrol boat, *Malaika.* Word had gotten out about the plutonium ship's change of course yesterday, and that, naturally, had complicated everything. "Plutonium Ship Off Course!" were the Friday morning headlines on half the world's newspapers. "Hijacking Suspected!"

Later, the hijacking theory had been all but confirmed when the *Yuduki Maru* had warned off the *Malaika,* proving that those aboard, whoever they were, were less than friendly. All of the publicity, however, made Operation Sun Hammer far more difficult. SEALs preferred operations set well out of the glare of media notice.

Master Chief MacKenzie leaned against the plot table with his arms folded, listening to the new lieutenant lay out the mission plan. Everyone in Third Platoon was there, gathered in the briefing room that was part of the CO's suite in headquarters. Also present were Captain Friedman of the Red Wolves light helo squadron, Captain Coburn, and their tactical staffs.

"Our overall plan has been approved by Admiral Bainbridge and his staff," Murdock was saying. "However, there's plenty of room yet for creativity in this thing. In particular, I want to hear your suggestions. After all, you guys're going to be in the water too."

Good, MacKenzie thought. *Draw them out and give them a say.* No military organization can afford to be a democracy, but the men, *these* men, responded well to an officer who cared what they thought.

The excitement in the room was rising, thick enough to cut with a SEAL's K-bar. First and Third Platoons had been notified early that morning that they were going after the hijacked Japanese plutonium ship.

Now they were working out just how they were going to pull it off.

"Well, I have to say I'm concerned about the approach, Lieutenant," Roselli said. "I'm wondering why we're doing it with CRRCs. If the objective keeps to that eighteen-knot speed, we're not going to have any leeway."

CRRCs—Combat Rubber Raiding Craft—were slightly larger versions of the traditional IBS. They could be dropped from aircraft by parachute or released by a submerged submarine, as was called for by the Sun Hammer op plan, and were powered by a silenced outboard motor. They had a top speed of about twelve knots, which meant that the SEAL assault force wouldn't be able to catch up with the target if they missed on their first try and it passed them by.

"What would you suggest instead, Chief?" Murdock asked.

"Come in astern by helo. Fast-rope onto the fantail. Short and sweet."

"And if the bad guys hear the helicopters' approach? We could find ourselves coming in over a damned hot LZ."

"Suppressive fire from an escorting gunship. Sir. Clear the deck with gas, small-arms fire, and buckshot so we don't risk breaching the cargo or hitting the hostages."

Roselli did have a point. Freighters like the *Yuduki Maru* were noisy enough astern that a helicopter, especially a silenced, covert-ops bird like the Model 500MG Defender II, could slip up their wake without being heard aboard.

"I agree that would make our approach easier, Chief," Murdock said. "Unfortunately, we can't guarantee the bad guys won't have lookouts on their fantail. Making the approach on the surface at least gives us a chance of getting aboard before they know we're there. And gentlemen, it's critical that we do just that. It'll let us take down some of the tangos silently, and maybe we can make some of them tell us where the hostages are being held and how many guys they have aboard. I think we'd all rather not have to fight our way aboard. Right, Chief?"

"Yes, sir," Roselli said.

"Other questions? Suggestions? Bitches?"

There were none.

"Okay, let's go over the approach again."

Sun Hammer's success depended on catching and boarding both the *Yuduki Maru* and the *Hormuz* in an ocean where Western assets were few and far between. While Murdock had considered staging the SEALs' assault out of Diego Garcia, the plutonium ship was expected to approach no closer to that island than thirteen hundred miles, probably sometime around noon local time on Sunday as it passed the Seychelles Islands. Thirteen hundred miles was well outside the range of any but the largest, midair-refueling-capable choppers like the Super Stallion.

The final decision had been to deploy the team from an American Los Angeles-class attack sub on station in the Indian Ocean, the U.S.S. *Santa Fe.* Helicopter support would come from a Marine Expeditionary Force now transiting the Red Sea; the U.S.S. *Nassau,* the MEF's amphibious assault ship, would provide a mobile landing field for the SEAL helos, but it would take a couple of days yet to get them into position off the Horn of Africa. The Indian Ocean was a very large and empty battlefield.

"What about the Greenpeacers, Lieutenant?" Magic wondered. "They see something goin' down, they might decide to get close. And get in the way."

During the past few days, the *Beluga* had closed to within thirty-five miles of the Japanese ship, though so far she'd not dared to come any nearer. That civilian ship could cause endless mischief, however, deliberately or accidentally, especially if they spotted a military operation unfolding and decided that the risk to the freighter's cargo outweighed all other considerations.

"Good point. Captain Friedman, you've got our perimeter security." The helicopter squadron, operating off of *Nassau*'s flight deck, would be available to provide airborne firepower and, of course, to bring in NEST personnel once the two ships had been secured. "Think you could block that Greenpeace ship if she started to get too close?"

Friedman grinned. "You just tell me where the line is, Lieutenant, and we'll dare them to step across. My boys won't have any trouble stopping a damned bed-sheet sailer."

"Question answered, Brown?"

"Affirmative, sir."

"Good. Now, let's take a look at our deployment once we get aboard. . . ."

Lieutenant Murdock, MacKenzie decided, was doing a pretty fair job leading the platoon through the briefing. Every one of them was with him, following along, making decent suggestions or asking intelligent questions, and no one was dragging his heels. Murdock could still stand to loosen up a bit, though. MacKenzie had the impression that the new lieutenant was pushing, pushing, trying to prove something to himself, or possibly to someone else, and while he was running himself into the ground, there was a very real danger that he would do the same to the platoon.

MacKenzie did not want to see that happen.

"Okay," Murdock said. "Once we're aboard the freighter, we have two main worries. We have to take down the terrorists, and we have to make certain the plutonium is secure. That means checking the stuff for booby traps and bombs, tampering by idiots, and outright theft. The NEST people will be concerned with stolen plutonium and subtle leakage. But we'll have to check for quick and dirty bombs. Needless to say, we'll want our best people on this. One slip and—"

"Shine on, shine on, *Evening Moon*," Doc Ellsworth sang, completing the thought. Most of the SEALs laughed at his gallows humor. "Evening Moon" was a literal translation of the poetic term "Yuduki," and if even one of those plutonium canisters in her hold was ruptured, she most certainly would, in a manner of speaking at least, "shine."

"That's right," Kosciuszko added. "We won't need a flare to

bring in our follow-up, 'cause we're going to be goddamn glowing in the dark."

2335 hours (Zulu −1)
U.S. Air Force C-130
En route to the Indian Ocean

Lieutenant Murdock leaned back in the C-130 Hercules's red-lit cargo deck, feeling the steady beat of the transport's four great engines, feeling his own excitement building, the pressure rising until he could scarcely contain it. *Combat!* He was going into combat again. The heady adrenaline rush was like a jolt from some powerful drug, sharpening the senses until every sound, every smell, the slightest detail of the men around him and their equipment stood out in his awareness with crystalline, supernatural clarity.

They were rigged out for an airdrop at sea, wearing wet suits and SCUBA tanks. Their personal combat gear was stowed in tethered, waterproof rucksacks resting on the deck between their feet, while their CRRCs and heavier stuff were in a separate paradrop package lying on a pallet near the C-130's cargo bay door.

Murdock studied each man carefully, without being too obvious in his appraisals. Thirteen men, thirteen different ways of dealing with the stress and the emotions that everyone felt as they approached combat. Bill Higgins, the Professor, had his legs stretched out and his ankles crossed atop his rucksack. He was holding a pencil flash in one hand and a paperback translation of Sun Tse's *The Art of War* in the other. Doc Ellsworth was also reading; he'd laid a wide strip of masking tape across the masthead of a recent issue of *Penthouse,* then used a magic marker to print in the title *Gray's Anatomy.* Bearcat Holt was sound asleep, his head back against the bulkhead and his mouth hanging wide open. Rattler and Boomer were talking quietly together in Spanish. Frazier was working a fist-sized lump of plastic explosives in his hands, kneading it like clay. Roselli and Nicholson both were stripping and cleaning their H&Ks. Magic Brown had a 9mm round in one hand and was turning it end over end between his fingers, almost as though it were a rosary or some kind of talisman. His eyes were fixed on something unseen beyond the Hercules's bulkhead. Jaybird was also staring into space, but with his arms crossed over his chest, an almost belligerent display. DeWitt, Kos, and Mac were all forward, talking together in tones drowned out by the C-130's engine noise.

They were good men, every one of them. He'd been pushing them all damned hard this week, and they'd responded well. If any men in the world could carry out this mission, these men could.

He just hoped that he was sharp enough to lead them. Usually, especially before combat, Murdock felt the supreme, egotistical, almost arrogant confidence of the athlete who knows he is ready to perform. This time, though, he felt . . . unsure of himself, despite the pre-combat excitement. It was an unfamiliar sensation. Was it his father's visit that had done this? Or was he simply nervous about jumping into action with thirteen men who were still near-strangers? He didn't know, and he didn't know how he could go about finding out . . . except, possibly, by surviving these next few hours.

"Lieutenant?"

He started. MacKenzie was standing over him, huge in his combat harness and rig. "Yeah, Mac?"

"Can I talk to you for a second?"

Rising, Murdock followed MacKenzie forward, to a place where they could talk without being overheard by the rest of the platoon.

"What's on your mind, Master Chief?"

MacKenzie's teeth gleamed briefly in the cargo hold's red lighting. "I just wanted to say, sir, that I think you've done a pretty fair job of pulling the guys together this last week. You've worked their tails off, and there's some of them that think you're a son of a bitch. But you're *their* son of a bitch, and they're pretty proud of that."

Murdock nodded. "Thanks, Mac. The hardest thing about this job, you know, is competing with Lieutenant Cotter. If the men don't follow *me* instead of him, this platoon doesn't have a chance in hell."

"Roger that, sir." He hesitated. "I, uh, just wanted to say one thing more. . . ."

"Spit it out, Master Chief. Off the record."

"These guys are not raw recruits, sir. Except for Jaybird, who hasn't pinned on his trident yet, they've paid their dues and they know their shit. Every man except Jaybird has been in combat."

"You're telling me to get off their backs and let them do their jobs."

MacKenzie's eyes widened slightly. "Well . . . yes, sir."

"Don't worry, Mac. I'd already reached the same conclusion. When we jump tonight, I'm not going out that door leading this platoon."

"No, sir?"

"Nope. I'm going out as *part* of the platoon. Part of the team."

"And the Teams." MacKenzie grinned. "Yes, *sir*!"

Hours later, the C-130 neared the planned drop site. The U.S.S. *Santa Fe,* motionless on the surface in a slight swell, signaled with an IR beacon, and the Hercules pilot replied in kind. They were going in at eight thousand feet so that they wouldn't need high-altitude breathing gear. The pressure on the cargo deck had already been adjusted to match the air pressure outside.

The Hercules crew chief passed the word that the sub was in sight and that the pilot was circling in toward the drop zone. Five minutes.

"Stand up!" Murdock called.

As one, the platoon stood up, looped swim fins over their right arms, gathered up their rucksacks, and made their way in two lines toward the rear of the aircraft, bunched up on either side of the paradrop package. There, the cargo ramp was coming down with a grumbling whine; beyond that opening, the night was darkness and the shrill thunder of wind and engines. Murdock felt the bite of cold, surprising this close to the equator.

"Check equipment!"

The equipment check was carried out in three phases. Each

man checked his own gear, making sure buckles were fastened, straps and weapons secure, equipment snug. Next, he checked the gear of the man in front of him in line, and finally he turned around and checked the man behind him.

"Sound off for equipment check!"

"One okay!" Kosciuszko called from the head of the port-side stick.

"Two okay!"

And so it went down the paired lines, until Murdock completed the litany with "Fourteen okay! This is it, SEALs. Stand in the door."

The Hercules's rear door was gaping wide now. Stars gave illumination enough that the waves a mile and a half below were intermittently visible, a glint of pale illumination in the darkness below the arc of the Milky Way. Murdock's heart hammered beneath his rebreather pack. It always pounded like this before a jump. Like more than one guy had said on similar occasions, jumping out of a perfectly good airplane is neither a sane nor a natural act.

A light on the forward bulkhead flashed from red to green. *"Go!"*

As one, the two lines of men grasped the equipment package and slid it aft on the cargo rollers set into the deck. With a heavy rumble, it slid down the ramp and into space, its static cord popping its drogue almost at once, the main chute appearing seconds later, then vanishing into the night.

Almost the moment the cargo was clear, Third Platoon rushed down the ramp after it, plunging headfirst into space. The mob rush allowed the platoon to free-fall close together, enabling them to stay together for the descent and splash down in a tight group.

The excitement that had been building inside Murdock exploded behind his eyes like a magnesium flare. The wind blasted at his face and wet suit as he spread his arms and legs and arched his back, assuming the classic free-fall position that actually let him turn his body into an airfoil and fly . . . at least for a few precious, fantastic moments. In the darkness, his companions were visible as mere shadows, sensed more than seen as their bodies occulted the stars around him. Free-fall was glorious, a buoyant weightlessness, transformed to literal and ecstatic flight by the lack of any fixed reference point save his own body suspended in space.

Together, they fell through the night until the luminous dials of their wrist altimeters read five hundred feet. Then they pulled their ripcords; Murdock could hear the pops and cracks of the other chutes around him an instant before his own parasail deployed, yanking him upright with a sensation that felt like he was heading straight back into the star-strewn sky.

His chute clear, he released his rucksack, letting it dangle at the end of its tether. Hauling on his risers, he guided the parasail into a gentle turn against the wind, killing his forward momentum. He could see the submarine now, a long, black shadow against the luminous sea.

He prepared for the landing, loosening the left side of his reserve chute, donning his swim fins, and readying his quick release by turning it to the unlocked position and removing the safety clip. One hundred feet above the water, he steadied his chute with his face into the wind and put his fingers over his Capewell Releases, which secured the parachute straps to his harness at his shoulders.

Moments later, he splashed into the water, pressing the left-side Capewell Release and releasing the chute before he was fully submerged. Underwater, he released the second Capewell, then hit the quick-release box to free the leg straps. The harness fell away, leaving him free in the ocean.

The *Santa Fe* rose like a black steel cliff from the sea, less than fifty yards away. Pushing his rucksack before him like a swim board, Murdock headed toward the sub. Around him, he heard the gentle splashes of other members of the unit.

Third Platoon, SEAL Seven, had arrived.

14

Sunday, 22 May

2220 hours (Zulu +3)
U.S.S. *Santa Fe*
North of the Seychelles Islands

For nearly eight hours after the SEALs had been plucked from the water off the coast of Somalia, the Los Angeles attack sub *Santa Fe* had been running south at her maximum speed of better than thirty-five knots. Her goal was a place on the charts, a featureless spot in the ocean where, if *Yuduki Maru* continued on her steady, northward course, submarine and freighter would meet.

The SEALs spent most of that time in the *Santa Fe*'s torpedo room, which had been vacated by the regular crew. The space was cramped to the point of claustrophobia, and the passage was monotonous. *Santa Fe*'s crew seemed to draw apart from the visitors, recognizing them as fellow professionals but unwilling to cross the wall of reserve that separated one group from the other. Submarine crews, like SEALs, were well known for their silence around people not their own.

For the last several hours of the passage, Murdock and DeWitt were guests of the Captain in the control room. Commander George Halleck was a lean, taciturn man, all creases and sharp edges. It was well past sunset on Sunday, though the only indication of day or night beyond the sub's steel bulkheads was the fact that the compartment was red-lit,

152

a measure that preserved the officers' night vision against the need to use the periscopes or to surface.

"We have sonar contact with your target, gentlemen," Halleck said. The three of them, plus Lieutenant Commander Ed Bagley, the boat's Executive Officer, were leaning over the control room's plot table, where a back-lit chart of the area rested under transparent plastic. The *Santa Fe*'s skipper tapped the end of a south-to-north line with his grease pencil. "About here. Course unchanged, still zero-one-two. Speed eighteen knots."

"They're making it easy for us," the boat's XO said with a grin. He was taller than the Captain, and heavier, with thick eyeglasses that gave him an owlishly unmartial appearance.

"How far?" Murdock asked.

"Approximately thirty miles," Halleck replied. "Exact range can't be determined by passive sonar, of course, but my best people have their ears on, and they're pretty sure of the number."

Passive sonar—listening for the engine noise of the target— was preferable to the more accurate and informative active sonar, because it didn't give away the sub's presence.

"Has anybody else tried approaching them?" DeWitt wanted to know.

"About the time we were fishing you boys out of the water," Bagley said, "they skirted within thirty nautical miles of the Seychelles Islands. Half the Seychellan navy turned out— three patrol boats, actually—but they didn't come closer than a couple of miles and no shots were fired. It was more like an escort than an attempt to stop them."

"There's also this," the Captain said, handing Murdock a black-and-white photograph. "That was transmitted to us by satellite an hour ago. The time stamp says it happened about an hour before that."

"Still after sunset," Murdock observed.

"Affirmative."

The "photograph" had actually been taken in radar, so details like hull numbers and slender masts were not visible and the water, daylight-bright, had the look of wrinkled metal. Still, the shot showed a remarkably detailed image of a ship, smaller than *Yuduki Maru* and riding lower in the water. Something like a white bed sheet had been stretched above her deck.

"That's *Hormuz*," Murdock said.

"So the Iranians rendezvoused with them?" DeWitt added.

"Actually, we don't know that for sure. If they did rendezvous, it was at a point where we had no satellite coverage, and our AWACS radar simply didn't have the resolution to be certain. They at least came very close, certainly within a mile or two. *Hormuz* is now five miles off *Yuduki Maru*'s starboard beam, traveling parallel to her course but quickly falling behind. She can only make nine or ten knots, top speed."

"I guess that confirms the Iranian connection, though, doesn't it, Lieutenant?" DeWitt said.

"I damn well guess it does." Murdock tapped the sheet in the photograph. "What's this? A tarp?"

"Probably," Halleck said, rubbing his chin. "A tarp or canvas rigged as an awning. Whatever they're doing, they don't want our satellites or recon planes to get a good look."

"The question, then, is whether they used that hole in our satellite coverage to transfer part of *Yuduki Maru*'s cargo to the *Hormuz*."

"Or if they moved soldiers from the *Hormuz* to the *Yuduki Maru*," DeWitt pointed out.

"We'll have to assume both," Murdock decided. "It'll be Plan Alfa."

In their planning sessions, they'd allowed for the possibility that *Hormuz* might rendezvous with the plutonium freighter before the SEALs could deploy. Plan Bravo would have sent Blue Squad aboard the *Yuduki Maru*, with Gold Squad waiting in their CRRCs as a backup. Alfa called for Blue to take the Japanese ship while Gold Squad boarded the Iranian *Hormuz*. It meant there would be no immediate backup for either team once they boarded the ships. The Fourth Platoon was now deploying to Masirah, just in case something went wrong in Third Platoon's assault.

Murdock suppressed the thought, and the surge of adrenaline that accompanied it. If something went wrong, the mission would be in the hands of Lieutenant Mancuso and Fourth Platoon.

It also meant that, in all likelihood, he and his teammates would be dead.

"We have one other joker in the deck," Halleck said. "Sonar has picked up another contact pacing the *Yuduki Maru*. It may be submerged."

"The Iranian Kilo."

"Looks that way. The sonar profile looks like a conventional sub. Stealthy, no reactor coolant pump noise or anything like that. She may be trailing the plutonium ship by another four or five miles."

"Have they heard us?"

"Not so far as we can tell. There's been no change in her course or speed since we picked her up."

"How big a problem is she for you, Captain?"

Halleck grimaced, then shrugged. "For us, not much. The big danger is whether she's there as escort, or as insurance."

"What do you mean, Captain?" DeWitt asked.

"He means that if we board the *Yuduki Maru* and take down the tangos before she reaches port, the Iranians might decide to put a fish into her."

"That's about the size of it," Bagley said. "Washington would have the devil of a time proving the ship hadn't been blown up by us, on purpose or by accident."

"And we get blamed for contaminating half the African coast," DeWitt said. "Cute."

"Will you be able to take her out?" Murdock asked.

"We won't, no," Halleck replied. "Not without letting those people aboard the freighter know we're out here. But the *Newport News* is already getting into position. They'll take care of the Kilo when you go aboard."

"Good." Murdock nodded. "How much longer to drop-off?"

Halleck consulted the large clock mounted on the bulkhead at the forward end of the control room. "I'd say another twenty minutes to get into position. We'll keep running ahead of them then, and you can leave any time after that."

"Can't be too much longer, or the separation between

Hormuz and the *Yuduki Maru* will become too great. We'd better get ready to swim then. If you'll excuse us, Captain?"

"Of course."

The platoon had been preparing for their swim for the past several hours, going over their rebreather apparatus, weapons, and other gear with the loving care and attention that had long been the hallmark of the SEALs. Each man was wearing a black wet suit and SCUBA gear, and his face had been completely blackened with waterproof paint. Weapons had been sealed, and explosive charges and detonators were stored in waterproof pouches. While they didn't want to sink either of the target ships, the theory was that if they couldn't capture them, the SEALs might at least slow them by damaging some critical piece of machinery.

That, at least, was the idea. The gap between theory and practice, however, was often turned into a yawning abyss by Murphy's Law. All the SEALs could do was try to be prepared for anything that might go wrong . . . and stay flexible enough to meet the problems they simply could not anticipate.

There are several ways to egress a submarine. Simplest would have been for Halleck to bring the *Santa Fe* up until just the top of her sail was above water, with the SEALs going out through the sail cockpit. *Yuduki Maru* had radar, however, and it was possible that even so small a target as that would be picked up at a range of less than ten miles, so the platoon egressed, as planned, through the after lockout compartment.

Because of the positioning of their water intakes, modern submarines cannot rest on the bottom as their World War II predecessors could. Besides, the ocean here was deep; they were over the Somali Basin, which plunged to better than five thousand meters—over three miles straight down. The *Santa Fe,* now traveling north some eight miles ahead of the *Yuduki Maru* and about ten miles ahead of the *Hormuz,* slowed to a crawl, maintaining just speed enough to maintain way, her conning tower scraping along just beneath the surface.

Two by two, because the chamber was too small for more, the men of SEAL Seven, Third Platoon, began locking out of the escape trunk. Murdock was last out, giving each man's gear a final check before he climbed the ladder into the narrow cylinder that was a floodable extension of the sub's pressure hull. He went out with MacKenzie, squeezing into the chamber opposite the big Texan and using the intercom, called a 31-MC, to alert the sub's crew that they were ready to go. Turning a valve flooded the chamber; when the water was above the side door, they pushed it open, emerging in a recess in the *Santa Fe*'s afterdeck. The other twelve men had already broken out the gear that had been stored there after their paradrop; four Combat Rubber Raiding Craft from the C-130's pallet canister had been rolled up, lashed together, and stowed in the deck compartment between the sub's outer and pressure hulls, along with the boat's engines and other necessary gear.

They worked swiftly and surely, in an almost total, inky darkness penetrated only incompletely by the small lights the men carried. Both the *Santa Fe* and the SEALs were still moving slowly forward, and the water pressure as the current boiled aft past the sail was like a stiff wind. Air bubbles tinkled and burbled in the darkness as they rose from SCUBA regulators. SCUBA gear was being used for this mission rather than rebreathers because the final approach would be on the surface, rather than underwater, and there would be no danger of the bubbles giving away the divers' positions.

In moments, the CRRCs were freed and inflated from pressure bottles, rising to the surface accompanied by their retinue of frogmen. Their lights were extinguished as they rode the rubber rafts toward the surface. In minutes, the four rafts were bobbing on a gentle swell on the surface. Stars peeped from among scattered clouds overhead. The horizon, visible only where the stars ended, was empty.

The SEALs rolled aboard their CRRCs and began unshipping the engines and securing their gear. SCUBA tanks, masks, and flippers were removed and stowed. Flak jackets and combat harnesses went on over wet-suit tops; radio headsets were slipped into place and plugged into belt Motorola units. They wore the SEALs' usual mix of headgear: floppy boonie hats, woolen balaclavas, or a dark green scarf folded into a triangle and worn over the head like a bandana. Under their swim fins, they wore thick-soled, rubber-cleated boots, specially designed footwear for climbing slippery steel. No words were spoken during the entire process, and radio silence was strictly observed save for the brief clicks of the necessary radio checks; each movement, each act had been practiced countless times by every man in the team. A hand signal, barely visible in the night, a thumbs-up, and the two sets of rafts began drawing apart, propelled by silenced engines that gave off little noise above a soft purr. The plan called for them to split into two groups of two, Murdock's group heading due south to intercept the *Yuduki Maru,* DeWitt's squad bearing to the southeast to close with the more distant *Hormuz.*

The Blue Squad rafts traveled side by side at twelve knots, meeting and breasting each swell. Murdock cradled a hand-held radar unit, intermittently sending out a pulse to check on the *Yuduki Maru*'s position. The signal, deliberately tailored to mimic that put out by aircraft search radars, would probably not be picked up at all by the freighter; if it was, it would be dismissed as another of the aircraft that had been prowling the skies around the hijacked plutonium ship for the past several days.

For the next fifteen minutes, *Yuduki Maru* remained steadily on course. Soon, the SEALs could actually see her, bow-on, her bridge brilliantly illuminated and with running lights to port and starboard, at her prow and at her masthead. Evidently, the hijackers were doing nothing to hide her presence. It was almost as though they were daring the SEALs to attack.

The lights provided the SEALs with one tremendous advantage, however. Guards on her deck would ruin their night vision every time they looked inboard; the SEALs, black-faced, in black garb, aboard black CRRCs, were all but invisible on the black water. The chances that shipboard guards would notice the approach of the SEAL boats were sharply reduced.

Three hundred yards from the *Yuduki Maru*'s bow, the two CRRCs began to separate. MacKenzie, Garcia, and Higgins in one boat steered for the freighter's starboard side. Murdock, Roselli, Brown, and Ellsworth made for the port. Stretched between the two rafts was a two-football-field length of lightweight, slender, but very strong wire rope; the CRRCs drew apart until they were two hundred yards apart and the cable was stretched taut between them. The range to the plutonium ship closed, more gradually now as the cable's drag slowed the CRRCs. The swell was growing worse, sending the rubber boats up each gentle but irresistibly passing mound of water, then sending them sliding man-deep into the trough that followed.

The *Yuduki Maru* loomed out of the night, her bow wake a ghostly white mustache shining in the darkness, her hull a black cliff towering over the rafts, her superstructure a bulky white castle riding the sky above the aft third of the ship. The freighter passed squarely between the two CRRCs, the throb of its engines booming out of the silence of the night.

Murdock killed the CRRC's engine as the wire rope snagged against the huge ship's bow. With a jerk, the rubber boat's course was reversed; the SEALs clung to handholds set into the gunwales as the *Yuduki Maru* began dragging them relentlessly forward at eighteen knots, a sleigh ride that carried them up and down the ocean swell with enough velocity to send a cascade of spray over the CRRC's bow. Inexorably, the raft was swung toward the freighter's side. The SEALs were ready as the rubber side thumped heavily against the ship's massive steel cliff, fending off the big ship with gloved hands. Brown secured the raft in place with a limpet magnet and a length of strong line. Wake and ocean swell combined to send the CRRC bobbing up and down at the *Yuduki Maru*'s side. Swiftly, Ellsworth dropped a hydrophone cable over the side; Roselli was already extending a long, telescoping aluminum pole with a hook on the end.

Fully extended, the climbing pole reached thirty feet, high enough that Roselli, supported upright by the others in the boat, was able to snag a deck stanchion with the rubberized tip.

"Solid," Roselli said, giving the pole a hard, downward tug. The rise and fall of the raft at the ship's side threatened to knock both SEAL and extension pole into the sea, but he hung on, riding the motion with practiced skill. The *Yuduki Maru*'s stern was only twenty yards astern, and the turning of her twin screws filled the air with a deep-throated throbbing.

Murdock nodded, then reached for the trigger for the hydrophone. This was a compact, battery-powered device designed to transmit data via a burst of high-frequency sound. Swiftly, he punched in a code group, three numbers that, transmitted through the water to the submerged *Santa Fe,* indicated that the SEALs had made contact with the *Yuduki Maru* and were going aboard.

On the other side of the freighter, MacKenzie and his people ought to be going through the same motions, but Murdock and the SEALs in his CRRC would operate as though they were alone. With the message transmitted and their gear ready, Murdock slapped Roselli twice on the shoulder and jabbed his thumb skyward. The chief nodded, then set one rubber-cleated sole against the *Yuduki Maru*'s hull, took a boost as the CRRC rose sharply beneath him with the next wave, and started walking up the ship's side, pulling his way along the climbing pole as though it were a rope and the sheer, steel-plated side of the freighter were simply a glossy black wall of rock.

As Murdock watched Roselli climb, he unslung his H&K subgun, then strapped it into position on the front of his combat web gear. He pulled the mud plug from the muzzle and breach, then racked back the charging lever to chamber the first round.

One way or another, the issue was about to be settled.

2311 hours (Zulu +3)
Freighter *Yuduki Maru*

Step by step, Roselli ascended the side of the *Yuduki Maru,* a human fly walking the sheer black cliff of the Japanese freighter.

His position was precarious, for the freighter's side bulged out over the raft, and as Roselli climbed the rigid extension pole, he was actually slightly head-down for part of the trip. Water slapped and boiled along the ship's side beneath him, and the first few feet were treacherously slick with a layer of slime. Once he was onto the part of the hull high enough above the water to be more or less dry, he still had to watch each step, for the steel plates were studded with rivets and made dizzyingly uncertain by the rise and fall of the vessel itself. Fortunately, the huge ship's motion in the water was far less than that of the raft at its side. Had the sea been much rougher, however, they would have been forced to come in by helicopter, as he had suggested back at Little Creek. An assault from the sea would have been out of the question.

All in all, however, Roselli had made more difficult climbs during training, scrambling hand-over-hand up dangling lines as instructors and other trainees played blasts of water from firehoses at him. Reaching the freighter's afterdeck, he paused to snap a hook attached to his web-gear harness to the stanchion rising just above his head. Then, swinging freely at the vessel's scuppers, he was able to use his hands to grab the edge and chin himself up.

As the new lieutenant had feared, there was a guard on the freighter's fantail . . . no, *two* guards. They carried AKM assault rifles, and leaning against the superstructure but within easy reach was the long, twin-handled tube of an RPG rocket launcher. There was light enough from the superstructure at their backs to illuminate both men. They were swarthy, one with a bushy, black beard, the other with at least a week's stubble showing on his face. They were wearing uniforms of some sort, nondescript brown or olive-drab clothing that could have belonged to almost any army in the world. One thing was clear. These two were not Japanese, which could only mean they had arrived off the *Hormuz.*

One, evidently, had just reached the fantail. Unslinging his AKM, he set it against the bench on which the other man was sitting. *"Salaam,"* the first man said. He reached for his left breast pocket. *"Segar mayl dareed?"*

"Teshakor meekonam," the seated man replied. He accepted a cigarette from the other. *"Kebreet dareed?"*

"Baleh. Eenjaw."

Roselli felt a small, inner chill. If they'd made their approach by helicopter, the bad guys would have been waiting for them. A single RPG round would have blown a helo right out of the sky as easily, as efficiently, as an American Stinger surface-to-air missile.

Not for the first time, Roselli wished he spoke Arabic . . . no, not Arabic. These men were Iranians and would be speaking Farsi. Whatever they were saying, it sounded like small talk. They appeared relaxed and slightly bored as they smoked and chatted, though both from time to time cast glances out beyond the railing and stanchions that circled the fantail. Once the seated man seemed to stare straight at Roselli, but the SEAL's blackened face and black balaclava, his eyes narrowed to slits to hide the whites and his motionlessness as he clung to the harness strap, all served to cloak him in invisibility.

He was careful not to meet the Iranian's eyes, however, even through narrowed eyes. The phenomenon had never been accepted by science, but Roselli, a combat veteran, was well aware that people could often *feel,* with what could only be described as a sixth sense, when another person was staring at them. Roselli had no idea whether or not this represented some kind of awareness beyond the usual five senses, or was simply a stress-induced heightening of hearing or smell to a near-magical degree, but he'd experienced it more than once himself. After his first quick appraisal, he kept his eyes lowered, staring at the deck close to the Iranians' feet rather than at the soldiers themselves.

He was not seen. The night-blind Iranians continued their conversation, puffing away at cigarettes that stank as powerfully as the mingled bilge-water stench and diesel fumes rising from the *Yuduki Maru*'s vents.

With one hand still clinging to the belaying strap, he used the other to unholster his sound-suppressed Hush Puppy pistol. Bracing the long barrel on the edge of the deck, he aimed carefully at the standing man first, then squeezed the trigger three times in rapid succession.

The *chuff-chuff-chuff* of the weapon, barely audible above the rumble of the engines, stuttered as sharply as a burst of full-auto fire, and the triplet of 9mm slugs caught the Iranian with a closely grouped volley that tore open his throat and crushed his skull, pitching him back and to the side as a startling pinwheel of scarlet arced from his head. Without pausing to confirm the first kill, Roselli shifted aim to the other man, who remained seated, the lit cigarette dangling from half-open lips, his expression still blank and uncomprehending. The SEAL fired three more rounds, and these were mingled with a trio of silenced shots from the *Yuduki Maru*'s starboard side.

The Iranian, pinned between volleys from opposite directions, lurched up high on his toes, groped with one clawed hand for the face that had vanished in a raw mask of blood, then crumpled to the deck a scant second after the first. An AKM clattered beside the bodies, then skidded to a halt. For a long second, there was neither movement nor sound beyond the throb of the freighter's engines.

Holstering his Hush Puppy, Roselli unsnapped a pouch at his belt, extracting a three-pronged grappling hook attached to a tightly rolled caving ladder. Securing the hook to another stanchion, he let the caving ladder unroll into the darkness below.

In a moment, he sensed the tug of someone climbing the ladder and knew the others in the CRRC were on their way up to join him.

15

In Washington it was mid-afternoon, but the overhead lights in JSOCCOMCENT had been turned off, giving the windowless room the feel of night. The only illumination came from the green-glowing phosphorescence of a large television monitor.

Congressman Charles Fitzhugh Murdock leaned forward, studying the monitor with keen interest. The image on the screen, an oblique view of the Japanese freighter *Yuduki Maru* glowing in pale, green-white light, was real-time, an infrared image transmitted from a satellite passing south over the Indian Ocean. The camera angle slowly changed as he watched.

"What is it?" he asked. Ten other men were in the room, civilians and high-ranking officers of several military services, clustered with him about the monitor. "What did I just see?"

A slender civilian first introduced to Murdock only as "Mr. Carter" pointed at ghost figures now slipping over the *Yuduki Maru*'s taffrail. "Those tiny flashes of light were gunshots, Mr. Congressman," he said. He was holding a telephone receiver in his hand and had been whispering into the mouthpiece at intervals ever since the drama had begun unfolding.

"Two terrs are down," a Navy captain, Paul Mason, said. "The rest of our people are climbing on board now."

Murdock suppressed the churn of acid fear in his belly those words raised. It was a lot worse than he'd feared, standing in this room ten thousand miles away, watching the action unfold on a television screen like the make-believe gunplay of some computer game.

General Bradley, the big, bluff Air Force officer who appeared to be in charge of this room, pointed at the screen. "Damn," he said, chewing on the end of an unlit cigar. "Can't we get a better view on this thing?"

Carter spoke quietly into a telephone, and Congressman Murdock realized he must be in direct communication with whoever was controlling the spy satellite. A moment later, the image of the ship expanded, the view zeroing in on the aft third of the ship. The glowing ghost figures of nine men, two of them prone on the deck, were barely distinguishable against the heat-glow of the ship itself. The imagery remained clear, but the satellite's motion was more apparent. The view kept slipping to the right, forcing the unseen controller to shift the camera angle left in compensation.

It had, Murdock reflected, taken all but an act of Congress to get him here, into this shielded, buried room within the Pentagon labyrinth, impregnable behind four separate security checkpoints. Captain Granger had been his passport into this underground shadow-world, and he'd had to do a fair amount of arm-twisting to pull it off. *Look,* he'd told Granger the day before. *The SEALs need a friend on the HMAC, someone who's willing to slug it out with Farnum and his kill-the-military cronies, and I'm it! But damn it, you've got to give me some cooperation on this. Let me see what it is I'm supposed to be defending. . . .*

Even yet, Murdock wasn't certain what strings Granger had had to pull to get him into this room. The very existence of this type of high-detail, real-time satellite imagery was still, three years after the collapse of the Soviet Union, a jealously guarded secret, one that most members of Congress were not privy to. The pictures were like magic, the freighter a ghost ship of green and white light, illuminated by her own heat. Moments before, he'd watched the approach of two tiny rafts to their far larger target, the heat from their laboring engines shining in the infrared image like tiny stars.

My son's down there, he thought, feeling as though he were watching from the satellite's vantage point hundreds of miles overhead. *My son's in one of those rafts, and I can't do a damned thing about it.*

He wasn't even certain that his son was leading this raid. Admiral Bainbridge had refused point-blank to disclose the names of the men assigned to the raid, and the source of his information, a mid-level staffer on NAVSPECWARGRU-Two's planning staff, had been unable to provide confirmation. When he'd confronted Blake, two days ago at the SEAL base in Little Creek, he'd been bluffing, hoping to get his son to admit to things the congressman had heard but been unable to verify.

But somehow, it was easier for him to *assume* that Blake was aboard one of those rafts. It was the uncertainty, the not knowing, that made the waiting hell.

He turned to Captain Granger, stiff and starched in his Navy dress whites. "I just want you to know, Ben, that whatever happens now, I'm grateful."

Granger glanced at him but said nothing, and Murdock sensed the resentment the former SEAL must still feel at the strong-arm tactics the congressman had employed to gain entrance to this inner sanctum. Granger, no doubt, had been forced to spend some political capital of his own to win this privilege for a mere congressional VIP. *I really called in all my markers on this one,* Murdock thought. *I just hope I can provide value for value next week when it comes time for the HMAC's vote.*

An electronic peep sounded from a speaker somewhere in the room's ceiling, startling in its intensity. "Foreman, Hammer Alfa," a voice whispered, and Murdock had his confirmation. Even through the hiss of static, he recognized his son's voice. "Sierra-Charlie. Moving."

"They're all aboard," Mason said, probably for Murdock's benefit since everyone else in the room apparently knew what was going on. "We're Foreman. Hammer Alfa is the *Yuduki*

Maru strike team. Sierra-Charlie is the code phrase meaning everything's on sched."

"How much longer we got on this bird?" Bradley asked.

"Three minutes, General," Carter replied. "It's going to be damned tight."

"KH-twelve-slash-nine will be over the horizon in fourteen minutes," a technician added. "There'll only be an eleven-minute hole in the coverage."

"Maybe so," Mason said. "But a hell of a lot can happen in eleven minutes."

"We'll still have voice communications, through our AWACS Sentry," Admiral Bainbridge said. He cast a hard glance at Murdock, then looked away. "Being able to see wouldn't help that much anyway."

He resents me, too, Murdock thought. *The hell with him. The hell with all of them. I just want my son to come out of this alive.*

He turned his full attention to the video-game action unfolding on the screen.

2316 hours (Zulu +3)
Freighter *Yuduki Maru*

Lieutenant Blake Murdock unhooked his harness, then chinned himself gently over the edge of the deck. Shadows moved on the starboard side of the fantail, forty feet away. MacKenzie materialized like a shadow out of darkness, an H&K MP5 clenched in black-gloved hands. Murdock signaled with a thumbs up, then unharnessed his own subgun. He could hear voices in the distance coming from somewhere forward, and a harsh bark of laughter. From elsewhere, higher up, came the metallic rattle of booted feet descending a ship's ladder, then the clump of a fast walk across a steel dock. *"Hajibaba! Kojaw meetavawnam jak paydaw konam?"*

Still, no excitement in the other voices, no sign that the SEALs had been spotted yet.

The two bodies and their weapons went over the stern, the splashes lost in the churning of the freighter's wake. Blood streaked the deck, but in the near-darkness it looked black, like grease or spilled coffee.

Murdock crouched alongside the superstructure, his H&K aiming up the covered port-side walkway that led past the bridge superstructure and toward the forward deck. More shadows slipped onto the deck alongside; Magic, Doc, and Roselli. MacKenzie, the Professor, and Boomer were all aboard to starboard.

Lightly, Murdock touched Roselli's shoulder and gestured toward the ship's bow. Weapon at the ready, Roselli nodded, then started forward along the walkway.

2317 hours (Zulu +3)
Oiler *Hormuz*

Jaybird rose above the sentry, a K-bar knife gleaming scarlet-black in the half-light, the guard lying on the deck with a six-inch gash through throat and windpipe, jugular and carotid. There was a very great deal of blood, but no one could have heard the man's muffled gurglings as Jaybird had lowered him to the deck.

The SEAL felt the first tremors of reaction and viciously suppressed them. With all his training, with all his mental preparation, the Iranian lying at his feet was the first man he'd ever killed, and for a trembling moment, the shock threatened to overwhelm him.

Then training reasserted itself. The man was an enemy who would have sounded the alarm if he'd heard Jaybird's stealthy approach from behind. Now he was a *dead* enemy; Jaybird's long hours of hand-to-hand had made the stealthy approach, the snatch, reach, and slash, almost instinctive. The SEAL wiped his K-bar on the man's pants leg and sheathed it. Behind him, Kosciuszko and Nicholson slithered over the ship's gunwales and onto her rusty deck.

The first thing Jaybird noticed about the ship was her stench. The *Hormuz* stank, a repulsive mix of diesel oil, dead fish, vomit, and unwashed bodies. Next he noticed the peculiar twist to her motion underfoot. Jaybird wondered if the ancient vessel's owners had really spent much effort making her seaworthy. The old, low-slung tanker wallowed in the worsening seas, and each swell threatened to break over the exposed quarterdeck and swamp her.

Gold Squad had approached *Hormuz* according to plan, with a length of lightweight wire rope snagging the vessel's prow and drawing the two CRRCs together roughly amidships. Now they were aboard, facing an unknown number of Iranian troops, possibly army, possibly *navshurawn,* as their marines were called.

"Hammer Bravo," Lieutenant DeWitt's voice whispered over his radio headset. "Go!"

That was the signal for the *Hormuz* assault team to move out. Holding his H&K shoulder-high and probing the darkness to his front, Jaybird moved with cautious, toe-first steps, flowing like a shadow against the rust streaks and flaking paint of the tanker's superstructure. Thirty steps forward took him to a safety-roped monkeywalk and the top of a ladder. Below was the *Hormuz*'s well deck, picturesquely called no-man's-land aboard a merchantman because its low freeboard shipped water in heavy weather. The area was cluttered with carelessly piled hills of hempen rope, rusty cable, a sloppily stowed derrick, and cargo pallets and crates. Hatches in the deck were propped open, revealing shafts of oily light from below; to his right, the railed walkway ran across the front of the ship's superstructure. A soldier in fatigues and a helmet leaned against the railing, staring across the well deck, his AKM slung muzzle-down across his back.

"Hammer Bravo-six, this is Bravo-three," he whispered into his lip mike, drawing back behind the corner of the superstructure. "One tango, O-1 deck forward."

"Take him down," came the answer.

"Rog."

Bracing the H&K high, Jaybird took a deep breath, then swung sharply around the corner of the superstructure, drawing down on the target's center of mass and squeezing the trigger simultaneously.

He'd deliberately set the weapon for semi-automatic fire; the sound-suppressed weapon hissed and spat with each tug of the trigger, slamming round after round into the Iranian, who staggered back a step, reached for his assault rifle, then collapsed onto the deck. His helmet hit the superstructure with a metallic clunk. Jaybird held his position, scanning left and right, watching for some reaction to the sudden sound.

Nothing. "Three," he snapped, identifying himself. "Clear. Moving."

A door in the superstructure four feet from the body opened onto a companionway with ladders leading up and down. Jaybird took the steps leading up, treading softly to the next deck . . . then continued beyond to the deck above that. The squad's meticulous studies of *Hormuz*'s deck plans back in Little Creek were paying off; Jaybird knew precisely where this companionway led, and what lay beyond it. At his back, Nicholson followed him up, covering his advance up the ladder.

At the O-3 deck, three levels above the main deck, the ladder ended at a passageway and a door leading forward. Jaybird was still halfway up the companionway when the door opened and a bearded man stepped through.

He was not wearing an army uniform, but a blue jacket over a striped T-shirt. He took two steps into the passageway and then saw Jaybird.

The SEAL's appearance—black-clad, with a dark bandana tight over his head and his face a horror of cold eyes staring from mingled green and black paint—bought Jaybird a full second of gape-mouthed silence. The Iranian's eyes widened, his mouth hung open . . .

And then Jaybird shot him, the reflex automatic, unthinking. Two coughs from his H&K drilled twin holes in the surprised Iranian's head, one above his left eye, the other through the bridge of his nose. The SEAL sprinted the last five steps, reaching the body scant seconds after it collapsed to the deck.

"Awn cheest?" a voice asked from beyond the half-closed door.

"Namedawnam," someone answered, and the door swung open. Another ship's officer took one step through . . .

Jaybird was on him in an instant, left hand grasping the

man's naval jacket with his forearm rammed against the windpipe, right hand wielding the H&K, the long, heavy muzzle roughly jammed against the Iranian's forehead.

"Tasleem shaveed!" Jaybird barked. Those SEALs who didn't speak Farsi had memorized useful key phrases before the mission. "Surrender!"

The man's eyes bulged in terror. *"Nazaneed! Nazaneed!"*

Jaybird shoved the man back into the compartment from which he'd just emerged. It was the ship's bridge, a wide area beneath a low overhead cluttered with pipes and conduits. Two other officers were there, one at the wheel, the other leaning above the bridge radarscope. Jaybird pushed his prisoner to the deck, then gestured with black-faced menace with his submachine gun.

"Dahstahraw boland koneed!" he ordered. The bridge officers complied, raising their hands over their heads. Nicholson came in at Jaybird's back, checking the radio shack and the captain's dayroom, both empty.

"This is Nickle," Nicholson said over his radio, returning to Jaybird's side. "Bridge secure. Three prisoners."

Jaybird moved to the opposite side of the bridge, keeping the prisoners covered as the other SEAL snapped several fast questions at the Iranian on the deck. That man was the oldest of the three and had the most gold braid on his cap and jacket—almost certainly *Hormuz*'s captain. After a brief exchange, Nicholson looked across at Jaybird.

"He says there's a crew of fourteen aboard," Nicholson said. "Claims the ship's a merchantman in international waters, that they're carrying a shipment of copra, timber, and kapok from Madagascar to Bandar Abbas, and that we're pirates."

With deliberate slowness, Jaybird raised his subgun until it was aiming directly at the merchant captain's face, then gradually tracked the muzzle down the length of the man's body until it was aiming at his groin. He allowed himself a smile, bared teeth startlingly white behind the grease paint. With a dramatic flourish, he flexed his forefinger over the trigger.

"Na! Na!" the captain cried, eyes wild and staring, sweat

glistening on his forehead and in his beard. "*Nazaneed! Kahesh meekonam!* I speak! I speak!"

Haltingly, in mingled bursts of Farsi and thickly accented English, the ship's captain admitted that there were ten soldiers aboard, members of a naval infantry brigade belonging to the Pasdaran, Iran's elite Revolutionary Guard. He knew of the Japanese plutonium ship, but insisted that none of the cargo had been transferred to the *Hormuz*. "Just soldier! Just soldier!" he insisted, looking from Jaybird to Nickle and back again. "We send soldier, other ship!"

"*Chand ast sarbawz?*" Nickle demanded. "How many soldiers?"

"*Chehel.*"

Nicholson blinked, then looked across at Jaybird. "Shit. He says forty."

"What, they put forty troops aboard the *Yuduki Maru*?" Jaybird licked his lips.

"We thought they might have reinforced the terrorists over there," Nicholson said. "But forty soldiers is a fucking army!"

"Yeah," Jaybird said. "And our guys are walking into a trap!"

2318 hours (Zulu +3)
Freighter *Yuduki Maru*

They'd been aboard the Japanese ship for less than seven minutes, splitting up and padding with cat's-stealth silence along the vessel's alleys and walkways. One by one, the Iranian guards they encountered were eliminated, silently and efficiently. So far, there'd been no sign of either Japanese terrorists or the *Yuduki Maru*'s original crew, but the ship seemed to be crawling with armed Iranian soldiers. The brown-fatigued soldiers were everywhere, lounging in small groups, standing lone watch in passageways, manning a pair of machine guns that had been mounted high up above the deck on the wings of the bridge.

Crouching in the shadows on the ship's starboard side, MacKenzie and Higgins studied the forward deck from beneath a white-painted deck ladder. By the light spilling from the bridge some thirty feet above his head, MacKenzie could make out at least a dozen armed men lounging on the ship's long forward deck.

"Hammer Alfa-six," he whispered over his mike, using Murdock's op call sign. "This is Alfa-one. I'm starboard side, aft of the main deck. I've got twelve tangos in sight, and I can hear more of 'em moving around above me. What the hell's going down?"

"Wait one."

"Rog." Murdock sounded tense. He must have just encountered another Iranian guard.

Damn, how many troops had boarded the plutonium ship off the *Hormuz*? Half, at least, must be asleep below decks, probably in the new quarters constructed for *Yuduki Maru*'s security contingent. Others were on watch throughout the vessel's interior. And there were still the original Japanese terrorists to consider. MacKenzie added up the likely numbers and arrived at a figure of between forty and fifty bad guys . . . not very good odds.

Still, the SEAL squad had the advantage of surprise, and they'd already whittled down the enemy strength somewhat. In Vietnam, he knew, it had been commonly claimed that five or ten SEALs could take on as many as two hundred enemy troops and expect to win, thanks to surprise, superior training, and superior technology.

He didn't savor challenging those kinds of odds here, however. Vietnam had been a different kind of war, with room for the SEAL teams to pick and choose their ambush sites, their battles, and their targets. Here, the SEALs were at a distinct disadvantage, hemmed in by the narrow confines of the ship.

And in Vietnam, they hadn't been worried about two tons of plutonium stored below decks either.

He glanced up, as though he could see through the overhead to the bridge wing thirty feet above his head. If someone could get to those machine guns, they might be able to command the deck below.

"Mac, Six. Looks like we've stepped into a nest of them." Murdock's voice in his headset was so low Mac had to strain to catch the words. There was a pause, and MacKenzie could almost hear the new lieutenant measuring the odds. "Okay, guys. This thing's too big not to give it a damned good try. Mac, you and your people get below to the engine room. Rest of you with me."

"Roger that. Moving." MacKenzie gestured to Higgins and started aft.

A sound, footsteps on steel, made him look up. An Iranian soldier was on the ladder eight feet above him, clattering carelessly down the steps. The man wore a helmet and carried an AKM slung over his shoulder. He was watching his own feet, but before he'd taken another step, he glanced up and his eyes locked with MacKenzie's.

The Texan was already in motion, bringing up his H&K, triggering a single, sound-suppressed shot that punched brutally into the Iranian's jaw and up through his brain. The man's boots flew out from beneath him and he pitched back against the ladder, his helmet hitting a step with the clang of something heavy and metallic striking steel. . . .

2319 hours (Zulu +3)
Freighter *Yuduki Maru*

Tetsuo Kurebayashi stood atop one of the low deckhouses on *Yuduki Maru*'s weather deck, striving to regain the peace he'd felt with the universe in the days before the Iranians had come aboard. The stars were the same, including the Milky Way, though their full glory was masked by a layer of broken clouds slowly moving in from the east. Still, he felt uneasy, about the mission, about the Eikyuni Shinananai Tori's new allies, even knowing that this reinforcement by the Iranian troops had been planned a full year ago, as Operation Yoake had first begun to take shape in Tehran and in the training camps in Syria.

The Iranians were barbarians, all of them, stinking with sweat and filth and the sharp spices in their food, distracted constantly by the demands of their religion, careless in their manners and courtesy. Their leader, a colonel in their Pasdaran outfit named Sayyed Hamid, was a member of one of Iran's most powerful families, and he was no better than the rest, a great pig of a man who cared nothing for the Ohtori or its goals, who treated Kurebayashi and his brothers as hirelings, as *mercenaries,* useful now so long as they stayed out of the way.

He didn't like the Iranians, and he wondered why Isamu Takeda, the Ohtori leader who'd conceived and engineered Yoake-Go from the group's base in Syria, had deigned to work with them at all. Other nations in that same part of the world would have paid any price for the cargo riding beneath the *Yuduki Maru*'s deck.

Kurebayashi heard a sound, a loud, metallic clang. Curious, he turned, staring aft across the freighter's tanker-like foredeck and the Iranians lying asleep or squatting in small groups. He couldn't see any—

No! There! On a ladder on the ship's starboard side, close against the superstructure, one shadow grabbed another and dragged it down. For a shock-frozen instant, Kurebayashi wasn't sure of exactly what had happened, but as he played it back in his head, he was pretty sure he'd seen an Iranian soldier sprawling back against the ladder, and another figure dressed in black grabbing him.

Commandos! It could be nothing else.

"Abunai!" he screamed in warning. Then he realized that not one in twenty of the Iranians aboard spoke a word of Japanese, so he snatched up his AKM, aimed it across the deck at the shadows moving next to the superstructure, and clamped down on the trigger.

Gunfire, urgent, insistent, and painfully loud, shattered the serenity of the night.

16

Bullets sparked and shrieked off the steel plating of the ship's superstructure as MacKenzie, Garcia, and Higgins dropped to their bellies. Mac could see the flicker of the muzzle flash against the darkness blanketing the ship's forward deck, could hear the characteristic flat crack of an AK on full-auto. On the well deck between MacKenzie and the gunman, Iranian troops were stirring, a hornet's nest awakened by the sudden, savage volley.

"Hammer Six!" Mac called. "This is One! It's going down!"

"Rog. I copy. Charlie Mike."

Charlie Mike: continue mission. Another burst of automatic gunfire screamed off the ladder four feet above MacKenzie's head. Levering himself up over the Iranian soldier's corpse, he aimed at the wink of the muzzle flash and triggered three quick bursts. The range was long for a subgun, even for an H&K. The hostile fire ceased, however, though there was no way to tell whether the enemy gunman had been hit or simply driven to cover.

"Let's move out," he snapped. Higgins and Garcia backed away from the ladder, then vanished through an open door into the superstructure.

Gunfire barked from the freighter's forward deck, as Iranians yelled at one another in urgent Farsi. MacKenzie switched to full-auto and loosed a long, sweeping burst, a pointed invitation to the hostiles to keep their heads down. Then he followed the others.

Inside the door, a companionway led down and aft, toward the *Yuduki Maru*'s engine room.

2320 hours (Zulu +3)
Bridge access
Freighter *Yuduki Maru*

Murdock was already on an interior ladder leading from the O-2 deck to the O-3 deck, with *Yuduki Maru*'s bridge just ahead. The chatter and crackle of automatic weapons fire was muffled inside the ship's superstructure, but still audible. Murdock signaled to Ellsworth, Brown, and Roselli. *Follow me!*

The door leading to the bridge was closed and unguarded. With no information on what was going on inside, Murdock silently signaled the others, having them take up positions on either side of the entryway. Reaching into one of his combat vest pouches, he extracted a flash-bang, grasped the arming pin, and nodded to Roselli.

The SEAL chief tried the lever on the door, which swung inward easily at his touch. Murdock yanked the flash-bang's cotter pin, flipped off the arming lever, and tossed the grenade through the opening.

An intense pulse of light, a rattling string of eight thunderclap detonations assaulted the senses as the flash-bang went off on the bridge. Roselli was through the door while the bulkheads were still ringing from the final blast, entering left to right with his H&K at the ready.

Murdock was immediately behind him, entering right to left. Smoke from the expended flash-bang wreathed the compartment. A shadow against the smoke resolved itself into an Iranian soldier leaning against a line of printers, his hands over his eyes, blood running from one ear. Murdock fired, a single round fired from chest-high that snapped through the man's throat, then punched a neat hole through the glass of the large bridge window at his back. Murdock fired again as the soldier collapsed, then swung to the right, weapon all the way up to his shoulder now. A second Iranian, rising from one of the track-mounted, sliding bridge chairs, staggered as a triplet of rounds from Roselli's H&K slammed him out of the chair and into the bridge console, arms flailing before he slumped to the deck in a spreading pool of blood. A Japanese seaman was kneeling behind the ship's wheel at the main control console, head turned to look back over his shoulder, his nose bloodied and his dark eyes wide with terror. Murdock had just dismissed the man as unarmed—a probable hostage—when another Japanese merchant sailor leaped behind the seaman, crouched, threw an arm around the man's throat, and held the muzzle of a SIG-Sauer P-220 automatic pistol against the man's skull.

"Tomare! Atoe sare!"

There was no time for negotiations. Clearly, the Japanese terrorist was unacquainted with SEAL marksmanship, a skill practiced constantly with a variety of weapons and from every position imaginable. More than enough of the terrorist's head was visible as he sheltered behind the hostage's body; Murdock shifted the aim of his H&K slightly and squeezed the trigger. The side of the tango's head exploded in a fine spray of blood and bone; the P-220 dropped from nerveless fingers and the terrorist slumped to the deck. The hostage let out a piercing scream and covered his eyes.

Movement behind the glass of the door leading to the starboard bridge wing caught Murdock's attention. Firing above the kneeling helmsman's head, he put three rounds through the glass and was rewarded by the sight of an Iranian twisting away, then falling against the outside of the door, leaving a smear of scarlet as he slumped below the bullet-holed window. Murdock heard the hard-voiced snap of sound-suppressed shots at his back. Ellsworth had just fired through the port wing door from his position at the entrance to the bridge, taking out the Iranian posted there.

Brown, coming in behind Roselli, had reached the bridge entrance to the communications shack. "Clear!" he yelled.

"Clear!" Roselli barked, standing astride the second dead Iranian.

"Clear!" Ellsworth called from the open door.

Murdock nudged the body of the first man he'd shot. The eyes were open, staring sightlessly at the overhead. "Clear! Roselli! Brown! Take the wings!"

Glass shattered in the forward bridge windows, and bullets whined and thudded among the overhead piping and wire conduits. Iranians on the forward deck could see the SEALs on the well-lit bridge easily and were firing at them as they rushed aft.

Then the machine gun mounted on the starboard wing of the bridge opened up, a long, raucous yammer shockingly loud after the harsh whisperings of the sound-suppressed H&Ks. Brown was wielding the weapon, a Type 62 GPMG on a pintel mount, sweeping the muzzle back and forth in broad arcs that lashed the forward deck with screaming lead. An instant later, Roselli opened up with the port machine gun, and the Iranians on the deck found themselves in a devastating, plunging cross fire. The wild shooting from the deck ceased, as a dozen Iranian soldiers scrambled for cover behind piles of wood, coiled cable, and any other cover they could find.

Murdock knelt beside the terrified Japanese helmsman. "You speak English?"

The man blinked at him, uncomprehending. *"Utsu na! Utsu na!"*

"Great," Murdock told him. "You're going to be all right, fella. Stay down."

The merchant sailor might not have understood the words, but he seemed to understand Murdock's tone and gestures. He lay flat on the deck. Murdock stepped behind him and, stooping down, dropped his knee into the small of the man's back, then grabbed his wrists. From the deck, the helmsman barked something, surprise mingled with hurt and anger in his voice, but Murdock swiftly secured the hostage's hands behind his back with a strip of white plastic that could be removed only with scissors or a knife. Each SEAL carried twenty-four of the disposable handcuffs in a vest pouch; standard operating procedure required them to cuff every non-SEAL they didn't kill. The helmsman was almost certainly a legitimate crew member of the *Yuduki Maru,* forced to steer the ship by his captors, but the short and sharp encounter with the tango holding a pistol to the guy's head could have been a charade, a way of planting one terrorist at least among the SEALs. Besides, with his hands tied, the guy was less likely to jump up at an inopportune moment and run into someone's line of fire.

"Sorry, fella," Murdock said gently, patting the hostage's shoulder and rising. "Until we can check your driver's license, we can't risk having you run loose."

Gunfire banged from the deck, was answered by a full-auto salvo from the starboard bridge wing.

"I don't know, Lieutenant," Ellsworth said. "Seems to me we weren't supposed to run into a fucking army on this tub." Another burst of gunfire from the deck punctuated his comment. Four more holes appeared in one of the slanted bridge windows, centered in small halos of crazed glass.

"You know what they say about Naval Intelligence, Doc. Contradiction in terms." He switched to the Pentagon's frequency. "Foreman, Foreman, this is Hammer Alfa."

Outside the bridge, gunfire flared and cracked in the night.

2321 hours (1521 hours Zulu −5)
Joint Special Operations Command Center
The Pentagon

"What is it?" Congressman Murdock said. "What's going on?"

None of the others with him in the room replied immediately. The atmosphere was charged with tension, and to make matters worse, the magic camera-in-the-sky pictures were gone now, the images lost when the satellite transmitting them had slipped below the horizon three minutes earlier. Murdock had only a hazy idea of how such things worked, but a staffer had patiently explained to him that morning that, while satellites could to a certain extent be repositioned in their orbits, those orbits were nonetheless dictated by certain laws of physics that not even Congress could rewrite. Once the KH-12 satellite transmitting those scenes had passed over the horizon at 3:18

P.M. Washington time, there would be an eleven-minute gap—until 3:29—when the only information coming to the Pentagon from the events unfolding aboard the *Yuduki Maru* would be the voice channels, monitored by an AWACS E-3A Sentry aircraft circling well to the north and relayed by communication satellite to Washington.

"Damn it," Congressman Murdock said again. "Someone tell me what's happening!"

General Bradley looked at him, and the corner of his mouth pulled back in a hard, quick, and humorless half smile. "Apparently, *Hormuz* was able to rendezvous with the *Yuduki Maru* sometime earlier today."

"Worst-case scenario," Mason added. "There are Iranian troops aboard that freighter. According to Hammer Bravo, it might be as many as forty men."

"Oh, God. Are we going to have to abort?"

"We'd rather not, Congressman," Admiral Bainbridge said, his voice cold. "We've gone to a hell of a lot of trouble to get our people onto those ships. Let's give them a chance, shall we?"

Though the air in the climate-controlled room was cool, almost chilly, Murdock found that he was sweating.

2323 hours (Zulu +3)
Bridge
Freighter *Yuduki Maru*

Bending over low to stay out of the line of fire, Murdock moved to the main bridge console, studying the array of computer terminals, instruments, and consoles.

The bridge arrangement of modern merchant ships had become more and more complex over the past decade, until they resembled something out of a science-fiction movie, but Murdock had been carefully briefed on the control systems layout of *Yuduki Maru*'s main console. At the extreme right of the main panel, next to a machinery monitoring station, was a terminal and display screen, the freighter's cargo-monitoring console. He checked to see that the display was on, entered some memorized commands on the keyboard, then studied the

glowing display of characters and graphics that filled the
screen.

The characters were Japanese ideographs, but he'd been
shown what to look for on the graphics, and what he saw was
immensely reassuring. *Yuduki Maru*'s cargo, stored in holds
one and two, was still secure. Radiation levels in the hold were
normal, there was no indication that the automated wash-down
foam had been triggered, and all of the cargo hold seals were
listed as intact. Apparently, no one had even tried to enter the
cargo holds, and that lifted an enormous weight from Murdock's
shoulders. One of several worst-case scenarios discussed back
at Little Creek was the possibility that the terrorists had mined
or booby-trapped the cargo.

If they hadn't been into the cargo hold, they couldn't have
tampered with the plutonium.

But Murdock was taking no chances. Still working by rote,
he entered another string of keyboard commands, and watched
as the characters on the screen shifted from Kanji characters to
English. With the United States insisting on a say in the
security of the plutonium, the freighter's computer security had
been programmed with both Japanese and English access, and
the SEALs had been given the appropriate codes before the
mission. He waited as a new screen came up, then began typing
in a series of memorized commands.

After another pause, the results of his work flashed onto the
screen and he nodded his satisfaction. The plutonium holds
were now under an emergency lock-down. Only a password
that Murdock had just typed into the security system—
Jaybird—would allow access. If the SEAL squad was wiped
out in the next few moments and the Iranians regained control
of the bridge, they would be unable to get past the security
overrides. Eventually, they might be able to break the code,
bypass the security lock-down, or cut their way in through the
weather deck and rifle the cargo by brute force, but all of those
attempts would take both time and special equipment not
available out here in the middle of the Indian Ocean.

"Lieutenant?" Ellsworth said. He was crouched by the door

at the back of the bridge through which the SEALs had burst moments before. "I think we're about to have company."

"On my way." He switched off the computer monitor, then hurried across the deck to where Doc was waiting.

Now everything was up to MacKenzie down in the engineering room.

2324 hours (Zulu +3)
Engine room access
Freighter *Yuduki Maru*

MacKenzie had led Garcia and Higgins down two levels, to what on a Navy vessel would have been called the third deck, somewhere close to the freighter's waterline. The passageway led fore and aft; forward, according to the deck plans and model the SEALs had studied, lay the cargo holds that—please God!—should be locked and secured. That, however, was the Lieutenant's responsibility. Three men could not secure *Yuduki Maru*'s cargo, but Murdock ought to be able to check it and lock it down from the bridge.

Instead, Mac led the way aft, toward the freighter's engine room. Somewhere ahead, a steel door clanged open. A moment later, a Japanese merchant sailor appeared, wearing shorts and a white T-shirt, running blindly down the passageway. An instant later he caught sight of the SEALs, of their black faces, menacing garb, and weapons, and he nearly collided with a bulkhead trying to stop.

"Tomare!" Higgins called. "Halt!" Several of the SEALs were fluent in more than one other language, but he was the only one in the platoon who spoke Japanese.

The seaman took a step back.

"Chikayore!" Higgins snapped. "Come forward!" Reluctantly, the man complied.

In seconds, they had the seaman on his face, his wrists cuffed with plastic ties behind his back, his ankles tied together. Higgins spoke to him, his voice coaxing. The hostage answered back, gesturing back down the passageway with his head and with rolling eyes.

"What's he say, Prof?"

"Okay, he says he's just a member of the crew," Higgins replied. "Says there's always a couple of Iranians on guard in the engine room. He also says something's got 'em pretty well stirred up right now. He decided to git while the gittin' was good."

MacKenzie nodded curtly. "Let's put 'em down then."

Leaving the seaman lying in the passageway, the SEALs headed for the engine room. The door was closed but unlocked, opening to Garcia's push.

Inside, a railed platform overlooked the engine room, a claustrophobic compartment filled with monstrous shapes: reduction gears, condensers, generators, and massive steam turbines like green-painted prehistoric monsters embedded in the ribbed, gleaming steel decks.

An Iranian soldier shouted warning as MacKenzie burst through the open door. The SEAL chief triggered a short burst from his H&K and the man went down, his AKM clattering off one of the engine housings and onto the deck. Another soldier lunged for cover, shouting something in Farsi. Garcia leaned into the railing and fired once . . . twice. The Iranian clawed at his back, then dropped to the deck. For a long moment, MacKenzie held his position, swinging his H&K's muzzle left and right, searching for further movement.

Nothing.

"Secure the door," MacKenzie told Garcia. "Prof, you're with me."

A steep metal ladder led from the platform down to the main engineering deck. MacKenzie, his H&K strapped to his combat harness, grabbed the railings and rode them twelve feet to the steel grating below. The engine room throbbed with the pulse of confined power, and in the distance aft, connecting with the turbines, he could see the ponderous revolutions of the reduction gears turning *Yuduki Maru*'s paired propeller shafts.

Mac and Prof carried out a lightning inspection of the engineering deck, checking the bodies and searching for tangos missed during their entry. They found no more terrorists, but they did discover four terrified Japanese crewmen hiding behind a massive generator mounting. MacKenzie covered them while Higgins tied their wrists, led them to the forward end of the compartment, where he tied their ankles as well, and then began questioning them.

"Shit, Mac," Higgins said, joining him again after a few moments. "These people all say there's forty or fifty bad guys on board! Some Japanese tangos, plus a shitload of Iranians!"

"I was beginning to get that idea." MacKenzie looked forward, past the humming hulks of the freighter's turbines. There were three doors in the forward bulkhead, two high up and to either side, and a third in the middle and on the same level as the engineering deck, leading forward to the boiler room. Garcia was still on the starboard side platform, guarding the door and watching over the engine room. The four civilians, tied hand and foot, lay on the deck next to the boiler room door.

Tactically, the SEALs simply could not now continue the mission as originally planned. Though SEALs liked to boast of a ten-to-one or better kill ratio in combat, there was no way, realistically, that the seven of them could face an unknown but very large force of heavily armed Iranians—now thoroughly aroused and hostile Iranians—and win. Despite the popular fictional image of SEALs as Ramboesque commandos who routinely took on impossible odds, the Teams were not suicide squads and they did not attempt hopeless missions. Their training, their experience, and their hard-won skills were too valuable to throw away in empty, heroic gestures.

"Hammer Six," he called. "This is One."

"One, Six. Copy."

"Echo Romeo secure. But Skipper, it's not gonna be secure for long. I've got some locals here who tell me we've just stepped smack in the cow patty big time."

"Roger that." There was a moment's hesitation, and MacKenzie could almost hear the wheels turning as Murdock considered his next order.

"Okay, Chief," Murdock's voice said. "Set for Kneecap, but do not initiate. Do you copy?"

"Roger. Set Kneecap, do not initiate."

"Keep me posted."

"Rog."

Kneecap was the code word for one of the SEAL team's contingency plans, a last-ditch, we've-got-to-get-out-of-Dodge measure to keep *Yuduki Maru*'s cargo out of Iranian hands. Two satchel charges, one apiece for each of the freighter's propeller shafts, would be enough to disable the *Yuduki Maru*, leaving her dead in the water. A second assault would then be mounted, as soon as additional SEAL or Marine forces could be mustered.

A final, more drastic option remained if Kneecap didn't work. If worst came to worst, the team could execute Headshot, blowing precisely placed holes in the freighter's sides and sending her to the bottom. In theory, specialized submarine recovery vehicles would be able to salvage the freighter's cargo before seawater corroded the cylinders containing the plutonium, contaminating the local waters with radioactivity.

That was definitely a last-ditch option, however. No one wanted to risk breaching or scattering the containment cylinders, for the scenario describing the spread of radioactive contamination through ocean currents from the Seychelles to Cape Town was too dreadful to easily contemplate.

"Prof!" he called. "It's Kneecap! You take the port shaft. I'll take the starboard."

Yuduki Maru's two propeller shafts ran from the reduction gears connecting them with the turbines, vanishing through watertight seals and bearings into the shaft alleys in the aft hull. An explosive charge positioned over the shaft bearings would break or bend the propeller shafts, rendering them useless, irreparable anywhere short of a major dry-dock overhaul.

MacKenzie reached into one of his waterproof satchels, pulling out a cable-cutting charge, a U-shaped pouch containing a half kilo of C-6 plastic explosive, multiple detonators, and an electronic firing trigger with a keypad for entering any time, in seconds, from one to 9,999.

He was halfway to the shaft bearing when the Iranians burst through the engine room's port-side entryway.

"Cover!" Garcia shouted from his perch on the starboard side. His H&K spat flame, striking sparks and shrill pings from the open door, then slashing into the first Iranian soldier in line and toppling him over the platform railing and onto a generator housing below. The next Iranian got off one brief, wild burst from his AK before Garcia's enfilade fire sent him tumbling in a bloody heap down the steel ladder. A confused babble of Farsi, shouted orders and queries, sounded from the passageway beyond.

MacKenzie dove for cover, crouching behind a massive reduction gear housing alongside one of the throbbing turbines. "Six, this is One! It's going down now. Hard!"

"Copy, One. What's your sit?"

MacKenzie could hear the hammer of a heavy weapon in the background as Murdock spoke. "Not good! Not good!" MacKenzie shouted over the tactical channel. "We need backup, and we need it fast!" Another burst of AK fire sang through the engine room. Sooner or later, overwhelming Iranian forces would root them out of here, with gunfire, grenades, or gas.

And then it would be all over.

MacKenzie dropped an empty magazine, then slapped home a fresh one. A single burst of AK fire snapped from the door, wild again, the rounds shrieking off steel. He guessed, judging by the yells and shouting voices outside, that the Iranians must be getting ready to try a rush.

The original plan to blow *Yuduki Maru*'s propeller shafts was out now. It would take minutes to plant the charges . . . and the SEALs now had only seconds.

What the hell was going on up on the bridge?

17

"I hear 'em on the ladder," Ellsworth said. "They're coming up the companionway."

"Flash-bangs," Murdock said, reaching for his combat vest as Ellsworth nodded and did the same. The metallic thumpings on the stairway behind the bridge were louder now, punctuated by shrill voices. The two SEALs yanked the pins on their stun grenades, paused, then tossed them in perfect arcs through the bridge door and into the square pit of the companionway outside.

Seconds later, the darkened corridors lit with pulsing flashes of dazzling light reflected from white-painted bulkheads, and the ear-hammering blasts of multiple concussions. When his ears stopped ringing, Murdock could hear the low groans and cries of stunned, wounded men.

"Together," he told Doc, and together they broke from cover, racing to the companionway and thrusting their H&Ks over the railing. Two decks down, and scattered halfway up the steps, a tangle of khaki-clad bodies was writhing in the uncertain illumination of a fallen emergency lantern, Iranian troops, the blood streaming from noses, mouths, and ears looking garishly black in the yellow light. Murdock flicked his selector switch to semi-auto and began triggering round after aimed round into the helpless targets. Doc joined in the slaughter until, seconds later, there was no more movement.

"Stay here," he told Ellsworth. "Yell if any more come."

"Will do, Skipper."

Murdock ducked back onto the bridge, ducking again as more bullets slammed through the shattered bridge windows, tunneling into the overhead soundproofing, spilling more shards of glass across the deck of the bridge. He crouched in the shelter of the console, as the Type 62 machine guns thundered from both wings.

Clearly, Operation Sun Hammer had gone badly sour. The four Americans on the bridge had stopped the Iranian thrust through the superstructure, and they had the Iranians on the forward deck pinned down for the moment, but others would be on their way soon, and there simply weren't enough SEALs aboard to neutralize the entire enemy force.

He switched channels on his tactical radio. "Foreman, Foreman, this is Hammer One. Do you copy?"

Somewhere to the north, the orbiting E-3A Sentry aircraft picked up his words, passing them along to the anxiously waiting men in the bowels of the Pentagon.

"Hammer One, Foreman copies" came the reply a moment later.

"Sheet metal," Murdock said, using the code phrase meaning that Hammer had just tried driving a nail into steel instead of soft wood.

For a long moment, Murdock heard only static. Outside, the gunfire had died down, but he could still hear the Iranians calling to one another in the darkness.

He had just told the mission directors back in the Pentagon that the mission, as originally planned, could not be completed, and what he was waiting to hear now was the code phrase "Alfa Bravo," the order to abort.

But what, he wondered, should he do if he heard Charlie Mike, ordering him to continue? Long before sunup, he and his men would all be dead or prisoners, and beyond executing Kneecap, they wouldn't be able to accomplish a damned thing.

Shit. If they ordered the SEALs to stay, there was a damned

good possibility that he was going to develop serious communications problems. *He* was supposed to have operational control on site, not the REMFs in Washington, but that wouldn't count for much if he ended up disobeying a direct order.

Come *on*! Come *on*!

2328 hours (1528 hours Zulu −5)
Joint Special Operations Command Center
The Pentagon

"Damn it," General Bradley said, chewing at his cigar. "They can't just jump ship! We'll have video back in another minute! They can't pull out now!"

To Congressman Murdock, it sounded as though Bradley were more concerned about not being able to see what was going on . . . almost like a child told that he couldn't watch his favorite cartoon.

"Doesn't sound like we have much choice, General," Captain Mason replied. He gestured at the main viewing screen, which showed a test pattern at the moment. "Murdock is our man on the scene. He has to make the call, one way or the other. And we have to back him."

There, it had been said. His son was in charge of Sun Hammer. Congressman Murdock closed his eyes, riding out a tremor of fear that rippled up his spine.

"In any case," Bainbridge said, "we have to give them our answer. *Now*."

Captain Granger laughed. "You gentlemen realize that there's not a lot we can do to enforce whatever order we give them? It really is their call."

"Tell them Alfa Bravo," Bainbridge said. His eyes glittered like ice in the phosphor light from the test pattern on the screen.

Mason picked up a telephone and began speaking into it rapidly.

As he was talking, another telephone on a console near the screen buzzed, and Carter picked it up. "Yeah . . . uh-huh." There was a pause. "Okay. We're ready." He kept the receiver in his hand, as he had before. "KH-twelve-five is coming over the horizon now," he told the others. "They're putting the feed through from NPIC now." Carter pronounced the acronym "en-pick," a word that stood for the National Photographic Interpretation Center, a joint CIA-NSA department located in Washington, D.C., that carried the responsibility for receiving and distributing all military satellite imagery.

The test pattern flickered out and was replaced by a slow-moving emptiness of rugged, black ripple patterns. It took Congressman Murdock a moment to recognize what he was looking at as the surface of the ocean. Under the control of unseen hands at some distant control center, the view slewed abruptly to one side, focusing once again on the *Yuduki Maru*. The angle was different this time, flatter, and from farther off. It was moving more quickly too, which meant, Murdock had been told, that the satellite shooting this was traveling in a lower, faster orbit.

Again, the *Yuduki Maru* was illuminated in soft-glowing greens and whites, an oblique view that picked out the flashes of gunfire on her long, forward deck in sharp pinpricks of light. It seemed strange to see the shots flickering in absolute silence.

"That's it," Bradley said, pointing. "A firefight. God, how are they going to get out of that?"

"What about the other group?" Murdock asked. "The ones on the *Hormuz*?"

"Normally," Mason said, "they would have been the backup to the strike on the plutonium ship. But they have their hands full with their own prisoners. The helos are still inbound. Another thirty minutes before they arrive at least." He shook his head. "I don't see that Hammer One has a choice. They have to get out."

"If," Bainbridge said quietly, "the Iranians let them."

2329 hours (Zulu +3)
Bridge
Freighter *Yuduki Maru*

"Hammer One, Foreman. Alfa Bravo. Repeat, Alfa Bravo. Confirm."

"Foreman, Hammer One confirms Alfa Bravo, Alfa Bravo.

Out." Murdock cut the channel. "That's it, people!" he yelled to the others on the bridge. "We're outa here!" Switching to the tactical frequency, he patched through to MacKenzie again. "Hammer One-one, this is Six. One-one, Six! Get out of there, Mac! We've got an abort and we're going over the side!"

2329 hours (Zulu +3)
Engine room
Freighter *Yuduki Maru*

"Roger that, Six. One copies." MacKenzie signaled Higgins and Garcia with a vigorous pumping of his fist. "Right, boys and girls! Time to get out of Dodge!"

Damn. With the Iranians pressing them, they'd not had time or opportunity to plant the charges that would cripple the Japanese freighter. Still, he might manage to salvage a portion of Kneecap at least. Murdock hadn't given any orders about that one way or the other, or even asked how far along they were planting their charges.

That left things pretty much up to MacKenzie. Rising from cover behind a reduction gear housing, he loosed a long, full-auto burst at the open door, forcing the Iranian troops at the port-side doorway to duck for cover. Higgins took the opportunity afforded by MacKenzie's covering fire to bolt for the starboard-side ladder and scramble up the rungs to where Garcia was crouched astride the watertight door's combing.

"Cover me!" MacKenzie shouted.

From his perch on the railed, overhead platform, Higgins responded with a three-round burst that sparked and sang off the doorway opposite his position. MacKenzie pulled out the timer on his satchel charge, stabbed the numeral nine twice, punched the start button, then tucked the canvas bag into the pistoning motion of a starboard reduction gear housing. He now had about a minute and a half.

"Moving!" he yelled, and with the word he was racing down a narrow passage between the hulking mountains of painted steel.

At the base of the ladder, he paused long enough to stoop next to the four Japanese enginemen who were still lying facedown on the deck next to the aft bulkhead. Swiftly, he used his diver's knife to slice through the plastic restraints on their wrists. Pointing fiercely at the center door, he shouted one of his few words of Japanese: *"Isoge!* Hurry!"

The crewmen needed no further encouragement. Scrambling to their feet, they dove for the passageway leading to *Yuduki Maru*'s boiler room. Lying flat on the deck, they probably would have been safe from the detonation of half a kilo of plastic explosives, but bits of metal and broken machinery would make a devastating shrapnel. Worse, MacKenzie had no idea what the Iranians might do to their hostages when they found them tied up and abandoned by the Navy SEALs, but a distinct possibility would be a mindless venting of their anger on helpless, trussed-up civilians. This way, at least, they would have a chance.

"God damn it, Mac," Garcia yelled from overhead. *"Move* your ass!"

MacKenzie swarmed up the engine-room ladder, joining the other two SEALs. By his watch, only seconds remained of the minute and a half on the timer.

"Go!" he snapped. "Go! *Go!"*

After dogging the watertight door shut, they raced down the passageway outside, retracing their steps. They were ten feet from the door when a loud crack echoed off steel bulkheads behind them, accompanied by the metallic clang of hurtling fragments. Instantly he felt a strange new sensation, an uncomfortable, uneven shudder transmitted through the deck plating.

"Feels like you frigged up the works real good, Mac," Garcia said.

"Yeah, but we only knocked out one screw." They stopped in the passageway next to the Japanese crewman they'd caught and tied earlier. As Garcia and MacKenzie watched the corridor approaches, Higgins cut the man free, speaking quietly to him in Japanese.

MacKenzie opened his tactical channel. "Hammer Six, Hammer Six! This is One."

"Six. Go ahead."

"Okay, Lieutenant. The bad guys are back in Echo Romeo, in force. We managed half a Kneecap before we split."

"Copy that, Mac. How badly is she hurt?"

"Can't say for sure, Lieutenant. But my guess is her port shaft is bent to hell."

"Rog. I can feel the cavitation up here. Okay, Mac. Good work. Make your way topside for E&E. Hold the boarding zone for three minutes. If we're not there by then, you're on your own."

E&E—Escape and Evasion. MacKenzie scowled at that sour thought. The mission had gone bad, a real clusterfuck. They would have to *run* . . .

"Yessir. Copy that." He glanced back at Higgins, who was helping the Japanese crewman to his feet. "Uh, Lieutenant? We have one of the hostages here."

"Good," Murdock's voice replied. "Bring him along if you can."

"That's what I was thinking." Questioning the Japanese crewman could reveal useful details about *Yuduki Maru*'s hijackers and might, possibly, give them a second shot at the freighter.

"Let's get the hell out of here," he growled at the others. Together, they started up another ladder toward the main deck.

2331 hours (Zulu +3)
Bridge
Freighter *Yuduki Maru*

Murdock looked at the terrified Japanese crewman still lying on the deck, hands bound behind him and his back dusted with broken glass. Blood streaked his forehead where he'd been cut by a flying shard. Murdock didn't want the SEAL force burdened by rescued hostages, but he also doubted that the terrorists or Iranians aboard would be lenient with anyone who had helped the U.S. intruders. Mac had one hostage already. Good enough. He would bring another.

"Doc!" he snapped. "You help this guy. We're taking him with us."

Ellsworth snicked a fresh magazine into his H&K. "Aye, Skipper."

Roselli and Brown joined them a moment later. "Port MG is spiked, Skipper," Roselli told him. "I yanked the operating rod and the bolt and chucked 'em over the side."

"Same on the starboard wing," Magic added.

"Okay, gentlemen." Murdock took a last look around the glass-littered, blood-splattered bridge. Was he forgetting anything? "Let's get the hell out of here."

2332 hours (Zulu +3)
Freighter *Yuduki Maru*

Tetsuo Kurebayashi poked his head above the deck hatch, staring aft toward the ship's superstructure. It was difficult to see much; it was dark and most of the superstructure lights had been smashed, including the lights on the bridge.

In fact, the bridge looked empty, the large, out-slanting windows eye-socket-empty and lifeless. The machine guns to either side, on the wings, were silent as well.

Had the American commandos been killed?

Kurebayashi was too much the professional to assume that. More likely, the attackers had withdrawn.

But what had they come here to accomplish in the first place? Kurebayashi had assumed their intent was to recapture the *Yuduki Maru,* but they'd seized the bridge and, according to the wild reports brought to him by the Iranians, other parts of the ship as well, then simply abandoned them.

Where had they gone . . . and why?

Cautiously, Kurebayashi rose, half expecting a sniper's shot from some darkened section of the bridge to slam him down, but no shot came. *"Tsuite koi!"* he called to the men crouched in the darkness around him. "Follow me!" When no one responded, he shifted to one of his fragments of badly accented Farsi. *"Akabeh man biaweed!"*

He started forward, his AKM thrusting ahead as he moved. Often, he'd been taught at the training camps in Syria and Libya, heroism in battle consisted of nothing more than keeping your wits about you when it counted . . . and in acting when others about you were *re*acting. At first, none of the Pasdaran hiding in the shadows moved, but as he continued his lone march toward the *Yuduki Maru*'s superstructure, others, first singly, then in small groups, began following. *"Isoge!"* he snapped, lapsing back into Japanese as he broke into a run. "Hurry!"

2333 hours (Zulu +3)
Port-side catwalk
Freighter *Yuduki Maru*
The rescued hostage was less than eager to maintain the SEALs' rapid pace, and twice Murdock had to tell Ellsworth to snap it up, to make the man *hurry*. He'd sent Magic Brown on ahead to flush any would-be ambushers, and ordered Roselli to bring up the rear, protecting their flanks from the Iranian and terrorist gunmen sure to be close on their heels. He stayed with Doc and the prisoner, pushing aft along the open walkway between *Yuduki Maru*'s superstructure and the side of the ship.

When Brown reached the fantail, Murdock gestured Doc and the hostage on, then doubled back to join Roselli. "Anything?" he asked the lanky SEAL.

"They're on our tail, Lieutenant," Roselli replied. "At least ten of 'em."

"Let's discourage them until the others get away."

"A pleasure." Crouched against the superstructure, Roselli raised his H&K, aiming into the darkness forward. Murdock stood behind, aiming over the other SEAL's head. Shadows moved against the darkness. . . .

"Now!" Murdock rasped, and he squeezed the trigger, loosing a hissing, full-auto burst at the half-glimpsed attackers. A shrill cry wailed from the forward deck. Gunfire barked and flashed in reply, and a bullet howled off steel a foot above Murdock's head.

"Shit, we're gonna get murdered here!" Roselli said.

"Just so they don't murder our guys in the water. Keep firing!"

He spent the last of his magazine, dropped the empty, and slapped in a new one, his last full mag. Thirty rounds . . . and then he'd be down to pistol and knife. He threw the selector switch to semi-auto.

A scream echoed from astern. Looking back over his shoulder, Murdock glimpsed one of the Japanese hostages flying through the air and into the phosphorescent glow of the ship's wake. Apparently, Doc had been forced to convince the guy to abandon ship; a black shadow followed the crewman— Doc in a perfect dive twenty feet into the sea below.

"Skipper!" Brown's voice sounded in his earphone. "We're in!"

"Our side's wet too," MacKenzie added. "You guys want to stay aboard and play with your new friends by yourselves?"

"Cast off!" Murdock replied. "Razor and me're right behind you!"

He snapped off several quick shots against targets felt more than seen. Murdock could almost feel the irresistible tug of the sea. From the beginning, SEAL training emphasizes that the sea is the SEAL's home, his advantage, his place of refuge, the place to go where the enemy cannot follow. "Okay, Razor," he called. "Over the side!"

"Right, Skipper! I'm—shit!" The deck lurched beneath their feet before Razor could finish the reply, and a dull, two-part ba-*BOOM* thundered in the night astern of the *Yuduki Maru*. Turning and staring aft, Murdock could just make out something like a vast wall of white spray, a geyser made dimly luminous by the faint luminosity of the sea itself, rising against the night.

"What in Jesus' name was that?" Roselli asked, his voice betraying his awe.

"Offhand," Murdock said, "I'd say it's that Iranian Kilo."

A second explosion thundered out of the darkness, accompanying a second towering geyser.

"That'll hold our playmates' attention for a bit," Murdock said. "Let's go!"

Together, they took three swift, running steps across the deck, catapulted over the railing, and dove head-first into the sea.

18

Monday, 23 May

1345 hours (Zulu −5)
NAVSPECWARGRU-Two Briefing Room
Little Creek, Virginia

"Once the order was given to abort Sun Hammer," Captain Coburn said, addressing the other officers in the room from the podium at the head of the table, "our people returned to their boats in the water and cut loose from the freighter. Lieutenant Murdock reported some shots fired from the ship's deck, but that the hostiles probably couldn't see much, if anything, on the dark water. Both CRRCs drew away from the *Yuduki Maru*, lowered a sonar transponder into the water, and awaited pickup by the attack sub *Santa Fe*."

Captain Paul Mason shifted uncomfortably against the hard wooden seat of his chair. His back was hurting badly already, and the session had just begun.

Most of the senior officers in the NAVSPECWARGRU-Two community were present for the briefing, along with Brian Hadley—the CIA spook from the National Security Council—and Kerrigan and his MIDEASTFOR staff. Kerrigan, Mason thought, would be sure to take the opportunity to scold the SEAL command for its failure yesterday, but it was clear that the SEALs were going to have a further part to play in this drama.

Otherwise, Kerrigan would never have bothered calling

them all together again to keep them up to speed on events in the Indian Ocean.

"At approximately the same time," Coburn continued, "at 2335 hours, the Iranian attack sub *Islamic Revolution* was destroyed by two wire-guided torpedoes launched some four minutes earlier by the U.S.S. *Newport News*. Our attack subs in the area had detected the *Islamic Revolution* closing on the *Yuduki Maru*. It is possible that the Iranians detected our operation, possibly by picking up the noises made by our SEALs while they were in the water." Coburn glanced up from his podium notes at Admiral Kerrigan. "The decision to sink the *Islamic Revolution* was made when the *Newport News* picked up the sounds of her outer torpedo doors opening, presumably in preparation for an attack against the *Yuduki Maru*. The attack was authorized by Vice Admiral Winston, CO-MIDEASTFOR, in Naples, after consultation with the National Security Council and the Joint Chiefs.

"As for SEAL Seven, the *Hormuz* Assault Team remained aboard the Iranian oiler until relieved by U.S. Marines flown in by helicopter off the U.S.S. *Nassau*. They returned by helo to the *Nassau*, where they are now. The *Yuduki Maru* Assault Team transferred to a Navy helicopter from the deck of the *Santa Fe* early this morning and were flown to the *Nassau*. With them were those two Japanese crewmen, who were flown to the *Nassau*, where they could be immediately debriefed by our intelligence people.

"So our current force disposition has all of our SEALs back aboard the *Nassau*, with II MEF. Their current position is some ninety miles off Ras Asir—that's the northeastern tip of Somalia, the Horn of Africa. The *Hormuz* and her crew are under Marine control and are heading north toward Socotra at nine knots. The *Yuduki Maru*, of course, remains in Iranian hands." He glanced at the faces of the men around the room, then nodded to Admiral Kerrigan. "Admiral?"

Kerrigan smiled as he took his place at the briefing room podium. He looked, Mason thought, like the proverbial cat that had eaten the proverbial canary, fat, sleek, and contemptuously pleased with himself. SEAL Seven's failure yesterday had let him score big in his campaign against Navy Special Warfare.

"Gentlemen," the Norfolk staff CO for MIDEASTFOR said. "The President has informed us through the National Security Council and the Joint Chiefs that the United States will act immediately and unilaterally to resolve the current crisis in the Indian Ocean. He has directed General Vonnegut of II MEF to prepare a plan for a Marine amphibious operation in order to seize the *Yuduki Maru* and restore her cargo to Japan before, ah, hostile radical forces can off-load it. This operation, code-named Deadly Weapon, will utilize the full assets of II MEF, which, as Captain Coburn has just told us, is currently positioned off the Horn of Africa.

"The failure of the Navy SEAL Team deployed to seize the *Yuduki Maru* demonstrates, I think, the necessity of relying on conventional military forces in situations bearing such serious international consequences as the hijacking of two-ton cargoes of plutonium. . . ."

Right, Mason thought, a little bitterly. *And it was the SEALs who bought you the time to mount your amphibious operation. The guess now is that the* Yuduki Maru *won't reach port in Iran before next Saturday.*

"As of zero-nine-hundred hours our time this morning," MIDEASTFOR's liaison continued, "*Yuduki Maru* was maintaining her original course at a reduced speed of about ten knots. She crossed the equator last night and is now eleven thousand kilometers due east of Mogadishu. Her destination still appears to be the Gulf.

"Iran has not yet made any public announcement about any of this. She has not admitted to the loss of one of her submarines, nor has she made any statement yet about the capture of the *Hormuz.* One notion we are still investigating is the possibility that the *Yuduki Maru* hijacking was carried out by an as yet unnamed dissident group within the Iranian military.

"One further disturbing development has been detected by our satellites. Five hours ago, well before dawn in the Persian Gulf, a large flotilla left Bandar Abbas, heading south. This flotilla consists of one guided-missile destroyer, the *Damavand,* two frigates, *Alborz* and *Sahand,* and four Combattante II-class patrol boats. Since this represents a considerable fraction of Iran's total naval force, we can only assume that Tehran is taking current events in the Indian Ocean very seriously indeed. What we do not yet know is whether this flotilla has been deployed to support the *Yuduki Maru,* or to combat the dissident forces that have hijacked her. From our perspective, it doesn't really matter which. It is the NSC's consensus that neither Iran nor an Iranian splinter group can be permitted access to *Yuduki Maru*'s cargo.

"In any case, the crewmen brought back by the SEALs may be able to shed new light on the situation. At this point in the proceedings, I'd like to turn the podium over to Mr. Hadley, who has some additional intelligence for us. Mr. Hadley?"

The CIA man took Kerrigan's place at the podium. "Thank you, Admiral. I have little to add at this point, except for an interesting development that was telexed back to Langley from intelligence officers aboard the U.S.S. *Nassau.*

"It turns out that one of the Japanese crewmen retrieved by Lieutenant Murdock's people is, in fact, one of the original terrorists who seized the *Yuduki Maru.*"

A stir ran through the listeners in the room. This was new, and unexpected.

"The man Murdock rescued from the freighter's bridge is who he claims to be, Jiro Kurosawa, a merchant marine employee of the company running the *Yuduki Maru.*

"The other man, however, who was intercepted near the freighter's engine room by, um, Chief MacKenzie, has been positively identified by Kurosawa as one of the new merchant seamen who produced concealed weapons last Wednesday and seized the ship.

"While the prisoner has not yet talked, his fingerprints were faxed to Langley, where they were matched with those of Shigeru Ota, a low-ranking member, a soldier really, of the Japanese Ohtori."

"Ohtori?" Kerrigan asked, interrupting. "What the hell's that?"

"A new and radical offshoot of the old Japanese Red Army. 'Ohtori' corresponds roughly to the West's 'phoenix.'"

"The fabulous bird reborn from its own ashes," Mason said.

He spoke softly, more to himself than to anyone else in the room, but Hadley heard him and nodded. "Exactly. The JRA was one of the more extremist terrorist groups of the seventies. They were behind a number of terrorist incidents but are probably best remembered for the Lod Airport Massacre in Israel in 1972, where they killed twenty-six people. In the early eighties their leader renounced violence as a political weapon, but they reportedly are still based in the Middle East. Ohtori may be a pro-violence splinter group with their own agenda."

"One working with the Iranians?" Admiral Bainbridge asked.

"Either with the Iranians, or with an Iranian faction," Hadley replied. "The JRA has reportedly been based in the Middle East ever since the early seventies, with training camps in Libya and Syria. Though they've been more closely associated with the PFLP and other Palestinian groups, it is possible that they've taken up the cause of the international Shi'ite revolution sponsored by Iran." Hadley ran one hand through his untidy fringe of white hair. "Whatever their goals, we can be certain that they are inimical to Western interests. They are anti-Israel, anti-American, and in favor of overthrowing the established order by armed revolution. It could be that they've decided to provide some additional arms to the revolution in the guise of the two tons of plutonium on that ship."

"What about the Greenpeace schooner," Admiral Bainbridge asked him. "What's her name? *Beluga.*"

"We've not been devoting satellite time to them, of course," Hadley told him. "But our AWACS radar surveillance pinpoints them still on *Yuduki Maru*'s tail, about twenty to thirty miles astern."

"Someone should warn them off," Captain Coburn pointed out. "I'd hate to see more civilians mixed up in this."

"Actually, they've been quite useful so far," Hadley said. "They called in the original report after *Shikishima* was sunk, and they've been filing position reports daily ever since."

"Sure, but we have satellites to tell us where the freighter is. And these people are going to draw a lot of unwanted publicity onto our operation."

"Actually," Hadley said, "while there was some legitimate concern over media publicity during Operation Sun Hammer, the Security Council has decided that *Beluga*'s presence in the area can become an asset."

"Christ," Mason said. "How?"

"First off," Hadley replied, "the *negative* publicity if we move in and order *Beluga* out of there could generate adverse world opinion. *Beluga* is registered to Greenpeace, but her owner of record is a German millionaire named Rudi Kohler. He's one of the top eight or ten people in the Green Party movement, a prominent antinuclear activist . . . and he's a big name in the European news media. Owns half a dozen major papers and news magazines in Germany, France, and Italy. We barge in and order *him* out of there, and I guarantee that we're going to be accused of censorship, police-state tactics, and probably wife-beating as well.

"On the other hand, if Kohler is present when the U.S. Marines seize the *Yuduki Maru* and prevent an eco-disaster, our role in this affair will be seen in a positive light."

"And what happens," Admiral Bainbridge said slowly, "if something goes wrong in front of these people? If the terrorists blow up the freighter, for example, and end up contaminating half of the East African coast?"

Hadley gave him a humorless smile. "In that event, Admiral, I'm afraid all of the public relations in the world won't help. And we'll have more to worry about than Rudi Kohler's newspaper syndicate.

"That's all that I have at the moment, if there are no further questions. I will, of course, pass on further developments as they become available." He stepped back from the podium. "Admiral Kerrigan?"

"Thank you, Brian." Kerrigan again changed places with the Agency man. "Okay, gentlemen. I'm sure you're all eager to know just what part the Navy Special Warfare community is going to play in Operation Deadly Weapon."

Here it comes, Mason thought. He had the distinct feeling that Kerrigan was setting up the SEALs as part of his own power play. The way he'd phrased it, "is going to play," suggested that NAVSPECWAR was now, at last, right where he wanted it.

"Since SEAL Seven's Third Platoon is already aboard the *Nassau,* they will be temporarily assigned to II MEF, under the command of General Vonnegut. They'll be pretty busy for the next few days as they undergo their mission debriefs. I will pass the word to Admiral Winston and General Vonnegut that they will be available for Deadly Weapon, if the site commanders deem their participation advisable. Yes, Admiral?"

"Ah, Admiral Kerrigan," Bainbridge said. "Wouldn't it be advisable to deploy additional Special Warfare groups to the region? Captain Coburn could have the rest of SEAL Seven in place by—"

"No, Admiral, it would not," Kerrigan said. "The Marines have their own special recon units, of course, and I very much doubt that your people could add much to the overall force picture. My staff will advise you of further developments. That is all."

With a gesture of his head, he gathered in his retinue of aides and staffers and vanished from the room. For several moments, a low buzz of conversation rumbled among the SEAL personnel who remained.

Kerrigan, it was clear, had just scored the victory over the Special Warfare community that he'd been searching for for years; SEAL Seven's failure aboard the *Yuduki Maru* had given him the leverage he needed to all but exclude the SEALs from Deadly Weapon.

Mason thought about the hearings on the U.S. Navy SEALs still going on up in Washington and wondered how much weight Kerrigan's faction now carried on Capitol Hill.

The entire future of the SEALs might have just been settled once and for all, and settled with all of the finality of a door slamming shut.

2310 hours (Zulu +3)
U.S.S. *Nassau*
Off Ras Asir, Somalia

"Hey, Skipper?"

"Hello, Mac. Whatcha got?"

Murdock was standing on *Nassau*'s port-side elevator, which had been lowered to the hangar deck position. At his back, through the cavernous maw opened in *Nassau*'s sheer, vertical side, lights glared from the overhead over a tangle of helicopters and AV-8 Harrier jumpjets. The aircraft were packed so closely that their order could have made sense only to the ship's "Mangler," the officer in charge of moving aircraft about the interior of the huge amphibious assault ship and up the elevators to the flight deck above. The sense of chaos was heightened by the men serving the machines, and by the dozens of low-slung "mules," vehicles that served as shipboard jeeps and tow trucks, skittering among the shadows.

It was more peaceful out here, Murdock thought, leaning against the elevator platform's safety railings beyond the spill of light from the glaring cavern of *Nassau*'s interior. Twenty feet above the dimly seen froth of the LHA's wake, he could hear the hiss of the water against the assault ship's hull, the powerful throb of her screws astern.

"I don't mean to disturb you, Lieutenant," MacKenzie said. He sounded hesitant.

"No problem, Chief. Come on out and enjoy the view."

The view was spectacular, and one Murdock never tired of. Though the ship itself cut off half of the sky, the other half, visible to port, was a glory of stars undimmed by city smog or street lights. Aft, half a mile astern in *Nassau*'s wake, the running lights of LPD 4, the U.S.S. *Austin*, added red, green, and white exclamation marks to the Milky Way's glowing message.

"Thanks, Lieutenant," MacKenzie said, walking up and delivering a salute that Murdock returned. He was wearing a chief's khaki uniform and flat black-billed cap with a CPO's anchor-and-USN insignia, both acquired at the ship's store just that afternoon. "I got the guys bedded down. Weapons stripped and cleaned, gear stowed. The ship's store was able to provide dungarees or khakis for everyone."

"That's good." Murdock plucked at his own new khakis, distinguished by the railroad ties on the collar, and by the officer's eagle, shield, and crossed-anchor insignia on the cap. "I was beginning to think we were going to be running around in our wet suits for the rest of the cruise."

Mac looked off into the darkness astern. "Hey, maybe you can tell me. Scuttlebutt says one of those slants we scooped up was a tango. Know anything about that?"

"Sorry, Chief. They haven't told me a damned thing."

It was true. Murdock had heard the same stories, spreading now among the enlisted men and junior officers aboard the *Nassau,* but no one had been able to confirm them, and when he'd asked the intelligence officers they'd simply smiled and politely told him that their investigations were continuing, and that he would be informed if there was anything about the rescued men he should know.

"I get the impression we've been sent to Coventry, sir."

"It's possible, Chief. I wouldn't worry about it, though. You and the men all did everything that was expected of you, and more." He grinned, though he didn't know whether MacKenzie could see his expression in the poor light. "If anyone gets the axe for the Sun Hammer screwup, it'll be me."

"Screwup, sir?"

"Hell, yeah, screwup. We didn't get the freighter, did we?"

"We locked up the Jap computer and we fucked up their starboard propeller shaft. That counts for something, sir, don't it? And we brought back those two slants. Even if neither one's a tango, that's bound to give G-2 some pretty solid intel on what's happening on that ship."

"Maybe. But we failed to carry out our orders, Chief. That's something CO-NAVSPECWARGRU-Two and CO-MIDEAST-FOR don't like to hear. Especially with so much riding on it."

He'd spent most of the past twenty minutes watching the stars and the ship's wake and wondering how this was all going to shake out. His father, conceivably, could use the episode as additional ammunition to force him out of the SEALs, if only because a congressman's son couldn't be permitted to embarrass his father; hell, Captain Coburn might be under pressure from half a dozen different directions right now, all urging him to dump Blake Murdock. Unless G-2 had more questions for him and the team tomorrow, he expected they'd all be heading back to CONUS by sometime tomorrow afternoon. From what he'd heard from the Marine officers aboard the *Nassau*, II MEF would be handling things from here on out.

"Well, if you ask me, Lieutenant," MacKenzie said, "you did a hell of a job out there. The guys think so too, all of 'em. I just thought you should know that." He saluted again, turned on his heel, and strode back onto *Nassau*'s hangar deck, leaving a stunned Murdock saluting empty air.

MacKenzie's respect, and the respect of the other SEALs of the platoon, meant more to him right now than an official commendation and "well done" from Admiral Bainbridge himself.

It was time, he decided, to stop thinking about his own future and make sure his men knew his feelings about them.

Turning away from the night, he followed MacKenzie back into *Nassau*'s brightly lit belly.

19

Wednesday, 25 May

1610 hours (Zulu +3)
Motor yacht *Beluga*
Indian Ocean, 380 miles southeast of
  Socotra

They'd crossed the equator in the wee hours of the morning on Tuesday, some thirty-six hours earlier. As they kept motoring north, sails furled, Jean had continued to hammer at Paul about what was happening, but neither Paul nor their hosts seemed to have any idea about what was really going on.

"It must be terrorists," Karl had said time after time. "It *must* be terrorists." But beyond the mute and tragic testimony of those bodies adrift in the oil slick a week before, there'd been no announcement, no official word of any kind except for continuing stories over the news networks about *Yuduki Maru*'s mysterious change of course. Other news bulletins, from Madagascar and the Seychelles, had reassured *Beluga*'s crew that it was indeed the plutonium ship they were still tracking on their radar, but the only solid reporting had been what they themselves had called in.

And Jean knew just how thin *that* information really was.

For several days now, Paul, Rudi, and Karl had been arguing among themselves about whether or not to take *Beluga* in close to the Japanese freighter in order to give her a visual inspection and, possibly, hail her crew. Paul and Karl were afraid that if the ship had been hijacked, they would be putting *Beluga* and all aboard at risk. One burst of machine-gun fire, and the yacht would be transformed into a sinking wreck, with everyone aboard her dead. Rudi continued to argue that terrorists wanted nothing more than a forum where they could air their political grievances . . . and who better to provide such a forum than Rudi Kohler? Although Rudi was *Beluga*'s master, however, he'd held back from simply deciding to take them in. Jean thought that, despite his reporter's zeal, he too was frightened of what they'd stumbled into.

The women, for the most part, kept out of it, though they speculated among themselves endlessly. The sunbathing sessions continued, though for short periods only and never in the middle of the day. In late May, the sun this close to the equator could be ferocious.

Terrorists. Jean wanted nothing to do with terrorists. She was still certain that she'd heard gunfire on Monday night, and the memory haunted her. Rudi insisted that she couldn't possibly have heard anything across thirty miles of open ocean. She'd heard *something*, though, just before midnight, a low, dull, double boom out of the north that might have been thunder . . . except that the sky had been perfectly clear.

The final decision had been to get closer, but not *too* close. According to the latest news reports—overflights by aircraft bearing the world's top news personalities were now daily, almost constant events—*Yuduki Maru* had suffered some kind of damage to her engines and was limping along now at about ten knots. During the night, *Beluga* had easily closed some of the distance between the two vessels, and the *Yuduki Maru* was now periodically visible as a dark speck on the northern horizon. According to Viktor, they were less than ten miles away.

"Jean!" Helga waved to her from the beach blanket she was sharing with Gertrude on *Beluga*'s sun deck. "Jean, come join us!"

Waving back, she climbed the short ladder to the sun deck. She was wearing bikini briefs and nothing else; somehow, during these past few days, she'd lost the shyness that had tormented her through the first couple of weeks of the cruise.

Was it the vague sense of danger focused on the plutonium ship
that had changed her? Or had the uncertainty simply let her
grow closer to the others, until they were more like family than
acquaintances? Dropping cross-legged onto the towel, she
accepted a bottle of sun block from Gertrude and began
lathering it on.

"So what's the word?" Helga wanted to know. "Anything?"

Jean had just come from *Beluga*'s tiny radio shack, their sole
link to the outside world via the sat-comm antenna atop the
mainmast.

"CNN just broke a story that American commandos tried to
board the plutonium ship the other day and failed," Jean
replied. "The Pentagon is denying it."

"What about . . . *them?*" Gertrude asked, jerking a thumb
forward toward the distant freighter. By now, everyone aboard
Beluga was assuming that the *Yuduki Maru* had been hijacked
by terrorists, but no one was quite willing to speak of that
possibility openly. The faceless hijackers, whoever they were,
remained *"them"* or *"those people."*

"Nothing," Jean said. "Though there was one interesting
related tidbit. It seems Iran is accusing the United States of
hijacking one of its navy ships. An oiler named *Hormuz.*"

"Ach," Helga said, disgusted. "Who is terrorizing who?"

"The White House and the Pentagon have both denied the
incident."

"Of course." Gertrude made a face. *"Militarists!"* She gave
the word, which meant the same in German as in English, the
full, throaty force of its German pronunciation, turning it into
a swear word. "When is your country going to learn that the
Cold War is over, that militarism is a thing of the past?"

Jean nodded toward the distant freighter. "Maybe when
those people learn it doesn't pay to use terror as a political
weapon."

"But what could be the point of capturing an Iranian ship?"
Helga wondered. "Did they get the wrong target, perhaps?"

Jean shook her head. "I wish I knew. None of it makes much
sense. . . ." She was staring thoughtfully toward the north,

where something was moving against the ultramarine surface of the sea.

"Jean?" Helga asked. "What is it?"

It was a ship . . . no . . . it was too small and much too fast to be a ship. It was bow-on, driving the white mustache of a sweeping wake before it as it slap-slapped across the waves toward the *Beluga* at high speed. In moments, however, it grew from a toy to a sleek, shark-lean craft at least twenty feet longer than the *Beluga,* with the huge, white sphere of a radar housing perched atop its deckhouse, and with a single turret on the foredeck sporting a long and wicked-looking cannon. A flag with three horizontal bars, green, white, and red from top to bottom, fluttered at the masthead—the flag of revolutionary Iran.

The women stared at the patrol boat, stunned by the suddenness of its appearance. The men remained motionless as well, all but Viktor, who dashed for the companionway going down to *Beluga*'s lower decks. By the time he reappeared, moments later, a bolt-action rifle in his hands, the Iranian craft had circled about and was drawing close to *Beluga*'s starboard side.

Soldiers, heavily armed and wearing khaki uniforms, lined the patrol boat's rail. When Viktor stepped onto the afterdeck with the rifle, a sharp burst of machine gun fire rattled from the craft's bridge, a warning volley that knocked splinters from *Beluga*'s mainmast and boom.

"Hör auf damit!" an amplified voice barked from the Iranian craft. "Drop the weapon!"

Reluctantly, Viktor let the rifle clatter to the afterdeck. Iranian soldiers were already vaulting the rail, boarding the *Beluga* both aft and forward in a rush of shouting, gun-waving men.

Jean screamed as a soldier grabbed her shoulder and shoved her roughly toward the well deck aft. "Get your hands off me!"

She was answered with a stinging slap across her back. *"Akab behraveed!"* She didn't understand, but the meaning was clear. She allowed herself to be dragged along.

The yacht's entire crew was herded aft. Resistance, even

verbal protest, was met with savage blows from fists or rifle butts. Helga struggled in the grip of two soldiers, one of whom was clutching at her naked breasts, and Karl lurched toward his wife and her attackers, fists clenched. *"Bastard! Nicht doch!"*

A single gunshot barked, propelling Karl forward. Blood splattered the white paint of *Beluga*'s deckhouse as he crumpled to the deck.

"Karl! *Nein!*" Helga tried to reach her husband, but her captors forced her into line with the others. Karl scrabbled weakly on the deck for a few more moments, clutching the wound in his chest, then lay still.

Jean and the other civilians all were in shock, uncomprehending, automatons shoved this way and that by the soldiers. Several of the boarders gathered around the women, leering at them and making jokes among themselves. Viktor tried to fight back when someone shoved him, and was clubbed to the deck with a blow from a rifle butt. The man who'd shot Karl was tall and muscular, sporting a thick black mustache that hid his mouth. He gestured at all of them with the automatic handgun in his fist.

"Kneel! All of you!" he snapped in English. "Here, in row! Hands on heads!"

Terrified, the prisoners obeyed as the soldiers prodded them into line on the deck. Jean found herself kneeling between a weeping, desperate Helga and one of *Beluga*'s crewmen as the black-mustached man, obviously the Iranians' leader, strode down the line, inspecting each of them in turn. With him, startlingly, was a Japanese man wearing olive-drab shorts and a short-sleeved floral-print shirt, and carrying an assault rifle as though he knew how to use it.

A Japanese . . . one of the plutonium freighter's crew? What in God's name was going on here?

The Iranian commander stopped in front of Gertrude. *"Amrikan?"* he asked.

"Nein," she said. *"Ich bin ein Deutscher."* She stopped, licked her lips, then tried again in English. "I am . . . German. My passport is in—"

The dark man cut her off with a sharp gesture, then

continued down the line. He stopped again at Helga, who was still crying uncontrollably, but said nothing. Instead, he looked her up and down, then turned and stared at Jean. She began trembling violently as she felt his eyes on her, and her legs grew so weak she could hardly hold her position. When he smiled at her, there was no humor in his eyes. "You," he said, moving in front of her. "You are certainly American."

How does he know? she wondered. Jerkily, she nodded.

Reaching out, he lightly brushed her bare, lotion-slick left breast with the backs of his fingers. She jerked back from the repulsive touch and nearly fell. Several of the watching soldiers chuckled unpleasantly.

"You Western woman really should learn modesty," the commander said thoughtfully. His English was excellent, though it carried a heavy accent. "By exposing your bodies in this shameful manner, you disgrace yourselves and your male relatives. You also present a considerable temptation for my men, who tend to regard such displays of female flesh as an indication of your moral character. Or lack of it."

The Japanese civilian whispered something to the commander, who nodded. Turning suddenly, the Iranian barked an order in Farsi. The soldiers advanced then, laughing, grabbing the women from the line, herding them forward toward the yacht's cabins. Rough hands groped and fondled Jean as she was propelled down the steps, grabbing at her breasts, buttocks, and thighs, tugging at the knots in the strings of her bikini bottom, then ripping the scrap of cloth away entirely. Gertrude screamed as a laughing Iranian soldier pranced about the galley, waving her briefs as trophy. Helga's bikini bottom had no ties, and they pinned her to the deck while one of them peeled the bottom off her thrashing legs.

Oh, Christ, they're going to rape us! she thought, but then the three naked women were shoved into a cabin and the door was slammed and locked behind them. The soldiers had already been here, rifling dresser drawers and smashing bottles of whiskey and gin discovered in the room's tiny bar.

Outside, she heard them shouting in Farsi and laughing as they went through the *Beluga,* smashing open every locked door in a joyful quest for loot. The Iranian officer was haranguing the male members of the crew, but she couldn't catch the words. Oh, God, what was he saying? What was he going to do to Paul?

Gertrude lay on the deck, trembling, trying to cover herself with her arms as she sank into shock. Helga, after a long moment, began stumbling about the cramped room, no longer crying but with a glazed expression fixed on her face as she began picking up torn and discarded articles of clothing and bits of broken glass. The room, Jean realized, had been the one occupied by Helga and her husband. "Karl," she mumbled half-aloud, "Karl doesn't like the mess. . . ."

Poor Karl . . .

Numb with terror, battling the shock that threatened to engulf her, Jean Brandeis sat on the bunk, her eyes fixed on the locked door. She had no illusions that any of them would be released, not after an incident that was nothing less than piracy on the high seas. There would be no phone call to the American embassy, no news report to the West save, possibly, a curt announcement to the effect that *Beluga* and her crew had been lost at sea.

She wondered how much longer they would be permitted to live, and what humiliation they would be forced to endure in whatever time was left.

1635 hours (Zulu +3)
Motor yacht *Beluga*
Indian Ocean, 380 miles southeast of
Socotra

Tetsuo Kurebayashi listened impassively as Pasdaran Colonel Ruholla Aghasi continued shouting at the men kneeling before him on the deck. Kurebayashi spoke English—that language was how he communicated with the Iranians who spoke no Nihongo—but the colonel's words were too rapid for him to follow more than a word or two, and Aghasi kept alternating between English and German, of which Kurebayashi spoke not a word.

Unlike Sayyed Hamid, however, that fat pig of a Pasdaran

colonel in charge of the Iranians aboard the *Yuduki Maru*, Aghasi was clearly a man of keen intelligence, who knew what he was doing and how best to achieve results. Though he couldn't understand the speech, he knew what Aghasi was saying, because Kurebayashi had come up with the idea and convinced the Iranian leader to try it just hours ago. Aghasi was the commander of a contingent of troops just arrived with the Iranian naval squadron; Kurebayashi had approached him, rather than the unimaginative Hamid, with his idea of seizing the Greenpeace schooner that had been dogging *Yuduki Maru*'s wake for the past three weeks.

The speech was having the desired effect. Aghasi, the Ohtori leader noted, was playing the game well, waving the confiscated scraps of the women's bathing suits in front of the male prisoners with evident relish, gesturing frequently toward the cabin where the women had been taken, and at those of his men who were lounging about the well deck now with weapons very much in evidence. Through threats and bullying, the colonel had already gotten two of the prisoners to admit that two of the women were their wives; the dead man, apparently, had been husband to the third. A pity that he had been the one chosen by Heaven to serve as an example to the others . . .

Still, those two would be enough.

Kurebayashi was a longtime student of American tactics. The Yankees had already tried a covert operation, slipping a small squad of commandos aboard the *Yuduki Maru* in an attempt to surprise her captors. That attempt had failed . . . though eighteen of the forty Iranian troops aboard had been killed or seriously wounded, and poor Shigeru Ota, one of Kurebayashi's Ohtori, had vanished in the fight. Their next move, he was certain, would be either another attempt to negotiate or an overwhelming show of force. Iranian sources had already reported the gathering of a sizable American naval task force south of the Arabian peninsula, between the *Yuduki Maru* and her destination; his guess was that they would try a frontal assault next, possibly behind the screen of a professional negotiator.

The Iranians, with their entire pathetic little navy, could not possibly hope to match the Americans ship for ship and gun for gun. The little *Beluga* and her activist passengers were the best weapon they could have to meet the Yankees' challenge, to force them to back down. All that was needed was some cooperation from the prisoners.

That part would be easy. Kurebayashi had studied in America, two years at UCLA. He knew Western men, and he knew something of their illogical ways of thinking, especially about women and sex. Kohler and Brandeis, he was sure, would do anything, *anything* to keep their wives from being gang-raped and tortured one by one before their eyes. Since it was Kohler's help they needed most, they would start with the dead German's wife, then move on to the American, saving Kohler's wife for last. The only real problem was that the process would take time, and Kurebayashi very much doubted that they had more than a few hours before the Americans struck.

But then, it was possible that the threat alone would be enough. He studied the prisoners through narrowed eyes. Yes . . . Aghasi's little speech was definitely having the desired effect. The American, Brandeis, was pale and sweating, on the verge of passing out right there on the deck. Kohler's eyes were squeezed shut, and he was moaning something to himself over and over in German. These men were already broken, Kurebayashi thought, clay to be molded in any way their captors saw fit.

Aghasi barked a question at the American. Slowly, a little jerkily, the man nodded, his hands still clasped on top of his head. Excellent. They had one ally, even if he was an unwilling one. Then Kohler agreed too, nodding his head enthusiastically as tears rolled down his cheeks.

Success . . .

20

Thursday, 26 May

1945 hours (Zulu +3)
Indian Ocean, seventy miles east of Socotra

It was evening, but the sun was still well above the western horizon when the first flight of four Marine SuperCobra gunships clattered in toward the *Yuduki Maru.* They came in low, skimming the waves, approaching out of the west so that the enemy's gunners—and their heat-seeking antiair weapons, if they had any—would be blinded by the sun. Half a mile behind the gunships, three big CH-53 Super Stallions of the 2nd Marine Aircraft Wing came in at higher altitude, each carrying a full load of fifty-five Marine combat troops.

Captain Ron Dilmore was strapped into the rear seat of Pickax One-three, one of the SuperCobras sliding into attack position west of the Iranian squadron. His gunner/copilot, in the front seat, was a skinny, blond kid from Kansas, Lieutenant Charles Mobely.

"So what's it gonna be," Mobely was saying over the ICS, the Cobra's intercom system. "Peace or war?"

"Aw, the Iranies are chickenshit, Mobe," Dilmore replied. "They'll take one look at us and—"

"Pickax One, Pickax One" sounded over Dilmore's helmet phones. "This is Rolling Prairie. Deploy in attack formation, but hold your fire. Repeat, deploy for attack but do not fire."

Rolling Prairie was the call sign for II MEF's Tactical

Command Team, buried away in the combat center aboard the *Nassau.*

"There they are," Mobely said. "I got the freighter and two . . . no, three warships. Looks like a destroyer has the freighter in tow."

"I see it, Mobe. Pick your targets. I'm gonna buzz the *Maru.*"

The SuperCobra held its approach, now less than fifty feet above the water, its rotor blast raising a wind-lashed fog of spray in its wake. Ahead, the Japanese freighter *Yuduki Maru* was wallowing forward in moderate seas, a long length of heavy towing cable stretched from the fantail of the destroyer to the freighter's bow chocks. Red-white-and-green flags flew from the mastheads of both vessels.

"Hey, Skipper!" Mobely called. "The *Maru*'s flying an Iranie flag!"

"I see it, Mobe." He put the SuperCobra into a gentle turn to port, circling the two vessels at a distance. So far there'd been no fire from either ship, though he could see armed men gathered on their decks. According to Prairie Fire's mission briefing, a team of Navy SEALs had managed to get on board the freighter and damage one of its screws, but had been forced to back off. How many Iranian soldiers were aboard? It looked like hundreds, though he didn't have time for an accurate count. Enough, certainly, to fight off a SEAL squad, and enough to make an airborne descent from helos, if not impossible, at least a very bloody business indeed.

"You getting all this, Mobe?"

"We're rolling, Skipper." The gunner/copilot was using a sophisticated camera mounted in the Cobra's chin turret to record the scene.

Damn. If the Iranians had raised their own flag over the *Yuduki Maru,* this could get real sticky, real fast. With that Iranian flag flying from her truck, the Japanese freighter was now, technically at least, Iranian property, and the American rescue mission could be construed as an invasion. Wryly wondering what the brass hats were going to make of this one, he opened a channel to Rolling Prairie and called in his report.

The other gunships began circling as well, while the troop-carrying Sea Stallions remained at a safe distance. After informing *Nassau* about the flags and tow cable, Dilmore was told to keep orbiting the freighter but to take no threatening action.

No threatening action? Add the SuperCobra's M197, a three-barreled, high-speed rotary cannon protruding from beneath its chin, to the rocket and minigun pods and TOW missiles slung from hardpoints to port and starboard, and you had one definitely threatening aircraft, even when it was squatting motionless on a flight deck. Circling its intended prey like some bristling, monster dragonfly, it was bound to make the people on those ships nervous.

The original plan, code-named Prairie Fire, called for the Marine helicopters to rush straight in, suppress any hostile fire from the freighter, and off-load the troops directly onto *Yuduki Maru*'s forward deck. It was thought that the sudden, demoralizing appearance of the gunships, coupled with the casualties the Iranian forces had already suffered during the SEAL raid earlier in the week, would be enough to force their surrender.

The raid had been almost ready to go the day before when word had been received from the Pentagon that the Iranian warships *Damavand; Sahand,* and *Alborz* had joined the plutonium ship and were now providing close escort, together with a number of small patrol craft. *Damavand,* a World War II-era British destroyer transferred to Iran in the 1970s, now had the *Yuduki Maru* under tow.

Delayed for twenty-four hours while options were reviewed and orders rewritten, Prairie Fire had finally been launched despite the new intelligence, but their mission profile now called for them to approach cautiously, to report everything they saw, to hold fire until specifically ordered otherwise. What had begun as a terrorist incident on the high seas could rapidly escalate into a major military confrontation between Iran and the United States.

"Hey, Skipper?" Mobely called over the ICS. "We've got something screwy coming in on channel four."

"Let's hear it." He flipped the channel select knob on his console.

". . . vessel *Beluga*! D-do not attack!" The voice was ragged with excitement, or more likely, Dilmore thought, with fear. "American forces, please, do not attack. This is Rudi Kohler, of the Greenpeace vessel *Beluga.* Soldiers and sailors of Revolutionary Iran, acting in the interest of world peace, have boarded the freighter *Yuduki Maru,* which was damaged several days ago in a terrorist incident, and have taken her in tow. This is a salvage and rescue operation as described under the international laws of the sea. The . . . the commander of the Iranian forces has asked me, as a representative of the organization Greenpeace International, to act as a neutral observer in this matter, to report what I see and hear to the world.

"American forces, please do not attack. . . ."

"Shit," Lieutenant Dilmore said, switching off. "A salvage operation! Who do they think they're kidding?"

"Pickax One, Pickax One, this is Rolling Prairie" sounded over Dilmore's helmet phones. "Hold fire, repeat, hold fire. This one's going up the chain. Confirm, over."

"Rolling Prairie, Pickax One," Dilmore replied. "Hold fire, roger." He dropped the helo into a shallow bank to starboard.

"What do you think, Skipper?" Mobely asked. "Was that message for real?"

"Hell, it sounded like he was reading from a prepared statement. I think the poor bastard had a gun to his head."

"Yeah. Who's this Kohler guy anyway?"

"I don't—"

"Ninety-nine aircraft, ninety-nine aircraft" sounded over the radio, interrupting.

"Uh-oh," Mobely said. The call sign "ninety-nine aircraft" was military shorthand for all aircraft aloft, and a general order to all of them probably meant an abort. "That was a little too fast for my liking."

"Quiet," Dilmore said. "I want to hear."

"Ninety-nine aircraft, scrub Prairie Fire. Repeat, scrub Prairie Fire and RTB."

RTB—Return to Base. The brass was calling off the attack before a single shot had been fired.

"Aw, *shit!*" Mobely said. "They're letting the bastards get away with fucking murder!"

"Maybe they know something about it we don't," Dilmore said. "Coming right to three-five-oh. Oops. What's that?"

"What's what?"

"Sailboat trailing the Iranians, six, maybe eight miles back."

"Hell, that's probably the Greenpeacers."

"Rog. Let's have a closer look, okay?"

"Fine. *You* explain digressing from the flight plan to the CO when we get back."

"*No problemo.* Hang onto your lunch."

The Marine SuperCobra dropped until its skids were practically skimming the waves, angling south toward the two-masted schooner motoring northward with its sails furled. Several men in civilian clothes stood on the aft deck, one of them at the wheel. As the helicopter circled at a distance, the men waved.

"That's the Greenpeace bunch?" Mobely asked.

"That's them. *Beluga.*"

"They look okay."

"Yeah. They could also have a guy with a machine gun pointed at 'em, hiding in that hatchway in the deck, telling 'em to smile and wave."

"Whatcha want to do?"

"Shit. We can't land. We can't attack a boat full of hostages, if that's what they are. I guess we wave back."

Circling once more, the SuperCobra then peeled off toward the west, following the other helos of Pickax back toward the U.S.S. *Nassau.*

Prairie Fire was, Dilmore thought, a total bust. The Iranians had just pulled a bit of legal chicanery that might let them get their hands on the plutonium, the operation had the blessing of some guy from Greenpeace, and Uncle Sam was going to come out of this with egg on his face . . . again.

Damn. Why couldn't those SEALs have done the job right when they'd had the chance?

1215 hours (Zulu −5 hours)
NAVSPECWARGRU-Two Briefing Room
Little Creek, Virginia

"Is the President aware that it will be a hundred times harder getting at the *Yuduki Maru* once it's in a hostile naval base?" Admiral Bainbridge asked. "It won't be a simple boarding operation at sea anymore. It'll mean a full-scale invasion."

They were gathered once again in the SEAL base briefing room. Captain Phillip Christopher, a staff aide for Admiral Kerrigan, had just brought the Special Warfare Command the news that Prairie Fire had been aborted. After Christopher had said his piece, Brian Hadley had informed them of the decision made by the President and the National Security Council to allow the Iranian squadron to pass the American ships now gathered south of Masirah unmolested.

"I'm sure the President has been advised of that fact by the Joint Chiefs," Hadley replied, but the CIA liaison officer didn't look happy. His once-neat gray suit was rumpled, and looking at the bags under his eyes, Paul Mason doubted that the man had had more than an hour or two of sleep in the past forty-eight. "For the moment, the military community is being asked to narrow its focus, to concentrate on the Greenpeace vessel *Beluga,* rather than on the Japanese freighter."

"Just what does Greenpeace have to say about all of this, Mr. Hadley?" Mason asked.

"They've not released an official statement yet," Hadley replied. "Privately, though, people at their European headquarters in Brussels have been discussing the situation with our ambassador there. They feel that there's a strong possibility that their people are being held hostage, that Kohler was being forced to make those statements against his will. They do not believe the story that Iran freed a hijacked ship any more than we do, and they certainly oppose having that plutonium diverted to Bandar Abbas." Hadley gave a grim smile. "Half of Europe is already panicking over what might happen if the Iranians decide to use the plutonium against their neighbors in the Gulf. They wouldn't have to build a bomb, you know.

Plutonium is the most deadly poison known to man. Dispersing a few *pounds* of the stuff as dust in the air or sea could render vast stretches of the Arabian Gulf coast uninhabitable, poison over half of Saudi Arabia's fresh-water supply, even contaminate the region's oil fields for centuries. Iran won't need to build an atomic bomb to become *the* power in the region. What we haven't been able to determine yet is whether this thing is being orchestrated from Tehran, or whether it's the work of a military cabal, a handful of military officers seeking a power base to overthrow the mullahs.''

"Hell, their four largest warships were protecting the *Yuduki Maru* this morning," Admiral Bainbridge pointed out. "If it's a cabal, it's a damned big one, one including their whole navy."

"We can't rule that possibility out," Hadley admitted.

"Haven't we learned anything from questioning the people aboard *Hormuz*?" Captain Coburn asked.

"Nothing definite," Hadley said. "Frankly, the officers and men aboard the *Hormuz* simply don't know that much. Their orders came from the Iranian Gulf Fleet Headquarters at Bandar Abbas."

"Who issued the orders?" Bainbridge asked.

"An Admiral Seperh Paydarfar," Hadley replied. "The Agency's still digging for information on Paydarfar, but he appears to be a fairly loyal senior fleet naval officer with good political connections in Tehran. No evidence yet that he might be involved in an anti-government plot.

"In any case, we think our best chance for detailed intelligence is going to come from the *Beluga*."

"That's a switch," Coburn said. Several of the other officers in the room laughed.

There was a long history of, if not outright animosity, then at least hostile wariness between Greenpeace International and the U.S. Navy. Greenpeace had publicly attacked the Navy on more than one occasion—for deploying nuclear weapons aboard its ships, for routinely dumping jet fuel at sea during carrier landing operations, even—and this one went back quite a few years—for purportedly training dolphins to plant explosives against the hulls of enemy ships. For its part, the Navy tried to maintain a good public relations profile by remaining aloof, despite what often appeared to be a leftist-organized campaign against the Navy's programs. It never admitted either way, for instance, whether or not nuclear weapons were stored aboard any given ship, and used simple "no comment" statements to avoid verbal engagements with antinuke protestors.

Leftist or not, Greenpeace was clearly now being used by the Iranians for reasons of their own, a situation that could not make the organization very happy. Greenpeace had taken the lead in the international battle against Japan's plutonium shipments, and now it seemed that the organization was actually giving its blessings to the diversion of two tons of stolen plutonium to a nation that was not exactly a trustworthy member of the international arena.

"I imagine the people at Greenpeace aren't exactly happy about this," Hadley said. "They stand to lose a very great deal of prestige and credibility if the Iranians decide to use that plutonium. Even if Tehran just uses the stuff to blackmail its neighbors, it will be remembered that one of Greenpeace's European spokesmen claimed the Iranians were just helping out."

"It's still possible the Iranians are on the level," Captain Christopher pointed out. "The Iranians the SEALs encountered on the freighter last Sunday could have been part of a terrorist faction or a coup, and the Iranian force could have regained control. They might still return the freighter and its cargo to the Japanese."

"Ha!" Bainbridge said curtly. "If that's true, why hasn't there been an official announcement from Tehran? Why haven't we heard from *Yuduki Maru*'s captain? Hell, they could have let the *Maru* go its way and taken the bad guys back to Tehran for a big show trial. No, this feels like Iran might be trying to play both sides in this. They're buying time until they can get their real plan, whatever it is, in place."

"So where does that leave us?" Mason wanted to know.

"It looks," Hadley said, a grin slowly spreading across his face, "as though Captain Coburn's people are going to get another shot."

"All right!" Captain Coburn said delightedly, smacking fist into palm. "The *Yuduki Maru* again?"

Bainbridge scowled. "I thought you said the President was ordering us to let the Iranians take the freighter into port."

"He did," Hadley said. "And we're not going after the plutonium ship. Not yet anyway. At least not until we can clarify the exact political situation. And to do that, we're going to need to take a closer look at the *Beluga.* . . ."

2230 hours (Zulu +3 hours)
Tactical Officer's Briefing Room,
U.S.S. *Nassau*
Indian Ocean, southwest of Masirah

"Wait a minute," Murdock said. "Let me get this straight. They're letting the bastards *pass*?"

Lieutenant Commander Robert Fowler, Intelligence Officer aboard the LHA *Nassau,* fixed Murdock with an icy stare. "Yes, Lieutenant. That is exactly what they're doing. The order was relayed down the chain of command from the President himself."

"Ah!" Roselli said from the other side of the room. "That explains it then."

"Belay that," Murdock snapped. The current U.S. President was not popular with most military personnel, partly because of various unpopular social changes he'd made in the armed forces since his inauguration, but partly too because of his erratic course in charting American foreign policy. Nonetheless, he *was* the Commander-in-Chief, and American military personnel were expected to keep their political convictions to themselves. High-ranking military officers had been broken for careless criticism of the President and his Administration.

More than that, though, the country simply could not afford to have a military that involved itself in politics. That path led to military dictatorship, as had been proven time and time again elsewhere throughout the world.

"Sorry, sir," Roselli said.

"*If* I might be allowed to continue," Fowler went on, "the Iranian squadron is continuing on course toward the Straits of

Hormuz, with the *Yuduki Maru* in tow. We now believe that they will escort the Japanese ship to their naval base at Bandar Abbas. The President has ordered that they be allowed to pass without interference."

"Fuck that," MacKenzie said, the vulgarity shockingly loud in the silence following the intelligence officer's words. Fowler and the SEALs in the compartment all turned and looked at him. "Ah, 'scuse me, sir," the chief added. "But that's just plain damned screwy! Those bastards get into Bandar Abbas, and it's gonna take nothing less than a Marine invasion to winkle them out!"

"That may be," Fowler said coldly. "Do you really want to be the one setting our foreign policy out here, Chief?"

"Uh, no, sir."

"Good. Then I suggest you keep your mouth shut and listen, or you'll find yourself bounced back to the States to sit this one out!"

"Hold on there, Commander," Murdock said suddenly, rising.

Flower looked at Murdock, eyebrows rising. "Huh? What is it now, Lieutenant?"

"Might I have a word with the Commander, sir? In private."

"Lieutenant, this is hardly the time—"

"These are my men, sir. And my responsibility. I respectfully suggest that if you have something to say to any of them involving order or discipline, you say *it through me*."

Fowler locked eyes with Murdock for a beat. "You're out of line, Lieutenant."

"No, sir. I don't think I am. Would you care to discuss the matter in private?"

Fowler stared at him for another moment, then took a deep breath and shook his head. "I really don't have time to discuss this matter, Lieutenant. Time is short and I have other briefings to deliver." He turned his gaze on MacKenzie. "Chief, if I was too harsh a moment ago, forgive me. The past few watches have been long ones."

MacKenzie grinned. "No problem, sir."

"Good. As I was trying to explain, the political situation over here is highly unstable. If we launch an outright attack on the Iranian squadron now, while they're claiming to be on an international rescue mission, well, it won't matter much whether they're hijacking that plutonium or not. The United States will be condemned all over the world . . . for interfering with that rescue, for putting our own prestige ahead of the lives of people in that region, for endangering the coastlines of countries from Saudi Arabia to South Africa if the *Yuduki Maru* is sunk, for acting like an out-of-control gunslinger when negotiation might have resolved the situation peaceably. The list goes on and on. Whatever you might think about his foreign policy statements lately, the President doesn't really have any other choice on this one. The draft for a formal resolution has been placed before the United Nations, but until we know for sure what's happening over there, our hands are pretty well tied."

Murdock raised his hand.

"What is it, Lieutenant?"

"Damn it, sir, we were aboard the plutonium ship. We brought back a freed hostage and a prisoner. What more do we need?"

"Frankly, Lieutenant Murdock, we need a clear picture of what the Iranians are thinking right now. Were the Iranians your people encountered aboard the *Maru* a revolutionary faction allied with Japanese terrorists? Or were they some kind of special action group working with the knowledge and approval of the mullahs in Tehran? We don't know, and until we do, our hands are tied.

"What we really need now, Washington feels, is a close look at what's going on aboard that Greenpeace yacht, the *Beluga*. If Kohler and the others aboard the yacht are telling the truth, then the Iranians have done our job for us, taking the *Yuduki Maru* back from the terrorists who hijacked her."

"With respect, sir," Roselli said, "that's a load of crap."

"That may be, Chief," Fowler said. "Personally, and speaking strictly off the record, I have to agree with you."

The man appeared to have resigned himself to comments from his audience. He was not, Murdock thought, used to

briefing SEALs, as nonconformist and as non-elitist a bunch as
Murdock had ever known.

"However," Fowler continued, "the Joint Chiefs have ordered a new mission, an intelligence-gathering operation this
time. They want you guys to go aboard the *Beluga* and find out
just what's going down. The operation will be code-named
Prairie Watch. If Kohler and the others are not hostages, you
are to ascertain that fact and leave, hopefully without upsetting
the diplomatic apple cart. If, as seems more likely from what
we know now, the Iranians are holding Kohler and his guests
prisoner, you'll proceed with a hostage rescue scenario."

"Yeah!" Magic Brown said. "That's more like it!"

The other men of Third Platoon sounded excited at the
prospect of getting another shot. Murdock wasn't sure that he
liked the sound of this mission, though. "What do we know
about the target, sir?" he asked. "We don't have models or— "

"The *Beluga* was built by Luxuschiff, a luxury yacht
manufacturer headquartered in Hamburg," Fowler said. "Detailed deck plans, including any modifications Kohler may
have had made at the Hamburg boatyards, are being transmitted to us via satellite. You should have them within the hour."

Murdock glanced at his watch. It was nearly 2300 hours.
"And when do you need our plans?"

For the first time that evening, Fowler smiled. "Lieutenant,
I'm afraid I'll need a copy by zero-nine-hundred hours tomorrow. I know that's stretching things tight— "

"I don't mind a little late-night work, Commander," Murdock
said. "But when is Prairie Watch supposed to go down?"

"Tomorrow night," Fowler told him. "Either late Friday
evening or early Saturday morning. We have to know which
way to jump in regard to the *Maru* by Sunday. Judging from
her speed under tow, she'll reach Bandar Abbas sometime
around midday on Sunday. We don't expect to be able to move
against her before she's in port. But we must take action before
the Iranians have a chance to remove her cargo. Your changing
the access code on the *Yuduki Maru*'s computer was a good
move, Lieutenant, but once they have the ship in port, all they

need to do is cut through the deck hatches with a shipyard-sized cutting torch. I'd guess we're looking at Sunday evening, at the latest."

"Then we'd better get busy," Murdock said. "Sir. We don't have a hell of a lot of time."

21

Friday, 27 May

2315 hours (Zulu +3)
Indian Ocean, 220 miles southeast of
Masirah

Beneath a black and overcast sky, the Marine CH-46E Sea
Knight skimmed across a black sea, its twin fore- and aft-rotors
pounding against the night. The transport helicopter was
running without lights, deliberately flying low to avoid enemy
search radar. Somewhere, a few miles to the south, the Iranian
squadron, the hijacked Japanese freighter, and the civilian
pleasure craft were all making their slow way north at a speed
of about eight knots.

Aboard the Sea Knight, the men of SEAL Seven's Third
Platoon sat in armored seats on the red-lit cargo deck, giving
their equipment and each other a thorough final inspection. Of
all the means of insertion into enemy territory, Murdock liked
helocasting the least. At least with other types of airborne
approaches, you got to use a parachute. . . .

"Three minutes!" the plane's crew chief yelled, holding up
three fingers for emphasis. The Sea Knight's rotors made so
much noise it was hard to talk and be understood, and Murdock
found it difficult to believe the enemy hadn't heard them from
the moment they'd lifted off from the deck of the *Nassau*. Of
course, helicopters from the Marine Expeditionary Force had
been probing and circling the Iranian force's perimeter all day,
partly to push them into some suitably revealing response, but

230

mostly to accustom them to the sound of nearby American helicopters.

Murdock nodded at the crew chief, then looked at each of the SEALs with him in turn. There were twelve men in all, with two men missing from the group, one from each squad. Magic and Nickle had been detached to serve as overwatch snipers and were following the big CH-46 in a smaller UH-1 helo trailing somewhere astern of the Sea Knight.

All of the men in the CH-46 were outfitted for a combat insertion, with black Nomex flight suits and hoods, fins, masks and UBA rebreathers, and with assault vests carrying full assault loadouts. Their faces, the only exposed skin on their bodies, had been heavily smeared with black paint. Their spirits, Murdock noted, were high; they were all keyed up, but with the grinning, joking intensity of men prepped for a mission and eager to see it through. Mac had seen to it that all of the men had had a good night's sleep. Murdock, DeWitt, and Mac, though, were all running a little shy on rack time. They'd been up most of the night before drawing up the op plans, orders, and loadout checklists for this mission. Both of them had caught a few hours that morning, however, and right now the adrenaline in his system had Murdock alert and wide awake.

The entire platoon had spent much of that afternoon studying the deckplans of the *Beluga,* until they knew every companionway and cupboard, every compartment and storage locker aboard, until they could have run through the yacht blindfolded if necessary. Of even more critical importance, they'd spent hours memorizing the faces of everyone known to be aboard: of the yacht's owner, Rudi Kohler, and his wife; of the Schmidts and the American couple, Jean and Paul Brandeis; and of the four Germans hired by Kohler as *Beluga*'s crew. The goal was to be able to recognize instantly any of these people, under any circumstances, from any angle, under any lighting.

They were ready.

Murdock locked eyes with MacKenzie across the Sea Knight's deck. The master chief grinned back in reply, his teeth impossibly white against his paint-blackened face, and returned a jaunty thumbs-up. It was difficult to put his finger on it, but Murdock sensed that something important had changed in his relationship with these men. He was accepted now, a part of the team. The change might have been occasioned by something as simple—and as complex—as shared combat aboard the freighter.

Carefully, Murdock gave his weapon a final check. For this raid, Gold Squad would be serving as backup, a just-in-case reserve against the possibility that Iranians might show up in force, perhaps from one of those escorting patrol boats, and they were armed accordingly, with sound-suppressed H&K MP5SD3 subguns and, just in case the platoon needed heavy fire support, an M-60 machine gun and M-16s with M203 grenade launchers attached.

Murdock and Blue Squad, on the other hand, had the primary task of boarding the yacht and taking down the terrorists, if any, a role known to SEALs as VBSS, or Visit, Board, Search, and Seizure. Marksmanship aboard a small and wave-tossed sailing vessel could be a problem even for the best shot, and there was the danger that high-velocity rounds that missed their target might punch through a thin, fiberglass bulkhead and kill a hostage in the next compartment. Though all of them carried H&K subguns strapped to the rear of their assault vests as secondary weapons, the boarding party's primary weapons would be their sound-suppressed Smith & Wesson Hush Puppies, each mounting an under-barrel laser target designator.

The problem was that the laser sights were relatively delicate and had to be perfectly aligned for them to do any good. The SEALs had checked their sight alignments aboard the *Nassau*; now pistols and attached laser sights were cradled in black, foam-padded, watertight cases. Murdock again tested each of his sight's connections, then closed up the case and secured it to his assault harness. It would have to ride out a pretty severe thump and he didn't want anything coming loose along the way.

"One minute!" the crew chief yelled, and Murdock signaled to the SEALs. Together, they stood up and made their way aft, as the Sea Knight's cargo ramp whined open. Because they were helocasting with bundles of gear, they would be using the open ramp instead of the small, square opening known as the "hellhole" in the Sea Knight's deck.

Chief Roselli, first in the stick, helped MacKenzie and Brown drag the team's bundled CRRCs to the ramp, then stood by, his swim fins looped over his arm, silently counting down the last few seconds to the jump point. The helo was traveling more slowly now; Murdock could sense the change in the pitch and speed of the rotors.

"Ready . . ." the crew chief warned. "Your target is now at bearing one-seven-four, range ten miles!"

"One-seven-four, ten miles," Murdock repeated.

A light at the front of the cargo deck winked from red to green, and the crew chief gestured sharply with his arm. "Go!"

MacKenzie and Roselli shoved the first CRRC bundle off the ramp, then the second. Roselli followed them, racing into the black gulf yawning beyond the open ramp.

"Go! Go! Go!" Murdock called, clapping Brown on the shoulder. Garcia was next, then Higgins, then Ellsworth, each man slipping smoothly into the place vacated by the man before him, taking a breath, and propelling himself into the night.

One after the other, each of the eleven SEALs went down the ramp, until finally it was Murdock's turn. The crew chief gave him a thumbs-up. "Good luck, SEAL!" The man yelled, and Murdock nodded. Stepping off the ramp's end, he dropped into space and plummeted toward the sea.

The Sea Knight was now traveling at a speed of less than ten knots, at an altitude of about fifteen feet. The blast from its twin rotors raised a swirling, wet mist above the surface of the water. Murdock splashed into the sea and, with practiced efficiency, donned and cleared his mask, slipped on his swim fins, and kicked his way toward the surface.

The other SEALs had already unshipped the four CRRCs and were busy inflating them. Murdock took his place in the first raiding craft, giving a hand to Garcia and Roselli in getting the outboard motor mounted.

It took only minutes to get all four boats inflated, to remove the UBA gear and fins, and to secure their equipment for the next phase of the mission. There was a brief delay as the engine on number three refused to start, but after several tries, Murdock signaled to the men to leave it. A CRRC could carry seven men, more if necessary; they would make the approach with all six men of Gold Squad on one boat, with Blue Squad traveling three apiece in the remaining two. Ten miles . . . running a little east of due south. With their engines purring softly beneath the overcast night sky, the three CRRCs began traveling south.

2356 hours (Zulu +3)
Greenpeace yacht *Beluga*
Indian Ocean, 230 miles southeast of
Masirah

Colonel Ruholla Aghasi leaned against the light wire railing of the schooner, studied the lightless sky for a moment, then produced a Turkish cigarette and lit it. A few meters away, an Iranian marine stood at the boat's wheel, studying the compass binnacle with an attentiveness that suggested the colonel's presence made him nervous.

Aghasi ignored the man, staring instead at the running lights of the Iranian ships visible on the horizon. The *Yuduki Maru* and the *Damavand* were currently about two miles ahead of the *Beluga* and to starboard, while the Iranian frigates and patrol boats were scattered carelessly about the horizon.

The sight of so many Iranian warships was reassuring somehow, and it took Aghasi a moment to decide why. Kurebayashi, the cold little Japanese terrorist, had motored across to the *Yuduki Maru* several hours before, and Aghasi, for his part, was delighted. He believed in this mission, believed in the promise for his nation resting in the *Yuduki Maru*'s vast cargo holds, but the Ohtori commandos disturbed him. Aghasi thought of himself as a moral man, a devout follower of the teachings of the Prophet, and the random, seemingly blind violence practiced by the members of some of the more extreme terrorist groups, such as Ohtori, sickened him. Worse, random terror, in his opinion, was counterproductive. It made enemies of potential friends and squandered the gains made for the Revolution by painting the terrorists and their allies as barbarians.

Ruholla Aghasi would have been a lot happier if the Japanese weren't involved in this mission at all. Possessing two tons of plutonium might indeed elevate Iran to the heady position of supreme military power in Southwest Asia and the Middle East, but the presence of the Ohtori—even if they had been necessary to carry out the initial hijacking—cast a sickly shadow over the entire endeavor.

A woman's muffled scream floated up from the open companionway leading below deck, followed by a man's laugh. He'd been dead serious when he'd lectured the women on their immodest dress a few days before; none of the nine soldiers or marines aboard the *Beluga* with him was used to the casual standards of dress so often adopted by Western women— especially by *rich* Western women—and it was proving increasingly difficult keeping his men under control. His request to Colonel Hamid, that the women be removed from the yacht and held elsewhere, or else put aboard a helicopter and flown to Bandar Abbas, had been ignored. There'd been no serious incidents aboard the *Beluga* yet, but that, Aghasi was convinced, was only a matter of time. The women had served their purpose in providing leverage over the men, and Aghasi was wondering if they hadn't already outlived their usefulness. The scream sounded again, louder, more urgent.

Angrily, he tossed his cigarette over the side. "Keep us on course," he told the helmsman, and then he stalked forward. Clattering down the steps to the lounge and galley, he brushed past five off-duty troops who traded knowing grins with one another as he passed, then squeezed into the narrow passageway that led to the *Beluga*'s staterooms. As he'd expected, several of his Pasdaran were clustered around the open door to the cabin where the women were being kept; Corporal Mahmood Fesharaki was holding one of the women, the American blond, by her waist, laughing as she beat at his chest with flailing fists.

"Mahmood!" he snapped. "Release her!"

"We weren't doing anything, Colonel," the man replied. "We just wanted her to dance with us."

"I said release her!"

Grinning, the Iranian corporal shoved the woman back into the cabin. Aghasi glanced at the three female prisoners incuriously. All of them were fully clothed now, at least after the lax fashion of Westerners, in long pants and pullover shirts, but obviously either their clothing was still too revealing, or the men had already made up their minds about their characters. Their obvious fear and vocal protests counted for very little.

"Return to your duties," he ordered.

"But we are off-duty, Colonel," a private said.

"Then find something else to do before I put you on duty! I will not tolerate this lax disregard for discipline and order!"

Reluctantly, but still grinning and nudging one another, the crowd began to break up.

The *Beluga* gave a sudden lurch to port, and Aghasi braced himself against a bulkhead to keep from falling. A loud thump sounded from outside, from above deck. . . .

Suddenly, Aghasi's eyes widened. Something was wrong. He didn't know what, but he could sense that all was not right aboard his tiny command. . . .

2358 hours (Zulu +3)
Greenpeace yacht *Beluga*
Indian Ocean, 230 miles southeast of
Masirah

They'd encountered the Iranian squadron right on schedule, and within moments, using AN/PVS-7 night-vision goggles, they'd spotted the *Beluga* some distance astern of the *Yuduki Maru* and closed in on her from port and starboard. Since the Iranian ships were traveling at close to the top speed of the outboard-driven CRRCs, the men of the SEAL assault team knew that they would have only one shot at this; if they missed, there would be no way to turn around and catch up with their target.

Boat one, with Murdock, Roselli, and Garcia, closed on the *Beluga* from starboard and toward her stern; boat two, with

MacKenzie, Higgins, and Ellsworth, came in from port up near the bow. The third boat, containing all of Gold Squad, followed the starboard-side assault team. They would hook on with Murdock's team, but not board unless they were needed.

Lying flat across the bow of the pitching rubber boat, Murdock studied the target carefully as they drew closer. He could see one man at the wheel and two others on watch, one beside the helmsman, the other on top of the boat house, leaning against the foremast. There was no way to guess how many more men were below decks; those he could see were wearing fatigues, evidently Iranian army uniforms, and the two men on watch carried German-made G-3 assault rifles.

Roselli, at the CRRC's silenced outboard motor, corrected the rubber boat's course, gauging the speed and direction of the much larger yacht. There was no need for words. Both the approach and boarding had been carefully planned earlier that day, and rehearsed time and time again, first with models, then with areas representing *Beluga*'s deck and compartments chalked out on *Nassau*'s hangar deck. With no wasted motion, with no noise at all save the soft purr of the outboard, they veered straight in toward *Beluga*'s starboard quarter. For Murdock, his face scant inches above the slap of the waves, it was an eerie sensation; he could look up and see the Iranian soldier and helmsman standing in *Beluga*'s well deck only a few feet away, brilliantly illuminated by his starlight optics, while they, obviously, had not yet seen the black-garbed commandos rushing toward them out of the night on the breast of a black ocean. Murdock had his Smith & Wesson out, the laser sighting device switched on, warmed up and ready. As they closed to within a few feet of *Beluga*'s hull, he flicked over the switch that engaged the laser and took aim.

Instantly, a dazzling pinpoint of ruby light appeared on the side of the sentry's head. Riding out the up-and-down bump of the CRRC beneath him, Murdock squeezed the handgun's trigger and the weapon coughed, a harsh sound masked by the growl of the yacht's own engine.

In the same moment, a second dot of light winked into existence on the forehead of the man at the helm. Garcia fired an instant after Murdock; both Iranians were dead instantly, and Murdock was clambering out of the CRRC and onto *Beluga*'s well deck a scant second or two behind the two bullets. The double thump-and-clatter of the falling bodies, the metallic crack of the G-3 rifle hitting the polished wooden deck, seemed impossibly loud in the near-silence of the night. Murdock took two long steps to *Beluga*'s now-untended wheel and grabbed it before the yacht could swing about into the wind. He kept the brilliant pinpoint of his Smith & Wesson's laser playing next to the companionway set into the yacht's deckhouse forward, holding his breath as he waited for alarmed Iranian soldiers to come boiling out onto the deck.

Nothing. Garcia came across the rail, his pistol in his right hand, a line from the CRRC clutched in his left. With a quick movement, he secured the boat by lashing the line to a cleat. As he finished the task, Roselli scrambled up into the yacht at his side.

Forward, the second sentry was already sprawled lifeless by the mast, as Mac, Doc, and the Professor came aboard over the bow.

"Prairie Home," Murdock whispered into his microphone, "this is Bedsheet. We're aboard and tucked in." They'd made it, clearing the upper deck of guards in mere seconds, and with no indication that the alarm had been given below.

"Awn cheest!" a voice cried from below decks. *"Ali! Bepaweed!"*

And then Murdock knew that his first assessment had been just a little premature.

22

Saturday, 28 May

0001 hours (Zulu +3)
Greenpeace yacht *Beluga*
Indian Ocean, 230 miles southeast of
Masirah

"Ali!" Colonel Aghasi called again, and again there was no answer from the sergeant on guard on *Beluga*'s well deck. Thoroughly alarmed now, he drew his pistol, a big, black Colt .45 automatic, and started toward the deckhouse companionway. "You men," he snapped at the five Pasdaran soldiers in the lounge. "With me, quickly!"

The soldiers were picking up their assault rifles when the commandos burst into the compartment.

The first two crashed through the aft companionway, figures scarcely human in black garb that completely obscured their features. Ruler-straight, needle-slender streaks of ruby light whipped about in the semi-darkness of the lounge and galley, and each time they brushed one of Aghasi's men there was a short, ringing *chuff* of sound. One after another, the Pasdaran infantrymen jerked wildly with a bullet's impact, arms and legs flailing as they spun, twisted, or pitched back off their feet. There were four left . . . then three . . . two . . .

A thunderous explosion sounded from forward, followed closely by the stink of burnt plastique. One of the men in the passageway screamed, then collapsed into the galley, just as Corporal Mahmood Fesharaki lunged through the door into the women's cabin. Two more nightmare apparitions appeared at the forward end of the passageway, dropping down into the yacht through a forward deck hatch blasted away by an explosive charge.

Chance spared Aghasi's life; he was lunging forward, the .45 in his right hand coming up, when the side of an Iranian soldier's head exploded a meter away in a fine mist of blood and pieces of skull. Something—a fragment of bullet or bone—struck Aghasi squarely on the inside of his wrist with the solid jolt of a hammer blow. His fingers went dead as the pain of a splintered bone lanced up his arm, and the pistol spun from his hand as though propelled by a kick. At the same instant, Aghasi's face and torso were painted by a grisly splash of blood and brain. Clutching his shattered wrist, he went to his knees as the last of the Iranian troops in the aft lounge died.

Then he was smashed down by a stunning blow to the back of his head. Blinking up from the deck, he saw one of the invaders looming over him, the night-vision goggles over his eyes giving him the glittering, black-chitin look of some monster insect. The long, heavy snout of a silenced automatic pistol swung toward him, and suddenly he was half blinded by the otherworldly dazzle of a laser tracking up his face.

"Don't . . . shoot!" Aghasi gasped in English, trying to squint past the laser's light. "Please! . . . "

"Harakat nakoneed!" the nightmare figure rasped in passable Farsi. The gaping muzzle of the sound-suppressed pistol, the ruby sparkle of the laser sight, did not waver. "Don't move!"

Gritting his teeth against the pain in his wrist, Aghasi managed a jerky nod. "Absolutely, sir," he replied, still in English. "I would not dream of moving."

A woman screamed nearby, and Aghasi squeezed his eyes shut, certain that the sound would make the invader kill him anyway. He felt a hot wetness spreading across his groin and realized with a burst of sickened shame that he'd just lost control and emptied his bladder. He could sense the commando's finger tightening on the pistol's trigger. . . .

0002 hours (Zulu +3)
Greenpeace yacht _Beluga_
Indian Ocean, 230 miles southeast of
** Masirah**

Murdock, the Smith & Wesson gripped firmly in both hands, held the red aim-point of laser light centered squarely on the prisoner's forehead. Garcia and Roselli squeezed past at his back. "Galley clear!" Roselli called. From the corridor leading to the sleeping compartments forward, MacKenzie answered with, "Passageway clear!"

Turning his full attention to the prisoner at his feet, Murdock revealed his teeth, a terrifying mimicry of a smile, he knew, from his paint-blackened, insect-eyed face. _"Rawst begueed,"_ he growled, before shifting to English. "Tell the truth! How many men with you?"

"Four and—ah, fourteen," the man admitted. He was wearing olive-drab fatigues, but the gold device on his collar was the rank insignia for an Iranian Pasdaran colonel. A lucky catch, if he could be made to cooperate. "Fourteen, plus myself! You've already killed some of—"

"Mac!" Murdock said, speaking into the slender microphone wired against his cheek. "We have fifteen tangos aboard total." Reaching up with one hand, he slid the starlight goggles up on his face, then glanced about the room. "I have five tangos down here, and one prisoner."

"Three tangos down here," MacKenzie replied. With three more dead on the upper deck, that made the total twelve.

Which left three unaccounted for.

He changed channels on his Motorola. "Backup, Backup, this is Bedsheet," he called. "We have three tangos loose. . . ."

0002 hours (Zulu +3)
UH-1 helicopter
Indian Ocean, 230 miles southeast of
** Masirah**

"No sweat," Magic Brown said, squinting into the eyepiece of his night sight.

"Bedsheet, Backup, we copy that," Nicholson murmured into his microphone. "Magic's got one of 'em lined up now."

They were aboard a UH-1 helicopter off the *Nassau*, hovering 150 yards off *Beluga*'s bow, at an altitude of eighty feet. The helo's right door panel had been slid back, and the two men were crouched behind an improvised firing platform on the cargo deck. Nicholson was serving as spotter with a hand-held nightscope, while Brown took aim through the scope mounted on his M1A1, a match-quality M-14 upgraded for use as a SEAL-sniper primary weapon.

From this almost-stationary vantage point, Magic could see almost all of the *Beluga*'s deck, including the still, sprawled form of the dead guard beside the foremast, and two more in the well deck aft. He could see the three CRRCs, two empty and tied alongside, the third occupied by Gold Squad and maintaining an overwatch position astern of the yacht. On *Beluga*'s starboard side, a live man's head and shoulders were protruding from a porthole. Evidently, he was trying to escape to the upper deck. The port was a tight fit, but a determined wiggle freed both arms, and then he was hauling himself through. The two airborne SEALs had been watching him intently for several seconds.

"C'mon, baby," Magic said softly. "Look at Poppa. . . ."

"I don't think it's a civvie," Nicholson said. "Look! I see a weapon."

"I see it," Magic said. The man was through, crouching on the wooden deck, and someone had just handed what looked like a G-3 assault rifle through the porthole. Still, it *could* be one of the civilian hostages, escaping with a captured rifle from the cabin where he'd been held captive. In the greens and grays of the starlight scope, it was difficult to determine whether or not he was wearing a uniform.

Suddenly he turned, his magnified face staring directly into Brown's scope, and the SEAL sniper had a clear look at his features. Definitely, he was not one of the civilians whose faces he'd memorized aboard the *Nassau*. Gently, almost lovingly, Brown caressed his M1's trigger. There was a single sharp report, and the upturned face in the nightscope exploded in a messy spray.

"Kill," Nicholson said. "Good shot, Magic."

"Yeah, that's one down," Magic said. "Now where're the rest of the bastards?"

0002 hours (Zulu +3)
Greenpeace yacht *Beluga*
Indian Ocean, 230 miles southeast of
Masirah

MacKenzie snapped off hand signals to Higgins and Ellsworth, then to Garcia and Roselli. *You two, that way! You two, over here!* Doc Ellsworth nodded as he crowded up against the bulkhead, his pistol in both hands, muzzle high. Luxury yacht or no, the *Beluga*'s central passageway was claustrophobic, especially when occupied by half a dozen SEALs in full gear, with weapons and combat loadout vests, and movement was made no easier by the bodies of three Iranian soldiers and their weapons lying on the deck.

Beluga boasted a number of cabins and staterooms on this deck. The owner's cabin was a large area forward, but the door was open and Doc had pronounced it clear when the bow team had first come in. Four more cabins were aligned two by two on either side of the passageway leading aft to the galley, while a companionway forward dropped to the next deck down, leading to a forecastle cubby for the yacht's crew, storage spaces, and a small engine room.

Two of the side-by-side cabins on this deck were open; one was filled with radio and computer equipment, including the electronic gear necessary for establishing a satellite communications link. Another room, empty when the SEALs broke in, had been occupied by the Iranians. The last two, opposite one another, were closed and locked from the inside. As MacKenzie gave silent, hand-sign directions, Doc and the Professor took up positions alongside the cabin door to port, while Garcia and Roselli took the cabin to starboard. Seconds before, Nicholson had radioed the VBSS team about the kill outside, warning them that at least one more tango probably occupied the starboard cabin.

Garcia and the Professor were both equipped as assault breachers, with shotguns instead of H&Ks. Standing to the sides of their respective doors, they took aim, then fired, the twin booms of the shotguns ear-splitting in the confined space below decks. The cabin doors were lightweight, hollow-core barriers designed for privacy and nothing more. One-ounce slugs smashed locking mechanisms and plywood, then punched through carpeting and fiberglass decks as the doors disintegrated into splinters and whirling sheets of wooden paneling.

On the starboard side, Roselli lunged through the door a blink behind the shotgun blast, his Smith & Wesson gripped in both hands, the aiming laser sweeping across the darkened room like a jewel-bright rapier. On the far bulkhead, a porthole had been opened; an Iranian stood there, a G-3 assault rifle aimed at the door.

The shotgun blast and the spray of splinters and wood chips had forced him to turn his head, and he was a split second late in firing—fortunately for Roselli, since the SEAL otherwise would have been dead as soon as he burst through the opening. Roselli tracked his pistol, the laser painting an unsteady line across the Iranian's chest. In the same, confused instant, one of the two other figures in the cabin, a big, lanky man in a lightweight safari jacket suddenly bolted toward the door.

Roselli held his fire as the hostage lurched between him and the soldier. The soldier fired an instant later, triggering a full-auto burst toward the door; the volley had been aimed at Roselli, but the bullets slammed into the bulkhead, the overhead, and the hostage's back. Roselli triggered three quick shots as the stricken hostage crumpled to the deck, slamming the Iranian back against the porthole.

On the other side of the passageway, Doc plunged into the stateroom through the storm of splinters loosed by Higgins's shotgun blast. A single Iranian soldier stood there, hiding behind a tall, attractive blond woman in a T-shirt and blue slacks. He had his left arm tight across her throat, gripping her so tightly that her scream was a silent, desperate gape as her hands clawed at his forearm; his right hand pressed the muzzle of a Colt .45 pistol against the side of her head.

"*Aslehetawnra beeandawzeed!*" he screamed, and the panic was evident in the harsh raggedness of his words. "*Goosh koneed va elaw meezanam!*"

Ellsworth wasn't sure what the man had said. He didn't speak Farsi, and the few phrases he'd memorized for this op were brief and strictly utilitarian. He suspected, though, that the Iranian had just rattled off a couple of those memorized phrases, things like "Drop your weapons," and "obey or I'll shoot." Strictly Wild West gunslinger stuff.

"Take it easy, fella," he said, his eyes glancing about the tiny compartment. Two more women were clinging to each other on the cabin's single bed. "Nobody's gonna hurt you! *Azyatee beh shomaw nameerasad!*"

The expression on the visible part of the Iranian's face went from desperation to blank puzzlement. The pistol in his hand didn't waver, but a fraction more of his head was visible now behind the woman's blond mane. Doc was holding his Smith & Wesson at waist level, a deliberately nonthreatening stance, but the laser was painting the wild straggle of the Iranian's hair. He dipped the muzzle a fraction of a degree, and the red dot of the laser aim-point slid onto the guy's face. The Iranian flinched, probably from the dazzle of the laser, and pulled farther behind the woman. Doc let the laser dot drift onto her hair, which sparkled under the beam's caress. "*Tasleem shaveed!*" Doc told him. "Surrender!"

"Eh?"

Doc squeezed the trigger. His pistol *chuffed,* punching the round effortlessly through the woman's hair and into the Iranian's left eye. The soldier spun backward and fell across the bed alongside the other two women. The blonde stood motionless on the deck, eyes squeezed shut, screaming now as loud as she was able.

"Shit," Doc said. "I didn't think my accent was that bad!"

The blonde stopped screaming, opened her eyes, then screamed again as soon as she'd had a good look at her rescuer.

"It's okay," he said, raising his voice. "It's okay! We're Americans!"

"Americans!" One of the women on the bed sprang forward, grabbing his arm. "Thank you, God! Americans!"

The other two women followed an instant later, and Ellsworth found himself surrounded. "Port cabin clear," he reported over his radio as the women crowded closer. "One tango down."

"One tango down, starboard cabin," Roselli added on the same channel. "And one hostage down too. Doc? We need you over here!"

"On my way, Razor." He had to roughly disentangle himself from the women to get out of the compartment. "Okay! Okay! Take it easy, ladies! We'll have you out of here soon."

He could hear the thunder of the Huey outside edging closer to the yacht.

0008 hours (Zulu +3)
Greenpeace yacht *Beluga*
Indian Ocean, 230 miles southeast of
Masirah

"Prairie Home, Bedsheet," Murdock called. Leaving the prisoner under guard, he'd emerged onto *Beluga*'s well deck and was standing again in the night, speaking via satellite link with the command center aboard *Nassau*. "Prairie Home, Bedsheet. Come in, Prairie Home."

He waited out the silence, listening to static. The Huey circled through the night, keeping watch against the appearance of Iranian patrol boats or other unpleasant surprises. Close by, Jaybird, who'd once professed to Murdock his experience with sailing vessels, had taken over the helm, while MacKenzie, Higgins, Roselli, and Fernandez mounted guard on *Beluga*'s upper deck.

Except for the muffled clatter of the helo, the night was quiet now. The nearest Iranian vessels, some three miles ahead now, seemed oblivious to the activity aboard the Greenpeace yacht. The continual flybys and perimeter intrusions throughout the past hours had paid off; the Huey was certainly registering on the Iranian warships' radar, but they'd apparently chosen to ignore it.

They would, no doubt, continue to ignore it, at least until *Beluga* showed some sign of trouble, an abrupt change of course, for example, or a rendezvous with an American ship.

"Bedsheet, this is Prairie Home," a voice crackled at last in his earplug speaker. "Authenticate Hotel, Alfa, one-niner-one."

"Prairie Home, roger. I authenticate: Victor, India, one-one-three."

"Roger, Bedsheet. Go ahead."

"Prairie Home, objective secured, repeat, objective secured. We have fourteen tangos down, that's one-four tangos down, one tango captured, all accounted for. We have one hostage dead during the takedown, one missing."

Murdock tried to dismiss the sour, dark burning inside he'd felt since he'd learned of Paul Brandeis's death minutes before, but it wouldn't go. The SEAL assault had gone down with stunning ferocity, speed, and precision. Forty seconds after Murdock had first opened fire on the *Beluga*'s helmsman, all but one of the Iranians had been dead, with no casualties among the SEALs. Of the hostages aboard, all three women, Rudi Kohler, and four of Kohler's employees found locked in the crew's cubby below decks were safe.

The single, wrenching tragedy in the takedown had been the death of Paul Brandeis, the American hostage who'd blundered into Roselli's line of fire and taken the full-auto burst meant for the SEAL. Doc hadn't been able to help the American, who'd probably been dead before he hit the deck. Murdock could still hear the wrenching sobs of Brandeis's widow, even out here on *Beluga*'s deck.

"Bedsheet, Prairie Home. That's a major well done! Now pack up and get the hell out of there!"

"Copy, Prairie Home," Murdock said. "We have some loose ends to tidy up first. This is Bedsheet, out."

Well done, right, he thought bitterly. *The hell of it is, the mission was well done! But damn it all! We came so close to pulling it off one hundred percent!*

There was always a terrible risk in hostage rescues, the near certainty that one or more of the civilians involved would get hurt or killed. Put one or more desperate, armed men in the company of a number of untrained and panicky civilians, then throw a SEAL assault team into the middle of it. No matter how well trained the attackers, no matter how expert their marks- manship, no matter how many hours logged in the fun house back at Little Creek or how advanced the technology of their weapons, the chances were still better than ever that someone— SEAL or terrorist, it didn't really matter—would deliberately or by accident cut down some kid or wife or husband. In the 1990s, the supreme example of how a hostage rescue ought to work remained the stunning Israeli raid on Entebbe in 1976. The Israeli paras performed brilliantly, but even there, two of the over one hundred hostages were killed and seven wounded during the fierce firefight in the air terminal building between Israeli troops and the PFLP terrorists.

Knowing the odds didn't help. Paul Brandeis had panicked and gotten in the way during the firefight; another hostage, Karl Schmidt, was missing—almost certainly dead, though Murdock hadn't had time yet to question the rescued civilians about that.

Yes, there definitely were several loose ends to wrap up here. Turning sharply, he strode across the deck and took the steps down the companionway two at a time.

23

0025 hours (Zulu +3)
Greenpeace yacht *Beluga*
Indian Ocean, 230 miles southeast of
   Masirah

Murdock sat behind a polished formica table across from the Iranian prisoner, who'd been propped up on one of the sofas that circled the lounge bulkheads. Doc was next to the prisoner, wrapping a bandage around his broken wrist. The man claimed to be Pasdaran Colonel Ruholla Aghasi and insisted that he was ready to cooperate in any way that he could.

Studying the man, Murdock was inclined to believe him, though training and common sense both urged caution. Senior officers did not change sides at a whim, nor were they as likely to be cowed by pain or threat as lower-ranking men who simply did what they were told.

None of the SEALs was feeling particularly friendly toward Aghasi at the moment. In choked, broken words, Gertrude Kohler had described the hijacking, Karl Schmidt's murder, and the threatened rape and torture of the women. Doc's hostility was clearest of all, a dark simmering behind his eyes as he tended to Aghasi's wound. Garcia was sitting quietly on the other side of the lounge, mounting guard with a sullen intensity that was disturbing. The rest were either forward with ex-hostages or up on deck.

Casually, Murdock gestured with the muzzle-heavy black-

249

ness of the Smith & Wesson in his hand. "Colonel, you say that you're willing to help us," he said quietly. "I don't see why I should believe you."

"Hell, *I* don't think you should trust him, Skipper," Doc said. He continued wrapping the roll of gauze bandage around Aghasi's wrist as he spoke, the action strangely at odds with the steel-hard anger in the SEAL's voice. "These sons-a-bitches gunned down two innocent people!"

"Take it easy, Doc. Let's hear him out."

"I . . . regret those deaths," the Iranian said. "I didn't want civilians to be hurt. This operation has not gone entirely to plan."

"Suppose you tell us about it, Colonel. Who killed Karl Schmidt? The Ohtori?"

That jolted the colonel. He reacted to the name Ohtori as though he'd been slapped. "N-no," he said. "One of my men shot him when he, when he attacked the soldier holding his wife. I did not order it. How . . . do you know of Ohtori?"

"Never mind, Colonel. It's my turn to ask the questions. How long have you been working with the Japanese?"

Aghasi swallowed. "Not long. To be truthful, this operation has been a mistake from the start. That is why I wish to cooperate."

Ellsworth tied off the bandage, then slipped the Iranian's hand into a gauze sling. "Maybe he'd like to cooperate from the bottom of the sea, Skipper. Should be safe enough. Even the sharks wouldn't want him. What d'you say?"

"Why don't you go check on Mrs. Brandeis, Doc?"

"Aye, aye, sir."

Aghasi looked pale, and he was sweating heavily. His uniform gave off the acrid bite of ammonia, a mingled stench of sweat and urine. "Your men are . . . frightening, Lieutenant."

"Frightening? Hell, you don't know what frightening really is. Right now, they just dislike you. You'd better pray you never get them *really* mad!" He gestured with the pistol again. "So. Why don't you like the Ohtori? Who decided to start working with them?"

The Iranian took a deep breath. "Do you know an Admiral Sahman? Or General Ramazani?"

"No. Should I?"

"Perhaps not. Sahman is second-in-command of the Iranian naval facilities at Bandar Abbas. Ramazani is one of our senior Pasdaran officers, a hero of the Iraqi War."

The "Iraqi War," Murdock knew, referred to the bloody struggle between Iran and Iraq from 1980 to 1988, a conflict that had claimed over a million dead on both sides.

"It happens that both Ramazani and Sahman oppose the mullahs in Tehran. Since the Shah was overthrown fifteen years ago, Iran has been held back, paralyzed. They believe, as I do, that an Islamic state can also be a *modern* state.

"In any case, they've kept their opposition secret while they built their own power bases and allied with other revolutionary groups. By now, they have connections with groups throughout the Gulf region, including the NLA."

The NLA, the National Liberation Army, was a brigade-sized band of Iranian rebels and defectors, perhaps 4,500 men in all, armed with captured or stolen equipment and operating out of southern Iraq. Murdock had seen the background and pre-mission intelligence on the NLA when he'd taken command of Third Platoon; the SEALs who'd gone in on Operation Blue Sky—the hostage rescue at the Basra airport—had been briefed on the possibility that they might encounter NLA elements in the Iraqi swamps.

"I believe Ramazani met the Ohtori through his NLA contacts," Aghasi continued. "The Ohtori are a . . . how is the English? A splintered fraction?"

"A faction. A splinter group."

"Yes, a splinter group of the old Japanese Red Army. They are strange people, absolute fanatics. . . ."

Murdock had heard plenty of the religious fanaticism of the Iranian Pasdaran, but he merely nodded. "Go on."

"Apparently, Ohtori established links with the NLA in Iraq. Both groups maintain training camps in that country. Now they are working with a splinter group within the Iranian military.

Their plan was for the hijacking of the Japanese plutonium ship."

"How does that help the NLA? Or the Ohtori, for that matter?"

"Power, of course. Political power. It provides the rebels with lever, with lever—"

"Leverage?"

"Precisely." Aghasi's face twisted in a wan, nervous smile. "The plutonium gives Ramazani a weapon strong enough, dramatic enough to induce the rest of Iran's military to join him."

"What weapon? An atomic bomb?"

Aghasi's eyes widened. *"Na!"* he said, momentarily lapsing back into Farsi. "No! Plutonium itself is dangerous enough. Packed in artillery shells, in a SCUD missile warhead . . ."

Murdock nodded impatiently. "I understand all of that. But is *that* what this thing is all about? A military coup? A power play by some of your officers?"

"It is more than a power play, Lieutenant. It is a first battle in the war for the soul of my people."

"Okay. So your side gets the plutonium. Your army joins your cause and overthrows the mullahs. Then what?"

"They install a military government in Tehran, under General Ramazani. They . . . they then have the, how you say, the advantage against our enemies in the region. Iran, Iran's people, will be secure at long last."

Murdock chewed on that for a long moment. He had the feeling that Aghasi was telling the truth as he understood it. He also had the impression, however, that Aghasi was holding quite a bit back. That bit about Iran being secure at last was a bit too pat, a bit too neat. Murdock could think of several other possible outcomes to the scenario Aghasi had just described. Iran's new rulers might decide to launch a preemptive strike on Iraq, for instance, using plutonium-loaded bombs and SCUD warheads.

The Iran-Iraq war had not been settled by the armistice of 1988. Far from it, in fact. That war had been only the most recent round in a bloody conflict of rival peoples that went back at least fifteen hundred years. Iraq had provided a safe haven for the NLA, hoping to use it one day to topple the Shi'ite regime in Tehran. From what he knew of the history of conflict in the region, Murdock doubted that the new ruling clique in Tehran would remain grateful for the help for long. If nothing else, a holy war with apostate Iraq would help unify the Iranian people and take their minds off the inevitable shortages and difficulties brought on by the change of governments.

And there was worse. Operation Blue Sky had been launched because some UN observers had discovered intelligence relating to Iraq's nascent atomic weapons program. What if Iraq was farther along toward an atomic bomb than American intelligence believed? Iran's attack using radioactive dust, possibly even the mere knowledge that they'd acquired the stuff, might be answered by a volley of Iraqi atomic warheads. Nuclear war at the head of the Persian Gulf could kill more millions, not to mention contaminating half the world's oil supply for generations to come.

"I notice," Murdock said at last, "that you refer to 'them' when you talk about Ramazani's coup, not 'us.' What's your part in all of this? Why are you here?"

"I was part of it. I suppose I still am. But . . . I no longer believe."

"What happened?"

The Iranian shrugged. "Lieutenant, I needn't remind you that my people have suffered a very great deal in the past fifteen years. I am a religious man, but I cannot honor the twisted fanatics who rule my country, who hold it trapped in an earlier century." He brought one long finger up to his head, tapping at his temple. "These eyes have seen the effects of their, their fanaticism. My own son, my Amin, was one of thousands of Iranian children who marched singing into the Iraqi minefields and machine-gun cross fires and mustard gas. That was eight years ago. He was thirteen then. It was the mullahs who commanded that the supreme sacrifice must be made, even to the sacrifice of our firstborn in their war against the Iraqi. It was then that I decided that I would do all in my power to fight the mullahs, the dictatorship that grips my nation. But . . ."

"But?"

The man sagged, and Murdock was aware of something behind those tired, tired eyes, a profound weariness. "I found myself working with fanatics once again, Lieutenant. It seems that I cannot escape them."

"Who? The Ohtori?"

He nodded. "Yes. These are men who . . . I don't entirely understand this, but I have heard that they believe they will be turned into stars if they die. The Prophet promises the faithful who die in *jihad* a place in paradise, but these men are, are monsters. You have a saying in your language, the ends justificate the . . . the . . ."

"The ends justify the means."

"Precisely so, yes. For these men, any act, no matter how terrible, is justified if it makes success for them in the end. The Ohtori leader who engineered the capture of this sailing vessel was ready to kill everyone aboard, to order my men to abuse the women, even to torture them if it would advance his cause. I spent a great deal of time last night wondering about this, wondering if I was fighting on the right side. On the side of Allah."

"And what did you decide?"

Again an eloquent shrug. "Nothing, Lieutenant, save that there are no easy answers to be found. And then I began to wonder if I was worthy of the martyrdom promised by Allah. That he did not permit me to die this night is, perhaps, an expression of his will."

Murdock pushed back from the table. "Colonel, I don't know about Allah, but I'd say that there's been enough martyrdom for one day."

"Ensha'allah."

Murdock knew that phrase, which could be heard in various related forms throughout the Islamic world. *As God wills.*

"Tell me, Colonel. What sort of radio schedule were you keeping aboard this vessel? How often were you supposed to check in?"

Aghasi pursed his lips. "There was no schedule, Lieutenant. We were ordered to maintain radio silence. Unless, of course, we came under attack. Then we were to call on a frequency of 440 megahertz, and a patrol boat would close to render assistance."

"And did you get that message off?"

"No, Lieutenant. Your attack was too swift."

Murdock stood. "Thank you, Colonel. You have been most helpful."

"What will become of me?"

"We'll arrange to fly you to one of our ships. Don't worry. You'll be well treated." As he spoke, though, Murdock's mind was racing ahead. If what this Pasdaran colonel had said was true, a startling opportunity existed for the Americans . . . *if* they could get their act together in time. Leaving Aghasi in Garcia's care, Murdock hurried from the cabin.

He needed to make another radio call to Prairie Home and, through them, to the Pentagon.

1045 hours (Zulu −5 hours)
NAVSPECWARGRU-Two Briefing Room
Little Creek, Virginia

"What is the single element that screws us up time and time again in this sort of op?" Captain Coburn demanded. He looked around the table, moving from face to face. "Intelligence! Or rather, the lack of *reliable* intelligence. I remind you that the last time we tried to go into Iran, during Operation Eagle's Claw, in 1980, we had no intelligence assets on the ground in that country at all."

"This is hardly a similar situation, Captain Coburn," Admiral Kerrigan said. "Besides, it was mechanical failure that doomed Eagle's Claw, that and the collision of a helicopter with an Air Force transport."

"You're talking through your brass hat, Admiral, and you know it," Brian Hadley said, grinning. "I was at Langley in '80, and I remember. The Company had been out of Iran ever since the Shah got booted out, and we were desperate to have some eyes and ears on the ground. If some young Navy officer had come up with an idea to walk into Tehran and tell us what was going on, I'd have fallen down and kissed his Corfams."

"Hmpf! Has anyone considered that Murdock might be hotdogging this thing?" Admiral Kerrigan demanded. "Good God, Captain, this whole idea reeks of romanticized John Wayne shit! Spies and traitors and the proverbial cavalry coming over the hill just in the proverbial nick of time!"

"Maybe so, Admiral," Captain Mason admitted from the other side of the table. "But the cavalry, as you put it . . . or in this case, the II MEF, is going in whether we approve Murdock's plan or not. And it *does* give us a hell of a lot better chance to pull this off."

"I, for one, resent the implication that my people are showboating a mission," Coburn said evenly. "These men are pros, Admiral. There are no 'hot dogs' in my command."

"Perhaps that was too strong a word, Captain," Kerrigan said. "But how are we supposed to coordinate a plan that your men keep changing in the field?"

Coburn grinned. "Are you suggesting, sir, that one lieutenant in a sailboat is about to upset something as big as Operation Deadly Weapon?"

"At this point, Captain, I'm not sure there's *anything* your people can't do . . . or screw up if they put half a mind to it." He said it with a wry half smile, and the other officers in the briefing room laughed.

Coburn felt himself relax a little. He'd been expecting a far bloodier battle with the MIDEASTFOR liaison, but Kerrigan's constant opposition to NAVSPECWAR operations appeared to have eased somewhat since the last time he'd been in this room. Obviously he still didn't like the special forces concept, but he at least was willing to work with the idea and had agreed that Deadly Weapon would lead off with NAVSPECWAR people. He seemed most concerned now with the possibility that intelligence data routed back from Murdock's team might force a last-second change in the U.S. Marine amphibious operations about to commence in the Gulf.

Today's planning session had actually been called by Brian Hadley, who was scheduled to meet with the President's National Security Advisor later that evening. He'd wanted an assessment by members of the Navy Special Warfare community about whether or not the idea radioed back by Murdock had a chance of working.

Except for Kerrigan and his people, of course, everyone in the room had thought Murdock's plan a wizard idea. And Kerrigan's opinion carried little weight here. Everyone knew he was down on the special-ops people, and he was consulted on the matter only because Deadly Weapon would fall under MIDEASTFOR's provenance.

But the SEALs were going to be a part of this, no matter what Kerrigan had to say.

"I suppose what I object to most," Kerrigan went on, "is this sense of making things up as we go along. Modern war can't be fought that way."

"On the contrary, Admiral," Hadley said. "Vietnam demanded flexible, adaptive battle plans, and every military option since has demonstrated the need for more flexibility, not less. We've got to know what we're getting into over there."

"I would have thought that the SEAL-Marine joint recon force was adequate to our needs."

"Maybe so," Coburn said. "I damn well hope you're right. But it seems to me that young Murdock is going to be the right man in the right place at the right time, and we'd be fools to yank him out now. This is too good an opportunity to throw away."

A rippling murmur of approval made its way about the table. Coburn had been as surprised as anyone else in Little Creek by Murdock's radio message, some eighteen hours ago, suggesting this last-minute change to Deadly Weapon. The former hostages, the Iranian prisoner, and all of the SEALs save four had been ferried by helicopter back to the *Nassau*.

But as of the last report, Murdock and three of his men were still aboard the *Beluga,* sailing in company with the Iranian squadron toward the port of Bandar Abbas.

It was expected that they would actually enter Bandar Abbas in another—he looked at his watch—eighteen hours now.

Just hours ahead of the planned Marine invasion of Iran.

"But how reliable is Murdock's information, do you think?" a captain on Kerrigan's staff wanted to know as the murmur died down. "His report says he got all of this from that captured Iranian colonel. Couldn't all of this be some kind of elaborate setup?"

"Up at Langley," Hadley said, "they're rating this one as a B-3."

"What's that supposed to mean?"

"It's how the CIA weights the reliability of data acquired from various sources. The letter gauges the reliability of the source, while the number reflects Langley's guess as to how accurate the information might be. B means usually reliable. That's not a put-down of your man, Captain Coburn. I don't think anyone ever gets tagged with an A, meaning absolute reliability. The 3 means the information is possibly accurate. It's not confirmed by other sources, so it's not a 1, and it's not possible to call something this fuzzy *probably* true, so we can't give it a 2. The point, gentlemen, is that we have here a reliable source giving us intelligence that quite possibly *is* accurate. We cannot afford to simply ignore what he says."

"Has anyone thought to consult with Congressman Murdock about this?" Kerrigan asked. "That's his son out there. I find it shocking that he was allowed to lead *two* dangerous assaults one right after the other, first against the *Yuduki Maru,* and then against the *Beluga,* and that now he's doing this."

"Lieutenant Murdock," Coburn said slowly, "is an excellent officer. He does not allow politics, personal feelings, or shall we say, family obligations to divert him from what he perceives as his duty. I am well aware of Congressman Murdock's interest in his son's activities. I'm also aware that neither Lieutenant Murdock, nor myself, nor the President of the United States himself for that matter, can allow personal feelings to jeopardize this operation. I'm sure, sir, that the congressman would be the first to agree if he were here."

"So what you're all telling me," Brian Hadley said at last, "is that this sneak-and-peek is a good idea. That we should plan this thing knowing we're going to have SEALs on the ground, or on the water actually, when we send in the Marines."

"Abso-damn-lutely," Coburn said. "These people'll be able to tell you things your spy satellites never dreamed of."

Hadley grinned. "I hope so, Captain. Because I happen to agree with you. This is too God-damned good an opportunity to throw away!" He began gathering up the charts and papers on the table in front of him and putting them into his briefcase. The naval officers rose, began gathering up their own papers, and started to leave.

"Captain Coburn?" Hadley said, looking up.

"Sir?"

"I wonder if I might have a word with you before you go?"

"Of course, sir," Coburn said. He glanced again at his watch. "I am on a pretty tight sched."

"I understand you're on your way over there."

"Yes, sir. First and Second Platoons will be taking part in the main landings."

"I just wanted to hear it from you, your assessment of young Murdock. He's been pushing pretty hard. Can we push him this much more?"

Coburn considered the question. "If he wasn't up to it, Mr. Hadley, I don't think he would have suggested it. Murdock always has the *Team's* best interests at heart, not his own."

"Hmm. That was my assessment, based on what I've heard. You know, don't you, that a lot of the SEALs' future is riding on this op?"

Coburn grinned at him. "Tell me something I don't know."

"Right now, a House investigative committee is going over your Murdock's after-action report on the Japanese freighter. They're explaining to each other how they could have done it better, and they're wondering if all the money they're giving NAVSPECWAR is being well spent. There's serious talk of disbanding the SEALs, Marine Recon, the Rangers, all of the SPECWAR people except the Green Beanies."

"Give us half a chance, Mr. Hadley. We'll show them that we can deliver plenty of bang for the buck."

"Yes. From what I've heard about your people, I have to agree." There was a knock at the door, and Coburn looked up. A young second class electrician's mate stood there, his SEAL Budweiser winking brightly in the overhead fluorescent lighting. "Hey, Chucker! Come on in."

"Helo's waitin' on the pad and ready to go, sir," EM2 Wilson called, gesturing with the rolled-up white hat in his hand. "Whenever you're ready."

"Let's haul ass then. Ah, if you'll excuse me, Mr. Hadley?"

"Of course." He nodded toward the enlisted SEAL. "That one of your people, Captain?"

"Sure is. A brand-new SEAL, just assigned to an open slot in First Platoon. Isn't that right, Wilson?"

"Yes, sir. Uh, begging the Captain's pardon, sir, but the helo jockey told me that if our asses weren't on board in five minutes we were gonna have to hitch a ride to Oceana."

"Then we'd better move. Mr. Hadley?"

"You've answered my questions." Hadley reached out and clapped Coburn on the shoulder. "Good luck over there, Captain."

"Thank you, sir. But believe me, it's not luck that counts in this game." He jerked a thumb over his shoulder, indicating EM2 Wilson. "It's guys like that."

He picked up his briefcase and headed for the door.

24

Sunday, 29 May

1612 hours (Zulu +3)
Greenpeace yacht *Beluga*
Off Bandar-é Abbas

The sun was merciless, glaring down from a brassy, cloudless sky. The yacht *Beluga* was still following along in the wakes of her larger Iranian consorts, but by this time she'd managed to drop back until she was nearly five miles astern of the *Yuduki Maru,* far enough to avoid inspection by curious soldiers or sailors aboard the freighter or the other ships, close enough that it was not obvious that she was hanging back.

Throughout the run north past Al Masirah, zigzagging northwest into the Gulf of Oman at the Tropic of Cancer, then north again through the oil-blackened narrows of the Strait of Hormuz, Murdock had noticed that the Iranian flotilla lacked almost any sense of order or convoy discipline. The *Damavand* continued plowing steadily ahead, towing the dead weight of the Japanese freighter. One or another of the frigates was usually within close support range, but the patrol boats scattered themselves all over the map, and by Sunday morning, two had vanished entirely, probably racing ahead to safe berths in Bandar Abbas.

The formation was made even more ragged by the presence of so many civilian vessels. The Strait of Hormuz was always crowded with commercial shipping, most of it the monster oil tankers bearing the flags of a dozen nations. The biggest were

261

VLCCs—Very Large Crude Carriers—steel islands as long as four football fields end to end, with dead weight tonnages of half a million tons or more. At any given moment, one or more of those monsters could be seen on the horizon from *Beluga*'s deck, entering the Persian Gulf riding high and light, or exiting the passage with full loads that seemed to drag those leviathan bulks down until their decks were nearly awash.

It was the seagoing traffic, of course, that invested the Strait of Hormuz with its singular strategic importance. More than once in recent memory, Iran had threatened to use its surface-to-surface "Silkworm" missiles purchased from China to close the strait to international shipping. So far, they'd refrained. Iran also used the Strait of Hormuz for access to the world's oil markets. But when it came to splinter groups like the NLA, or bands of disaffected military leaders who might actually *welcome* the political chaos such a shutdown of the economy might bring, all bets were off, and anything was possible. General Ramazani and his fellow plotters might easily decide to close the Strait of Hormuz permanently, leaving them free to pursue their own military objectives without fear of Western intervention in the Gulf. A couple of tons of radioactive plutonium distributed among the warheads of SCUD or Silkworm missiles and detonated across the shipping channel off Ra's Musandam would do just that. Alternatively, clouds of plutonium dust released from Iran's Gulf islands of Abu Musa and Tunb could close the channel and leave the port of Bandar-é Abbas open.

The situation might even allow Iran's new rulers to practice some good old-fashioned blackmail, *threatening* to close the strait or to poison the Saudi oil fields unless their demands were met. Murdock had a realistic enough understanding of modern international politics to know that the chances of closing ranks against such threats were nil. Japan and much of Europe still depended on the Gulf for nearly all of their oil imports. Hell, even the United States, given its zigzag record in foreign policy over the past couple of years, might cave in and pay rather than risk having the Strait of Hormuz closed. Murdock was frankly amazed that the go-ahead had been given for Deadly Weapon.

Threading their way north past the civilian traffic, the SEALs stuck with the *Yuduki Maru*. The Iranian radio-silence order worked to their advantage, of course, as did their straggling. With luck, the SEALs would be able to sail the *Beluga* all the way into Bandar Abbas, allowing them to provide II MEF with an eyewitness report on the defenses and preparedness inside the port.

Jaybird Sterling had the helm again. The young SEAL trainee did indeed know how to handle a pleasure craft like the *Beluga,* and he'd been standing watch-and-watch at the wheel with Murdock since he'd volunteered to stay aboard. The other two SEAL volunteers were Razor Roselli and Professor Higgins. During Saturday's early morning hours, the former hostages had been bundled up in life jackets and transported two by two in one of the SEALs' CRRCs to a point well clear of the *Beluga,* then hoisted aboard a hovering Sea King sent out from the *Nassau* for the recovery. Colonel Aghasi had made the trip as well, along with eight of the VBSS team SEALs.

Murdock, Roselli, Higgins, and Sterling had remained aboard, ready to make a quick getaway over the side with their diving gear if their cover was too closely probed, but otherwise continuing to report on the Iranian squadron's position and disposition throughout the next thirty-six hours. Higgins had programmed *Beluga*'s on-board satellite communications gear to track a MILSTAR relay satellite, giving them secure and untraceable communications with both *Nassau* and the Pentagon.

Now Murdock emerged from below deck into the baking heat of the Gulf sun and walked back to the helm. There was a somewhat lonely emptiness to the sky; American helicopters had continued to dog the Iranian squadron day and night until an hour earlier, when the freighter had officially entered Iranian territorial waters.

Now the four SEALs were alone.

"Looks like we're getting pretty close," he told Jaybird.

"For sure, Skipper. Maybe we should get shined up and squared away for inspection, huh?"

"Shit, Jaybird," Roselli called from the top of the deckhouse. "You look just fine to me!"

"You both need haircuts," Murdock replied, and the others laughed. None of the SEALs looked very military at the moment. All of them had removed their black gear and wet suits and were wearing pieces of uniforms scrounged from the Iranian dead before they'd been put over the side Saturday morning. Jaybird had stripped to the waist; just since yesterday, his California-boy tan had darkened to the point where his skin was as swarthy as that of any Iranian. To aid the disguise, he kept his pale, sun-bleached blond hair covered by a black Navy watchcap. Roselli and Higgins both wore Iranian tunics that, unbuttoned and with the shirttails dangling, gave them the unkempt appearance of a pair of modern-day pirates . . . or a Pasdaran boarding party. Murdock had relieved Aghasi of his peaked officer's cap and tunic, complete with colonel's insignia, and aviator's sun glasses before packing the Iranian off aboard the helo. He hadn't had time to grow the colonel's bushy mustache as well, but to complete the deception he'd smeared his upper lip with a finger laden with camo paint. The disguise wouldn't fool anyone up close, of course, but through binoculars at a range of twenty meters or more, it ought to get by. The SEALs were banking on that peculiar aspect of human psychology that allowed people to see what they *expected* to see, rather than what was actually there.

Raising his own binoculars to his eyes, he carefully swept the horizon from west to east.

They were well into the northern portion of the Strait of Hormuz now. That wrinkled-looking mass of bold gray mountain rising to the north was Iran. Almost due west was the rocky, mountainous island of Qeshm, largest island in the Gulf, with its odd, cone-shaped rain reservoirs and impoverished-looking, ramshackle coastal villages. Through his binoculars, Murdock could pick out the anachronistic intrusion of radar dishes and blockhouses marking an Iranian Silkworm missile battery mounted on the erosion-streaked side of a barren hill. Camouflage tarps had been stretched between poles, shielding

SAM sites and vehicle parks from the blazing sun . . . and from the probing eyes of American satellites.

Dead ahead, some fifteen miles across the sun-dazzled water, the port of Bandar-é Abbas—known simply as Bandar to the locals—rose between sea and mountains in blocks and tiers of white stone. A beneficiary of the wars, both trade and military, of the 1980s, Bandar was a large and modern city with a population of just over 200,000. Though the typically squalid tent cities and slums of most Middle Eastern cities cluttered Bandar's fringes, Murdock could make out the gleaming facades of several modern buildings above the noisome tenement hovels of the low-rent districts. Every building seemed in need of paint, however, and the dhows, fishing boats, and motor craft lining the waterfront were uniformly battered, sunbaked, and coated with ancient layers of filth and grime.

Farther west, Bandar-é Abbas's airport buildings were visible as gray and white blurs shimmering in the desert heat. Murdock could just barely pick out the shapes of several military aircraft there—F-4 Phantoms and F-5E Tiger IIs, for the most part, sold to Iran before the revolution—as well as the larger bulk of an Iran Air 727.

Returning his attention to the city's waterfront, Murdock examined several port facilities. One fronting the downtown area was clearly a commercial port and ferry dock; others were marinas occupied by high-sterned, lateen-rigged dhows and fishing smacks. Most of the military facilities appeared to be northwest of the city, tucked in behind the lee of Qeshm Island and the hook of the headland on which the city was built.

And that, clearly, was where *Damavand* was taking the Japanese freighter. Through the binoculars, Murdock identified a small shipyard between Bandar-é Abbas and the port of Dogerdan to the west, with dry-dock facilities, the looming skeletons of hammerhead cranes, the squat cylinders of POL storage tanks, and the long, low tent-roofed shapes of warehouses and machine shops. Numerous yard and service craft lay alongside sun-bleached wharfs; larger ships, a destroyer and a pair of frigates, were tied up alongside a fueling pier.

Patrol boats and landing craft were everywhere, almost too numerous to count.

Shifting the aim of his binoculars again, he studied the stern of the *Yuduki Maru.* A large number of Iranian soldiers were visible on her upper deck, and the sounds of gunfire, single shots and full-auto, carried faintly across the open water. Many of the soldiers were firing off whole magazines into the sky, celebrating their victory over the Great Satan and his minions. It was unlikely that they'd been told anything about the politics of their mission, other than that it would be a blow against the hated Americans.

"Better get your celebrating done now, you sons of bitches," Murdock said softly. "You might not have the chance later."

"Hey, Skipper," Roselli called from his perch atop the deckhouse. "What do the rules of war say about you wearing a Pasdaran colonel's uniform?"

"Oh, not a whole lot, Chief. The usual hearts-and-violins stuff about piracy, hanging from the neck until dead, drawing and quartering . . ."

"Yar!" Roselli growled. "We be pirates!"

"Aye," Higgins added, clambering up out of the companionway. "Break out the skull and crossbones!"

"You guys're pirates, all right," Murdock replied, continuing to study the *Yuduki Maru* through his binoculars. It looked like a deck crew forward was casting off the tow from *Damavand,* though from this angle it was a little hard to be sure. No doubt they'd decided that it made better propaganda for the freighter to be taken into her berth under her own steam, even if she did have to limp along on one screw.

Higgins joined him on the well deck. "Skipper?"

"Yeah, Prof. What's up?"

"I'm not sure," the slightly built SEAL replied, "but I think it involves us." Higgins had been manning the yacht's communications shack almost continuously since they'd taken *Beluga,* not only transmitting intelligence, but also eavesdropping on the Iranians. The radio-silence orders had applied to all of the ships in the squadron, but there'd been plenty of traffic coming out of Bandar-é Abbas, and from other warships in the area.

"Okay, you know I don't have much Farsi," Higgins said. "Just Arabic. But I could follow enough to know that they've been trying to raise us for the past five minutes or so. If I had to take a guess, I'd say they started out by telling us where to go, then started telling us to heave to."

"Okay, Prof, thanks. It's nothing we weren't expecting."

"Stick with the radio silence then?"

"Absolutely. Damned thing's bust, right?"

"Can't hear a thing, Skipper."

"Good. Hang tight a sec." Pulling a notebook from his pocket, Murdock began writing quickly, filling three pages with his observations of the port approaches, the military aircraft on the runway, the ships and patrol boats in the harbor, the Silkworm and SAM batteries on Qeshm. Tearing off the pages at last, he handed them to Higgins. "You read all that?"

"Sure. No sweat."

"Transmit that ASAP, coded burst through MILSTAR. Repeat it until you get an acknowledgment."

"Aye, aye, Skipper."

"And keep your primary ready. This'll get hot damned quick."

"Yes, sir." Higgins took the papers and descended back into the cool darkness of *Beluga*'s below-deck spaces.

Murdock glanced up at Roselli. "You hear all that, Razor? We may have company soon."

Roselli patted the captured G-3 rifle. "Ready to rock and roll, Skipper."

Raising his binoculars again, Murdock swept the harbor. Motion on the water to one side of the freighter caught his attention. "Uh-oh," he said, focusing on the blurry white mustache of a high-speed wake. It looked like a speedboat was coming toward them bow-on, racing out from the naval facility. "Okay, you pirates. Just make sure your powder's dry and your cutlasses are within reach. That company's about to pay us a visit."

In minutes, the Iranian craft was close enough that Murdock could easily make out its details. During the Tanker War in the Gulf during the early 1980s, the Western press had consistently called these fast little attack craft "speedboats," implying that the grenade and rocket attacks on the oil tankers of various nations were being carried out by men in outboard-motor pleasure craft.

That sleek, low shape was no pleasure craft, Murdock knew. It was a long, low, dagger-lean "Boghammer Boat," one of some forty high-speed military patrol craft acquired by Iran from Sweden for naval operations in the Gulf. Though not originally armed, they could carry as many as ten or twelve commandoes, armed with machine guns, RPGs, and shoulder-fired rocket launchers. As he studied the group of three Iranians standing in the Boghammer's enclosed pilothouse, he could see at least two pairs of raised binoculars staring back at him.

He hoped none of those men knew Aghasi personally, for the camo paint on his upper lip didn't do much to change the differences in height, weight, or age between Murdock and the Iranian.

It only had to get them close enough.

"Keep her steady," Murdock told Sterling. The Boghammer cut past *Beluga*'s bow, then whipped past the starboard side, throwing up a choppy, froth-edged surge of dirty water as it slowed. Engine growling, the Iranian patrol boat slipped down *Beluga*'s starboard side, crossed astern, and began moving up the port side from aft. Murdock counted eight men aboard, two of them officers, all armed. An American-made M-60 machine gun had been raised on a makeshift mount in the well deck forward of the deckhouse. One of the soldiers nervously fingered the blunt-snouted tube of an RPG-7, a Russian-made weapon almost certainly captured in years past from the Iraqis. Most Iranian military hardware was still American-issue, weapons and gear left over from the days of the Shah.

One of the officers was standing on the Boghammer's afterdeck, a loudhailer in his hand. Raising it to his lips, he elicited a piercing yowl of feedback, then began calling to *Beluga*'s crew across the narrowing stretch of water.

"What's he saying, Skipper?" Jaybird asked.

"Haven't the faintest idea," Murdock replied. For answer, he raised an arm and waved the Boghammer closer.

At Murdock's command, Jaybird throttled back, bringing the yacht to a near-idle. The Iranian speedboat drifted closer, then closer still. One man stood on the bow, ready to leap across with a line. Another lineman stood aft, while the officer with the loudhailer took up a position amidships.

"Higgins? Roselli?" Murdock asked, not taking his eyes off the Iranians. "You both ready to go?"

"Sure are, Skipper," Higgins answered from the shadows in *Beluga*'s open companionway.

"Just say the word, Skipper," Roselli added. He was standing by the mainmast now, holding the G-3 in a casually relaxed and non-threatening pose. From the corner of his eye, Murdock could see Jaybird's H&K, tucked safely out of sight below *Beluga*'s port-side gunwale. His own H&K was lying on the deck at his feet.

"Roselli," he said, a stage whisper through smiling, clenched teeth. "You've got the MG forward. Stand ready. . . ."

"Az kodawm vawhed hastid?" the Iranian officer demanded, lowering the loudhailer. He sounded angry, and his dark eyes flashed as he waved it at Murdock. *"Kaf kardam!"*

Smiling, Murdock shook his head, then gestured for the officer to come on board. Glowering, the Iranian stepped onto the Boghammer's gunwale. . . .

"Now!" Murdock yelled, dropping to the deck, scooping up his H&K, and rolling back to his knees as he brought the weapon to his shoulder. By the mainmast, Roselli whipped the G-3 into firing position and triggered a short, full-auto burst that chopped into the Iranian behind the machine gun and punched him back against the Boghammer's pilothouse windscreen. Murdock sent three rounds slashing into the officer, who tried to complete his leap to the *Beluga*'s afterdeck, faltered, then tumbled into the water between the two boats. Sterling put the *Beluga*'s wheel hard over, sending the larger yacht smashing into the Boghammer's side with a grinding crash.

Murdock shifted targets smoothly, cutting down an Iranian soldier holding a G-3 rifle, then another whose weapon was still slung over his back. Higgins emerged from *Beluga*'s companionway, firing into the Boghammer's pilothouse, while Sterling, armed now, advanced to *Beluga*'s gunwale, firing down into the patrol boat's after well deck.

Murdock estimated that five seconds passed between the first shot and the last. He and Roselli scrambled aboard the Boghammer to bring it under control, checking the bodies sprawled from bow to transom for signs of life. Two badly wounded and unconscious men were dispatched with single shots through their heads. The SEALs were in no position to tend to prisoners.

"Can you run it, Chief?" Murdock asked Roselli as he studied the simple controls in the pilothouse.

"Aw, shit, Lieutenant. I could run this blindfolded. Throttle, gearshift, and wheel . . . that's all there fuckin' is to it!"

"Good man. I want you to go over this boat with a magnifying glass, okay? Find and fix anything we broke in that firefight."

"Right, Skipper."

Returning to the afterdeck, Murdock crossed back to the *Beluga*, where Sterling was finishing tying off a stern line, securing the Boghammer to the yacht. "Jaybird!"

"Yeah, Skipper?"

Murdock put one hand on Sterling's sweat-slick shoulder, and with the other pointed west across the water toward the rugged coast of Qeshm. "Looks to me like we might have a beach over there at the foot of those hills. Think this tub has the oomph to haul herself and the speedboat into the shallows?"

"Sure thing, Skipper."

"Do it. If she's too sluggish, Roselli can help from the Boghammer. Higgins!"

"Yessir!"

"You'n me just got assigned the grunt detail. Let's start hauling our gear over to the Boghammer."

"Aye, aye, Skipper. You get in the 'Hammer and I'll start passing to you, okay?"

"Affirmative."

In the blazing, late-afternoon heat, the two men began

moving all of the SEAL weapons and equipment to the smaller boat.

"Looks to me like you've got this thing pretty well thought out," Higgins said, passing a SEAL rebreather across *Beluga*'s rail to Murdock.

"Nah," Murdock replied, taking the UBA and stowing it in the Boghammer's aft well deck. "I'm making it all up as we go along."

"Yeah," Higgins said. "I was afraid you were gonna say that."

Murdock decided to take a chance. "So? How do I stack up so far against Lieutenant Cotter?"

Higgins reached for a bundle of swim fins, masks, and weight belts. "Well, I'll tell you, sir. The L-T'd have had this thing scoped out a week in advance, everything planned down to the last detail. He wasn't one to make it up on the fly, know what I mean?"

"Yup." Murdock suppressed a flash of irritation. He *had* asked for the comparison. . . .

"But I'll tell you what," Higgins continued. "Whatever plan he'd have come up with, I guarantee you it wouldn't've been this much *fun*!"

As they continued loading their gear aboard the Boghammer, Murdock wasn't sure whether he'd just been complimented or not.

25

Boghammer patrol boat
Northeastern coast of Qeshm

"Damn," Sterling said as he leaped off the *Beluga* and onto the Boghammer's after well deck. "I really hate trading this sweet beauty for a stinkpot, skipper!"

"I like the bed-sheet navy too, Jaybird," Murdock replied, casting off the stern line. *Beluga* rested where she'd been run aground several hours earlier, in a shallow cove several miles from the village of Qeshm at the eastern tip of the island. "But you've gotta admit, she's one of a kind, while this Boghammer is going to be one among forty. And right now, we can't afford to stand out in the crowd!"

"Besides," Higgins said, grinning, "it's kind of nice to be in something that'll give us a bit of speed!"

"Roger that," Murdock said, casting a wary eye toward the darkening sky. An Iranian helicopter droned low over the water several miles to the south, but didn't appear interested in Qeshm. So far they'd been damned lucky. The Boghammer must have been sent out to investigate when the *Beluga* failed to respond to instructions over the radio; sooner or later, someone ashore was going to realize that the Boghammer had never reported back, and that the *Beluga* had failed to dock in Bandar-é Abbas, or wherever they'd been ordered to go. The military bureaucracy—*any* military bureaucracy—was slow and cumbersome enough that it would have trouble tracking down a covert team as small as four SEALs in one small boat, and the Iranian bureaucracy was considerably more disorganized than most. Still, Iranian aircraft were bound to spot the yacht sooner or later, and any determined search by patrol boats or helos would discover her resting place on Qeshm Island almost at once.

And if they figured out which Boghammer boat was missing . . .

Jaybird and Roselli had taken a step to further confuse the Iranians. The Boghammer had a hull number painted on both sides of her bow. It *looked* like the number 10, with a slanted "1" followed by a small "0," but Professor Higgins knew the Iranian numerals well enough to translate the number as 15, and he knew that, unlike Iranian script, their numerals were read left to right. He and Roselli took brushes and black and white paint found in a storage locker aboard *Beluga*, mixed up a gray that closely approximated the gray color scheme of the Boghammer, and, standing in waist-deep water, had carefully painted out each "0" on her hull. They'd then replaced the numeral with another black "1," transforming the Boghammer from number 15 to number 11.

The likeliest action by the Iranian port authorities once Boghammer 15 failed to report in, Murdock was guessing, would be to send out patrols looking for the missing craft. With luck, no one would notice that there were now *two* Boghammer 11s, especially at night and within the bustle and confusion of a major naval shipyard facility.

"Okay, Razor," Murdock called. "Let's get away from the scene of the crime. I don't want you guys to have to paint another fake number on our sides."

"You got that right, Skipper," Roselli called back as he eased the throttle forward, eliciting a deeper growl from the engine. "Scraping and painting's for the *real* Navy. I joined the SEALs so I wouldn't have to do that shit!"

Smoke fumed from the Boghammer's engine vents as her screw churned the water aft to white froth. Veering sharply away from the beach, they began moving into deeper water.

Murdock and Higgins turned to the task of testing out the connections on their HST-4 sat comm and the KY-57 encryption set, the "C-2" communications element that would let them stay in touch with both II MEF and Washington. Before abandoning the *Beluga,* Higgins had transmitted a final set of intelligence data over the yacht's small sat-comm unit, including Murdock's impressions of the port facilities as seen through binoculars from Qeshm. The island provided an excellent OP, just eleven miles south of the port, but to get the detailed intelligence Deadly Weapon would need, the SEALs would have to get a lot closer than that. The transmission had been insurance against the possibility that the four SEALs would be killed or captured while trying to penetrate the Iranian port.

As darkness fell across the Gulf, the lights of Bandar-é Abbas gleamed like brilliant pearls on a necklace stretched across the northern horizon. Once clear of the beach, Roselli opened up the Boghammer's throttle, the knife-pointed prow came up out of the water above a boiling white streak of foam, and they jolted into the passage between Qeshm and the mainland at twenty-eight knots.

2130 hours (Zulu +3)
U.S.S. *Austin*
In the approaches to the Strait of Hormuz

The *Austin,* LPD 4, was a bulky, hybrid-looking vessel, half transport, half carrier, known officially as an Amphibious Transport, Dock. With a crew of four hundred and berthing facilities for nearly a thousand Marines, she was part of II MEF's assault transport contingent—the backbone of the Marine Expeditionary Force—which included the *Nassau* and the helicopter carrier *Iwo Jima.*

All together, II MEF comprised a Marine air-ground task force, or MAGTF, comprised of fifty ships and over 52,000 Navy and Marine personnel, the largest and most powerful of all Marine task forces. Under the overall command of FMFLANT—Fleet Marine Force Atlantic—II MEF drew its forces from the 2nd Marine Division, the 2nd Marine Aircraft Wing, and the 4th and 6th Marine Expeditionary Brigades. The

force, which had been on maneuvers in the Med during the
opening scenes of the *Yuduki Maru* drama, had transited the
Suez Canal and passed south through the Red Sea, emerging in
the Gulf of Aden south of the Arabian Peninsula. After the
abortive attempt to reach the *Yuduki Maru* at sea, the task force
had been routed into the Gulf of Oman, closely following the
Iranian squadron, dogging their formation with helicopters,
AV-8 Harriers, and F/A-18 Hornets. They were massed now in
international waters just outside the Strait of Hormuz, ready to
strike with the entire, staggering might of a reinforced Marine
division.

And the very tip of that titanic Army-Navy spearpoint was
now on *Austin*'s well deck, preparing to get under way.

"Captain Coburn?"

Phillip Coburn straightened up from the bundle of equipment
he'd been checking. "Here!"

A commander in Navy khakis approached him across the
crowded, metal grating of the deck. "Commander DiAmato,
sir," the officer said, saluting. "They said to pass this on to
you."

DiAmato handed him a sheaf of papers. Awkward in his
black gear, wet suit, and full rebreather rig, Coburn accepted it
and started reading. It was an intelligence update, the latest
condensation of data from satellites, reconnaissance aircraft . . .
and from the SEALs already in the approaches to Bandar-é
Abbas.

Metal clanged and gonged in the cavernous space around
him and echoed with shouts and the whine of overhead hoists.
Austin's well deck was completely enclosed, a vast, echoing
cave of gray-painted metal, overhead pipes, and a central well
that could be flooded in order to facilitate the launch of various
vehicles and small craft. Normally, this was where Marine
LCMs or the odd-looking, tracked LVTs were loaded before
letting them swim out through the huge doors set into the
transport's stern. This time, however, the well deck was
occupied by several craft that made even the boxy LVTs look
ordinary.

Three were Mark VIII SDVs. "SDV" stood for Swimmer

Delivery Vehicle, but SEALs referred to the contraption as a "bus." Each was twenty-one feet long, with a beam and draft of just over four feet, and looked like a blunt, overfed torpedo. Hatches in the side gave access to the interior; two SDV crewmen, a pilot and a navigator, manned a cramped compartment forward, while four more SEALs could snuggle in aft, squeezed in side by side.

The three SDVs were being loaded now; their twelve passengers were the ten men of SEAL Seven's Third Platoon who'd returned early that morning from the *Beluga* mission plus EM2 Wilson and Captain Coburn.

Coburn finished reading the message printout, then handed it back to DiAmato. "Looks like nothing much new," he said. "At least we know where they've stashed the damned target."

"I'd just like to know how a captain rates getting to go out on a joyride," another voice boomed from behind.

Turning, Coburn saw the craggy features of Rear Admiral Robert Mitchell, the commander of the Navy component of the MEF.

"Excuse me, Admiral," Coburn said, saluting. "I didn't know you were aboard the *Austin*."

"I just heloed over from the *Nassau*." Mitchell returned the salute, then extended a hand. Coburn took it. He'd known Bob Mitchell all the way back in Annapolis; the fact that Mitchell was a rear admiral now while Coburn was still a captain was proof of the adage that special forces assignments slowed a man's Navy career track.

"Heard you were about to go and wanted to see you off," Mitchell continued. Planting fists on hips, he stared at the nearest SDV, suspended above the flooded well deck from an overhead hoist. "You know, I still think it's nuts for a captain to go joyriding like this. How'd you pull that off?"

"Ah, I told Admiral Winston I'd hold my breath until I turned blue," Coburn replied easily. "Besides, I'm still dive-rated. Just because I've got four stripes doesn't mean I'm senile. You need flag rank for that."

Mitchell laughed. "Sounds like even CO-MIDEASTFOR

has trouble managing SEALs. Housebreaking you guys must be a bitch."

"Hey, if you want housebroken, send in the Marines. They can break *anything* if they put their minds to it."

"As a matter of fact, we're planning on doing just that little thing." Mitchell extended his hand again. "Good luck, Phil."

"Thanks, Admiral. See you in Bandar!"

Minutes later, Coburn was tucked into the passenger compartment of SDV #1. He was rigged out in the SEALs' new UBA Mark XV gear, an advanced underwater life-support system that used a computer to regulate the rebreather's gas mix. With the Mark XV, a SEAL could dive deeper and stay deep longer than he could with the old Drager LAR V system; he wore a full-face mask that allowed him to communicate by voice, either through an intercom jack or by radio, though the range of radio communications was sharply limited within the radio-wave-absorbing medium of the sea.

Seated next to Master Chief MacKenzie, and just ahead of HM2 Ellsworth and HT1 Garcia, Coburn plugged his breathing system into the boat's air supply, a measure that would extend the range of his own rebreather gear, then waited as water flooded the cramped compartment. It was dark, and the confines were downright claustrophobic. Coburn chuckled to himself as he thought of the ongoing budgetary war that continued to keep the Navy divided into separate, rival camps. Many years earlier, the submariners, seeking to expand their control over a portion of the Navy's appropriations, had managed to push through a rule with Congress that established that *only* they could build and operate "dry" submarines, underwater craft that provided a shirtsleeve environment for their operators. As a result, arms of the service that could use small, covert entry or reconnaissance craft—arms like the SEALs and the Marines—had to rely on "wet" submarines like the Mark VIII.

For that reason, SDV operations were sharply limited in range. The Mark VIII could manage about six knots on its electric batteries and had an endurance of six hours, so the SDVs had to be piggybacked to within eighteen nautical miles of the target—three hours in, three hours back—with the further disadvantage that the SEALs aboard were going to be tired long before they even got there. That narrow-minded bean-counting was a typical example of the bureaucratic idiocy that plagued those military circles high enough in the Washington hierarchy to be contaminated by the politics of that town.

Usually in SEAL SDV missions, ferry duty fell to one of the few dry submarines equipped to carry SDVs in special hangars on their decks. Unfortunately, none of the subs so equipped had been available on such short notice, which meant that *Austin* had been tasked with carrying the SEALs in to a drop-off point eighteen miles south of Bandar-é Abbas. *Austin*'s captain, Coburn thought, as well as the skippers of her escorting warships, must be sweating bullets about now, wondering if the Iranians were about to launch a preemptive strike against the task force. The Iranians *had* to figure that the American MEF was here for more than a show of force, that they weren't going to just stand by and watch while the Iranians rifled the *Yuduki Maru* of her cargo.

What was their response going to be? There was no way of telling. All the SEALs could do was plan it the best they could, then Charlie Mike.

A few yards away, MacKenzie stood on the steel deck grating and watched Coburn talking with the admiral. He'd learned that Coburn was joining the platoon only a few hours earlier, when the captain had met the team in a briefing room and explained the nature of the mission.

MacKenzie didn't like this twist, not one bit. Captain Coburn was a capable officer, but damn it, the guy was getting a bit old for this sort of thing. Coburn was fifty years old and had served in Nam. Three hours in a wet suit, breathing reprocessed air, was incredibly draining, especially for an old guy.

The chief protested, of course, and he'd been slapped down. Coburn had grinned to rob the rebuke of its sting and pointed out that if he, Coburn, was over the hill, Master Chief MacKenzie couldn't be far behind.

MacKenzie grimaced at the thought. He was forty-five . . .

but at least he'd been active in the Teams' diving proficiency drills and PT over the years. When was the last time the Old Man had swum two miles, with fins, in seventy minutes? Or run fourteen miles in 110?

He decided he would stick close to Coburn throughout this mission . . . just in case.

2345 hours (Zulu +3)
Captured Boghammer patrol craft
Off Bandar-é Abbas

With her powerful engine barely ticking over, the Boghammer growled past the huge, gray bulks of a dozen Iranian military craft, most yard tenders and oilers, but a few heavily armed patrol boats as well. The sailors on the decks of those craft watched the sleek craft incuriously if at all; Boghammers were common enough in all parts of the harbor that it should not excite curiosity.

So far, the Iranian shipyard and naval facilities appeared quiet. No alarm had sounded, no heavily armed patrol boats were dashing about. Their most serious test had come as they'd approached a massive boom guarding the hundred-yard-wide opening to the shipyard's inner harbor. Half expecting to be turned aside without the necessary password or code, they'd motored slowly toward the boom, only to see the central section slide open for them, allowing them to pass inside. Guard towers rose on either side of the opening; the boom floated on the water's surface but was clearly the support for a heavy antisubmarine net. Guards patrolled everywhere, but none paid more attention to the Boghammer than a casual wave or salute.

Inside the harbor, most activity seemed lethargic. Except for a few armed guards in evidence ashore, the only men visible were lounging and talking on the decks of their ships. Most of the base was dark, save for patches of illumination cast by street lights along the waterfront.

The single area of intense activity appeared to be centered on the forward deck of the freighter *Yuduki Maru,* which had been drawn up, port side to, at a long pier close by the shipyard's dry-dock area and launching way. Tarpaulins had been stretched across the forward deck in an obvious attempt to block out surveillance by American spy satellites, and a construction crew could be seen by the flaring, actinic light of cutting torches hissing on the forward deck.

"Could be they're running into some computer trouble," Murdock said. All four of the SEALs were inside the Boghammer's pilothouse, peering out through the salt-encrusted windscreen at the activity on the huge freighter. "Without the right password, they're not going to get through the cargo hatches."

"So their only option is cutting their way through solid steel," Roselli said, standing at the boat's wheel. "That should take 'em a while, even with dockyard facilities."

"All night at least," Higgins said.

"That was the idea," Murdock said.

"What the hell is the new password, anyway?" Roselli wanted to know.

Murdock grinned. "'Jaybird.' It was the only thing I could think of at the time."

"Ha! Well, they sure won't hit on that by trial and error. It must be giving them fits!"

"I just hope they don't think the Japanese crewmen are giving them the wrong information," Sterling said. "Things could go a bit hard on them."

"Shit, Jaybird, you want we should go in and give them the keys to the stuff?" Roselli asked.

"I didn't say that."

"Anyway, they know we were up there on the bridge long enough to change the codes. They're probably just mad as hell they didn't get one of us to tell them what it was!"

Murdock leaned over, studying the armed men arrayed along *Yuduki Maru*'s side. More soldiers were on the pier alongside, where workers were preparing to sway several bulky propane tanks up to the ship's deck in a cargo net. "What would you guys say . . . twelve armed guards on board?"

"About that," Roselli agreed. "Twelve in sight anyway. And another fifteen or twenty on the dock. Ramazani probably has every Pasdaran soldier he feels he can trust in this burg sitting on top of his prize."

"And they're positioning that hammerhead crane over there to offload the stuff," Sterling added. "If we're gonna do something, we'd better do it damned fast."

Higgins glanced at his watch. "Patience, son. The SDVs ought to be here in another hour."

"If they stuck to sched," Roselli added. "Hey, Sterling?"

"Yeah?"

"How *did* you get the name Jaybird?"

The SEAL trainee groaned and the other SEALs laughed. With her engine set just one notch above idle, the Boghammer cruised slowly and ever deeper into the Iranian harbor.

26

Monday, 30 May

Freighter *Yuduki Maru*
Bandar-é Abbas shipyard

Tetsuo Kurebayashi had been unable to sleep. Despite the years of self-discipline and self-denial, despite the rigors of his Ohtori commando training, the excitement, the overwhelming sense of fulfillment of a mission accomplished blended with the heady anticipation of another mission about to begin, left him wide awake.

Besides, it was noisy within the steel confines of the hijacked freighter. A small army had come aboard as soon as they'd been safely tied up to the dock, and the Iranian construction personnel were now hard at work, attempting to cut through the reinforced steel containment walls that surrounded *Yuduki Maru*'s precious cargo.

Dressing, he'd gone up to the vessel's bridge. Iranian soldiers had finished removing the machine guns ruined by the American commandos but had not replaced them. Instead, grim-looking Iranian Pasdaran stood guard with automatic weapons. The compartment still showed the signs of battle— the soundproofing tiles overhead shredded by hundreds of bullet holes, the teletype printers and several consoles smoke-stained and pocked by stray rounds, most of the glass in the large, slanted bridge windows missing. A brown stain on the tile deck marked where an Iranian soldier had died.

Glancing around once, Kurebayashi stepped through the door and onto the open starboard wing of the bridge.

Isamu Takeda was already there, leaning against the railing.

"A, Isamusama," Kurebayashi said, startled. *"Sumimasen!"*

"Please, Tetsuosan," the Ohtori leader replied, also speaking Japanese to maintain a sense of privacy from the nearby Iranian troops. "Join me."

"Hai, Isamusama!" Kurebayashi gave the requisite, respectful bow, raising his eyes no higher than the collar of Takeda's military-style blouse. "You honor me."

"We have come a long way from the streets of Sasebo, *neh*?"

Clearly, Takeda was in a reflective mood. Kurebayashi grunted an assent, joining his leader against the wing railing. It had been a long time, almost fifteen years, since they'd met one another in the rock-throwing riots staged to protest the American military presence in the home islands. That had been at the very beginning, when Ohtori was first being born from the fallen ideals and promise of the Japanese Red Army.

It had taken that long to find a weapon suitable for bringing the American imperialists to their knees.

"The general tells me it will take a little time yet to reach our goal," Takeda said. He nodded toward the activity on *Yuduki Maru*'s deck. The flare of cutting torches cast monstrous, flickering shadows across the steel.

"After waiting this long," Kurebayashi said, "I suppose we can wait a few hours more. The arrangements are made for our share?"

"Yes. It will be flown to Bangkok tomorrow night, then placed aboard a ship to be smuggled into Yokohama." He smiled easily. "It will be most poetic, don't you think? The Western devils brought down by the demon they first unleashed upon our people seven sevens of years ago."

"Hai, Isamusama! It is justice, and partial payment as well."

"I know how you feel about working with the Iranians, Tetsuosan," Takeda went on. "But it is proper *naniwabushi, neh*?"

In Japan, the practice called *naniwabushi,* meaning to get on such close personal terms with someone that he was obligated to generosity, was basic to any good businessman's repertoire. Terrorism too was a business, sometimes even a profitable one, certainly one to be pursued with the dedication and attention to detail of any corporate endeavor. By planning the capture of the *Yuduki Maru,* by penetrating the security measures put in place by the freighter's owners and actually executing the takeover, Ohtori had placed a tremendous obligation upon Ramazani and the other plotters within Iran's military. As payment, Ramazani had promised Ohtori two hundred kilos of plutonium—one tenth of the cargo locked away in the freighter's hold. This mission, Operation Yoake, had yet one final act to unfold, one that would find consummation at Yokosuka some three months hence.

Yokosuka, just twenty-eight miles south across Tokyo Bay from the Japanese capital, once one of Imperial Japan's first naval bases, had for five decades been the largest U.S. Navy shore facility in the Far East, covering five hundred acres and including the headquarters for COMFLEACT, the Commander of Fleet Activities, which oversaw the logistics and maintenance for all U.S. Navy forces in the western Pacific. Just a few kilos of highly radioactive plutonium, dispersed by a remotely detonated car bomb, would be more than enough to render the entire area uninhabitable for the next several centuries. And that would be only the beginning. Two hundred kilos would provide blast-scattered death enough for *many* car bombs, many places around the world. The blast that had shaken the World Trade Center in New York City over a year ago would be utterly forgotten, a mere shadow of the horror, blood, and lingering death that was to follow.

It would be . . . what was the American term? Payback. Yes, it would be payback indeed for the horrors of Hiroshima and Nagasaki. To drive that particular point home, the attack was planned for the sixth of August, some sixty-eight days hence.

Kurebayashi looked away from the dazzle of the torches and work lights, staring instead at the black water slowly rising and falling along *Yuduki Maru*'s starboard side. Turning and leaning over the railing to peer into the darkness aft, he saw one of the sleek Iranian patrol boats motor slowly past the freighter's stern, at the very edge of the illumination spread by the work lights ashore.

All was quiet, but Kurebayashi was ill at ease. He'd been thinking a lot lately of the black-garbed commandos who'd risen from the sea and so nearly overturned Yoake. He was fairly sure that they'd been American SEALs—though both the U.S. Marines and the Army Special Forces used UBA equipment when necessary. The SEALs had a well-deserved reputation throughout the world's freedom-fighter underground as ruthless, efficient, and implacably deadly foes.

He didn't believe for a moment that the Americans were going to let Ohtori and the Iranians walk away with two tons of plutonium. If they were going to try again to stop the theft, it would have to be now, before *Yuduki Maru*'s steel-lined vaults were breached, before the plutonium could be scattered to waiting terrorist cells around the world.

Kurebayashi felt a small chill down his spine at the thought.

"If you agree, I will inspect our sentries," he told Takeda.

"Of course, Tetsuosan."

He bowed again, then left the Ohtori leader on the bridge wing. According to the schedule, Hotsumi and Masahiko were on duty on the fantail, while Seito stood guard over *Yuduki Maru*'s crew, locked away now in the aft crew's quarters. Throughout the voyage north to Bandar-é Abbas, the Ohtori gunmen had maintained their own watch independently of the Iranians. These Pasdaran were too lax, too ill-disciplined to maintain a proper military watch.

And there was a very great deal at stake.

0040 hours (Zulu +3)
Bandar-é Abbas shipyard

Roselli had guided the Boghammer across the harbor, approaching at last a deserted pier in a remote and poorly lit part of the waterfront. There, they'd shut down the engine and tied the patrol boat to a ramshackle bollard. One by one then, with the others standing watch, they'd donned their black gear and UBAs, tested them, and checked once more their weapons and equipment. At 0015 hours precisely, they'd rolled over the side of the Boghammer, moving stealthily in the shadows beneath the rickety pier, donned fins and face masks, and slipped beneath the ink-black surface of the water with scarcely a ripple to mark their passing.

It was a two-hundred-meter swim from the pier where they'd left the Boghammer to the dockside construction area where *Yuduki Maru* had been moored. They navigated by compass and by counting the strokes of their swim fins.

Halfway across, Murdock could hear sounds transmitted through the water from the target, the clank of steel on steel, the thump of something heavy being dropped. Sound propagates through water much more efficiently than it does in air, and far faster. It felt as though they must be nearly on top of their target.

They continued swimming. As the noises grew louder, Murdock cautiously moved to the surface until the upper half of his head broke the water, rising just enough to give him a frog's-eye view of the target. *Yuduki Maru*'s stern rose like a black wall against the glare of lights on the dock side. The dazzling flare of a cutting torch shone like a brilliant star.

Submerging again, Murdock had waited until the other three SEALs moved close enough that he could signal by touch. They were dead on course, and only about thirty meters short of their target.

Moments later, they'd swum up against the slime-slick bottom of the *Yuduki Maru,* where she rode at her moorings in twenty-one feet of water. Reaching into a pocket of his loadout vest, Murdock extracted a small metallic case the size of a pack of cigarettes, nudged the transmit switch with his gloved thumb, then positioned the device against the freighter's hull.

The homer was part of the specialized VBSS loadout, originally brought along against the possibility that they would need to mark the *Beluga* for a second boarding attempt. He heard nothing when he turned it on, of course; the high-frequency chirps emitted by the device were well above the human auditory range.

But someone equipped with the right equipment would be

able to pick up the signals, and home on them. Murdock and the other SEALs allowed themselves to sink to the muck of the ill-defined harbor bottom, and waited.

SEALs were very, very good at waiting.

0052 hours (Zulu +3)
SDV #1
Outside the Bandar-é Abbas shipyard

With a dwindling whine of its electric motor, the lead Mark VIII SDV settled gently to the muddy bottom, closely followed by the other two. Moving carefully in the cramped darkness, MacKenzie switched on his own rebreather, then disconnected the life-support line that had been feeding him off the bus's bottled air.

The long three-hour run north from the drop-off point had been routine. There'd been a few tense moments as they cruised past the island of Larak, a few miles east of Qeshm. The SDV's pilot had reported over the plug-in intercom that sonar had detected a rotary-wing aircraft hovering overhead, and moments later, they'd heard the telltale throb of approaching propellers. An Iranian patrol boat was passing overhead.

There was no telling what the helicopter had seen—or even if it had seen anything at all in the darkness. All three SDVs had powered down until they were only barely making way, traveling in near-perfect silence; the patrol boat had passed close overhead, circled a time or two, then headed off toward the west.

With sonar reporting the area clear again, the three SEAL minisubs had continued on their way. The Mark VIII featured a sophisticated Doppler Navigation System, or DNS, that allowed pinpoint navigation even in waters as foul and choked with mud as those of the Gulf. It also mounted an OAS, or Obstacle-Avoidance Sonar subsystem, allowing the subs to keep track of one another and to avoid obstacles—sunken hulks, coral heads, or the structural pylons of Gulf drilling rigs—even when the water was almost completely opaque.

At 0041 hours, the SDV's pilot had alerted the passengers over the intercom: A high-frequency sonar signal had been picked up on the predicted bearing. MacKenzie had allowed himself to relax a little at the news. Murdock and the others were okay. They'd penetrated the harbor, located the *Yuduki Maru,* and planted the sonar homer.

Now it was up to the rest of Third Platoon.

MacKenzie dragged the passenger compartment hatch back, then carefully extricated himself from the grounded bus. He had to operate almost entirely by feel; it was past midnight, and even at high noon, the visibility in the silty waters of the Gulf was never more than a few feet. A shimmering glow suffused from the surface overhead, creating a kind of ceiling to the watery world. There were floodlights up there, MacKenzie decided, illuminating the surface of the water at the harbor entrance. By that glow he could just make out the vague shadow of a net hanging vertically in the water above him.

The luminous dial of his depth gauge showed a depth of forty feet, well within the safe working range for Mark XV UBA gear. Carefully, he moved aft along the side of the SDV and opened the hatch to the cargo compartment. Other divers appeared in the water around him. Together, they broke out a small sled, a raft stretched across two small pontoons, to which their equipment and heavy weapons had been lashed. It took a moment to valve air from the sled's ballast tanks until it assumed neutral buoyancy. Then Holt and Frazier assumed positions to either side of it and began guiding it with gentle, flippered kicks toward the net. The other SEALs followed.

MacKenzie marked the net with two red-glowing chemical lights, their glow too dim to reach the surface but bright enough here to let the SEALs see what they were doing. Brown, Kosciuszko, and Fernandez produced cable cutters, and together they went to work on the submarine net.

In moments, they'd cut a six-foot gap through the net, marking the opening with the chemical lights. Leaving the three SDVs parked by the net, the twelve SEALs one by one slipped through the opening and into the inner harbor.

MacKenzie checked the luminous dial of his watch. It was 0058 hours. They were behind sched and would have to hurry. He wondered how Coburn was holding up, but when he caught sight of the Old Man sliding through the opening in the net, he looked okay. MacKenzie assigning himself as the captain's dive buddy, touched Coburn in query and received a jaunty OK hand signal in reply.

So far, so good.

Kosciuszko was holding a black device the size of a paperback book before him as he swam, studying the LED readout on a tiny screen. Sensitive to the frequencies used by Murdock's homer, the hand-held sonar would guide the SEALs to their target.

With firm, thrusting kicks that felt good after three hours of immobility in the SDV, MacKenzie and the others began swimming through the jet-black murk.

He thought he could already hear the water-transmitted clangs and bumps of construction work somewhere ahead.

0112 hours (Zulu +3)
Beneath the freighter *Yuduki Maru*
Bandar-é Abbas shipyard

In Vietnam SEALs had learned the art of patience, deliberately assuming uncomfortable positions in order to stay awake and alert for hour after dragging hour while waiting at the side of a jungle trail for the appearance of an enemy column.

Such extreme measures weren't necessary here, waiting in the black murk beneath the *Yuduki Maru,* though each of the four men was alert to the signs of drowsiness in himself and in the others. Drowsiness here, twenty feet beneath the surface, could be a symptom of CO_2 poisoning, due to malfunction, chemical exhaustion in their Drager LAR V rebreather rigs, or simply from working too hard.

Each move they made was slow and deliberate; the bottom, obscured in drifting silt, was a tangled, potential deathtrap of concrete blocks, discarded truck tires, broken glass, empty packing crates, and slime-covered railroad ties, jumbled together in a kind of chaotic obstacle course. They'd taken up a bottom watch position, the four of them within touching distance, resting back-to-back so that they could see in all directions. There was little to see. They were underneath the wooden pier, close to one of the massive, algae-shaggy pilings that descended from the dim glow at the surface into the tarry muck of the bottom, and visibility was effectively zero.

In fact, while swaddled in his wet suit and dive gear, the only sense Murdock still had was hearing, and he was focusing all of his attention on the sounds echoing through the black water around him. The heavy-equipment noises from the *Yuduki Maru*'s deck had ceased, but loud thumps and bumps continued to transmit themselves through the water at irregular intervals, and occasionally he could hear the creak and pop of wood shifting as men moved on the pier directly above his head.

And then he heard another sound . . . one that made him reach back and urgently tap the other SEALs. It was a metallic, tinkling noise, a *bubbling* that came in short bursts of noise, followed by silence.

The SEALs' rebreathers were silent, giving off no air bubbles. What they were hearing was almost certainly a SCUBA rig . . . no, two rigs, judging from the one-two, pause, one-two rhythm of the noise.

Iranian divers . . . and they were coming toward the SEALs.

0115 hours (Zulu +3)
Inside the Bandar-é Abbas shipyard harbor

Coburn didn't realize that he was in trouble until the thought struck him, with all of the impact of religious revelation, that he'd somehow forgotten what the mission was.

He'd been swimming steadily ahead through the silt-laden water, checking his wrist compass occasionally to maintain the assigned heading of three-two-zero degrees, but mostly relying on the dimly sensed shadows of the other SEALs around him. He was working harder than he'd expected. His muscles were still up to the task the SEALs had set for themselves, but Coburn found he was having to fight for air as he swam harder and harder, trying to keep up. The effort was much like that of Hell Week, a demanding test of stamina and willpower as the recruit's reserves were drained completely, then challenged by yet another seemingly impossible task.

He was thinking about Hell Week when he realized that he'd

lost sight of the other divers. That in itself was not surprising, the silt in the water had been growing steadily thicker as the team moved deeper into the harbor, until the water was so murky that his dive buddy could have been six feet away and remained invisible. The shock came when he stopped to think about what to do next and realized that he didn't know why he was here. A training mission? Yes, that must be it . . . though he had the nagging feeling that this operation was far more important then the usual SEAL qualification dive.

He shook his head, trying to clear it. How could he forget what he was doing in the middle of an exercise? There was a reason for that, but he couldn't remember what it was.

His head hurt, the pain throbbing with his accelerated heartbeat, and he was having trouble clearing his ears. The full mask squeezed uncomfortably against the borders of his face. His thinking felt . . . muddy, somehow.

And God! He was feeling so tired, so *sleepy*. . . .

27

0115 hours (Zulu +3)
Beneath the freighter *Yuduki Maru*
Bandar-é Abbas shipyard

Murdock strained to catch the tinkling gurgle of the enemy's
SCUBA rigs. Had the SEALs been discovered already? There
was no way to tell. Possibly the Iranians had picked up the
telltale pings of the sonar homer, though the high-frequency
device had been designed to avoid the usual sound channels
used by conventional sonar ears. More likely, it was a routine
patrol, checking the *Yuduki Maru*'s bottom for mines or
listening devices, or sweeping the area for any signs of enemy
frogman activity. The bad guys had to be a bit nervous after
that first attempt to take the freighter back by seaborne assault.

Silently, Murdock spoke to the others with touch and
shadow-shrouded gesture: *Roselli and Higgins, go* that *way . . .
Jaybird, come with me.* Splitting into two teams of two, the
SEALs circled left and right. It was always difficult to tell the
source of underwater sounds, but the SCUBA bubble noise was
sharp enough that the SEALs could localize it to the general
direction of the shore. Most likely, the enemy divers had gone
in near *Yuduki Maru*'s bow and were approaching now along
her bottom. Murdock drew his Mark II Navy knife and sensed
Jaybird doing the same.

The sounds were closer now and sharper. *That* way. Moving
out from under the pier, Murdock scraped along inches beneath

the steel ceiling of the freighter's keel, trying to localize what he was now certain were the noises from two SCUBA regulators. They needed to be careful in their identification, since it was quite possible that the two SEAL teams could blunder into one another by mistake. Shadows moved a few feet in front of him, materializing out of the drifting silt. . . .

Yes! Those were no SEALs, not with dark gray wet suits and the bulky, steel cylinders of air tanks strapped to their backs. Evidently, they were checking *Yuduki Maru*'s bottom, for one swam close to the hull, dragging his hand across the surface, while the other hung a few feet back. Both carried bangsticks, meter-long rods tipped with shotgun shells, weapons designed to kill sharks but equally effective against men.

Murdock touched Jaybird to make sure he saw, then lunged forward with three hard kicks to his fins. Exploding out of the muck beneath the ship, he collided with the lead Iranian frogman, left hand blocking the other's bangstick hand, knife hand spearing for the throat. Jaybird hit the second diver an instant later, rolling him over and carrying him toward the bottom.

Bubbles angrily hissed and gurgled in the water. Murdock's knife slashed the rubber of the Iranian's hood, then penetrated to the flesh below. Blood, ink-black in the almost nonexistent light, formed an expanding cloud about both men. The bang-stick slipped from the man's fingers, though he continued struggling in Murdock's grasp. Gradually, those struggles died away . . . and then the frogman floated limp and unresisting in the water, just as Roselli and Higgins loomed out of the shadows from astern, knives at the ready.

Murdock glanced up. Jaybird had killed his man as well, slitting the man's throat like an expert.

Turning the bodies over, the SEALs closed the regulator valves shut, stopping the flow of air from the tanks. Men on the pier following the divers' progress by their tell-tale bubbles on the surface might wonder at having lost the bubbles . . . but they would wonder a lot more if the rhythmic bubble patterns turned to two steady streams that no longer moved. The SEALs had just purchased a little more time while the people on the surface assumed that their divers had moved beneath the ship . . . ten or fifteen minutes, perhaps. After that . . .

Damn, where were the guys off the SDVs?

0116 hours (Zulu +3)
Inside the Bandar-é Abbas shipyard harbor

Coburn's breaths were coming in short, panting rasps now. The pain in his head was almost unendurable, and he had to stifle an urge to yawn inside his mask.

Damn this Hell Week shit. Push a guy until he's so damned tired he doesn't know whether he's coming or going, until he's about to fall asleep on his feet. Maybe it's time to ring the fucking bell, to get out now while the getting's still good.

Compass heading . . . what was his heading? Holding the wrist compass up before his mask, he tried to focus on the numbers. Two-three-zero . . . he needed a heading of two-three-zero. Damn! He was *way* off course! The next marker in the exercise was *that* way! How much time had he lost?

He had to keep moving, keep working. He wasn't going to quit, wasn't going to ring the damned bell. But God, he was so *sleepy*! . . .

A hand descended on his arm, yanking him to one side. Angrily, Coburn turned to fend off this unexpected attack from behind. The other diver was much bigger than he, and stronger. Coburn reached for his knife . . .

. . . and the move was expertly blocked. The other SEAL positioned himself so that his face mask was six inches from Coburn's. The SEAL captain found himself looking into MacKenzie's worried eyes.

MacKenzie. What was *he* doing here? He was supposed to be in the Persian Gulf, going after that Japanese freighter.

Then Coburn remembered where he was, and the realization was at once terrifying and embarrassing. He floated there in MacKenzie's grip, almost limp, as the SEAL master chief reached out and snagged another diver out of the gloom.

Ellsworth, the platoon's corpsman. Coburn watched as MacKenzie signaled to Ellsworth with his free hand, forming a "C," an "O," then holding up two fingers.

CO_2. Coburn's symptoms of the past few minutes began to make some kind of sense. He'd been breathing awfully hard since they'd left the SDVs, partly because the long night swim was hard work, partly because—he made himself admit the fact now—he'd been excited. Maybe *too* excited. He'd started breathing so hard that he hadn't been ventilating his lungs properly . . . or possibly he'd simply not been giving his rebreather's CO_2 absorbent time to purge all of the carbon dioxide from his gas mix.

He wanted to kick himself.

MacKenzie pointed toward the surface and Doc nodded. The only treatment for carbon-dioxide poisoning was to abort the dive at once. Coburn felt MacKenzie handing him off to Ellsworth.

Together, they started for the surface.

0118 hours (Zulu +3)
Beneath the freighter *Yuduki Maru*
Bandar-é Abbas shipyard

Murdock and the other three SEALs had dragged the bodies of the two Iranians to the bottom and wedged them securely among the broken concrete blocks and discarded rubber tires beneath the pier, then returned to their back-to-back watch position. How long before the bad guys topside decided to come looking for their missing frogmen?

If the SDV team didn't show up damned quick, he would have to start thinking about what the four of them could do on their own.

Not that they'd be able to do a hell of a lot. A four-man Rambo-type assault was a possibility, but not a good one. SEALs got results by working as a team according to a carefully worked-out plan, not by going in with guns blazing in some kind of wild, death-or-glory banzai charge. Besides, though they were armed, they had no grenades, no explosives, and once on board they would be outnumbered at least ten to one. Getting themselves shot would accomplish exactly nothing.

The smart move would probably be to return to the Boghammer and try to raise Prairie Home on the sat comm. Presumably, the air assault portion of Deadly Weapon was still under way, even if the SDV attack had been aborted.

Or was it? It wouldn't be the first time that a nervous Pentagon or an indecisive Administration had gotten cold feet and called off a major attack at the last possible second. Maybe the SDV SEALs and the airborne assault had both been called off, but nobody had bothered to inform the four SEALs already in the harbor.

It was a lonely thought.

Then as if on cue, other divers materialized silently out of the inky water, familiar shadow-shapes in SEAL black gear vests and Mark XV UBAs. It was too dark to recognize features behind those full-face masks, but MacKenzie's big-boned lankiness was a welcome sight indeed.

Murdock counted them as they gathered around, and realized with a small stirring of alarm that there were only ten men in the group. The last sat-comm transmission from Prairie Home had said that there would be twelve. Who was missing?

There was no time to find out. With swift, silent efficiency, the SEALs parceled off into two groups. As in the first assault against the freighter, they would go aboard in two groups, both of them on the starboard side this time, to avoid being seen from the pier.

Unpacking their gear from the cargo sled, the SDV SEALs extended their hooked painter's poles and unshipped their weapons. In moments, the first two SEALs were on their way up the *Yuduki Maru*'s side.

0121 hours (Zulu +3)
Inside the Bandar-é Abbas shipyard harbor

Doc Ellsworth broke surface close beneath a wood-and-concrete pier extending west from a massive stone jetty. Coburn surfaced a moment later, and Doc guided him to the algae-caked bulk of one of the pier's bollards.

This appeared to be a fueling pier. A Combattante II-class patrol boat was tied up alongside, and the sailors aboard were passing fuel lines across from the jetty.

The Combattante II was a French-made boat, about 155 feet long, weighing 249 tons, and carrying a complement of about thirty men. Originally equipped with harpoon missiles, the Iranian Combattantes were now armed only with one rapid-fire 76mm cannon in a turret forward and a 40mm antiaircraft gun aft. Doc was less worried about the patrol boat's armament than he was about the men working on her afterdeck.

But Doc's first thought was for his patient. As Coburn clung gasping to the bollard, Ellsworth pulled off the SEAL's mask, then examined his face closely in the dim light. There was a lot of bloody mucus hanging in clots from Coburn's nose . . . probably from a ruptured sinus. No froth at the nose or mouth, which was damned good because then Ellsworth would have to consider the possibilities of embolism or lung squeeze. Chances were, Coburn had been breathing so hard he'd popped a sinus.

Hard breathing almost certainly meant CO_2 poisoning. The symptoms were subtle, but included drowsiness and loss of concentration, confused thinking, and sometimes the headache that might be associated with the dilation of the arteries in the victim's brain.

"How do you feel?" he whispered in Coburn's ear, just loud enough to be heard above the lapping of the water at the pier and the voices of the working party nearby. "Head?"

"Head hurt like a bastard for a while there," Coburn said. "It's better now."

"Tingling in your hands? Nausea? Chest pains?"

Coburn shook his head. "Negative."

His speech was taut and coherent. MacKenzie had spotted Coburn's trouble in time. The insidious thing about CO_2 poisoning was the way it crept up on you, robbing you of your concentration and mental clarity, while making you breathe harder . . . which in turn made the condition worse. A two percent excess of CO_2 in the gas mix was enough to trigger harder breathing. Ten percent caused unconsciousness, while fifteen brought on spasms and rigidity. Death was usually from drowning.

One thing was sure. They didn't dare risk letting Coburn dive again. Doc gestured toward the shore, where rocks and mud rose from the water at the point where the pier met the land. They could take shelter there, without having to worry about clinging to the bollard. They would also be able to unstrap their H&Ks and have them ready, just in case. "Let's get comfortable."

Together, they started moving toward the shore, keeping to the shadows beneath the pier.

0121 hours (Zulu +3)
Freighter *Yuduki Maru*
Bandar-é Abbas shipyard

MacKenzie was first up the freighter's side, hauling himself from the water hand over hand along the painter's pole. The last time he'd done this had been at sea, safely shrouded by the anonymity of night. This time it was night . . . but the glare of lights from the shipyard facilities ashore and from the work area on *Yuduki Maru*'s forward deck was bright enough that he could imagine himself etched clearly against the ship's side.

In fact, his combat blacks provided camouflage enough against the ship's black side, and the SEALs had chosen their approach carefully, coming in over the quarter where they were unlikely to be noticed by casual observers ashore. Still, guards in a passing patrol boat or sailors aboard one of the other ships in the harbor could easily look the wrong way at the wrong moment. They *might* assume that the divers emerging from the water were part of the "salvage work" going on aboard the Japanese freighter . . . or they might sound an alarm. Security lay in moving swiftly, with no waste motion and no delays in the open.

As he reached the top of his climb, hanging from the freighter's gunwale, he could hear voices coming from the deck above his head.

"Dokokara kimashita ka?"

"Ah, Osaka kara kimashita. . . ."

Japanese. At least two of them.

Clinging one-handed to the painter's pole, MacKenzie drew his Smith & Wesson Hush Puppy. The team wasn't bothering with laser sights this time; the gadgets were too sensitive to salt-water immersion.

This one was going to have to be quick, crude, and dirty.

0121 hours (Zulu +3)
Fueling dock
Bandar-é Abbas shipyard

Doc helped Coburn in a clumsy side-kick as they made their way along from piling to piling, always staying in the shelter beneath the pier. As they passed beside the patrol boat, they could hear the voices of Iranians on the dock and aboard the vessel, calling to one another in Farsi. Doc concentrated on staying afloat. Both men were burdened with weapons and gear, and it was a struggle just keeping both of their heads above water. Moments later, they cleared the patrol boat. They were less than ten yards from the shore now.

Across the water toward the north, less than one hundred yards away, the *Yuduki Maru* lay tied up to the construction pier, bathed in light from shore and from her own forward deck. As he moved through the water, Doc could see her aft starboard quarter . . . and two tiny, black figures dangling against her hull near the fantail.

Shit! If anyone on the fuel dock looked that way . . .

0121 hours (Zulu +3)
Freighter *Yuduki Maru*
Bandar-é Abbas shipyard

Twelve feet to MacKenzie's left, Kosciuszko clung to the second painter's pole, pistol in hand. MacKenzie exchanged silent nods with the other SEAL, wordlessly counting down with a three . . . two . . . one . . . *now!*

Pulling themselves fully erect, MacKenzie and Kosciuszko reared over the freighter's fantail gunwale, balanced back against the gripper hooks at the tops of their poles, weapons tracking and firing in a blurred succession of rapidly triggered shots. The sound-suppressed gunfire sounded like a ragged chain of heavy blows, scarcely louder than the slaps and thuds of bullets striking flesh. The two Japanese guards were caught

in intersecting lines of fire, struck again and again and again
before they'd even had time to fall. Their assault rifles clattered
onto the deck; one man crumpled where he stood; the other
stumbled back three steps, half turned, and very nearly went
over the rail before dropping to his knees, then collapsing onto
his back, arms outflung in a spreading pool of blood.

MacKenzie swung himself over the rail and took a kneeling
position, standing guard while Kos attached and unrolled two
caving ladders. In seconds, two more SEALs were on the
fantail . . . then two more. Kosciuszko and Nicholson hauled
away hand-over-hand at a line, dragging the platoon's heavy
weapons up the ship's side. Moments later, MacKenzie had his
M-60 machine gun, a one-hundred-round ammo box snapped
onto its receiver and the first round already chambered.
Kosciuszko too had a 60-gun, wielding the massive weapon in
his huge hands like a carbine.

As the other SEALs came aboard, they dispersed immediately, every man already briefed on his deployment. Fernandez
and Garcia stopped long enough to draw their M-16/M203
combos from the heavy weapon pack, tuck some grenades into
their pouches, and load up. Magic Brown picked up his M-21
rifle and nightscope, while Scotty Frazier grabbed a shotgun.
Doc's beloved full-auto shotgun remained on the deck un-
claimed.

The rest of the SEALs carried their standard loadouts, H&K
MP5s with Smith & Wesson Hush Puppies as backups.

Silently, MacKenzie willed the SEALs to move faster. They
didn't have much time now at all.

0122 hours (Zulu +3)
Freighter *Yuduki Maru*
Bandar-é Abbas shipyard

Murdock dropped into a crouch at MacKenzie's side. "What's
the word, Chief?" His whisper was scarcely audible above the
soft scufflings of the moving SEALs.

"Hey, L-T." It was the first time Murdock had been called
that since joining SEAL Seven. "Welcome aboard."

He looked around at the silently moving SEALs. "Who's OIC? DeWitt?"

"You are, I guess. Coburn brought us in, but he's out of the game. Diving casualty."

"Aw, shit! What happened?"

"Maybe CO_2 poisoning. I'm not sure. Doc's with him."

DeWitt joined them, clutching his H&K against his chest. "Hey, Lieutenant," he said. "I'm damned glad to see you."

"Glad to see you. Mac tells me Coburn is scratched. I don't know the plan. You two'd better take the lead."

MacKenzie considered this, then nodded. "I think so too." He glanced at DeWitt. "Lieutenant?"

"Affirmative. But stay with me, L-T, huh? I'll feel a lot better with you at my back."

Murdock grinned. "You'll do fine, 2IC. Where are you supposed to be?"

"Bridge."

Murdock nodded. "The bridge again. Okay, let's move it!"

It took a few seconds more to sort out the last-minute details. Roselli and Higgins were posted on the fantail, guarding the SEALs' escape route, manning the sat comm, and providing the rest of the team with a ready reserve. Jaybird would partner with Murdock. Tactical radios were set to the proper frequencies. By the time Murdock was set, the rest of the platoon had already dispersed, leaving him, the three SEALs off *Beluga*, Lieutenant j.g. DeWitt, and Chucker Wilson on the fantail.

DeWitt gestured forward. *That way.*

0125 hours (Zulu +3)
Bridge access ladder
Freighter *Yuduki Maru*

With his AKM slung over his shoulder, Kurebayashi was on his way back up the ladder toward the bridge. After completing an inspecting tour of the freighter, he still felt uneasy. The atmosphere held that undefinable tension, a charge that was nearly electric in its intensity, that often presaged a storm.

The air was dry, however, and the sky clear. Perhaps, Kurebayashi told himself, it was simply his nerves.

For a long time now, he'd been questioning his own motives, and his future. What was it he wanted from the Ohtori? What did he expect to accomplish?

Martyrdom, certainly . . . but Kurebayashi questioned the popular idea that he and those with him would be transformed into stars if they successfully fulfilled their vow and brought low the American giant. Oblivion seemed a likelier fate, and Kurebayashi had found himself dreading that possibility. To be snuffed out, never to know whether all of his pain and sacrifice for the cause thus far had borne fruit . . . the very idea was repellent now, even though he and his comrades had discussed the possibility countless times before.

Or was it simply that he was afraid? The thought shamed him, burning more than the fear of oblivion as he turned the corner on the landing just below the bridge access corridor. He stopped for a moment, steeling himself. Perhaps if he spoke again with Takeda, he would feel better.

At the top of the steps, two Iranian Pasdaran stood guard, lounging in the passageway, their red scarves much in evidence. One looked down at Kurebayashi, smirked, then said something in Farsi to his companion. The other laughed unpleasantly.

Barbarians . . .

Silenced gunshots chuffed from some unseen source above and behind Kurebayashi's head. The laughing soldier's eyes bulged as crimson flowers blossomed at his throat, the bridge of his nose, his forehead. The other was still trying to raise his G-3 rifle when a trio of 9mm slugs punched a three-inch triangle through his chest, centered on the middle of his breastbone. His mouth gaped to shout a warning; three more hissing rounds slammed into his face in a wet spray of blood and bone.

Kurebayashi did not wait to identify the attacker, did not even pause to analyze what had just happened. Dropping straight to the landing on the steps, he rolled onto his back, dragging his AKM around as he fell. Shadows flitted across the top of the companionway. Someone was up there in the passageway over his head, moving toward the bridge.

Carefully, he raised his rifle, waiting for a target to move into his line of sight.

0126 hours (Zulu +3)
Bridge access passageway
Freighter *Yuduki Maru*

Chucker Wilson studied the passageway ahead, empty now save for the bodies of the two Iranians sprawled on the deck beneath twin smears of scarlet on the bulkhead they'd been leaning against. The bridge door between them was closed, and there'd been no sign that anyone on the other side of that massive steel bulkhead had heard.

Lieutenant Murdock slapped his shoulder; it had been swift-triggered three-round bursts from their H&Ks that had brought down the guards. And now the way was clear. At their backs, Lieutenant j.g. DeWitt and Jaybird Sterling stood up, getting ready to advance.

Captain Coburn had been right. Wilson knew he wasn't cut out for any job with the fleet, anymore than he was cut out for a job as a civilian. It was good to be back with the Team again, back where he belonged.

Murdock started toward the bridge door, and Wilson followed, four feet behind.

Somewhere in the back of Wilson's mind, an alarm bell was going off. Something was *wrong*. . . .

0126 hours (Zulu +3)
Bridge access ladder
Freighter *Yuduki Maru*

Kurebayashi could hear the footsteps moving across the deck, soft and muffled, but identifiable nonetheless as stealthy footsteps. In another two seconds, the American commando— this must be the work of the Yankee SEALs—would be visible through the open companionway at the top of the steps.

Ever so slightly, his finger tightened on his AKM's trigger. . . .

28

Wilson knew what had set off the mental alarms. The L-T was advancing toward the bridge door, his H&K held stiffly in front of him with the muzzle covering the door and the two bodies. In a moment, he would step past a companionway, the rail-guarded opening in the deck giving access to a ship's ladder and the next deck down.

And Murdock's attention was so completely focused on the bridge door, he didn't appear to even be aware of the companionway. If there was someone down there, out of sight but ready with a weapon . . .

There was no time for finesse or even for a radioed warning. With the telescoping butt stock of his own H&K already pressed high against his shoulder, Wilson lunged forward, shoving past a startled Murdock, pivoting sharply to face into the open companionway.

There was someone down there, sprawled on the landing with an assault rifle already raised. Wilson squeezed his trigger as the muzzle flash from the other weapon obscured the enemy soldier's face. His H&K's sound-suppressed burst mingled with the bone-rattling crack-crack-crack of an AKM; he felt something pluck at his thigh, felt something else nudge him hard in the side, but he held his stance, triggering two more quick three-round bursts. The guy on the landing jerked sharply as though kicked, rolled to one side trying to rise, then shuddered and collapsed. Only then did Wilson notice that he was Japanese.

MacKenzie, with his big M-60 slung around his neck, and Bearcat Holt appeared on the landing moments later, probing the body for signs of life.

"That's a dead tango," MacKenzie said, but the words sounded far away and muffled.

Murdock helped Wilson to the deck. "Son of a bitch, Chucker," Murdock whispered harshly in his ear. "Did you think I was going to leave my back open?"

It was only then dawning on Wilson that he'd been hit. There was still no pain, but his side felt numb, as though he'd taken an injection there full of novocaine, and his leg felt hot, sticky, and wet.

"Thought . . . you weren't gonna check your tail." Holt knelt at Wilson's side and began breaking out a first-aid dressing. Gunfire exploded in the distance.

"That tears it," Murdock said. "We're out in the open now."

"Okay!" DeWitt snapped. "Let's hit the bridge!"

Wilson wondered why everyone sounded so very far away.

0126 hours (Zulu +3)
Forward deck
Freighter *Yuduki Maru*

As the first chatter of automatic weapons fire echoed across the freighter's deck, a SEAL fire team was just moving into position beneath the ladder on the starboard side of the ship's superstructure forward. Chief Ben Kosciuszko and Rattler Fernandez just had time to take cover behind a wooden crate on the deck when the gunfire from topside brought all work forward to an immediate halt.

Someone yelled a warning in Farsi, and then soldiers with readied weapons were trotting aft toward the deckhouse. Kosciuszko eased his M-60 around and squeezed the trigger. Full-auto thunder pounded across the steel deck, hammering down three of the lead Pasdaran soldiers and scattering the rest.

Fernandez raised his M203, sighting at the clutter of propane tanks and cutting equipment stacked up in the center of the deck.

"Hey, Chief," Fernandez yelled above the M-60's thunder. "This ship has pretty thick decks, right?"

"Ten inches of steel, Rattler. I don't think you can hurt 'em with your toy."

"Let's find out, man." He triggered the 203, which loosed its 40mm grenade with a hollow-sounding thump. The projectile slammed into an acetylene tank and detonated; the entire front half of the ship lit up in a savage, yellow glare, as white flames clawed at the sky. Men were screaming, lying prone and pounding on the deck as flames ate their backs, or running madly to escape their own blazing clothing and skin.

The survivors, completely demoralized, ran for cover or dove headlong over the railing, preferring the cool black of the water to being burned alive on deck.

A single automatic rifle barked challenge from the bow, and Kosciuszko opened up in reply.

0126 hours (Zulu +3)
Fuel dock
Bandar-é Abbas shipyard

Gunfire exploded in the night, full-auto bursts cracking across the black water from the direction of the *Yuduki Maru*. From their vantage point in the stinking mud beneath the shore end of the fuel pier dock, Coburn could see tiny figures running along the freighter's forward deck, or on the pier at the ship's port side. It looked like all hell had broken out aboard the Japanese freighter, with flames engulfing part of the deck halfway between the bow and the superstructure, accompanied by the familiar chatter of a pig, an M-60 machine gun.

"What's happening with the Combattante?" he asked. Cautiously, Doc crawled out from beneath the pier, looking down the line of wooden pilings to the moored patrol boat. "Shit," he said. "Looks like trouble."

Coburn duck-walked through the mud to Doc's side, to a point where he could see the patrol boat's stern alongside the massive pilings of the fuel pier. Steel pipes threaded their way across the dock, and beyond them, embedded in concrete, were several storage tanks.

The gunfire and explosions aboard the *Yuduki Maru* had certainly captured the attention of the Iranians aboard the gunboat. Coburn couldn't see the craft's forward turret, but the open 40mm mount was being rapidly swung around, as Iranian sailors yelled at each other and pointed. Soldiers were trotting across the pier now, looking for firing positions. Gunfire from the patrol boat would slash into the Japanese freighter's side if the bad guys dared open up. Any SEALs caught on deck would be sitting ducks.

"You thinkin' what I'm thinkin'?" Doc asked.

"Wouldn't be one bit surprised." Coburn fished into his black gear and pulled out a hand grenade. Doc too produced a grenade, holding the arming lever shut as he worked the cotter pin free.

"Those POL tanks look good," Coburn said. POL—petroleum, oil, and lubricants, in this case diesel fuel—an ideal target.

"A SEAL's wet dream," Doc said.

"On my mark now, three . . . two . . . one . . . go!"

Together, they let fly, sending the grenades arcing high above the pier, then bouncing with a stony clatter on the concrete among the fuel pipes. *"Bepaweed!"* someone screamed, and then the night dissolved in thunder. Diesel fuel gushed across the concrete from ruptured lines and tanks.

Coburn pulled out a second grenade, a canister this time, with AN-M14 and INCEN TH3 stenciled on the side. The AN-M14 was an incendiary grenade, packed with thermite and given a two-second fuse delay. He exchanged glances with Doc, pulled the pin, and let fly.

The thermite burst amid the pooling fuel oil at 2200 degrees, hot enough to burn through steel. Thunder rolled again, and this time the sky turned to flame.

0127 hours (Zulu +3)
Bridge
Freighter *Yuduki Maru*

They'd waited outside the bridge until they heard gunfire rather than bursting in at once, figuring that the battle might offer a

diversion for the bridge assault team. Taking up positions on
either side of the door, Murdock and MacKenzie counted down
silently as the gunfire built to a crescendo of thundering noise.
There was a deck-jolting concussion—what were the guys
playing at out there?—and then Murdock went through the
bridge door first, his H&K stuttering softly as he tracked its
muzzle across a startled Iranian soldier, punching the man back
against a bank of computer consoles. MacKenzie was right
behind him, swinging the deadly gray bulk of his M-60 as
lightly as Murdock's H&K, and when his finger closed on the
trigger, the bridge rang with the hammering, rapid-fire detonations of that machine gun.

Half glimpsed as he swept the bridge were flames lighting
the night outside—one blaze on *Yuduki Maru*'s own forward
deck, other greater, brighter fires erupting two hundred yards to
starboard, lighting the night in an unfolding glory of yellow
and orange that caught a large patrol boat in silhouette.

Murdock didn't pause to admire the view, however. He
tracked left and killed another man by the teletype machines,
then pivoted back to cover Mac. Three Iranian naval officers,
one with ornate gold braid on his white uniform, tried to scatter
for cover as MacKenzie's searing fusillade scythed through
them. One down . . . two . . . three . . . Another man, an
army officer, grabbed for his holstered pistol, then seemed to
dissolve in red mist and fragments as MacKenzie's weapon cut
him down as well.

"Wheeoo! Rock and roll!" MacKenzie yelled into the sudden
silence as his finger came off the trigger. "Just a-playin' in the
band!"

"Yeah, you left 'em dead in the aisles," Murdock replied,
stepping closer to the dead naval officers, probing them with
his foot. "Watch it with that thing, huh? We still have to get this
ship out of . . . uh-oh."

Murdock froze, his H&K aimed at the figure standing alone
on the *Yuduki Maru*'s starboard bridge wing. The man was
holding a pistol, but the muzzle was pointed uselessly at the
overhead. Possibly the guy hadn't had time to aim . . . or
maybe he was trying to surrender. He was Japanese, which

meant Ohtori. Another Ohtori prisoner would be a real bonus for the intel boys. "Easy there, guy," Murdock called. "Drop the weapon. Ah . . . *buki o sutero!* Drop your weapons!"

"Put it down!" MacKenzie added, his voice sounding as loud as the full-auto mayhem of a moment earlier. "Now!"

The Japanese terrorist wavered for a moment, the pistol aimed at the sky in a trembling, uncertain hand. Suddenly, he snapped the muzzle down against his right temple and jerked the trigger. There was a crash and the man's head snapped over against his shoulder, the left side of his skull suddenly gone soft beneath a wet mat of disarrayed hair. The pistol fell over the railing; the terrorist dropped to his knees, then fell full-length on the deck.

"Son of a bitch!" Jaybird said, coming up behind Murdock. "Was he crazy?"

"Worse," Murdock said. "He wanted to die for his cause. Hard to fight people like that."

"Well, better them than us," MacKenzie said. "Let's make sure the rest of them do the same. C'mon, Jaybird. Help me set up this pig over there."

Together, Jaybird and MacKenzie braced the M-60 on a smashed-open section of the bridge window.

There were bodies all over the freighter's forward deck, visible now as the flames dwindled. It looked like someone had touched off some propane tanks; the only fire now was from burning scraps of wooden crates, but it was bright enough to give MacKenzie a perfect view of the deck. A soldier took aim at the bridge and fired, the bullet going wide. MacKenzie answered with a burst that sent the man toppling sideways into the water. Wild shots were coming from the shore, but nothing coordinated or effective.

For the second time, Murdock approached the bridge computer console, tapping in memorized commands. The computer was giving readouts in Japanese again; obviously someone had been working with it recently, trying to access the cargo locks. Switching it back to English, Murdock scrolled rapidly through various user logs and menus. Good. His password was still in place . . . and the cargo hold had not been breached.

He let go a low, heartfelt sigh of relief. This op would have been immeasurably more complicated if the bastards had managed to break into the hold. He keyed his Motorola. "Prof! This is Murdock!"

"Copy, L-T," Higgins's voice replied. "We're set up and ready to go."

"Call 'em in," Murdock told him. "Tell 'em the package is safe!"

"Ro-*ger*! I'm on it!"

The lieutenant glanced across the bridge to where Wilson was lying on a fire blanket on the deck. He looked unconscious. "Also tell 'em we need medevac for a casualty."

"Right, L-T."

"Razor."

"Here, L-T."

"Where's 'here'?"

"On the fantail, L-T. With Prof."

"Head on down to the engine room. I'll have Mac meet you there. I want you two to go over the engines of this tub. Find out if we can get her under way again."

"Roger that, L-T. On my way."

"Mac, you hear that?"

"Sure did, Skipper." The big Texan somewhat reluctantly yielded his M-60 to Holt, who'd done all he could for the wounded Chucker. Roselli's original rating before he'd joined the SEALs had been a machinist's mate, while MacKenzie was a master chief engineman. He wanted his two best snipes in the freighter's engine room before he even thought about backing off from the Bandar Abbas dock.

"Jaybird?"

"Yeah, L-T."

"You take Mac's pig for him. Holt, you're with me. I want to check out the ship's con before we try moving her."

"Aye, aye, Skipper."

"Right, L-T."

They had a busy several minutes ahead of them now.

0130 hours (Zulu +3)
Fuel dock
Bandar-é Abbas shipyard

Cautiously, Doc peered past a stack of crates toward a vast and well-lit expanse of concrete fronting a row of machine shops and storage buildings. Coburn knelt beside him, his face still a nightmarish mix of blood and greasepaint.

"What's the word, Doc?"

"I don't like it, Captain. Too open."

Another explosion boomed in the night at their backs. The fueling dock was still burning furiously, the livid orange flames adding to the light bathing the waterfront strip. Hundreds of Iranians had descended on the area and were fighting the blaze now. Doc and Coburn had hidden behind a pile of concrete pipe sections as the fire trucks and soldiers hurried past, then slipped deeper into the shipyard, putting as much distance between themselves and their handiwork as they could.

Now they were about eighty yards from the water, and still some two hundred yards or more from the *Yuduki Maru*'s pier. Doc could see the forward half of the Japanese freighter, revealed in the gap between two small buildings. The fires on her deck appeared to have died down.

Damn! The ship was still too far for the short reach of their tactical radios. Each time Doc tried, he heard only garbled bursts of noise and static.

Coburn pointed to a line of military vehicles parked beside a storehouse, apparently untended. "There's transport."

"Yeah. . . ." Doc's voice sounded less than certain.

"We've got to get to the *Maru*'s pier," Coburn said. "In a jeep we can just drive up to the dock like we own the place."

"And maybe get nailed by our own guys when they think we're the Iranian cavalry." But Doc had to agree that riding would get them where they needed to go faster than by shank's mare. And though he'd said nothing to the patient about it, Coburn was not in good shape. The immediate effects of the CO_2 poisoning had been banished by getting rid of the rebreather, but the SEAL Seven commander could well have internal injuries. Doc wouldn't be able to know that for sure, though, until he had Coburn back aboard the *Nassau*. Where other ships had a sick bay, the LHA had no less than three well-equipped hospitals with a total of six hundred beds and all the high-tech medical wonder gadgets you could ask for.

But for any of that to do any good, Doc had to get his patient off the beach and aboard the *Nassau*. "Okay," he said at last. "We'll give it a try."

Ellsworth and Coburn moved together, sticking to the shadows at the perimeter of the field, circling the well-lighted part until they reached what appeared to be a small motor pool. Doc selected a vehicle, a military jeep of obvious American manufacture, handed Coburn his H&K, and slid in behind the wheel.

"No keys," Coburn said.

"No problem," Doc replied. Drawing his knife, he used the hilt to smash the face plate off the ignition block assembly. Selecting two wires, he cut and stripped them with his knife, then brought the bare ends together. The engine ground, then caught as Doc pumped the gas.

Coburn watched the process, which took less than five seconds, dubiously. "Your record says you're a country boy, Doc."

"Yup, that's me. Just a sweet, simple country boy—"

"—trying to get along in the big city, yeah," Coburn said, finishing the old line for him. "I've heard that one before. Remind me never to trust you with my car."

Doc gunned the engine once, put the jeep in gear, and pulled out of the motor pool area. "Hey, I'm just a laid-back kind of guy," Doc replied easily. "You can trust me with your car, your money, your girl—"

"Yeah, you're laid back like a rattlesnake. I don't know if . . . watch it!"

Doc had seen the danger at the same instant, a line of Iranian soldiers moving along the catwalk atop a massive, concrete structure that looked like a dry dock crib. He increased the jeep's speed slightly. "Don't sweat it, Captain. We're Iranians too, remember? This here is an oh-ficial Iranian government vehicle."

But the men on the catwalk evidently were not convinced. Muzzle flashes popped and stuttered as the Pasdaran infantry opened fire. Bullets sparked off the pavement and slammed into the jeep's side.

"Right," Coburn said. Twisting in his seat, he aimed his H&K and loosed a long, full-auto burst. "Unauthorized use subject to heavy penalty!"

Doc spun the jeep's wheel, sending the vehicle hurtling down a narrow alley between two warehouses. They emerged on the waterfront, driving along a broad, concrete wharf. Startled Iranian soldiers and dock workers dove left and right, scattering from the jeep's path.

"I hope you're a better corpsman than you are a driver," Coburn yelled. Then a burst of machine-gun fire slammed into the jeep from the front, shattering the windshield and shredding the right front tire. Doc felt the jeep going out of control, the rear skidding wildly to the left, and he fought to keep the vehicle from flipping over. Smoke exploded from beneath the hood, and the engine died. Still spinning now, they skidded another ten feet and slammed hard into a bollard rising from the water's edge.

"Damn, the pedestrians are getting worse every—" He stopped. Coburn was slumped over in the passenger's seat, fresh blood bright against his scalp. "Shit!"

Half standing in the wrecked jeep, Doc grabbed his H&K from the back seat, thumbed the selector to full auto, and cut loose at a squad of advancing Pasdaran. Two collapsed on the pavement and the others scattered. Doc glanced back over his shoulder; the *Yuduki Maru* was still a good fifty yards away.

"The sea is your friend," Doc said. He'd meant the words, drilled into SEAL recruits throughout their BUD/S training, to be ironic, but right now he was well aware of the truth behind them. He checked Coburn, finding a strong pulse. It looked like a round might have grazed his scalp, knocking him unconscious, though Doc wanted to give him a thorough look-over. There was no time for that now, though. Another bullet slammed into the side of the jeep. "C'mon, Captain," he said, dragging Coburn's limp body from the passenger's seat and draping him over his back in an awkward fireman's carry. "Let's us go for a swim!"

With Coburn still over his shoulders, Doc leaped off the wharf and into the cold, dark embrace of the harbor once more.

29

The helicopters had launched nearly an hour earlier, but they'd been orbiting over the Gulf since that time, well out in international waters. Devil Dog Flight consisted of six UH-1 Hueys, "Slicks" off the *Nassau* and the *Iwo Jima*. Each carried a Blue/Green Team, a joint SEAL/Marine Recon boarding party of fourteen men, and they came in low and fast, close behind a flight of two Marine SuperCobras. The Cobras clattered across the *Yuduki Maru*'s deck, less than twenty feet above her steel deck, then wheeled across the dockyards and waterfront buildings beyond.

Automatic gunfire chattered from a dry dock; there was a rippling flash, and then a bundle of living flames slashed from the lead Cobra, lighting the sky with their contrails. The rocket barrage struck a catwalk running along the side of the dry dock, flinging shards of metal and fragments of bodies far across the compound.

By now, the entire shipyard was in chaos. A siren wailed its mournful ululation against the crump and rumble of exploding ordnance. Somewhere in the distance, antiaircraft batteries were going off with a stolid-sounding *crump-crump-crump*, apparently at random and apparently without actually bothering

315

to aim at anything. Green tracers drifted across the sky above
the horizon.

Over the shipyard, however, the American forces appeared
to have won a momentary control. Flames continued to boil
into the sky from the fuel dock, which was now blazing from
one end to the other. The fire had spread to the patrol boat as
well, and fresh explosions continued to rack the sadly listing
vessel's frame as fuel and ammo stores detonated. Ashore, men
were running everywhere, some armed and moving with
purpose, but most scattering in desperate bids to find shelter or
simply to *leave,* as quickly as possible. Very few stood their
ground and attempted to duel with the circling Cobras. Those
who did were cut down almost at once, by rocket salvos, or by
ratcheting fusillades of 7.62mm minigun rounds, sprayed from
the helos' chin turrets so quickly the tri-barreled cannons
sounded like chain saws.

The lead Huey, meanwhile, circled the *Yuduki Maru* once,
trying to draw fire from her deck or from the pier alongside.
When no one accepted the offer, the Slick came in at a hover,
twenty feet above the forward deck, tail low; from its open
cargo doors, ropes and black-faced men descended with
stomach-wrenching drops.

The technique was called "fast roping," and it was a quick
way of getting from an airborne chopper to the ground . . . or
to the deck of a ship. The first men thumped onto the deck and
moved clear, H&Ks held at the ready. More men followed,
sliding down the rope on gloved hands.

The men hitting *Yuduki Maru*'s deck now were drawn from
Marine Force Recon and SEAL Seven, First Platoon, and were
part of the Maritime Special Purpose Force, or MSPF. Designed, in the language of the Pentagon, "to optimize forces
available to conduct highly sensitive and complex special
missions," the MSPF was trained to conduct raids deep in
enemy territory, to reinforce U.S. embassies or other facilities
at need, to extract important people or documents, and to
conduct hostage rescues. The theory was that, more often than
not, when a crisis situation went down it would take two or
more days to move the Army's Delta Force into position, but

the U.S. Navy and the Marines nearly always had units positioned somewhere close by, allowing MSPF insertion at virtually a moment's notice.

SEALs and Recon Marines had been practicing joint MSPF exercises for a number of years now, and though the traditional Navy-Marine rivalry continued to run deep, this particular collaboration had been used with outstanding success on a number of occasions.

As soon as the first fourteen men were down, the Huey cast off the ropes, dropped its nose, and roared off into the darkness as its prop wash lashed the water below. The second Huey came in right behind the first, and fourteen more men roped their way to the freighter's deck.

The other Hueys deposited their loads of Blue/Green commandos ashore, dropping them into open areas that blocked avenues of approach to the pier from inland. Other helos clattered overhead, big Marine Super Stallions, each loaded with fifty-five combat troops and their gear, bound for LZs along the roads leading from the shipyard to Bandar-é Abbas and other coastal towns. They were protected by AV-8 Harrier jumpjets, wondrous aircraft that swooped and stooped like great birds of prey or slowed to a magical, helicopter-like hover. An Iranian armored battalion was reported to be somewhere near Bandar, and the MEF's Marine Air contingent was committed to stopping those tanks from reaching the shipyard. Meanwhile, Harriers and SuperCobras staged a surprise raid at the Bandar-é Abbas airport, turning a dozen military planes into twisted, blackened skeletons, and savaging twenty more with shrapnel and machine-gun fire. More air support was already on the way, a flight of Marine F/A-18 Hornets off the *Iwo Jima,* rigged for their role as close ground support with cluster bombs and laser-guided ordnance.

Soon, the *Yuduki Maru* was an eye of relative peace in an expanding storm of violence.

0140 hours (Zulu +3)
Freighter *Yuduki Maru*

Murdock crossed the steel deck to where one of the newcomers was giving orders to his men. There was no easy way to separate the Marines from the SEALs in the MSPF. All wore black gear with full assault loadouts; all wore full-head safety helmets and had their faces heavily blacked. Most carried H&K subguns, though a few varied the routine with M-16/M203 combos, or with combat shotguns. The only real outward difference was in their backup weapons; SEALs carried 9mm handguns, while Marines favored the venerable .45 Colt.

Watching them as he approached, Murdock could tell that they were working as a well-rehearsed, well-practiced team.

The officer in charge of the unit turned toward Murdock. "Captain Cavanaugh," he said, extending a gloved hand. He didn't salute, not when enemy snipers could be watching the scene from the buildings in the distance. "U.S. Marine Corps."

"Semper Fi,"" Murdock replied, taking the Marine's hand and firmly shaking it. The rank of captain in the Marines was equivalent to Murdock's rank of Navy lieutenant. "Welcome aboard!"

"A real pleasure. You the OIC?"

"That's me!"

"I was told to report to you, sir," Cavanaugh said. "We thought maybe you boys might need some help!"

"Good! We could use it." Murdock pointed toward the burning fuel dock. "Listen! I've got two guys ashore. Probably back that way. One of them may be injured. Think you could spare some of your boys to go look for 'em?"

"No problem, sir. That fuel dock fire was their idea?"

Murdock cocked an eyebrow. "I wouldn't be a damned bit surprised."

He was interrupted by a loud cheer from the top of *Yuduki Maru*'s supestructure, a cheer that was taken up by the MSPF team members on the deck. Turning and looking up, Murdock saw the American flag rising up the freighter's main truck in a series of short, jerky movements, illuminated by the lights from shore. He wondered if one of his SEALs had brought the flag, or if it was courtesy of the Marines.

"Okay, make yourself at home, Captain," Murdock told Cavanaugh. "We're seeing what we can do about getting under way."

"Aye, aye, sir," Cavanaugh said. Then his teeth shone brightly against his black face. "You guys did a real good job, Navy. Almost as good as the Marines!"

Murdock grinned back. "Just don't let me hear any shit about the Marines always being first to hit the beach!"

Yuduki Maru was secure. SEALs, and now Marines as well, continued to move through the freighter's passageways and compartments, ferreting out remaining pockets of Iranians or Japanese terrorists, but it looked as though this part of the battle had been won. Minutes earlier, DeWitt and Frazier had killed an Ohtori gunman standing guard outside the crew's quarters. They'd found the captive Japanese merchant marine sailors and officers locked inside, including the stolid Captain Koga, a prisoner aboard his own ship. Murdock had ordered that the crew be kept locked up, at least for the moment. It was safer that way, without having to worry about Ohtori gunmen hiding among the former hostages . . . or about civilians blundering into the middle of a firefight.

Gunshots continued to bang and thump in the surrounding darkness, but for the moment, at least, it appeared that the *Yuduki Maru* was firmly in American hands. A Huey Medevac chopper had touched down on a clear stretch of the dock side a few moments before. They'd have Wilson aboard and on his way to the *Nassau* in another few minutes.

Roselli trotted across the deck. "Hey, L-T!"

"Whatcha got, Razor?"

"Me'n Mac have been going over the engine room and boilers. Except for that twist to the starboard shaft, everything's shipshape. We can have her up to steam and ready to move out in twenty."

"Do it. How much trouble is that bent shaft gonna cause us?"

"Some, especially when we're maneuvering inside this damned, tight-ass harbor. Course, if you don't mind us denting some fenders on the way out . . ."

"Dent all the fenders you want, just so we get this scrap heap to the Gulf of Oman."

"I've got a good engineman in my platoon," Cavanaugh said. "I can have him lend a hand."

"Outstanding."

"L-T, this is Prof" crackled in Murdock's earphone.

"Copy, Professor. Go ahead."

"We've got VIPs inbound, Skipper. ETA two minutes. They say we should clear the deck."

"Roger. Who is it?"

"They say it's NEST, L-T. Looks like the show's going to be taken out of our hands." Higgins sounded annoyed.

"That's okay, Professor. We've *done* our part."

The black, unmarked Huey dropped toward *Yuduki Maru*'s forward deck two minutes later, right to the tick.

NEST—the Nuclear Emergency Search Team—was an elite and high-tech government unit set up under the auspices of the Department of Energy in 1975. Its mission was to search for and identify lost or stolen nuclear weapons or SNM— Special Nuclear Materials—and to respond to nuclear bomb or radiation-dispersal threats. Most of its activities were highly secret, for obvious reasons; one indication of the unit's efficiency was the very fact that few people *had* heard of it, though in the past twenty years it had responded to many hundreds of alerts. In the United States, NEST teams were based at the Nevada Test Site and at Andrews AFB. Overseas, a team was permanently stationed at Ramstein Air Base in Germany; the NEST coming in to the *Yuduki Maru* now would be a special field detachment from the Ramstein group, deployed to II MEF when the emergency first began.

Murdock watched as the helicopter lowered itself gently to the deck, its skids just off the steel. Twelve men climbed out, six of them swaddled in bulky white antiradiation garments, anonymous behind the helmets that made them look like lunar astronauts. The others wore nondescript Army fatigues, without emblems or rank insignia. One of them strode purposefully toward Murdock as the Huey lifted off with a roar.

"You Murdock?"

"Yes, sir."

"Smith. Senior NEST control officer. What's the situation?"

"As far as we can tell, sir, the cargo's intact and secure. We stopped the bad guys before they could breach the hold."

"We'll be the judge of that, Lieutenant," the man said. "I want you to keep your people well clear of the cargo area. Only those personnel absolutely essential to the defense of this vessel are to be on this deck. Your men will stand by until we can tow this vessel clear of Iranian waters."

"Tow, sir?"

"Yes. One of the destroyers with the Marine force offshore will work its way in as soon as the enemy batteries on some of the Gulf islands are neutralized. We should rendezvous with the *Recovery* in the Gulf of Oman sometime late tomorrow."

Recovery, the ARS 43, was a WWII-era vessel fitted out for diver support, salvage, and ocean tug duties.

An explosion thumped in the distance, followed by a burst of muffled gunfire. "Pardon my saying so, sir, but that's a dumb-ass idea. The whole, damned Iranian army's going to be all over this place before too much longer, and we *don't* want to risk an attack on this ship! We can be out of here in twenty minutes."

The NEST officer looked startled. "The ship is ready to sail?"

Murdock looked at his watch. "Twenty minutes, sir."

"But are you sure it'll make it? I was told some Navy SEALs caused a lot of damage to its engines and it had to be towed."

"I've got good men on it down in the engine room now, sir," Murdock said, a little stiffly. "We have one good screw, and the con's all right. We'll take her out on her own steam."

The NEST officer didn't look happy, but he was obviously tempted by the idea of getting clear of Bandar-é Abbas in twenty minutes instead of several hours.

"What about those Iranian gun and missile batteries on the islands?"

Murdock grinned. "Sir, I imagine the SEALs and Marines are on top of that right now."

He was guessing, but Murdock was sure he was right. He'd participated in too many planning sessions and simulations to believe that the planners for Operation Deadly Weapon had failed to arrange a safe path clear of the enemy coast.

"Very well," Smith said at last. "You will make all preparations to get this ship under way as soon as possible."

"Yes, sir. As soon as two of my men show up."

"Eh? What's that? What do you mean?"

"I've got two men ashore, sir. They didn't make it back after liberty. We can't sail without them."

DeWitt, standing nearby, turned suddenly away, stifling a laugh. Jaybird grinned broadly and nudged a smiling Roselli with his elbow.

The NEST officer sputtered. "You—you can't do that! The cargo on this vessel—"

"Is of the utmost importance and takes precedence over all other considerations, yes, sir. I wouldn't worry, Mr. Smith. One of the missing men is my commanding officer. The other is one of my most steadfast and dependable men. I feel sure they'll turn up soon."

The officer gave Murdock a black look, then spun on his heel and stalked toward the *Yuduki Maru*'s deckhouse. Murdock shook his head as he watched him go. The plutonium shipment *did* have absolute priority, of course, and if Doc and the Old Man didn't show up fast, the *Yuduki Maru* would have to sail without them.

But it had been fun giving that stiff-assed DOE prick's tail a good twisting.

Roselli stepped closer. "Still no word about Doc and the captain, sir?"

"Not yet. The Marines'll keep looking, though, even if we have to pull out."

"I'd like to volunteer for a shore party, L-T. I could help look for 'em. I know how Doc thinks."

Murdock gave a lopsided grin. "I hate to break it to you, Razor, but they don't have bars in Iran. Alcohol's illegal here, remember?"

"Poor Doc," DeWitt said, shaking his head. "We *can't* leave him here, Skipper. He'd die of thirst!"

"We'll leave it to the Marines," Murdock said. "I need you here, Roselli, watching those engines with Mac."

"Yes, sir." Roselli looked crestfallen.

"Ahoy the *Maru*!" a voice called from the shore. "Man in the water, starboard side!"

Murdock, Roselli, DeWitt, and Jaybird all raced for the freighter's starboard rail. Murdock couldn't see anything against the black water . . . no! There! And *two* heads, not just one!

Roselli and Jaybird were already stripping off their load-bearing vests. Stepping up on the railing, they vaulted smoothly over the side, Jaybird going in feet-first, Roselli cutting a perfect and strictly-against-regs dive. Murdock leaned against the rail and watched. It looked like Coburn was wounded, with a lot of blood on his face and head despite his immersion in the water. Doc had one arm across the captain's chest and was pulling him along with a slow but powerful sidestroke.

In seconds, Roselli and Jaybird had reached the two swimmers. Jaybird took Coburn and started hauling him toward the shore, while Roselli helped a clearly exhausted Ellsworth. Marines and SEALs splashed off the side of the wharf to lend a hand, and others gathered at the side of the water. DeWitt was already on his radio, ordering the medevac chopper to hold up for one more. By the time Coburn was hauled from the water, a couple of corpsmen had reached the dock with a Stokes stretcher. It was hard to tell from here, but Murdock was sure he saw Coburn moving his arms as he was fastened down. He was conscious, and that was a damned hopeful sign.

Murdock had to grip the rail to avoid showing the weakness that swept through him. *Coburn and Doc were okay!* Until that moment, he'd not realized how worried he'd been about his people.

Turning, he strode back toward the *Yuduki Maru*'s deckhouse.

Fifteen minutes later, he stood on the freighter's bridge, peering out through paneless windows at the Blue/Green Team members ashore and on the forward deck. Smith glowered over his shoulder to his right, while a still-damp Jaybird stood behind the wheel and Holt manned the engine-room telegraph. Roselli had joined MacKenzie and several MSPF snipes below in the engine room, but Higgins had transferred his satellite gear to the freighter's bridge and was watching with professional interest. The other SEALs, less Doc, Chucker, and Captain Coburn, were scattered about the ship. The medevac chopper had lifted those three out several minutes earlier.

Murdock picked up a microphone and pressed the switch. "Now hear this, now hear this," Murdock said, and the words boomed from loudspeakers all over the ship. "Make ready to get under way."

A rifle shot popped from somewhere ashore, but he scarcely noticed it. The Marine perimeter now enclosed the entire shipyard, and the last report from the air contingent had placed the nearest organized Iranian forces just outside of Bandar-é Abbas proper, a good three miles down the coast.

"Cast off forward," he ordered, and the Marines manning the forward line tossed it across to their fellows on the pier. A pair of SuperCobras thundered overhead, keeping watch.

Murdock walked to the starboard bridge wing and checked aft. With the freighter tied portside-to and bow-on to the shore, and with only one engine working, maneuvering in this tight harbor would be tricky. He was glad it was the starboard screw that was off-line, though, and not the port.

It occurred to him that this was his first command—at least if you didn't count the little *Beluga* or the Boghammer patrol boat. He'd had classes in ship handling at Annapolis, of course, and during his senior year he'd conned a guided-missile destroyer out of Norfolk on a training exercise.

This, however, was completely different.

"All back," he said, and Holt moved the telegraph handles to reverse. "Back her down easy. Starboard helm . . . just a touch."

Yuduki Maru's engine rumbled through the deck beneath their feet. Slowly, slowly, the freighter moved astern. With the rudder to starboard, the ship's bow pressed in toward the pier, while her stern moved away. Moving to the port wing, Murdock checked aft. The ship's stern was now five feet from the pier, the stern line stretched nearly taut.

He'd given the freighter room astern to maneuver. "Forward on the engine," he said, and Holt rammed the telegraph handle to the forward position. "Keep your helm starboard."

The freighter's slow, backward drift halted, then reversed itself. Tugging on the stern line until the pier gave an ominous creak, the *Yuduki Maru* started to swing, her bow moving out from the pier now in a tight circle. When the still-smoldering ruin of the fuel pier lay dead ahead, Murdock gave his next order. "Cast off stern lines!"

Free now of the shore, *Yuduki Maru* slid forward, barely making way. Slowly at first, then faster and with more confidence, the plutonium ship eased clear of the dock, gliding past the fuel dock and the wreckage of a half-sunken patrol boat. Reaching past the helm to the console, Murdock thumbed a large red button, giving a deafening blast from *Yuduki Maru*'s air horns.

And from the Marines watching ashore came a rising, answering growl of noise, a thunderous cheer as the *Yuduki Maru* put to sea once more.

"Okay, gentlemen," Murdock said to the others with him on the bridge. "Let's go home."

EPILOGUE

0950 hours (Zulu −5)
House offices
The Capitol Building, Washington, D.C.

Congressman Charles Fitzhugh Murdock read the paper, prominently stamped SECRET at top and bottom, for the third time, tears glistening at the corners of his eyes. His boy was coming home.

And the timing couldn't have been better. Every newspaper in the country was cheering the recovery of the Japanese plutonium ship, even though the whole story would probably never be made public.

Iran was officially condemning the incursion, of course, but private channels between Tehran and Washington had already established that the entire hijacking incident had been the work of a dissident element within the Iranian military. The two ringleaders were already dead, Ramazani in front of a firing squad only hours ago, Admiral Sahman on the bridge of the *Yuduki Maru* during the raid. Iran was holding off its military forces; the last of the Marines ashore ought to be back aboard the ships of II MEF within the next several hours. The public story was that terrorists had taken the ship to Bandar-é Abbas, and that American Marines had liberated the vessel. That story didn't bear too much close scrutiny, but it would be good enough for now. The Administration wanted to play down America's involvement in what amounted to an invasion of another country, *especially* one that they were still trying to mend fences with. Perhaps the Iranians would be grateful, eventually, for the help rendered by the Americans in uncovering the coup.

Japan was grateful, of course, for the recovery of their ship and its cargo, though whether that would translate as an advantage at the next round of trade talks remained to be seen. Murdock was well aware of the concept of *naniwabushi,* and expected that Tokyo would show its gratitude when the time came. Certainly, they'd already agreed to suspend the controversial plutonium shipments while security policies were reviewed and overhauled. *Yuduki Maru* was officially in Japanese custody again now. Captain Koga had reassumed command as soon as his vessel had passed the last of the Iranian-owned Gulf islands, cruising slowly past Silkworm missile batteries now in the hands of SEALs and U.S. Marines. Even the Greenpeace vessel *Beluga* had been recovered from where the SEALs had beached her on Qeshm Island and was being towed by a Navy frigate to Dahran.

So everyone had come up winners, except for the Ohtori terrorists.

And, of course, the two civilians killed aboard the *Beluga* and their wives. The horrible thing about terrorism was its blind, terrible *randomness.*

The upshot of it all was, though, that the country was being swept by a mad swell of flag-waving approval for the U.S. military. Though the public had a notoriously short memory, enthusiasm for the armed forces always crested in the wake of a fast, successful operation like this one, and Congressman Murdock was already planning on how to turn that to his political advantage. The House Military Affairs Committee's final debate and vote was set for tomorrow morning. Murdock had no doubt now that Farnum's attempt to kill the SEALs and the other Special Warfare units would be easily defeated.

Until this week, Congressman Murdock himself had never realized how well, how smoothly the SEALs could work with other military units, units such as the Marines. While there was duplication among the services, it was impossible to select any one unit out from among all of the rest as less worthwhile, less useful, or less efficient than the others. And America needed those SPECWAROPs people. The pace, the scope, the very nature of modern warfare *demanded* their use, and their support. At this point, Murdock would have voted to dismantle the regular military services if it would have meant keeping the elite, professional warriors of the Special Warfare forces.

Well, that was a bit extreme, perhaps, since the point of the SPECWAR people was that they could support and augment the regular forces. He sighed. Why was it America always axed her own military as soon as the current war was won, as though there were no possibility of there ever being another one?

But the important consideration, the only consideration right now, was that Blake was safe, and that he was on his way home. Tensions had been so strained between them lately. The elder Murdock wanted desperately to close up that gulf between them, to make things right again.

He knew now that the way to accomplish that was to stop trying to ride Blake about his career decision, to let him go his own way. That was the hard part about being a parent, of course, watching the kids go their own ways, watching them make mistakes.

Or watching them do the right thing, even when Dad thought it was wrong. Murdock grinned.

It was obvious that Blake Murdock had found his place with the SEALs.

WHEN YOU ARRIVE IN FANTASYLAND . . .

1. Consult the **Map**. Find your starting point.
2. Open the **Toughpick** section at random to select your tour. . . .

- **Smells** are everywhere and strong, and, except for those of ENCHANTRESSES and INCENSE, unpleasant. Even DANGER has a Smell—the REEK OF WRONGNESS⊙. There is something in the chemistry of the land that makes Smells. It is probably a fallout effect of MAGIC, but see also SOCKS and TROUSERS.

- **Socks** are never worn in Fantasyland. People thrust their feet, usually unwashed, straight into BOOTS.

- **Sorcery** is sometimes a general word for MAGIC, usually connected with *wiles*⊙, but also sometimes a technical term, referring to that part of Magic entailing the storage and use of POWER. In the latter case, the Sorcerer becomes a sort of battery.

- **Speech.** On some Tours it is necessary to adopt a highfalutin' form of Speech. Instead of saying "I will go out and take a look" you have to say "I shall now walk forth and examine things without." This is tiresome to have to keep up. Even more tiresome are those PANCELTIC TOURS where you have to keep remembering to say "Och aye" and "Top of the marnin' te ye." But these are the Rules.

    See also LANGUAGES.

THE
TOUGH GUIDE
~TO~
FANTASYLAND

Diana Wynne Jones

DAW BOOKS, INC.
DONALD A. WOLLHEIM, FOUNDER
375 Hudson Street, New York, NY 10014

ELIZABETH R. WOLLHEIM
SHEILA E. GILBERT
PUBLISHERS

First Printing, December 1998
1 2 3 4 5 6 7 8 9

For Hannah M. G. Shapero

With particular thanks also
to Chris Bell and Paul Barnett

THE MAP OF FANTASYLAND

GREAT NORTHERN BARRIER

SEA OF DA'AR TENERMEN

IER NEHIR

SEA OF CANISPA

NUNEATON

RIVER GISTRI

CA'EA PURT'WYDYN

BAY OF DOGS

DARK CITADEL

THE SMOKING MOUNTIAN OF G'WD

RIVER LAVOG

IMPERIAL WAY

RIVER NEBADU

RIVER SMEALT

RUIN

GAN'ASH

MARSHES

HOW TO USE THIS BOOK

What to do first

1. Find the MAP. It will be there. No Tour of Fantasyland is complete without one. It will be found in the front part of your brochure, quite near the page that says

> For Mom and Dad for having me
> and for Jeannie (or Jack or Debra or Donnie or ...) for
> putting up with me so supportively
> and for my nine children for not interrupting me
> and for my Publisher for not discouraging me
> and for my Writers' Circle for listening to me
> and for Barbie and Greta and Albert Einstein and
> Aunty May

and so on. Ignore this, even if you are wondering if Albert Einstein is Albert Einstein or in fact the dog.

This will be followed by a short piece of prose that says

> When the night of the wolf waxes strong in the
> morning, the wise man is wary of a false dawn.
> Ka'a Orto'o Gnomic Utterances, VI ii

Ignore this too (or, if really puzzled, look up GNOMIC UTTERANCES in the **Toughpick** section). Find the Map.

2. Examine the Map. It will show most of a continent (and sometimes part of another) with a large number of bays, offshore islands, an inland sea or so, and a sprinkle of towns. There will be scribbly snakes that are probably RIVERS, and names made of CAPITAL LETTERS in curved lines that are not quite upsidedown. By bending your neck sideways you will be able to see that they say things like "Ca'ea Purt'wydyn" and "Om Ce'falos." These *may* be names of countries, but since most of the Map is bare it is hard to tell.

These empty inland parts will be sporadically peppered with little molehills, invitingly labeled "Megamort Hills," "Death Mountains," "Hurt Range," and such, with a whole line of molehills near the top called "Great Northern Barrier." Above this will be various warnings of danger. The rest of the Map's space will be sparingly devoted to little tiny feathers called "Wretched Wood" and "Forest of Doom," except for one space that appears to be growing minute hairs. This will be tersely labeled "Marshes."

That is mostly it.

No, wait. If you are lucky, the Map will carry an arrow or compass-heading somewhere in the bit labeled "Outer Ocean" and this will show you which way up to hold it. But you will look in vain for inns, rest-stops, or villages, or even roads. No—wait another minute—on closer examination, you will find the empty interior crossed by a few bird tracks. If you peer at these you will see they are (somewhere) labeled "Old Trade Road—Disused" and "Imperial Way—Mostly Long Gone." Some of these routes appear to lead (or have led) to small edifices enticingly titled "Ruin," "Tower of Sorcery," or "Dark Citadel," but there is no scale of miles and no way of telling how long you might take on the way to see these places.

In short, the Map is useless, but you are advised to keep consulting it, because it is the only one you will get. And, be warned. If you take this Tour, you are going to have to visit every single place on this Map, whether it is marked or not. This is a Rule.

3. Find your STARTING POINT. Let us say it is the town of Gna'ash. You will find it down in one corner on the coast, as far away from anywhere as possible.

4. Having found Gna'ash, you must at once set about finding an INN, Tour COMPANIONS, a meal of STEW, a CHAMBER for the night, and then the necessary TAVERN BRAWL. (If you look all these things up in the **Toughpick** section, you will know what you are in for.) The following morning, you must locate the MARKET and attempt to acquire CLOTHING (which absolutely *must* include a CLOAK), a SADDLE ROLL, WAYBREAD, WATERBOTTLES, a DAGGER, a SWORD, a HORSE, and a MERCHANT to take you along in his CARAVAN. You must resign yourself to being cheated over most prices and you are advised to consult a local MAGICIAN about your Sword.

5. You set off. Now you are on your own. You should turn to the **Toughpick** section of this brochure and select your Tour on a pick-and-mix basis, remembering only that you will have to take in all of it, so that it is no use going straight to CONCLUSION. Management Rules will not allow you to do this until you are on your third brochure. With this proviso, you can take anything in any order you please. The Rules are clearly stated in every case and the OFFICIAL MANAGEMENT TERMS (OMTs) have been thoughtfully included in *italics*⊛ where necessary. All items in CAPITALS AND SMALL CAPITALS can be found in **Toughpick**.

6. Have a good Tour. Thank you for choosing to go with our MANAGEMENT.

What to do next:

Consult **Toughpick**.

Toughpick

Adept. One who has taken what amounts to the Postgraduate Course in MAGIC. If a MAGIC USER is given this title, you can be sure she/he is fairly hot stuff. However, the title is neutral and does *not* imply that the Adept is either GOOD or EVIL. Examine carefully each Adept you encounter and be cautious, even if she/he seems friendly. See COLOR CODING for the best way of telling friends from enemies.

Alleys are the most frequent type of ROAD in a CITY or TOWN. They are always narrow and dark and squishy, and they frequently dead-end. You will escape along them when pursued and also be AMBUSHED there.

See also REFUSE and SQUALOR.

Alligator. Probably extinct in Fantasyland and now to be found only in a mummified state hanging from the rafters of a WIZARD's workroom. If the Alligator is present, it is a sure sign that the Wizard is friendly.

Altars are of three types:

1. In TEMPLES. These are for SACRIFICES, so they will be waist-high and long enough to contain the supine body of a VIRGIN. The stone top will have grooves for blood, and the whole will be covered with *dry brown stains of a troubling kind*⊚ from former Sacrifices.

2. In the open, usually on a hilltop. These are of marble and quite simple but handsome, because they are always devoted to a GOOD deity. The size and shape varies, but the general effect is of unassuming potency.

3. In RUINS. These Altars are underground or inside a *pyramidal structure*⊚. They will sit on a dais at the further, darker end, and be about the size of a laundry hamper, in stone. Approach these with care. Though they undoubtedly hide or contain SECRETS or QUEST OBJECTS you need, they will be set about with magical booby traps that are still operative even after a thousand years. You need to disarm these first, and then possibly the thin shade of the enraged deity after that.

Ambushes will be of four kinds, and you will have them all.

1. By BANDITS, of the CARAVAN with which you are traveling. This will happen early on in your Tour. It will have been carefully set up, usually by a SPY masquerading as a CARAVAN

GUARD. In some narrow place with high sides (*rocky defile*⊙) or where there is thick forest on either side of the route, Bandits will first shoot all the Guards and then come pouring down to overwhelm the Caravan. This is where you will part company with the Caravan since nearly everyone but you will be killed. You will just be left for dead.

2. By ·LEATHERY-WINGED AVIANS a little later on, at night in a high place. This will be your first light brush with the forces of EVIL (you can tell the Avians are Evil because they SMELL). You will fight them off quite easily, but you may be left with a festering wound.

3. By the forces of Evil, upon a group of people you either care about or were depending on for help. You will come upon the evidence of this Ambush some time after the midpoint of your Tour. It will be in a ravine. Here you will find the corpses of your brutally murdered friends being eaten by scavengers. Your rage and grief will be enormous—the more so as you had hoped that this party had made it through to the CITY/WIZARD/KING for help. You must dig graves and proceed.

4. By you, on the forces of Evil. This will be near the end of the Tour, when at last you will be able to turn the tables on the ENEMY, by lying in wait at the top of cliffs beside a *rocky defile*⊙. With luck, you will have help here both from the GOOD King and from assorted Other PEOPLES, usually DWARFS, who will be experts in the art of rolling boulders down on

[icon] the soldiers of the DARK LORD as they pass below. You, with your now considerable experience of Ambushes, will then attack and finish them off. This will be one of your first victories against the forces of Evil. You will throw up afterwards, but basically you will feel good.

Amulet. One of many magical protective items to be found throughout Fantasyland. This kind is usually small, made of metal, amber, or semiprecious stone, and adapted for hanging round the neck. You may be given yours; you may pick it up among other TREASURE; or you may [icon] be forced to obtain one from a MAGIC USER. On many Tours, an Amulet is essential and you must acquire one before going on to the next part. Where not essential, Amulets are still useful, since they can give warning of danger (usually by growing very hot) and, if specially powerful, can either invoke the aid of a God or WIZARD or render the owner invisible.

See also INSCRIPTION, INVISIBILITY, QUEST, and TALISMAN.

[icon] **Ancient Engineering Projects** tend to litter the landscape in some parts of the continent. Most of them are quite mysterious and all of them are made of some substance not known to the present inhabitants, often of a greenish color, or a matte black, though white is not unknown. They will be gigantic. Most of them will be pillars that touch the clouds, but ROADS and broken BRIDGES are common too. It is unknown

quite what challenge caused earlier peoples to make things that were so very large. Most of them are no use to anyone.

See also RUINS.

Anglo-Saxon Cossacks live in the STEPPES and breed HORSES. They try to look like Horses themselves by wearing their hair in ponytails. They ride often, expertly and acrobatically. In fact, they show off rather. Regardless of the fact that winds continually sweep the Steppes, they wear little but sleeveless VESTS and scanty TROUSERS. These people are tough. But, despite riding since early infancy, not one Anglo-Saxon Cossack ever has bandy thighs. Something in their genes prevents this. They are organized normally in CLANS under a supreme chieftain but do not seem to fight among themselves. Nor do they fight other peoples much. Everyone knows better than to mess with them. If called on to fight for GOOD, they muster eventually, but it takes time. Then they are formidable cavalry. Oddly, since their way of life is nomadic, they live in stone fastnesses and rarely use TENTS. On most Tours they are a dreadfully masculine society. Their women wear long skirts and are trained to be wimps.

Animals. See ENEMY SPIES, FOOD, and TRANS-PORT. Apart from creatures expressly designed for one of these three purposes (and this includes HARES and RABBITS), there appear to be almost no animals in Fantasyland. Any other animal you meet will be the result either of a WIZARD'S BREEDING PROGRAM or of SHAPE-SHIFTING. You may on the other hand *hear* things, such as roaring, trampling, and frequently the hooting of owls, but these are strongly suspected to be sound-effects only, laid on by the Management when it feels the need for a little local color.

See also DOMESTIC ANIMALS and ECOLOGY.

Animal Skins are much in use and are of four kinds:

1. Trappers' furs. These are occasionally brought south in bundles. As there appear to be no animals to be trapped, it is likely that these skins are either cunning manmade imitations or imported from another world.

2. Furs worn by NORTHERN BARBARIANS. It is possible that these are also false or imported. Another possibility is that the animals providing these furs are now extinct (see ECOLOGY) and that the famous fur loincloths are handed down from father to son.

3. Leather for BOOTS, VESTS, etc. is again of mysterious origin. (See DOMESTIC ANIMALS.) There are not enough cows to go round, but the leather has to come from *somewhere*.

4. Skins of which the TENTS of DESERT NOMADS are made. Here the source is obvious. Nomads breed HORSES: the Tents have to be made of horsehide. In fact, it is entirely probable that Horses provide all four kinds of Animal Skin.

Apelike Cannibals are small, weak, white, and horrible, but where they exist they occur in great numbers, all bundled together like maggots. They have small clawed hands and small sharp fangs, and it is by sheer numbers and persistence that they overwhelm the unwary Tourist, whom they will then eat raw. They live underground, but not very far underground, often in places like deserted farmhouses where travelers would not expect attack; though they seem to fear daylight, they will come out at dusk as soon as those in the farmhouse have relaxed. Just occasionally they will attack a CAMP or a strayed Tourist in open country. They have the look of degenerate humans. Possibly they have strayed into Fantasyland *via* H. G. Wells's Time Machine.

Apostrophes. Few NAMES in Fantasyland are considered complete unless they are interrupted by an apostrophe somewhere in the middle (as in Gna'ash). The only names usually exempt from apostrophes, apart from those of most WIZARDS, HEROES, and COMPANIONS on the Tour, are those of some COUNTRIES. No one knows the reasons for this. Nor does anyone really know how an apostrophe should be pronounced, though there are theories:

1. You ignore the apostrophe and simply pronounce the word. (Here Gna'ash = Gnash.)

2. You leave a gap or lacuna where the apostrophe occurs. (Here Gna'ash = Gna-ash.)

3. You make a kind of clucking-sound to

stand for the apostrophe. (Here Gna'ash = Gna**glunk**ash.) Persons with insecurely mounted tonsils should adhere to one of the other two theories.

Apprentices are people who are training for a trade or skill, which means they are usually quite young and bad at what they do. Most of the time they are like nurses during an operation, being there only to hand the master his tools. They seem to have to do this for a good many years before they get to do anything more interesting, and it is therefore not surprising that some of them get restless and either try to do the interesting stuff themselves or simply run away and join the Tour. The Rules state that if an Apprentice tries to do the interesting stuff on her/his own it will blow up in her/his face. If she/he runs away, she/he will learn all sorts of things very quickly and also probably prove to be the MISSING HEIR to a Kingdom. Surprisingly, very few Apprentices do run away. If you have one on your Tour, you are in for an eventful time.

Aristocratic Feudalists. There are several branches of this PEOPLE:

   1. Bad. Here the COUNTRY is organized into peasants and lords and usually ruled by a bad KING or REGENT. The peasants will live in HOVELS and do all the work. The lords will have all the money and oppress the peasants by taxing, beating, and imprisoning them and

exercising unlimited *droit du seigneur*. The
lords will live in CASTLES or MANSIONS, but will
spend much of their time at Court, wearing
sumptuous clothes, and jockeying corruptly for
the King's favor. Court will be very elaborate.
And everything will be worse if the country is
ruled by a bad QUEEN. Usually the arrival of
the Tour is the signal for the peasants to revolt.

2. Good. This country has the same setup,
except that a GOOD King rules it. The lords
are therefore honest, polite, and kind to their
underlings, and the underlings are prosperous
and jolly and do not mind pulling their fore-
locks to the gentry. They will turn out in great
numbers if the Country goes to WAR, and
fight valiantly.

3. Indifferent. This has the same setup, but
the King is a nonentity, or is lost, or has failed
in his duties. The peasants here will be poor
because of crop failure and the lords poor because the peasants are. Generally the Management has little interest in this country. The
Tour will pass through very quickly unless one
of its number happens to be the MISSING HEIR
or a poverty-stricken lord from this place. In
the latter case, the Tour will visit his broken-
down MANSION.

In all three types, the Tourist should, if possible, go straight to Court. That is always where
the interest lies.

Armor is, in the opinion of the Management,
cheating. This is why it is allowed only to the

ARMIES of bad KINGS and MINIONS OF THE DARK LORD, as well as the DARK LORD himself. Warriors of the Dark always wear plate Armor, colored black, though whether the color is painted on, stove-blacked on, or intrinsic to the metal is not known. No Tourist should attempt to acquire or wear Armor, unless it is sanctioned by being of special metal, found in a PALACE treasury or DWARVEN FASTNESS and needed urgently for some special purpose. This Armor will be of chain mail of incredible lightness, and it will always be, by lucky chance, an exact fit.

🖎 **Army.** There are strict Rules about this. Only bad KINGS and the DARK LORD are allowed to raise an Army at the start of a Tour. This will always be vast in numbers. It will trample over everything and devastate the country as it

marches, and will get bigger and worse as the
Tour goes on. This Army will also use MAGIC
in unfair ways. The GOOD are allowed to raise
a proper Army to combat the bad one only
when it is almost too late, right at the end of
the Tour, and the Good Army will somehow
avoid either trampling crops or eating off the
countryside—probably because the Army of
the Dark Lord has eaten it all already. Neither
Army will have prostitutes and other camp followers: these are reserved for MERCENARIES
only. The Rules also state that the two Armies
are very evenly matched, although the Good
Army is only about half the size of the other
one. Do not worry, however, if you find your
side apparently defeated. Your Army may be
killed to a man, but Good will triumph all the
same.

Aspect. The Aspect of a GODDESS OR GOD is
the deity manifesting itself through a human by
making her/him take on an often shadowy form
representing that deity. This can be an ANIMAL
or other shape, or sometimes just a kind of
light. Deities tend to do this when they want
to speed up the action a bit. It is often quite
hard on the human and a great shock to any
onlookers.

Assassins, Guild of. The second most frequent
guild after the THIEVES' GUILD. Indeed, it is
possible that these are the *only* two, and that
in Fantasyland crime is the sole organized activ-

ity. Be that as it may, the Assassins are numerous and widespread. They are said to be very good at their job, which is of course killing people for money, and to proceed on all occasions with strict regard to law and protocol. Each member will have trained for years in rather a large number of ways of murdering humans (it is not known whether they also accept commissions to rub out ELVES, GIANTS, etc.) and will be distinguishable by a uniform (often black) or a badge. From one-third of the way through your Tour onwards, you may expect someone to have paid an Assassin to slaughter you. The traditional venue of this murder is a townhouse (Assassins, for some reason, do not operate in open country) or WHARF, so be on your guard in these places. But do not lose sleep over it. As the Assassin approaches you will get a *sense of wrongness*⊙ or *feeling of being watched*⊙, and this should alert you in time. Once alert, you will find it surprisingly easy to kill this practiced killer. He will die protesting that you broke some Rule or other.

Astrology. Fantasyland has *strange constellations*⊙ which MAGES and astrologers frequently consult, often with the help of an instrument called an *astrolabe*⊙, which in our world is a primitive sextant but in Fantasyland is probably a zodiacal ready-reckoner. However, the Management is very reticent about the constellations that comprise their ZODIAC and about what each of them means, either alone or in conjunction. Consequently a Mage or an astrologer can tell you just what she/he feels like. Usually the Management pays these people to tell you in obscure terms what the STARS say is going to happen in the way of WARS and CATACLYSMS on the Tour, and therefore any prediction they make is bound to come true, provided you can understand it.

See also PROPHECY.

Average Folk are any people inhabiting the continent who are not specifically mentioned in the list of PEOPLES. They are not precisely normal all the same. Those who are not ASSASSINS, BEGGARS, or THIEVES will be INNKEEPERS, MERCHANTS, or Peasants, and therefore they are busy trying to either rob you, rub you out, or cheat you. The rest will be fully occupied being taxed out of existence or dealing with a variety of magical nuisances. Otherwise they are rather like you, give or take a few hideous sores, gnarled hands, and suspicious scowls. Do not expect help or sympathy from any of them.

Axe. The only allowable cutting weapon apart from a SWORD. To be allowed one you must be a NORTHERN BARBARIAN, a DWARF, or a BLACKSMITH; most Tourists have to make do with a Sword. WOODSMEN, of course, have Axes too, but not as WEAPONS.

Beware, when the landscape is of surpassing
beauty, of the needle in the haystack.

Ka'a Orto'o, Gnomic Utterances, XXI vi

Backlash of Magic is when a SPELL is either
foiled or bungled and the MAGIC recoils. This
usually ends up in the face of the one who cast
the Spell, often fatally; but occasionally, particularly if the Spell was very large, the Backlash
goes on to spray everyone in the vicinity or
even travel in waves across the continent. This
can be very dangerous. The Rules state that
there is no way of stopping Backlash.

Backpacks are fairly unobtainable, since they
do not form part of the regulation equipment
 for Tourists. The Rule is that the correct form
of luggage is a SADDLE ROLL or Saddlebag.
When, however, you have got through all available supplies of HORSES, you will find yourself
forced to manufacture a Backpack from blankets and harness. Expect to have to do this any
time from halfway to two-thirds of the way
through your Tour. This makeshift luggage will

prove quite trouble-free. It will not fall to pieces and drop your lunch the way it would if you did the same thing in your own world. It should last you easily to the end of the Tour.

Bale. Merchandise of any description (although the Management seldom describes it) is always in Bales, presumably waterproof since you will mostly see Bales on a WHARF. Crates are almost never used. This is peculiar as timber seems readily available, more so than waterproof fabrics. (See BUILDINGS and CLOAKS.) We put this down to custom or Rules. Bales on Wharfs are always being unloaded by very noisy dockworkers of all sexes.

See also WINE.

Bandits roam the hillier parts of the country in large gangs that seem fairly well organized. They are easily able to plant a SPY or a false GUARD in any CARAVAN (see also CARAVAN GUARD) to lead it into a prepared AMBUSH. Expect to be attacked by Bandits early in the Tour. They will leave you for dead, possibly taking one of your COMPANIONS prisoner before they do. In this case you must prepare to rescue her/him from the clearing where the Bandits are preparing for a mass rape. You need have no compunction about killing as many Bandits as you can. Male or female, they are the dregs. Nor will they seem very organized when you burst into the clearing. You may steal their HORSES and proceed with the Tour.

Two questions about Bandits remain unanswered. These are:

1. Where are Bandits recruited from? The Management is vague on this point, but sometimes indicates that Bandits are outcasts, on the run for crimes committed in their home towns or villages, or that they are unattached MERCENARIES.

2. What do the Bandits do with the large amount of loot they regularly cull from Caravans? The Management is vaguer still on this point and has never so far indicated the whereabouts of any receivers of stolen goods willing to deal with Bandits, but since the Bandits cannot eat JEWELERY or BALED cloth, such outlets must exist.

Both these questions may have the same answer. The Bandits are employed by the Management to make the early stages of the Tour more interesting.

Barbarian Horde. This will be lots and lots of wild-seeming people advancing under a cloud of dust in order to devastate more civilized parts. They are a bit like locusts, except that they kill people directly. Tourists should take cover at once when the tell-tale dustcloud is sighted, but should not otherwise be too concerned. These Barbarians never harm Tourists and are, in fact, mostly innocent victims. They have usually been stirred up by some God or the DARK LORD. They will often go home quietly when talked to seriously.

See also NORTHERN BARBARIANS.

Barbary Vikings wear horned HELMETS and fur CLOAKS; otherwise you could mistake them for NORTHERN BARBARIANS. They swagger hugely, quarrel hugely, drink hugely, and boast hugely. The thing they like best is killing people, particularly lots at once. If a Barbary Viking goes berserk, he will kill even *more* freely. Stand clear if one does.

All of them are excellent seamen. Their BOATS have square sails and lines of SHIELDS down the sides. Quite often, the Management employs them as PIRATES because they are good at raping and looting and burning, but on some Tours they appear as allies of a rather willful kind, and will even take Tourists for a sail. At home, which is somewhere quite northerly, they have a KING, who is GOOD and to whom they are violently loyal, and their womenfolk whom you scarcely see at all because they are all at home breeding warriors. Barbary Vikings are even maler than ANGLO-SAXON COSSACKS.

Bards are best thought of as musical MAGIC USERS. On former Tours they tended to be diffident people, forced to roam the continent in ragged finery, scraping a poor living by playing and singing in INNS and FAIRGROUNDS. They were not always honest. When their MUSIC

proved to have enormous power, they were na-
ively astonished and usually blamed their
HARPS. Nowadays the Management is alerted
to the powers of Bards and has taken to collecting bardic youngsters into halls or troupes
under a master, for stringent professional training. Bards are now required to dress smartly,
to play the Harp and at least two other instruments, to have on tap (and sing to professional
standards) all available songs and invocations,
to memorize all LEGENDS, ballads, and *old
lore*☜, to recite epics, and to know a fair number of SPELLS. Thus they frequently join Tours
as a powerful COMPANION. You can ask your
Bard to open PORTALS and assuage DEMONS
and do almost anything musical. She/he will
often dredge from memory vital pieces of
KNOWLEDGE that even your Tour MENTOR has
missed. Bards are so potent that it is possible
they all go on in old age to become MYSTICAL
MASTERS. After all, Mystical Masters had to
begin somewhere.

Barons occur among most of the ARISTOCRATIC
FEUDALIST Peoples. They are a kind of lord
who is not a good thing. Most of them live in

huge old (*moldering*☜) Halls or CASTLES, from
which they oppress the peasantry, attack and
imprison Tourists, and have dealings with either
DEMONS or the less pleasant MAGIC USERS.
They have great numbers of ancestors, and
their residences are likely to be full of the
GHOSTS of these forebears, most of whom were

as unpleasant as the present Baron and all of whom met with bad ends. GOOD Barons are almost unknown. If they are Good, they will have another title to add to the "Baron."

Bar Service has not yet been invented. Drinks and other orders are traditionally brought to you at your table in the INN by barmaids. This is an enlightened arrangement by the Management because it prevents unemployment among young unmarried women and probably also keeps up the birthrate.

See also EUNUCHS, MAIDS, and WAR.

Bath is something all Tourists crave for quite soon. After very few days of slogging along in all weathers and sleeping in your clothes, you will be ready to kill for a Bath. You will crave to wash your hair. The Management is reasonable on this issue. Before long, you will find either a deep POOL in a RIVER of icy water (*icemelt*⊛; see also HYPOTHERMIA, COMMON COLD, and CHILBLAINS) or an INN with a heated bath-house. You will be able to leave your clothes, money, weapons, and SECRETS on the bank or bath-house bench and wash in perfect safety. Management Rules state that no one ever steals your clothes/valuables or AMBUSHES you while you are immersed in a Bath. Any lurker will wait until you have finished. Take care, however. Baths are the occasion for SEX with one or more of your FELLOW TRAVELLERS. No matter how irritating you have found her/him up to then, after or during the Bath you will find her/him irresistible. It is probably something in the WATER.

Bays nibble the coastline all over and have three uses:

1. For having fishing VILLAGES where you might hire a small BOAT, provided the villagers are not all out sailing against the sunset.

2. For being washed up in after a shipwreck. This kind of Bay is always a long way from anywhere, rather sandy, and without fresh WATER. Never mind. If you are washed up here, it will be because some vital QUEST OBJECT or Information (see KNOWLEDGE) is waiting nearby in a CAVE for you to discover.

3. For going down to in order to meet SCALY FOLK. This Bay will be rocky and picturesque, the more so because you will probably have to

wait for either Moonrise or dawn before the Scaly Folk condescend to emerge from the sea. Be patient. They too have vital Information.

Bed. This is something all Tourists will soon miss acutely. And when, after days of sleeping outside on the ground, you finally arrive somewhere where there are beds, prepare yourself for disappointment. Beds in Fantasyland are always made of rope wrapped around a frame, with a mattress of straw on top. You will spend the night oozing between the holes among the ropes. And being prickled.

Beer always foams and is invariably delivered in tankards. The Management is not concerned with the taste of it. That is your funeral.

Beggars are to be found in all major CITIES, always wearing rags and often with hideous deformities. They will pester Tourists for money from the City gates onwards. As soon as the City comes under SIEGE, however, all Beggars vanish. The Management has prudently withdrawn them for use in other Cities along the Tourist routes. This makes sense. Beggars would only be in the way during the fighting.

Beginnings. Fantasyland, like so many other places, had its Beginnings at a time when no one was around to see it. Nevertheless, quite a lot is known about it. Unlike our world, Fantasyland was definitely made by Gods, working alone or in teams of three, or in whole panthe-ons. This accounts for some of the peculiarities of the place, since the Rule states that one Goddess or three Gods invariably make some kind of mistake, as a result of being distracted during the act of creation; and a pantheon of GODDESSES AND GODS tends to disagree and quarrel, causing mistakes likewise. This, at the very least, lets EVIL in. After this, according to the ELVES, the deity/deities who created Fantasy-land took time off to make the Elves and then let a certain amount of evolution happen. Opin-ions vary as to when and how humanity arrived, but the majority seem to favor the notion that humans were imported from another planet or universe.

Betrayal is a word widely used on the Tour. It can mean:

1. One of your COMPANIONS lets you down. You can tell by their COLOR CODING who this is going to be.

☎ **2.** An ENEMY SPY tells the BANDITS or the MINIONS OF THE DARK LORD where you are. Which is what you would expect.

3. An employee of the DARK LORD shows 🖫 the ENEMY how to get into the CITY.

4. A COURTIER or rival PRINCE frames the heir to the crown and causes him to be exiled for crimes he did not commit.

Expect all of these things in the course of the Tour, whatever you think Betrayal means.

Bets are laid by soldiers on dice, by everyone on GLADIATORS, and by WARRIOR WOMEN on almost anything. Management Rules state that no Tourist will lay a Bet unless he is the SMALL MAN. No Tours so far have been founded on the outcome of a Bet, and only in rare cases are they started by one.

See also GAMING.

Birds. There are remarkably few Birds in Fantasyland, either in WOODS or on moorland. The reason is probably that, when any Bird is seen, it is promptly shot by a Tourist desperate for something else to eat besides STEW. Otherwise Birds are of three main kinds:

1. The occasional carrier pigeon, for use when no MAGIC USERS are around to exercise MINDSPEECH.

2. Trained hawks/eagles in the employ of EYRIE CLANS. These Birds are larger than their wild cousins (which do not exist), with larger heads. This is because they are telepathic. They have formidable intelligence and acute eyesight, and usually fight to the death beside their owners.

3. ENEMY SPIES, which are nearly always crows. The ENEMY here exercises remarkably little intelligence. In the virtual absence of all other Birds, the crows are nearly always spotted as SPIES and it rarely seems to occur to any MINION OF THE DARK LORD to disguise these crows as friendly eagles.

See also BREEDING PROGRAMS, ENEMY SPIES, and FOOD.

Birthright. This is what at least one of the party on the Tour will be looking for and it may indeed turn out to be the main QUEST OBJECT. It is a little on the lines of people from North America and Australia coming to Europe to find out about their families, but more complicated. There are two kinds of Birthright quested for:

1. Magical. The person in search of Magical Birthright will have inklings of TALENT, but no more. In order to become a proper MAGIC USER she/he will have to seek out a powerful MAGE or WIZARD and try to learn from them. Mere family will not do, unless a parent turns out to be the Wizard, the DARK LORD, or an ENCHANTRESS. And it usually turns out that the Mage/Wizard is no help either. The seeker will have to go through difficult and frightening experiences that make her/him develop her/his Talent out of sheer terror.

2. Family. Here the person seeking Birthright is always a Royal heir. If you are an ordinary person do not expect to discover your family, unless of course you are a MISSING HEIR and had no idea that you were. If you are of Royal birth, then finding out who you are may well happen quite early in the Tour. You will have to spend the rest of it honing your skills as a ruler and collecting lost items of Royal regalia, all of which will proclaim your Birthright. See also ORBS, RINGS, SCEPTERS, and SWORDS.

On some Tours both kinds of Birthright are

being sought, occasionally by the same person. This is where it can get complicated.

Black Arts. All MAGICS of an unpleasant and antisocial nature. They are often to do with killing and enslaving things and normally require a SACRIFICE as preliminary, or at least a lot of blood. The mark of Black Arts is that the blood is not willingly donated. Practitioners will either trick Tourists and others into donations or seize them and cut them, often with a knife that looks rather unpleasant. There will then be a lot of mumbling and GESTURES around a PENTAGRAM, during which there will be *a sense of wrongness*⊕ or *a feeling of extreme cold*⊕; in extreme cases, *terror blooms*⊕. This usually heralds the arrival of a DEMON which is about to get out of control. Practitioners can be of all grades of expertise, from the feeble person who merely wishes for a little power (and gets steadily more corrupted) to the high ADEPT who regularly summons Demons and enslaves ARMIES. Some of them will be adherents of the DARK LORD. Some of them will have set up on their own. Tourists may expect to meet someone who is into the Black Arts at fairly infrequent but regular intervals along the way.

See also NECROMANCY and REEK OF WRONGNESS.

Blacksmiths are much in evidence, hammering in forges and sometimes even shoeing HORSES. The Rules state that a Blacksmith is huge and

IRON AND SON,
SHOES FOR MEN
AND BEASTS.

 brawny but wise and gentle in nature. For this reason Blacksmiths make excellent foster-fathers, either to young Tourists or to MISSING HEIRS. If someone from either of these classes of person needs to reforge a broken SWORD, the Blacksmith can show her/him how. But the Rules also state that two out of three Black-smiths have a sexy teenage daughter, who will attempt to seduce her foster-brother(s). When this happens, the only course for the fosterling is to leave at once on a QUEST. On his travels, he will soon realize that this young lady is not for him.

Blankets are to Fantasyland what sleeping bags are to our own world. They are what you will sleep in. Blankets seem very warm. No Tourist ever has more than one. And they seem quite waterproof. It is usually only towards dawn that rain gets through them to the sleeper beneath. All the same, those booked for the Tour must steel themselves for spending many nights shivering. And then the next night, since even in Fantasyland Blankets do not dry in twelve hours when rolled up behind the saddle.

Boats are always quite small and built of wood. This is to make it easier for them to sink in a Storm, be caught by Pirates, or overturned by a Sea Monster.
   The rigging of Boats is puzzling. Small ones seem to be fore-and-aft rigged in a more modern manner than large ones, which always seem to have more of an antique cross-rig. Perhaps this is again so that Pirates can catch them more easily, but it does make problems in contrary winds. Helpful Wizards are forced to spend long hours standing either before the mast or in the prow, making wind get into the sails.
   See also Galleys and Ships.

Bogs are water-sodden parts of the Terrain put there to slow you down when the Forces ≋

of the Dark are chasing you. The mud will often be very deep. You could lose HORSES here. You will also nearly lose a COMPANION, who will sink in the mire up to her/his shoulders and have to be pulled out using a makeshift arrangement of rope. After that, you will soon be out of the Bog. Bogs are quite small, unlike the MARSHES, which are another matter.

Booths are always there where commerce is going on. They are a cross between a TENT, a SHOP, and a MARKET stall, and are sort of halfpermanent. People in them sell everything except FOOD; some of them are barber's stalls—expect to have to bargain even for a haircut. Storytellers have Booths, too, and it is here that you will be directed if the Management wishes you to learn a handy LEGEND. It is not known why everyone has Booths instead of something more permanent and rainproof.

Boots. In Fantasyland these are remarkable in that they seldom or never wear out and are suitable for riding or walking in without the need of SOCKS. Boots never pinch, rub, or get stones in them; nor do nails stick upwards into the feet from the soles. They are customarily mid-calf length or knee-high, slip on and off easily and never smell of feet. Unfortunately, the formula for making this splendid footwear is a closely guarded secret, possibly derived from nonhumans (see DWARFS, ELVES, and GNOMES).

Bows and Arrows are used by ELVES, defenders of a CITY under SIEGE, and WOODSMEN. Tourists are discouraged by the Management from using these WEAPONS, probably because it is so easy to miss with them, whereas anyone can swing a SWORD. Crossbows, being more accurate, are used almost exclusively by bad people.

Bread is quite well known in Fantasyland, but you will seldom get much of it and it will never be fresh. You might be given some to sop up your STEW in an INN of an evening, but in the morning, just as that day's baking should be ready, the Rules state that you will make a hurried departure, having time to grab up only a piece of stale loaf and a hunk of cheese.

Breeding Programs—official or unofficial—are quite common, and affect both ANIMALS and people. It is something everyone accepts. Expect to see the results of the following at any time on your Tour:

1. Animals.

(a) By non-MAGIC USERS, ANGLO-SAXON COSSACKS, DESERT NOMADS, EYRIE CLANS, and WOODSMEN all breed either HORSES or BIRDS for greater intelligence, endurance, and, in the case of Birds, MINDSPEECH. Their methods are secret, but it is suspected that magical enhancement is often used. The OMT for this is *traditional methods*.

(b) By WIZARDS, who never seem able to refrain from tinkering with genes. Bad Wizards have enormous fun building beasts out of bits and pieces of other creatures, adding wings to bears and lions and snakes and extra legs to birds, and then fangs and slime to the result. The CITADELS of these Wizards are usually surrounded by ill-smelling breeding pits, where all sorts of infant monstrosities are hopping and flopping. GOOD Wizards quite often do the same sort of tinkering, but the results are rarely described as monstrous, nor as stinking in a breeding pit. Somehow a Good Wizard can cross an eagle, a bear, a lion, and a lizard without the creature being anything but well proportioned, fragrant, and comely. Such beasts are always friendly to humans too (see ECOLOGY). This explains why there are so few large beasts of a normal type in Fantasyland. They have all been captured long ago and interbred with other species.

2. People.

(a) By Royal Families, who are of course mainly concerned that their son/daughter marry only someone else who is Royal. Royalness seems to be a gene, but one which is recessive and easily overwhelmed by common genes. For this reason Royal marriages are always arranged ones. Most of the spirited PRINCESSES joining your Tour will be doing so because a Royal marriage has been arranged for them against their wishes. But there are a few Royal Families where other genes are being preserved and strengthened by judicious marriage. These traits will usually have to do with the hereditary ability to speak to GODDESSES AND GODS, hold the SWORD of the Kingdom, or perform major state MAGICS. Ironically, these traits often manifest in long-lost offspring whose descent is far from pure (see MISSING HEIRS).

(b) By families of MAGIC USERS intent on preserving or enhancing the family TALENTS. For some reason this is rarely done by coercion or arranged marriage. Someone of the opposite sex and the correct Talent always comes along at the right moment.

(c) By WIZARDS again. Bad Wizards tinker with humans and Other PEOPLES to breed them with several more arms and legs or unwholesome dispositions, or both. Sometimes they do this to make convenient SLAVES, sometimes to make better bodies for themselves. Good Wizards will have done this too, but always in the far past. Whole races claim to owe their existence to the Breeding Program of a long-dead Good Wizard.

Bridges. The inhabitants of Fantasyland seem to have a distrust of Bridges, maybe because they provide an easy way for an invading ARMY to cross to a VILLAGE on the other side of the RIVER. This is a great inconvenience to the Tourist. The Rule is that, when being pursued by the forces of the Dark, you are going to need to cross a Bridge, and there will be no Bridge. While the Tour is waiting to find a way across, the forces of the Dark have time to catch up. Even if there is supposed to be a Bridge on the route, you are likely to arrive to find it broken—whereupon the forces of the Dark gain steadily again. The only Bridges sure to be still in place are ANCIENT ENGINEERING PROJECTS, and they will be huge, with, as soon as you get to the middle, a tendency to develop a small but impassable gap right at the apex.

Brigands. See BANDITS.

Building Materials bear little relation to what is available locally. Thus all ordinary houses are made of wood and plaster, even if there is no forest for miles, and all major BUILDINGS are of stone, regardless of the fact that Fantasyland appears to have no quarries. In the case of Wizards' TOWERS, the stone is always of some notable color, such as red, black, or blue. Possibly this is a side-effect of the no-entry spells that the Rules state must always be present. Northern-based WIZARDS and ENCHANTRESSES favor ice as a Building Material, and often have fantastic PALACES carved magically out of glaciers.

ANCIENT ENGINEERING PROJECTS are made of another substance entirely. This seems no longer obtainable.

Buildings. The Rule is that all ordinary houses are made mostly of timber, with a tendency to lean off the true. Those in CITIES always have the upper story jutting out over the street so that the occupants can empty chamberpots on passers-by. PALACES and TEMPLES are probably made of stone, but this is so ornamented that no Tourist can be sure. The Rule is that the Tour slams to a stop while the Management draws your attention to every pillar and most gargoyles. No interior, except in HOVELS, is ever simple. The Rules further state that all Buildings seem larger inside than out. Passages, stairs, and halls abound, and every Building you enter will have at least one mysterious shut door leading to somewhere that does not fit the groundplan. Windows are glazed and often have diamond panes, making it hard to see the painted decorations on the walls and very difficult to see out at all.

See also BUILDING MATERIALS, CASTLES, CITADELS, and TOWERS.

Certain Sages encountered the hero Somplac one day, who challenged them with the words, "Which is mightier—the mind or the sword?" To which the Sage Algeron answered, "What the sword does, the mind has already accomplished." "True," replied Somplac, "but my answer is more cutting." And he sliced off the left big toe of Algeron.

Ka'a Orto'o, Gnomic Utterances, V xvi

Camps are of two kinds:

1. For ARMIES and MERCENARIES. These consist of many orderly rows of TENTS, with the commander's tent in the middle and sentries regularly patrolling the outskirts. There will be provision carts and the cookhouse Tent (making STEW) in one quadrant, and pickets for HORSES in another. The odd thing here is that, when you look down upon the ENEMY camp from a convenient hillside, you will be able to tell the size of the Army not by counting Tents but by the numbers of cooking fires you see. When you enter the Camp, cooking fires are not in evidence unless required to be scattered, set fire to Tents, and thereby cause the numerically hugely superior Enemy to panic.

2. For Tourists. You will have one of these every night, either in the open under a windy rock or in woodland under dripping TREES. Here you will picket and feed Horses, light a fire and cook Stew, and spread your bedroll and sleep. First, however, you must dig a latrine pit, and the MAGIC USER among you must set WARDS to keep you all safe at night. Tourists often make the mistake of leaving the latrine outside the Wards, and occasionally the Horses too. This means that you could lose a COMPAN-ION and several mounts to MUTANT NASTIES or other marauders in the night. It is often simpler to arrange to be awake in turns. Whichever, you are going to be glad to sleep under any roof before long.

Capital Letters at the beginnings of words are used liberally by the Management according to Rules that transcend human understanding and may under no circumstances be questioned (see TABOO).

Caravan Guards are men drawn from all PEO-PLES, though human is preferred, and set to ride with a MERCHANT'S CARAVAN and protect it from BANDITS. They are of four kinds:

1. Unattached MERCENARIES. These are quite nice guys. Some of them even have NAMES. Tourists need not, however, trouble to get to know this class of GUARD. They will all be killed when the Bandits attack.

2. Unattached nobles or PRINCES. You should

cultivate these. They will survive the Bandits' attack and then act as your guides for the next phase of your Tour.

3. Bandits in disguise. This is a frequent class of Guard. They will lead you into an AMBUSH and there is nothing you can do to stop them (see also ENEMY SPIES). Tourists should, however, remember that this Ambush always happens early in a Tour and is therefore usually survived. The Tourist will merely be left for dead.

4. Unattached and/or penniless Tourists. You may find you have to take service as a Guard in order to proceed with your Tour. If you are strong and know how to use a SWORD it helps, but Merchants seldom check on fighting skills. And your service will last only until the Bandits attack and leave you for dead.

Caravans in Fantasyland are not the colorful conveyances of Gypsies. They are always a cumbrous train of wagons, wains, and HORSES with CARAVAN GUARDS, and carry merchandise and occasional passengers along prescribed routes for profit. Probably very few make it to their destinations, given the frequency of BAN-DITS and other marauders. Tourists, however, are always booked into a Caravan. Any other mode of travel is said to be even less safe. It is therefore odd that most Tourists find themselves in much less trouble as soon as the Caravan has been AMBUSHED and they are free to proceed on their own.

Castles occasionally adorn the heights for pictorial effect, but the Management usually arranges for you to see round only the obligatory Castle at the center of a TOWN or CITY. These are edifices with *frowning battlements*, slit windows, and multiple defensible spiral stairways inside. They contain few or no comfortable rooms, but this does not matter. You will be there under SIEGE, along with the last remaining defenders. These will be running out of arrows and preparing boiling oil to pour through holes in battlements and above the portcullis. When things have got to this pass, most Tourists will be able to depart through the cellar by means of a SECRET PASSAGE; the

doomed defenders will be remarkably decent—
even jolly—about the fact that you are deserting them like this in their hour of need.

Cataclysm. There has always been at least one
of these in Fantasyland, usually in the far past;
it reduced the country to a primitive state. But
stay alert. A Cataclysm during the present Tour
is not to be ruled out, particularly if one of your
COMPANIONS annoys or challenges a WIZARD.

Caverns are large underground systems with
RIVERS running through them. They can be entered from SECRET PASSAGES, behind WATER-
FALLS, and from holes in the hillside. At first
there will be large grottoes with stalactites, followed, when your torch fails, by areas that glow
on their own. Shortly you will come upon a
major center of population, which can be of
Other PEOPLES or of troglodytic humans. Here
you will be prudent to buy a BOAT (or steal
one if the Cavern Dwellers are hostile), load
yourselves, your wounded, and any provisions
aboard it, and set off down the underground
River. Your least favorite COMPANION will
probably die at this point. After quite a few
days you will come out in a Hidden VALLEY,
often occupied by DRAGONS. This is the main
way in which male Tourists get to meet Dragons and you should not miss the experience.
Even if there are no Dragons, all Tourists must
expect to spend some days in a Cavern at some
point in the Tour.

Caves are smaller systems than CAVERNS and are usually entered from somewhere beside a Blocked MOUNTAIN PASS. You will stumble upon a Cave either under a snowdrift or behind a jut of rock just as night falls and you are too exhausted to continue. There will be a stony front CHAMBER big enough for HORSES and a cooking fire for STEW, and a further Chamber at the back which you will not discover straight away. When you do, you will find it contains either the missing ORB or SCEPTER you wanted or a carefully wrapped pile of parchment SCROLLS which will give you the KNOWLEDGE you needed. The Management has directed you to this Cave on purpose.

Chamber is the regular word for your room at an INN and for rooms in any other old buildings. This may be to distinguish them from ordinary houses (*the room at the back of the hovel appeared to be a sleeping space⊕*) or PALACES. But even here the throne room can be a Chamber, as in *silence fell throughout the whole vast Chamber⊕*. CAVES have Chambers, too, if you are proposing to sleep in them, and TORTURE is generally done in a specially designated Chamber. Perhaps the Management just likes the word.

Chickens are seen only after they have been cooked and then only in PALACES, where the Rule is that you eat chicken drumsticks with your fingers and then throw the bones to the

dogs. Eggs are very rare. The hens of Fantasyland do not seem to lay very well. They seem
to be bred in unseen Palace poultry yards
purely for the pot.

Chilblains are unheard-of, however inclement
the WEATHER. This is probably because the
Management lives mostly in California.

Children are not commonly found on a Tour.
If a Child appears and seems to wish to take
part, be very wary. She/he is likely to be either
a God or the MISSING HEIR to a Kingdom. In
either case this will make the Child unpredictable and capricious. She/he will unquestionably
involve you in a great deal of trouble. See
THIEVES' GUILD for the only exception to this
Rule.

Citadels are very strong BUILDINGS of thick
black stone made for defense. They are tall,
with few and slitty windows. Spiral staircases
lead to a battlemented top with a very wide
view. Most Citadels are at the center point of
a CITY and are where you will all retreat when
the ENEMY has got inside the City walls and is
burning and sacking there. Naturally you will
not need to surrender. Down inside the Citadel
are SECRET PASSAGES *carved from the living
rock*⊙ through which you can escape into a
CAVERN. Usually you will have to leave quite
a few defenders behind. Just occasionally, the
Citadel will belong to an Evil WIZARD. In this

case it will be all alone, perched on a black crag that proves to be *honeycombed with passages*⊛, and the Tour will get in through these.

See also CASTLES and CONFRONTATIONS.

Cities occur at the rate of one, or at the most two, to every COUNTRY. They are usually where the ruler lives and they are surrounded by high stone walls. For these reasons, they are going to be under SIEGE around the time the Tour arrives in them. Prepare for HARDSHIP as soon as you see the walls in the distance. But first prepare for a lot of noise and people (see BEGGARS) and horsedrawn traffic. There will also be multiple ALLEYS (where all the HORSE droppings get pitched), many squares, and some fine houses. The CASTLE or PALACE of the ruler will be on a hill in the exact center, with TEMPLES somewhere near. The heads of malefactors or enemies of the state will be on stakes somewhere—you may recognize one of them as having belonged to a GOOD man you encountered earlier and rather liked—or perhaps there will be picked-clean skeletons hanging in cages along the sides of the streets, performing the same function as street-lamps except after dark. (See also EXECUTIONS.) It is usually quite easy to get into a City through the gates in the walls, but not so easy to get out. When you wish to get away, you will find the gates are shut at sunset and are guarded at all times; you will need to bluff your way through or adopt a disguise. But this does not apply to Siege. The

Rule is that, in a Siege situation, you will be glad to stay there and help until eventually you escape, leaving the plucky citizens to their fate.

See also CITY OF CANALS, CITY OF WIZARDS, OLD RUINED CITY, and WALLED CITY.

City of Canals. This CITY is usually on a south or south-facing coast and under the governance of MERCHANT FEUDALISTS at their most crooked. The City is pretty old and seems to have grown up from settlements on a great number of islands in a large RIVER delta; after a while, the channels between island and island have become the canals (*dark*⊕, *scummy*⊕) and on their banks houses have been built upon houses, mostly of timber (*rotting*⊕), with WHARFS on top of that and BRIDGES on and around those. The result is a labyrinth of watery ways known only to the inhabitants, who mostly get about in old, cranky BOATS. The ruling MERCHANTS always live somewhere at the center in very beautiful houses built of imported stone. They are totally ruthless about wringing their money's worth out of the poorer folk and everything else, and their laws are draconian. Not surprisingly, the THIEVES' GUILD is very strong here; one of the Merchants is probably its Guildmaster. Murders are frequent, and bodies drift up and down the canals along with other REFUSE. The whole City SMELLS.

It is essential that Tourists find some kind of native guide in this place, or their throats will be cut before nightfall (see DANGER), but, with any luck, the Management will have thought of this and one of the Tour COMPANIONS will turn out to have been born here. Failing that, there will be a young lad to help (see THIEVES' GUILD). As a Tourist, you will be here to wring some QUEST OBJECT or SECRET out of the paranoiacally defended home of the beastliest of the Merchants. You will be so lucky. But then Tourists always are.

City of Wizards is normally quite a GOOD thing, since only Good WIZARDS seem able to live together. This CITY will be on a hill in some place that is hidden/hard to get to and surrounded by inviting green lands tilled by non-Wizard underlings, who also perform all domestic chores. Houses will be of stone, often white, and their shapes gracious but odd. Perspective and distances will be a bit strange too. If the effect of all this is rather stately, the City will be full of white-robed MYSTICAL MASTERS, out of whom no one will be able to get any sense. If the effect is more homely, the Wizards will be more like human beings and may quarrel a lot—in fact, they will seldom agree on anything. If the place is organized as a college, do not expect anything but Wizardly bickering.

There have been Cities of EVIL Wizards in the past. Tours will occasionally come across the sites of these, reduced to glassy slag during the ultimate disagreement.

Clans. EYRIE CLANS (obviously), DESERT NO-
MADS, and OTHER CONTINENTALISTS are always
organized in Clans. ANGLO-SAXON COSSACKS
and BARBARY VIKINGS sometimes are, and at
times most other countries have them one way
or another. Clandom is supposed to be a very
close and special bonding. Certainly a member
of a Clan can call upon all other members in
an emergency and they will come flocking in to
help. But the easiest way to think of it is as a
civilized word for TRIBE, where the obligations
are just the same. In the VESTIGIAL EMPIRE,
the word for Clans or Tribes in Houses, because the Empire is even *more* civilized. Houses
have Politics where Clans do not. Clans and
Houses both give rise to ELITE.

See also POLITICS.

Cliff Dwellings. See EYRIE CLANS, though some
Other PEOPLES have them too. The average
Cliff Dwelling is high up, and approached by a
rocky hidden staircase of prodigious length.
When you finally gasp your way to the top, you
will be instantly challenged by an alert sentry
carrying an outsized BIRD. If he is satisfied that
your business is important enough, he will then
lead you through a hitherto unnoticed gap in
the rock. Within, a natural CAVE will have been
infinitely enlarged to make rooms, passages,
galleries, and storeplaces, most—but not all—
with cunningly disguised windows in the cliff
face. It will be very chilly (see HEATING), but
only you will notice the chill. The place will be

organized like a barracks, but the FOOD is always better than the Fantasyland norm. You will get butter, honey, fresh BREAD, and probably not STEW. The Dwellers, though austere, will be friendly and you can take a well-earned rest from DANGER and HARDSHIP here.

Cloaks are the universal outer garb of everyone who is not a Barbarian. It is hard to see why. They are open in front and require you at most times to use one hand to hold them shut. On horseback they leave the shirt-sleeved arms and most of the torso exposed to wind and WEATHER. The OMTs for Cloaks well express their difficulties. They are constantly *swirling and dripping* and becoming *heavy with water* in rainy Weather, *entangling with trees* or *swords,* or needing to be *pulled close around her/his shivering body.* This seems to suggest they are less than practical for anyone on an arduous Tour. But they do have one advantage. Female Cloaks usually add a wide frilly hood, male cloaks a wide plain one, and neither of these adjuncts ever gets blown from the head or lets water in round the edges. So at least your head is dry.

It is thought that the real reason for the popularity of Cloaks is that the inhabitants like the look of themselves from the back.

Clothing. Although this varies from place to place, there are two absolute Rules:

1. Apart from ROBES, no garment thicker than a SHIRT ever has sleeves.

2. No one ever wears SOCKS.

See also CLOAKS, COSTUME, and KNITTING.

Coats do not exist in Fantasyland—CLOAKS being universally preferred—but TURNCOATS do.

Coinage has various names, according to which Tour you choose, and will seem to be made of gold, silver, and copper. Adjust to inflation and think of it in dollars: a gold coin = $5, a silver coin = $1, and copper coins are cents. This system is easier than most European currencies.

See also MONEY.

Color Coding is very important in Fantasyland. Always pay close attention to the color of the CLOTHING, hair, and eyes of anyone you meet. It will tell you a great deal. Complexion is also important: in many cases it is coded too.

1. Clothing. Black garments normally mean EVIL, but in rare cases can mean sobriety, in which case a white ruffled collar will be added to the ensemble. Gray or red clothing means that the person is neutral but tending to Evil in most cases. Any other color is GOOD, unless too many bright colors are worn at once, in which instance the person will be unreliable. Drab color means the person will take little part in the action, unless the drab is also torn or disreputable, when the person will be a lovable rogue.

2. Hair. Black hair is Evil, particularly if combined with a corpse-white complexion. Red hair *always* entails magical POWERS, even if these are only latent. Brown hair has to be viewed in combination with eyes, whose colors are the real giveaway (see below), but generally implies niceness. Fair hair, especially if it is silver-blonde, *always* means goodness.

3. Eyes. Black eyes are invariably Evil; brown eyes mean boldness and humor, but not necessarily goodness; green eyes *always* entail TALENT, usually for MAGIC but sometimes for MUSIC; hazel eyes are rare and seem generally to imply niceness; gray eyes mean POWER or healing abilities (see HEALERS) and will be reassuring unless they look silver (silver-eyed people are likely to enchant or hypnotize you for their own ends, although they are not always Evil); white eyes, usually blind ones, are for wisdom (never ignore anything a white-eyed person says); blue eyes are always GOOD, the bluer the more Good present; and then there are violet eyes and golden eyes. People with violet eyes are often of Royal birth and, if not, *always* live uncomfortably interesting lives. People with golden eyes just live uncomfortably interesting lives and most of them are rather fey in the bargain. Both these types should be avoided by anyone who only wants a quiet life. Luckily, it seldom occurs to those with undesirable eye colors to disguise them by ILLUSION, and they can generally be detected very readily. Red eyes can *never* be disguised. They are EVIL and surprisingly common.

4. Complexion. Corpse-white is Evil, and it grades from there. Pink-faced folk are usually midway and pathetic. The best face-color is brown, preferably tanned, but it can be inborn. Other colors such as black, blue, mauve, and yellow barely exist.

So, if your acquaintance is wearing green and is blue-eyed and brown-faced, she/he will be OK. *Caution:* Do not apply these standards to our own world. You are very likely to be disappointed.

Combat Ring. See PRACTICE RING and SCHOOL OF WEAPONRY.

Common Cold. This is one of many viral nuisances not present. You can get as wet, cold, and tired as you like, and you will still not catch cold. But see PLAGUE.

Common Tongue. See LANGUAGES.

Companions are chosen for you by the Management. You will normally meet them for the first time at the outset of the Tour. They are picked from among the following: BARD, FEMALE MERCENARY, GAY MAGE, IMPERIOUS FEMALE, LARGE MAN, SERIOUS SOLDIER, SLENDER YOUTH, SMALL MAN, TALENTED GIRL, TEENAGE BOY, UNPLEASANT STRANGER, and WISE OLD STRANGER. Most parties will have at least one of these and may also occasionally include one or two of the Other PEOPLES, usually small ones.

Conclusion. For this you will have to undertake the third (or possibly the fifth) Tour of the trilogy. If you do not immediately book for the whole set, you may well find yourself stranded halfway across the continent without having completed your QUEST or discovered your BIRTHRIGHT. And the DARK LORD will still be a menace. A little extra money will soon dispel these inconveniences, and you may then have the pleasure of seeing the continent torn asunder in the Final CONFRONTATION. This is a spectacular sight and should not be missed.

Confrontations. These will occur with mounting intensity as the Tour proceeds, and will fall into one or other of the following classes:

1. Small Friendly Confrontations. This will be when you meet your Tour COMPANIONS and the MERCHANT in whose CARAVAN you intend to travel. Later, you meet a friend aboard the Slave GALLEY or in contest as a GLADIATOR. You then encounter TRAVELING FOLK and a SEER or Astrologer (see ASTROLOGY). You have an argument with your SWORD or an ORB. You chat up a SLAVE of the opposite sex. You hire a Necromancer (see NECROMANCY). You receive reports from a Good SPY. You encounter an old General of the VESTIGIAL EMPIRE/ the WEAPONMASTER. You have solemn meetings with EYRIE CLANS/WOODSMEN and telepathic BIRDS. A HERBWOMAN/HEDGE WIZARD/ HEALER comes to your rescue in the MOUNTAINS. A BARD recites to you a vital LEGEND.

2. Small Hostile Confrontations. This term refers to the intruder with a DAGGER in your CHAMBER in the INN, the AMBUSH by BANDITS, and your first brush with the forces of the Dark. You also spot a SPY. Later there are PIRATES on the INLAND SEA and a MINION OF THE DARK LORD on the OTHER CONTINENT. You are brought before an ENCHANTRESS. You are almost killed by a hostile COURTIER/beard a fat PRINCE/have to spend time with a BARON. You are caught by a prehensile TREE. You face down GUARDS and torturers. You are captured by GOBLINS and their chieftain insults you. You come up against WERES, who are not open to reason.

3. Small Ambiguous Confrontations. You meet your Tour MENTOR and the UNPLEASANT STRANGER. You are cheated by a FERRYMAN or RIVER Travelers. You have a run in with DWARFS, GNOMES, and DESERT NOMADS. You try to get MONEY from a COUNCIL. You meet a GHOST/ELEMENTAL. You are captured by MARSH DWELLERS and have LANGUAGE problems. You come upon a NUNNERY and talk to the survivor. You try to persuade ISLANDERS that their ISLAND is about to be inundated. The Tour enters a VILLAGE and is rendered uncomfortable by the attitude of the Dwellers. You make the mistake of looking into a Prophetic POOL.

4. Medium-Sized Friendly Confrontations. You meet your first KING or the VESTIGIAL EMPEROR. Later you talk to a DRAGON or friendly DEMON. You stay the night with a Good WIZARD, who shows you some remarkable pieces of KNOWLEDGE. You find ELVES, a college of WITCHES, enter a CITY, or attempt to understand a MYSTICAL MASTER. You persuade a HIGH PRIESTESS to help you and your COMPANIONS. You arrive at the STEPPES/SNOWBOUND NORTH and run into crowds of ANGLO-SAXON COSSACKS/BARBARY VIKINGS/NORTHERN BARBARIANS. You are told home truths by a STONE CIRCLE.

5. Medium-Sized Hostile Confrontations. You face a HIGH PRIEST and his deity, a RE-

GENT, a bad or puppet KING. You try to get the better of an Evil COUNCILOR. You reject the overtures of a bad QUEEN. You face and repulse hostile MAGICS. You fall foul of RELIGION in the FANATIC CALIPHATES. You come face-to-face with an Evil WIZARD or a red-eyed MINION OF THE DARK LORD. You fight a MONSTER or two. You confront the ENEMY in a SIEGE.

6. Medium-Sized Ambiguous Confrontations. You encounter loose lumps of MAGIC or guardians of a QUEST OBJECT or enter the HIDDEN KINGDOM and attempt to make sense of its inhabitants. You try to argue with a WOOD.

7. Large Friendly Confrontations. You and your COMPANIONS tout for support among the GOOD rulers. There is a long and verbose COUNCIL of WAR.

8. Large Hostile Confrontations. There is allout WAR between GOOD and EVIL. You face

down the strongest of the MINIONS OF THE
DARK LORD.

9. The Final Confrontation, or Last Battle.
You get your chance to finish the DARK LORD
at last. In the process a large part of Fantasyland
gets destroyed.

Cook. Presiding over all KITCHENS is the Cook,
who can be male or female, although males pre-
dominate in CASTLES and PALACES and females
in INNS. Every single one of them has a filthy
temper. This gets worse in direct proportion to
the amount of cooking they do, and is clearly
even worse if the Cook is required to cook
something else besides STEW. Any scullion or
Kitchen helper in reach during these trying
times is bound to have an awful experience.
But there is a bright side. Cooks divide into fat
and thin. Fat Cooks are really kindly underneath, in which case the Kitchen helper has
extra food to look forward to. Thin Cooks, on
the other hand, are mean right through. In this
case the Kitchen helper can look forward only
to an evening without supper and maybe a
beating too.

Costume. It is a curious fact that, in Fantasyland,
the usual Rules for CLOTHING are reversed.
Here, the colder the climate, the fewer the garments worn. In the SNOWBOUND NORTH, the
BARBARIAN HORDES wear little more than a fur
loincloth and copper wristguards (see CHIL-
BLAINS and HYPOTHERMIA). However, as one

progresses south to reach the ANGLO-SAXON COSSACKS, one finds VESTS and BOOTS added to this costume. Further south still, the inhabitants of the VESTIGIAL EMPIRE wear short SKIRTS and singlets and add to this a voluminous wrapper on cold days. Thereafter, clothing steadily increases in thickness and quantity, until one finds the DESERT NOMADS in the tropics muffled to the eyebrows in layers of ROBES (see HEATSTROKE).

Council. Although other Councils exist, this term refers primarily to the group of twelve or so unpleasing men who rule the MERCHANT FEUDALISTS, because they do not trust one another enough to let one person do the ruling. The OMT for these is *corrupt,* but they are also cruel and greedy, and they will combine to get rid of anyone who seems to threaten their power. Most Tours do this, so be prepared for Councils to have you Assassinated or put in PRISON on sight. You will find the Council meeting in a lavish CHAMBER⊛ with a breathtakingly ornamental ceiling and gold everywhere. Likely they will be eating and drinking gourmet stuff as well, and each member will have different gorgeous ROBES, covered with JEWELS and gold EMBROIDERY. Some will be piggishly (*swinishly*⊛) fat, some thin and wrinkled, but it makes no difference. They are all pure poison. Above all avoid being owed MONEY by them: you will never get it.

Councilors are those who advise a KING. Nine-tenths of them are EVIL. These will be of youngish middle age, with nothing aside from the REEK OF WRONGNESS🄬 to give away the fact that they report directly to the DARK LORD. They will be busy giving the King bad advice and generally messing up the COUNTRY, and they will not welcome the Tour at all. After making efforts to send it on its way, they will normally contrive to have every Tourist imprisoned. You must escape and *unmask*🄬 the Councilor concerned. The other tenth of Councilors are GOOD and grave and elderly. Many of them have been soldiers. You can rely on them to *understand*🄬 when the monarch does not.

Countries have ill-defined boundaries, but on the whole correspond to each of the PEOPLES listed, although under various names at the whim of the Management. Most will be ruled by KINGS, TYRANTS, REGENTS, CLAN Chieftains, or members of a priestly caste. The exception is any country of the MERCHANT FEUDALISTS, where the ruling class trusts one another so little that they rule as a COUNCIL. Do not expect democracy anywhere. Do not expect, either, to find one Country bordering on another: there are always large empty/ungoverned areas in between, where there will be forests, WASTE AREAS, or even VILLAGES. No ruler since the VESTIGIAL EMPIRE seems to have got her/his act together sufficiently to claim this spare land.

Courtiers are mainly extras hired by the Management for all scenes in PALACES. Male and female Courtiers will be standing or strutting about, wearing the richest and most exaggerated fashions, and staring or gasping at the manners and dress of the Tourists. Courtiers never sit down. They whisper in groups, trying to gain the favor of the monarch. Very few of them are nice people. If they are, they will be quite young, with NAMES like Daren or Lynthelle, and they will help you a lot with the strange customs at Court. Nasty Courtiers have sneering names like Blyfil and Myrna. If you learn their Names it will be because the man will challenge you to a duel (and possibly POISON his sword-tip) and the woman will make bitchy remarks and spread rumors. Myrna often turns out to be a MAGIC USER too. She will cast SPELLS to make all Tourists look like fools and to seduce any male Tourists.

Crone. On most Tours a ragged old woman, sometimes of a wild and sinister demeanor, tends to crop up by the wayside in moments of stress, *hobbling*⊕ and *cackling*⊕. If the Tour has lost its way, she will misdirect it, usually throwing in a few GNOMIC UTTERANCES of a depressing nature as she does so. If the Tour takes in a public EXECUTION, this Crone will be present at it *busily knitting*⊕. Since KNITTING is not a normal mortal skill, it is clear that this old lady is an ASPECT of some GODDESS or other.

Crystal can be almost any color. It can be set in a RING, suspended on a chain as a pendant, or be just a lump on its own. It is Fantasyland's equivalent of the telephone, with attached vision. Through Crystal, most MAGIC USERS and some ordinary people can communicate with the WIZARD of their choice over quite long distances. The operator simply leans over the Crystal and concentrates. Shortly a small but extremely clear image of the Wizard forms within it and can be heard to speak. Crystal usually takes over where MINDSPEECH leaves off.

See also CRYSTAL BALL.

Crystal Ball. You look into one of these and see *vapours swirling like clouds*⊶. These shortly clear away to show a sort of video without sound of something that is going to happen to you soon. It is seldom good news.

See also CRYSTAL and PROPHECY.

Cups are goblets that look rather like golf trophies. You can tell they are important because nobody tries to drink out of them. This is actually silly, because the least a Cup can do is negate POISON. Cups either turn up in hoards of TREASURE or are carefully hidden, packed in a casket, under an ALTAR or somewhere similar. Just occasionally, an ENCHANTRESS will flourish one at you. You will want to take it away from her. This Cup is your QUEST OBJECT. It has Powers, though these are often vague and not always demonstrated. Probably it is best to think of a Cup as a sort of superGrail.

Curses are longstanding ill-wishings which, in Fantasyland, often manifest as semisentient. They have to be broken or dispelled. The method varies according to the type and origins of the Curse:

1. Curses on lands. These can be caused either by defects in the KING or lord or by direct malevolence of the DARK LORD. Usually the land turns to Waste in various ways but, if it is a true Curse, there will be a slimy lump of miasma somewhere, or a MONSTER exuding EVIL. You have to find this and torch it.

2. Curses on families. These will have been put on generations ago, causing the family to lose money, to give birth to cripples, and generally to be low and disheartened. These Curses are difficult. The correct way to raise one is to get the person who did it to take it off. But she/he is probably dead by now. Sometimes a descendant can do as well. If not, the best thing is to force the family into some noble deed on behalf of a God. The God can then remove the Curse.

3. Curses on BUILDINGS. You can tell when a Building (usually a MANSION) is Cursed: it will feel cold as a grave, and some of the roof will be missing, and pieces will keep dropping off on you. This type of Curse probably takes a PRIEST or WIZARD and an exorcism to raise.

For some reason, DEMONS usually have a hand in this sort of Curse.

4. Curses on RINGS and SWORDS. You have problems. Rings have to be returned whence they came, preferably at over a thousand degrees Fahrenheit, and the Curse means you won't want to do this. Swords usually resist all attempts to raise their Curses. Your best source is to hide the Sword or give it to someone you dislike.

5. Curses on people. Here the one laying the Curse has obtained your toenail, one of your hairs, or your true NAME, and possibly also made a wax image of you which she/he proceeds to mistreat. You will have racking pains and monstrous bad luck until you find the missing bit of you and get it back.

6. Curses with conditions. These are the easy kind. The Curser has probably stated that the Curse will be lifted only when the INLAND SEA is dry. You just have to arrange for this to happen.

Doras II was a somewhat absent-minded king. It is said that, when Death came to summon him, Doras granted Death the usual formal audience and then dismissed him from his presence. Death was too embarrassed to return until many years later.

Ka'a Orto'o, Gnomic Utterances, LIV iii

Daggers are of three main kinds:

1. A slender stabbing WEAPON worn on the belt, in the boot, or up the shirt-sleeve as back-up to the SWORD, or as the thing with which your assailant intends to kill you. Everyone uses these. They are like knives with a narrower blade.

2. Ceremonial. This is fancier and is usually worn as part of a uniform (*outmoded*⊙) and will not have changed its pattern for centuries. Be careful when you see someone with one of these. It indicates that she/he is about to attack you when you have no weapon yourself. You will, after a bout of unarmed combat, be forced to kill this person with her/his own ceremonial Dagger.

3. Mercy blades. These are spare Daggers carried in a special place by most MERCENARIES and WARRIOR WOMEN and by some DESERT NOMADS; they use the Daggers to kill themselves or their friends when survival is out of the question. Expect at least once on the Tour to have to finish one of these people off with her/his own mercy blade, usually at the person's own request.

Danger is everywhere in Fantasyland. You will be in Danger from the first step you take on your Tour, starting with the intruder with a knife on your first night, then running through ASSASSINS and DEMONS on to WIZARDS and bad QUEENS and finally the DARK LORD—not to speak of AMBUSHES in between and subtle Dangers devised by ENCHANTRESSES. You will spend a lot of time fleeing. In order not to live in a state of perpetual abject Terror, you must remember that in Fantasyland Danger has an actual SMELL. (REEK OF WRONGNESS is the general OMT for it.) Watch for this Smell. HORSES are good at detecting it. When there is any threat to safety, they have *their heads up scenting danger*OMT. Learn to recognize what the Horses are sniffing and from then on you can relax until the moment you smell it.

Dark Lady. There is never one of these—so see DARK LORD instead. The Management considers that male Dark Ones have more potential to be sinister, and seldom if ever employs a female in this role. This is purely because the Management was born too late to meet my Great Aunt Clara.

Dark Lord (*dread lord*ⓞ). There is always one of these in the background of every Tour, attempting to ruin everything and take over the world. He will be so sinister that he will be seen by you only once or twice, probably near the end of the Tour. Generally he will attack you through MINIONS (*forces of Terror, bound to his will*ⓞ), of which he will have large numbers. When you do get to see him at last, you will not be surprised to find he is black (see COLOR CODING) and shadowy and probably not wholly human. He will make you feel very cold and small. Actually, when it comes down to it, that is probably all he will do, having almost certainly exhausted his other resources earlier on. You should be able to defeat him, with a little help from your COMPANIONS, without too much effort. However, the Rules state that at this stage you will be exhausted yourself and possibly wounded by MAGIC. So be careful.

Demons are less frequent on the Tour than they used to be. Most of them have followed VAMPIRES and WERES over to the Horror Tour, possibly because people evoke them more there. Nevertheless, quite a few remain and must be treated with caution or, preferably, shunned. The Management itself is quite good at shunning. It is often very hard to discover what any given Demon looks like, apart from a general impression of large size, huge fangs, staring eyes, many limbs, and an odd color; but all accounts agree that Demons are very powerful, very MAGIC (in a nonhuman manner), and made of some substance that can squeeze through a keyhole yet not be pierced with a SWORD. This makes them difficult to deal with, even on the rare occasions when they are friendly. Demons are sometimes found batting about loose, but mostly they appear to live elsewhere entirely and must therefore be evoked by NAME (often hard to pronounce) and confined within a PENTAGRAM or MAGIC circle while they are given their orders. Tourists are advised to leave all this sort of thing to WIZARDS and never, ever attempt to bargain with a Demon themselves. The Rule is that all Demons are cheats.

Desert occurs very suddenly some way south— usually, but not always, at the edge of the grassy plain where the crows will SPY on you (see BIRDS). It is of course very hot and dry there, and the sand dunes roll away to the horizon *like waves of a frozen sea*. When you reach the Desert, be prepared to be in it for days and to experience at least one sandstorm, either magical or natural, before you run out of WATER. Some time after that, but not until then, you will encounter someone from the DESERT NOMADS, who will usually gallop away without talking to you. Never fear. She/he has only gone to warn the rest of the CLAN that they have visitors.

One odd fact about the Desert is that, considering the unrivalled opportunities it gives for ILLUSIONS, mirages are nearly nonexistent here. No WIZARD seems yet to have got to work on this.

Desert Nomads occupy the hot parts to the south, which is either DESERT or rather parched grass. For some reason this is ideal TERRAIN for breeding HORSES, of which all Nomad CLANS have huge numbers. The Clans move from place to place, each in their own areas, with their wondrous TENTS, flocks, and Horses, but tend to muster at least once a year for religious reasons. Desert Nomads usually have a GODDESS and are always hot on RELIGION. They also have lots of wisdom and KNOWLEDGE, much of which is in the head of the SHAMAN allotted to each Clan. Tourists will come to this PEOPLE to learn. But be prepared for two peculiarities. First, unlike the northerly Clans, Desert Nomads allow their women to do everything the men do. Second, both sexes are always *swathed from head to foot*◉ in ROBES, though they may have all sorts of finery underneath. They seem to have a TABOO on legs: no Nomad ever show her/his legs in public, even when riding flat out astride a STALLION.

Domestic Animals are as rare as wild ANIMALS. In most cases their existence can be proved only by deduction. Thus, sheep must exist, because people wear wool, and so must cattle as there is usually cheese to eat. Cats are seen in company with WITCHES and CRONES, often in large numbers, but seldom elsewhere, and there have been sightings also of solitary pigs; possibly in Fantasyland cats are herd animals whereas pigs are not. Goats are seen oftener (and may even provide the cheese) and dogs are frequent but often rather feral—the arrival of the Tour party at a VILLAGE is usually greeted by barking dogs. Dogs are also kept in numbers by KINGS and nobles, where their job is to be scavengers: you throw bones on the floor and the dogs fight for them. These hounds cannot be kept for hunting (except perhaps for hunting men and MUTANT NASTIES), as there are no Animals to hunt.

The thoughtful Tourist might like to pause here and consider, since ANIMALS are so rare, what exactly the meat is that the Management puts in its STEW.

Donkeys are rare and are reserved for the use of MONKS and humble but friendly WIZARDS. In each case the relevant APPENTICE or NOVICE will follow on foot.

Dragons are very large scaly beings with wings and long spiky tails, capable of breathing fire through their mouths. They can be almost any color or combination of colors, though green, red, and black are preferred. They are always very old. Most of them seem to have flown to Fantasyland aeons ago across the void. This migration was almost certainly to get away from our world, where people would insist that they were dangerous MONSTERS that had to be exterminated.

Dragons, as all Fantasyland knows, are no such thing. They quite like people, provided you can get their attention. They are very wise and can do MAGIC of a type not known to other MAGIC USERS. But they do not have human emotions. This can cause misunderstandings, if Tourists are trying to make friends with them. Female Tourists are best at this. Dragons seem to be in tune with the female mind. A friendly Dragon will airlift female Tourists to the OFF-SHORE ISLAND where most Dragons live. A male Tourist will have to wait to meet Dragons until he has been through the CAVERNS that lead to the Hidden VALLEY, where Dragons also live; or until the Dragons have joined the forces of GOOD for the Final CONFRONTATION.

Even then, the relationship is likely to be a bit edgy. This is because Dragons can, if they want, eat people.

Dreams. While you are on the Tour, your psyche is in the care of the Management, who will when necessary provide you with Dreams. You should always attend to these, particularly when they are repeated the next night in the same form. They occupy the same slot as LEGENDS. They will be telling you something you need to know for the next phase of your Tour, but they will not be doing so very clearly. You will need to think a bit.

See also PROPHECY and VISIONS.

Dukes. This is the highest form of lord, often one of the KING's family. Very few of them are GOOD and most of them are wicked uncles at the very least. The few Good Dukes are always frantically busy and *beset with cares of state*⊙. The Rule is that all Dukes, Good or EVIL, are always forty years old or more.

See also REGENTS.

Dungeons are the first thing to be built when anyone is planning a large BUILDING. Even TOWN Halls tend to have them. The Rules state that Dungeons are damp and small and a long way underground. If the Tourist being confined is lucky, there will be a small barred window too high up to reach, through which the contents of the moat trickle, and old (*fetid*⊙, *filthy*⊕) straw on the ground. There will be a thick door (locked) with a small shutter in it where what passes (only just) for FOOD can be thrown in at prisoners, generally dropping tantalizingly an inch out of reach, and there will always be rings in the walls carrying chains and sometimes old bones too. It is all designed to make you feel low. There may even be *scutterings*⊕ that could be rats (but see ANIMALS). Do not, however, let this get you down. The average stay in such a place is, for Tourists, twenty-four hours. If the Dungeon is a pit of the type called an oubliette, on the other hand, you are justified in slight melancholy. It will be several days before someone lowers a rope to you and hauls you out.

See also PRISON.

Dwarfs are short, muscular, bearded PEOPLE much given to mining and forging. They mostly live hidden inside hills, where they do their mining. Until recently, almost no female Dwarfs had been sighted, but now they are seen quite often. They do not have beards, but seem to be squat like the males. All Dwarfs, perhaps through living so long immured in DWARVEN FASTNESSES, have a very old-fashioned, surly demeanor. They bow a lot, but also grumble. They recite long epics about the marvelous deeds of their ancestors. The advantage of their old-fashioned ways, however, is that they are very honorable and always keep their word once they have been induced to give it. They

will join the forces of GOOD and supply
ARMOR, but before this the Tour may well have
a difficult time with them. Dwarfs will take all
Tourists prisoner for trespassing in their Fastness, and it will involve much persuasive talking
to get them to be friendly.

Dwarven Fastness. A wondrous place. It normally occupies the whole inside of a MOUN- ▲
TAIN. It has concealed gates, often protected by
RUNES. Inside, there is gallery after gallery
carved out of the Mountain, usually ornamented with Dwarven sculpture and JEWELS. It
will be lit by torches or glowbaskets. There
never seems to be any domestic quarter for females, children, or cooking: it is all fabulous
hallways. The place is so many-leveled and lab-
yrinthine that Tourists easily become lost there.
As they blunder along, DWARFS will capture
them and drag them to the Central Hall, which
is often rougher and more workaday than the
rest of the place. Possibly the Dwarfs keep most
of it as a historical monument. On occasions,
the Fastness will be deserted, long-abandoned.
Here a MAP or guide is essential.

Dwell is the word used throughout the Tour
meaning to live somewhere. The inhabitants are
always *Dwellers*⊙⊤.

Energies are far-reaching things. The Sage
Morinden once fetched himself a lemon from a
distant galaxy and felt much refreshed.

> Ka'a Orto'o, Gnomic Utterances, XIII i

Eating Implements are minimal. The most
usual provided is a SPOON for STEW. Otherwise
you are expected to use your knife or DAGGER
to eat with.

Ecology. The Ecology of Fantasyland is in a
bad way. It is full of empty niches. To start
with, there are few or no bacteria. We can see
this by the way REFUSE and other pieces of
SQUALOR lie about in heaps which fail to rot
down. To add to this, there are few or no IN-
SECTS (except for fleas, some localized bees, numerous silkworms somewhere in the FANATIC
CALIPHATES, and clouds of mosquitoes in the
MARSHES). Both these empty niches mean that
all crops will be poor; perhaps this explains the
crop failures more usually blamed on MAGIC or
the personality defects of KINGS. There are also
very few BIRDS. In the absence of bacteria and
Insects, one might expect plants and Birds to
adapt so that Birds do the pollinating as well

as their normal task of spreading the seeds, but this is not the case. The one species that seems to be moving into the niche normally occupied by Birds is the LEATHERY-WINGED AVIANS, but these are predators, not seed-feeders or pollinators. (And, in the absence of ANIMALS, we have to ask what exactly the Leathery-Winged Avian feeds on. Perhaps we should conjecture the existence of lots of juicy little bats? These would come forth silently at night and therefore remain largely unobserved.)

So there is no means of improving the soil, or of pollination, or of seed-spreading. Constant magical irradiation seems to have destroyed it all. It seems to have destroyed also any large wild predator mammals and most ruminants. This is a pity. These larger Animals would ordinarily do their part by spreading dung and carrying seeds in their coats. In their absence, we should not be surprised that so many TREES have become mobile: they have to move about in order to find more fertile ground and shed their seeds in it.

Plants might be expected to adapt to these conditions by evolving to become wind-pollinated. Few of them have. In the empty heathlands left by the shrinking of the VESTIGIAL EMPIRE, just where we might expect wind-pollination to happen, Tour after Tour reports sparse vegetation and no food ANIMALS or BIRDS. Clearly not enough plants are getting pollinated to support small creatures here, which in turn would support larger ones. The food chains are in a bad way.

We come to the reasons for all this in the WASTE AREAS left desolate by the WIZARDS' War. There was fierce magical pollution here and its effects are still seeping out into the rest of the continent. Tourists who visit these sites report that the magical irradiation has resulted in hungry slimes, dark twisted plants that try to eat people in a variety of ingenious ways, and numerous highly active Animals with a taste for human flesh. This is most encouraging. All these living things—along with MONSTERS and MUTANT NASTIES—are flourishing and spreading with a strength and vitality that suggest that in time to come they will move out into all the vacant ecological niches. Fantasyland will become filled with aggressive plants and vicious animals. Humans will find themselves near the bottom of every food chain. All will be well. Unfortunately, it will be several hundred years before this happens.

Economy. The Economy of Fantasyland is as full of holes as its ECOLOGY. Most areas seem self-sufficient in a hand-to-mouth, depressed way, and very poor, since WEATHER and magical pollution seem regularly to cause a shortage of food crops. But some areas, notably among the MERCHANT FEUDALISTS and the FANATIC CALIPHATES, appear to carry on considerable trade by sea and land. Both areas support large ARMIES, either MERCENARY or conscript. This shows that both have healthy trade balances. But it is hard to know where their trade comes from. PIRATES on both the open sea and the INLAND SEA make sure that few SHIPS arrive at their destination, and on land BANDITS intercept most CARAVANS. Neither Pirates nor Bandits seem to recirculate the wealth they acquire. Yet there is considerable wealth in places, for the THIEVES' GUILD is never out of business and frequently possesses itself of remarkably valuable purses and artifacts. CITIES where the Guild operates all seem to thrive. Where does the wealth come from? Now add to this the facts that two-thirds of the continent is out of action as a producer of wealth, by reason of the polluted WASTE AREAS, and that large quantities of precious metal are also out of circulation under DRAGONS, in lost treasuries, or by reason of being enchanted into an unusable condition; and the mystery deepens. Add to this again the very small signs of any INDUSTRY, and one begins to ask oneself just how the Economy is maintained. The VESTIGIAL EMPIRE seems central to the mystery. Here we have a large civilized area in the center of the landmass, with a vigorous Economy, large building programs, faultless engineering, and full employment. But no Industry. How is this managed? One has to suppose that regular paying Tours from other worlds secretly support the whole tottering edifice.

See also IMPORT/EXPORT.

Elementals fairly frequently adopt visible form and sometimes even show off to Tourists. A typical Elemental is seen as a whirling cloud of dust, in or just outside the Desert. It is not clear whether this is an earth or an air Elemental. Perhaps it can be either. Elementals exist for many other things besides the earth, air, fire, and water that the Tourist will know from her/his own world, and in all categories are much more numerous. Ice Elementals are common, IRON not unknown, and Fog or MIST ones have been sighted. WIZARDS will often summon an Elemental to help in their work. The preferred, but most dangerous, kind are FIRE Elementals, which can take the form of a human or ANIMAL made of flames. These, like all Elementals, are mischievous and unreliable, and can easily set everything in sight ablaze if not carefully controlled.

Most Elementals can take on quasi-human form, but Tourists are advised to refrain from chatting with them. You might put ideas into their quasi-heads that would be hard to dislodge. For instance, if you expressed pleasure in a cool breeze the Elemental would thereafter follow you around for weeks blowing half a gale.

Elite are the people who, while not being PRINCES or PRINCESSES necessarily, are nevertheless destined for great things. They have star quality. Most of them will have sprung from humble-to-medium backgrounds, and will have had Sorrows. Usually they have been cast out of a CLAN, but some of them have simply been orphaned at an early age. In neither case will they tell you their troubles until you know them really well. Meanwhile, the events the Gods have chosen them for will be catching up with both of you. If an Elite joins your Tour, expect a lot of INCIDENTS.

See also MISSING HEIRS.

Elves claim to have been the first PEOPLE in Fantasyland. They are called the Elder Race. They did not, they claim, evolve like humans, but sprang into being just as they are now. Certainly there seems to be no such thing as an Elvish ancestral ape, or if there was it existed too long ago for any sign of it to remain. The Elves' claim is borne out to some extent by the well attested fact that their flesh is less gross and substantial than that of humans. This fineness of substance seems to be what makes them IMMORTAL (although not invulnerable: they can be killed). In looks, Elves are taller and more slender than any humans, and very beautiful. Most of them appear youthful. Only rarely does an Elf show signs of age. Then she/he is very wise. The majority have flowing blonde or ash-blonde hair and huge blue-green eyes, though the odd few are dark (see COLOR CODING). A dark Elf, even if not allied with EVIL, is likely to be even more stand-offish and equivocal in her/his attitude to humans than a fair one; but *all* Elves feel themselves superior to humans and make it very clear that they do not operate by human rules.

This is true, in that all of them can do some MAGIC, surround themselves at will with a silver or blue-green nimbus, and move freely in and out of other dimensions. But their most impressive Magic is always communal. In groups, Elves can create warded magical space, conjure meals, hollow out hills, and put on spectacular displays of riding through the air. Much of this group Magic is done by singing. All Elves sing, usually in beautiful unearthly voices. (See MUSIC and WARDS.)

Elves generally live in some sort of magical side-skewed reality, sometimes called Otherwhere or Elsewhere, which can be reached only through certain spots in WOODS, MOUNTAINS, Hidden VALLEYS, and even underwater, making them elusive and hard to encounter or study. Much of their customs, economy, and way of life is still obscure. All that is known is that Elves owe allegiance to powerful KINGS and QUEENS, who can at times be rather frightening. But Elves have made a contract with the Management that ensures that the Tourist will encounter Elves at least once on a Tour. Here you may be in for a treat. Despite fleshly differences, Elves can interbreed with humans. They may even be the only Other PEOPLE who can. And offspring seldom result, since the Elven birthrate was always low and has become lower in recent times.

In fact, Elves appear to have deteriorated generally since the coming of humans. If you meet Elves, expect to have to listen for hours while they tell you about this—many Elves are great bores on the subject—and about what glories there were in ancient days. They will intersperse their account with nostalgic ditties (*songs of aching beauty*⊙) and conclude by telling you how great numbers of Elves have become so wearied with the thinning of the old golden wonders that they have all departed, departed into the West. This is correct, provided you take it with the understanding that Elves do not say anything quite straight. Many Elves have indeed gone West, to Minnesota and thence to California, where they have great fun wearing punk clothes and riding motorbikes.

Embroidery is very frequent on CLOTHING, banners, hangings, and cushions, and badges are Embroidered on most uniforms. A lot of it is beautiful, and there is so much of it that there must be the equivalent of factories devoted to making it. But no Tour is ever taken round these. The only people the Tourist will see actually engaged in Embroidery will be ladies of high birth. And they can't do all of it. Can they?

Enchantment. This is the Management's term for manipulative MAGIC. Under its influence you will feel nice, become dreamy, and find yourself doing something you would not otherwise do. Enchantment can be worked for both GOOD and EVIL ends. For Good, it tends to be used to make trusted GUARDS leave their posts at crucial times. For Evil, it is used to make Tourists walk into a trap set by the MINIONS OF THE DARK LORD or even the DARK LORD himself.

See also ENCHANTRESS and SPELLS.

Enchantress is another word for "seductress," only with more punch. The one assigned to your Tour will be very beautiful, with red or black hair and probably a startling bosom, all of it magically enhanced. She will have you captured (*in her toils*⊕), usually by MAGIC, just over halfway through the Tour—whereupon she will proceed to seduce you if you are male; if you are female she will do something bitchily enchanting to you instead.

Enemy. The marvelous thing about Fantasyland is that you nearly always know exactly who your Enemy is. Everything is black and white— there is none of the grayness that afflicts enmities in our world, where you are always having to concede that there may be some good in someone you hate. Here, Enemies are always rotten bad and also out to get Tourists, quite unequivocally. Most Enemies will of course be MINIONS OF THE DARK LORD, but some will be power-crazy WIZARDS and bad KINGS or QUEENS. You will be able to spot them at once, even if they have not yet attacked you, by their REEK OF WRONGNESS⊕. Even Enemies who are trying to be inconspicuous may be detected in this way—for instance, the UNPLEASANT STRANGER at the INN and the SPY among the CARAVAN GUARDS. All will have the Reek.

Enemy Spies are planted on every Tour and are of two kinds:

1. BIRDS, normally flocks of black crows

which will follow the Tour in open spaces such as moorland and WASTE AREAS. In DESERTS these may be replaced by vultures. Both are easy to spot but hard to defeat or avoid. They are particularly vexatious if you are trying to get somewhere secretly.

2. Humans (see also UNPLEASANT STRANGER) are planted at INNS, usually by BANDITS, and in Courts by the DARK LORD or one of his MINIONS. These are sometimes harder to detect. Most have the REEK OF WRONGNESS⊙, but a few will not know that it is the Dark Lord to whom they are reporting and so will not Reek. In Court, the Tourist should be wary of all who seem innocent, even if that person is the Crown PRINCE.

See also CARAVANS and SPIES.

Eternal Quest. See QUEST, ETERNAL.

Eunuchs are found very frequently, particularly in the FANATIC CALIPHATES, but also in most TEMPLES and quite often attached to WIZARDS. Wherever a KING has more than one wife, Eunuchs will abound. There are so many of them in some quarters that it must be quite a problem for the Management to maintain the birthrate high enough to provide ARMIES for bad Kings, puppet Kings, and the DARK LORD. Eunuchs do not fight. Their function is to be fat and effeminate and to thwart Tourists wherever possible by trying to POISON them. One theory is that Eunuchs are recruited from the unwanted children of barmaids (see BAR SERVICE).

Evil (OMTs include *taint of Evil, Evil imperiling the realm, ancient Evil grips, Evil scheme, the Evil in men's souls, Evil springs eternal, the stench of Evil*) is generally around somewhere in Fantasyland and seems to cast quite a blight. It has two states, active and passive. In the active state, it is rampant, embodied in puppet KINGS, ARMIES of UNDEAD, MONSTERS, and creeping pollution of the countryside, and it is out to get all Tourists (who are by definition

GOOD). In its passive state it ponds in deserted spots, where it lies around waiting to be aroused by the unwary. The active state is usually connected with the DARK LORD, and must be overcome in the course of the Tour. The passive, when not connected with a predecessor or avatar of the Dark Lord, is either fallout from the WIZARDS' War or the work of some God way back at the BEGINNING of things. When it is in this form there is not much to be done about it but stay clear.

Executions are frequent in any COUNTRY not ruled by a Good KING. They take place in public in a holiday atmosphere. People flock to Executions and bring their CHILDREN, and sales of snacks and drinks are vast. Methods of Execution are various but are generally designed to be as much of a spectacle as possible. Thus burning at the stake is a great favorite, along with impaling, crucifixion, disemboweling, etc., while suspending the victim in a cage to starve is also very popular. Hangings and beheadings, being over rather swiftly, are generally done only in batches of ten or more. Some Tours will generally include an Execution in their schedule, but on most Tours the Management wishes to spare its Tourists the sight of anything so painful. You will be irritated to find you have just missed it.

The approach to the CITY will be flanked with stakes and crosses carrying fresh corpses; its streets will be lined with severed heads or rows of throttled dangling bodies; its walls will be hung with desiccated cadavers or skeletons in small iron cages; and outside there will be large charred patches smelling of mutton chop. But you will be too late to witness anyone actually dying.

See also TORTURE.

Export. See IMPORT/EXPORT.

Eyrie clans live in CLIFF DWELLINGS in northerly parts of the continent, where the sexes are rigidly segregated. The men live like commandoes and train BIRDS to be their lifelong companions. The women do nothing much; indeed, Tourists may not meet any of the women. The men will be very austere and humourless and not inclined to trust Tourists, but in the end they will offer their help on the side of GOOD. They make excellent scouts.

Felt hats should be worn only before harvest time, when there is danger of bird droppings in the hair. Never wear fur boots in a marsh, and don a cloak only at great need. Do not attempt to dress like a Barbarian.

Ka'a Orto'o, Gnomic Utterances, XIV ix

Fairground. This is like a MARKET, except that it is much, much bigger and planted somewhere right in the middle of nowhere so that everyone can get to it. There will be rows and rows of TENTS and BOOTHS, often arranged in streets, and vast areas off to one side for HORSE trading. There will also be a profusion of JUGGLERS, Harpers (see BARDS), and other performers, all of whom will get in your way when you are trying either to find someone you urgently need to meet or to escape from SPIES and pursuers. Be sure that, if the Tour takes you to a Fairground, it will be for one of these two things. Usually it will be both.

Fanatic Caliphates generally occupy the east-southeast of the continent, where the climate is

quite hot. When the Tour brings you to these
COUNTRIES, you are warned to watch your
tongue. They are all fanatics here in the worship of particularly demanding Gods, and are
prone to torture/imprison/execute anyone they
regard as an unbeliever. It is this worship which
enables the ruler (usually a bad KING or a TY-
RANT) to hold his people subject to his every
word; and it is also fertile ground for the DARK
LORD, who will have planted at least one puppet King here. Apart from this, the Caliphates
are generally even noisier and dirtier than the
rest of the continent (*clamor*ᴼᴹᵀ is expressive
here), but a lot richer, which you can see at
once if you walk in their MARKETS (here the
OMT is *bazaar*), where they are selling carpets
and silks. Everyone will be shouting about bar-
gains and thinking of MONEY. But MERCHANTS
here are thoroughly under the thumb of the
King/Tyrant and will report your presence at
once (and even before that if they think you
have blasphemed). You will then be hustled to
the PALACE. The wealth of the Country is particularly apparent in the Palace, which will be
breathtakingly ornamented in a frenzy of gold,
lacy jeweled carvings, wildly patterned pave-
ments, and many-colored cushions and hangings. There will be hundreds of well dressed
SLAVES. Here the King/Tyrant will ask you politely what you want (these people are seldom
rude) and, when you reveal which QUEST
OBJECT/item of KNOWLEDGE you are looking
for, will take the same reasonable line as the

rest of his people: "What's in it for me?" You will get nowhere unless you can answer this to everyone's satisfaction, and even then you will have to steal what you need. The Caliphates do not consider it cheating to cheat foreigners and unbelievers. You will then be pursued by fanatic soldiery or PRIESTS. Some Tour members will get wounded or killed.

Fantasyland is all the country on the MAP, usually a whole continent complete with OFFSHORE ISLANDS, and sometimes including also the OTHER CONTINENT, when this lies near enough to be reached either by Slave GALLEY or on Dragonback. There is plenty of room in it for numerous COUNTRIES, for much space to have been laid waste by earlier WIZARDS' WARS, and for still more space to be emptied by the shrinking of the VESTIGIAL EMPIRE. The WEATHER in both these emptied spaces is likely to be peculiar. The Management of course reserves the right to alter the shape and name of the continent at will and to move MOUNTAINS about whenever necessary. There will, however, always be the usual features present, as discussed in this **Toughpick** section.

Farmhouses are among the few BUILDINGS which are not larger inside than out—in fact, they are usually smaller. Outside, they are thatched, timbered, and pleasantly large-looking. Inside, there will be room only for the KITCHEN, which is the family living room, and bedrooms for the farmer, his wife, and four children. Tourists invited to stay the night usually sleep in the stable loft.

Farming obviously takes place, since produce appears in the MARKETS and the Tour will sometimes take you past cultivated fields. But most fields will have been trampled or burnt by ARMIES, or else parched by magical drought. Dairy farming seems very rare. This probably accounts for the extreme dullness of most meals in Fantasyland (see STEW, FOOD, STEW, SCURVY, STEW, etc.).

Farseeing can be performed by a MAGIC USER with or without CRYSTAL, though it often takes a trance without. Here the operator lies on her/his back under a fur rug, often in some place of POWER, and during some hours sees things that are happening several hundred miles away. It is said to be very draining. The operator usually requires a hot, sweet drink afterwards.

Fellow Travelers. These are people who join the Tour for a short while and then leave or get killed. If they have NAMES and characters, then you will be sorry to lose them, otherwise not.

See also COMPANIONS.

Female Mercenary. This will be a COMPANION on your Tour. She is usually tall, thin and wiry, silent, and neurotic. SEX scares her. This is because she either came from a NUNNERY or was raped as a child. Or both. Somehow this inspired her to become a MERCENARY and she is very good at her job. You can rely on her absolutely in a FIGHT. She can usually kill two people at once while guarding your back in between. The rest of the time, she will irritate you with lots of punctilious WEAPONS cleaning and a perpetual insistence that a proper watch be kept. Mostly, she will have no Magic TALENTS, but sometimes, in an emergency, she will come up with a GIFT or a VISION. You will end up grudgingly admiring her.

Ferry is a raft-like craft for crossing RIVERS. It can be rowed or pulled across on ropes, but in either case the FERRYMAN must be paid. Since the Rules state that you need a Ferry only when the forces of Dark are on your heels, the price is usually exorbitant.

Ferryman is the only important FERRY operator. All the other rowers and haulers are extras. A Ferryman is traditionally surly, reluctant, and frightened. This is probably because the Tour usually hauls him out of bed near dawn with urgent demands to be taken over the RIVER right *now*. He will overcharge you horribly in revenge. He will sometimes also blight the crossing by making various ominous and depressing remarks; but he will, on the offer of more money, swear not to reveal that you have used his Ferry. He will of course tell the forces of Dark everything as soon as they gallop up in pursuit.

Fever is something that follows a wound: it never has any other cause (except possibly PLAGUE, which you will not catch). It will cost the Tourist a day or so of sweating and strange DREAMS before someone fetches a HEALER. Then a drink of herbal tea will have you right in no time.

Fights follow the same Rules as CONFRONTATIONS and INCIDENTS. They get larger and more frequent as the Tour goes on. You will first *blood your sword*⊕ in the AMBUSH mounted by the BANDITS, and follow that by further practice upon LEATHERY-WINGED AVIANS. You will then Fight an Assassin in a TOWN or CITY and so proceed by increments to your bout in the arena as a GLADIATOR. By the end of the Tour, you will be leading the front-line charge against the forces of Dark quite happily, killing soldiers, UNDEAD, and DEMONS almost with abandon.

Fire. One of the very few things most forces of the Dark find hard to combat. One of the standard ways to defeat the DARK LORD or his MINIONS is to engineer a mighty explosion in the place where he/they are holed up, then let everything burn for days. Of course, before this the Dark Lord will have set Fire to large parts of the countryside, so it is only fair.

See also ELEMENTALS.

Firestarting is one of the basic Magic TALENTS, and often manifests at an early age. This must be dangerous (see BUILDING MATERIALS), but the inhabitants of Fantasyland have learned to take it in their stride. The Firestarter has only to concentrate for a candle or fuel in a grate to burst into flame. It is a lowly Talent. Young MAGIC USERS often apologize that this is all they can do. And thank goodness it seems confined wholly to candles and grates. We are probably lucky that in our own world it is not nearly so common.

Fish is caught all along the coasts and often in the INLAND SEA, with much palaver about putting to sea in small wooden BOATS, mending nets, and so on. It is unloaded as picturesquely as possible on to WHARFS. But it is very seldom eaten, and almost never by Tourists, except just occasionally as a variant on STEW. One conjecture is that it is carted inland to manure fields ravaged by ARMIES, WIZARDS, droughts, and demonic invasion. But this has never been confirmed. Also, trout (*plump and gleaming*ᴼᴹᵀ)

may be caught in a RIVER, almost always by
the FEMALE MERCENARY, who tickles out the
fish *with a cocky glint in her eye*⊙; the fish are
then gutted with a thumbnail and cooked on
a spit over the campfire. They taste delicious,
although burnt on the outside and raw in the
middle.

Fleas. See LICE.

Food. See STEW, SCURVY, STEW, WAYBREAD,
(also known as Journey Cake), and STEW—
though there are occasional BIRDS, FISH, RAB-
BITS, and pieces of cheese. Generally the diet
is an unvaried one, although MARSH DWELLERS
can work wonders with ROOTS. Desserts are
unknown except occasionally in the Courts of
KINGS. Tourists who suffer from diabetes
should be quite safe.

Foreseeing. Foreseeing is done by those MAGIC
USERS with the GIFT of looking into the future,
quite often MYSTICAL MASTERS. It is done un-
asked. Indeed, most people would rather not
know. But, unlike the other forms of PROPH-
ECY, this is usually very obscure, although quite
accurate. Tourists should not lose sleep over it.
Whatever is Foreseen is going to happen
anyway.

Forest of Doom. This is usually the home of
mobile and prehensile Trees. There will be
giant SPIDERS too, and Dwellers near the center

who will want to SACRIFICE any stranger to their God. It is best to avoid the place if possible. But the Management usually insists on sending you there. An OLD RUINED CITY is sometimes situated in the heart of this Forest.

See also WOODS.

Forts usually occur in MOUNTAINS. Generally they are guarding a pass, but sometimes they are just there. They are about equally divided between manned and deserted. In all cases they are sort of square and blockish, with many additional geometric features for which the Management seldom gives reasons. The Rule is that if a Fort is manned, then it will be attacked by the forces of the Dark. If it is deserted, then some SECRET vital to the Tour QUEST is concealed there.

Frostbite is unknown, even in the extreme frozen north. This is convenient for Tourists, who will be compelled to suffer HARDSHIPS of cold when visiting the north, and also probably accounts for the fact that the NORTHERN BARBARIANS wear little besides a furry loincloth.

See also CHILBLAINS and HYPOTHERMIA.

Fruit is probably a luxury item. It is seldom served at INNS and usually makes its appearance only at feasts in the courts of KINGS.

See also SCURVY.

> Gardens are fraught with risk. King Doras II fell over a flowerpot in his garden after seeing a vision of seven future kings.
>
> Ka'a Orto'o, Gnomic Utterances, 1 ix

Galley. A large, cumbrous SHIP moved by both sail and banks of oars. Usually, but not invariably, it belongs to the FANATIC CALIPHATES, who may be using it for trade. Or maybe not, because the only things most Galleys seem to contain are rows of benches for GALLEY SLAVES.

Galley Slave. The only opportunity, if you are a man, of reaching any of the OFFSHORE IS-LANDS is to become a GALLEY Slave. It is one of the two main occupations open to you once you are enslaved (see also GLADIATOR). You will be captured and sold into slavery on an average halfway through the Tour and will then very shortly find yourself chained to a bench belowdecks (*noisome*⊙) and probably to a large heavy oar too. (There is no toilet provided, hence the OMT.) You have to sit there all the time, even when the galley is under sail. You will be given just enough food and drink to keep you alive. There will be an overseer (*brutal*☜) who will encourage you with a large leather whip, as well as someone else to beat time as you row. You will find it hard work. You will acquire blisters and scars as well as muscles. But do not despair. Next to you on the bench there will be a future friend, generally of giant stature, and, as soon as your muscles are properly hardened, you will be able to cut your • chains and, with the help of this LARGE MAN, slaughter your employers and leap overboard. You may then have to swim some way to an island. If you are lucky, a SEA MONSTER will arise from the deep and offer you a lift, but even without this help you will reach land in a day or so. In some cases, you may find that you have not reached an island at all, but some other land. This will be the OTHER CONTINENT and the Tour will proceed as normal there.

Games are few, usually only dice, cards, and chess.

GUARDS, soldiers, and Thieves are all addicted to dice, which they normally play only when drinking. This is a convenient habit, since it will often enable you to slip past them, either into or out of a PRISON, FORT, or TOWN, whenever you need to. Often the dice have been crafted from unusual materials, like human vertebrae, and they may have RUNES on them in place of the normal spots.

Card games are always fraught affairs, since inevitably the fall of the cards has some *miasma of meaning* ☞ that goes far beyond the game ♣ itself; players are likely to look over their shoulders nervously before reluctantly muttering "Snap."

Chess seems to be played by the upper classes. That is to say, you will find KINGS, rich MERCHANTS, and the like all possess very handsome chess sets, but you will almost never see them playing with them.

Psychiatrists may find matter for grave concern in the almost total absence of other Games, particularly among children, but the reason is easy to find. From the cradle up, the inhabitants are in the serious business of keeping alive in spite of the best efforts of the DARK LORD, WIZARDS, bad Kings, DEMONS, and maverick MAGIC, and have no time for fripperies.

See also GAMING.

Gaming is done with dice by soldiers and SPIES. Dice are traditionally loaded. Tourists are not advised to try it.

See also GAMES.

Gay Mage may be one of your COMPANIONS on the Tour. He will be very beautiful and he will dress in gorgeous colors. He will have long hair ⚠ which may be silver-blonde. He will *ache with sensitivity*☞. He will not like to fight or to be • angry with people. Despite all this, he will be surprisingly strong, competent, and determined, and he will be very good at MAGIC indeed. He will fall in love while on the Tour and suffer other disasters, but this will not impair his efficiency in the least. You will find him giving you a back rub and aromatherapy late in the Tour at some point when he ought to be dead. A valuable Companion.

Geas is the word for the Rules governing PANCELTIC TOURS. On normal PanCeltic Tours it is something magically laid on you that you must do or not do. This can be a nuisance, because the Geas takes no account of the feelings you may have about whatever is laid on you. For instance, you can be under Geas to marry the next person you see with violet eyes, or to kill every third red-haired man, or to visit every COUNTRY on the MAP, and you will do those things. You may weep and curse, but do them you will.

Gestures are the invariable accompaniment to the performing of MAGIC. The Management here takes the reasonable line that, without Gestures, most people would not know that Magic was being done. So all WIZARDS wave their arms about a lot. Many Gesture with their STAFFS. Some flick their fingers. In extreme cases, the Gesture leaves a *green glowing trace in the air*⊙ᴍᵀ.

Ghosts come both singly and in battalions. Single Ghosts are met in MANSIONS and out of doors, but very seldom in CASTLES, PALACES, or other places where people might have come by sticky ends. This is because Ghosts on the whole seem to exist not as a result of the way they died but because of unfinished business. This applies particularly to Ghosts in battalions, who will be waiting in a large cemetery or graveyard for someone to call them up to fulfil their vows. Single Ghosts will be feeling vengeful about some legal or magical matter they have had to leave to their descendants. Tourists should be careful of all Ghosts. In Fantasyland, Ghosts can interact with living substance and do real damage. Single Ghosts can hurt or bespell you. The called-up battalions usually fight like living soldiers but are, for obvious reasons, very difficult to kill.

Giants are seldom seen these days. They may be invisible (see INVISIBILITY). If you think you see a Giant, it will usually prove to be a very large human or the result of a BREEDING PROGRAM. There are, however, confirmed sightings of a whole race of gentle Giants. Tours occasionally stumble on these.

Gifts is another word for TALENTS. It is used by people who feel reverent about MAGIC.

Gladiator is the second of two professions open to male Tourists when they are taken prisoner and sold as a SLAVE (see also GALLEY SLAVE). You need not be muscular for this, though it helps; it is better to have a brain and to have recently been in WEAPONS training at a SCHOOL OF WEAPONRY (the Management usually arranges for this to have been the case). Once enslaved, you will be taken to the pitlike pens at the back of the arena, where you will be lightly chained but not underfed or too badly treated, since your owners wish you to give the audience a decent show. You may even be allowed exercise. During this time, you will hear rumors about the other Gladiators, the professionals, one of whom will be said to have defeated all comers. Naturally, when your time comes to fight, this will be the man you have to meet. With luck, you will by this time have had a few early bouts, either with other professionals or with a mutant ANIMAL or two, and your skills will be honed. But this fight will be the big one. Often, freedom will be the reward. The Rule is: if you are offered freedom, then you must kill your professional; but, if you are just put to fight him, you will get the best of it and the man will become your friend. The two of you will then escape together.

But, either way, you have to fight him, in glaring heat (this is the Rule) and in front of the local TYRANT and a huge crowd. Usually your opponent will have superior WEAPONS. But thanks to your earlier training you are able, at the last gasp, to pull a fast one on him and win. The crowd will then wish you to take his place as their HERO. This can be awkward, but do not worry. The Rule is that you can escape during the next day or so.

Gnomes are a small, brown, rather childish PEOPLE who tend to live beneath the roots of TREES or under hillsides. They come out of their earthy warrens to capture Tourists for no real reason. Since they have some knowledge of MAGIC they can make life uncomfortable and be hard to escape from. Nor do they always understand that humans need to eat and drink. Captured Tourists are advised to work hard at finding out what the Gnomes want, or think they want, and then talking them out of it. The average time this takes is about forty-eight hours. By this time you are very hungry and thirsty indeed.

Gnomic Utterances. These are traditional, and are set at the head of each section of the Guidebook. The reason for them is lost in the mists of HISTORY. They are culled by the Management from a mighty collection of wise sayings probably compiled by a SAGE—probably called Ka'a Orto'o—some centuries before this Tour begins. The Rule is that no Utterance has anything whatsoever to do with the section it precedes. Nor, of course, has it anything to do with GNOMES.

Goblins are the smaller unmutated form of ORCS, and quite as unpleasant. They are *mis-shapen*⊙ ugly humanoids with long nails and teeth. Usually they have green scaly skins and pointed ears. They live underground in MOUNTAINS and WOODS and are likely to pour out of these dens in hundreds and attack the Tour without warning. They have a habit of keeping on coming, however many you kill, so you will find you have to keep cutting Goblins to pieces until your arm aches. If there are enough Goblins, they will capture you at this stage and haul you underground. It will be some days before your COMPANIONS manage to rescue you. Be prepared for a bad few days. Goblins enjoy TORTURE and are rather good at it. Some Goblins are cannibals too.

Goddesses and Gods operate in ones, threesomes, or whole pantheons of nine or more (see RELIGION). Most of them claim to have made the world, and this is indeed a likely claim in the case of threesomes or pantheons: Fantasyland does have the air of having been made by a committee. But all Goddesses and Gods, whether they say they made the world or not, have very detailed short-term plans for it which they are determined to carry out. Consequently they tend to push people into the required actions by the use of coincidence or PROPHECY, or just by narrowing down your available choices of what to do next: if a deity is pushing you, things will go miserably badly until there is only one choice left to you.

Deities are also much given to manifesting and taking part in the action themselves. They manifest, according to their natures, as a CHILD, a bright light, a silver beam, a demonic creature, or a superhuman human, and in this form will tell you what your next move must be. They have to do this. Because of the Rule that all Goddesses and Gods fade when not worshipped (see IMMORTALS), each deity has constantly to make it quite clear to humans that She/He exists. You may therefore expect to meet at least one deity during your tour. The experience is generally awe-inspiring and usually instructive, though you may come away from it feeling rather bullied.

See also ASPECT and BEGINNINGS.

Good means everyone and everything on your side. This of course includes Tour COMPANIONS—in spite of irritating quirks—DRAGONS, DWARFS, ELVES, and, once you have talked to them seriously, GNOMES. It means about half the GODDESSES AND GODS. Most other things are the ENEMY, and EVIL. If you find something/someone that is neither, such as a HORSE or a neutral God, you may safely ignore them.

Government in Fantasyland is another word for KING or TYRANT. Most AVERAGE FOLK seem to get on perfectly well without any of it.

See also POLITICS.

Grimoires are books of Evil SPELLS. Tourists should avoid looking into or even touching them except in true need. Most of them behave like conscious entities and are out to entrap. You can tell which they are, because their leather covers are either black or the *glabrous hue*⊗ of human skin. Sometimes this smokes a little when fingered. Grimoires will often flutter their pages enticingly, or fall open at a Spell that entraps; but it is also quite customary for the page you need to be blank when you first look at it, or to blank itself as you try to read. If you really need to consult a Grimoire as part of your QUEST for KNOWLEDGE, you need a shielding Spell, a coercion Spell, and a Spell that enables you to remember what you saw without having nightmares for the rest of the Tour. It is best to let your Tour MENTOR or a WIZARD handle it.

Guards are the TOWN Watch and quite useless. They always arrive too late to quell a TAVERN BRAWL or riot. This is because there are too few of them and all of them are stupid. Tourists will be glad of both these facts at the point when they are trying to leave the Town unseen.

Guilds. See ASSASSINS, GUILD OF and THIEVES' GUILD.

Guns are banned on most Tours. If a Tourist succeeds in smuggling a Gun through from our own world, the Management will usually arrange for it not to work for some reason. On most Tours gunpowder does not explode. If you really feel you must bring a Gun (and who is to blame you, given the trials and DANGERS of the Tour?), your best chance of getting away with it is to import something antique such as a musket or a flintlock pistol.

Hard on your port a bit
Down on your right a bit
That's how to make a hit
Down with the rest of it.

Barbary Viking Song*

Hardship is intrinsic to all Tours. Be prepared to be cold, tired, wet, wounded, and, above all, sleepless, and still to have to slog on. For some reason, sleep is the thing the Management is least prepared to allow you. But you will lose more than sleep before the CONCLUSION. Be prepared to have to go about SAVING THE WORLD with one leg or your soul missing. Until you have done this, you will not know what Hardship is.

Hares are a distinct species from RABBITS, which they superficially resemble—about as close to a Rabbit as a monkey is to a human—but the Management will always try to kid you

*The Management regrets that it was unable to find a Gnomic Utterance that was sufficiently irrelevant. It was forced to resort to doggerel instead.

that they are the same thing. Hares do not dig burrows, but spend all their life above ground, running very hard. This is probably why they so often end up in Tourist traps. Because of their lifestyle, Hares taste bitter and their flesh is so tough that they should be hung for at least two days after slaughter. The Management, however, will want you to eat the Hare that same evening and will therefore call it a Rabbit. That night's STEW will be unpleasant and very hard to chew.

Harp. A triangular stringed instrument, often MAGIC. Even when not Magic, a Harp is surprisingly portable and tough and can be carried everywhere on the back of the BARD or Harper in all weathers. A Harp seldom goes out of tune and never warps. Its strings break only in very rare instances, usually because the Harper is sulking or crossed in love. This is just as well as no one seems to make or sell spare strings. If Magic, a Harp makes its player able to do most things a WIZARD can do, only few Harpers seem to realize this. Perhaps this is a pity, because almost no Harp, Magic or not, will respond to anyone who is not GOOD.

Harper. See BARDS, HARP, and PANCELTS.

Healers are the medics of Fantasyland, but even more highly venerated. Usually they deserve respect. They are slender, mild-mannered people who dare not kill or offer violence because this would destroy their Healing Powers. Any Healer who reverses the flow of energy to hurt instead of heal is said to suffer terribly. A Healer will show a GIFT at an early age, whereupon she/he will be taken and trained in a Hall, which seems to be something like a MONASTERY, and will emerge around the age of twenty able to close Wounds with a touch of the finger, dispel FEVER by concentrating, and mend bones by going into a light trance. A Healer may also know HERBS and save her/himself the fatigue of falling into a trance by applying leaves and ointments instead. Some ointments even mend broken bones. Healers appear to derive their POWER and some of their training from the hand of the GODDESS, and are often very devout people. All this makes you see that medicine in our world has a long way to go.

Heating is open fires or nothing, except in MONASTERIES, TEMPLES, and the PALACES of sick KINGS, where a charcoal brazier is allowed to the abbot, HIGH PRIEST, or King. Sometimes the inside of an ANCIENT ENGINEERING PROJECT will be kept inexplicably warm by *some preternatural agency beyond the ken of Man*, indicating that the ancients knew a thing or two about central heating.

Heatstroke is rare but, since it is caused by the sun and not by bacteria, it can happen. Expect to be smitten by it in the DESERT. It will cause you only a day or so of acute discomfort.

Hedge Wizard. A MAGIC USER who received little or no training or was not intelligent enough to qualify for the College of Wizardry (see INVISIBLE COLLEGE), but who has decided to make a living out of it all the same. Most Hedge WIZARDS are small, shabby and self-deprecating. They are to be met trudging around the land touting for custom. Tourists often feel sorry for them, and this is a snare. Few of them are EVIL, but they will land you in trouble anyway, because their SPELLS are likely to be weak or incomplete and will fail you just when you need to rely on them. Consult a Hedge Wizard only when no other help is around.

See also HERBWOMAN.

Heirs. See MISSING HEIRS.

Helmets are allowed only to the following, and never to Tourists:

1. GUARDS, particularly of the TOWN Watch, so they can shove the Helmet back and scratch their heads.

2. Vestigial Imperialists (See VESTIGIAL EMPIRE), so that it can be surmounted by a plume of dyed horsehair.

3. BARBARY VIKINGS, to carry the necessary horns.

4. The forces of the DARK LORD, so that they can have the visors down and behave like automata (*faceless*ⓞⓜⓣ).

5. Foreigners, so that they can be a peculiar foreign shape.

6. Just occasionally ARMIES, if the Management is intending to pour boiling oil on the besiegers.

Heraldry is rampant, passant, and even couchant, but the exact rules are vague. Generally the Management is happy to paint an ANIMAL or plant of one color on a field of another and leave it at that.

Herbs are plentiful in Fantasyland. All the most useful and curative plants seem to have escaped the magical pollution that has so blighted ANIMAL life and, what is more, whole crops of hitherto unknown healing Herbs are also available, growing freely on hillsides and the banks of streams just where and when they are needed. All HHEALERS and HERBWOMEN are well versed in their uses and habitats (*lore*⊚ᴹᵀ). If you are wounded, one of these can soon put you right with a poultice of crushed leaves.

Herbwoman. Said to be the female equivalent of a HEDGE WIZARD, but this is seldom the case. She is never rich, but she can be any age, and the older she is the more likely she is to be an accomplished midwife. She will usually wear HOMESPUN Robes. If young, she may join your Tour. A Herbwoman will have had little or no formal training, but she will have received enormous amounts of *lore*⊛ from her predecessors, and anything to do with the natural world is an open book to her. She will be quite a powerful WITCH and often able to Heal when normal HEALERS have given up. She is also likely to have LEGENDS and other KNOWLEDGE you need.

See also HERBS.

Heroes. These are mythical beings, often selected at birth, who perform amazing deeds of courage, strength, and magical mayhem, usually against huge odds. The Rule is that the Hero is always Out There. If you get to meet a so-called Hero, she/he always turns out to be just another human, with human failings, who has happened to be in the right place at the right time (or the wrong place at the wrong time, more likely). Tourists, too, may perform amazing deeds and quite normally end up SAVING THE WORLD, but cannot qualify as Heroes because they are not Out There.

Hidden Kingdom. Usually reached through CAVERNS or after an arduous trek into the heart of the central massif, this is often the object of the Tour QUEST and much of the Tour will be devoted to getting directions to find it. When you get there you will discover it is very beautiful and very orderly. The Dwellers will be either MYSTICAL MASTERS or ELVES, or both. The ruler, who will be grave, wise, and comely, will talk to you long and seriously about MAGIC and your aims in life. People will play fine, restful MUSIC. You will be able to relax and feast. One good thing about this place is that they will either not serve STEW or, if they do, it will be strangely spiced and vegetarian. For a few days, you will think this is the perfect place, but after that you will be anxious to leave because it is really very boring. The Dwellers want you gone too. They find you unrestful. So they will give you a magical preview of what you do next (see PROPHECY) and fresh supplies of WAYBREAD and send you on your way to SAVING THE WORLD.

Hieroglyphs can be the form of writing used in the OTHER CONTINENT, or else a difficult and unpleasant alternative to RUNES. WIZARDS write Hieroglyphs a lot on floors and in the air. You need help to read them.

See also GRIMOIRES and SCROLLS.

High King is the top KING of whatever number of COUNTRIES, dukedoms, and principalities the Management pleases. He is a northerly phenomenon and does not occur on all Tours.

When he does, he is always GOOD, rather conscientious, and terribly overworked. You will often witness the start of his reign about halfway through the Tour. There will be a long and tedious ceremony in which all lesser rulers swear oaths to the High King. He will then be the one who has to muster an ARMY to fight the forces of the DARK LORD.

High Priest is nearly always, EVIL, either on his own account or on behalf of the DARK LORD. Sometimes he is fat, thick-lipped, and corrupt, sometimes tall, thin, shaggy-browed, and corrupt. He will be wearing ROBES of enormous richness and a medallion round his neck that can shoot MAGIC at people. He has not cut his fingernails in years. Mostly he does not believe in his God, but cynically uses both the God's powers and his own considerable Magic skills to his own ends, which are (a) getting rich, (b) being cruel, and (c) acquiring catamites and concubines. The younger members of the Tour are not safe from him. He is particularly dangerous because he can call on two kinds of Magic and after that hundreds of fanatic soldiers and worshippers, who may pursue the Tour party for miles.

See also RELIGION, SCROLLS, and TEMPLES.

High Priestesses are always devout and always head the worship of female deities. They are:
   1. Of the Triple Goddess. The High Priestess is good-looking, with a nice figure and a warm

and motherly nature. She will give you excellent advice and any other help you need.

2. Of any other Goddess. This High Priestess is tall, thin, and austere. In her view, nothing comes before her duty to her deity. Consequently, you have to convince her that her deity wants what you need. Then she will put the large resources of her TEMPLE/COUNTRY at your service. On occasion, however, the DARK LORD has got in before you, often by pretending to be the GODDESS, and convinced the High Priestess she needs to support him. You will have to persuade her otherwise, often by trickery. But she has not got where she is by being stupid, so you will have your work cut out.

History is generally patchy and unreliable. Any real information about past events is either lost or contained in a SCROLL jealously guarded in a MONASTERY or TEMPLE. All that can be ascertained with any certainty is:

1. That there once was an Empire that ruled the continent from coast to coast (give or take a few enclaves of ELVES, GOBLINS, and the like), but that this shrank to one CITY a long time before the era of the current Tour, leaving only a few ROADS, perhaps some of the less ancient ANCIENT ENGINEERING PROJECTS, and much deserted country.

2. That there was once a WIZARDS' War which probably occurred earlier still. The result of this is that large tracts of land are still magically devastated (see WASTE AREAS).

See LEGENDS, as more reliable sources of information.

Homespun (*servicable*⏺) is probably a kind of tweed worn by those who are not rich. The cloth seems to be a sort of mud color.

Horse-Breeding is practiced by both the ANGLO-SAXON COSSACKS in the mid-north and the DESERT NOMADS in the south. They are not in competition with one another and their activities do not result in a glut of horseflesh. In Fantasyland, the mortality rate for HORSES is even higher than that for MONSTERS and humans. Despite these grim statistics, both races are said to love their Horses passionately.

Horses are of a breed unique to Fantasyland. They are capable of galloping full-tilt all day without a rest. Sometimes they do not require food or water. They never cast shoes, go lame, or put their hooves down holes, except when the Management deems it necessary, as when the forces of the DARK LORD are only half an hour behind. They never otherwise stumble. Nor do they ever make life difficult for Tourists by biting or kicking their riders or one another. They never resist being mounted or blow out so that their girths slip, or do any of the other things that make horses so chancy in this world. For instance, they never shy and seldom whinny or demand sugar at inopportune moments. But for some reason you cannot hold a conversation while riding them. If you want to say anything to another Tourist (or vice versa), both of you will have to rein to a stop and stand staring out over a VALLEY while you talk. Apart from this inexplicable quirk, Horses can be used just like bicycles, and usually are. Much research into how these exemplary animals come to exist has resulted in the following: no mare ever comes into season on the Tour and no STALLION ever shows an interest in a mare; and few Horses are described as geldings. It therefore seems probably that they breed by pollination. This theory seems to account for everything, since it is clear that the creatures do behave more like vegetables than mammals. It also explains why the ANGLO-SAXON COSSACKS and the DESERT NOMADS appear to have a monopoly on horse-breeding. They alone possess the secret of how to pollinate them.

See also HORSE-BREEDING.

Hovels are small squalid dwellings, either in a VILLAGE or occasionally up a MOUNTAIN, and probably most resemble huts. The people who live in Hovels are evidently rather lazy and not very good with their hands, since in no cases have any repairs ever been done to these buildings (*tumbledown*☜, *rotting thatch*☜, etc.) and there is no such thing as a clean Hovel. Indoors, the occupants *eke out a wretched existence*☜, which you can see they would, given the draughts, smoke, and general lack of house-cleaning. This need not alarm you. The Tour will not require you to enter a Hovel that is inhabited. If you enter one at all, it will be *long-deserted*☜ and there will be sanitary arrangements out the back.

Hypothermia is a very rare condition, but may be experienced by the unlucky Tourist, usually when crossing a MOUNTAIN (see MOUNTAIN PASS, BLOCKED). The cure is swift, involving hot soup and the attentions of a HEALER in an icy cave.

> Insights are always valuable, even if they only show you your duodenal ulcer.
>
> Ka'a Orto'o, Gnomic Utterances, V xciii

Idol. A statue of a bad or EVIL God, usually found in a TEMPLE, but occasionally carried through the streets by fanatical worshippers (see also IMAGE). It will be covered with gold, JEWELS, and caparisons, and be very ugly. The most appalling RITES and SACRIFICES will be held in front of it. On occasion an Idol will be hollow and thus usable by GOOD people as a convenient place to hide, notably if they were about to be the subject of one of those appalling Rites and Sacrifices. Oddly, through all the centuries during which they have had it, the Idol's worshippers have never noticed that it is not solid, and thus haven't a clue where you might have vanished to.

On the rare occasions when the hollowness *is* known about, the hollow space is of course used by PRIESTS to create special effects, such as a thunderous voice issuing from the Idol, the rolling of its eyes and the belching from its mouth of flames to terrify and convince its worshippers.

Illusion is an important branch of MAGIC. In fact, some Tours work on the assumption that all magic is really Illusion, or the art of making one thing/person seem like something quite different. Even where this is not the case, forms of Illusion play a large part. These are:

1. An appearance put on something from outside. Here the MAGIC USER makes thin air, a table, or an ARMY look like, respectively, a flight of butterflies, the REGENT, or a bank of MIST.

2. Something is done to the mind of the onlooker to make her/him see thin air, a table, or an Army as butterflies, the Regent, or a bank of Mist. This is where it can get edgy. Nasty Illusions can be planted permanently in a mind so that the person has a case of perpetual magical DTs. Worse still, the person can spend the rest of her/his life thinking she/he is an elephant or a bat.

3. Most Illusion is probably a mix of the two kinds.

Image. A statue of a GODDESS OR GOD, only here—unlike the case with and IDOL—the deity is said to be GOOD. There will be RITES but not SACRIFICES.

Immortals are fairly common in Fantasyland. There are three kinds:

1. GODDESSES AND GODS, who exist forever unless people stop believing in them.

2. ELVES and DARK LORDS, who live forever unless someone kills them.

3. Humans who are:

(a) Cursed and have to spend Eternity drearily Questing and/or hating everything. (See CURSES and QUEST.)

(b) MAGIC USERS. These generally find plenty to occupy the long years and mostly have rather a good time.

P

POISON

Imperial Citizens are so civilized that they have given up WAR in favor of POLITICS and POISON. The Management considers this effete and will direct you to feel contempt for most of these people, except the Emperor, until you come upon the elderly man who retains the old virtues of the Empire. A former General, he is totally trustworthy and warlike and scorns politics too. He will become a staunch supporter of the Tour and of great help either on the QUEST or in SAVING THE WORLD.

Imperial City. See VESTIGIAL EMPIRE.

Imperious Female is a Tour COMPANION you probably hate at first. She is rather finely dressed and may have the SERIOUS SOLDIER as her bodyguard. She will sweep into the INN at the STARTING POINT and behave as if what she wants is the only thing of importance to anyone. Before long, however, you will see that she is really *driven by huge anxiety*OMT. She has some KNOWLEDGE or SECRET with her that preys on her mind, usually by suggesting her duty is SAVING THE WORLD. You will then discover she is a WITCH or of Royal birth or both. After that she will earn your respect by not complaining at any of the HARDSHIPS of the Tour, and then by rescuing everyone from either an attack by DEMONS or the efforts of a bad KING to imprison you all. And after that, she will indeed Save the World, with a little help from her friends.

Import/Export of goods clearly happens, or there would not be BALES on WHARFS. But most goods seem purely local, except perhaps in the FANATIC CALIPHATES and among the MERCHANT FEUDALISTS, where things from overseas do occasionally appear. It is not known what the Caliphates send in exchange or where these goods are sent.

See also ECONOMY.

Incense is much used, probably because all SMELLS in Fantasyland are significant in some way. It seems to have a strong effect on everyone, particularly Tourists. When EVIL, Incense is used by ENCHANTRESSES and WITCHES and in TEMPLES; the OMTs are *heavy, soporific, seductive,* etc. When GOOD, it will be used by the GAY MAGE and referred to by what it was made from, as *lavender, camomile, aniseed, pine,* etc.

Incidents should happen at regular intervals on every tour. You should not be able to travel more than fifty miles without something happening. Usually they start small and work up to big.

1. Small Incidents include: AMBUSH (by BANDITS or LEATHERY-WINGED AVIANS); BETRAYAL; arrest by Imperial GUARDS; attack by prehensile TREES; SEX with a Tour COMPANION; an encounter with a WIZARD/DRAGON/MINION OF THE DARK LORD/Fortune Teller; bad WEATHER; crossing a RIVER; an arrow shot suddenly from nowhere (it will miss everyone and stick in a tree); stealing something from a MONASTERY/TEMPLE; a near-fatal visit from VAMPIRES in the night; stumbling into a QUICKSAND. . . .

2. Medium-Sized Incidents can be: magical STORMS; attack by small APELIKE CANNIBALS or inferior DEMONS; being caught in crossfire during a WIZARDS' argument; capture by an ENCHANTRESS/PIRATES/PRIESTS/NORTHERN BARBARIANS; being hunted by MINIONS OF THE DARK LORD or PRIESTS; losing your FOOD supply; visiting a KING; becoming lost in CAVES; imprisonment/TORTURE; being enslaved as a GLADIATOR and having to FIGHT in the arena. . . .

3. Medium-Big Incidents often concern: large DEMONS; SIEGES/battles, but not of a conclusive nature; intervention of DRAGONS/WIZARDS/GODDESSES AND GODS/STONE CIRCLES; entrapment by a Puppet KING; confrontation with an ENCHANTRESS/high MINION OF THE DARK LORD;

losing your soul/SWORD/COMPANIONS; major MAGIC, resulting in earthquakes/volcanic activity/other large destructions; the opposition stealing your QUEST OBJECT. . . .

4. Big Incidents are anything involving the end of the DARK LORD/world/both together. You do not get these until you have taken at least two previous Tours.

Industry. Apart from a bit of pottery and light metalwork, or some slagheaps around the domain of the DARK LORD, most Tours encounter no Industry at all. Even EMBROIDERY factories are kept well out of sight.

See also ECONOMY.

Information. See KNOWLEDGE.

Inland Sea. There is always one of these somewhere around the midpoint of the continent. Tourists must expect to have to embark upon it at some stage in the Tour. It has PIRATES, but few or no SEA MONSTERS. Because it is shallower than the OUTER OCEAN, voyaging on it will be very choppy. Also, maybe because the land is all round it, it is extremely susceptible to both normal STORMS and STORM CONTROL. Expect a miserable voyage ending in capture and enslavement, or in shipwreck, or at the very least a frantic race in which your MAGIC USER tries to keep your SHIP ahead of the pursuit.

Innkeepers are all so alike that the Tourist may be pardoned for thinking she/he has not moved from one INN to the next. Innkeepers are tall, fat, male, aproned, busy, and normally jovial. They are there to serve and shout orders to barmaids. They take everything in their stride, from STRANGE RACES and TAVERN BRAWLS to peculiar requests from Tourists with awkward SECRETS to conceal. They seldom otherwise intrude on the action. They are always too busy. It is not known when these admirable men find time to eat or sleep.

Inns exist in TOWNS and CITIES, but seldom outside them, except at crossroads that are miles from anywhere. They are quite large buildings, mostly of wood, and are always larger upstairs than downstairs. Downstairs there is space for only the taproom and bar— a low-ceilinged CHAMBER with a fireplace at each end, the bar at one side, and many tables and benches—and a KITCHEN off the back; but upstairs there is space for innumerable *sleeping chambers* for the Tour party plus whatever room the INNKEEPER and his staff use, all arranged around long corridors so that people can creep from one to the other and intruders can invade the rooms of Tourists either to search their baggage or to menace them with DAGGERS. There are also extensive cellars, but these are only rarely brought into the action. Outside, there will be a yard and stables for the HORSES. Sometimes, the prudent Tourist will stay in the stable with her/his Horse. It is generally a lot safer. Quite a lot of INCIDENTS tend to happen in Inns.

See also BAR SERVICE and PATRONS OF INNS.

Inn Signs are always *crudely painted*⊙. Art— except the sort of obscenely decadent art you may encounter on a TEMPLE wall and turn away from with an embarrassed wince—does not seem to be studied by the inhabitants of Fantasyland, possibly because they are usually so busy fighting and coping with magically induced CATACLYSMS. Do not be surprised to find that every Inn Sign creaks loudly. This is a form of aural advertising.

(The gloomy wall tapestries in MANSIONS might be thought of as another form of art seen in Fantasyland, but most observers agree, having studied these tapestries, that, whatever they are, it is not art.)

Inscriptions are widespread. Tourists will need to keep someone on hand who can *decipher*⊙ such things. They can be in RUNES, HIEROGLYPHS, or ordinary writing, but the Rule is that they are always hard to read. Although only about forty percent of Inscriptions prove to be important, you can never tell until you know what they say. Inscriptions occur:

1. On AMULETS and COINAGE. Only about half of these are significant. If an Amulet is Inscribed with the NAME of its maker, this is some guide to its MAGIC strength and effi-

ciency. Your Tour MENTOR will know. Coinage
will have a picture of the last or current KING
and an Inscription that gives his name and
dates. It is surprising how often this King's profile will resemble that of a young woman on the
Tour, and thus give you a clue to her identity.

2. In stone, on DWARVEN FASTNESSES, CITA-
DELS, and TOMBS. Two-thirds of these are the
equivalent of GNOMIC UTTERANCES and say sad
things about Dying or threatening things about
regretting it should you try to barge inside.
These simply set the mood. The other third will
contain valuable KNOWLEDGE or MAGIC formulae for entering. Again, your Tour MENTOR
will know.

3. In GRIMOIRES and SCROLLS. These always
stand out in some way, often by being in another language, but again only about one-third
will contain Knowledge. The rest will be threats
or sad remarks by copyists.

Insects are almost nonexistent, possibly as a result of the WIZARDS' War (see also ECOLOGY).
Parasitic insects such as LICE and bedbugs have
mostly been stamped out—although fleas are
still popular—and only HOVELS occasionally
manifest houseflies. Small numbers of bees
must exist, since honey is often served by
friendly WIZARDS and people who live in CLIFF
DWELLINGS, and so must silkworms, because so
many persons wear silken garments. Otherwise,
almost the only recorded Insects are the mos-

quitoes all Tourists complain of in the
MARSHES (*in stinging clouds⊕*).

Invisibility can be induced by RINGS, CLOAKS,
and MAGIC headgear, and also by competent
MAGIC USERS either on themselves or a third
party. It seldom occurs to more than one person at once. In essence, Invisibility inhabits that
dubious ground between ILLUSION and true
Magic. In its minor forms it is a SPELL that says
"Don't notice me," which directs the eye of the
beholder away from the operator, who is not
really Invisible at all. Most Tourists can avail
themselves of this Spell when escaping from a
CITY. Median forms of Invisibility will make
the operator's body wholly transpicuous, but
that body will cast a shadow and appear in any
MIRROR. Avoid bright lights and reflecting surfaces in these cases, where the Invisibility is
really an Illusion. True Invisibility renders the
body and its shadow unseeable. This is the rar-
est and most magical kind. Tourists should bear
in mind that all cases of Invisibility are Spells
of sight only, and do not affect sounds, SMELLS,
and touch. The City GUARD will be able to hear
you, smell you, and feel you. Tiptoe past, and
do not cough, bump into anyone, or sweat
too much.

Invisible College is used for training WIZARDS
and usually occupies a prime site in some major
CITY. Once you have penetrated its invisible
exterior, you will find it has the usual features

of an Oxbridge college—dining hall, buttery, library, towers, lecture rooms, tutors, and even students—but all a little skewed. The Rule here is that, if something magical could possibly go wrong, it will. Be prepared for the Universe to split and for colored explosions, levitating towers, and tutors in ANIMAL form.

See also APPRENTICES, CITY OF WIZARDS, and HIDDEN CITY.

Iron is around in great quantities (this often causes distress to various magical beings), but it is impossible to get to see iron being mined or smelted. The Management doubtless knows why this should be, but Tourists and AVERAGE FOLK are left to conclude that it is All Very Magical.

Islanders are always unusual in some way; this is the Rule. It comes of being descended mostly from PIRATES. At the very least, they are likely to know MAGIC that is not like any other. They tend to build unusually constructed harbors, often defended by Magic. Their SHIPS trade from here. Most Islanders have a strong commercial bent, but under attack they always run about uselessly, and when tidal waves threaten their ISLANDS they have no idea what to do.

Islands are moved about by the Management at will. Sometimes they are in the INLAND SEA, in which case one or more may be the abode of a reclusive WIZARD, and sometimes they are strategically placed at the center of several sea routes, in which case they are usually the seat of a HIGH KING. Islands further out to sea are traditionally at risk from huge tidal waves generated by underwater volcanoes.

See also ISLANDERS.

Just when you think the taxes are all paid and there is nothing more to worry about is the time you should leave home secretly. This is just the time when everyone will ask you for money.

Ka'a Orto'o, Gnomic Utterances, XIV clvi

Jewelery. The Rule is that it all has magical purpose. The Management takes the very reasonable line that no one is going to wear or carry something just because it is pretty or beautifully made. Your pendant will always be an AMULET, your brooch a TALISMAN, and your necklace will be of CRYSTAL which will enable you to communicate with distant friends. If you pick up a piece of Jewelery by the roadside or in a MARKET it will, whatever it looks like, turn out to have some MAGIC. Take care, however. By far the majority of Jewelery is EVIL or, if not Evil, will have conditions attached to its use. For instance, a Ring can either put you under the influence of the DARK LORD or grant wishes while aging you ten years for every wish. In Fantasyland, even Jewelery you have owned for years will turn out to be something of this kind. If you are lucky, your mother's Ring will merely bring out your latent TALENT. But don't bank on it. Be careful particularly of Jewelery pressed upon you by a dying stranger.

See also JEWELS.

Jewels can, provided they are large enough, be QUEST OBJECTS. Huge rubies, massive sapphires, enormous emeralds, and other great big gems unknown in our world can all be imbued with potencies of various kinds, lost, and then Quested for. Diamonds, oddly, are not much desired, but the rest are eminently collectable. Their exact powers are at the discretion of the Management. Just a few of them have sentimental value only.

See also JEWELERY.

Jokes are against the Rules, except for very bad cumbersome jokes cracked by GUARDS, MERCENARIES, Other PEOPLES, and servitors. (It is believed that the Management in fact thinks these are very good jokes, and treasures them.) Everyone else must be deadly serious, although the SMALL MAN, some WIZARDS, and most bad KINGS are allowed to have a sense of humor—and see also THIEVES' GUILD.

Journey is of course your Tour. No discovery or action can take place in Fantasyland without a good deal of traveling about. This is in the

Rules. The Tour will be set up so that you will find at the outset you need to go to a CITY on the other side of the continent. Once there, you will find you need to go to the extreme south. And so on. You can count on the worst conditions for doing so. (See HARDSHIP, which the Management seems to find synonymous.) (See also LANDSCAPE, ROADS, and TERRAIN, of which you will see lots.) (Oh, and HORSES, which you will have to ride, BOOTS, which you will need when all your Horses are dead, and DARK LORD, who will be trying to stop you every mile of your Journey.)

Journey Cake. See FOOD and WAYBREAD.

Jugglers are normally hired as extras by the Management and will exhibit their skills in most MARKETS and often also in PALACES. They will be there purely for local color and your entertainment. In rare cases, the Tourist will need to hide in a troupe of Jugglers and even learn juggling skills. You can tell when you are going to have to do this because the Jugglers will have NAMES.

Justice does not exist as such. In some CITIES there will be officials called Justices, but the name means nothing. You will have to pay them and they will then sell you a favorable verdict. Do not look for Justice even in the Court of a Good KING. With the best of intentions, the King will be forced to judge against you and may even order you horribly executed. It is better to steer clear of legal matters entirely.

> Kinship is a bondage dragons feel more keenly
> than men. Their mothers-in-law live longer.
>
> Ka'a Orto'o, Gnomic Utterances, 1 iii

King's Men are the elite soldiers who surround
 any KING. You will encounter three sorts:

   1. Good. These usually guard a Good King,
but on rare occasions you will find them guarding a King that nobody knows is bad. They are
very smart and well trained and their drill is as
crisp as any you will see. But they are human.
At some point you will encounter them in a
relaxed mood, joshing their captain, swearing
merrily and recounting touching anecdotes
about their young children. They are the salt of
the earth, like their King, but there will probably be a time when they have to arrest you.
When this happens, they will tell you how much
they regret it and not give you any chance to
escape. You will have to rely on outside help
for that.

   2. Bad. These guard either a bad King or a
feeble one. Outwardly they may seem like the
GOOD guards, but in reality they are cruel and

coarse. You can tell they are because they swear nastily and their quarters are a mess. When these arrest you, they will find every opportunity to kick you or twist your arm. They will lick their lips when they hear you are to be put to the TORTURE, and ask to watch.

3. Automata. These are always in full ARMOR and HELMETS (with the visors down). This is because they are not human any more. The DARK LORD has made their wills his own and they behave as if they are clockwork, often in unison. They keep coming at you while you are killing them. Usually these GUARDS are in the employ of a puppet King or a MINION OF THE DARK LORD, but sometimes there are whole ARMIES of them directly under the command of the Dark Lord. It is hard to see why the Dark Lord goes to the trouble of enslaving so many minds, unless the aim is to produce ideal soldiers, in which case a good Sergeant is probably cheaper and quicker.

Kings come in four kinds:

1. Puppet Kings. These are EVIL entirely under the power of the DARK LORD, usually through the use of some magic-psychic device such as a glowing RING or a CRYSTAL BALL. You can detect them by the empty look in their eyes and by the fact that their followers behave like automata (see KING'S MEN). They will be very dangerous and must be either tricked or released from their bondage to the device.

2. Bad Kings. These manage to be EVIL entirely on their own. They are harder to detect, because they often have the air of quite pleasant people and, indeed, usually have some good traits of character, such as strength of mind and intelligence. The main way of discovering they are bad is to see how polite they are. Truly Evil Kings are *very* polite. They will offer you all sorts of luxuries and attempt to divert you from the Tour by every courteous ploy they can think of. Only when you refuse will they show their true colors, after which they will imprison you.

3. Good Kings are rough diamonds and the salt of the earth. They are easy to detect by their bluff manner and the lack of riches or protocol in their Court. The very best Good Kings always have their crowns on crooked.

4. Long-lost Kings. These are Kings who have been hidden or mislaid soon after birth. They are normally rather young and will be using the Tour to acquire both experience as rulers and various items of Royal regalia (SWORD, SCEPTER, RING, CUP, etc.) which have been lost at least as long as they have. There is, however, a subsection of long-lost Kings who have been magically deprived of their THRONES. This will have been done either by the implating of false memories or, in extreme cases, by transplanting the monarch to another body. In these cases the throne will be held by a usurper. Otherwise the same Rules apply. There is obviously a bit of an overlap between long-lost Kings and MISSING

HEIRS, but you can generally tell the difference when you see one: a Missing Heir is almost inhumanly naive.

Note that many Kings have a curious relationship with the patch of land they happen to be entitled to rule. If they are absent too long or failing in their duties, crops will not grow, cattle will die, and there will be general bad luck. COUNTRIES where a formerly good King develops a serious personality problem will in sympathy evolve a malign micro-climate, entailing drought in winter, snow in summer, and rain during the harvest. This may be one reason why the choice of FOOD in Fantasyland is so limited.

Kitchen. The place where STEW gets made. In CASTLES, INNS, and PALACES there are always large greasy stone Kitchens, usually with an open fire where cauldrons of Stew are boiling and the occasional CHICKEN is roasting. Kitchens are presided over by both male and female COOKS, though the Cook in an Inn is regularly female; all have the vilest possible tempers.

There will be a lot of shouting and much hurrying about with enormous platters. Helpers in a Kitchen have a miserable time and may often be hit over the head with ladles, etc., for failing to wash dishes quickly enough. Most Tourists will at some time in the Tour get a stint as a Kitchen helper, mostly when MONEY runs out but sometimes as a disguise or because a MAGIC USER has decided to punish them. When this happens, examine the Cook carefully to determine her/his COLOR CODING. Some turn out to have hearts of gold under the apron and the shouting. Some are just swine, in which case you can only suffer.

Knitting. It is possible that Knitting has not yet been invented in Fantasyland—at least so far as mortals are concerned (see CRONE). The complete absence of SOCKS and sweaters suggests that the inhabitants have concentrated instead on EMBROIDERY and weaving.

Knowledge can, in rare cases, be your QUEST OBJECT, but only if it is very important, such as the one fact or PROPHECY which will be essential if you are to go about SAVING THE WORLD. Very often, this Knowledge appears in pieces, which the Tourist must collect and assemble in the correct order, and then endeavor to understand before action can be taken. Sometimes there is the added twist that the Knowledge has been collected without your knowing it. In this case, you must have an inspiration before recognizing it. A friendly WIZARD or TOUR MENTOR can help here. They will madden you, but they will give hints.

> "Laugh long, live long," was the saying of the Sage Grometherus. He took poison to prove it and died chuckling.
>
> Ka'a Orto'o, Gnomic Utterances. XXXIX i

Landlords are always INNKEEPERS. The term is never used for those who own property for rent.

Landscape. During a Tour, both Tourists and Management will be kept too busy to examine the Landscape much. The Management will draw your attention to a view only when it is likely to prove a threat. Thus a WOOD will be mentioned if the TREES or WOODMEN are going to be hostile, MOUNTAINS will figure if you are going to have to cross them in bad WEATHER, and steep-sided gorges are delineated when you are about to be AMBUSHED there. If you want to know what the average Landscape is like, consult the cover of any brochure. Here you will see a range of spiky Mountains in the distance, from which a tall WATERFALL descends adorned with a rainbow at its crest. There will

be huge and intensely gnarled Trees in the fore-
ground, and both these features will dwarf the
line of horsemen making its way across a misty
green plain towards the Mountains. The sky is
orange and purple. *This* is what Fantasyland
really looks like. This is what entices Tourists
to enroll for Tours.

Languages are seldom as numerous or as difficult to learn as those of our own world. Most
Tours arrange for all inhabitants to speak the
same Language or else for most people to know
the Common Tongue, even if they speak some
other tongue to their families. The exception to
this is the OTHER CONTINENT, where the Tourist will have to master a little of the Language.
On some Tours, the Management will arrange
for a convenient translation SPELL to be cast
just as the Tourist is entering the world. But
none of this applies to MAGIC. The Language
of Spells is usually highly obscure. Sometimes
it is the same as the Old Tongue, sometimes
not. The Old Tongue is what the really important SCROLLS will be written in (possibly in HI-
EROGLYPHS or RUNES), and you will need a
translator for that. There is only one of it. Evidently the former inhabitants spoke only the
one Language. This seems to make it very potent. Just occasionally, when a Tourist is truly
beleaguered by Magic, either trying to get
through a magic door that will not open or
about to lose to someone EVIL, the Old Tongue
has a way of suddenly making itself known.

Then the Tourist will find her/himself crying out strange words. But do not expect this to happen much.

See also CAPITAL LETTERS and SPEECH.

Large Man may not join the Tour until encountered aboard the Slave GALLEY. He is very calm, very strong, and not at all stupid. In some cases he will have been a BLACKSMITH, which accounts for the ease with which he severs the chains in the Galley. He is often a BARBARY VIKING as well, in which case he will enjoy killing people, preferably more than one at once. In some cases, he is also ELITE, and the Gods take an interest in him; from the moment he joins the Tour, things start to get busy.

Last Battle. See CONFRONTATIONS.

Leathery-Winged Avians usually attack the party early in the Tour, always at night and generally on an exposed hilltop. You can tell they are about to attack because of the SMELL (see also REEK OF WRONGNESS⊛ and DANGER). They will be beaten off quite easily, but it will be a good scrap. They have probably been sent by a MINION OF THE DARK LORD to feel out the strength of the party, and will not reappear. Since it is always dark when they attack, it is hard to get much idea of their appearance, but they are thought to be about four feet from wingtip to wingtip, with sharp claws and teeth (*razorlike*⊛). Where they inflict a wound, that wound will fester instantly. As to their origin, they seem to be some WIZARD's attempt to create pterodactyls (see BREEDING PROGRAMS and ECOLOGY).

Legends are an important source of true information. They always turn out to be far more accurate than HISTORY. Listen and attend carefully if anyone recounts you a legend. The person telling it may be an old HERBWOMAN, a BARD, a bad KING, one of your COMPANIONS, or just someone in an INN. But no matter how improbable the story, it will always turn out to be the exact truth and only by following it accurately can you hope to succeed in your QUEST. The Management will never allow anyone to tell you a Legend unless it is going to be important for you to know.

Lice seem to be extinct in Fantasyland, possibly because of the good management of the Management. Fleas, by contrast, infest most BLANKETS and all BEGGARS—they are among Fantasyland's very few INSECTS.

Lighting—unless Magical (see MAGELIGHT and WITCHLIGHT)—is nearly always primitive and inconvenient, unless magically supplied. There are, in order of frequency:

1. Torches, which are used particularly in PALACES, CASTLES, and DUNGEONS, but also in the streets. These consist of a hefty stick with something flammable at one end. They are not at all convenient, since they are always *flaring*⊙ and *guttering*⊙ and must constitute a considerable FIRE risk in TOWNS where buildings are mostly of wood. They frequently blow out (the Rule here is that they do so at the worst possible moment) or simply burn away and plunge you into darkness while you are underground.

2. Candles, either solitary or in candelabra. These are used in INNS and other indoor places. Again there is risk of fire during TAVERN BRAWLS, but brawls very seldom do that amount of damage.

3. Rocks deep underground which glow with an eerie light of their own. Fortunately, these are often found moments after your torch has burnt out.

4. Glowbaskets. These are popular in some areas and may be magical. Usually they are a handwoven basket hung high on a wall and filled with something that glows with a *soft greenish light*⊙. The contents of the baskets may be either some form of mutant glowworm or stones, possibly chipped from the rocks that glow underground.

5. Lanterns—which, in the absence of electricity, might be supposed to be the most practical form of shielded light—are surprisingly uncommon and used mostly on the infrequent carriages (see TRANSPORT).

6. SWORDS.

Little People come in all sizes, from knee-high right up to the shoulder of the average human, and in a variety of breeds. The general Rule is that the smaller kinds are more like humans, while the larger ones get hairier and hairier, beginning with hairy feet and ending as hairy everything. All of them live in secret retired places, in either WOODS or MOUNTAINS, and come out only to join the Tour and help in SAVING THE WORLD. They are surprisingly cheerful, efficient, and brave, and usually win through where humans fail. If you have one or more on your Tour, count yourself lucky. Apart from anything else, Little People are allowed to make JOKES.

Martas V. Tyrant of Do'olge'ethly, always cut one hair from his head every day—no more, no less. This, it was said, greatly prolonged his reign, since everyone was waiting to see him with a full haircut.

Ka'a Orto'o, Gnomic Utterances. CLI vi

Mage. A fully qualified MAGIC USER who is either in the wings or taking only a camero role in the action. Bit-part Mages are usually present as a team. The exception to this is the GAY MAGE, who is on his own and a Tour COMPANION.

Magelight or Magefire is so common among MAGIC USERS that it is probably what an APPRENTICE WIZARD learns to do on his first day. The operator simply thinks, and a small ball of bluish or white light appears either on the hand or hovering in the air, at the shoulder, above the head, or on the end of the STAFF. Magelight has two uses: it gives light in dark places, and it shows that the maker can do MAGIC. When a more powerful Magic User overwhelms the one making the light, the Magelight normally flickers and dims away. Thus it is also a sort of

Magic meter. It is otherwise not good for anything much, but it would be nice to be able to do it.

See also WITCHLIGHT.

Magic has slightly different Rules for every Tour. Tourists had better find out swiftly which Rules apply or there could be problems. Luckily the Management seldom or never changes the Rules in mid-Tour, but it has been known to reserve one or two extra SECRETS for a nasty surprise later on. Even when the Rules are very clear, a Tour will have several different systems of Magic in operation. This is because Magic is an impure art. You will have to contend with at least three of the following kinds:

1. Magic that exists like liquid in a reservoir. Here the operator simply attaches a sort of magical hose and draws off what she/he needs. Attaching the hose often takes a trance to do, whereupon the operator also becomes the hose. HEALERS use this method.

2. Magic that is rather like electricity. Here the process is a longer one. The Magic has first to be generated or acquired by invocation; then it must be shaped or fed into the machinery (this is usually done with diagrams, RUNES, and incantations); and finally it must be plugged in to operate by GESTURE or word of POWER. (See SPELLS.)

3. Mind Magic. This is quicker. The operator simply *concentrates*ᴼᴹᵀ. This system applies to FARSEEING, FIRESTARTING, FORESEEING, MIND-

SPEECH, TELEKINESIS, TELEPORTING, and most SHAPESHIFTING.

4. Thought magic. Here the operator can, simply by having very powerful ideas, send out physical feelings that wound, cure, or transform another person. The red-eyed MINIONS OF THE DARK LORD do this when pursuing Tourists. The OMT is *baleful influence*. The afflicted Tourist will feel cold, weak, and contaminated, and may take days to recover. The Rules forbid Good WIZARDS to do this back to the forces of Dark, although they could, quite easily. They have to leave this to a humble Tourist, who will confront the DARK LORD and pour thoughts of GOOD at him. It is very effective. The Dark Lord usually finds this as painful as a bath of acid.

5. Sympathetic Magic. This is when the operator takes a piece of something/someone, such as a wood splinter or a nail clipping. Sometimes this is made into a small model, and named if necessary. The piece is then moved about like a computer mouse and the bigger object/person will do exactly the same, just like the mouse pointer. Many CURSES act this way. To become free, you have to repossess the piece. Alternatively, the piece of you that is used is nothing physical, but instead your NAME. Repossessing this can be more difficult.

6. Magic with a price. Here the operator has to pay in some way for the Magic used. This may be selling her/his soul to a DEMON, or simply becoming very tired. Setting WARDS seems to act this latter way.

7. Nature Magic. This often involves HERBS, though it can also be done by attuning to TREES and breezes and things. The operator uses the correct natural object and the result follows.

8. Pattern Magic. Here the Magic lies like threads in a design. The operator perceives this by WITCH SIGHT, takes up the threads and tugs.

9. MUSIC.

10. Alien Magic. DEMONS, DRAGONS, ELVES, GNOMES, GODDESSES AND GODS, and MARSH DWELLERS all have Magic that works in a quite different way from any of the above. The Rules are not known.

Magician. A MAGIC USER who knows about the mechanics of SPELLS. Get him to check your SWORD.

Magic Objects can be almost anything, but the important ones are usually QUEST OBJECTS too. There are two kinds:

1. Objects that have been bewitched or bespelled. This can be a temporary SPELL on a BUILDING or a coal scuttle or a BOOT, to make it behave in a startling way; or it can be an enchantment carefully crafted to be permanent. Spells on SWORDS, RINGS, and JEWELS are normally of this kind.

2. Objects that contain their own Magic. This is done by

(a) making the Object of some substance,

such as CRYSTAL, that gives off Magic like radioactivity. ORBS are like this.

(b) Making the Object in a certain way; for instance, SCEPTERS, STONE CIRCLES, and some SWORDS are Magic because they are the shapes they are. If a Tourist is stupid enough to twist a gem out of a Scepter or remove a STONE from a henge or hammer out the rib down the center of a Sword, none of them will work properly.

Magic Users. Anyone capable of using MAGIC. They range from the untaught or APPRENTICE or NOVICE right through to WIZARDS and DARK LORDS. Most have NAMES that describe their status or speciality, such as ENCHANTRESS, MAGE, Necromancer (see NECROMANCY), but they all have in common the fact that they were born with magical TALENTS/GIFTS. Some never come to very much, but most go on to years of rigorous training and studies. The result nearly always seems to be that their lives get incredibly prolonged. Wizards live for thousands of years. It seems that the longer a person marinades her/himself in Magic, the longer she/he lives. Only HEALERS seem to be exempt from this Rule.

Maids. These are well built young women (*buxom*⊙ᴹᵀ and *sweating*⊙ᴹᵀ) who wait at table or act as barmaids in the taprooms of all INNS. Traditionally, they are always in a hurry because there are too few of them and too many patrons, all of whom are shouting for service;

they are further distracted by the INNKEEPER bawling incomprehensibly at them.

See also BAR SERVICE and EUNUCHS.

Managment is the body who has arranged this Tour for you. It has made up the Rules for your comfort and convenience, so that no Tourist will ever be taken by surprise or shocked by an unexpected INCIDENT. Management reserves the right to alter the Rules in accordance with current fashions, and will admit absolutely no complaints or responsibility. It wishes you a safe and happy Tour of Fantasyland.

Management Directives occurs when the Management requires heavenly choirs to add to the usual OFFICIAL MANAGEMENT TERMS (OMTs). This is when the Tour gets particularly *doom-laden,* usually in the lead-up to the CONCLUSION. Then the OMTs go into overdrive and start saying things backwards. Typical MDs are *Grim were they and of awesome countenance,* or *Wan was that dawn and spectral the Sun,* or *High and frowning were the walls but undaunted was the assault thereon,* or *Sang they with eagerness and sang their swords with them.* Anyway, you'll know one when you see one.

Mansions are rare and usually rather tumble-down BUILDINGS. They are where lords and BARONS live. Their chief features are wall tapestries, oak staircases, an elderly butler, a gallery of family portraits, and GHOSTS. Expect to

Map • **164**

be uncomfortable in any Mansion. The four-poster beds will certainly be damp. However, you will be spared from having to sleep much in yours thanks to haunts, Vampires, and other Incidents.

Map. See Introduction for description. We must emphasize again here that no tour is complete without a Map. Further, you must not expect to be let off from visiting every damn' place shown on it.

Markets are a feature of every Town of any size. They comprise stalls and Booths and lots of Smells and shouting. It is where you go for local color, though you may buy cooked food in insanitary wrappings if you feel so inclined (see Squalor). Stalls sell mostly food, Booths clothing, armor, and jewelery. There are also plentiful fresh vegetables on sale. You might as well buy some, as no one else seems to eat the things. This is the place where you will come for your Sword, Clothing, and possibly your Horse. You will be cheated. If you need a jobbing Magician to test your Sword (this is strongly advised: see Swords) you will find him here in a Booth in one corner.

Marsh Dwellers are the Basques of Fantasy-land, entirely different from other Peoples and quite as anxious to be independent. They can be human or Other. In either case, they are smallish, brownish, a little twisted (perhaps rheumatically, since they DWELL in such a wet place), with thin limbs and wild brownish weedy hair. They worship an entirely different God, who requires much drumming and lots of SACRIFICES (which involve impaling the victim on a stake), and they use a form of MAGIC that no one else can use. They are expert at lurking entirely unseen until the Tour party is thoroughly lost in the MARSHES, whereupon they will spring out and capture everyone. They will then keep everyone prisoner in a pit, under a net, inside a fence of long thorns, or just unable to move because of Magic, until the ritual hour for Sacrifice has come. Tourists are advised to attempt to persuade these people not to kill them before this hour arrives. This is not easy, since the Marsh Dwellers speak a strange LANGUAGE, but usually an interpreter is provided, almost *but not quite* too late to be of use. After that, there will be apologies and then a feast of ROOTS.

Marshes are an area in the southern-central part of the continent where everything suddenly goes wrong and different. The Management has usually thoughtfully provided you with a BOAT shortly before you enter the Marshes; if not, you should acquire one soonest. The land here becomes mostly WATER, winding sluggishly in multiple channels between banks and islands too soggy to bear your weight. Generally, unpleasant drooping Trees clutch at you as you punt past and brakes of gigantic rushes look *ineffably menacing*ⓞⓜⓓ; all this adds to your confusion about which is north and also harbors millions of mosquitoes (*in stinging clouds*ⓞⓜⓓ) which will eat you alive. You will at this stage be lost, foodless, and without WATER. You will not dare to drink from the muddy channels—and with good reason. Strange squriming things swim there, and sometimes there are predators. On some Tours, the overhanging Trees are replaced by small thorny bushes, but the only difference is that the mosquitoes come out at night when you attempt to CAMP on a muddy ISLAND, and by day a cruel wind sweeps over everything. In both cases you will be overwhelmed by *dread*ⓞⓜⓓ and a *sense of danger*ⓞⓜⓓ. After a few days of it all, you will almost be glad when the MARSH DWELLERS take you prisoner. They will at least drag you to the only firm ground in the area.

Mayor. The head of the Town COUNCIL and usually a bumbling idiot. Quite often he is a MINION OF THE DARK LORD, but only a minor one. Keep out of his way.

Mentor. A Tour official who will be at your service until halfway through the Tour, when you will unaccountably lose him. Before that he will guide you, tell you what to do in the face of strange customs, and even sometimes instruct you in how to perform minor MAGICS. He will be several hundred years old and will probably have a long white beard; this will give him the right to be bossy, smug, tiresomely philosophical, and infuriatingly secretive about all-important facts. You will be glad to see the back of the old idiot. Unfortunately, you won't have. He will reappear, smugger and bossier than ever, near the end of the Tour, just when you thought you were doing rather well on your own.

See also MYSTICAL MASTERS.

Mercenaries are soldiers for hire who fight WARS they are not really interested in for (a) pay and (b) the raping and looting they get when a CITY falls. Their aim is to survive to enjoy this part, so they are mostly very good soldiers indeed, although they are sometimes rather rough-and-ready-looking in their CLOTHING. Either male or female (see FEMALE MERCENARY), they are drawn, it is stated, from all over the continent, but when you get down to enquiring you find that most of them come from places that are hardly on the MAP—unless they are female captains, in which case they are from a distant NUNNERY. Their leader is always male and mostly has the total loyalty of all these rough types. And they are very well organized. They spend the summers in paid fighting and retire to winter quarters until the fighting starts again in the spring. Here even the roughest types will carve exquisite statuettes in the long winter evenings after they have finished the day's training. Some even read books. The people who employ Mercenaries are normally the more corrupt of the MERCHANT FEU-DALISTS, until there is War throughout the land. Then the Mercenaries join the rest of the forces of GOOD. Do not be put off by all the drinking and fighting Mercenaries do. They are going to be on your side in the end.

Merchant Feudalists are organized in clusters of little COUNTRIES, mostly along the coast, each ruled by a COUNCIL. These trade with one another and are among the few PEOPLES who seem to trade overseas as well. Spices, silks, and olives are mentioned by the Management here. There is no unity among Merchant Feudalists. They all want to see their neighbors dead or reduced to penury. By the judicious use of POISON and MERCENARIES they often do.

Merchants—when freelance—travel from an unknown place in the south northwards to another uncertain place. They own CARAVANS loaded with BALES. And they love MONEY. This must be the reason so many of them travel, because nearly all of them fall by the wayside, victims of BANDITS or other AM-BUSHES, and the rest must know the risk. But they keep coming. Individual Merchants are *portly*⊙⊙, warmly dressed, and rather prone to trust hired GUARDS on small evidence. While alive, they drive a hard bargain. Many of them travel with young female relatives. This is unwise. See SLAVES, FEMALE.

Mindspeech is the regular term for Telepathy among MAGIC USERS. Almost everyone with a spark of TALENT is able to do it with both humans and ANIMALS. The Tourist may be disconcerted at first when a voice speaks out of nowhere soundlessly inside her/his head, but it will shortly come to seem quite natural. And do not be alarmed in case the Mindspeaker might be able to read your inmost thoughts: usually this is not so, or, if it could be done, the Magic User has sworn not to. Only the DARK LORD breaks this Rule: he will meanly try to read your weaknesses and worst fears and use them against you.

Mines are strategically placed in most hills of any stature that are some distance from anywhere civilized. They are of two kinds:
1. Made by DWARFS. The Rule here is that the Mine is either long deserted or at most is inhabited by a few survivors who will make confused claims to have been driven out/decimated by humans/other Dwarfs/MINIONS OF THE DARK LORD. Inhabited or not, this Mine will be very complex, with many levels of galleries, beautifully carved and engineered. What was being mined here is not always evident, but

at least some of the time it will appear to have
been JEWELS, since it is customary to find unwanted emeralds, etc., still embedded in the
rock of the walls. Metal will also be present, but
only when made up into armor and weapons
(*wondrous*⊛).

2. Man-made. This type of Mine appears to
exist for punishment only. It is where prisoners
of the DARK LORD or recalcitrant male SLAVES
are sent to work. The Mine will abound in
whip-wielding overseers (*brutal*⊛), chains for
the inmates, crude ladders and props, and carts
to carry the Mine produce *rumbling through the
passages*⊛. The miners will be working very
hard, but just exactly what they are mining is,
as with **1,** something the Management is very
coy about. Since miners die here in droves, it
is possible that the substance mined is dangerous. It could be uranium.

Minions of the Dark Lord are all over the
place. The DARK LORD has been busy planting
them for years. They can be either male or female. All will be carefully supplied with the
means to slaughter tourists appropriate to
their station.

1. Males are bad KINGS, puppet Kings,
DUKES, POWER-hungry usurpers, most HIGH
PRIESTS, ambitious MERCHANT FEUDALISTS,
BARONS, COURTIERS, fat PRINCES, EVIL WIZ-
ARDS, REGENTS, all ENEMY SPIES, and anyone
who suddenly conquers a CITY just as the Tour

arrives. We must add to this GOBLINS, TROLLS, and random Other PEOPLES.

2. Females are ENCHANTRESSES, Evil WITCHES, some HIGH PRIESTESSES, and most bad QUEENS.

3. EUNUCHS, MUTANT NASTIES, and carefully selected MONSTERS.

4. UNDEAD or Demonic persons, most of them red-eyed, wearing black, and riding black *steeds⊙*. These persons always have formidable MAGIC and usually operate by night. By day, they rely on brain-dead human soldiery (such as bad KING'S MEN) to keep up the pursuit.

Minstrel used to be a grand term, equivalent of BARD or Harper. These days it mostly refers to the humbler form of musician who plays busily (and probably hungrily) in a gallery all through a feast.

See also MUSIC.

Mirrors are somewhat infrequent, despite the fact that glass is used for windows. Many of them are made of polished metal and are the property of rich people or ENCHANTRESSES. Do not expect to find one in an INN. Where mirrors exist, of whatever material, they are not commonly used for combing the hair in. They will be employed for PROPHECY or FARSEEING or, less frequently, as the way in from our own world to start the Tour, or simply for travel. Glass mirrors are almost exclusively used as a

device for spotting VAMPIRES or other ENEMIES
in disguise.

Missing Heirs occur with great frequency. At
any given time, half the COUNTRIES in Fantasyland will have mislaid their Crown PRINCESS/
PRINCE, but the Rule is that only one Missing
Heir can join your Tour at once. Yours will
join as a COMPANION selected from among the
CHILD, the TALENTED GIRL, or the TEENAGE
BOY, and as part of your QUEST you will have
to get them back to the Kingdom where they
belong. This can be a right nuisance. All Missing Heirs shine with innocence (some of them
quite dazzlingly) and most have very little
brain, which means that they will not pick up
any hints as to their true status. You have to
do this for them. In addition, they all have a
lot of inborn Royal Qualities such as chivalry,
extreme (and embarrassing) honesty, a tendency to give away everything to BEGGARS, and
a natural desire for the best of everything for
everyone. Since they usually have at least one
untrained Royal TALENT too, they can be quite
a handful. When the ORB, SCEPTER, SWORD,
etc., start accepting them, this usually makes
things worse. But do not despair. Their characters improve at once as soon as they get back
where they belong.

Heirs go missing for a variety of reasons:

1. The THRONE was usurped and the False
Monarch ordered the Heir killed. Faithful servi-

tors hid her/him with a poor family instead. See BLACKSMITH.

2. The previous Royal Heir secretly married an unsuitable girl, who fled with her child back to her family. See BLACKSMITH again.

3. A GODDESS OR GOD, for inscrutable reasons, removed and hid the Heir.

4. A WIZARD, for equally inscrutable reasons, did the same.

5. The Royal Family has for centuries been obliged to hide from the DARK LORD, who killed all the previous generation before the latest Heir could be told of her/his BIRTHRIGHT.

6. All the Royal Family has died out except for the most distant branch, which consists only of the Missing Heir, living in poverty and ignorance of her/his BIRTHRIGHT. See BLACKSMITH yet again, plus KING, QUEEN, and QUEST.

Mist is almost never due to natural causes. It is usually one of the following:

1. WEATHER CONTROL (see STORM CONTROL).

(a) At sea, when it will have been made by a WIZARD, either to cover the approach of PIRATES or to cover your escape from Pirates.

(b) On land, when it is always a bad sign. It will have been made by an Evil MAGIC USER in a ravine to cover an AMBUSH. In open country, it conceals the approach of a hostile ARMY.

2. The *exudations*⊕ of ancient EVIL. These creep out like a *miasma*⊕ from places where the BLACK ARTS have once been performed.

This can date either from the WIZARDS' War or from the BEGINNING, when it will have been made by mistake by some God. It may also hang over the OLD RUINED CITY as a sign that the erstwhile inhabitants were not a good thing.

3. Lumps of loose MAGIC. This kind of Mist can be various colors, the most favored being red and green (see COLOR CODING). It comes rolling in of its own accord and, when it engulfs the Tour, you will find all sorts of peculiar things happening. Its usual trick is to give you a vision of some unhappy event in your childhood, but it can cast any kind of ILLUSION the Management wishes.

4. A sign of any Magic being worked. You will find a Wizard making GESTURES and the result will be first a Mist, followed quite soon by the magical effect desired. For instance, *the mists rolled aside to reveal a doorway in the cliff*⊙ᴹᴰ.

5. A sign that there is a PORTAL to some other world. If a MIRROR dissolves into Mist, you can be sure that you have to go through it.

6. A sign that you have accidentally strayed into a PANCELTIC TOUR.

Monasteries. Thick stone buildings on a steep hill. They are full of passages, cloisters, and tiny cells, all with no HEATING, and inhabited by MONKS, mostly elderly and austere, some rather addled in their wits. At the Monastery's head will be an Abbot, who is often portly and sly. These establishments have three uses:

1. For SCROLLS (see also TEMPLES). Any Scroll containing information vital to the Tour QUEST is likely to be jealously guarded in a Monastery. It is not advisable to say that you have come to look at this Scroll. If the abbot is really sly, he will find two dozen ways of putting you off. You will probably have to steal the Scroll. In cases where the Monks are willing to let you consult their Scroll, you will find that the keeper of Scrolls has recently lost his reason and the Scroll with it. You will have to search through the disordered (*smelling mustily of old books*☜ and *filled with the plangent scent of ancient minds*☜) library by night.

2. For sanctuary and rest. In this case, you will come pounding up to the Monastery at dusk, with the forces of Dark hard on your heels. You will have to hammer at the huge (*oaken*☜) door a lot, but they will let you in. Once inside, you are safe. This kind of Monastery has religious WARDS that really work. But the problem comes when you have to get out again (see SECRET PASSAGES and UNDERGROUND PASSAGES).

3. For sacking. Here you come pounding up to the building with the forces of the Dark half a day behind, only to find it a heap of smoking stones. But there will be one survivor (see NUNNERY for the rest of the Rule).

Money. There is always a question as to how a Tourist acquires Money. The Management does not permit one to bring gold or travelers' checks on a Tour. Usually a Tourist arrives with just enough to buy equipment but, if not, the Rule is that you must hire yourself on as a ⊏⊐ CARAVAN GUARD or some other kind of menial (see KITCHEN). Later in the Tour you may have to hire out likewise as a sparring partner at a ⊖ SCHOOL OF WEAPONRY. Any other funds must be supplied by discovering TREASURE or by theft; note that, whenever you need them, there will be a plentiful supply of EVIL (or at least degenerate) people and/or fat MER- CHANTS from whom you can steal with a blithe conscience.

Monks inhabit MONASTERIES and are mostly extras hired by the Management. Those with NAMES are likely to be either MENTORS or, very rarely, Tour COMPANIONS. Treat all Monks cour- teously, however. Many of them have KNOWL- EDGE you will be glad to hear.

Monsters are likely to live in WASTE AREAS, CAVES, and OLD RUINED CITIES. You can usu- ally detect their presence by SMELL (see also DANGER and REEK OF WRONGNESS⊙⊙). Most of them have something snaky about them. All have prodigious jaws and teeth and tend to drool. They are normally rather large and prone to attacking Tourists around or after twi- light. The most dangerous kind are those who have the MAGIC or the ability to live half the time in some spirit world. This makes them difficult to kill. The usual practice is to disable the Monster if possible and then run.

See also LEATHERY-WINGED AVIANS and SCALY FOLK.

Moon(s). There is usually only one moon visible, as in our own world. This has given rise to the theory that Fantasyland is an Earth-Alternate, but that may be a false idea since there have been rare sightings of other moons in the sky, often two or three at once and in some cases pink or red or blue. One hesitates to query these sightings. Sometimes a cluster of moons hang forever in the same position in the sky, revealing that Astronomy is not the Management's strong point.

Mountain Pass, Blocked. The Rule is that, any time you need to get from one side of the MOUNTAINS to the other, the pass across is blocked. The pass will be a narrow rift high in the Mountains, and by the time you have climbed up there, either with the forces of the DARK LORD hard behind you, or knowing you have only so long to get to the other side before the forces of Darkness get there first, you will find the pass . . . impassable. Usually the Management applies this Rule by prudently sending you off in winter, so that the pass is snowbound; on occasion, though, the blockage can be a landslide or a fall of rocks. In some cases, you can go down and round the long way, but mostly you just have to bash on through. Somehow.

See also HARDSHIP and HYPOTHERMIA.

▲▲▲ Mountains are always high and mostly snowcapped. There seems to have been no ice age in Fantasyland, so the Mountains rise tens of thousands of feet into pointed, *jagged peaks*⊛, which have evidently never suffered erosion. They are full of *rocky defiles*⊛ and paths so steep you have to dismount and lead the HORSES. Almost certainly there will be at some stage a ledge along a cliff that is only a few feet wide with an immense drop on the other side. This will be covered with ice. Snow will be sweeping across it. The Rule is that you are always in a hurry at this stage.

Mountain Tribes. See DWARFS, EYRIE CLANS, GNOMES, GOBLINS, and STRANGE RACES.

 Mules are the sterile and sexless offspring of a HORSE and a DONKEY and are sometimes used as pack animals on the Tour. The Management, however, is confused as to the nature of Mules and will often refer to them blithely as *mares*. This is probably because Horses in Fantasyland breed by pollination. (See HORSES for a fuller exposition of this important theory.)

Music is very important, always GOOD, and probably MAGIC, especially if played on a HARP. It seems that DARK LORDS are tone-deaf. They have never been known to employ Music as a WEAPON, or to strike fear and desolation into anyone by means of a bespelled tune. The utmost they ever rise to is chanting in TEMPLES. This is lucky because, on the side of Good, Music has enormous power. It can amplify SPELLS, summon supernatural help, and inspire superhuman courage. On some Tours it is the only vehicle for GOOD Magic.

See also ELVES, PANCELTS, and SONG.

Mutant Nasties. These, as opposed to MONSTERS, are monstrous beings created by some form of evil Wizardry. They can be magically enlarged and blended ANIMALS, or humans reduced to bestial form. It is standard practice for a WIZARD who is setting out to rule the world to surround himself with monstrous mutant helpers as a first step. Other Mutants are left over from the demise of earlier Wizards.

See also BREEDING PROGRAMS and LEATHERY-WINGED AVIANS.

Mystical Masters. Your TOUR MENTOR is likely to be one of these, on special assignment. Mystical Masters, male, female, and (possibly) neuter or something else, all wear long white ROBES and operate on the side of GOOD. One or more of these will appear to all Tours from time to time in order to give instructions. These instructions will be so obscure that they will be impossible to follow until too late, but afterwards you will feel good that you knew all along.

Narope, daughter of the Moon Queen of Semirond, bathed daily in the milk of fifty camels. She then applied two magnums of rosewater to counteract the smell. Her mother soon tired of the expense all this entailed and sold her to a Nomad when she was fifteen. No one minded, Narope least of all. Despite the milk of camels, she might never otherwise have found a husband.

Hag'git'ta Onch'a Beggiz, Anecdotes, CLI iiii*

Names are very potent in Fantasyland. People with no Names always get killed (unless they are powerfully EVIL and have a Name That Must Not Be Spoken, in which case they get killed anyway, but a lot later). Of those who have Names, almost nobody tells anyone else what their Name *really* is, for fear of its being used in a SPELL to enslave them. MAGIC USERS have to be particularly careful of this. But MERCENARIES also tend to call themselves things like Bald Eagle and Silversword, presumably for the same reason (or maybe because their

* The Management gives no reason or apology for deserting Ka'a Orto'o here.

true Names are Joe Coward and Jill Doe). MISSING HEIRS are always called Names like Triggs and Dumpling: when they find their Names are really PRINCE Tornalorn or PRINCESS Diore, they stop being Missing. This shows how important Names can be. AVERAGE FOLK, SAGES, and some Tourists, however, adopt the expedient of cutting out half their Names and filling the gaps with APOSTROPHES, as in Ka'a Orto'o. Then, unless you know what was in the gap, you can't enslave them. This is the true reason why so many Names in Fantasyland contain Apostrophes.

Many folk—ELVES and DEMONS particularly—are given hugely long Names so that they can be conveniently shortened in this way. Demons, indeed, would have a bad time otherwise. As soon as a Magic User learns a Demon's Name, that Demon has to do anything the Magic User wants.

On some Tours the same prudent coyness applies to MAGIC OBJECTS. The exceptions are SWORDS, who seem very proud of being known to be really Excalibur or Widowmaker.

Necromancy is, in Fantasyland, the art of raising the dead, and you need a specialized MAGIC USER to do it. You must expect to need to consult someone who is dead about two-thirds of the way through your Tour. You must hire or call in a favor from a Necromancer, who will do things with little pots of smoke over the grave and then summon the dead person in words that vibrate the earth and the air. After this, a misty version of the corpse (or sometimes one not misty enough for comfort) will arise, bringing with it a cold blast of air and a strong graveyard SMELL. This simulacrum will be able to speak and will have all the memories of the dead person. You must ask it what you want to know. But take care to ask the right questions. Usually such a rite cannot be repeated, and the dead are often as literal-minded as computers.

See also BLACK ARTS.

Nomads. See DESERT NOMADS and NOMAD TENTS.

Nomad Tents have peculiar acoustics, possibly because they are usually constructed of skins over a framework of wood. Perhaps this makes them more like houses. Be that as it may, you will find that you can hold a secret and private conversation in one of these tents without any danger whatsoever of anyone overhearing you. The TENTS of MERCENARY captains and KINGS often display the same properties. Like so many of the marvels of Fantasyland, the secret of these soundproof tents has not yet been imparted to this world.

Northern Barbarians dwell in the snowy part behind the northern MOUNTAIN range. They are very barbarous and tend to kill strangers on sight. This is because the males spend their time in longhouses honing their fighting skills. It is not certain what their females do. Northern Barbarians do not feel the cold. They wear only a fur loincloth and copper wristguards. Their real clothing is their WEAPONS. But they are not stupid savages, only savages. They use skis and sledges for getting about in the snow and this, given the state of TRANSPORT generally, must be the equivalent of having invented the wheel. When Tourists visit here, they are advised to defeat all barbarians who attack them. Then the Barbarians will respect them: it is the only LANGUAGE they understand. The Tourists must then go on to prove the SHAMAN a fraud. After this, the Chieftain will offer the Tour anything it needs.

See also BARBARIAN HORDES.

Novice is a term in frequent use. There are not only Novice PRIESTS and Priestesses and Nuns: you will also encounter Novice HEALERS and Novice BARDS, and sometimes also Novice MAGES. This reflects the religious awe in which all these callings are held in Fantasyland. Novices are always young, frequently skinny and undernourished, and clad in ROBES (*skimpy*ⓄⓂⒹ) appropriate to the calling they are learning. Most of them behave as if they have either taken vows of chastity and silence or are very stupid. They do little but agree with the Priest/Bard/Mage to whom they are assigned, and they are utterly loyal to this person. If a Novice behaves in any other way, suspect her/him either of having been got at by the forces of EVIL or of being in fact an APPRENTICE who might at any moment do something foolish with a SPELL. Alternatively, she/he might be a MISSING HEIR.

Nunneries. The Rule is that any Nunnery you approach, particularly if you are in dire need of rest, Healing, or provisions, will prove to have been recently sacked. You will find the place a smoking ruin littered with corpses. You will be shocked and wonder who could have done this thing. Your natural curiosity will shortly be satisfied, because there is a further Rule that there will be one survivor, either a very young NOVICE or a very old nun, who will give you a graphic account of the raping and burning and the names of the perpetrators. If old, she will then die, thus saving you from having to take her along and feed her from your dwindling provisions; if a Novice, she will either die likewise or prove to be not as nunnish as you at first thought, in which case you may be glad to have her along.

Onions much attracted the Sage Algeron, who used to declare that onions were like the eyes of demons. Some say it was a demon who took off his left big toe.

Ka'a Orto'o, Gnomic Utterances, CCCIX xv

Official Management Term (OMT) appears in this Guide where necessary and in *italics*. OMTs are forms of words which the management has dreamed up for use every time a certain thing, fact, sensation, or person is mentioned. Thus STEW is *thick* and *savory*; HISTORY is *lost*; at the point where the party of Tourists is about to be attacked *the very air seemed doom-laden*; and a constant COMPANION on the Tour will be *the rat-faced little man*. OMTs perform the same function as music in films.

Offshore Islands exist in some quantity, some having human inhabitants and one at least being the abode of DRAGONS. Unfortunately, the only ways to reach these islands are somewhat hazadous for Tourists:

1. If male, you must be captured by PIRATES and sold as a GALLEY SLAVE. You may then

row to the vicinity of an island, saw through
your chains, kill your owners, and swim there.
(Note that this is impracticable for female
Tourists as female SLAVES are reserved for Another Fate.)

2. If female, you must befriend a Dragon and
get flown to the Isle of Dragons.

Yes, it is clear that only males get to visit the
human islands and only females find their way
to the Dragons. This is the tough, sexist way
the Management wrote the Rules.

Old Ruined City can be in a WOOD, in the
DESERT in a dry ravine, or hidden in the MOUN-
TAINS. It can be an ANCIENT ENGINEERING PROJ-
ECT, or just RUINS. You will do quite a lot of
Traveling looking for it if you want it as a
QUEST OBJECT. Otherwise your Tour will stumble upon it by accident. Either way, it is *beset
with Dangers*℠. It will be full of residual
MAGIC of an antique and unpleasant kind. The
former inhabitants will have set up traps and
magical burglar alarms which are still in place
after many centuries. These will be nastiest and
most active near the TOMB or TEMPLE. Some
of the party will have to deactivate these while
fighting off hostile tribes, and the rest must go
after the SECRET behind the ALTAR.

Old Tongue. See LANGUAGES.

Omens. See PROPHECY.

Orbs are strange things with a double purpose. On one hand they are part of a KING's regalia; on the other they are *numinous*⊚ objects with minds of their own. In appearance, they are a large ball, the size to fit the hand of an adult male, and they are often made of some very obscure CRYSTAL. This lights up, gives orders, attacks enemies, and communicates with other Kings and the DARK LORD. If they are your QUEST OBJECT they will play hard to get, but end up, almost with a sign, beaming with colored light in the hand of the true heir. You feel the Orb has been having fun hiding. So willful are Orbs that it seems likely that they are in reality the positronic brains of dismembered robots, imported from the SF Tour.

Orcs are a newer and better mutation of GOBLINS, even nastier and always in the service of the DARK LORD.

Other Continent. This is the second major landmass. It is sometimes brought into play on the Tour, but only if the MAP shows it as fairly close to the continent where the Tour began. Things there are generally much the same as on the first continent but described as *exotic*⊚, as are its inhabitants, the OTHER CONTINENTALISTS. Probably the main difference will be the FOOD (*highly spiced*⊚). You may expect at least one CONFRONTATION there, normally with a female in rather scanty clothing.

Other Continentalists live (*dwell*ⓞⓜⓣ) on the OTHER CONTINENT. They are seldom dissimilar from PEOPLES on the first continent except that, for some reason, they are always members of CLANS. This is so even when the inhabitants evidently belong to the FANATIC CALIPHATES, which they often do, and wear turbans and eat spiced food. This means there is always likely to be a blood-feud and Clan WAR, during which the Tourist must keep her/his head down and try to arrange a passage back to the first land-mass, which is normally not difficult. Otherwise, Other Continentalists are mild, reasonable people, although some Tours find they have more than their fair share of seductive older women. In rare cases, the People here are savage xenophobes (see XENOPHOBIA), in which case the Management will get you out of here, quick.

Other Peoples. See PEOPLES and STRANGE RACES.

Outer Ocean. This is on the MAP, but it is out of bounds for the Tour. You can see that it is from the little drawings all over it. The Management does not know what, if anything, lies beyond this Ocean, and the Cartographer felt free to doodle in the space.

Politics is when you sell your daughter to bandits and your daughter and yourself are then
both set free.

Ka'a Orto'o, Gnomic Utterances, XXXI ii

Palaces are where all rulers and some DUKES
live. The Rule is that all Palaces are large and
ornate inside, and reached by a triumphal avenue and a long flight of steps. Otherwise they
can be of any architectural style. The Management will stop you as you reach the Palace
and force you to look at the rows of windows/
columns/statues/gilded carvings/domes/fretted
towers/lacy spires, and the effect of the gigantic
doorways guarded by soldiers. You will have
to observe the several wings, courtyards, and
gardens. A further Rule seems to be that all
this magnificence is of stone, unless it belongs
to an ENCHANTRESS or a northerly WIZARD, in
which case it will be built of ice. The more
normal stone kind has plainly taken many ma-
sons and sculptors many moons to make. Sometimes the Management gives you potted
HISTORY here, and shows how some parts are

old and some newer. Inside, a Palace follows
the Rule for BUILDINGS and is even larger, with
many long corridors, ballrooms, CHAMBERS,
and galleries. Some Palaces are an actual maze
in which Tourists may get lost. The THRONE
room is usually, but not invariably, the largest
and most imposing room of all. There will be
paintings, pillars, lackeys, and SLAVES, not to
speak of COURTIERS. In more northerly Palaces, banners are hung from high ceilings.
There will be at least one INCIDENT in every
Palace, usually more. Tourists seldom leave
Palaces peacefully by the front entrance.

See also HEATING.

PanCeltic Tours are normally taken separately
from the rest of Fantasyland. Here the MAP
will be of only one COUNTRY, which has a
Welsh name, and show TOWNS called things like
Dun Bhlaioinaidbth (pronounced Dublin) or Glas
Uedhaoth (pronounced Glasgow) and rather

more MOUNTAINS. The Tour will, however, take place in the usual way, except that POR-RIDGE will largely replace STEW and there will be rather more MAGIC. But the WEATHER will be a great deal worse. When it is not raining, everywhere will be hidden (*shrouded*) in MIST. If you go on one of these Tours, you will not always find it easy to know either what is going on or what people are talking about. The Mist seems to get into everyone's brains.

PanCelts are frequently red-haired. They wear plaids and have NAMES you must consult the glossary in order to pronounce. By the Rules (pronounced GEAS) which govern them, they have to call ELVES Shee (pronounced Sidhe) and refer to the ENEMY as Shadow. Otherwise they are nice people who drink a lot of the water of life (pronounced Uisce) and love to tell you LEGENDS by firelight. They also fight a lot and rather well, since both men and women train hard from the age of ten. But there is no such thing as an ordinary PanCelt. Each of them is either a MAGIC USER or a BARD or a Druid (prounced like a sneeze), or sometimes all three (in which case you pronounce it Merlin). They are governed by strong and beautiful QUEENS called things like Maebdh Aeiolaien (pronounced Mad Eileen) or strong and serious KINGS called, for instance, Daibhaeaidhaibh MacAeraith (pronounced Dave mate), and they appear to worship the Welsh Bard Taliesin. It is in this Bard's honor that they all sing so much, even more than the Shee/Elves do. And, like the Elves, they are prone to go on about how very much better things were in the Old Days, when a HERO could walk in one day from Caer Dibdh to the sea by taking a short cut through Tir n'an og (pronounced The Many-Colored Land).

Patrons of Inns are mostly AVERAGE FOLK with a sprinkling of STRANGE RACES, and are put in the INN to make the barmaids too busy to serve you and to provide loud conversation shortly followed by a TAVERN BRAWL. In some cases they also show suspicions and *growl*⊚ when you talk to them. All of this is known by the management as "atmosphere." But you should listen to what they say over their tankards of BEER. They will always have the latest rumor, and this will give you a hint about what the DARK LORD is up to now.

Peasants. See AVERAGE FOLK.

Pentacle. See PENTAGRAM.

Pentagram or Pentacle. A five-pointed figure essential in many forms of ritual MAGIC. It can ☆ be drawn both on solid surfaces and in the air. In the latter case, it will *hang there, glowing*⊚.

Peoples are of two kinds, human and other:

1. Humans are ANGLO-SAXON COSSACKS, ARISTOCRATIC FEUDALISTS, AVERAGE FOLK,

BARBARIAN HORDES, BARBARY VIKINGS, DE-
SERT NOMADS, EYRIE CLANS, the folk of the
FANATIC CALIPHATES, ISLANDERS, MERCHANT
FEUDALISTS, NORTHERN BARBARIANS, OTHER
CONTINENTALISTS, RELIGIOUS FEUDALISTS, TRAV-
ELING FOLK, denizens of the VESTIGIAL EMPIRE,
WAR AND WORSHIP PEOPLE, WARRIOR
WOMEN, and WOODSMEN. We should perhaps
also include the PANCELTS, although they generally have their own Tour. WIZARDS and other
MAGIC USERS are mostly thought to be human
too, but that was long ago and seems to have
worn off. BANDITS, MERCENARIES, PIRATES,
and SLAVES are said to be drawn impartially
from among the Peoples, but all four types exhibit occasional exotic individuals not easily accounted for. Oh, and tourists are mostly
human, too.

2. Other are APELIKE CANNIBALS, DWARFS,
ELVES, GIANTS, GNOMES, GOBLINS, LITTLE
PEOPLE, MARSH DWELLERS, ORCS, SCALY
FOLK, SEA PEOPLES, TROLLS, WERES, and those
simply designated STRANGE RACES. Not all of
these are friendly to Tourists.

Person. As a QUEST OBJECT, a person is very
hard to find. She/he will not be located until
two-thirds of the way through the Tour. When
found, she/he will be all you expected, but un-
satisfactory in some way. If a parent or a WIZ-
ARD, she/he will not be able to give the
comfort, instruction, or SECRET you needed and
you will spend the rest of the Tour looking for

these instead. In rare cases, the Management has you on by having the Person there all along, as a Tour COMPANION. Then the rest of the Tour will be spent helping this person with the business she/he was on the Tour to perform. See BIRTHRIGHT.

Pirates range the seas in force, though most of them operate individually. When not BARBARY VIKINGS, Pirates are drawn from all populations. The sole qualifications are that they must be rough and ruthless, with a penchant for dressing gaudily. This usually includes pierced ears. The Rule is that Pirates always have the fastest SHIPS, except for Barbary Vikings; so, if the Tour takes you to sea and the lookout reports a Pirate in the offing, expect to be overhauled, grappled and boarded. Nervous Tourists will be pleased to know that this is a mere INCIDENT, however. Pirates are always beaten off after a bloody swordfight, unless you have not yet been enslaved. Then you will be captured and sold. See GALLEY SLAVE and SLAVE.

Place. If a place is a QUEST OBJECT it is invariably a long way away, Hidden, or obscure. In some cases it can be a small crag designated as a meeting-place with persons in urgent need of help. Usually it is a CITY, HIDDEN KINGDOM, ISLAND in a lake, OLD RUINED CITY, STONE CIRCLE, or SECRET VALLEY. In all cases, you will reach it to find the Tour by no means stops here. There will be an interval while you acquire Arcane KNOWLEDGE or SELF-KNOWLEDGE, and then off you will go again to do something about what you learned.

Plague *visits*⊛ certain areas unpredictably and kills a lot of people. Though this is not surprising, given the amount of REFUSE lying about, the relative absence of bacteria/viruses suggests that the cause may be magical. Indeed, on investigation, this usually proves to be so. The DARK LORD or a MINION has tried to stamp out a TOWN or CITY. Tourists need not be alarmed. The Dark Lord will not proceed against any Tours with such underhand tricks. No Tourist catches Plague. The normal pattern is for the Plague to have visited ten or so years before your Tour, when it will have killed the parents of at least one of your COMPANIONS. Very rarely, you will enter a City *in the grip*⊛ of Plague and be forced to pick your way among hideously blotched (*disfigured*⊛) corpses lying in the streets. But it will not be catching.

Poison is in use a lot, primarily by EUNUCHS, MERCHANT FEUDALISTS, and denizens of the VESTIGIAL EMPIRE. Tourists should watch everything they eat or drink around all these kinds of people. They are experts and have Poisons not known in our world. Most Poisons work swiftly, turning the victim a variety of strange colors as they do their stuff; but the most dangerous are the slow Poisons to which only the poisoner has the antidote. You can be enslaved by one of these, because the poisoner will always offer the antidote once a day provided you do what she/he wants. Usually this type of Poison is administered in a drink, but if they hold you down and inject you there is nothing you can do. The Management, fortunately, seldom allows this to happen, possibly because hypodermics are so hard to obtain.

Politics occur only in the VESTIGIAL EMPIRE and on some PANCELTIC TOURS. The Rule is that they are always very complicated and involve issues most Tourists have never heard of. A typical piece of Politics would be:

House/CLAN Frumpus, who worship Ad and trade in leather, have intermarried with House/Clan Trumpus, who worship Bagel and wish for leather concessions in their sheep business, and are allied with House/Clan Dorpus, whose head is a weak person and who trade in perfume and skins and worship Vinus, against Houses/Clans Drumpus, Corpus, and Bremo, who trade in skins, wine, and pottery and worship Bagel, Ord, and Vinus. Because of Bagel- and Vinus-worship (see RELIGION), Houses/Clans Drumpus, Dorpus, and Trumpus also have a secret understanding against the others. Only one senator can be elected here. While the Houses/Clans maneuver, there is also great jockeying for headship inside the Houses/Clans, and people merrily POISON each other. . . .

Anyway, it eventually cancels down to the head of House/Clan Frumpus, because he is on two sides at once, having to sell himself sheepskins and then Poison himself, leaving the four deities glaring at one another.

Pools. Any Pool is likely to be *numinous*ᴼᴹᵀ or Enchanted. Some give you strange Visions when viewed by moonlight, some just give you strange Visions. A few have additional virtues, such as healing or granting longevity. Some can lead you astray.

The Rule is that, of all prophetic objects (see Prophecy), only Pools are allowed to give false information—and even they will base their misinformation on true facts. If a Pool is a Quest Object, it follows the Rule that you have not completed your Quest by finding it. Often there is something under its surface, such as the transformed body of a Royal heir or a Monster, or both, which will give you Knowledge that requires further action.

Porridge. See PanCeltic Tours.

Portals can be Mirrors, Pictures, Standing Stones, Stone Circles, Windows, and special gates set up for the purpose. You will travel through them both to distant parts of the continent and to and from our own world. The precise manner of their working is a Management secret.

Power means either ruling a lot of people or very strong MAGIC. In Fantasyland, the two tend to be synonymous.

Practice Ring or Combat Ring is a sanded circle used for sparring and WEAPONS practice; usually it has a paling around it. It can be found attached to any SCHOOL OF WEAPONRY, outside MERCENARIES' winter quarters, and quite often on the outskirts or aggressive TOWNS and VILLAGES. It is always well kept. Fighting is important. Expect at some stage of the Tour to have a practice bout during which your opponent is out to kill or maim you.

Priests will be attached to a small local TEMPLE. Some are austere and unpleasant, but most are quite decent people. HIGH PRIESTS are another question altogether.

Princes are of three kinds:
  1. Acknowledged heirs to thrones. These Princes are bad lots, fat, greedy, willful, and cruel at best, usually noted for their *pasty*⊕ or *puffy*⊕ faces and their rude, discontented manners. In some way, these will have managed to disguise their natures in front of their Royal father the KING, who will think the world of them. At their worst, Princes will either be under the thumb of the REGENT, who will have sold his soul/services to the DARK LORD, or the Prince himself will be a MINION OF THE DARK LORD. In this case, there is no nasty sort of

cruelty and slyness these Royal heirs will not stoop to. They recognize those of better natures at once and attack them with everything they have.

2. Unacknowledged heirs. These are:

(a) Princes who have been thrown out by their Royal father. These will have been framed by a Chancellor or younger Prince (who will be fat, see above) and disinherited for crimes they did not commit.

(b) Lost heirs (see MISSING HEIRS), who have been stolen or removed for safety at their births. These will not have a notion of who they really are, but will find out in the course of the Tour.

Both (a) and (b) are invariably basically GOOD, but hasty, naive, and with a lot to learn, which the Tour will mostly teach them. Both will be seeking their BIRTHRIGHTS.

3. Ruling Princes. These rule slightly lesser COUNTRIES and are normally average to good in their natures. Sometimes they are even better than good Kings, from having a Princely nature.

Princesses come in two main kinds:

1. Wimps.

2. Spirited and willful. A spirited Princess will be detectable by the *scattering of freckles across the bridge of her somewhat tiptilted nose*⊕. Spirited Princesses often disguise themselves as boys and invariably marry commoners of sterling worth. With surprising frequency these commoners turn out to be long-lost heirs to Kingdoms (see PRINCES).

Prison is really a lot of DUNGEONS in one place, plus a fairly grisly TORTURE Chamber. It will be reached by a stone stair, dampish, lit by torches in brackets on the walls, and guarded by sadistic soldiery. Most of these GUARDS are rather careless: they think no one can escape. All Tours tend to prove this assumption wrong.

See also KING'S MEN.

Prophecy is used by the Management to make sure that no Tourist is unduly surprised by events, and by GODDESSES AND GODS to make sure that people do as the deity wants. All Prophecies come true. This is a Rule (but see POOLS). The methods used are various:

1. A SEER or MYSTICAL MASTER suddenly gives tongue. This is always unwelcome and usually obscure. The most obscure pronouncements strongly resemble GNOMIC UTTERANCES. A typical example might be: *I see the white eagle flying into the Sun with the red lion in his beak.*

2. Crystal Gazing. This method is without sound and can therefore be misconstrued. See CRYSTAL BALL.

3. DREAMS and VISIONS. These usually give vivid scenes without explanations.

4. Looking into MIRRORS or POOLS/bowls of magically enhanced water or ink. These give limited sights of the future, again without sound but usually in full color.

5. Casting RUNES or other counters. Here the result must be read by an expert, but it is always very detailed and explicit.

6. Cards, called Tarot by the Management. here a Fortune Teller will lay out the cards for a reading and explain as it proceeds. A typical layout might go: *Ace of Winds, that's for Talent, and the Wandering Minstrel suggests the Talent is wild; the Queen of Dreams and Knave of Voids are a threat to you; but the King of Castles can withstand it; and here are the Ace and Ten of Jewels in support.* Some packs have up to ten suits, plus wild cards and trumps. Many of them appear to contain only aces and court cards.

7. Omens. These can vary from a sudden blast of wind at a foolish act to a Tour COMPANION becoming suffused with kingly golden light.

8. ASTROLOGY, which is used mostly for large-scale Prophecy to do with SAVING THE WORLD.

Query all results when crystal-gazing. You
never know who may have been looking over
your shoulder.

Ka'a Orto'o, Gnomic Utterances, IX ix

Queens ruling in their own right are rare, but
they do occur. When they do they are:

1. Totally useless because dominated by a
male lover or COUNCILORS, or both.

2. Good, but incapacitated by MAGIC or scru-
ples or both. In the most extreme cases, this
Queen will sit on her throne perpetually in a
state of blanched preservation. Tourists requir-
ing favors of her will need only one look to
know that here is something else they have to
put right before they can get on with the real
business of the Tour. When rescued, such
Queens can put things in order with commend-
able briskness.

3. Good. This Queen will be a MAGIC USER
and terribly conscientious. In her case the Tour
will reveal something highly amiss with either
her COUNTRY or the whole continent. The
Queen will often have to join the Tour to put

this right (see SAVING THE WORLD). You will have to spend the Tour worrying about the Queen's safety.

4. Old-fashioned bad. This kind of Queen is totally in control. She has everybody terrified of her, possibly through Magic. And again possibly through Magic, she will be beautiful (see COLOR CODING, but there is an exception to the usual Rule here: such Queens can be red-haired to show how willful and bad-tempered they are). Her Country will be the most abject and oppressed of any on the Tour. Since she is very cruel, this will not bother her at all. She will just order in a few more peasant youths to ravish and then dismember. Naturally, she is very sexy. She will demand SEX with most

Tourists and one of you will slight her. She will have you put to the TORTURE and then, after you escape, pursue you for the rest of the Tour. The only thing to do is to kill her, but you will not like to strike a woman.

5. A bad mother. This Queen is really ruling for her young son (see CHILDREN), but she will be so anxious to go on ruling that she will be bringing the lad up to be wholly dependent on her. This Queen is a dangerous sentimental bitch, because she will claim that everything she does is for the sake of her Child. She will try to POISON anyone who gets in her way. Only a powerful AMULET will help you here. Naturally no Tourist will want to have anything to do with this Queen, but it will usually be necessary to release the young KING from her clutches before you can proceed on the Tour. The local God may well insist on it.

Quest. Many, possibly most, Tours are organized as a Quest. This is like a large-scale treasure hunt, with clues scattered all over the continent, a few false leads, MYSTICAL MASTERS as game-show hosts, and the DARK LORD and the TERRAIN to make the Quest interestingly difficult. The Management selects a QUEST OBJECT (of which Tourists are normally informed either at their STARTING POINT or no later than six INCIDENTS after) then adds the various INCIDENTS, CONFRONTATIONS, and FIGHTS plus a STEW of all the other items you find listed here in **Toughpick.** Places where clues to the Quest

Object can be found are listed in the appropriate entries, but Tourists should stay alert both to statements made by, say, dying GOBLINS and to the behavior of the DARK LORD: much can be learned from what he does not want you to do. You should then have a thoroughly eventful Tour without ever feeling truly at a loss. The Rule is that Tours will always succeed in a Quest, so the Management will give you hints if you go off in the wrong direction (see PROPHECY). In order to be assured of your future custom, the Management has a further Rule: Tourists, far from being rewarded for achieving their Quest Object, must then go on to conquer the Dark Lord or set about SAVING THE WORLD, or both. And why not? By then you will have had a lot of practice in that sort of thing and, besides, the Quest Object is usually designed to help you do it.

Quest, Eternal. See ETERNAL QUEST.

Quest Objects can be various, but are quite strictly defined by the Rules. They are:

1. Material objects.

CUPS, JEWELS, ORBS, RINGS, SCEPTERS, STONES, and SWORDS.

2. Places.

HIDDEN KINGDOMS, ISLANDS, OLD RUINED CITIES, POOLS of enchantment, STONES, TEMPLES, VALLEYS, and, less frequently, Fountains (which may double up as Fountains of Youth).

3. PERSONS.
See APPRENTICES, HARDSHIP, and PRINCES.
4. KNOWLEDGE.
Usually for BIRTHRIGHT or MAGIC or both.
5. Most rarely of all, SELF-KNOWLEDGE.

Quicksand. This is a hazard that can occur anywhere. Blundering into a Quicksand counts as a
small INCIDENT; usually there is no Bog handy.
Basically, the sandy ground underfoot turns out
to be bottomless and everyone starts to sink.
Most people make it back to firm ground, but
at least one HORSE (*eyes rolling in frenzy*⊚)
and one unlucky Tourist will sink and have to
be rescued either by the strength of the LARGE
MAN or by everyone hauling on ropes.

Run far and fast when a wizard frowns. If he smiles, run harder. Above all refrain from laughing when he laughs. But if he weeps, you may join in courteously.

Ka'a Orto'o, Gnomic Utterances. IX x

Rabbits. Plump furry rodents who live in burrows underground. These have been thoughtfully introduced by the Management as a FOOD source on the Tour. They are quite rare, to judge by the number of times the Management pretends you have caught a Rabbit when you have really caught a HARE, and so may have been introduced only very recently. Rabbits, when they have no natural predators (of which there are none except humans in Fantasyland), always spread uncontrollably and become a pest. This they have evidently not yet had time to do.

Reek of Wrongness is the OMT for the sensation you get when you encounter a POOL of EVIL, or when you have been set up for an AMBUSH or BETRAYAL. It is possible that local conditions do give such things a noticeable SMELL.

See also DANGER.

Refuse of a thankfully unspecified kind is obligatory in the streets of TOWNS and CITIES. Sometimes it lies about in such heaps that you will feel it fortunate there are so few germs in Fantasyland.

See also ECOLOGY.

Regents. These are hale men in their early forties, often DUKES, who have charge of a Kingdom while the monarch (usually a KING, but sometimes a QUEEN, here indistinguishable from a spirited PRINCESS) is too young to rule. Nine-tenths of them are EVIL. They have the young ruler under their thumbs in a variety of unpleasant ways, and do not intend to give up ruling even when the monarch comes of age. Most of them plot to kill her/him then. Nearly all of them are bluff, pleasant, and richly dressed, so Tourists may have trouble discerning their true Evil until proof is supplied. Luckily the Management will supply it as soon as the Tour is settled in the PALACE and is just about to go to sleep for the night. The Regent must then be unmasked and the young monarch freed from her/his toils; but this will not be easy. The Regent is up to most tricks and will fight back hard. In some cases, the Regent will not be hale, but sickly and careworn. Be careful of Regents who are like this. They are worse than the healthy kinds.

Religion is varied and widespread. The Rule is that, even among rational peoples, all adherents are extremely devout and in many places worship is fanatical. The exceptions to this Rule are all Other PEOPLES, who do not appear to have Religions; NORTHERN BARBARIANS, who believe only in spirits and themselves; and BARBARY VIKINGS, who believe in nothing. Anywhere else, you have to be careful what you say about GODDESSES AND GODS. There are three sorts of Religious beliefs:

1. One God. This belief is generally represented as the newer Religion, but only if the one God is masculine. Often, this male God is supposed to be the Sun, but sometimes he just *is*. Even when his worshippers see him as benign, they tend to hate women and MAGIC USERS (especially WITCHES, who are both). At their worst, they become extremely cruel: they make strict and arbitrary laws and stamp out all other beliefs as heresy. They also have a tendency to build a lot of oppressive TEMPLES.

If, on the other hand, the one God believed in is female, she will be a GOOD deity and her worshippers nice people. They will worship her out of doors or in small shrines, with singing and very charming festivals. The exceptions here are the WAR AND WORSHIP PEOPLE, whose Goddess is highly puritanical and appears to be an ASPECT of Nature at its worst. This probably reflects the state of the ECOLOGY.

2. Three Gods. This is supposed to be the older, gentler belief. Certainly, those who believe in threesome Gods simply get on quietly with their devotions, not attempting to convert or persecute anyone else. Opinions differ as to the constituents of this Triad. Some Tours give it as being a Mother, Father, and Son, others as Mother, Father, and Daughter. The Triad that most Managements opt for, however, is VIRGIN, Mother, and CRONE.

3. Many Gods. This entails the worship of whole tribes of Gods, good and bad, who sometimes quarrel bitterly among themselves. The Rule here is that people always believe in the whole lot of Gods, but devote themselves, often quite fanatically, to just one. On some Tours, these Gods are spread out over several countries, to which they act as patron deities, but most Tours have the pantheon gathered into one CITY for convenience. This City will boast a TEMPLE for each God, each with its band of fervent and fanatical worshippers. Tourists should not miss the religious processions here, which abound in quaint customs: leaping, dancing, cutting oneself, throwing oneself under the cart with the God in it, chanting, walking backwards, and many more things. Just occasionally, a particularly savage God worshipped in this City turns out to be in fact a DEMON imprisoned under a Temple. Where this is the case, the Management will always arrange for Tourists to descend and view the Demon in its pit.

There are two further absolute Rules for Religion:

(a) All Gods fade away when their worshippers stop believing in them.

(b) However benign and Holy a belief is, or however zealously fanatics torture you, you as a Tourist will never, ever become a convert to any Religion you meet on a Tour.

See also IDOL and IMAGE.

Religious Feudalists have the same arrangements with HIGH PRIESTS as ARISTOCRATIC FEUDALISTS have with bad KINGS, only in this case the ruler is the HIGH PRIEST. The inhabitants will go in terror of being accused of heresy, losing sons to the priesthood and daughters to the lusts of the clergy. This usually lasts until the Tour comes along and shakes them up. But expect one or two people you liked to get crucified or burnt alive at the stake before you can reform this COUNTRY.

Rings are as dangerously magical as SWORDS. Tourists should avoid putting on any Ring. If you have to acquire one as part of your QUEST, the safest way to wear it is on a thong round your neck. The Rules for Rings are as follows:

1. Rings with large carved stones, usually green, although sometimes a big ruby will do. These are fairly harmless, since the carving is the crest or totem of the owner's family. The main thing these do is to prove your right to a Kingdome or lordship. Often the wrong person recognizes it. Then you are in Trouble.

2. Rings with CRYSTAL stones. These need only be raised in anger for the Crystal to shoot FIRE and POWER and blast the people in front of you. This is awkward if you happen to lose your temper with a friend. And a further trouble is that these Rings need recharging frequently and will often not work when you really need them to.

3. Rings with a dead black stone. These are usually *accursed*⊕ in some way and will either drain your spirit or allow the DARK LORD to take over your mind. Avoid these, no matter what other useful things they do.

4. Rings with any other kind of stone. Most of these will have belonged to WIZARDS or ELVES and the very least they will do is allow you MINDSPEECH with someone unexpected. Those with blue-green stones will either transport you abruptly elsewhere or put you in touch with some GODDESS. Some need only be turned around on the finger for unexpected things to happen. If you must wear one of these, avoid fidgeting with it. You may suddenly turn into a DRAGON.

5. Plain Rings with RUNES on the inside. Avoid these like the PLAGUE. The Rule is that, the plainer a Ring is, the more powerfully MAGIC and *accursed*⊚ it will be.

Rites take place in TEMPLES, on hilltops at full MOON, and in other places designated by tradition at the start of the Tour; they especially take place in front of IDOLS (gorily) and IMAGES (with a certain twee impressiveness). If GOOD, Rites involve singing, a procession, and a ceremony both charming and solemn. If EVIL (and these are in the majority), they take place in darkness and involve chanting, SACRIFICE, and bloodshed. All are religious services to honor or placate a deity. The Rules allow the Tour to interrupt Evil Rites but never Good ones.

Rivers are frequent and wide. As so many Tours take place in winter, they are also usually *swollen*⊚ and *turbid*⊚. The near absence of BRIDGES makes them rather a nuisance to the Tourist. You will have to cross them, which may mean going miles to find either somewhere shallow enough to ford or, conversely, a FERRYMAN. It will be night when you find one of the latter, and he will be very surly about getting you across; he may then betray you to the forces of the Dark who are following you. On the bright side, Rivers are long, deep, and wide, and there are often BOATS plying up and down them. If your Tour happens to lie down- or up-

River, then you can save much time and effort
by hitching a lift on a Riverboat. River folk
may likewise betray you, but they are, unlike
Ferrymen, cheerful and colorful, and some are
even GOOD (see COLOR CODING and TRAVEL-
ING FOLK).

Roads in Fantasyland are not good. Tourists
have frequent cause to complain. There are several types of Road, each with its characteristic
inconvenience:

1. Ancient magical ways, normally engineered from some black rocklike substance im-
pervious to wear. These are so old that only
short stretches remain. The rest has been torn
up or buried in some ancient CATACLYSM. This
can be exasperating. You are just beginning to
make some decent mileage on this blacktop-
like surface when it stops, and you are back to
a snail's pace again.

2. ANCIENT ENGINEERING PROJECTS. These
are wider than an eight-lane highway, dead
straight, and made of cobbles that *preternatu-
rally* show no sign of aging. Though hardly
ever used today—they are characterized by
wind-swept emptiness—they were clearly built
to allow a traffic of horse-drawn carts, four
lanes in each direction, traveling at seventy
miles per hour.

3. Old trade routes. These are long-disused
and normally serve to do little more than point
you in the right direction. If you try to follow
them you are quite likely to get lost when the

route peters out into pathless moorland or even MARSHES. If the route is obvious, you will find no shelter along it, and no WATER.

4. Vestigial Roads of the VETIGIAL EMPIRE. These cover quite a lot of the country and were once good roads made of stone blocks, but, in places from which the Empire has withdrawn, no maintenance has been done for centuries and most of the stones are missing or broken. It rains a lot along these roads and the going gets rough. If you are lucky you may find tumbledown remnants of old guardposts along the way, and these will provide some shelter; but don't count on it. As these roads approach what now remains of the Empire they are discovered to be in better repair and, closer to the Imperial capital, the guardposts are intact and well manned. Though this means you are safe from BANDITS you are not safe from the GUARDS, who at the sound of hooves will come out with demands for toll and bribes, and generally attempt to hassle you.

5. Unpaved roads. These are the norm. They are always muddy and full of deep ruts from the passage of MERCHANTS and previous Tours. They lead through dangerous WOODS and abound in *rocky defiles*⊙ ideal for AMBUSH. Nobody ever maintains these, despite frequent representations to the Management, and you have to use them because they are the only way to get about. Some Tourists lose patience and ride across country, but this is not recommended because it is the surest way to get attacked by APELIKE CANNIBALS.

Robes are the only garments, apart from SHIRTS, ever to have sleeves. They have three uses:

1. As the official uniform of PRIESTS, Priestesses, MONKS, Nuns (see NUNNERY), and WIZARDS. The OMT prescribed for the Robes of Priests and Nuns is that they *fall in severe folds;* of Priestesses that they *float;* and of Wizards that they *swirl.* You can thus see who you are dealing with.

2. For KINGS. The OMT here is *falling in stately folds.*

3. As the garb of DESERT NOMADS. The OMT has the Robes *covering them from head to foot.* (See DESERT NOMADS for a discussion of a possible TABOO here.)

Roots appear to be edible only in the MARSHES, where the Marshfolk find them by some means unknown to everyone else and dig them up to offer Tourists. These Roots are long, gluey, pallid, gritty, and mud-covered. But they make a change from STEW and WAYBREAD.

Ruins of former days, like ANCIENT ENGINEERING PROJECTS, litter Fantasyland. Only the large kind are important to the Tour, and even most of these will be just setting the mood. You are not expected to be happy on this Tour. The Ruins make you think of the sad losses of former days. But cheer up. Just occasionally you will find TREASURE in a Ruin.

Runes are an intensely magical form of writing. Anything written in Runes is going to be a SPELL.

1. In GRIMOIRES. If the Spell is in Runes it will do its best to leap up and hit the Tourist reader, or at the very least sort of scintillate. In such cases, Runes have a way of translating themselves, so you may learn the Spell without wanting to.

2. In INSCRIPTIONS on rock. These are useful. Runes incised into cliffs reveal the presence of a hidden doorway or, particularly if inscribed on STONE CIRCLES, show that supernatural protection is available. Just occasionally, though, they show that entry is forbidden. Ask your Tour MENTOR.

3. In Fortune Telling. Here the Runes are written on little wooden buttons and thrown. The patterns they fall into are as important as the individual meaning of each letter. The Management, however, reserves the right to alter the significance of both without notice. See PROPHECY.

4. In Spellcasting. MAGIC USERS draw Runes all over PENTAGRAMS and around MAGIC circles as a prelude to important Magics. Some ADEPTS draw them inside other shapes, even more potently. Most WIZARDS incorporate Runes into the GESTURES they use, in which case they will briefly appear *glowing in the air*⊚. We see from this that Runes do not need to make words in order to be powerful. The OMT here is *Runes of Power*.

5. Hidden. These Runes have to be made visible either by a Magic User passing her/his hands across them, by the application of heat, or by the light falling on them in a certain way. Runes of this kind tell anyone their message after that. But Wizards can leave hidden Runes written on walls that are only visible *glowing in the air*ᴼᴹᵀ to other Wizards. Hidden Runes are always extremely important.

6. Written on Rɪɴɢs and Swᴏʀᴅs. The Runes always make words and nearly always mean trouble. Avoid any artifact with Runes on it, even if the Runes prove only to spell the maker's name.

Settle for what you can get, but first ask for
the world.

    Ka'a Orto'o. Gnomic Utterances, C iv

Sacrifice is made both in TEMPLES and as an
aid to the BLACK ARTS. In its minor form it
involves cutting the throat of an ANIMAL, usually a goat. The major and preferred form is of
course the ritual killing of a human, preferably
young, female, and beautiful. This is normally
done in a dim reddish light—to the accompaniment of chanting—and on an ALTAR. The victim is roped down, ritually raped, and then
disemboweled. Someone has to stand at one
end of the Altar to catch the blood, which has
many uses in RELIGION and MAGIC. This kind
of Sacrifice is frequently interrupted by a rescue
party. Uninterrupted Sacrifices are much more
sinister and complicated. Here the Tour will
come upon the scene only after the Sacrifice
has been performed, to find the *ritually muti-
lated*⊙ corpse hanging piteously in its ropes on
the Altar. A pause is usually allowed here,
while you bury the corpse.

Saddle Roll is what the Rules state you have
to have for luggage; Saddlebags are the only

alternative. This is fine until your last HORSE is killed.

See also BACKPACKS.

Saga. This is another word for your Tour, particularly if it goes on for several brochures.

Sage. A wise and Holy man who died a long time ago. No one modern qualifies.

Saving the World is something many Tours require you to do. You have to defeat the DARK LORD or WIZARDS who are trying to enslave everyone. It is about the same as a QUEST, except there is always a WAR, a personal CONFRONTATION, and a CATACLYSM before you succeed. Thousands of troops and DEMONS must be annihilated. The CITADEL or base of EVIL must be destroyed (*razed*ⓞ). This usually triggers a semi-natural disaster. Sometimes large parts of the world you are saving go up in smoke.

Scaly Folk—apart from Dragons—are numerous and of all sizes from knee-high to a towering ten feet or more. They divide into lizard kinds, who live on land in warm climates, and fishy-snaky kinds, who live in the sea. These latter always have a tell-tale web between their fingers. All walk upright like humans. All are intelligent and many can do MINDSPEECH. Quite a few are very wise as well. If, however, the Management calls them *subtle*ⓞ this means they are not friendly to Tourists. Scaly Folk can appear as servitors or as advisors with useful KNOWLEDGE, but for some reason they never become COMPANIONS on the Tour. This may be because they are cold-blooded.

Scenery. See LANDSCAPE and the cover of any brochure. The Tour will pass through a lot of Scenery, but no one will have much time to admire it.

Scepters are, in Fantasyland, much more than mere regalia. They are a Royal version of a WIZARD'S STAFF, made vastly more potent by being impregnated with Royal powers over generations of monarchs. Luckily they respond only to one of Royal blood. But, since they are so potent, someone has usually taken the Scepter away and hidden it. The Tour will QUEST to recover it. Sometimes it is far away in a cave or underground fastness, only happened upon by accident; sometimes it is concealed by cunning MAGIC in the PALACE itself. In this case, the Tour must infiltrate the Palace and deceive the REGENT or usurper into letting them search the place. This search is made more difficult by the fact that Scepters can disguise the way they look and slot into the furniture as if they were part of it. Normally only when the hand of the true heir (likely a MISSING HEIR) is laid upon it will a Scepter reveal itself. It will be a sort of golden truncheon with a large STONE or CRYSTAL at the top. Some have little wings near the bottom.

School of Weaponry is to be found in most TOWNS belonging to ARISTOCRATIC FEUDALISTS and outside any MERCENARY winter quarters. It will be in a house that is impressively neat, well maintained (often with vines trained up the walls), and very civilized. There will be a bare gymnasium with a good floor and an outside PRACTICE RING with a superb surface: everything in apple-pie order, in fact. A huge variety of training WEAPONS will hang from walls in neat rows. But the instruction and training given, though wholly excellent, will be very expensive. The Rule here is that the Tourist will not be able to afford any lessons and so will be forced to act as a sparring partner for pupils at the school. Be prepared to receive painful blows and many bruises. But it will pay off. In a remarkably short time you will be able to defeat the School's star pupil and give a good account of yourself to the WEAPONMASTER himself. You will be glad of this when you are enslaved and forced to fight as a GLADIATOR.

Scrolls are important sources of information about either HISTORY or MAGIC, and are only to be found jealously guarded in a MONASTERY or TEMPLE. You will usually have to steal your copy. Against this inconvenience is the highly useful fact that the Information in the Scroll will be wholly correct. There is, for some reason, no such thing as a lying, mistaken, or inaccurate Scroll.

Scurvy. Despite a diet consisting entirely of STEW and WAYBREAD, supplemented by only the occasional FISH, you will not suffer from this or any other deficiency disease. It is possible that while on the Tour, you absorb Vitamin C through the pores of your skin.

Sea Monsters are always vast, of whatever kind. You will see the odd Kraken, a Leviathan or so, and a sea serpent in huge loops, each one capable of wrapping itself around a SHIP. Most of them do no permanent harm: you will be only shipwrecked, and after clinging to a spar for a few days you will come to land.

Sea People can be normal SCALY FOLK, but there are quite a few other kinds. The most common of these are the quasi-human:

1. Mermaids and mermen (*Merfolk*⊛). These seem to have given up tempting mariners to their deaths and are generally friendly.

2. SHAPESHIFTING people. These often manifest as seals, but in some cases can be whales, dolphins, or fish. The Management refers to them impartially as *Selkies;* this means "seals," but must here be considered a technical term. Selkies are often fey and as hard to understand as MYSTICAL MASTERS, but if they appear in human form it is always because they have something important to tell you. See BAYS for where to contact them.

Seasons in Fantasyland appear to be the normal Spring, Summer, Autumn (sometimes called Fall by the Management), and Winter, but few Tours get to see them all. The Management tends to start you out in late Autumn, by tradition, and you will then experience only Winter. Your perceptions are messed up anyway, because you will be traveling into hot climates and cold, as well as traversing many magical microclimates. You may as well give up wondering what the Season is and think of it all as WEATHER.

Secret. A Secret of some sort is quite usual on a Tour. There are four main kinds:

1. Objects that must be kept Secret. These are stolen SCROLLS, RINGS, AMULETS, and most other QUEST OBJECTS. You will not want ENEMIES to know you have these. Some, like ORBS and SWORDS, insist on shining in public and have to be muffled in blankets. Oddly, most Objects try to reveal themselves in INNS.

2. Personal Secrets. Some COMPANIONS will not want their gender or their Royal birth known (see BIRTHRIGHT). Others will be of a nation or calling that could get them killed. For instance, WITCHES must generally be Secret in RELIGIOUS FEUDALIST Countries. Or Other PEOPLES will have to go to great lengths to conceal their hairiness from xenophobes (see XENOPHOBIA) in the FANATIC CALIPHATES. Or the entire Tour will for a while have to pretend allegiance to a bad KING for safety, and their real allegiance must be kept Secret.

3. Magical Secrets. These are either SPELLS or formulae necessary to the QUEST, which must usually be wrested from a WIZARD or a GRIMOIRE, or Magical Rules withheld by the

Management for a later surprise. This is where you will find your Tour MENTOR especially maddening, because she/he will know all along.

4. Vital Secrets. These are Secrets that cost lives. They can be the Secret way into a PALACE or CASTLE (see, for example, SECRET PASSAGES); the mustering of a Secret ARMY by the DARK LORD; the Secret substitution of the true PRINCE by a lookalike; the Secret conquest of a CITADEL/COUNTRY; a crucial and Very Secret weakness in the Dark Lord; or Secret KNOWLEDGE about the way the Gods made the world.

Secret Passages. No CASTLE, CITADEL, PALACE, or TEMPLE is complete without a lot of these, and very useful they are too. Although many Secret Passages are in the cellars or DUNGEONS, so that the release and escape of prisoners can be easily effected, there are usually just as many within the thick walls of the upper stories. The upper Passages will be reached by pressing in a certain place on a wooden or stone wall carving, whereupon a narrow door will creak open to reveal a ladder-like stair. This will take you to the Passages in the walls of the COUNCIL Chamber and bedchambers, each provided with its concealed spyhole and listening space. If you go this way, you are bound to hear something important about your QUEST or Mission or discover that someone you thought friendly is plotting your downfall. You may also find your boyfriend making love to the QUEEN. Be careful not to rush away then in a state of shock:

the Secret Passages are a maze and you will soon become lost. Usually the Management has thoughtfully provided you with a COMPANION on this jaunt who knows the Passages like the back of her/his hand, and you will be able to leave at once by the underground route through the SEWERS.

Tourists should note, however, that Secret Passages are useful to the forces of EVIL too. Be wary of what you say inside any BUILDING with thick walls. Someone is usually standing at the spyhole listening in. SECRETS are safe only when told inside a TENT.

See also UNDERGROUND PASSAGES.

Seer. A Talented old man or young woman able to see into the future (see PROPHECY and TALENT). They are either blind with *white eyes* or tend to wear a symbolic blindfold. Having the GIFT of SIGHT does not make Seers at all happy. Young female Seers are usually morbid and neurotic. Old men seem to have adjusted better, probably from having learned there is nothing they can do about what they *See*.

Self-Knowledge is, on rare occasions, a QUEST OBJECT. It is seldom found, and then only by PRINCES. Tourists are not expected to acquire it.

Serious Soldier is a rather boring Tour COMPANION, although a very efficient one. He is even better at his job than the FEMALE MERCE-

NARY and speaks even less. He is usually on the Tour to guard someone, and has no interest in it otherwise. Nevertheless you will miss him when he is killed.

Sewers. Despite the presence of so much RE-FUSE and SQUALOR, most CASTLES and CITIES seem nowadays to have Sewers. Their use, apart from the obvious one, is to provide access to or escape from the interior. Be warned. Many Tours make use of Sewers in preference to SECRET PASSAGES. Opportunities for WASH-ING afterwards are not always provided. Do not worry, though: most often, within half a day, all trace of stench will have vanished from you and your CLOTHING, almost as if the Management had forgotten about it.

Sex is obligatory at some stage in the Tour. The Rules differ according to whether you are male or female. If male, your partner will be either an ever-youthful WITCH or some other beautiful and obliging female, possibly a female SLAVE. In any case you will not be obliged to feel any emotion and no offspring will result. If female, you are required to have strong feelings for your partner, who will usually be worthy of your regard. Again, there will be no offspring. Female Tourists should note that they will not menstruate during the Tour. Both sexes will be glad to know that sexually trans-mitted diseases are unknown.

See also BATH.

Shaman is another word for "charlatan" in Fantasyland. This pretended MAGIC USER will be dirty and strung about with little hairy bags. He will mumble a lot and produce useless information. An honest Shaman is unknown, although many seem to believe in their own powers. An exception to this is the Magic User you will find among the DESERT NOMADS. She/he will sometimes be called a Shaman, but this is only because the true job description—MAGICIAN-SEER-PRIEST-HEALER-and-any-other-odd-magic—is a little long-winded. When you meet this person, you will see that she/he is in no way to be compared to the usual kind of Shaman.

Shapeshifting is frequent among both WERES and MAGIC USERS. The usual form taken is that of a WOLF (see also WEREWOLVES), but lions, eagles, serpents, owls, and cats are common too. In all cases the Rule is that the Shapeshifter cannot stay too long in ANIMAL form without actually becoming that Animal and losing touch with her/his human thoughts. There are two schools of Shapeshifting:

1. Illusory. Here the shifter either pretends to have or has thrust upon her/him the appearance of an Animal. You will drop to all fours but not lose your clothes. It is very important not to believe in this ILLUSION—otherwise you may go for days on hands and feet and get blisters and a cricked neck. A better form of this is to take the appearance of a piece of furniture. You will be far less ready to believe you are a table or a cupboard.

2. Actual. Here you really are the Animal or thing. In this case it is better not to become furniture. You will end up being an armchair for the rest of your life. There are two methods here:

(a) Change on land from human to Animal. This is normally swift and painless, though some Weres seem to suffer rather as their faces turn inside out. However, the most you will feel is discomfort and disorientation, shortly replaced by a wonderful sense of SMELL or the realization you can fly. The problem here is your clothes. They will not Shift with you and must be discarded. When you change back you will be naked.

(b) Change at sea. This often involves donning or discarding the skin of a seal, dolphin, or walrus. This skin must be stashed carefully on the beach. If someone gets hold of it you will not be able to turn back.

There is an absolute Rule that any wounds sustained in another form go back with you into human form.

Shields are of four kinds:

1. Big oblong ones used by soldiers of the VESTIGIAL EMPIRE to protect them in fighting.

2. Round ones hung along the sides of SHIPS run by BARBARY VIKINGS.

3. Large, hastily assembled protection for ARMIES attacking WALLED CITIES.

4. Psychic.

No one else uses a Shield at all. This is odd, given the amount of fighting that goes on.

Ships. The Rule is that PIRATE SHIPS are faster than anything—except that BARBARY VIKINGS, when on the side of GOOD, can overtake even Pirates.

See also BOATS and GALLEYS.

Shirts are always of thin material with long, floppy sleeves. They are normally worn without UNDERWEAR, and do not seem very warm. If you are prone to feel the cold, you are advised not to visit the SNOWBOUND NORTH (see FROSTBITE, HYPOTHERMIA, and WEATHER).

Shops have not been invented yet, even in the VESTIGIAL EMPIRE. Visit the MARKET instead.

Siege is when the ENEMY surrounds a CITY or TOWN (especially a WALLED CITY) and tries to break down the walls. The Rule is that no besieger is ever content just to CAMP round the City and starve the defenders out. Tour schedules do not allow time for this. Instead, the Enemy throws soldiers under SHIELDS, battering rams, and Siege engines at the walls continuously, while the defenders shoot arrows from the walls and repel from the battlements soldiers scaling Siege towers and ladders. A lot of people on both sides get wounded. The defenders eventually run short of arrows but not of FOOD and Pluck. No one is forced to eat rats or HORSES. But the Enemy eventually breaches the walls and rampages around the City, killing, raping, and looting. No Siege is ever called off. Tourists, however, always, escape through SE-CRET PASSAGES.

Sight is the TALENT of being able to *See*⊙ⓂⓉ into either the future or the past, or in a more general divinatory way into the workings of MAGIC or human politics and emotions. It is useful, but it can be a great burden to the possessor.

See also SEER.

Silk is worn quite frequently by the richer classes. It follows that somewhere in the land there must be a considerable and sophisticated silk industry (for instance, the OMT to describe the silk dresses of most female SLAVES is *diaphanous,* which argues considerable refinement among the producers), but the Tour will never take you anywhere near places where silkworms are cultivated. The Management wishes to keep some secrets.

See also INSECTS.

Sing is used in a technical sense. This is because MUSIC is so powerful in Fantasyland that no one can really just Sing a SONG without risking a Magical result.

The most frequent use of Singing is to speed a dead person's soul on its way. On some Tours no one is properly dead without it (see UN-

DEAD). Otherwise Singing is an invocation, a SPELL, or a way of summoning nature MAGICS for some purpose. Tourists should be careful to avoid humming a casual tune. You may find you have summoned an ELEMENTAL, a STORM, or a selection of GODDESSES AND GODS.

Skirts are of four kinds, all reaching to the ankle or below:

1. Coarse HOMESPUN, as worn by peasant women to show that they will be taking no real part in the action.

2. SILK, worn by women of high birth to show that they are malicious and/or demanding.

3. SILK, worn by women of *very* high birth to show that they are helpless pawns.

4. Gauzy, split to the hip, showing the wearer to be a SLAVE and/or dancing girl, or else a WITCH in seduction mode.

Slaves, Female are of three kinds, probably:

1. Tourists who have been captured by PIRATES or BANDITS. The Rules here state that such females must be lightly chained, loaded as soon as may be into a fairly small SHIP, and ferried to the OTHER CONTINENT. From this description you will see that this is the way female Tourists must proceed in order to take in that part of the Tour (see GALLEY SLAVE for the male route). Arrived at the Other Continent, you will be put up for auction in the Slave MARKET. You may well be annoyed to find how little your new owner pays for you, but this is

the Management's way of protecting you from rape, beatings, and other hardships. Your purchaser will bring you to her/his villa (a building of one story, mostly built of wood and covering a lot of ground) and there you will be put to work. You may even learn some useful skill, such as pastry-making or weaving. Alternatively, you might use the time to learn the alphabet of this continent (see HIEROGLYPHS) or study MAGIC. Make full use of this opportunity. Shortly, the villa will be raided by a CLAN that is feuding with your owner, and burnt down. You may use the resulting chaos to escape and continue your Tour.

2. Beautiful young women. You will find these in droves in the FANATIC CALIPHATES and sometimes in the PALACES of bad KINGS. Their duties are light and pleasant and are: looking beautiful, bathing and massaging visitors, singing and dancing, and, for male Tourists, providing company in bed. None of them seem unhappy in their work and they show no desire to escape. It is not usually possible to discover their life stories, but sometimes one will tell you that her father was a MERCHANT and that she was kidnapped by BANDITS somewhere many hundreds of miles away and was forced to watch her father being killed before she was carried off. Few seem to have been born to slavery.

Often male Tourists will sympathize with the plight of such Slaves, nobly reject their offer of free, no-holds-barred SEX, insist on assisting

Slaves, Male • 236

them to escape from the exploitative tyranny
under which they have been existing, and then,
having obviously done them a Good Turn, have
free, no-holds-barred SEX before stranding
them in the middle of nowhere to make their
way thousands of miles back to their own
COUNTRY.

3. Drudges. These exist, but are seldom seen.
There must be someone who does the dusting,
polishing, and laundry required in a large PAL-
ACE, as there must also be some occupation
needed for beautiful young Slaves who are no
longer beautiful or young, but you will not get
to meet any. In fact, the only time you will
become aware of drudges will be when you
need to escape the Palace. You will still not
meet one, but you will find a closet where
drudges' clothes are hanging. When you put
these on, you will gain the same INVISIBILITY
as the drudge, and can simply walk away. Why
all the drudges did not do exactly this is a SE-
CRET of the Management.

Slaves, Male are used by bad KINGS, FANATIC
CALIPHATES, and some WIZARDS in large numbers as GUARDS, attendants, fan-bearers, wait-
ers, and entertainment, and for SEX. Bad Kings
and Fanatic Caliphates always have their male
Slaves in matching sets, as in *a litter borne by
four gigantic ebony slaves®, fanned by two
beautiful young boys®, a troupe of slender
young acrobats®, the door guarded by two
seemingly identical Barbarian slaves®,* etc. A

Wizard tends to have his Slaves more mis-
matched but rather more attentive, unless he
intends to rule the world, in which case he will
try to be like a bad King.

See also EUNUCHS.

Slender Youth. A TOUR COMPANION who may
be either a lost PRINCE or a girl/PRINCESS in
disguise. In the latter case it is tactful to pretend you think she is a boy. She/he will be igno-
rant, hasty, and shy, and will need hauling out
of trouble quite a lot. But she/he will grow up
in the course of the Tour. In fact she/he will be
the only Companion who will change in any
way. Quite often, she/he will soon exhibit a
very useful TALENT for MAGIC and end up by
hauling everyone else out of trouble. But this
will not be until midway through your second
brochure.

Small Man can be a very funny or very tiresome Tour COMPANION, depending on how this
kind of thing grabs you. He gambles (see GAM-
ING), he drinks too much, and he always runs
away. Since the Rules allow him to make
JOKES, he will excuse his behavior in a variety
of comical ways. Physically he is stunted and
not at all handsome, although he usually
dresses flamboyantly. He tends to wear hats
with feathers in. You will discover he is very
vain. But, if you can avoid smacking him, you
will come to tolerate if not love him. He will

contrive, in some cowardly way, to play a major part of SAVING THE WORLD.

Smells are everywhere and strong, and, except for those of ENCHANTRESSES and INCENSE, unpleasant. Even DANGER has a Smell—the REEK OF WRONGNESS℠. There is something in the chemistry of the land that makes Smells. It is probably a fallout effect of MAGIC, but see also SOCKS and TROUSERS.

Snowbound North is the COUNTRY beyond the most northerly MOUNTAINS where the NORTHERN BARBARIANS live. It is quite often the place where the DARK LORD chooses either to sequester himself or to plant a MUTANT NASTY of huge proportions whose magical exudations poison the whole continent. Therefore it is a very important place and the Tour will unfailingly call there. Do not expect a pleasant time. You will have to gatecrash a PALACE of ice and/or torch the Nasty. And contend with deep snow, blizzards, and Barbarians.

See also CHILBLAINS and HYPOTHERMIA.

Socks are never worn in Fantasyland. People thrust their feet, usually unwashed, straight into BOOTS.

Songs in Fantasyland perform the same function as LEGENDS. If you are made to listen to the words of a Song, this is because they contain KNOWLEDGE you need. The tune is not important.

See also MUSIC and SING.

Sorcery is sometimes a general word for MAGIC, usually connected with *wiles*⊕, but also sometimes a technical term, referring to that part of Magic entailing the storage and use of POWER. In the latter case, the Sorcerer becomes a sort of battery.

Speech. On some Tours it is necessary to adopt a high-falutin' form of Speech. Instead of saying "I will go out and take a look" you have to say "I shall now walk forth and examine things without." This is tiresome to have to keep up. Even more tiresome are those PANCELTIC TOURS where you have to keep remembering to say "Och aye" and "Top of the marnin' te ye." But these are the Rules.

See also LANGUAGES.

Spells can do almost anything. They usually involve chanting, GESTURES, and ritual, but these range from a simple, silly rhyme to hours of invocation accompanied by the drawing of symbols, according to the complexity required. Some Spells require HERBS and outlandish ingredients like fish-feathers. Many can be readied beforehand and cast with a final word, and quite a few of these can be seen floating through the air before they roost on the victim and take effect. This sort of half-life in Spells can be dangerous, particularly if the Spell is written down. It can enter the mind of its own accord.

See also ENCHANTMENT, MAGIC, and GRIMOIRES.

Spiders are rare. This is fortunate because they are always of enormous size and venom. They lair in certain WOODS and in CAVES, where shorter and slighter Tourists may be seriously inconvenienced by their gigantic webs made of sticky, rope-thick strands. Often only a special SWORD will cut these webs, and it usually takes two or more Tourists to defeat the Spider. The reason for the monstrous size of Spiders in Fantasyland is that their former prey, INSECTS, no longer exists (see also ECOLOGY), so that Spiders have been forced to evolve into something big enough to entrap DWARFS, GNOMES, and small succulent humans.

Spies are as much part of life in Fantasyland as they are in our own world. The ARISTOCRATIC FEUDALISTS, FANATIC CALIPHATES, MERCHANT FEUDALISTS, and VESTIGIAL EMPIRE have Spies everywhere. Many HIGH PRIESTS and some PIRATES also maintain them. BANDITS plant one on every CARAVAN. And the DARK LORD and his MINIONS have Spies in all KINGS' courts. (See also BIRDS and UNPLEASANT STRANGER.) The majority of Spies will of course report by MAGIC, sometimes in MINDSPEECH, but usually by some Farspeaking device such as a RING, a

CRYSTAL, or an ORB. Tourists must be prepared to be watched every inch of their way.

See also ENEMY SPIES.

Spoon. About the only EATING IMPLEMENT you are allowed apart from your own knife or DAGGER.

Sport. The only real Sport is FIGHTS. Those who can, train fiercely and take on everyone. Those who can't watch GLADIATORS and lay BETS.

See also GAMES and GAMING.

Squalor is the OMT for "local color." Mostly it occurs in TOWNS and SMELLS rather strong (*noisome*⊚, *unspeakable*⊚), but it is in fact wholly innocuous and just there for show.

Staff. The magical implement of nearly all WIZARDS. Staffs are about five or six feet long and often twisted or *carven*⊚ with some kind of head or face at the top end. Bad Wizards tend to have Staffs that are black and made of no easily recognizable substance. The face at the top will be nasty and may bite or give electric shocks. GOOD Wizards have Staffs made from real, honest wood. Both kinds can ignite with blue MAGELIGHT when necessary. Depending on the Rules for MAGIC on this particular Tour, a Staff can contain all a Wizard's SPELLS, leaving him helpless without it; or be simply a convenient conduit for Magic; or have a life of its own.

Stallions are always ridden by KINGS and other important people. You get the impression that no one of any standing would be seen dead on a mare or a gelding. Luckily, the Stallions are quite docile about it. (See HORSES for the reason why these impressive beasts are so easy to control.)

Standing Stones. See PORTALS, QUEST, STONE CIRCLES, and STONES.

Stars are quite unlike those of Earth. For one thing, they seem to predict the future much more accurately than our own.

See also ASTROLOGY and ZODIAC.

Starting Point is where you commence your Tour. Having proceeded through your PORTAL to Fantasyland, you will find yourself either on the MAP in the neighborhood of a small to medium TOWN, such as Gna'ash (immediately see SQUALOR), or in rather poor circumstances, usually those of a menial in a KITCHEN or an APPRENTICE to a BLACKSMITH (see SQUALOR again) in an unimportant corner of the continent. If you are in Gna'ash, you must at once set about acquiring COMPANIONS and equipment on your own. If you are in menial circumstances, you will be contacted by your Tour MENTOR (normally an elderly male MAGIC USER with much experience) who will tell you what to do, which is almost certainly to discover you are a MISSING HEIR and, after three brochures, to claim your rightful THRONE.

Steppes are miles and miles of rolling grassland that suddenly happen some way south of the SNOWBOUND NORTH. They are a marvelous place for breeding HORSES, and the ANGLO-SAXON COSSACKS do not find themselves able to live in TENTS, the Management has carefully strewn the grasslands with large outcrops of rock suitable for CITADELS and Dwellings. The result is *austerely picturesque*☞. The sole drawback here is the wind, which brings continual squalls of sleet and snow.

Stew (the OMTs are *thick* and *savory*, which translate as "viscous" and "dark brown") is the staple FOOD in Fantasyland, so be warned. You may shortly be longing passionately for omelette, steak, or baked beans, but none of these will be forthcoming, indoors or out. Stew will be what you are served to eat every single time. Given the disturbed nature of life in this land, where in CAMP you are likely to be attacked without warning (but see BATH) and in an INN prone to be the center of a TAVERN BRAWL, Stew seems to be an odd choice as staple food, since, on a rough calculation, it takes forty times as long to prepare as steak. But it is clear the inhabitants have not yet discovered fast food. The exact recipe for Stew is of course a Management secret, but it is thought to contain meat of some kind and perhaps even vegetables. Do not expect a salad on the side.

Stone Circles are on some Tours quite a feature of the WASTE AREAS. Most are simple circles, but some can instantly turn into a maze when entered by the unwary. They can be GOOD or EVIL, and are given COLOR CODING accordingly. A Good STONE Circle will be of either white or bluish stones, which may have a RUNE carved on them somewhere to confirm this allegiance.

Inside such a Circle a Tourist may travel to another place or be safe for the night from the forces of Dark, which will sniff round the edges but be unable to enter. Further to this, Good Stone Circles are a powerful aid to magically induced KNOWLEDGE, and sometimes even to SELF-KNOWLEDGE. You can sometimes have quite an argument with one. After a night of defending your motives, you will come away wiser. Bad Stone Circles are of black stones, *shine with an unwholesome sickly light*◉, and are imbued with the REEK OF WRONGNESS◉. Avoid entering these.

Stones. Some QUESTS prefer a spot marked by a Stone as the QUEST OBJECT. Such Stones can be on: an ISLAND, in which case the Tour will be met by ELVES, MYSTICAL MASTERS, or special guardians; a crag, in which case the Quest goes on after an interval for meditation and SELF-KNOWLEDGE; or in a remote spot or CAVE—this Stone will have an INSCRIPTION which ought to clarify things. Nearly all Stones are Quest Objects in the second brochure only. You will need to book another Tour after finding them.

Storm Control can be exercised by most WIZ- ARDS and many other MAGIC USERS, but even the most EVIL of these is remarkably conventional: rain, hail, snow, dust, ice, and wind are the only kind of STORMS raised. These are, of course, useful in their places, but not one Storm-raiser shows half the invention of, let us say, Moses. Rains of frogs, showers of blood, and Storm-borne locusts are practically unexploited.

Storms are of three kinds. Not surprisingly, hardly a day passes without a Storm of some kind.
1. Natural (see WEATHER). These are all the usual kinds, including dust-storms. The Rule is that a Storm occurs when you least need it to. Storms at sea are likely to throw up both MONSTERS and whirlpools (*maelstroms*⊙).
2. Magical (see STORM CONTROL). Here a

WIZARD will have produced the MAGIC to make a natural-style Storm at the time and place it is needed. These are actually less inconvenient than the normal kind, unless the WIZARD is your Enemy, but also rather more severe.

3. Storms of MAGIC. These are quite unpredictable to everyone. They occur when the lumps of loose Magic and/or the BACKLASHES to major SPELLS get out of control. They can be very violent and may last for days, during which time the very fabric of existence quakes, MAGIC USERS become sick or fall over, colored lights manifest, sparkling MISTS swirl, and ANIMALS and plants are flung for many leagues. The Rule is that these Storms avoid major centers of population.

Strange Races whose individuals are both aggressive and expendable turn up here and there in CAVES, TAVERN BRAWLS, and aboard PIRATE Ships. They can be of any shape and size the Management chooses. Their main function is to get killed and to bleed blood of an unspecified *strange color*⊕. Just occasionally, a Tourist succeeds in making friends with one of these PEOPLES, whereupon she/he will discover that Strange Races are almost human.

Swords. You are advised to choose your Sword with great care and, if possible, have it thoroughly checked by a jobbing MAGICIAN before undertaking ownership. Swords are *dangerous.*

This does not simply mean that you can stab yourself in the foot with one without due care (though some Swords do that too, if crossed): it means that all Swords in Fantasyland are dangerously magical in some way. Here are the hazards you should look out for and avoid if possible:

1. Swords with RUNES. Runes are almost always a sign that your Sword is:

(a) Designed only to kill DRAGONS.

(b) Designed for some other specific victim, such as GOBLINS or UNDEAD.

Both (a) and (b) are likely to let you down if you are attacked by ordinary humans.

(c) Designed for some other purpose entirely, so that when drawn it will proceed to raise a STORM or—Gods protect you!—try to *heal* your assailant.

Be wary of Runes, even if they appear to say only "Made in Gna'ash."

2. Swords with Souls. These will contain:

(a) The soul of someone formerly alive or, worse,

(b) A soul of their own.

Swords of both (a) and (b) types are prone to argue with you in MINDSPEECH whenever you are trying to use them to fight with. Since the Rules clearly state that all Swords are extremely old, your Sword's soul will be old, too, and probably set in its ways. It will interrupt you and impair your concentration with antiquated advice. Or it could even be a pacifist; it will then declare that it has given up killing, and go all bendy.

 (c) A highly aggressive soul. This kind of Sword tends to take over the user at unexpected moments, put her/him through impeccable but obsolete Martial Arts movements, and end up beheading people on rather slender grounds. This can be awkward. The relatives of the beheaded person may not be pleased, and there is a strong possibility the wielder may dislocate a joint through being forced to adopt an unaccustomed fighting posture.

3. Swords with appetites. These feed on:

(a) Blood.

(b) Lifeforce.

(c) Souls.

The preferred provender of any given Sword depends upon the whim of its maker. Some Swords are partial to all three and may, if not regularly fed, turn and feed on their owners. Fortunately, these Swords can be distinguished (and then quickly avoided) by their dead black unreflective coloration, their extreme coldness to the touch, and their unlovable habit of welding themselves to the hand of their future owner. Needless to say, by the time that has happened, it is too late. You are stuck with a hungry Sword.

4. Swords that give signals. This class of Sword heralds the approach of enemies by:

(a) Running with blood.

(b) Groaning or singing.

(c) Shining with an unearthly light or bursting into flame.

This causes at least two kinds of trouble. In the first place, if there are ten enemies to one of you, you will certainly want to hide rather than face them, but the activities of your Sword will rapidly betray your hiding-place. In the second place, the enemies of your Sword may not be your enemies at all, and it can cause you much embarrassment by dripping, shouting, or shining in front of your friends. If you must own a sword of this class, it is better to opt for Swords that

(d) Merely turn icy cold. You can always wear a glove.

5. Swords that are something else. These will *look* like Swords, but are in reality made of some other substance entirely:

(a) Star metal. This is like steel, but brighter. It not only holds a wicked edge, but can cut through *anything*. This has its uses but, before you learn what these are, you may have lost a finger and several toes. Besides, this Sword will be continually slicing through its scabbard and plunging point-down into the earth. And it will go in a long way.

(b) Forged of pure spirit, though goodness knows *how*. This Sword will usually resemble a bar of light, and like a genuine bar of light it is probably most useful as a torch for frightening nocturnal creatures with (see LIGHTING). Rumor has it that it operates like a laser, but most experienced Tourists agree that it does this only in the Final CONFRONTATION with the DARK LORD.

(c) A DEMON. The Demon will be standing very straight with its arms by its sides and be further disguised by ILLUSION. But it will have its demonic powers intact and, unless you know its NAME, or have other means of controling it, it will get you in the end.

(d) Glass. This is quite common, unpractical as such a sword might seem. It may be best to snap it off to a razor-sharp splinter straight away and use it as you would your DAGGER. Unfortunately, such Swords tend to belong to MYSTICAL MASTERS, who might object to this.

(e) CRYSTAL. This must be a telepathic device in disguise.

6. Swords in stones. Avoid these at all costs. Usually such Swords are easy to spot because they will be up to half their length inside a rather large boulder, but Illusion may have been used to make the boulder look like a pebble on the very point. And they will be offered to you cheap because nobody else will want them. Resist the bargain. The sole use of such Swords is to acclaim you KING of some godforsaken Kingdom or other.

7. Swords that are incomplete.

(a) With a notch or missing bit. This type will be pressed on you as an heirloom that has seen much service. It may even have belonged to your father. But there is a high probability that the missing fragment will turn up embedded in someone's head, arm, or leg and you could be accused of murder.

(b) Broken into two or more pieces. This Sword will probably be given to you as useless. Or you will find it on a corpse in a forest clearing. Get rid of it at once. Before the Tour has lasted much longer, you will be required to reforge the bugger for a special purpose of a dangerous and frightening nature. First you will have to spend nearly a year learning metalwork and forging and then you will have to do the unpleasant thing the Sword has set you up for. It is not worth it.

8. Swords that contain your own magical powers. This is a stupid place to put your powers, but it can happen accidentally. This is why swords are so dangerous. If this has happened, seek magical aid at once and have the Sword unzipped. If you have pumped the Sword full of your powers on purpose, there is no hope for you.

9. Swords that are gaudy. These can be very tempting, what with wavy patterns down the middle, bright metalwork, and big stones in the hilt. Do not be fooled. This pretty Sword could be:

(a) A dress Sword for Court that will not keep an edge. It will certainly break or crumple in serious use.

(b) CURSED, in any number of ingenious ways.

(c) Dangerous because of the big precious stones in the hilt. This keeps the Rule that all

JEWELERY in Fantasyland has some magical purpose. The big red stone could poison you. The large green stone could hypnotize you. And the great yellow stone is certainly a means for the DARK LORD or a MINION to whisper things to you that control you to their ends (*fell purposes*⬚). (See also MAGIC OBJECTS.)

10. Swords that seem quite innocuous. These can still turn out to be any of the above without warning.

We would advise against buying or using a Sword, except that in Fantasyland this would make you look as if you were walking in traffic with no clothes on.

Tes'rac was an ordinary man who was no happier than the King. Tes'rac suggested to the King that they change places to prove it, but the King declined on the grounds that it was self-evident.

Ka'a Orto'o, Gnomic Utterances, II v

Taboo is something that is so sacred and so terrible that it cannot be changed, touched, or mentioned. This is why you will find no entry in **Toughpick** for the Rules.

Talent is the technical term and OMT, although GIFT is sometimes preferred as a variation, for the inborn ability to do MAGIC. If it is a general ability for all Magic it is *High Talent*. If it is an ability to perform only one or two types of Magic, then it is used in the plural, as *His Talents were Firestarting and Mindspeech*. This OMT is never used of any other ability except MUSIC, which in Fantasyland counts as a magical Talent.

Talented Girl. This young lady has almost constant employment as Tour COMPANION. The reason is that she not only has enormous poten-

tial as a MAGIC USER, which is something she
has to learn about in the course of the Tour,
but is good-looking with it, if you don't mind
girls who are tall and skinny or else unusually
short. She will have either red or fair hair and
blue or green eyes (see COLOR CODING) and a
highly spirited and resourceful personality to go
with these. This quite often causes her to argue
with her Tour Companions. She is usually
pretty opinionated, or will be as soon as she
gets her confidence. Sometimes she will join the
Tour quietly at the start, having set out to seek
her fortune from the INN, but more often she
will join from a VILLAGE or a PALACE. If she
comes from a Village, she will have had some
training from a local HERBWOMAN or BARD.
When she comes from a Palace, she will be a
PRINCESS or a Good QUEEN, and may or may
not be trained. In all cases, there will be much
still for her to learn. She is usually the Companion who must acquire the SECRET that will enable the Tour to succeed in SAVING THE WORLD.

Talisman. The same as AMULET, only Talis-
mans do not hang round your neck.

Tarot. See PROPHECY.

Tavern is either in a cellar or open to the street,
and mostly serves only bad cheap drink and
very greasy STEW. MERCENARIES love Taverns,
but the Management disapproves. The OMT is

low. Most Tourists will enter a Tavern only in order to get disgustingly drunk for the first time, but be careful: about twenty percent of Taverns harbor an Assassin with a contract for you. Avoid Taverns unless you really want a terrible hangover or a bout of unarmed combat. Stick to INNS.

Tavern Brawl. This will break out without warning in any crowded TAVERN or INN early on in the Tour. The Rule is that everyone in the taproom almost instantly joins in, and the ferocity of the fighting is normally extreme. SWORDS, chairlegs, and tankards may be used impartially. There will be a lot of shouting and crashing. The amount of actual injury is, however, usually minimal, unless members of STRANGE RACES happen to be present, in which case there will be large quantities of blood (*some of it an odd color*⊛) and possibly a death or so, along with extensive breakages. Do not be alarmed. Be guided by the INNKEEPER, who will take it in his stride. If you feel like joining in, you may; but, if not, the Management will have arranged for you to find yourself either quickly underneath a table or else drawn gently by the elbow to a place of safety. The Rules also state that the next morning there will be little or no sign of the mayhem of the previous night.

Teenage Boy is a very young Tour COMPANION. He will grow larger. Even to start with he is quite big, thin, and gangly. This is because he

is a MISSING HEIR or a thief (see THIEVES'
GUILD) who has not had a decent start in life.
He is very good-hearted and moderately clever,
and a bit of a lunk with it. He will tend to
throw up after FIGHTS; and this will not change,
however big he grows. He will go on to inherit
riches and/or a Kingdom and still be the same.

Telekinesis is the magical ability to move objects about without touching them. It is done a
lot, but it is not given this name. In fact, there
is no OMT for Telekinesis.

Telepathy. See MINDSPEECH.

Teleporting is when a MAGIC USER moves himself (and sometimes other people) from one
place to another without touching the space in
between. It is a very useful art which we have
yet to learn in this world.

Temples are richly architectured marvels. All
Tourists should attempt to take in the gran-
deurs of at least one Temple, even though the
Management will arrange for you to be very
busy while you are there. Temples cover a great
deal of ground and also occupy the skyline with
ranks of sumptuous domes, painted, gilded, and
carved with images, with minarets and twisty
towers and sometimes steeples as well. They
have gargoyles on every wall and colored roofs
with fretworked edges. Temples go deep under-

ground too, in a labyrinth of DUNGEONS, TREA-
SURE rooms, and SECRET PASSAGES. Each is
enormously wealthy, some of them by highly
questionable means.

The layout of a Temple is traditional. There
will be an elaborate facade, sometimes frighten-
ingly carved, with a gate in it guarded by fanatics.
Inside the gate will be at least two forecourts,
one thronged with people delivering offerings
and/or protection money, the other thronged
with Temple Prostitutes. PRIESTS will patrol
here, looking for trouble, thieves, and pretty
women to abduct as SLAVES. There may then
be an inner court, smoking with small
SACRIFICES.

Beyond that will be the public Temple, very
large, with *ornate pillars* and elaborately tiled
floor. It will be dimly lit. Chanting will be going

on. There will be an IDOL or IMAGE of the God here, but this may well not be the Image you are looking for—if you need to steal anything from Temple, be *sure* that this is not the Image you need. You will have to penetrate beyond, where the building becomes steadily more confusing and secret. First will come the quarters for NOVICES and GUARDS (*austere*⊕, *ascetic*⊕), then quite comfortable quarters for qualified Priests, and then the inner Temple. This is where the true, dark, fanatical worship goes on and the serious Sacrifices get made. The Idol here may be lit by a red light. This is the one you must look for if you need to steal any of its sacred regalia or JEWELS. If, however, it is a SCROLL you have to steal, you must go on, to the inner parts where the library (*musty*⊕) is to be found. A long way further inside from here, you will find the place where the HIGH PRIEST has made himself very comfortable indeed. Here also you will find the rooms for his concubines and catamites. This is the part you will have to get to if you need to rescue a COMPANION from his clutches. Go carefully. There are often magical traps.

Surprisingly, some Temples are not EVIL. You can tell because the High Priest will not have made himself comfortable. However, GOOD Temples are rare. And take care again. Some Evil High Priests are not above having falsely ascetic quarters to make people think they are holy. In such cases, expect an inner

ring of initiates who will resent your foray and
try to kill you.

Tents are soundproof canvas structures that are
hauled along when ARMIES or MERCENARIES
are on the march. Good KINGS and their generals have large Tents, quite modestly furnished
with a lamp, a bed, and a table covered with
maps. Bad Kings and Mercenary captains have
carpets and real furniture (*of nearly barbaric
splendor*⊚) and dangling golden chandeliers.
Their Tents are often divided into several
rooms, for the use of servants, concubines, and
prisoners; most of these are also fully furnished.
It is hard to see how this lot gets carried from
CAMP to Camp, but somehow it does.

See also NOMAD TENTS.

Terrain varies enormously in Fantasyland, and
with great abruptness. You can go from tilled
land to magical WASTE AREA in a few steps,
or from MARSHES to STEPPES in the same way.
What is constant is that the going is terrible.
Thus, in tilled land, the ROAD will be all muddy
ruts, while on the Steppes there will be no
Road and a strong keen wind; expect snow in
any MOUNTAINS, stasis in the Marshes (even by
BOAT), roots and tangled vegetation in a WOOD,
BOGS and steep hills near RIVERS, areas of
gravel and boulders elsewhere. Perhaps worst,
in the magical Waste Areas your way will be
blocked by seeping slimes, ILLUSIONS, land-
slides, and magical MISTS. Only in the small

area now occupied by the VESTIGIAL EMPIRE
can you expect to travel with any freedom.

Thieves' Guild. The best organized body of
people in the continent. Thieves' Guilds exist
in all CITIES and can usually pass messages reli-
ably between branches, although each City appears to have its own independent hierarchy.
The Thieves' Guild exists to transfer wealth but
not to distribute it. Its members are pickpock-
ets, burglars, robbers, fences, and housebreak-
ers, but never muggers. The Guild claims to be
a body of artists. All its members profess horror
at violence (but are quite proficient fighters all
the same) and pride themselves on bringing off
robberies in apparently impregnable TREASURE
stores, on picking locks, and on climbing
smooth walls. The Guild is organized into masters, journeymen, and APPRENTICES, with an
anonymous Hidden Head, or Guildmaster, who
rejoices in such NAMES as The Faceless Man or
The Gentleman. You will be taken to see this
person at some point when your Tour visits a
City. You will be blindfolded and led along
strange-smelling passages to an upstairs venue
evidently concealed between two or more
houses. The man's face will be veiled by MAGIC
or masked. But meanwhile you will have made
the acquaintance of a very young Apprentice
thief. In return for the Guild's helping the
Tour, the Hidden Guildmaster will ask you to
look after this Child because he shows promise,
and you will take him with you when you leave

on the rest of the Tour. He will become an excellent and useful Tour COMPANION, and even make JOKES. There is always an unspoken suggestion that this young thief is the son of the Hidden Guildmaster.

Thrones are the elaborate seats that KINGS, QUEENS, Evil WIZARDS, and Emperors sit in. They are usually of metal or stone and placed on a platform in the Throne Room. Metal Thrones are either of gold or of some metal symbolic of the ruler's nature. Thus a cruel and unforgiving King will have a Throne of IRON. A lovely young Queen will have one of silver. The metal will be worked *with consummate artistry*⊗ into beasts, flowers, and abstract designs all over, and may be jeweled as well. Stone Thrones tend to be carved into ANIMAL shapes or austerely simple. Both kinds must be chilly and uncomfortable. It is therefore surprising how many rulers spend their leisure hours sitting on their Thrones, alone in the Throne Room, often wearing their Crowns as well. This is a convenient habit: when you are ready to overthrow an Evil King or Wizard, you at least know where to find him.

Time taken on the Tour is often vague. Only if there is a public festival which happens all over the continent will you be able to tell how long you have taken getting anywhere. You may be slogging happily along and find yourself surprised that you have had *months of travel*⊗.

Or you may think you have been a year on the way and find it has been only days. The Management likes to keep you guessing.

Tombs. There are few or no churchyards in Fantasyland, so Tombs tend to have to be in peculiar places. The Rule is that, wherever a Tomb is, it is always intensely sinister and normally visited at night. Tombs are:

1. On a hill outside of TOWN. Here there are always many Tombs. Tourists will visit by moonlight and become appalled by hootings, rustlings, and groaning. These are sound-effects only, unless there is reason to expect a GHOST or VAMPIRES. You will be alerted to these by a *sense of dread*⊕ or *a cold chill down the spine*⊕. This will be followed by sight of a *white flitting shape*⊕.

2. In one of the few churches. Here the Tomb is in a side chapel and will be approached when moonlight makes *strange-colored patterns on the floor*⊕ from the stained-glass windows. Expect to be terrified here, too.

3. On its own in open country. Here you will *decipher*⊕ an INSCRIPTION that makes it clear that the occupant of this Tomb has KNOWLEDGE that you need. You must then engage a Necromancer (see NECROMANCY) who will raise something that looks uncomfortably like a decaying corpse to answer your questions. Even in broad daylight, this is a harrowing experience.

4. Somewhere in a catacomb. Here you will

pass through UNDERGROUND PASSAGES lined
with skulls and hipbones, to the accompaniment
of rustlings and gurglings, until you reach an
inner CHAMBER. Expect to get colder with
every yard you go. In the Chamber there will
be either a single Tomb with an INSCRIPTION
you need to read, or a whole roomful, each
with a statue of its contents. You will probably
need to raise and talk to these occupants, too.

5. In a RUIN or OLD RUINED CITY. Just occasionally the Ruin looks like a Pyramid. More
often it is an antique sort of TEMPLE. You will
have to descend into this, either by stairs or by
an excavated pathway, with the *sense of
doom*◍ growing about you, and proceed by
flaring torchlight to the center of a tangle of
passages. There will be *the dust of ages*◍
everywhere, but the age-old booby traps will
still be in place. The Tomb will be in the middle
of the central Chamber in front of an ALTAR
and both will try to flame you or get you bitten
by snakes. In some cases the buried person will
manifest and try to stop you in person. She/he
will definitely be of a STRANGE RACE and glowing unpleasantly. You have to disarm this antique MAGIC. The thing you are looking for will
usually be behind or under the Altar. Do not
waste time on the Tomb. It is there for misdi-
rection only.

6. In a Barrow. Here, once you get inside,
the corpse will be lying on a slab in the middle.
Probably your arrival will trip the SPELL that
arouses it. It will seem confused and attempt to

equate your party with a set of marauders it knew centuries ago. It will try to kill you with its grave furniture. It may also attempt to take over your body for its own use. Barrows are the most unsettling Tombs of all.

Torture is obligatory at some stage on the Tour. Generally this takes the form of being tied to rings in the wall almost too high for you to reach, and then being flogged. But on occasions worse things happen. Tourists usually find the Management blanks their minds to the details afterwards.

    See also CHAMBER, EXECUTIONS, and PRISON.

Tour is everything here in **Toughpick,** plus any of a few variations the Management has devised. Most Tourists will need to spend up to six months recovering after they reach home.

Tour Mentor. See MENTOR and MYSTICAL MASTERS.

Towers (*brooding*⊙, *dark*⊙) stand alone in WASTE AREAS and almost always belong to WIZARDS. All are several stories high, round, doorless, virtually windowless, and composed of smooth blocks of masonry that make them very hard to climb. The Rule is that there is also a strong no-entry SPELL, often backed up by a guardian DEMON. In addition, Towers are subject to COLOR CODING: black for EVIL Wizards and blue, white, or red for GOOD or neutral ones. Black Towers tend to cast a blight of Evil on the surrounding TERRAIN: days before you reach them, you will have been able to tell they are near by the dead grass and TREES.

You will have to go to a Tower and then break into it at some point towards the end of your Tour. Usually by then you will have an AMULET or TALISMAN that will act as a key, but sometimes you may have to climb the Tower and force an entry on the roof. Inside, the Tower keeps the Rule about BUILDINGS and is much bigger, with many more floors, each of which suffuses your party in acid MISTS or ILLUSION, or turns you into something nasty.

You have to stop this by breaking the central Spell. Hacking it apart with SWORDS usually suffices. This brings out the Demon. When you have dealt with the Demon, the Wizard himself will appear. If Evil, he will hurl far more subtle Spells at you. You will need to know a SECRET to stop him. If Good or neutral, he is quite likely to appear in a crystal box apparently asleep, and you will have to wake him. This can take days. Towers are quite arduous matters.

Towns are smaller than CITIES and do not always have walls; some may have palisades instead. A Town will be under the power of a lord, but will have a MAYOR for day-to-day ruling. Otherwise the Rules for Cities apply. Expect at least one INCIDENT here.

Transport. Because of MAGIC and bad ROADS, Transport is very primitive. Here, though, are some general notes:

1. By land, if you do not ride a HORSE, you must go by cart or wagon. Both of these have wooden wheels and no springs. Carriages are known, but very rare, even in TOWNS. They have slightly more springing but are distressingly likely either to break down or be waylaid by BANDITS. Tourists who ride in a carriage complain how chilly they are despite sheepskin coverings inside. Ladies and Evil WIZARDS prefer to travel instead by litter. This is a kind of curtained bed that can be slung between Horses, but most often is carried by a team of strong servitors or SLAVES. Litters are most frequently encountered in CITIES.

 2. By WATER, whether sea or RIVER, you must go by small wooden BOAT, FERRY, RIVER-BOAT, or SHIP. Whichever of these craft you find yourself on, be assured that one of the following will occur:

(a) It will sink, possibly because of attack by a SEA MONSTER; Sea Monsters are attracted by Tourists as mice are by cheese, although it is a lot easier to understand how the mice know the cheese is there than how the Sea Monsters know the Tourists are there. Perhaps Tourists possess an identifying SMELL to which Sea Monsters are unusually sensitive. Even if there is no Sea Monster in the region, the Ship is likely destined for the bottom: why captains take Tourists on board at all is a mystery, in this context, unless they are confident of cleaning up on the Insurance.

(b) You will be attacked by PIRATES, who will hack to death or hang all the crewmen who have no NAME and possibly the grizzled but kindly Captain as well, so that you can pause for a restorative tear or two before trying to reconcile yourself to the fact that you are now a SLAVE, bound to be either a GLADIATOR or a GALLEY Slave, if male, or towards An Even Worse Fate, if female (except that it will not be all bad because one of the people who rapes you/to whom you will be obliged to offer sexual favours will turn out to be somewhat fanciable and GOOD at heart, not to mention an exquisite lover, and will in due course help you escape).

(c) You will be betrayed to the forces of the DARK LORD as soon as you have been either delivered to your destination or thrown off the vessel in disgust by the crew.

(d) The Ship proves to be able to fly through the air rather than merely chug through the water. This will of course obviate your inborn tendency, as a Tourist, to seasickness: instead you will discover airsickness.

Travel by Water is not to be recommended, but you will certainly do it nevertheless—and more than once.

See also TELEPORTING and TRAVELING FOLK.

Traveling Folk are quite common. They are of two kinds:

1. Land travelers, who go about in TRIBES in gaudily painted carts. These people are merry, colorfully dressed, dishonest, and knowledgeable. When you meet an encampment of them, they will cheat you, cure your wounds, feed you a variant of STEW, and then hustle you off to the cart of their oldest lady, who will tell you something about the future you need to know (see PROPHECY). After that you will spend time feasting and chatting with the rest. Listen carefully. Land Travelers know LEGENDS and SONGS which always turn out to be important.

2. RIVER travelers are equally gaudy, cheery, and dishonest. They have brightly painted BOATS which ply up and down Rivers and are navigated by *close-knit families*. Tourists can either pay for a lift in the Boat, usually with the last of their MONEY, or stow away. In both cases the River travelers will be very grudging about it (although retaining their cheeriness) and force you to help in the chores. You will peel endless vegetables for STEW, haul ropes, and possibly do laundry as well. They will get even more grudging if the pursuing forces of the Dark catch up and try to damage the Boat. They will often tip you ashore and then tell the DARK LORD exactly where you went. Before that, they will have given you valuable Information either about the TERRAIN to come or in the form of a LEGEND. It is normally worth putting up with their clannishness (see CLANS) just for this.

Treasure lies about in piles in Fantasyland, provided you know where to look. You should search for the following sources:

1. TOMBS, on which there is usually a CURSE.

2. DRAGONS' lairs, where the difficulties of removing the Treasure are obvious.

3. Deserted DWARVEN FASTNESSES, where the Treasure is likely to be in the form of ARMOR of a make and fabric unknown to the present day (but which nevertheless fits you perfectly), or WEAPONS.

4. TEMPLE treasuries, where most of the Treasure will be MAGIC items, some of them unexpectedly dangerous, such as RINGS and CRYSTALS which put you in immediate touch with the DARK LORD.

5. The Treasure houses of KINGS. Except in the case of Puppet Kings and REGENTS, you are advised to let the King make his own selection of Treasure and give it to you freely. He knows the magical conditions that go with each item.

6. The cellars of ruined TOWERS/CITADELS, etc. Here only about half the Treasure will prove lethal.

Note that the Rule is that no Treasure in the form of MONEY can be retained for long, and that the only use it will be is to buy yourself an ARMY or pay your MERCENARIES.

Tree Homes are mostly what TREES are for, except when the tree is prehensile. ELVES, GNOMES, and WOODSMEN all use them.

Trees are unchancy in Fantasyland. There are four kinds:

1. Dwelling places.

(a) As a house built among the branches, in which case you should watch for a rope ladder suddenly descending.

(b) As a domicile inside the trunk of the Tree, in which case the Tree will be very large but the space inside will be larger still, as in a BUILDING.

(c) As a space under the roots. Here the dwellers are always hostile and usually DWELL much further underground than you bargained for.

2. Hostile Trees.

(a) Prehensile. These will grab you with their branches and try to eat you.

 (b) Mobile. These will quietly move about and get in your way. They may also try to eat you. In extreme cases they will attack BUILDINGS.

(c) Poisonous. Avoid any drips from these.

(d) All these things at once. Run away.

3. Former People. You can tell this kind because their branches make expressive noises and they tend to bleed if you snap a twig off. Tourists please note that meditating in a WOOD can cause *you* to become a Tree too, unless great care is taken. Once a Tree, you are likely to stay that way for quite a while, because Trees live at a slower rate than humans.

4. Supernatural. These are:

(a) A God (see GODDESSES AND GODS). This Tree will be huge and old and in the heart of the WOOD, whence it will control most things that go on in the Wood and often make demands to its worshippers for the SACRIFICE of Tourists.

(b) Inhabited by a Tree spirit. This type is also big and old, and the spirit may not be very friendly, particularly if one of your COMPANIONS carries an AXE. But most such spirits can be bargained with for help when needed. Caution: Do not ask a Tree spirit to go far from its Tree or it and the Tree will both die. Otherwise it will give any help within reason.

(c) An Ash Woman. She will look exactly like a real woman and try to seduce male Tourists lost in a Wood, but if you go round behind her you will find she has no back. She is the shell of a female imprinted on a bent piece of bark. Ash Women can be dangerous. If you find a strange woman in a Wood, always go round behind her and check before getting seduced.

Tribes are what Barbarians have instead of CLANS. Each has a Chieftain and a SHAMAN, and its members (probably) share a surname, such as Jones, or Sons of Thog.

Trolls are said by some to be a silicon lifeform. They do certainly tend to turn to stone in daylight, however this might happen. They are huge knobbly beings, not very bright, who will attack Tours in moorlands and hilly places. They are also said to live under BRIDGES (when, on the PANCELTIC TOUR, they are often called Kelpies). Formerly you needed only to keep them fighting until sunrise, but nowadays Trolls seem to have become desensitized to daylight and must be destroyed by MAGIC or just driven off, preferably by SWORDS. This is difficult, because they are hugely strong.

Trots, The. One of the many nuisances that do not exist in Fantasyland. See ECOLOGY.

Trousers are worn by both males and females who are taking part in the action. (NB: They are almost never referred to as "pants" or "breeches.") These garments have to be tough, since they are designed to be lived in day and night for some weeks, and so are usually made of leather or thick wool.

See also SMELLS.

Tunnels. The inhabitants of Fantasyland appear to have been, in the recent past, obsessive diggers of Tunnels of all kinds—not only SEWERS. The walls of all large BUILDINGS are *honeycombed*. Tunnels and UNDERGROUND PASSAGES can be trusted to radiate underground from all CASTLES, CITADELS, CITIES, ISLANDS in lakes, MANSIONS, MONASTERIES, PALACES, and TEMPLES; many RUINS have them too. Nearly all of them at once plunge impractically beneath the nearest RIVER or stretch of WATER and are thus slimy and liable to flooding. Quite a number provide habitats for unspecified slimy critters, and many SMELL. It is hard to see what has prompted this undoubtedly useful obsession with Tunneling, unless it is an understandable desire to escape from DANGER. One conjecture is that the inhabitants of Fantasyland have not long ago interbred with DWARFS and so find that Tunneling is in their blood.

A curious thing about the Tunnels in Fantasyland is that, although often the Management has omitted to supply you with any obvious source of LIGHTING, you are almost always able to see where you are going and what you are doing.

Turncoats are people who change to the side of the DARK LORD in mid-Tour. This can happen to anyone except CHILDREN, Gods, and the TALENTED GIRL. Turncoats are particularly dangerous because they have no REEK OF WRONGNESS⊕. You will have got to know them as a friendly COMPANION, Good KING, Tour MENTOR, etc., and you will trust them with your life/ QUEST OBJECT/SECRET without suspecting that they now operate on behalf of EVIL. Such people will have been taken aside during the Tour and been blackmailed, threatened, put to the TORTURE, fed POISON, hypnotized, enchanted by a MAGIC OBJECT or simply been made an offer they couldn't refuse. After this they will be working very seriously for your downfall. But take heart. The Rule is that only one person becomes a Turncoat at a time. The Management does not allow everyone in Fantasyland to turn against you at once.

Note that the term Turncoat is never used to describe a person who leaves the cause of the Dark Lord to join yours. This is reasonable. Your side is in the right. People who join you are merely becoming converted.

See also BETRAYAL, MINIONS OF THE DARK LORD, SPIES, and UNPLEASANT STRANGER.

Tyrants. Tyrants are like bad KINGS, only truly atrocious. Most of them seem to rule in the FANATIC CALIPHATES, but they are not unknown among the ARISTOCRATIC FEUDALISTS if things have got out of hand there. They may be REGENTS. Tourists can tell when a COUNTRY is ruled by a Tyrant because the ROAD to the main CITY will be lined with impaled corpses and severed heads will be stuck above the City gates. Expect to be imprisoned and put to the TORTURE here.

Undo nothing. You could freeze to death.
Saying of the Desert Nomads

Undead. Remarkably few people stay dead when killed in Fantasyland. This may be because it is necessary for a correctly qualified MAGIC USER to SING a person's soul to rest. Without this formality, there is trouble. Even with it, the DARK LORD is likely to come along and raise an ARMY of corpses. The difficulty here is that they cannot be killed a second time, but walk mechanically about minus various limbs, rising up each time they are knocked down, until they are either hacked to pieces or discharged of MAGIC by a MYSTICAL MASTER or Good WIZARD. Expect to encounter at least a squad of Undead from quite early in your Tour. Individual Undead may be met in Barons' MANSIONS, OLD RUINED CITIES, and other desolate places at any time. Unless they have been deliberately summoned by the Tour MENTOR for KNOWLEDGE, they are nothing but bad news. In extreme peril, Tourists too can summon Undead in some numbers, but only on the third leg of the Tour, near the CONCLUSION.

See also NECROMANCY and ZOMBIES.

Underground Passages are usually there when you need them. No FORT, CASTLE, MONASTERY, or TEMPLE is without one. Thus your escape from an uncomfortable situation or PRISON is assured. Traditionally, the Underground Passage will be down some stone steps from the cellar or DUNGEON, where you may have to clear away some rubble, and then it will be wet and slimy (*dank and dripping*⊙ᴹᵀ) with puddles underfoot, because it always takes you under the nearest RIVER. It will bring you out a good healthy distance from the DANGER you were escaping, usually into a clump of very prickly undergrowth. This is how the Management takes care of its Tourists.

Underwear is optional and largely nonexistent. It is believed that some form of loincloth or drawers is sometimes permitted, but the Management is naturally coy on this subject. Bras are certainly unknown, but in the case of dancing girls may be replaced by sequined things with tassels.

Unicorns are exceedingly rare. Each one you meet will tell you that it is the last one. Their horns, however, are to be found quite often, and you may use them both for healing and as a magic wand. The rumor that Unicorns still acknowledge VIRGINS is probably false.

Unpleasant Stranger is a TOUR COMPANION whom no one likes or trusts. Usually the Stranger is male and neither young nor old. He can be either sly and ingratiating or *gruff and taciturn*⊛, and sets everyone's back up and teeth on edge. He will be dressed well but unremarkably. His hair will be dark. This piece of COLOR CODING often, but not invariably, makes it clear that the Stranger is a SPY for BANDITS or for the DARK LORD, but in his case you have to wait and see. If he is a Spy for Bandits, then you will not have to wait long; if for the Dark Lord, then you have him for most of the Tour. But in some cases he is a dispossessed or long-lost KING, embittered by his past, in which case you will have misjudged him. A fairly sure rule of thumb is to look at the Stranger's hair. If it is greasy, he has to be a Spy. If it is simply *unkempt*⊛ or *graying*⊛, or both, he is on the side of GOOD and the Dark Lord is his personal ENEMY; he will be a great help in the Final CONFRONTATION by drawing the Dark Lord's attention to himself while the rest of you work at SAVING THE WORLD.

Vengeance is seldom rewarding. You should negotiate payment in advance. The Assassin Huggi forgot this maxim but fortunately did not live to regret it.

> Ka'a Orto'o, Gnomic Utterances, V xxiii

Valleys are places of importance. They are:

1. The sites of major battles that either take place on the present Tour or took place in the past. If the battle is here and now, the Valley will have been carefully chosen as the site. It will be green and attractive until after the battle, when it will be trampled and *littered with* *dead and dying*⊛. If the battle was in the past, the Valley will be a sad place, where *the old agony still clings*⊛. Sensitive Tourists will find it quite distressing.

2. Hidden and Enchanted, and likely your QUEST OBJECT. Here the Valley will be more than just green. It will be a paradise of wildflowers and stately old TREES. Any WATER will flow melodiously or stand and reflect the view harmoniously. The sky will be azure, the breeze dulcet. The Management really does you proud here. You will feel as if you are home at last. Some of your COMPANIONS may well stay here for good. The rest of you will absorb whatever the ENCHANTMENT has to give you and then depart, yearning. Later, you will kick yourself for leaving.

Vampires are increasingly rare on the Tour. They have been attracted over to the Horror Tour by offers of better pay. Where they appear, you will find up-to-date Vampires wear expensive sunglasses and wish to drain you of energy rather than blood.

Vegetables are seldom eaten except as a component of STEW. This is odd, because every MARKET has piles of glossy legumes on display. Raw vegetables are unknown as part of a meal. The inhabitants insist on everything being cooked, usually for hours, and would certainly faint at the sight of lettuce.

See also ROOTS and SCURVY.

Vest. A sort of V-necked sweater without sleeves, made of leather and usually worn over a SHIRT.

Vestigial Emperor is nearly always a small, ordinary man (this shows how the VESTIGIAL EMPIRE has shrunk) rattling about in an enormous PALACE. He shows little interest in restoring the former glories of his Empire, but concentrates instead on harmless occupations like botany and gardening. His gardens are always very fine. He will be suave and hospitable to Tourists. But do not underestimate him. That ordinary appearance hides a keen political brain and an up-to-the-minute grasp of local POLITICS. You will find him very proud and snobbish if you chance to want to marry his daughter, but if you want material aid or an ARMY he will tell you at length how pacific and penniless he is. If you work at it, you can marry his daughter *and* get an Army out of him, but it will take some time and probably an unprovoked attack on the Empire to convince him.

Vestigial Empire. The most civilized part of the continent. You can even get decent FOOD and a BATH here. This Empire occupies an area usually slightly larger than most other COUNTRIES and you will know you are in it because the ROADS will be well made and patrolled by Imperial GUARDS in HELMETS and SKIRTS. Rest-houses line the way, a day's march apart. The LANDSCAPE will be full of prosperous farmlands, vineyards, and olive groves, and you may even see a little light INDUSTRY, such as pottery and carpetmaking. White villas crown the hills—in fact, most Buildings in the Empire are white. When you reach the Imperial City, you will find TEMPLES and colonnades as well as streets of decent houses, drains, and public Baths. The aura of civilization extends to daily life too. The Vestigial Empire is the only Country on the standard Tour to have POLITICS. It has a parliament and a senate and many noble CLANS to jockey for power. This keeps all Imperialists very busy, very noisy, and very likely to POISON one another. They also have time to spare to overcharge most Tourists, since they understand MONEY in a truly civilized way. If you can survive this, you should enjoy the Vestigial Empire. It has a touch of home about it.

Villages almost never appear on any MAP, but are quite frequent on most routes; one may even be your STARTING POINT, provided it is sufficiently far from anywhere else. Villages usually consist of one street with houses scattered along it, a lot of barking dogs, a smithy (see BLACKSMITHS), and, if you are lucky, an INN. People who live in Villages tend to be very parochial and suspicious even of GOOD visitors. This is because their life is a constant struggle against poverty and SQUALOR as well as magical drought and other WEATHER. They will have a lot of rather strange beliefs about MAGIC being dangerous and girls needing to wear SKIRTS, but their hearts are in the right place. You will be quite sorry when MUTANT NASTIES emerge from the hinterland and kill them all.

Virgins are much in demand for various reasons:
1. For SACRIFICE on an ALTAR to a bad God (see GODDESSES AND GODS). The Virgin has to be female, young, good-looking, and wearing white.
2. For WITCHCRAFT. Some schools of WITCHES

hold that a Witch retains her POWERS only so
long as she is a Virgin. This is probably a myth
and causes much unhappiness on most Tours.

3. For sale to a rich person. Most BANDITS
and PIRATES go to surprising lengths to ensure
their most beautiful young female captives remain Virgins until they are sold as SLAVES. This
more than doubles the price they can get.

4. For tempting UNICORNS. The mode of attraction, whereby a Unicorn is brought to lay
its head in the lap of a young girl, is probably
no longer effective.

5. For tempting DRAGONS. Again a female
Virgin is needed, but this practice is long
outmoded.

6. AS TALENTED GIRLS. These are very

likely, towards the end of the second third of the Tour, to come across a male Tourist in his BATH and turn implausibly to jelly (*a surge of some deep, hitherto unknown emotion swept through her*ⓞⓜⓣ). Thereafter they have a sprightly step, a jaunty gleam in the eyes, a yet more tiptilted nose, and a private life over which the Management generally draws a discreet veil.

7. Nobody wants a male Virgin at all. Young boys, yes, but there is no stipulation about Virginity. In fact, some experience is preferred.

Visions. Tourists without TALENT can often be obtuse about how the Management wishes them to act. DREAMS will be tried first. If the unTalented Tourist still refuses to decide to do the right thing, she/he will be accorded a Vision. This will sometimes show the consequences of her/his present reluctance to act, but most often will be a graphic sight of things happening elsewhere which need to be set right at once. Visions can show CITIES burning, ISLANDS sinking, and ARMIES marching, but may also show more domestic scenes in PALACES where the beleaguered young QUEEN is being forced into marriage with her Evil COUNCILOR. Such sights will galvanize any Tourist.

See also PROPHECY.

When you obtain a talisman of great worth, you should exchange it quickly for a bag of beans. Protection is nothing like as valuable as climbing to the sky.

Ka'a Orto'o, More Gnomic Utterances,

XXXII il

Walled City. If a City has walls around it, particularly if those walls are spectacularly strong, high, and thick, and if its gates are marvels of sevenfold beaten bronze, then you can BET large odds that it will be under SIEGE before you have been in it three days.

Wand, Rare. Another term for STAFF.

War. Long ago there was of course the WIZARDS' War, usually accounted the Ultimate Conflict, but war naturally goes on all the time in Fantasyland. It follows the Rules for CONFRONTATIONS, FIGHTS, and INCIDENTS by starting smallish and ending up with the whole continent on a War footing. There is usually dreadful slaughter before the finish. And, like all Wars, this one solves very little. The Tour party has to go in alone and finish the DARK

LORD off, either during the main fighting or after it is over. But never fear: GOOD will triumph in the end, though at considerable expense. After the War, there will be a brand new WASTE AREA ready for the next Tour to visit.

War and Worship People were once a much larger PEOPLE than they are now. These days they are limited to one remote VALLEY, and some Tours do not even call there. It is easy to see why. Among this People, women spend their days as PRIESTESSES in exclusive service to their GODDESS and occupy any houses there are. Men live apart in Halls and devote their energies to being Warriors. Each sex despises the other. There is some yearly arrangement whereby the sexes can get together for one night. Usually there is a feast at which a potent drink is served. This reduces cultural inhibitions just enough so that the next generation can be conceived. Possibly these days the drink is less potent, or maybe the arrangement is flawed. One serious problem is that neither sex seems to have time either to cultivate fields or to look after children. At any rate, this People is definitely on the decline.

Wards are magical protections. They have to be invoked by a MAGIC USER (usually tired out after a day's travel) who concentrates at four points of a circle, or draws a circle in the earth with a stick, or SINGS. After this, the CAMP will be safe from predators and the forces of EVIL

for one night. But do not expect the Magic
User to help with the chores afterwards. The
Rules state that this form of MAGIC is hard
work.

Warrior Women. The country where these ladies live is almost the only one you will not
visit on your Tour. They do not like intruders
or men. Rumor has it that there are no men in
this country, even for breeding with. Where the
next generation comes from or who looks after
it is anyone's guess. But the Warrior Women
themselves are out and about a lot. They are
far more soldierly than male soldiers, and do a
lot of swaggering, sweating, screwing, drinking,
and betting, as well as fighting. Some are huge
and coarse with very hairy armpits, but most
are quite slender and comely. They are all naturally very strong. If you want your arm broken,
try insulting a Warrior Woman. Nevertheless, it
is possible to become quite friendly with them,
provided no one treats them like women.
Rumor has it that they are all gay. This may be
true, but SEX with a Warrior Woman is often
provided on a Tour and should not be missed
by either men or women.

Washing. Do not expect to wash often. Do not
expect warm WATER. Do not expect to wash at
all in most INNS. Washing of yourself and
clothes will be done mostly in RIVERS and
streams. Expect to feel gritty afterwards.

But see also BATH.

Waste Areas occupy large parts of the main landmass. Each has a different origin:

1. A KING's personality defects. Here the land reflects the King and parches dry or simply refuses to grow crops. The inhabitants are forced to leave. This Waste is full of derelict farms and often has very unreliable WEATHER.

2. Overtaxation. Here the LANDSCAPE looks like the first kind, but seems quite lush. The peasantry have all sold up because they were unable to pay the extortionate taxes demanded by their lord.

3. A recent visit by the DARK LORD or his ARMIES. Ashes and corpses are left in their wake. Again, land and farms are empty, though there may be a few pitiful survivors to tell you what happened (see NUNNERY).

4. One-time lands of the VESTIGIAL EMPIRE. As the Empire shrank, the lands were simply left empty. Before that they must have been perilously overcropped. All that is left now are miles of tussocky grass, broken ROADS, and stumps of BUILDINGS overgrown with bushes and weeds. There are almost no BIRDS or ANIMALS here; MUTANT NASTIES, WERES, and MONSTERS have usually moved in. Tours need to go warily in this Waste.

5. Remains of the WIZARDS' War. Go even more warily here. This Waste is still full of magical pollution. There are areas of glassy slag and creeping MIST. The vegetation is weird and often a strident green. It will eat you. Twisted TREES, in particular, are quite clever at acquiring human prey. Slimes and mosses will try to absorb your flesh. Thorns will poison you. Rocks are likely to try to kill you. And any Animal seen will be frightfully mutated into something intelligent, vile, and predatory.

≈ **Water.** You may drink from or wash in any Water, however scummy, while on the Tour, except in the MARSHES, where it is full of wriggly things. Water in Fantasyland does not harbor germs. The only other Water it is unwise to touch will be either near the home of an ECHANTRESS or on the trail left by a WIZARD. This may turn you into things or show you disturbing pictures.

But see BATH and SEX.

Waterbottles. Heavy leather bags for taking water along in on a JOURNEY. They customarily hang by the saddle. Most of them have slow punctures. They always prove to be emptier than you thought, and invariably prove to be quite empty a day or two after you started crossing a desert.

Waterfalls are generally very tall and thin (see LANDSCAPE). If the Management draws your attention to a Waterfall, it will not be for its scenic value. It will be because there are CAVES or a hiding-place or a secret colony of friendly folk behind it. You will have to turn sideways and slither along the rock to reach it.

Waybread or Journey Cake is a flat cake, infinitely nutritious and weighing almost nothing, on which Tourists may sustain themselves for long periods. In appearance, it seems to be halfway between a ricecake and a ship's biscuit, and in substance it is truly remarkable since those eating it are never hungry and absolutely never suffer from any deficiency disease (see SCURVY). In some areas there is also a kind of grass capable of being eaten instead of Waybread, but this seems to grow only when your Waybread has run out. It is strange that the inhabitants, given the remarkable properties of Waybread and grass, do not choose to live entirely on one or the other. The reason must be that neither tastes of anything very much. After a month of eating them you will even be glad of STEW.

Weaponmaster. The ex-GLADIATOR or MERCENARY who runs the SCHOOL OF WEAPONRY. The Rules state that he will be in late middle age but extremely fit, with iron-gray hair, broad shoulders, and a scar somewhere on his face. In his day he has been a legend. Nor has he lost any of his skills. So good is he that he will seldom take on any of his pupils unless they show extreme promise. He leaves tuition to helpers and sparring partners, so how he keeps himself fit is a bit of a mystery. He may look forbidding, but this is just to hide his nice nature. When you have been in his School long enough to show promise, you will become his friend. He will give you tips that are invaluable in the arena. You will try to persuade him to come with you on the Tour, but you will seldom succeed. If you do, though, he will be a valuable COMPANION.

Weapons. Essentially, see AXE, BOWS AND ARROWS, DAGGER, GUNS, and SWORDS. In addition, spears, pikes, and halberds may be used by militias, tridents by GLADIATORS, and scythes and cudgels by AVERAGE FOLK. A few exotic Weapons, such as throwing-stars, are sometimes permitted to FEMALE MERCENARIES. The GAY MAGE may use a crossbow, but otherwise crossbows are reserved for bad people. Magical Weapons were banned after the WIZARDS' War, but may still be in evidence—their use is a sure sign that the wielder is EVIL.

Weather is always wrong for what you are doing at the time. It varies from heat/drought, if you must travel quickly, to heavy rain, if you need just to travel. If you need to sleep rough, there is always a frost; invariably, if you have to cross MOUNTAINS, there will be a thunderstorm or blizzard. Some of the reason for this is that, despite obvious drawbacks, the Management nearly always arranges for Tours to set out in late autumn or early winter (see SEASONS). The rest is natural perversity. Weather is, too, remarkably apt to reflect the emotions of the Tour party. It is sullen and gray if the party is quarreling among itself, bright and springlike if everyone is happy. It is also very susceptible to MAGIC, particularly at sea, where STORMS can be raised in instants (see STORM CONTROL), and in DESERTS, where dust-storms can be created almost as quickly. The general advice here is to keep smiling and avoid annoying WIZARDS.

Weres. These are people who change from human to ANIMAL form either at will or involuntarily under the full MOON (see SHAPESHIFTING). Few can take more than one sort of Animal form, but the Animals chosen are various. There are reports that a Were beagle has been sighted. Not all Weres are unfriendly to Tourists, but most are.

See also WEREWOLVES.

Werewolves and other WERES still prowl the WASTE AREAS, but in decreasing numbers. Most of them have gone over to the Horror Tour in search of better working conditions and more prey. However, the sight of an apparent man or woman suddenly shortening in the body, elongating in the face, and then dropping to all fours while she/he grows a lot of rank gray hair is still a great Tourist attraction and should not be missed. But have your silver weapon ready. A Were will spring before the change is complete. You should not let her/him take you by surprise.

See also SHAPESHIFTING and WOLVES.

Wharf. The OMT here is *scummy* and refers to both the wood or stone surface of the Wharf and the water beside it. Wharfs are full of picturesque SQUALOR.

See also BALES, BOATS, FISH, SHIPS, and THIEVES' GUILD.

 Wild Hunt. This crosses the paths of Tourists scarily at unpredictable intervals, often through the sky and nearly always at night. It is very *numinous*⊙⊤ and also *doom-laden*⊙⊤. Otherwise no one knows quite what to make of it. Normally all that can be distinguished of it is the barking of many hounds, the galloping of many HORSES, and the one rider, horned and masked, at its head. Possibly none of it is fully within the control of the Management, since its appearances often occur arbitrarily, and perfectly well conducted Tourists who witness it tend thereafter to become *numinous* and *doom-laden* themselves.

Wine is always served in tankards like BEER (and may well foam in the same way). It is traditionally kept in leather containers. No one knows why bottles are not used. Glass exists. Most windows are glazed. But the inhabitants seem to prefer wine tasting of Animal skin.

Wise Old Stranger. Usually a MAGIC USER and possibly your Tour MENTOR. In neither case should a Tourist be rude to him, though he will often be extremely irritating. If he is not your Mentor, his MAGIC will not be so powerful and his personality may well be timid, but it is still inadvisable to cross him; he will anyway die desperately trying to save you and your COMPANIONS during a magical attack. You just have to be patient. If, however, this person is female, you are stuck with her. She may be old as the hills, but she is also tough as old boots and could well outlive everyone else on the Tour. And she is so Wise you want to hit her.

Witchcraft is the Herbal and more personal end of MAGIC. It can be either EVIL or GOOD.

See also HERBS, HERBWOMAN, and WITCHES.

Witches are special and probably at least the equal of WIZARDS. They come in several kinds:

1. GOOD. These are the commonest type. Most of them seem to be, at most, in their early thirties, and they are often good-looking and extremely well dressed. All of them have commanding personalities and great skill in MAGIC, but from time to time they show an endearing lack of confidence in themselves. This is because they are alienated from normal society. Witches of this type normally live in a College or Hall sited in a remote spot, along with numerous other Witches and governed by strict Rules and an even stricter Mother Superior. This establishment will have sent the Witch forth with instructions to perform a task, such as SAVING THE WORLD, that she feels to be almost beyond her power. You may become quite friendly with this type of Witch, but do not attempt to have SEX with her unless she invites you. A condition of her POWERS may be that she remains a VIRGIN. But you never know.

2. Bad. (See ENCHANTRESS, which is really the same thing.) This kind seems younger than Good Witches, but it is not the case. They always prolong their life, looks, and youth indefinitely by their arts.

3. Freelance. These are rarer and tend to be:

(a) Mature ladies who have decided to strike out on their own, in which case they look like bad Witches or are fat, overdressed, and silly-seeming. In very rare cases they may be retiring and ugly. They live in CITIES and can usually be persuaded to join your cause.

(b) A very young Witch in search of more Magic or adventure, who will probably join the Tour. You may not realize she is a Witch until there is a magical attack of some kind (see IN-

CIDENT) and she is forced to help. Then she counts as a COMPANION.

Witchfire is the insubstantial burning substance which MAGIC USERS can cast at ENEMIES. It also appears at sea during STORMS. This makes it clear that the phenomenon is akin, at least, to St. Elmo's Fire.

Compare MAGELIGHT and WITCHLIGHT.

Witchlight. Really just another word for MAGE-LIGHT or WITCHFIRE. In the case of Witches, this light can flame from the hair and surround the hands. Some manifestations of MAGIC are clearly sex-linked.

Witch Sight is the ability to see through ILLU-SIONS and to spot Magical events, invisible persons, ELVES, and the nimbus surrounding a Spellworking. It is a truly useful GIFT. All MAGIC USERS seem to have it. In some cases it entails the ability to see patterns that others cannot perceive. Tourists without it must regard themselves as seriously disabled.

Wizards are normally intensely old. They live solitary lives, mostly in TOWERS or CITADELS, or in a special CITY which has facilities for study. They will have been studying MAGIC for centuries and, alas, the great majority have been seriously dehumanized by those studies. Two-thirds have become EVIL, possibly agents of the DARK LORD. The remaining GOOD one-third have become eccentrics or drunks or just very hard to understand. Evil or Good, Wizards are the strongest MAGIC USERS of all except for the DARK LORD and GODDESSES AND GODS, and can usually be distinguished by the fact that they have long beards and wear ROBES.

You need to distinguish Wizards: if crossed, most Wizards get childishly offended and exact terrible revenge. Angry Wizards are likely to throw lumps of LANDSCAPE hither and thither, move MOUNTAINS, wave WEATHER systems about (see STORM CONTROL), hurl DEMONS, flood or bury CITIES, and pollute whole COUNTRIES with sleeting Magics. This is how the Wizards' WAR seems to have come about: too many Wizards got too annoyed at once.

As a result, full-scale Magic Wars have been prohibited by the Rules. Nowadays most Wizards are bored. Evil ones have to occupy their time with BREEDING PROGRAMS and plans to reign over the world. Good Wizards could not do this, and so the Tours have come as a godsend to them. Some Good Wizards can accompany the Tourists as MENTORS, and all of them have fun bossing the show and delivering PROPHECIES or cryptic advice. And the Management in its turn is grateful to the Wizards, both for making the Tours so interesting and for obligingly putting all the Landscape back together again after each Final CONFRONTATION, so that the next Tour may visit Fantasyland and find it whole and entire, as if as always.

See also Apprentices and Hedge Wizard.

Wolves can sometimes be heard howling in the winter wastes, but are not actually present. No Wolf has ever attacked a Tour party. If you see a Wolf, it will be either a normal Were or one of the shapes your Tour Mentor can assume at will. The color of its eyes will tell you if it is friendly or not. Werewolves in Fantasyland tend to be red-eyed. A Wizard or other Magic User will, in Wolf shape, either retain her/his normal eye color or have silver eyes.

See also Color Coding and Shapeshifting.

Woods are frequent, and some of them are just Woods where you Camp. Others are different. You can tell which because, from the moment you enter the *other* type of Wood you will have *a sense of being watched*ᴼᴹᵀ. There are two basic kinds:

1. There are Dwellers, human or Other, who are up Trees watching you. Expect an arrow here that will just miss you and stick in either a treetrunk or a Fellow Traveler who has not been allotted a Name. This will be followed either by ladders descending from above or by the Dwellers themselves, unheard and unseen, surrounding the Tour party and preventing escape.

2. The Wood is a sentient entity—ground, vegetation, Animals, and all. Here the Wood is watching you. It will shortly herd you by vegetable means inwards to its very heart, where there will be a mound or a Tree. You have to get into communication with this type of Wood as soon as possible, or it will get angry and either attack you or just make sure you fail to get out and starve to death. When you do succeed in talking to it, you will gain profound wisdom from it. Woods are one of the few places where SELF-KNOWLEDGE is often acquired, but you usually have to earn this by having a bad time first.

See also FOREST OF DOOM.

Woodsmen live in WOODS and can be either human or Other. They seldom join a Tour, but are often met in the course of it. Frequently they are hostile and suspicious to begin with. You may have to work hard to get them on the side of the Tour. Mostly they simply want to go on living privately. This is particularly true if they are nymphs or satyrs, who are the only kind of Woods people to DWELL on the ground. All other types live up TREES and come down on long rope ladders to parley. Most of them are wonderful trackers and make very useful scouts in the ARMY of the GOOD. The majority also have trained BIRDS, which are telepathically bonded to their owners—this makes the Woodsmen's scouting even more effective. Quite a few Woodsmen are also MAGIC USERS, often of a strange and powerful kind, having imbibed the *secrets of Nature*℠ from the

Woods over the centuries. Tourists are advised to be very polite to Woodsmen, however extraordinary they might look.

Many human Woodsmen have mutated into skinny, silver-haired Elflike beings, but should never be mistaken for ELVES. Elves would object. They live in Woods up Trees too, and wish to remain distinct.

Xerostomia, otherwise known as extreme dryness of the mouth, has many causes but only one cure: the nearest inn.

Ka'a Orto'o, Gnomic Utterances, 1 i

Xenophobia is displayed by most of the PEOPLES of Fantasyland. If they have a supernumerary appendage, as they quite often do, you will be treated as a freak for having only the requisite two of whatever it is. However, they are unlikely to SACRIFICE you for this small fault; more likely they will befriend you in a patronizing fashion and thereafter make sly digs about the fact that you are inferior. Which, you will deduce halfway through the second brochure, you probably are: where can you store your JEWELS without that second navel?

If the Peoples have the usual number of appendages, they normally express their xenophobia by enslaving you.

Yield gracefully when someone pushes in front of
you. You can then stab them in the back.

Ka'a Orto'o, Gnomic Utterances, X xv

Year King. Rarely seen on the Tour these days,
the Year King rules for but a year before being
made the subject of a hideous SACRIFICE. Nevertheless, there are lots of volunteers for the
post, possibly because of the positive effect a
lusty Year King can have on the LANDSCAPE
and even the COUNTRY as a whole, possibly
because of all the fun he is allowed to have
creating that positive effect.

Yogurt. The health-conscious Tourist's alternative to STEW. Yogurt is served on the one occasion when you are ravenously hungry and
would *murder* for a nice filling bowl of STEW.
Nevertheless, you smile politely and make ap-
preciative noises, because the person serving it
to you is an attractive member of the opposite
sex and, after the meal (if such it can be called),
you plan to take a BATH.

Zero bears no relation to infinity, even in magic.

Ka'a Orto'o, Gnomic Utterances, CVI i

Zodiac. The constellations of Fantasyland are quite different from those we see in our own skies. Nevertheless, ASTROLOGY follows a very similar system. Expect Doom when the Angry Red Planet is in the Eye of the Shovel. Do not be frightened if the Morning Star is widdershins to the Rabbit, because this is likely a sign of Good Fortune. The Management is allowed to make such stuff up as it goes along until the sky is positively crowded out with improbable constellations and multiple conjunctions. The MOON, often full or *gibbous*<small>OMT</small> for months on end, will play a large part in all this.

Zombies. These are just the UNDEAD, except nastier, more pitiable, and generally easier to kill. When you slash your SWORD across their stomachs—which you will inevitably do—they watch their impossibly decayed intestines pour out in a glob, and then look at you with *an expression of ultimate pathos*<small>OMT</small> before crumpling at the knees. Naturally they SMELL quite strongly.

FANTASY ANTHOLOGIES